Anonymous

Branson's Agricultural Almanac

Anonymous

Branson's Agricultural Almanac

ISBN/EAN: 9783337334475

Printed in Europe, USA, Canada, Australia, Japan

Cover: Foto ©Andreas Hilbeck / pixelio.de

More available books at **www.hansebooks.com**

Vol. 3.] 27th YEAR OF PUBLICATION. [No. 7.

BRANSON'S
AGRICULTURAL
ALMANAC

FOR THE YEAR OF OUR LORD
1894,

And, until the 4th of July, the 118th year of American Independence.

Carefully Calculated for the Latitude and Longitude of Raleigh, by

LEVI BRANSON, A. M., D. D.

LEVI BRANSON, Publisher, Raleigh, N. C.

POSTMASTERS ARE AUTHORIZED AGENTS FOR THIS ALMANAC.

TIME.

The calculations of this Almanac are made in mean solar or clock time, which is indicated by a well regulated clock or watch, and does not correspond with the sun precisely, except on four days of the year.

Apparent time is that which makes the Sun come to the meridian at 12 o'clock. No good clock will run with the Sun; if set with the Sun on the 2d of January, the clock will seem to be one minute too fast on the 3d of January.

To adopt the calculations of this Almanac to apparent time, use the minutes in the column marked "Sun slow" or "Sun fast;" add them when fast, subtract them when slow.

The calculations are made for the Latitude and Longitude of Raleigh, N. C., but the times, phases, &c., will vary only a few minutes for any part of North Carolina, South Carolina, Georgia, Tennessee or Virginia.

RISING AND SETTING OF THE SUN.

The Almanacs generally used have made the rising and setting of the Sun together equal twelve hours. This is incorrect. During some portions of the year the Sun changes so rapidly in Right Ascension and Declination that it makes a material change in the Diurnal Arc during the day. The times here given have been rigorously calculated and compared with the authority, and are true to the nearest whole minute.

TWELVE SIGNS OF THE ZODIAC.

The Head and Face sign.   ♈ Aries the Ram........Ar.

♊ Arms.
Gemini .... Gem.
Twins.

♌ Heart.
Leo .... Lion
Lion.

♎ Reins.
Libra .... Lib.
Balance.

♐ Thighs.
Sagittarius .. Sag.
Bowman.

♒ Legs.
Aquarius ..... Aq.
Waterman.

♉ Neck.
Taurus .... Tau.
Bull.

♋ Breast.
Cancer ...... Can.
Crab.

♍ Bowels.
Virgo .... Vir.
Virgin.

♏ Loins.
Scorpio .... Scorp.
Scorpion.

♑ Knees.
Capricornus .Cap.
Goat.

The ♓ *Pisces* the Fishes......Pisc.

To know where the sign is, find the day of the month, and against the day in the column marked Moon's Signs you have the sign or place of the Moon, and then find the sign; it will give you the part of the body it is supposed to govern.

SIGNS.

Spring Signs.	Aries, or Ram. Taurus, or Bull. Gemini, or Twins.	*Autumn Signs.*	Libra, or Balance. Scorpio, or Scorpion. Sagittarius, or Bowman.
Summer Signs.	Cancer, or Crab-fish. Leo, or Lion. Virgo, or Virgin.	*Winter Signs.*	Capricornus, or Goat. Aquarius, or Waterman. Pisces, or Fishes.

SIGNS OF THE PLANETS.

☀ Sun.	⊕ Moon.	♀ Venus.	♂ Mars.
♃ Jupiter.	♄ Saturn.	☌ In conjunction.	☐ Quadrature.
☿ Mercury.	⛢ Uranus.	♆ Neptune.	☊ Ascending Node.

MOON'S PHASES.

⊕ New Moon.   ☽ First Quarter.   ⊕ Full Moon.   ☾ Last Quarter.

ELECTROPOISE—See page 43.

CHRONOLOGICAL CYCLES AND ERAS.

Dominical Letter	G.	Julian Period	6607
Epact	23	Jewish Era	5654
Golden Number	14	Era of Nabonassa	2641
Solar Cycle	27	Olympiads	2670
Roman Indiction	7	Mohammedan Era	1311

MOVABLE FEASTS OF THE CHURCH.

Epiphany	Jan. 6	Palm Sunday	March 18
Septuagesima Sunday	Jan. 21	Easter Sunday	March 25
Sexagesima Sunday	Jan. 28	Whit Sunday	May 13
Quinquagesima Sunday	Feb. 4	Trinity Sunday	May 20
Shrove Tuesday	Feb. 6	First Sunday in Advent	Dec. 2
Ash Wednesday, or Lent	Feb. 7	Ascension Day	May 3
St. Patrick's Day	March 17		

THE FOUR SEASONS.

	D.	H.
Spring commences	March 20,	10 A. M.
Summer commences	June 21,	6 A. M.
Autumn commences	September 22,	8 P. M.
Winter commences	December 21,	3 P. M.

MORNING STARS.

Mercury will be Morning Star......April 10, August 8, and November 27.
Venus will be Morning Star from............February 15 to November 30.
Jupiter will be Morning Star from ....January 4 to December 22.

EVENING STARS.

Mercury will be Evening Star about.....February 25, June 23 and October 19.
Venus will be Evening Star till............Feb. 15, then Nov. 30 to Dec. 31.
Jupiter will be Evening Star till...........June 4—Dec. 22 to Dec. 31.

ECLIPSES.

In the year 1894 there will be four Eclipses—two of the Sun and two of the Moon, and a transit of Mercury over the sun's disk.

I. A partial Eclipse of the Moon March 21st, not visible in North Carolina.

II. An Annular Eclipse of the Sun April 6th, not visible in North Carolina.

III. A partial Eclipse of the Moon September 15th, visible more or less in North and South America. Moon enters shadow 3:35 A. M., leaves shadow 5:27 A. M.

IV. A total Eclipse of the Sun September 29th, not visible in North Carolina.

A Transit of Mercury over the Sun's disk November 10th, visible generally to North and South America. The Transit comes on at 10h. 56m. A. M., and goes off at 4h. 12m. P. M. It commences on the Eastern limb of the Sun.

TIDES.

The time of tide can readily be found for the following places by adding the hours and minutes opposite the names to the time when the Moon is South on the day to which the tide is sought. The time when the Moon is South is given in the Calendar for every day. The next tide can be found very nearly by adding 12 hours and 29 minutes to the time of the one previous.

The tides are given in local time—add 12 minutes for Eastern Standard.

	H. M.		H. M.
Boston	11 12	New York	8 13
Sandy Hook	7 29	Old Point	8 17
Baltimore	6 33	Washington City	7 44
Richmond	4 32	Hatteras Inlet	7 04
Beaufort	7 26	Bald Head	7 26
Southport	7 19	Wilmington	9 06
Charleston	7 26	Savannah	9 33

HERSCHEL'S WEATHER PROGNOSTICATOR

For Foretelling the Weather through all the Lunations of the Year.

This table and the accompanying remarks are the result of many years actual observation, the whole being constructed on a due consideration of the attractions of the Sun and Moon, in their several positions respecting the Earth, and, by simple inspection, it shows the observer what kind of weather will most probably follow the entrance of the Moon into any of its quarters, and that so near the truth as to be seldom or never found to fail.

If the new moon, first quarter, full moon, or last quarter, happen—	IN SUMMER.	IN WINTER.
Between midnight and 2 in the morning............	Fair	Hoar frost unless the wind be S. or S. W.
Between 2 and 4 morning	Cold, with frequent showers............	Snow and stormy.
Between 4 and 6, morning	Rain	Rain.
Between 6 and 8, morning	Wind and rain........	Stormy.
Between 8 and 10 morn'g	Changeable	Cold rain if wind be W.; snow if E.
Between 10 and 12 morning	Frequent showers.....	Cold and high wind.
Between 12 o'clock at noon and 2 in afternoon......	Very rainy..........	Rain and snow.
Between 2 and 4, afternoon	Changeable...........	Fair and mild.
Between 4 and 6, afternoon	Fair	Fair.
Between 6 and 8, aftern'n	Fair if wind N. W.; rainy if S. or S. W.	Fair and frosty if wind N. or N. E.; rain or snow if S. or S. W.
Between 8 and 10, aftern'n	Ditto	Ditto.
Between 10 and midnight.	Fair	Fair and frosty.

OBSERVATIONS.—1. The nearer the time for the Moon's change, first quarter, full and last quarter are to midnight, the fairer will be the weather during the next seven days.

2. The space for this calculation occupies from 10 at night until 2 next morning.

3. The nearer to midday or noon the phase of the Moon happens, the more foul or wet weather may be expected during the next seven days.

4. The space for this calculation occupies from 10 in the forenoon until 2 in the afternoon. These observations refer principally to the Summer, though they affect Spring and Autumn nearly in the same ratio.

5. The Moon's change, first quarter, full and last quarter, happening during six of the afternoon hours, i. e., from 4 to 10, may be followed by fair weather, but this is mostly dependent on the wind, as is noted in the table.

6. Though the weather, from a variety of irregular causes, is more uncertain in the latter part of Autumn, the whole of Winter and the beginning of Spring, yet, in the main, the above observations will apply to those periods also.

7. To prognosticate correctly, especially in those cases where the wind is concerned, the observer should be in sight of a good vane, where the four cardinal points of the heavens are correctly placed.

FARM AND GARDEN.

FARM AND GARDEN WORK FOR JANUARY.—Plant peas, beans, beets, onions, Irish potatoes, horse radish; sow turnips, spinach, lettuce, radish, parsley, carrots, salsify. Plant early peas; artichokes must now be dressed, also asparagus beds; this is the proper time to sow early spring tomatoes, etc.

Prepare land for the next crop, if not done. In the low country, if mud marsh or rushes are used, this is a good time to haul out and spread in the alleys, and throw upon it a slight listing. Repair fences, plow, ditch, drain and manure. You can sow oats for a first crop.

FARM AND GARDEN WORK FOR FEBRUARY.—Continue to sow peas, and such vegetables as were omitted in January. Plant pole beans, first crop (in the low country); full crop Irish potatoes, beets and carrots; dress artichokes and asparagus. Tomatoes, peppers and cucumbers sow in hot beds; put out mangoes.

This is considered the opening month of the planter's year. Continue preparing as in January. Sow oats for a full crop in the low country; plant Irish potatoes; make up sprout beds for sweet potatoes. Plant root crop of sweet potatoes.

FARM AND GARDEN WORK FOR MARCH.—Plant bush squash, pumpkins, water and muskmelons, okra, Guinea squash or egg-plant, sugar beets, carrots, beans, peas, radishes, lettuce, corn, celery (first crop), tanyah and mangoes in the low country and elsewhere as soon as danger from frost is over.

This is the first planting month for cotton, corn and rice. Plant your high lands first; leave the low lands for April. Plant rice about the 20th of the month.

FARM AND GARDEN WORK FOR APRIL.—Whatever has been omitted in March, do not neglect any longer. Sow green glazed cabbage, pickling cabbage, full crop of cauliflower and brocoli, okra, tomatoes, peppers, beets, carrots, leeks, melons, cucumbers, celery.

Full crops of corn, cotton and rice should be put in during this month. Plant your lowland corn. Commence early to hoe your young cotton, and thin out to stand. Plant pumpkins for a field crop.

FARM AND GARDEN WORK FOR MAY.—Plant snap beans and squashes. Sow cabbages for winter use, cauliflower, brocoli, celery, beets, carrots, salsify. Plant cucumbers, melons and pumpkins for late crop. Gather herbs for drying; always dry gently in the shade.

Look well to your hoeings and plowings. Continue to plant corn in low lands. Sow first crop of early cow peas. Rice planting is generally postponed until June, as the birds are very bad in May, and the May bird is exceedingly destructive.

FARM AND GARDEN WORK FOR JUNE.—Sow full crops of cabbages for fall and winter use. Cauliflower and brocoli may yet be sown, also a few carrots. Continue to sow tomatoes, okra, radishes, snap beans. Transplant leeks; pull and dry onions, garlic and eschalots. A few cucumbers and melons plant for a late crop, and a few ruta baga turnips.

Keep constantly at the plow and hoe; this is the most important grass month! If the vines from your sweet potato sprout-bed are fit you can draw and plant out first good rain. Sow cow peas between your corn hills and rows. The end of this month is a good time to put in the first crop of standing field peas.

FARM AND GARDEN WORK FOR JULY.—Sow cabbages, but protect from hot sun when young. Water at night. Plant snap beans and a few Irish potatoes. Continue to sow radishes, lettuce, endive, cresses, mustard and small salading. The early Dutch turnip is the best to sow for the first crop; follow with the yellow Swedish or ruta-baga.

Now do not omit to sow full crops of standing cow peas. Sow a few turnips, carrots and beets as field crops, though the hot suns are apt to destroy them; should they escape they will be fine; the next month is the best for these crops.

1st Month. ***JANUARY, 1894.*** ***31 Days.***

Moon's Phases.

	D.	H.	M.			D.	H.	M.	
New Moon,	6	9	59	p. m.	Full Moon,	21	10	3	a. m.
☽ First Quarter,	14	7	10	p. m.	☾ Last Quarter,	28	11	42	a. m.

Day of Month.	Day of Week.	Sun rises.		Sun sets.		Sun slow.	Sun's decline south.		ASPECTS OF PLANETS AND OTHER MISCELLANEOUS MATTER.	Moon's place.	Moon rises or sets.		Moon south.	
1	Mon	7	10	4	58	4	22	58	NEW YEAR'S DAY.		rises.		morn	
2	Tue	7	10	5	0	5	22	53	♀ in ☊. Gen. Wolf b. 1727.		3	30	8	29
3	We	7	10	5	1	5	22	47	☌ ♂ ☽. Cicero b. B. C. 106.		4	32	9	17
4	Thu	7	10	5	1	5	22	41	Arnold invaded Va. 1781.		5	32	10	6
5	Fri	7	10	5	2	6	22	34	☌ ☿ ☽. Richm'd burnt 1781.		6	29	10	57
6	Sat	7	10	5	3	6	22	27	Epiphany.		sets.		11	49
1.	Epiphany.								Day's length 9 hours 55 minutes.					
7	***G.***	7	9	5	4	7	22	19	Liberia colonized 1822.		5	17	eve	
8	Mon	7	9	5	5	7	22	11	Battle New Orleans 1815.		6	19	1	28
9	Tue	7	9	5	6	8	22	02	Napoleon III died 1873.		7	21	2	15
10	We	7	9	5	6	8	21	53	☌ ♀ ☽. ♀ greatest brilliancy.		8	25	2	59
11	Thu	7	9	5	7	8	21	44	☿ in aphe. Alex. Hamilton b. 1757		9	28	3	41
12	Fri	7	9	5	8	9	21	34	Vicksburg fortified 1861.		10	31	4	23
13	Sat	7	9	5	9	9	21	24	George Fox died 1690.		11	35	5	6
2.	First Sunday after Epiphany								Day's length 10 hour s 1 minute.					
14	***G.***	7	9	5	10	10	21	13	□ ♄ ☉. Com. Maury b. 1806		morn		5	51
15	Mon	7	9	5	11	10	21	2	♃ sta, Jackson b. 1767.		0	43	6	39
16	Tue	7	9	5	12	10	20	51	☌ ♃ ☽. Com. Gibbon d. 1794.		1	55	7	33
17	We	7	8	5	13	11	20	39	Dr. Franklin born 1706.		3	10	8	32
18	Thu	7	8	5	14	11	20	27	☌ ♆ ☽. Bulwer Lytton d. 1873.		4	27	9	36
19	Fri	7	8	5	15	11	20	14	Gen. R. E. Lee born 1807.		5	39	10	44
20	Sat	7	8	5	15	11	20	1	John Howard died 1790.		6	44	11	50
3.	Septuagesima Sunday.								Day's length 10 hours 9 minutes.					
21	***G.***	7	7	5	16	12	19	48	Mayor Holden died 1875.		rises		morn	
22	Mon	7	7	5	17	12	19	34	Henry VIII born 1547.		6	32	0	53
23	Tue	7	6	5	18	12	19	20	♀ sta. Wm. Gaston died 1844.		7	49	1	49
24	We	7	6	5	19	12	19	5	Pres. Johnson impeached 1868.		9	0	2	41
25	Thu	7	5	5	20	13	18	50	♂ in ☋. Fayetteville settled 1749		10	8	3	28
26	Fri	7	4	5	21	13	18	35	Battle of Newbern 1864.		11	13	4	13
27	Sat	7	3	5	22	13	18	20	☌ ♄ ☽. Mozart born 1756.		morn		4	56
4.	Sexagesima Sunday.								Day's length 10 hours 21 minutes.					
28	***G.***	7	2	5	23	13	18	4	☾ ☌ ☿ ☽. Tripple Alli. 1668.		0	18	5	40
29	Mon	7	2	5	23	13	17	48	☌ ☿ ☉ sup. Kansas ad. '61.		1	22	6	25
30	Tue	7	2	5	24	14	17	31	☿ gr. Hel. Lat. Harper d. 1883		2	25	7	12
31	We	7	2	5	25	14	17	15	☌ ♂ ☽ Corn laws abol. 1849.		3	26	8	1

WEATHER CONJECTURES.—JANUARY—1, 2, 3, 4, 5, fair if wind N. or N. E.; rain or snow if S. or S. W.; 6, 7, 8, 9, 10, 11, 12, 13, fair if wind N. or N. E.; rain or snow if S. or S. W.; 14, 15, 16, 17, 18, 19, fair if wind N. or N. E.; rain or snow if S. or S. W.; 20, 21, 22, 23, 24, 25, 26, 27, 28, cold high wind; 29, 30, 31, cold high wind.

FARM AND GARDEN.—Continued.

FARM AND GARDEN WORK FOR AUGUST.—Transplant all kinds of cabbage, cauliflower and celery. Sow carrots and beets, turnips of all kinds, spinach, lettuce, radishes and onions.

Now sow full crops of field turnips, carrots and beets, and such other crops as were omitted last month; strip fodder. Early rice will be fit to cut the last of this month. Look to it. This is a good time to plant vines of the first slips, in order to procure seed potatoes for the next year's crops.

FARM AND GARDEN WORK FOR SEPTEMBER.—Now sow full crops of all kinds—turnips, onions, carrots, beets, cabbages, lettuce, cresses. Look after your mushroom beds. Hoe and thin your turnips.

Continue to sow field turnips, carrots and beets. Southern seed is always better than the imported; those from the latter are apt to run to seed early in the spring, unless it be English seed. Prepare land for sowing rye in October. Pick cotton; harvest corn.

FARM AND GARDEN WORK FOR OCTOBER.—You may make two sowings of cabbage this month, and, if of English seed, they will not " run " in the spring. Sow lettuce; hoe turnips and thin; put out leeks and onions; sow principal crop of spinach; earth up celery.

Continue picking your cotton as it blows. Sow early rye, wheat and barley. Dig your sweet potatoes when the weather becomes cool and you expect frost.

FARM AND GARDEN WORK FOR NOVEMBER.—Sow your first crop of peas and a few turnips. Plant out onions raised from seed in August and September. Plant Windsor and long-pod beans. Dress asparagus and artichokes.

Sow full crops of rye, barley, wheat and other small grain. Harvest your sweet potatoes.

FARM AND GARDEN WORK FOR DECEMBER.—Plant peas of all kinds; set out onions, garlic, eschalots and cabbage. Sow a few lettuce, spinach, carrots and radishes. You may try a few Irish potatoes.

Finish picking cotton; get out crops of rice, and prepare for market. Commence plowing, ditching, draining and manuring as early as possible for next year's crop.

ANECDOTE OF DR. CLOSS.

When quite a young man he was sent by Conference to preach to the plain, illiterate fishermen on our coast south of Cape Hatteras. At one of his earliest appointments he was accosted by a rude, rough sailor, who requested that he would preach his father's funeral.

"Is your father dead?" asked Mr. Closs.

"Oh, yes, he's been dead more'n a year, but nobody han't preached his funeral."

"Well," said Mr. Closs," "I'll give notice to-day that at my next appointment one month hence I'll preach Billy Wilkins' funeral."

Notice was accordingly given, and at the next "meeting" a large crowd greeted the young preacher. He ascended the pulpit, a sort of story-and-a-half affair, securely boxed in to prevent the escape of any preacher who might enter it ere the benediction was pronounced, and after giving out his hymn and praying, and just as he was about to announce his text, he felt a nervous jerking at his coat tail. Somewhat surprised at the unusual occurrence, he looked around and down at the figure of a man who was thus attracting his attention, and beheld Jim Wilkins, the son of the deceased, in a stooping position behind the pulpit, with one hand on the skirts of the preacher's coat and the other wound away around towards his hip-pocket, and as Mr. Closs stooped to catch the message, Jim, in a hoarse whisper, said:

"Parson, you know this is dad's funeral, and I want you to do your level best." And producing a "tickler" of what might have been whisky, said, "wont you take a drap to help you on in the good work?"

It is said on the authority of Mr. Closs that he declined and proceeded with the funeral discourse. JOHN B. NEATHERY.

2d Month.   FEBRUARY, 1894.   28 Days.

Moon's Phases.

	D. H. M.		D. H M.
New Moon,	5 4 36 p m.	Full Moon,	19 9 8 p. m.
First Quarter,	13 5 34 a. m.	Last Quarter, 27 7 20 a. m.

Day of Month.	Day of Week.	Sun rises.	Sun sets.	Sun slow.	Sun's decline south.	ASPECTS OF PLANETS AND OTHER MISCELLANEOUS MATTER.	Moon's place.	Moon rises or sets.	Moon south.
1	Thu	7 1	5 27	14 16	37	Peace Conference 1865,	♐	4 23	morn
2	Fri	7 1	5 28	14 16	40	♄ sta. Prof. Dana born 1814.	♐	5 16	9 43
3	Sat	7 0	5 29	14 16	22	☐ ☿ ☉. At.on Ft.Donaldson '63.	♑	6 3	10 34

5. Shrove Sunday.   Day's length 10 hours 31 minutes.

4	*G.*	6 59	5 30	14 16	4	♀ in Peri. Guiteau sent'c'd 1882	♑	6 42	11 24
5	Mon	6 58	5 31	14 15	46	☾ ♂ ☿ ☽. Carlyle d. 1881.	♒	sets.	eve.
6	Tue	6 58	5 32	14 15	28	SHROVE TUESDAY.	♒	6 18	0 57
7	We	6 57	5 33	14 15	9	ASH WEDNESDAY—LENT.	♒	7 21	1 40
8	Thu	6 56	5 34	14 14	50	♂ ☿ ♀. Fall of Roanoke Isl. '62	♓	8 25	2 23
9	Fri	6 55	5 35	14 14	31	Gen. Hancock died 1886.	♓	9 29	3 5
10	Sat	6 54	5 36	14 14	11	☐ ♃ ☉. Treaty of Paris 1763.	♓	10 36	3 49

6. First Sunday in Lent.   Day's length 10 hours 44 minutes.

11	*G.*	6 53	5 37	14 13	51	Charleston evacuated 1865.	♈	11 44	4 36
12	Mon	6 53	5 38	14 13	31	☽ ♂ ♃ ☽. Seymour d. 1886.	♈	morn	5 26
13	Tue	6 52	5 39	14 13	11	♂ ♅ ☽. Fer. Wood d. 1881	♈	0 55	6 21
14	We	6 51	5 40	14 12	51	Gibbon died 1794.	♈	2 9	7 22
15	Thu	6 50	5 41	14 12	30	☌ ♀ ☉ inf. Durham fire 1881.	♉	3 21	8 26
16	Fri	6 49	5 42	14 12	9	Judge Battle buried 1879.	♉	4 28	9 31
17	Sat	6 48	5 43	14 12	9	☿ sta. Peace with England 1815	♊	5 26	10 34

7. Second Sunday in Lent.   Day's length 10 hours 57 minutes.

18	*G.*	6 47	5 44	14 11	48	☽ ☿ in ♌. Luther b. 1546.	♊	6 11	11 32
19	Mon	6 46	5 45	14 11	27	♅ sta. A.W.Venable d. '76	♋	rises	morn
20	Tue	6 45	5 46	14 10	41	Battle of Olista, Fla., 1864.	♋	6 35	0 26
21	We	6 43	5 47	14 10	23	☿ greatest brilliancy.	♌	7 45	1 15
22	Thu	6 42	5 48	14 10	1	WASHINGTON born 1832.	♌	8 54	2 2
23	Fri	6 41	5 48	14 9	39	☌ ♄ ☽. ☿ in Peri. Rom. 3:10–23	♍	10 1	2 47
24	Sat	6 40	5 48	13 9	17	☌ ☿ ☽. Guttenburg d. 1468.	♎	11 7	3 32

8. Third Sunday in Lent.   Day's length 11 hours 10 minutes.

25	*G.*	6 39	5 49	13 8	54	☾ ☿ gr. Elon. E.	♎	morn	4 18
26	Mon	6 38	5 50	13 8	32	☌ ♀ B. ♀ gr. Hel. L. N.	♏	0 12	5 5
27	Tue	6 37	5 51	13 8	9	Longfellow born 1807.	♏	1 14	5 54
28	We	6 36	5 52	13 7	47	☐ ♅ ☉. Dr. Wingate d. 1879.	♐	2 14	6 42

WEATHER CONJECTURES.—FEBRUARY—1, 2, 3, 4. cold high wind; 5, 6, 7, 8, 9, 10, 11, 12, rain; 13, 14, 15, 16, 17, 18, expect rain; 19, 20, 21, 22, 23, 24, 25, 26, fair if wind N. or N. E.; rain or snow if S. or S. W.; 27, 28, stormy.

BRANSON MAXIMS.

1. All men have faith in something, hence they work expecting results.—*Branson*.

2. Some men have faith in the laws governing mind; obeying those laws they attain to mental power.—*Branson*.

3. Some men have faith in the laws of health, and hence by obeying those laws they secure physical health and happiness.—*Branson*.

4. The man who has faith in the laws governing the spirit life, can realize that "the law of the Lord is perfect, converting the soul."—*Branson*.

5. The Christian religion leads a man towards the highest cultivation of all his best capabilities.—*Branson*.

6. The man who has *full faith* in *all* God's laws, and renders a perfect obedience, has peace flowing as a river, and a joy that is complete.—*Branson*.

7. To give advice unsolicited is so delightful; it magnifies our self-esteem. To receive advice unsolicited is humiliating; it minifies our self-esteem.—*Branson*.

8. A man in whose mind his own country is not *first*, is a man who himself is not *worthy* to be first in another country.—*Branson*.

9. Our State is a diamond; let us polish it well.—*Branson*.

10. The *mind crop* is the greatest crop that can be raised on any farm or in any State.—*Branson*.

11. The *mind crop* in North Carolina is better than ever before.—*Branson*.

12. The *mind crop* should be planted early and cultivated better than cotton or tobacco.—*Branson*.

13. The stronger the *homes*, the stronger the *country* in which the homes are found.—*Branson*.

14. The greatest possibilities of a man are on his native heath; if he is great on another heath, he is still less than a native ought to have been.—*Branson*.

15. It is strange how freely we *give away* our *own* knowledge, and how freely we *pay high prices* for the knowledge we obtain from others.—*Branson*.

16. Living in obedience to spiritual *laws* brings spiritual *blessings*.—*Branson*.

17. *Do* your duty, then *wait*.—*Branson*.

18. Work for your *country*, and God will work for *you*.—*Branson*.

19. Much of our best work is unsuspected by *ourselves*, and even by the *recipients*.—*Branson*.

20. Individual comfort, State wealth, make a happy people.—*Branson*.

21. Never keep people unnecessarily waiting.—*Mrs Branson*.

22. Be happy; life is short.—*Branson*.

23. To *sleep sweetly*, recline a few moments on your *left* side; then turn *slowly* onto your right side. Try it.—*Branson*.

24. Live with happy people, and you are likely *to be* happy.—*Branson*.

25. Do not keep a *burr* in your *throat*, nor a bit of *malice* in your *heart*.—*Branson*.

26. If you are *good* this world is *good enough* for you; if you are *mean*, then it is *too good* for you.—*Branson*.

TWENTY-FOUR CITIES AND TOWNS OF NORTH CAROLINA WITH POPULATIONS OF OVER 1,500.

Wilmington, city	20,056	Washington, town	3,545
Raleigh, city	12,678	Greensboro, city	3,317
Charlotte, city	11,557	Elizabeth City, town	3,251
Asheville, city	10,235	Reidsville, town	2,969
Winston, city	8,018	Oxford, town	2,907
New Berne, city	7,843	Salem, city	2,711
Durham, city	5,485	Statesville, city	2,318
Salisbury, city	4,418	Edenton, town	2,205
Concord, city	4,339	Wilson, town	2,126
Fayetteville, town	4,222	Hickory, town	2,223
Henderson, town	4,191	Beaufort, town	2,007
Goldsboro, city	4,017	Morehead City	1,623

3d Month. **MARCH, 1894.** *31 Days.*

Moon's Phases.

	D.	H.	M.		D.	H.	M.
New Moon,	7	9	10 a. m.	Full Moon,	21	9	2 a. m.
First Quarter,	14	1	19 p. m.	Last Quarter,	29	3	19 a. m.

Day of Month.	Day of Week.	Sun rises.	Sun sets.	Sun slow.	Sun's decline south.	ASPECTS OF PLANETS AND OTHER MISCELLANEOUS MATTER.	Moon's place.	Moon rises or sets.	Moon south.
1	Thu	6 34	5 55	12	7 24	☌ ♂ ☽. Czar Nicholas d. 1858.	[illegible]	3 9	morn
2	Fri	6 32	5 56	12	7 1	Bishop Andrews d. 1871.	[illegible]	3 58	8 27
3	Sat	6 30	5 57	12	6 38	☿ stationary.	[illegible]	4 41	9 18
9.	Fourth Sunday in Lent.					Day's length 11 hours 30 minutes.			
4	*G.*	6 28	5 58	12	6 15	☌ ♀ ☽. INAUGURATION DAY.	[illegible]	5 16	10 6
5	Mon	6 26	6 0	12	5 52	☿ gr. Hel. Lat. N. John 3: 18.	[illegible]	5 45	10 52
6	Tue	6 24	6 0	11	5 28	Massacre Alamo 1836.	[illegible]	6 12	11 37
7	We	6 23	6 1	11	5 5	♀ sta. Bible Soc. f'rmd 1804	[illegible]	sets	eve
8	Thu	6 22	6 1	11	4 42	First U. S. Cong. 1787.	[illegible]	7 26	1 3
9	Fri	6 20	6 2	11	4 18	Merrimack sunk Cumberland '62	[illegible]	8 26	1 47
10	Sat	6 18	6 3	10	3 55	Dr. Bennet Perry d. 1882.	[illegible]	9 35	2 33
10.	Fifth Sunday in Lent.					Day's length 11 hours 47 minutes.			
11	*G.*	6 17	6 4	10	3 31	Benj. West died 1820.	[illegible]	10 47	3 23
12	Mon	6 16	6 5	10	3 7	☌ ♃ ☽. Mrs. Mordecai d. 1886.	[illegible]	morn	4 17
13	Tue	6 14	6 6	9	2 44	Mrs. C. W. D. Hutchings d. 1873	[illegible]	0 1	5 15
14	We	6 13	6 6	9	2 20	☌ ☿ ☉ inferior. Acts 16:31.	[illegible]	1 13	6 17
15	Thu	6 12	6 7	9	1 56	Cæsar assass. B. C. 44.	[illegible]	2 20	7 20
16	Fri	6 11	6 8	9	1 33	Battle of Averasboro 1865.	[illegible]	3 19	8 22
17	Sat	6 9	6 9	8	1 9	ST. PATRICK'S DAY.	[illegible]	4 7	9 20
11.	Palm Sunday.					Day's length 12 hours 2 minutes.			
18	*G.*	6 8	6 10	8	0 45	Suez Canal completed 1869.	[illegible]	4 45	10 14
19	Mon	6 6	6 11	8	0 22	O'Kelly born 1741.	[illegible]	5 17	11 4
20	Tue	6 4	6 12	7	north	☉ ent. ♈. SPRING COM.	[illegible]	5 43	11 52
21	We	6 3	6 12	7	0 26	Moon partly ecl. invisible.	[illegible]	rises	morn
22	Thu	6 2	6 13	7	0 49	♀ gr. bril. Stamp Act 1765.	[illegible]	7 42	0 37
23	Fri	6 0	6 14	6	1 13	☌ ♄ ☽. GOOD FRIDAY.	[illegible]	8 47	1 22
24	Sat	5 59	6 15	6	1 37	☌ ♅ ☽. Queen Elizabeth d. 1603	[illegible]	9 54	2 8
12.	Annunciation—Easter Sunday.					Day's length 12 hours 18 minutes.			
25	*G.*	5 58	6 16	6	2 0	EASTER SUNDAY.	[illegible]	11 0	2 55
26	Mon	5 57	6 17	6	2 24	☿ sta. EASTER MONDAY.	[illegible]	morn	3 44
27	Tue	5 55	6 18	5	2 47	Lord Bacon born 1627.	[illegible]	0 3	1 35
28	We	5 53	6 18	5	3 11	Dr. J. T. Leach died 1883.	[illegible]	1 1	5 27
29	Thu	5 51	6 19	5	3 34	☿ in ☊. Brit. Mus. f'nd 1753	[illegible]	1 52	6 19
20	Fri	5 50	6 20	4	3 57	☌ ♂ ☽. Bat. Somerville, Ky., '63	[illegible]	2 37	7 9
31	Sat	5 48	6 21	4	4 21	Mrs. Mary Bayard Clark d. 1886.	[illegible]	3 15	7 58

WEATHER CONJECTURES.—MARCH—1, 2, 3, 4, 5, 6, stormy; 7, 8, 9, 10, 11, 12 13, cold rain if wind be from West; snow if East; 14, 15, 16, 17, 18, 19, 20, look for rain and snow; 21, 22, 23, 24, 25, 26, 27, 28, cold rain if wind be West; snow if East; 29, 30, 31, snow and stormy.

"JESUS, LOVER OF MY SOUL."

"Jesus, lover of my soul,"
  Rose the words, sweet and clear,
From the lips of a little child,
  Drifting fast to the other world.

"Let me to thy bosom fly,"
  She repeated, o'er and o'er,
While her sweet brown eyes beheld
  Visions on the other shore.

"While the nearer waters roll,"
  And her voice was fainter still,
But her echo rang more clear
  Far beyond the heavenly hills.

"While the tempest still is high,"
  When the angels took her home,
And Jesus bade her sing the rest
  As she stood before the throne.

"Hide me, O my Saviour, hide,"
  Thus we sang while bending low
O'er the empty casket left
  For its precious gem had flown.

"Till the storm of life is past,"
  Came these words from trembling lips
As the sweet, white lids were closed
  Over eyes with love once lit.

"Safe into the haven guide,"
  We sang the hymn soft and low,
While we laid our darling's form
  Far beneath the drifting snow.

"O receive my soul at last,"
  Swelled this plea from aching hearts
As we turned in blinding tears
  From that low and sacred spot.

But the Saviour heard our cry
  Ere we reached our darkened home,
And he gave us strength to say,
  "Thy will, O Lord, not mine be done."

And as we sat that night alone,
  And thought of her safe in the fold,
We sang her hymn with happy hearts,
  "Jesus, lover of my soul."

October 5, 1893.   L. H.

"I HAVE LIVED," says the indefatigable Dr. Clarke, "to know that the great secret of human happiness is this—never to suffer your energies to stagnate. The old adage of 'too many irons in the fire' conveys an abominable falsehood; you cannot have too many. Poker, tongs, and all—keep them all going."

☞ Shoes for Men, Boys, Ladies and Children, cheap at WHITING BROS.

4th Month. **APRIL, 1894.** *30 Days.*

Moon's Phases.

	D.	H.	M.			D.	H.	M.	
New Moon,	5	10	51	p. m.	Full Moon,	19	9	54	p.m.
First Quarter,	12	7	24	p. m.	Last Quarter,	27	10	12	p.m.

Day of Month.	Day of Week.	Sun rises.	Sun sets.	Sun slow.	Sun's decline north.	ASPECTS OF PLANETS AND OTHER MISCELLANEOUS MATTER.	Moon's place.	Moon rises or sets.	Moon south.
13.	Low Sunday.					Day's length 12 hours 35 minutes.			
1	*G.*	5 47	6 22	3	4 44	☌ ♀ ☽. ALL FOOLS DAY.	[illegible]	3.46	morn
2	Mon	5 46	6 23	3	5 7	Richmond surrendered 1865.	[illegible]	4 14	9 30
3	Tue	5 44	6 23	3	5 30	☌ ☿ ☽. Richmond evacuated '65	[illegible]	4 37	10 14
4	We	5 42	6 24	3	5 53	☌ ♀ with [illegible].	[illegible]	5 0	10 57
5	Thu	5 41	6 25	3	6 15	☉ ecl. invis. at Washington.	[illegible]	5 23	11 41
6	Fri	5 39	6 26	2	6 38	Battle of Shiloh 1862.	[illegible]	sets	eve
7	Sat	5 38	6 27	2	7 1	Island No. 17 surrendered 1862.	[illegible]	8 33	1 17
14.	Second Sunday after Easter.					Day's length 12 hours 52 minutes.			
8	*G.*	5 36	6 28	2	7 23	☿ in Aphe. 7th Crusade 747.	[illegible]	9 49	2 10
9	Mon	5 35	6 29	1	7 45	☌ ♃ ☽. Gen. Lee sur. Ap. C. H. '65	[illegible]	11 3	3 8
10	Tue	5 34	6 30	1	8 8	☿ gr. Elon. W. Benton d. 1858.	[illegible]	morn	4 10
11	We	5 33	6 31	1	8 30	☍ ♄ ☉. Ft. Pulaski sur. '62.	[illegible]	0 13	5 14
12	Thu	5 31	6 31	fast	8 52	Fort Sumter attacked 1861.	[illegible]	1 14	6 16
13	Fri	5 30	6 32		9 13	Raleigh sur. to Gen. Sherman '65	[illegible]	2 5	7 15
14	Sat	5 28	6 33	0	9 35	Pres. Lincoln assassinated 1865.	[illegible]	2 46	8 9
15.	Third Sunday after Easter.					Day's length 13 hours 7 minutes.			
15	*G.*	5 27	6 34	0	9 56	Andrew Johnson inaugurated '65	[illegible]	3 20	8 59
16	Mon	5 25	6 34	0	10 18	French evacuated Mexico 1867.	[illegible]	3 48	9 46
17	Tue	5 24	6 35	1	10 39	Dr. Ben. Franklin died 1790.	[illegible]	4 11	10 31
18	We	5 23	6 36	1	10 50	☌ ♄ ☽. Bat. Cerro Gordo '47	[illegible]	4 13	11 15
19	Thu	5 22	6 37	1	11 20	D'Israeli died 1881.	[illegible]	4 57	morn
20	Fri	5 21	6 38	1	11 41	☌ ♅ ☽. 1st newspaper U.S. 1704	[illegible]	rises	0 1
21	Sat	5 20	6 39	1	12 1	Norfolk Navy Yard cap. 1861	[illegible]	8 43	0 47
16.	Fourth Sunday after Easter.					Day's length 13 hours 22 minutes.			
22	*G.*	5 18	6 40	2	12 22	R. C. Badger died 1882.	[illegible]	9 49	1 35
23	Mon	5 17	6 41	2	12 42	♀ in ☊. S. A. Douglas b. 1831.	[illegible]	10 48	2 26
24	Tue	5 15	6 41	2	13 1	Dr. McKee died 1875.	[illegible]	11 43	3 17
25	We	5 14	6 42	2	13 21	Bank of England incor. 1694.	[illegible]	morn	4 10
26	Thu	5 13	6 43	2	13 40	♀ gr. Elon. W. Mark 6: 12	[illegible]	0 31	5 1
27	Fri	5 12	6 43	3	13 59	C. C. Barbee died 1876.	[illegible]	1 12	5 50
28	Sat	5 11	6 44	3	14 18	☌ ♂ ☽. Gen. Wolf killed 1759.	[illegible]	1 45	6 38
17.	Rogation Sunday.					Day's length 13 hours 35 minutes.			
29	*G.*	5 10	6 45	3	14 37	☿ gr. Hel. Lat. S. John 14:1-3	[illegible]	2 14	7 23
30	Mon	5 9	6 46	3	14 55	Louisiana ceded 1803.	[illegible]	2 39	8 6

WEATHER CONJECTURES.—APRIL—1, 2, 3, 4, look for snow-storm; 5, 6, 7, 8, 9, 10, 11, fair and frosty; 12, 13, 14, 15, 16, 17, 18, frost if wind N. or N. E.; rain or snow if S. or S. W.; 19, 20, 21, 22, 23, 24, 25, 26, frost if wind N. or N. E.; rain or snow if S. or S. W.; 27, 28, 29, 30, fair and frosty.

ANECDOTE OF DR. CLOSS.

At another time he was on the Granville Circuit, and near one of his churches resided a sister Jones. Her house was the home of all Methodist ministers, and though she was not wealthy they were ever welcome. She had a room adjoining the sitting-room which was known as the "preacher's room," and as it was secluded from the rest of the house, and the good sister was lacking in pantry accommodation, she stowed under the bed therein her goodly store of pickles and preserves. She had a mischievous boy of thirteen years who had a sweet tooth and who sometimes made raids on his mother's sweetmeats. She accordingly kept an eye on John and on her hoarded treasures for company occasions.

It so happened that Bro. Closs stopped at the close of a summer day at sister Jones' house. It was about dusk, and so he left his horse to be taken to the stable, and went in without knocking. Whoever heard of anyone knocking at a country house in those days? He entered the sitting-room and went at once to the preacher's room, and, North Carolina like, left the door open behind him.

He removed his coat and bathed, and then bethought to spend a few moments in prayer. He knelt most reverently by the bedside and poured out his soul in thanksgiving and prayer, when just then sister Jones entered the sitting-room and seeing the door to the "preacher's room" ajar, she naturally suspected her son John guilty of his usual misdemeanor, and tipping in with cat-like tread, she saw in the dim and uncertain light of the room the form of Bro. Closs by the bedside, and so raising aloft her strong right hand she let fall the palm thereof on the bald head of her pastor, exclaiming in a high key:

"Oh, you rascal, I've caught you again—stealing my preserves."

Bro. Closs arose from his devotions—solemnly assured her that he was not "John," and that he was not even thinking of stealing her preserves, and was forgiven.

Bless the memory of that blessed man, and when we have done with earth and earthly things may we meet him in the home of the blessed.

Yours,   JOHN B. NEATHERY.

BEAUTIFUL LIVES.

Beautiful lips are those whose words
Leap from the heart like songs of birds,
Yet whose utterances prudence girds.

Beautiful hands are those that do
Work that is earnest and brave and true,
Moment by moment the long day through.

Beautiful feet are those that go
On kindly ministries to and fro,
Down lowliest ways if God wills it so.

Beautiful shoulders are those that bear
Ceaseless burdens of homely care,
With patient grace and daily prayer.

Beautiful lives are those that bless,
Silent rivers of happiness,
Whose hidden fountains but few may guess.

I AM NOW an old man. I have seen nearly a century. Do you want to know how to grow old slowly and happily? Always eat slowly; masticate well. Go to your food, to your rest, to your occupations, smiling. Keep a good nature, and a soft temper everywhere. Never give way to anger. A violent tempest of passion tears down the constitution more than a typhus fever.—*Waldo, in "Looking Toward Sunset."*

5th Month. ***MAY, 1894.*** ***31 Days.***

Moon's Phases.

	D.	H.	M.			D.	H.	M.	
New Moon,	5	9	33	a. m.	Full Moon,	19	11	34	a. m.
First Quarter,	12	1	12	a. m.	Last Quarter,	27	2	56	p. m.

Day of Month.	Day of Week.	Sun rises.	Sun sets.	Sun fast.	Sun's decline north.	ASPECTS OF PLANETS AND OTHER MISCELLANEOUS MATTER.	Moon's place.	Moon rises or sets.	Moon south.
1	Tue	5 8	6 47	3	15 13	☌ ♀ ☽. Apian Way const. 312 B.C	♓	3 2	morn
2	We	5 7	6 48	3	15 31	Samuel H. Young died 1882.	♓	3 25	9 32
3	Thu	5 6	6 49	3	15 49	♂ ☌ ☉. ASCENSION DAY.	♓	3 47	10 18
4	Fri	5 5	6 49	3	16 6	☌ ☿ ☽. Dr. Wm. G. Hill d. '77	♈	4 12	11 6
5	Sat	5 4	6 50	3	16 24	Bonaparte died 1821.	♈	sets	11 58
18.	Sixth Sunday after Easter.					Day's length 13 hours 48 minutes.			
6	***G.***	5 3	6 51	4	16 40	☌ ♃ ☽. Dr. Somers d. 1882.	♉	8 44	eve
7	Mon	5 2	6 51	4	16 57	♂ ♆ ☽. M. C. Doub d. 1876.	♉	10 0	1 59
8	Tue	5 1	6 52	4	17 13	Battle of Palo Alto 1846.	♊	11 7	3 4
9	We	5 0	6 53	4	17 29	Battle Spottsylvania C. H. 1864.	♊	morn	4 9
10	Thu	4 59	6 54	4	17 45	CONFEDERATE MEMORIAL DAY.	♋	0 3	5 10
11	Fri	4 58	6 54	4	18 0	Queen Mary died 1694.	♋	0 47	6 6
12	Sat	4 57	6 55	4	18 16	Battle of Raymond 1863.	♌	1 22	6 57
19.	Whit Sunday—Pentecost.					Day's length 14 hours 0 minutes.			
13	***G.***	4 56	6 56	4	18 31	Battle Brazos, Texas, 1865.	♌	1 51	7 44
14	Mon	4 55	6 57	4	18 45	Battle Resaca, Ga., 1864.	♍	2 15	8 29
15	Tue	4 54	6 58	4	18 59	☌ ♄ ☽. Dan'l O'Connell d. 1847	♍	2 38	9 13
16	We	4 53	6 59	4	19 13	Battle Champion's Hill 1863.	♍	3 1	9 57
17	Thu	4 53	7 0	4	19 26	☌ ♅ ☽. John Penn born 1741.	♎	3 25	10 42
18	Fri	4 52	7 1	4	19 40	☿ in ♌. Matamoras tak. '46	♎	3 50	11 29
19	Sat	4 52	7 1	4	19 52	☌ ☿ ☉ sup. Prov. 11: 2.	♏	rises	morn
20.	Trinity Sunday.					Day's length 14 hours 11 minutes.			
20	***G.***	4 51	7 2	4	20 5	Mecklenburg Independ. 1775.	♏	8 38	0 18
21	Mon	4 50	7 3	4	20 17	Columbus died 1506.	♐	9 36	1 10
22	Tue	4 49	7 3	4	20 29	☿ in peri. Buchanan b. 1791.	♐	10 26	2 2
23	We	4 48	7 4	4	20 40	☿ gr. bril. Livingston d. 1886.	♐	11 9	2 54
24	Thu	4 48	7 5	3	20 52	CORPUS CHRISTI.	♑	11 45	3 44
25	Fri	4 48	7 5	3	21 2	♂ ♃ ☿. Col. Tucker died 1882.	♑	morn	4 32
26	Sat	4 47	7 6	3	21 13	☌ ☿ ♆. John Calvin died 1564.	♒	0 14	5 17
21.	First Sunday after Trinity.					Day's length 14 hours 20 minutes.			
27	***G.***	4 47	7 7	3	21 23	☌ ♂ ☽. St. Petersb'g fn'd 1703	♒	0 40	6 0
28	Mon	4 46	7 8	3	21 33	♀ in aph. N. Webster d. '43	♓	1 4	6 43
29	Tue	4 46	7 9	3	21 42	Gen. Winfield Scott d. 1866.	♓	1 25	7 25
30	We	4 45	7 10	3	21 51	FEDERAL DECORATION DAY.	♓	1 47	8 8
31	Thu	4 45	7 11	3	21 59	♂ ♀ ☽. Johnstown disaster 1889	♈	2 11	8 53

WEATHER CONJECTURES.—MAY—1, 2, 3, 4, frosty; 5, 6, 7, 8, 9, 10, 11, changeable; 12, 13, 14, 15, 16, 17, 18, very rainy; 19, 20, 21, 22, 23, 24, 25, 26, frequent showers; 27, 28, 29, 30, 31, changeable.

THE LAW OF CHASTITY.

We are not surprised to learn that Hon. W. C. P. Breckinridge will have opposition when he again offers for Congress. Mr. Breckinridge has been sued for breach of promise, and we do not pretend to say that Miss Pollard has a case against him. We do not know and we do not intimate that he made the young woman a promise of marriage. But the public believes that Mr. Breckinridge has sinned against the social law—the law of chastity—and he must clear his skirts of this charge before he can hope to regain the confidence of the people.

There was a time when the public winked at immorality of this kind among men, and there are those who still do so. But the time has now come when the better class of the American people demand that public men shall be clean in their inner life, and they will not tolerate in office men who are impure and unchaste.

There is but one code of morals and it applies with equal force to both sexes. Chastity in man or woman is the immediate jewel of the soul and it is as binding upon one as upon the other. We long to see the day, and we believe that we shall see it, when society will as surely frown upon the unchaste man as it now frowns upon the unchaste woman, when no guilty man may obtrude his offensive presence into the society of pure woman.—*Richmond State.*

SUICIDE NOT HEROIC.

Suicide, as an escape from the earthly consequences of one's own misdeeds, is much affected nowadays, and it must be confessed that if escape is all that is desired no surer expedient could be adopted. But if one cares for character or name, it is the least worthy of all expedients.

When a man loses his fortune which he has hardly earned, necessity compels him to go to work to earn another, or at least he tries to keep himself out of the poor-house. But when he loses his character, which is worth more than fortune, he has a more imperative motive for re-earning what he foolishly parted from. True it is easier to build up a shattered fortune than regain a good name, but the greater prize is worth the greater effort.

Besides, to quit life at such a time is to repudiate every obligation imposed by natural affection to parents, wife and children, who have the right to demand that no taint be put upon them. The individual himself may escape by suicide. But the children he has brought into the world cannot. He simply handicaps them in the struggle for existence and slips away, leaving them a heritage of shame. To live down wrong-doing and right one's self after having wandered so far out of the one true way is hard to do, but the manly man will not hesitate to live and undertake the task.—*St. Louis Post-Dispatch.*

A DRUNKARD'S WILL.

I leave to society a ruined character, a wretched example, and a memory that will soon rot.

I leave to my parents the rest of their lives, as much sorrow as humanity, in a feeble and decrepid state, can sustain.

I leave my brothers and sisters as much mortification and injury as I well could bring upon them.

I leave to my wife a broken heart, a life of wretchedness and shame, to weep over my premature death.

I give and bequeath to each of my children poverty, ignorance, low character and a remembrance that their father was a monster.

DRESSING PRETTY NECKS.

It is frequently noticeable that the slender woman covers her neck with illusion when wearing a low-cut dress, but even a beautiful neck is often more lovely if fitted over with a seamless yoke of transparent or semi-transparent material. A tiny edge of ruffle may finish the yoke at the neck, or it may be drawn full with a dainty, narrow ribbon, or, again, it may simply disappear under a necklace.—*St. Louis Star Sayings.*

6th Month. **JUNE, 1894.** *30 Days.*

Moon's Phases.

	D.	H.	M.			D.	H.	M.
New Moon,	3	5	48 p. m.		Full Moon,	18	1	58 a.m.
First Quarter,	10	8	5 a. m.		Last Quarter,	26	4	54 a.m.

Day of Month.	Day of Week.	Sun rises.	Sun sets.	Sun fast.	Sun's decline north.	ASPECTS OF PLANETS AND OTHER MISCELLANEOUS MATTER.	Moon's place.	Moon rises or sets.	Moon south.
1	Fri	4 44	7 11	2	22 8	☌ ♃ ♆. Prov. 10:17.		2 38	morn
2	Sat	4 44	7 11	2	22 15	☿ gr. Hel. Lat. N. Prov. 5:21.		3 11	10 39
22.	Second Sunday after Trinity.					Day's length 14 hours 28 minutes.			
3	*G.*	4 44	7 12	2	22 23	☌ ♆ ☉. ♃ ☽. ♃ ☉.		3 51	11 40
4	Mon	4 43	7 12	2	22 30	☌ ☿ ☽. A. L. Woodall k. '86.		sets	eve
5	Tue	4 42	7 13	2	22 36	DeSoto died 1542.		9 53	1 53
6	We	4 41	7 13	2	23 43	Patrick Henry died 1779.		10 42	2 58
7	Thu	4 41	7 14	1	22 48	Robert Bruce died 1329.		11 21	3 58
8	Fri	4 41	7 14	1	22 54	Battle Cross Keys 1862,		11 53	4 52
9	Sat	4 41	7 15	1	22 59	Georgia chartered 1732.		morn	5 42
23.	Third Sunday after Trinity.					Day's length 14 hours 34 minutes.			
10	*G.*	4 41	7 15	1	23 4	Dutch landed in N. Y. 1620.		0 19	6 28
11	Mon	4 41	7 16	1	23 8	Salem witchcraft 1692.		0 43	7 12
12	Tue	4 41	7 16	0	23 12	☌ ♄ ☽ Tr. Ch. Durham dedic. '81		1 5	7 56
13	We	4 41	7 16	slow	23 15	☌ ♅ ☽. Maryland chart. 1633.		1 28	8 40
14	Thu	4 41	7 16		23 18	1st persecution by Nero 64.		1 54	9 26
15	Fri	4 41	7 17	1	23 21	Magna charta 1215.		2 22	10 14
16	Sat	4 41	7 18	1	23 23	□ ♂ ☉. Luther excom. 1520.		2 55	11 4
24.	Fourth Sunday after Trinity.					Day's length 14 hours 37 minutes.			
17	*G.*	4 41	7 18	1	23 24	Bat. Boonville, Mo., 1861.		3 34	11 56
18	Mon	4 41	7 19	1	23 26	Battle Waterloo 1815.		rises	morn
19	Tue	4 42	7 19	1	23 27	Alabama sunk 1864.		9 6	0 48
20	We	4 43	7 19	1	23 27	♀ gr. Hel. Lat. S. Rev. 22:17.		9 44	1 39
21	Thu	4 43	7 19	2	23 27	☉ enters ♋. SUMMER COM.		10 15	2 28
22	Fri	4 43	7 19	2	23 27	♃ sta. Bat. Weldon R. R. 1864		10 43	3 14
23	Sat	4 43	7 19	2	23 26	☿ gr. Elon. E. Prov. 11:12.		11 7	3 57
25.	St. John Baptist.					Day's length 14 hours 36 minutes.			
24	*G.*	4 43	7 19	2	23 25	ST. JOHN'S DAY.		11 29	4 39
25	Mon	4 43	7 19	2	23 24	☿ in ♉. Gen. Morgan k. '63.		11 49	5 20
26	Tue	4 44	7 20	3	23 22	Thos. Bashford d. 1881.		morn	6 2
27	We	4 44	7 20	3	23 19	Jeff. Lovejoy died 1877.		0 12	6 45
28	Thu	4 44	7 20	3	23 16	Vicksburg bombarded 1861.		0 37	7 31
29	Fri	4 45	7 20	4	23 14	☌ ♀ ☽. Henry died 1852.		1 5	8 25
30	Sat	4 45	7 20	4	23 10	☌ ♆ ☽. Joe Smith killed 1844.		1 41	9 20

WEATHER CONJECTURES.—JUNE—1, 2: changeable; 3. 4. 5. 6. 7. 8. 9. expect fair weather, 10, 11, 12, 13. 14. 15. 16, 17. changeable; 18, 19, 20, 21, 22, 23. 24. 25. fair weather; 26. 27, 28, 29. 30, cold with frequent showers.

GOVERNMENT OF NORTH CAROLINA—1893-'97.

EXECUTIVE DEPARTMENT.

Elias Carr, of Edgecombe County, Governor; salary $3,000 and furnished house, fuel and lights.

R. A. Doughton, of Alleghany County, Lieut. Gov. and Speaker of the Senate.

Octavius Coke, of Wake County, Secretary of State; salary $2,000 and fees; $1,000 additional for clerical assistance.

Robert M. Furman, of Buncombe County, Auditor; salary $1,500; $1,000 additional for clerical assistance.

Samuel McD. Tate, of Burke County, Treasurer, salary $3,000.

John C. Scarborough, of Johnston County, Superintendent of Public Instruction; salary $1,500; $500 per annum additional traveling expenses.

Frank I. Osborne, of Mecklenburg County, Attorney General; salary $1,000; Reporter to Supreme Court; salary $1,000.

Francis H. Cameron, of Wake County, Adjutant General; salary $600.

J. C. Ellington, of Johnston County, State Librarian; salary $1,000.

T. P. Jerman, of Warren County, Chief Clerk to Auditor; salary $1,000.

S. F. Telfair, of Beaufort Co., Private Secretary to Governor; salary $1,200.

C. L. Hinton, of Wake County; Executive Clerk; salary $600.

W. P. Batchelor, of Wake Co., Chief Clerk to Sec. of State; salary $1,000.

H. M. Cowan, of Chatham County, Chief Clerk to Treasurer; salary $1,500.

Ernest B. Bain, of Wake County, Teller; salary $750.

R. L. Burkhead, of Wayne County, Clerk for Charitable and Penal Institutions; salary $800.

C. M. Roberts, of Vance County, Superintendent of Public Buildings and Grounds; salary $850.

STATE BOARD OF EDUCATION.

The Governor, Lieutenant Governor, Secretary of State, Treasurer, Auditor, Superintendent of Public Instruction and Attorney General constitute the Board.

UNIVERSITY OF NORTH CAROLINA.

(Chartered 1789, Founded 1793, Opened 1795.)

Located in Chapel Hill, 28 miles N. W. from Raleigh. Is non-political and non-sectarian. Gives free tuition to sons of all ministers, to candidates for the ministry, to public school teachers and to young men under bodily infirmity. Loans and scholarships for needy young men of talent and character. Offers four general courses of study with wide range of electives, six brief courses, a normal course for teachers, also special courses in law, medicine and engineering, and an unlimited number of optional courses. · There were 400 students in 1893-'94.

FACULTY.—George Tayloe Winston, A. M., LL.D., President; Kemp Plummer Battle, A. M., LL.D., Professor of History; Francis Preston Venable, Ph. D., F. C. S., Professor of Chemistry; Jos. Austin Holmes, B. S., F. G. S. A., State Geologist; Collier Cobb, A. M., Professor of Geology and Mineralogy; Joshua Walker Gore, C. E., Professor of Natural Philosophy; John Manning, LL.D., Professor of Law; Thomas Hume, D.D., LL.D., Professor of the English Language and Literature; Walter D. Toy, M. A., Professor of Modern Languages; Eben Alexander, A. M., Ph., Professor of the Greek Language and Literature (on leave of absence as Minister to Greece); William Cain, C. E., Professor of Mathematics and Engineering; Richard H. Whitehead. M. D., Professor of Anatomy, Materia Medica and Physiology; Henry Horace Williams, A. M., B. D., Professor of Mental and Moral Science; Henry V. Wilson, A. M., Ph. D., Professor of Biology; Karl P. Harrington, A. M., Professor of the Latin Language and Literature; Howard Burton Shaw, A. B., B. C. E., Instructor in Mathematics and Engineering; Edwin A. Alderman, Ph. B., Professor of the History and Philosophy of Education; Herbert C. Tolman. Ph. D., Professor of Sanskrit and Acting Professor of Greek; A. J. Edwards, Assistant in Chemical Laboratory; De Berniere Whitaker, Assistant in Physical Laboratory; Charles Baskerville, B. S., Instructor in Chemistry and Assaying; James T. Pugh, A. B., Instructor in Latin; J. W. Gore, Secretary and Registrar; W. T. Patterson, Bursar; Prof. Alexander, Librarian; F. C. Harding, A. B., Student Librarian.

7th Month. **JULY, 1894.** *31 Days.*

Moon's Phases.

	D.	H.	M.			D.	H.	M.	
New Moon,	3	0	37	a. m.	Full Moon,	17	4	54	p. m.
First Quarter,	9	5	6	p. m.	Last Quarter,	25	3	58	p. m.

Day of Month.	Day of Week.	Sun rises.	Sun sets.	Sun slow.	Sun's decline north.	ASPECTS OF PLANETS AND OTHER MISCELLANEOUS MATTER.	Moon's place.	Moon rises or sets.	Moon south.
26.	Sixth Sunday after Trinity.					Day's length 14 hours 35 minutes.			
1	G.	4 45	7 20	4	23 6	☌ ♃ ☽. Bat. Gettysburg 1863.		2 27	10 28
2	Mon	4 46	7 20	4	23 1	♂ gr. Hel Lat. N.		3 25	11 30
3	Tue	4 47	7 20	4	22 56	⊕ in Aphe. Luke 11:9.		sets	eve
4	We	4 47	7 20	4	22 51	☌ ☿ ☽. INDEPEND. DAY.		9 18	1 42
5	Thu	4 48	7 19	4	22 46	☿ in Aphe. Monroe died 1831.		9 51	2 41
6	Fri	4 48	7 19	5	22 40	♀ sta. Battle Carthage 1861.		10 21	3 34
7	Sat	4 49	7 19	5	22 33	Mrs. Surratt hung 1865.		10 46	4 23
27.	Seventh Sunday after Trinity.					Day's length 14 hours 29 minutes.			
8	G.	4 50	7 19	5	22 26	Dr. Wm. Closs died 1882.		11 9	5 9
9	Mon	4 50	7 19	5	22 19	☌ ♄ ☽. Siege of Malta 1565		11 33	5 53
10	Tue	4 51	7 18	5	22 12	□ ♄ ☉. Blackstone b. 1723.		11 58	6 38
11	We	4 52	7 18	5	22 4	☌ ♂ ☽. Bat. Rich Mount'n 1861		morn	7 24
12	Thu	4 52	7 18	5	21 55	☌ ♀ ♆. Battle Boyne 1690.		0 24	8 11
13	Fri	4 53	7 17	6	21 47	Draft riot in New York 1863.		0 56	9 1
14	Sat	4 53	7 17	6	21 38	Great Chicago fire 1873.		1 34	9 52
28.	Eighth Sunday after Trinity.					Day's length 24 hours 22 minutes.			
15	G.	4 54	7 16	6	21 28	Napoleon at Elbe 1814.		2 19	10 44
16	Mon	4 55	7 16	6	21 18	Mrs. Lincoln died 1882.		3 10	11 35
17	Tue	4 55	7 15	6	21 8	I. J. Young died 1885.		rises	morn
18	We	4 56	7 15	6	20 58	Kirk cap. Yanceyville 1870.		8 18	0 24
19	Thu	4 57	7 14	6	20 47	♅ sta. ☌ ♀ ♃. Math. 24:13.		8 47	1 11
20	Fri	4 57	7 13	6	20 36	☌ ☿ ☉ inferior. 2 Cor. 5:1.		9 11	1 56
21	Sat	4 58	7 13	6	20 24	Battle Bull Run 1861.		9 34	2 38
29.	Ninth Sunday after Trinity.					Day's length 14 hours 13 minutes.			
22	G.	4 59	7 12	6	20 12	Atlantic Cable laid 1865.		9 54	3 19
23	Mon	5 0	7 12	6	20 0	harlotte Cushman born 1816.		10 15	4 0
24	Tue	5 1	7 11	6	19 47	☌ ♂ ☽. J. G. Holland b. 1819.		10 38	4 41
25	We	5 2	7 11	6	19 34	☿ gr. Hel. Lat. S.		11 3	5 25
26	Thu	5 3	7 10	6	19 21	♂ in Peri. Prov. 12:2.		11 35	6 13
27	Fri	5 3	7 9	6	19 8	☌ ♀ ♅ Gemini. Prov. 13:2.		morn	7 6
28	Sat	5 3	7 8	6	18 54	☌ ♃ ☽. Reign of terror 1794.		0 15	8 4
30.	Tenth Sunday after Trinity.					Day's length 14 hours 3 minutes.			
29	G.	5 4	7 7	6	18 40	☌ ♀ ☽. Poland dissolved 1794.		1 6	9 8
30	Mon	5 5	7 6	6	18 25	☿ sta. Wm. Penn died 1718.		2 9	10 15
31	Tue	5 6	7 6	6	18 10	☿ ☌ ☽. Pres. Johnson d. 1875.		3 25	11 21

WEATHER CONJECTURES.—JULY—1, 2, cold rain; 3, 4, 5, 6, 7, 8, fair; 9, 10, 11, 12, 13, 14, 15, 16, fair; 17, 18, 19, 20, 21, 22, 23, 24, fair weather; 25, 26, 27, 28, 29, 30, 31, changeable.

PUBLIC WORKS AND INSTITUTIONS IN NORTH CAROLINA.

THE N. C. INSTITUTION FOR THE DEAF AND DUMB AND THE BLIND.

The North Carolina Institution for the Deaf and Dumb and the Blind is located at Raleigh, and comprises two separate departments—one for the whites, in the northwestern part of the city, the other for the colored in the southeastern part of the city.

OFFICERS.—W. J. Young, Principal; John G. B. Grimes, Steward; Samuel McD. Tate, *ex officio* Treasurer.

BOARD OF TRUSTEES.—R. S. Tucker, President; B. F. Park, C. D. Heartt, John R. Williams, Dr. H. C. Herring, James A. Briggs, B. F. Montague.

The Institution has a full corps of teachers in the deaf-mute and blind departments at both buildings. The buildings can accommodate about 250 pupils. The course of instruction includes eight years. Applications for admittance of pupils should be made to the Principal.

NORTH CAROLINA INSANE ASYLUM.

Situated in the vicinity of Raleigh, and will accommodate 300 patients.

RESIDENT OFFICERS.—Dr. Wm. R. Wood, Superintendent; Dr. Francis T. Fuller, First Assistant Physician; Dr. William H. Cobb, Jr., Second Assistant Physician; William R. Crawford, Jr., Steward; Mrs. M. E. Whitaker, Matron.

BOARD OF DIRECTORS.—John B. Broadfoot, Cumberland County, President of Board; R. R. Cotton, Halifax County; Dr. Geo, A. Foote. Warren County; Capt. J. B. Burwell, Wake County; Capt. J. D. Biggs, Martin County; Dr. Geo. L. Kirby, Wayne County; Maj. J. B. Broadfoot, Cumberland County; Dr. R. H. Speight, Harnett County; B. F. Boykin, Esq., Sampson County.

EXECUTIVE COMMITTEE.—Capt. J. B. Burwell, Dr. Geo. A. Foote, Capt. B. F. Boykin.

OFFICERS.—Hon. Samuel McD. Tate, Treasurer *ex officio;* W. T. Smith, Esq., Keeper of Records.

STATE HOSPITAL, MORGANTON.

OFFICERS.—P. L. Murphy, M. D., Superintendent; Isaac M. Taylor and C. E. Ross, Assistant Physicians; F. M. Scroggs, Steward; Mrs. C. A. Marsh, Matron.

DIRECTORS.—James P. Sawyer, Buncombe County, President; I. I. Davis, Burke County; J. P. Caldwell, Iredell County; J. G. Hall, Catawba County; Dr. H. T. Bahnson, Forsyth County; Dr. G. H. P. Cole, Henderson County; E R. Hampton, Jackson County; J. C. Mills, Burke County; G. W. F. Harper, Caldwell County.

EASTERN N. C. INSANE ASYLUM.

OFFICERS.—Dr. J. F. Miller, Superintendent; Dr. W. W. Faison, Assistant Physician; Capt. Daniel Reid Steward; Mrs. B. V. Smith, Matron; John W. Wilson, Engineer; John Pate, Farmer; Mrs. Victoria Bryan, Seamstress.

EXECUTIVE COMMITTEE.—Dr. J. W. Vick, Johnston County, Chairman; L. H. Costex and John F. Southerland, Wayne County.

BOARD OF DIRECTORS.—Dr. J. W. Vick, Johnston County; Dr. N. M. Culbreth, Columbus County; J. L. McLean, Robeson County; W. F. Roundtree, Craven County; H. E. Dillon, Lenoir County; L. H. Costex, Wayne County; Jno. F. Southerland, Wayne County; Dr. M. B. Pitt, Edgecombe County; Theophilus Edwards, Greene County.

BUREAU OF LABOR STATISTICS.

B. R. Lacy of Wake County, Commissioner, salary $1,500; Logan D. Terrell, Wake County, Clerk, salary $900. Office in the Supreme Court Building.

Trunks, Bags, Valises and Umbrellas at WHITING BROS.

8th Month.   *AUGUST, 1894.*   **31 Days.**

Moon's Phases.

	D. H. M.		D. H. M.
New Moon,	1 7 15 a. m.	Full Moon,	16 4 8 a. m.
First Quarter,	8 4 57 a. m.	Last Quarter,	24 0 31 a. m.
		New Moon,	30 2 56 p. m.

See Advertisement COLLEGE OF PHYSICIANS AND SURGEONS. Page 29.

Day of Month.	Day of Week.	Sun rises.	Sun sets.	Sun slow.	Sun's decline north.	ASPECTS OF PLANETS AND OTHER MISCELLANEOUS MATTER.	Moon's place.	Moon rises or sets.	Moon south.
1	We	5 6	7 5	6	17 55	South America disc. 1498.		sets	eve
2	Thu	5 7	7 4	6	17 40	Black Hawk war 1832.		8 18	1 20
3	Fri	5 8	7 3	6	17 24	☐ ☾ ☉. Columbus left Spain 1492		8 45	2 12
4	Sat	5 9	7 2	6	17 8	Tilden died 1886.		9 10	3 1

31. Eleventh Sunday after Trinity.   Day's length 13 hours 51 minutes.

5	G.	5 10	7 1	6	16 52	♂ ♄ ☽. T. H. Briggs d. 1886.		9 34	3 47
6	Mon	5 11	7 1	6	16 35	♂ ♂ ☾. Cromwell d. 1658.		9 59	4 33
7	Tue	5 11	7 0	5	16 19	Hampton, Va., burned 1861		10 26	5 19
8	We	5 12	6 58	5	16 2	☿ gr. Elon. W. Luke 5:23		10 56	6 7
9	Thu	5 14	6 56	5	15 44	Battle Cedar Run 1862.		11 32	6 56
10	Fri	5 13	6 55	5	15 27	Daguerre died 1851.		morn	7 47
11	Sat	5 14	6 54	5	15 9	W. H. Harrison d. 1880.		0 15	8 39

32. Twelfth Sunday after Trinity.   Day's length 13 hours 38 minutes.

12	G.	5 15	6 53	5	14 51	George IV. born 1762.		1 4	9 31
13	Mon	5 16	6 52	5	14 33	☿ in ♌. Nat. Turner ins. 1831.		1 59	10 21
14	Tue	5 17	6 51	4	14 14	♀ in ♌. Gen. Grimes ass. 1880.		2 59	11 9
15	We	5 18	6 50	4	13 55	Gen. Lafayette visits U.S. '24		4 2	11 54
16	Thu	5 19	6 49	4	13 36	California discov. 1536.		rises	morn
17	Fri	5 19	6 48	4	13 17	Mt. Cenis Tunnel opened 1871.		7 39	0 37
18	Sat	5 20	6 46	4	12 58	☿ in Peri. Atlantic Hotel dest. '79		8 0	1 18

33. Thirteenth Sunday after Trinity.   Day's length 13 hours 41 minutes.

19	G.	5 21	6 45	3	12 38	☿ gr. bril. Cæsar died 14.		8 20	1 59
20	Mon	5 21	6 44	3	12 18	Benj. Harrison born 1833.		8 43	2 40
21	Tue	5 22	6 43	3	11 59	♂ ♂ ☽. J. C. Slocum d. 1881.		9 8	3 23
22	We	5 23	6 42	3	11 38	Capt. Cook com. voyage 1768.		9 36	4 9
23	Thu	5 24	6 40	2	11 18	Battle Pope's forces 1862.		10 12	4 59
24	Fri	5 25	6 39	2	10 57	♂ ☿ ☽. Math. 5:5.		10 57	5 54
25	Sat	5 26	6 38	2	10 37	♂ ☽☽. Gr. proce. in Raleigh '70		11 53	6 54

34. Fourteenth Sunday after Trinity.   Day's length 13 hours 9 minutes.

26	G.	5 27	6 36	2	10 16	Battle of Crecy 1746.		morn	7 58
27	Mon	5 27	6 35	1	9 55	Sir Rowland Hill died 1879.		1 1	9 2
28	Tue	5 28	6 33	1	9 34	♂ ♀ ☽. First Cable mess. 1858.		2 17	10 5
29	We	5 28	6 32	1	9 12	☿ gr. Hel. Lat. N. Prov. 16:1.		3 38	11 3
30	Thu	5 29	6 31	0	8 51	♂ ☽ ☽. 2d bat. Manassas '62		sets	11 57
31	Fri	5 30	6 30	0	8 29	Great earthquake 1886.		7 10	eve

WEATHER CONJECTURES.—AUGUST—1, 2, 3, 4, 5, 6, 7, wind and rain; 8, 9, 10, 11, 12, 13, 14, 15, rain; 16, 17, 18, 19, 20, 21, 22, 23, expect rain; 24, 25, 26, 27, 28, 29, fair; 30, 31, changeable.

N. C. BOARD OF RAILROAD COMMISSIONERS.

COMMISSIONERS.—J. W. Wilson, Burke County, Chairman, term expires April, 1899; E. C. Beddingfield, Wake County, term expires April, 1897; T. W. Mason, Northampton County, term expires April, 1895; salary $2,000 each; H. C. Brown, Surry County, Clerk, salary $1,200.

Special sessions of the Court are held at Raleigh. Special sessions are also held at other places, under such regulations as made by the Commission.

Offices of the Commissioners are located in the Agricultural Building.

NORTH CAROLINA GEOLOGICAL SURVEY.

Jos. A. Holmes, State Geologist; H. B. C. Nitze, Assistant State Geologist. General offices of the Survey, Raleigh, N. C.

OFFICERS N. C. STATE PENITENTIARY.

A. Leazar, Superintendent State Prison, salary $2,500; W. J. Hicks, General Supervisor, salary $1,800; J. M. Fleming, Warden, salary $900; Wm. Ledbetter, Deputy Warden, salary $500; Dr. J. W. McGee, Physician, salary $500; Jos. J. Bernard, Bookkeeper, salary $900,

BOARD OF DIRECTORS.—A. B. Young, Vice-President, Concord, N. C.; T. J. Armstrong, Rocky Point, N. C.; Frank Stronach, Raleigh, N. C.; Dr. I. E. Green, Weldon, N. C. One vacancy.

N. C. AGRICULTURAL EXPERIMENT AND FERTILIZER CONTROL STATION
AND STATE WEATHER SERVICE, RALEIGH, N. C.

OFFICERS.—H. B. Battle, Ph. D., Director and State Chemist; F. E. Emery, M. S., Agriculturist; Gerald McCarthy, B. S., Botanist and Entomologist; W. F. Massey, C. E., Horticulturist; C. F. von Herrmann, Meteorologist; B. W. Kilgore, M. S., F. B. Carpenter, B. S., W. M. Allen and C. B. Williams, B. S., Assistant Chemists; Alex. Rhodes, Assistant Horticulturist; Roscoe Nunn, Assistant Meteorologist; A. F. Bowen, Secretary.

Offices and Laboratories in Agricultural Building, Raleigh; farm, stables and dairy at the Experiment Farm, adjoining State Fair Grounds. Visitors invited. Many interesting and valuable bulletins free on application.

NORTH CAROLINA COLLEGE OF AGRICULTURE AND MECHANIC ARTS.

BOARD OF TRUSTEES.—W. S. Primrose, President of the Board, Raleigh; W. F. Green, Franklinton; D. A. Tompkins, Charlotte; Henry E. Fries, Salem; N. B. Broughton, Raleigh; W. R. Williams, Falkland; J. B. Coffield, Everett's; W. R. Capehart, Avoca; W. E. Stevens, Clinton; J. H. Gilmer, Greensboro; J. F. Payne, Alma; J. R. McLelland, Mooresville; C. D. Smith, Franklin; R. W. Wharton, Washington.

EXECUTIVE COMMITTEE.—W. S. Primrose, Chairman; W. F. Green, N. B. Broughton, Henry E. Fries, W. E. Stevens, J. H. Gilmer.

FINANCE COMMITTEE.—N. B. Broughton, Chairman; J. H. Gilmer, W. E. Stevens.

FACULTY AND OFFICERS.—Alexander Q. Holladay, President; W. F. Massey, C. E., Professor of Horticulture, Arboriculture and Botany; W. A. Withers, A. M., Professor of Pure and Agricultural Chemistry; D. H. Hill, A. M., Professor of English; B. Irby, M. S., Professor of Agriculture; W. C. Riddick, A. B., C. E., Professor of Mechanics and Applied Mathematics; R. E. L. Yates, A. M., Adjunct Professor of Mathematics; F. E. Emery, B. S., Assistant Professor of Agriculture; Charles M. Pritchett, B. S., Instructor in Mechanics; Charles B. Park, Instructor in Practical Mechanics; C. B. Williams, B. S., S. E. Asbury, B. S., Instructors in Chemistry; B. S. Skinner, Assistant in Agricultural and Horticultural Practice; L. T. Yarborough, B. E., Assistant in Mechanics; F. T. Meacham, B. E., Dairyman; C. D. Francks, B. E., Preparatory Department; Professor Withers, Secretary of the Faculty; Professor Hill, Bursar; Benj. S. Skinner, Superintendent of Farm and Steward; Mrs. Sue C. Carroll, Matron; J. B. Dunn, M. D., Physician.

9th Month. **SEPTEMBER, 1894.** *30 Days.*

Moon's Phases.

	D.	H.	M.			D.	H.	M.	
☽ First Quarter,	6	7	54	p. m.	☾ Last Quarter,	22	7	23	a. m.
○ Full Moon,	14	11	13	p. m.	● New Moon,	29	0	35	a. m.

Day of Month.	Day of Week.	Sun rises.	Sun sets.	Sun fast.	Sun's decline north.	ASPECTS OF PLANETS AND OTHER MISCELLANEOUS MATTER.	Moon's place.	Moon rises or sets.	Moon south.
1	Sat	5 31	6 28	1	8 7	Battle of Sedan 1870.	♎	7 35	eve
35.	Fifteenth Sunday after Trinity.					Day's length 12 hours 55 minutes.			
2	*G.*	5 31	6 27	1	7 45	☌ ♄ ☽. Bat. Fairfax Ch. 1862.	♎	7 59	2 23
3	Mon	5 33	6 25	1	7 23	☌ ☿ ☉ sup. Cromwell d. 1658.	♎	8 24	3 11
4	Tue	5 34	6 24	1	7 1	☌ ♅ ☽. Gen. Morgan killed 1864	♏	8 55	3 59
5	We	5 35	6 22	2	6 39	☽ Congress met 1774.	♏	9 30	4 49
6	Thu	5 35	6 21	2	6 17	May Flower sailed 1620.	♐	10 11	5 40
7	Fri	5 36	6 19	2	5 54	Independence of Brazil 1822.	♑	10 58	6 33
8	Sat	5 36	6 18	3	5 31	Montreal surrendered 1760.	♑	11 52	7 25
36.	Sixteenth Sunday after Trinity.					Day's length 12 hours 39 minutes.			
9	*G.*	5 37	6 16	3	5 9	Battle of Eutaw 1781.	♑	morn	8 16
10	Mon	5 38	6 15	3	4 46	Battle of Lake Erie 1813.	♒	0 50	9 4
11	Tue	5 39	6 14	4	4 23	Battle of Brandywine 1777.	♒	1 51	9 50
12	We	5 39	6 12	4	4 0	Battle of Chepultepec 1847.	♓	2 54	10 34
13	Thu	5 40	6 11	4	3 37	○ □ ♆ ☉. Battle Quebec 1759.	♓	3 57	11 16
14	Fri	5 41	6 10	5	3 14	☽ p'tly ecl. vis. at Wash'gton.	♓	4 56	11 58
15	Sat	5 42	6 8	5	2 51	♂ sta. Sheriff Nowell d. 1882.	♈	rises	morn
37.	Seventeenth Sunday after Trinity.					Day's length 12 hours 23 minutes.			
16	*G.*	5 43	6 6	5	2 28	Senator Hill died 1882.	♈	6 48	0 39
17	Mon	5 44	6 5	6	2 5	♀ in Peri. Ephe. 4:32.	♈	7 10	1 22
18	Tue	5 44	6 4	6	1 41	♆ sta. Surrender of Quebec 1759	♉	7 37	2 7
19	We	5 45	6 2	6	1 18	Battle of Iuka, Miss., 1862.	♉	8 11	2 56
20	Thu	5 45	6 1	7	0 55	☌ ♆ ☽. New York panic 1873.	♊	8 52	3 49
21	Fri	5 46	6 0	7	0 32	☾ ☿ in ☊. Ephe. 6:2.	♊	9 44	4 47
22	Sat	5 47	5 58	8	0 8	☉ ent. ♎. AUTUMN COM.	♋	10 47	5 48
38.	Eighteenth Sunday after Trinity					Day's length 12 hours 8 minutes.			
23	*G.*	5 48	5 56	8	south	Neptune discovered 1846.	♋	11 59	6 51
24	Mon	5 49	5 54	8	0 39	Monterey surrendered 1846.	♌	morn	7 52
25	Tue	5 50	5 53	9	1 2	Battle of Montreal 1775.	♌	1 17	8 51
26	We	5 51	5 52	9	1 26	Philadelphia surrendered 1777.	♍	2 34	9 45
27	Thu	5 51	5 50	9	1 49	☌ ♀ ☽. □ ♃ ☉. Eph. 6:11.	♍	3 50	10 36
28	Fri	5 51	5 49	10	2 12	● ☉ total ecl. invis. at Wash'tn	♎	5 3	11 24
29	Sat	5 52	5 47	10	2 36	MICHAELMAS DAY.	♎	sets	eve
39.	Nineteenth Sunday after Trinity.					Day's length 11 hours 53 minutes.			
30	*G.*	5 53	5 46	10	2 59	Battle Peebles' Farm 1864.	♎	6 24	0 59

WEATHER CONJECTURES.—SEPTEMBER—1, 2, 3, 4, 5, changeable; 6, 7, 8, 9, 10, 11, 12, 13, fair if wind N. W.; rainy if S. or S. W.; 14, 15, 16, 17, 18, 19, 20, 21, fair; 22, 23, 24, 25, 26, 27, 28, wind and rain; 29, 30, fair.

NORTH CAROLINA AGRICULTURAL SOCIETY.

OFFICERS.—President, Julian S. Carr, Durham, Durham County.
VICE-PRESIDENTS (Permanent).—Hon. Kemp P. Battle, Orange; Gov. T. M. Holt, Alamance; W. G. Upchurch and R. H. Battle, Wake.

FOR STATE AT LARGE.—S. B. Alexander, Mecklenburg; B. M. Collins, Warren; A. T. Mial, Wake; H. E. Fries, Forsyth; R. P. Rheinhart, Catawba; Charles M. McDonald, Cabarrus; J. A. May, Haywood. The Presidents of all county fairs.

COR. SEC. AND MANAGER.—H. W. Ayer.

NORTH CAROLINA DEPARTMENT OF AGRICULTURE.

W. F. Green, Chairman, Franklinton; W. R. Williams, Falkland; J. B. Coffield, Everetts; W. R. Capehart, Avoca; W. E. Stephens, Clinton; J. H. Gilmer, Greensboro; J. F. Payne, Alma; Dr. J. R. McLelland, Mooresville; H. E. Fries, Salem; C. D. Smith, Franklin   John Robinson, Commissioner Agriculture and Immigration. T. K. Bruner, Secretary. Inspectors—George S. Terrell and P. C. Enniss.

STATE NORMAL AND INDUSTRIAL SCHOOL AT GREENSBORO, N. C.

This school was chartered by the General Assembly of 1891. The first session was opened in the fall of 1892. The following constitute the officers and Faculty for 1893-'94:

BOARD OF DIRECTORS.—J. C. Scarborough, President, Wake County; E. McK. Goodwin, Secretary, Wake County; B. F. Aycock, Wayne County; Hugh Chatham, Surry County; R. D. Gilmer, Haywood County, A. C. McAlister, Randolph County; M. C. S. Noble, New Hanover County; W. P. Shaw, Hertford County; J. M. Spainhour, Caldwell County; R. H. Stancell, Northampton County.

FACULTY.—Chas. D. McIver, A. B., Litt. D., President, Pedagogics and Civics; Mrs. S. M. Kirkland, Lady Principal; P. P. Claxton, A. B., Pedagogics and German; J. Y. Joyner, Ph. D., English Literature and Methods of Teaching Arithmetic; Gertrude W. Mendenhall, B. S., Mathematics; Dixie Lee Bryant, B. S., Geology, Biology and Physical Geography; Mary M. Petty, B. S., Chemistry and Physics; Viola Boddie, L. I., Latin and French; Annie M. Graves, M. D., Physiology and Hygiene; Maud F. Broadaway, Physical Culture; Lucy H. Robinson, History and Reading; ...., Vocal Culture; Melville Vincent Fort, Industrial Art; Edith A. McIntyre, Domestic Science; Sue May Kirkland, Habits and Manners; E. J. Forney, Bursar, Business Department; Fannie Cox Bell, Director of Observation and Practice School; Mrs. W. P. Conway, Matron.

There was an attendance of 223 girls the first year, representing 70 counties.

CLERKS U. S. CIRCUIT AND DISTRICT COURTS.

W. C. Brooks, Elizabeth City; George Green, Newbern; W. H. Shaw, Wilmington; James E. Reid, Asheville; H. C. Cowles, Statesville and Charlotte; Samuel L. Trogdon, Greensboro; N. J. Riddick, Raleigh.

ABOUT DR. WM. CLOSS.

The mere mention of the name of Dr. William Closs will awaken a train of happy thoughts in the minds of thousands of people in North Carolina. He was one of those grand old pioneers and patriarchs of Methodism in the State, whose memory should be cherished for aye. His zeal for his church, his love for his fellow-man, and his earnest and constant desire to see all brought under the influence and saving power of the Christian religion knew no bounds. With a heart full of faith, with an industry that never tired, with a diligence that never swerved, and with a judgment that seldom erred, he was a man to be admired—yea, venerated. Possessed of commanding stature, quick, penetrating eye, with a massive forehead, an earnestness that attracted every hearer, and with a magic voice that fascinated and charmed, he towered above his associates and left the impress of his intellect and peerless preaching of pure gospel on thousands of grateful, regenerated hearts.—*Communicated.*

10th Month.   **OCTOBER, 1894.**   *31 Days.*

Moon's Phases.

	D. H. M.		D. H. M.
☽ First Quarter,	6 7 5 p. m.	☾ Last Quarter,	21 1 47 a. m.
☽ Full Moon,	14 1 32 p. m.	☽ New Moon,	28 0 48 a. m.

See Advertisement COLLEGE OF PHYSICIANS AND SURGEONS. Page 29.

Day of Month.	Day of Week.	Sun rises.	Sun sets.	Sun fast.	Sun's decline south.	ASPECTS OF PLANETS AND OTHER MISCELLANEOUS MATTER.	Moon's place.	Moon rises or sets.	Moon south.
1	Mon	5 54	5 44	10	3 22	☿ in Aphe. Capt. White d. 1885	♓	6 52	eve
2	Tue	5 55	5 43	11	3 43	S. L. Riddle died 1886.	♓	7 24	2 38
3	We	5 56	5 41	11	4 9	Samuel Adams died 1803.	♈	8 3	3 30
4	Thu	5 57	5 40	11	4 32	Battle Germantown 1777.	♈	8 49	4 23
5	Fri	5 58	5 39	12	4 55	☽ A. J. Partin died 1880.	♉	9 41	5 16
6	Sat	5 59	5 38	12	5 18	Battle Altoona Pass 1864.	♉	10 38	6 3

40. Twentieth Sunday after Trinity.   Day's length 11 hours 37 minutes.

7	G.	5 59	5 36	12	5 41	Battle Saratoga 1777.	♊	11 39	6 58
8	Mon	6 0	5 35	13	6 4	Battle Fort Pickens 1861.	♋	morn	7 45
9	Tue	6 1	5 34	13	6 27	♀ gr. Hel. Lat. N. Chig.fire '71	♋	0 43	8 29
10	We	6 2	5 32	13	6 50	Gen. Stuart raid Pa. 1862.	♌	1 45	9 12
11	Thu	6 3	5 30	13	7 12	Samuel Wesley died 1837.	♌	2 47	9 54
12	Fri	6 4	5 29	14	7 35	Gen. Robert E. Lee died 1870.	♍	3 49	10 35
13	Sat	6 5	5 28	14	7 57	☽ ☿ ♌. Prof. Wise lost 1879.	♍	4 51	11 18

41. Twenty-first Sunday after Trinity.   Day's length 11 hours 21 minutes.

14	G.	6 6	5 27	14	8 20	☽ ♂ ☉ ☽. Bat. Hastings 1066.	♎	5 56	morn
15	Mon	6 7	5 25	14	8 42	☽ Bank of Paris 1857.	♏	rises	0 3
16	Tue	6 8	5 24	15	9 4	Napoleon at St. Helena 1815.	♏	6 12	0 51
17	We	6 9	5 23	15	9 26	Burgoyne surrendered 1777.	♐	6 52	1 44
18	Thu	6 9	5 21	15	9 48	☿ gr. Elon. E. Prov. 24:17, 18.	♐	7 41	2 41
19	Fri	6 10	5 19	15	10 10	Battle Hatcher's Run 1864.	♑	8 40	3 42
20	Sat	6 11	5 18	15	10 31	☽ ♂ ☉. Grace Darling d. 1842.	♑	9 49	4 45

42. Twenty-second Sunday after Trinity.   Day's length 11 hours 5 minutes.

21	G.	6 12	5 17	15	10 53	☾ ☿ gr. Hel. Lat. S.	♒	11 3	5 46
22	Mon	6 13	5 16	16	11 14	Hon. Thos. Kenan d. 1843.	♒	morn	6 44
23	Tue	6 14	5 15	16	11 35	♃ sta. C.W.D.Hutchings d. '83	♓	0 19	7 38
24	We	6 15	5 14	16	11 56	Daniel Webster died 1852.	♓	1 34	8 29
25	Thu	6 16	5 12	16	12 17	John F. Hanff died 1883.	♈	2 47	9 17
26	Fri	6 16	5 11	16	12 37	Hogarth died 1765.	♈	3 56	10 3
27	Sat	6 17	5 10	16	12 57	♂ ♀ ☽. Bishop Doggett d. 1880.	♉	5 5	10 50

43. Twenty-third Sunday after Trinity.   Day's length 10 hours 51 minutes.

28	G.	6 18	5 9	16	13 18	☽ Dr. Milburn in Raleigh '83.	♊	6 16	11 37
29	Mon	6 19	5 8	16	13 38	Battle White Plains 1776.	♊	sets	eve
30	Tue	6 20	5 6	16	13 57	☿ sta. Gambetta b. 1838.	♋	5 59	1 19
31	We	6 21	5 5	16	14 17	Gen. Scott retired 1861.	♋	6 41	2 12

WEATHER CONJECTURES —OCTOBER—1, 2, 3. 4. 5. expect fair weather; 6, 7, 8, 9, 10, 11. 12. 13. fair if wind N. W.; rainy if S or S. W.; 14, 15. 16, 17, 18, 19, 20, look for much rain; 21, 22, 23, 24, 25, 26, 27, 28, fair; 29, 30, 31, fair, Indian summer weather.

THE STORY OF JIM JONES.

Jim Jones, he was a candidate for office—so he was;
He'd been workin' clean from daylight in the Democratic cause;
He'd heard about the salary an office-holder draws—
So he went in for an office in the mornin'!

He brushed his old black beaver an' he polished up his boots;
He got him twenty packages of Georgia-made cheroots,
An' they missed him from the village an' political disputes—
For he went in for an office in the mornin'!

But the office wasn't comin', an' they told him for to wait;
The road was kinder crooked when he thought it kinder straight;
But Jones—he kept a'swingin' on the Democratic gate,
"For," said he, "I'll ketch the office in the mornin,!"

Soon the Congressmen had smoked up every one o' his cheroots,
An' the mud had worn the polish from the leggins of his boots,
An' the office jes' got mixed up in political disputes,
An' Jones—he kinder weakened in the mornin'!

So he boarded of a freight train that was runnin' by the rule,
For he didn't have a dollar, an' was feelin' like a fool;
An' then he went to plowin', with a mortgage on his mule—
An' he cussed out every office in the mornin'!   F. L. S.

SIAMESE TWINS AGAIN.

They were natives of Siam. After traveling all over the world and accumulating a large fortune, they married two sisters (Gates) in Wilkes County, and after settled in Surry County on a large farm not very far from Mt. Airy, about 1845 or '50. They were said to have been fine farmers, very industrious and quite well skilled in doing many kinds of manual labor, such as cutting down trees, loading and driving the wagon, plowing, &c. They had a kind of double house, and one family lived in each end. They each had eight or ten children, which they educated liberally. I think two or three were mutes and were educated at the North Carolina Institution for the Deaf and Dumb and the Blind in Raleigh. My friend Z. W. Haynes, a mute teacher, married one of the daughters, and now lives in Raleigh. He will be able to correct any mistakes I may have made in this short article. After settling down to private life they were known by the name of Bunker—Chang Bunker and Eng Bunker.

A neighbor of mine once visited them and told me that they slept on a large double bed—the twins in the middle and the wives on the outside. The families did not entirely agree after they grew to be numerous, so the husbands bought another farm adjoining and then alternated themselves between the farms—a week at each one. Having lost their negroes and much other property by the war, they set about regaining and put themselves on exhibition at Barnum's in New York, where I saw them in 1865 or '66. There are many other things of peculiar interest about them which I hope Prof. Z. W. Haynes will be pleased to tell us.   LEVI BRANSON.

"God be thanked for books. They are the voices of the distant and the dead, and make us heirs of the spiritual life of past ages. Books are the true levelers. They give to all, who will faithfully use them, the society, the spiritual presence of the best and greatest of our race. No matter how poor I am. No matter though the prosperous of my own time will not enter my obscure dwelling. If the sacred writers will enter and take up their abode under my roof, if Milton will cross my threshold to sing to me of Paradise, and Shakespeare to open to me the worlds of imagination and the workings of the human heart, and Franklin to enrich me with his practical wisdom, I shall not pine for want of intellectual companionship, and I may become a cultivated man though excluded from what is called the best society in the place where I live."—*Channing.*

11th Month. **NOVEMBER, 1894.** *30 Days.*

Moon's Phases.

	D.	H.	M.			D.	H.	M.	
☽ First Quarter,	5	10	7	a. m.	☾ Last Quarter,	19	9	0	p. m.
Full Moon,	13	2	41	a. m.	New Moon,	27	3	46	a. m.

Day of Month.	Day of Week.	Sun rises.	Sun sets.	Sun fast.	Sun's decline south.	ASPECTS OF PLANETS AND OTHER MISCELLANEOUS MATTER.	Moon's place.	Moon rises or sets.	Moon south.
1	Thu	6 22	5 4	16	14 36	Gen. McClellan in com'nd 1861.	♐	7 31	eve
2	Fri	6 23	5 4	16	14 55	N. and S. Dakotas adm'ted 1889	♐	8 28	3 59
3	Sat	6 24	5 3	16	15 14	Battle Hohenlinden 1800.	♐	9 27	4 50
44. Twenty-fourth Sunday after Trinity.						Day's length 10 hours 37 min.			
4	*G.*	6 25	5 2	16	15 32	☽ Geo. Peabody died 1869.	♑	11 29	5 38
5	Mon	6 26	5 1	16	15 51	Kepler died 1630.	♑	11 30	6 23
6	Tue	6 27	5 0	16	16 9	Lincoln elected 1860.	♒	morn	7 6
7	We	6 28	4 59	16	16 26	☌ ♅ ☉. Braxton Craven d. 1882.	♒	6 32	7 47
8	Thu	6 29	4 58	16	16 44	Milton died 1694.	♓	1 33	8 28
9	Fri	6 30	4 56	16	17 1	☿ in ♌. Dr. Lovic Pierce d. '79.	♓	2 34	9 10
10	Sat	6 31	4 56	16	17 18	Transit of ☿ invis. at Wash'gt'n.	♓	3 38	9 54
45. Twenty-fifth Sunday after Trinity.						Day's length 10 hours 23 minutes.			
11	*G.*	6 32	4 55	16	17 34	Wm. E. Pell died 1870.	♈	4 45	10 41
12	Mon	6 33	4 55	15	17 51	Dr. J. L. Craven d. 1885.	♈	5 56	11 33
13	Tue	6 34	4 54	15	18 7	Fall of Meteors 1833.	♉	rises.	morn
14	We	6 35	4 53	15	18 22	☿ in Peri. Herschell born 1738.	♉	5 32	0 30
15	Thu	6 36	4 53	15	18 38	Battle Campbell's Station 1863.	♊	6 30	1 32
16	Fri	6 37	4 52	15	18 53	Sherman's march 1864.	♊	7 39	2 36
17	Sat	6 38	4 51	15	19 7	Suez Canal opened 1869.	♋	8 54	3 40
46. Twenty-sixth Sunday after Trinity.						Day's length 10 hours 11 minutes.			
18	*G.*	6 39	4 51	15	19 21	☾ Mt. Ætna eruption 1832.	♋	10 10	4 40
19	Mon	6 40	4 50	14	19 35	☿ sta. Mason&Slidell cap.'61	♌	11 24	5 35
20	Tue	6 41	4 50	14	19 49	Eruption Mt. Vesuveus 1857.	♌	morn	6 26
21	We	6 42	4 49	14	20 2	Telescope invented 1790.	♍	0 36	7 14
22	Thu	6 43	4 49	14	20 15	♂ sta. France an Empire 1852.	♍	1 45	8 0
23	Fri	6 44	4 49	13	20 28	Gen. Bragg defeated 1863.	♍	2 53	8 45
24	Sat	6 45	4 48	13	20 40	☌ ♄ ☽. Aunt Abbey House d. '81	♎	4 2	9 31
47. Twenty-seventh Sunday after Trinity.						Day's length 10 hours 1 minute.			
25	*G.*	6 46	4 47	13	20 52	☌ ☿ ☽. Isaac Watts d. 1748.	♎	5 11	10 19
26	Mon	6 47	4 47	12	21 3	♂ in ♌. Bishop Marvin d. 1875.	♏	6 18	11 9
27	Tue	6 48	4 46	12	21 14	● ♀ ☌ ☽. B. F. Moore d. 1877	♏	sets	eve
28	We	6 49	4 46	12	21 25	☌ ☿ ♅. Irving died 1859.	♐	5 22	0 55
29	Thu	6 50	4 46	11	21 35	☌ ♀ ☉ sup. Seaton Gales d. '78.	♐	6 16	1 49
30	Fri	6 51	4 46	11	21 44	SAINT ANDREW.	♐	7 14	2 41

WEATHER CONJECTURES.—NOVEMBER—1, 2, 3. 4. frost unless wind be S. or S. W.; 5. 6. 7. 8. 9. 10, 11. 12, cold high winds; 13. 14. 15, 16, 17. 18, cold winds, perhaps snow; 19, 20. 21. 22, 23. 24. 25. 26. fair and frosty if wind N. or N. E.; rain or snow if S. or S. W.; 27. 28, 29. 30, snow and stormy.

12th Month.   **DECEMBER, 1894.**   **31 Days.**

Moon's Phases.

	D.	H.	M.			D.	H.	M.
First Quarter,	5	7	7 a. m.	Last Quarter,	19	6	7 a. m.
Full Moon,	12	2	37 p. m.	New Moon,	26	9	11 p. m.

Day of Month.	Day of Week.	Sun rises.	Sun sets.	Sun fast.	Sun's decline south.	ASPECTS OF PLANETS AND OTHER MISCELLANEOUS MATTER.	Moon's place.	Moon rises or sets.	Moon south.
1	Sat	6 51	4 46	11	21 54	Battle Austerlitz 1805.		8 16	eve

48. First Sunday in Advent.   Day's length 9 hours 54 minutes.

2	G.	6 52	4 46	10	22 3	John Brown executed 1857.		9 18	4 17
3	Mon	6 53	4 46	10	22 11	Illinois admitted 1818.		10 19	5 0
4	Tue	6 54	4 46	9	22 19	☽ ♀ in ♎. Alabama adm'td '18		11 20	5 42
5	We	6 55	4 46	9	22 27	Van Buren b. 1782.		morn	6 22
6	Thu	6 56	4 46	9	22 34	Hastings born 1782.		0 21	7 2
7	Fri	6 56	4 46	8	22 41	♂ ☿ ♌. Heb. 2:3.		1 22	7 44
8	Sat	6 57	4 46	8	22 47	Dr. A. T. Bledsoe died 1877.		2 25	8 29

49. Second Sunday in Advent.   Day's length 9 hours 48 minutes.

9	G.	6 53	4 46	7	22 53	Milton born 1608.		3 31	9 18
10	Mon	6 59	4 46	7	22 58	Dr Columbus Mills d. 1882.		4 42	10 13
11	Tue	7 0	4 46	6	23 3	Fredericksburg bomb. 1862		9 57	11 13
12	We	7 1	4 47	6	23 8	Cromwell Protector 1653.		rises	morn
13	Thu	7 2	4 47	5	23 12	Drake sailed 1577.		5 20	0 18
14	Fri	7 3	4 47	5	23 15	☿ in Peri. HALCYON DAYS BEGIN		6 35	1 24
15	Sat	7 3	4 47	4	23 19	♂♃☽. Bat. Nashville 1864		7 55	2 28

50. Third Sunday in Advent.   Day's length 9 hours 44 minutes.

16	G.	7 4	4 48	4	23 21	Boston Tea Party 1773.		9 13	3 28
17	Mon	7 4	4 48	3	23 23	Poet Whittier born 1807.		10 26	4 22
18	Tue	7 5	4 49	3	23 25	☽ in ♎. Sir Hum. Davy b. 1778		11 37	5 12
19	We	7 6	4 49	2	23 26	Rome burnt 69.		morn	5 59
20	Thu	7 7	4 49	2	23 27	South Carolina seceded 1860.		0 46	6 44
21	Fri	7 7	4 50	1	23 27	⊙ ent. ♑. WINTER COMMENCES		1 54	7 29
22	Sat	7 8	4 50	1	23 27	♀ ♃ ⊙.		3 1	8 16

51. Fourth Sunday in Advent.   Day's length 9 hours 43 minutes.

23	G.	7 8	4 51	slow	23 26	♂♂☽. Henry W. Grady d. 1889		4 8	9 5
24	Mon	7 9	4 51	0	23 25	♂ ♄ ☽. Dr. Wm. Little d. 1879		5 15	9 56
25	Tue	7 9	4 52	1	23 24	CHRISTMAS DAY.		6 18	10 48
26	We	7 9	4 53	1	23 22	♀ ☽. Battle Trenton 1776		7 15	11 42
27	Thu	7 10	4 53	2	23 19	♂ ♃ ☿. Kepler born 1571.		sets	eve
28	Fri	7 10	4 54	2	23 16	♀ in Aphelion. Rom. 10:10.		6 6	1 25
29	Sat	7 10	4 54	3	23 13	♂ ♀ ⊙ sup. 1st John 3:1,2.		7 8	2 12

52. Sunday after Christmas.   Day's length 9 hours 44 minutes.

30	G.	7 11	4 55	3	23 9	Battle Savannah 1778.		8 9	2 56
31	Mon	7 11	4 56	4	23 4	Battle Murfreesboro 1862.		9 10	3 38

WEATHER CONJECTURES.—DECEMBER—1, 2, 3, 4, snow and storm; 5, 6, 7, 8, 9, 10, 11, stormy; 12, 13, 14, 15, 16, 17, 18, fair and mild; 19, 20, 21, 22, 23, 24, 25, stormy; 26, 27, 28, 29, 30, 31, fair and frosty if wind N. or N. E.; rain or snow if S. or S. W.

See Advertisement of A. S. LEE, Page 41.

COLLEGE OF PHYSICIANS AND SURGEONS,
RICHMOND, VIRGINIA.

HUNTER McGUIRE, M. D., LL. D., President.
JOSEPH A. WHITE, A. M., M. D., Secretary.

A THREE YEARS' GRADED COURSE,
Comprising the Following Departments:

MEDICINE, THOMAS J. MOORE, M. D.,
Chairman.

DENTISTRY, LEWIS M. COWARDIN, M. D., D. D. S.,
Chairman.

PHARMACY, T. A. MILLER, Ph. G.,
Chairman.

The next regular session of the College of Physicians and Surgeons, Richmond, Va., will begin October 2, 1894, and continue six months. The Course will consist of Recitations, Didactic and Clinical Lectures—special attention being devoted to Laboratory Work—Demonstrations on the Cadaver, etc., and Clinics, according to the grade of the student.

IN DENTISTRY AND PHARMACY Every Facility is Afforded for Thorough Practical and Laboratory Instruction.

THIS COLLEGE has been established in Richmond, Virginia, the historic city of the South, in order to give SOUTHERN MEDICAL, DENTAL AND PHARMACY STUDENTS the same high grade facilities in a Southern climate as are offered by similar institutions beyond the Potomac. Everything being equal, high grade, able instructors, clinical advantages, there is every reason for Southern students to patronize home institutions. The corps of professors and teachers has been selected from among the prominent men in Virginia and North Carolina; the grade of the School has been placed high enough to make a graduate proud of his diploma; and the laboratory and clinical facilities all that could be desired. No expense has been spared to gain this end. The laboratories are large and well equipped for thorough instruction in Chemistry, Histology, Pathology, Physiology, Bacteriology, Pharmacy, and Mechanical Dentistry.

THE VIRGINIA HOSPITAL, with a frontage of 110 feet, adjoins the College buildings, and, with a thoroughly organized DISPENSARY, affords ample clinics and bedside instruction.

THE RICHMOND EYE, EAR, THROAT AND NOSE INFIRMARY, at 217 Governor Street, also adds to the clinical advantages.

*Attendance upon three full courses of lectures** is required of an applicant for graduation in Medicine or Dentistry, and credit is given for courses taken at any accredited Medical School; moreover, this School accepts certificates of proficiency in any branch from any regular College requiring a graded course of three or more years.

For catalogue and particulars as to fees, board, clinical advantages, hospital accommodations, etc., apply to the Secretary,

Dr. JOSEPH A. WHITE,
200 E. FRANKLIN STREET, RICHMOND, VA.

*A three years' course is required for several reasons: Firstly, in the interest of higher medical education; secondly, because it is demanded by the Association of American Medical Colleges, of which this school is a member; and thirdly, because some States have already passed laws making three years of study necessary before a license can be granted to practice.

THE EDUCATION OF POOR BOYS.

By Dr. John F. Crowell, President of Trinity College, N. C.

The first thing that a poor boy needs in order to get an education is an inspiration that he is worth something to himself. Call it ambition, self-esteem or anything else; it is after all the sense of present and future worth of his native powers that affords the point of departure for him. Whence that sense of personal worth we may not know, or how it comes may be a mystery, but it comes as certain as fate. The dull and hopeless Anthony Trollope, whom his father occasionally knocked down with the family Bible, at last broke the crust of his apparent stupidity, and felt his strength like a young eagle.

The second thing needed is confidence in others. A Baltimore young man, about half a century ago, went to a man of wealth and asked him for the use of a few thousand dollars with which to begin business. "What security have you to give?" asked the merchant. "My own personal honor, sir." The loan was made and so was the fortune of the young man. This incident suggests a third essential besides confidence of others, to the getting of an education by a poor boy, that is, integrity and intelligence. No one will care to help to educate a young man whose character is unsound. Nor will any man in his right senses do much for a lazy, loafing young man—I speak of poor young men. Character is better than collateral. The measure of credit which character can command is simply enormous. I met a manufacturer the other day who told me of a merchant who had failed and settled with his creditors for 50 cents on the dollar, with receipts in full. Then some one turned around and offered the creditors 75 cents on the dollar for the other half of the unpaid debt from which the creditors had released their insolvent debtor. Such was the confidence which he had in the man who had failed but not impaired his power to restore himself in business nor lost his integrity in the time of trial.

Integrity, to define more strictly, means wholeness of character. It must be above price; it must be kept entirely out of the market, for as soon as it or a part of it becomes for sale, then men will not be willing to trust it unless it is plastered over with bonds and mortgages, and the poor young man has none of these. Integrity means truthfulness in act, word and thought alike. A liar is a curse to the human family, because it becomes its destroyer. So, then, as a woman guards her honor, must a man guard this part of his possessions called integrity of character, above suspicion of evil.

Diligence comes of a purposeful life. To what purpose can a young man be living who simply eats, drinks, sleeps and breathes the open air on the street corner, as if he had a perfect right to it? Indolence is vice, or the next step to it. He who will not use opportunities is not the one upon whom to spend money. A poor, indolent young man is a prospective pauper, a criminal potentially. If he can be shaken out of his lethargy, his age will be the richer, for poverty may then be a spur to effort. Senator Simon Cameron, who began very poor and became rich, said of his son Don, that he, the father, had one advantage which Don wanted in starting life; that advantage was in being poor. Poverty is nothing to be ashamed of; but on the other hand it is nothing to boast of. I have known young men who made fools of themselves coddling the notion that their poverty entitled them to future greatness. There is about as much virtue in that as there was in the pious dirtiness of the mediæval monks.

A poor young man usually works his way by earning enough to support himself for a time at school or college. If he is a clerk, let him be ambitious to be the best clerk in the store; if a mechanic, let him prove that he is not excelled; if a book agent, let him know that he is carrying the golden treasures of knowledge to thousands to whom the wisdom of the ages would never have come but for him, I thank God for the book agents that have visited the distant rural home of my youth, where the fountains of history were opened to me and the treasures of philosophy were sought in quiet devotion.

Be the best that you can be, young men, then men and women will risk money on you, if you want them to, in your effort to get an education. For every dollar you earn with diligence, integrity and earnestness, you can borrow ten. Every college will trust you to pay your tuition. But be careful about a

(Continued on page 34.)

SUPERIOR COURTS OF NORTH CAROLINA FOR 1894.

(Having all the changes made by the Legislature of 1893.)

JUDGES.

Name.	District.	Residence.
George H. Brown,	1	Washington.
Henry R. Brown,	2	Newbern.
Jacob Battle,	3	Rocky Mount.
Spier Whitaker,	4	Raleigh.
Robert W. Winston,	5	Oxford.
Edward T. Boykin,	6	Clinton.
James D. McIver,	7	Carthage.
Robert F. Armfield,	8	Statesville.
Jesse F. Graves,	9	Mount Airy.
John Gray Bynum,	10	Morganton.
W. Alexander Hoke,	11	Lincolnton.
George A. Shuford,	12	Asheville.

SOLICITORS.

Name.	District.	Residence.
John H. Blount,	1	Hertford.
G. H. White (col.),	2	Newbern.
John E. Woodard,	3	Wilson.
Edward W. Pou, Jr.,	4	Smithfield.
Edward S. Parker,	5	Graham.
O. H. Allen,	6	Kinston.
Frank McNeill,	7	Rockingham.
Benjamin F. Long,	8	Statesville.
W. W. Barber,	9	Wilkesboro.
W. C. Newland,	10	Lenoir.
J. L. Webb,	11	Shelby.
George A. Jones,	12	Franklin.

Time of Holding Courts.

FIRST JUDICIAL DISTRICT.

Spring—Judge Armfield.
      Fall—Judge McIver.

Beaufort—‡Feb. 19th, May 28th, Nov. 26th.
Currituck—March 5th, Sept. 3d.
Camden—March 12th, Sept. 10th.
Pasquotank—March 19th, Sept. 17th.
Perquimans—March 26th, Sept. 24th.
Chowan—April 2d, Oct. 1st.
Gates—April 9th, Oct. 8th.
Hertford—April 16th, Oct. 15th.
Washington—May 7th, Nov. 5th.
Tyrrell—April 23d, Oct. 22d.
Dare—April 30th, Oct. 29th.
Hyde—May 14th, Nov. 12th.
Pamlico—May 21st, Nov. 19th.

SECOND JUDICIAL DISTRICT.

Spring—Judge Graves.
      Fall—Judge Armfield.

Halifax—‡March 5th, May 14th, Nov. 12th.
Northampton—April 2d, †Aug. 6th, Oct. 1st.
Bertie—Feb. 5th, April 30th, Oct. 29th.
Craven—‡Feb. 12th, May 28th, Nov 26th.
Warren—March 19th, Sept. 17th.
Edgecombe—April 16th, Oct. 15th.

THIRD JUDICIAL DISTRICT.

Spring—Judge Bynum.
      Fall—Judge Graves.

Pitt—Jan. 8th, March 5th, †April 2d, Sept. 17th, †Dec. 3d.
Franklin—Jan. 22d, April 16th, Oct. 22d.
Wilson—‡Feb. 5th, June 4th, Oct. 29th.
Vance—Feb. 19th, May 21st, Oct. 1st.
Martin—March 19th. Sept. 3d.
Nash—April 30th, Nov. 19th.

FOURTH JUDICIAL DISTRICT.

Spring—Judge Hoke.
      Fall—Judge Bynum.

Wake—*Jan. 8th, †Feb. 26th, *March 26th, †April 23d, *Sept. 24th, †Oct. 22d.
Wayne—Jan. 22d, April 16th, Sept. 10th, Oct. 15th.
Harnett—Feb. 5th, Aug. 6th, †Nov. 26th.
Johnston—March 12th, Aug. 27th, Nov. 12th.

FIFTH JUDICIAL DISTRICT.

Spring—Judge Shuford.
      Fall—Judge Hoke.

Durham—Jan. 15th, March 26th, June 4th, Oct. 8th.
Granville—Jan. 29th, April 23d, July 23d, Nov. 26th.
Chatham—Feb. 12th, May 7th, Sept. 24th.
Guilford—Feb. 19th, May 28th, Aug. 27th, Dec. 10th.
Alamance—March 12th, May 21st, Nov. 12th.
Orange—March 19th, Aug. 6th, Oct. 29th.
Caswell—April 9th, Aug. 13th, Oct. 22d.
Person—April 16th, Aug. 20th, Nov. 19th.

SIXTH JUDICIAL DISTRICT.

Spring—Judge Brown.
      Fall—Judge Shuford.

Pender—March 5th, Sept. 10th.
Greene—Feb. 26th, Aug. 13th, Nov. 26th.
New Hanover—†Jan. 22d, †April 16th, †Sept. 24th.
Lenoir—May 7th, Nov. 12th.
Duplin—Feb. 19th, Aug. 6th, Dec. 3d.
Sampson—Feb. 5th, Apr. 30th, Oct. 8th.
Carteret—March 19th, Oct. 22d.
Jones—March 26th, Oct. 29th.
Onslow—April 2d, Nov. 5th.

SEVENTH JUDICIAL DISTRICT.

Spring—Judge Bryan.
      Fall—Judge Brown.

Columbus—Feb. 26th, July 16th, Nov. 5th.
Anson—†Jan. 8th, †Apr. 30th, *Sept. 3rd, †Nov. 26th.
Cumberland—Jan. 22d, †May 7th, July 23d, †Nov. 12th.
Robeson—Jan. 29th, *May 21st, Oct. 1st.
Richmond—Feb. 12th, June 4th, Sept. 17th, Dec. 3d.
Bladen—March 20th (Tuesday), Oct. 23d (Tuesday).
Brunswick—April 9th, Sept. 10th.
Moore—March 5th, *Aug. 13th, †Aug. 20th, *Dec. 10th, †Dec. 17th.

Insure against Loss by Fire in the N. C. Home Ins. Co. Raleigh, N. C.

SUPERIOR COURTS—Continued.

EIGHTH JUDICIAL DISTRICT.

Spring—Judge Battle.
                    Fall—Judge Bryan.

Cabarrus—Jan. 22d, July 23d.
Iredell—Feb. 5th, May 21st, Aug. 6th, Nov. 5th.
Rowan—Feb. 19th, May 7th, Aug. 20th, Nov. 19th.
Davidson—March 5th, Sept. 3d, †Dec. 3d.
Randolph—March 19th, Sept. 17th.
Montgomery—April 2d, Oct. 1st.
Yadkin—April 16th, Oct. 15th.

NINTH JUDICIAL DISTRICT.

Spring—Judge Whitaker.
                    Fall—Judge Battle.

Alexander—Jan. 22d, July 23d.
Rockingham—Jan. 29th, July 30th, Nov. 5th.
Forsyth—Feb. 26th, May 21st, Aug. 6th, Dec. 3d.
Wilkes—March 5th, Sept. 3d.
Alleghany—April 9th, Sept. 17th.
Davie—April 9th, Sept. 24th.
Stokes—April 23d, Oct. 22d.
Surry—March 19th, Oct. 8th.

TENTH JUDICIAL DISTRICT.

Spring—Judge Winston.
                    Fall—Judge Whitaker.

Catawba—Feb. 19th, July 23d.
McDowell—March 5th, Aug. 20th.
Burke—March 19th, Sept. 3d.
Caldwell—April 2d, Sept. 17th.
Ashe—April 9th, Sept. 24th.
Watauga—April 23d, Oct. 8th.

Mitchell—April 30th, Oct. 15th.
Yancey—May 14th, Oct. 29th.

ELEVENTH JUDICIAL DISTRICT

Spring—Judge Boykin.
                    Fall—Judge Winston.

Union—Jan. 29th, Aug. 20th.
Stanly—Feb. 19th, Sept. 17th.
Mecklenburg—†March 5th, †June 4th, †Sept. 3d, †Dec. 17th.
Gaston—March 19th, Oct. 1st.
Lincoln—April 2d, Oct. 15th.
Cleveland—April 16th, Aug. 6th, Oct. 22d.
Rutherford—April 30th, Nov. 5th.
Polk—May 14th, Nov. 19th.
Henderson—May 21st, Nov. 26th.

TWELFTH JUDICIAL DISTRICT.

Spring—Judge McIver.
                    Fall—Judge Boykin.

Madison—Feb. 26th, July 30th, †Nov. 19th.
Buncombe—†March 12th, †Aug. 13th, †Dec. 3d.
Transylvania—April 2d, Sept. 3d.
Haywood—April 9th, Sept. 10th.
Jackson—April 23d, Sept. 24th.
Macon—May 7th, Oct. 1st.
Clay—May 14th, Oct. 8th.
Cherokee—May 21st, Oct. 15th.
Graham—June 4th, Oct. 29th.
Swain—June 11th, Nov. 19th.

*For criminal cases.
†For civil cases alone.
‡For civil cases alone except jail cases.

CRIMINAL COURTS.

NEW HANOVER COUNTY.—Oliver P. Meares, Wilmington, Judge; Benjamin R. Moore, Wilmington, Solicitor. Court begins January 1st, March 19th, May 21st, July 16th, September 17th, November 19th.

MECKLENBURG COUNTY.—Oliver P. Meares, Judge; George E. Wilson, Charlotte, Solicitor. Court begins February 12th, April 9th, August 13th, October 8th, December 3d.

BUNCOMBE COUNTY.—H. B. Carter, Asheville, Judge; E. D. Carter, Asheville, Solicitor. Court begins January 22d, April 23d, July 23d, October 22d.

U. S. CIRCUIT AND DISTRICT COURTS.

WESTERN DISTRICT.—R. P. Dick, Greensboro, Judge: *Greensboro*—Circuit and District—April 2d, October 1st. *Statesville*—Circuit and District—April 16th, October 15th. *Asheville*—Circuit and District—April 30th, October 29th. *Charlotte*—Circuit and District—June 11th, December 10th.

EASTERN DISTRICT.—A. S. Seymour, Judge: *Elizabeth City*—District Court—April 16th, October 15th. *Newbern*—District Court—April 23d, October 22d. *Wilmington*—Circuit and District Court—April 30th, October 29th. *Raleigh*—Circuit Court—June 4th, November 26th.

SUPREME COURT.

SUPREME COURT meets first Monday in February. Examinations on Friday and Saturday before. First District, February 5th; Second District, February 12th; Third District, February 19th; Fourth District, February 26th; Fifth District, March 5th; Sixth District, March 12th; Seventh District, March 19th; Eighth District, March 26th; Ninth District, April 2d; Tenth District, April 9th; Eleventh District, April 16th; Twelfth District, April 23d. End of Docket, April 30th.

Last Monday in September. Examinations Friday and Saturday before. First District, September 24th; Second District, October 1st; Third District, October 8th; Fourth District, October 15th; Fifth District, October 22d; Sixth District, October 29th; Seventh District, November 5th; Eighth District, November 12th; Ninth District, November 19th; Tenth District, November 26th; Eleventh District, December 3d; Twelfth District, December 10th, etc.

Chief Justice: James E. Shepherd, Beaufort County; Associate Justices: Armistead Burwell, Mecklenburg County; Alphonso C. Avery, Burke County; Walter Clark, Wake County; James C. MacRae, Cumberland County. Salaries, $2,500 each. Frank I. Osborne, Attorney-General and Reporter; salary $2,000. Thomas S. Kenan, Clerk; salary $300 and fees. R. H. Bradley, Marshal; salary $800. J. L. Seawell, Office Clerk.

(CONTINUED FROM PAGE 30.)

dishonest memory; one that forgets obligations or even settles down to the abominable heresy that after all the world owes you a living and that the institution can thank fortune for having had the chance to educate you.

The financial means for a poor young man aspiring after an education are the least difficult to obtain, if the young man has character and can prove that there is something in him. Given character and grit, and he will wedge his way through without asking odds. But he must deny himself of some things in order to make sure of other things. If an education is really what he seeks, let him if possible lay other things aside except so far as they contribute to his main purpose. This is a hard lesson to learn—the long-continued concentration of energies in the line of a well-settled purpose. The majority of men do otherwise; as Emerson says, The key to all ages is imbecility. Most poor young men lack encouragement from their surroundings. Their friends seldom understand them, and were it not for their mothers the world would be far poorer in greatness than it is. It takes pluck to break through the shell of uninspiring environments such as envelope the life of many a country hero. Custom often turns up its nose at the one who attempts to rise above his fellows in his attainments. We fool ourselves in thinking that we Americans are entirely free to emerge from one class to another. Our ignorant democracy, in frowning down aspirations after something above the common level, is no less contemptible than any aristocracy of Europe. We rave at Russia; we pity her in our ignorance of the fact that a peasant boy of talent and real worth has an open way to honor and glory even into the ranks of social and political life; the Universities are open to him, the academies welcome him for his worth. But who has not found the notion extant that a man's social standing may be estimated from the price he pays for board! Yet I do not agree with Dickens, that we are a nation of gluttons.

The chances are, I think, in favor of poverty in the long run. What by eating themselves to gout, and by softening themselves with luxury, or working themselves to pieces in business, the wealthy have not many generations of success to their credit. And yet they have and may hold the field on the one invariable condition—*self-denial*. That virtue to the rich is what the sacrifices of poverty are to the poor, both serving as the needed spur to higher aims. Knowledge was sweeter than sleep to him who read by the light of the pine-knot on the hearth. But that was a necessity to him and of that he made a virtue. To the rich young man, the invitation to the feast or the reception means much small talk from people who have left their individualities at home. The social pressure to go is great enough to test his strength of self-denial. All credit then to wealthy young men who fight it off for higher things. The wise young man of wealth finds better company in books in which individuals are let loose. But the poor young man need not assert himself against such inducements; he saves that much energy of resistance at least. The solitude of poverty is congenial to him. Chances and risks are counterparts, and poverty ever has its opportunities and its dangers.

Education never ends. After the trial of abstinence, to the poor student comes the flush of success. It makes him unsteady, it is apt rather to do so. His solitude has been his armory; his contact with men to get a livelihood has been the battle-field of his life, and the touchstone of his creed. Where should a poet live? asks Longfellow. In the city. Others say in the country. The ages say—with humanity, past, present and future. But when we see a class of present society capture a genius that was once poor, then there is a crisis at hand. It is only when his attainments shall have made him notorious that the social world, so-called, wishes to touch elbows with him. Until poverty is sugared over with greatness, society would feel quite uncomfortable to find him in its pew at church. That world laid hold on poor Burns and made him a guzzling gauger. Genius cradled in poverty can rarely stand the discipline of luxury; it is much less liable to survive it than the rich to survive poverty. The reason, it seems to me, is this: that genius, once led out of poverty into luxury, cuts off its communion with the ages and lives with those who live in and for the present alone. But that is not education, that is abduction. Of it this age must beware.

ELECTROPOISE !!! See page 43.

County.	County Town.	Clerk Superior Court.	Chairman County Commissioners.	Register of Deeds.	Sheriff.	Treasurer.	Chairman Board Education.	Superintendent of Schools.
Alamance,	Graham,	J. I. White,	S. H. Webb,	J. H. Watson,	J. A. Hamilton,	J. A. Dickey,	H. J. Stockard,	Rev. W. S. Long.
Alexander,	Taylorsville,	I. B. Pool,	R. M. Stevenson,	J. L. Gwaltney,	I. W. Watts,	H. J. Burke,	I. P. Matheson,	W. M. Smith.
Alleghany,	Sparta,	W. E. Cox,	W. E. Harden,	J. N. Edwards,	W. S. Gambrill,	W. S. Gambrill,	W. R. Gentry,	T. J. Carson.
Anson,	Wadesboro,	I. C. McLauchlin,	E. D. Gaddy,	S. A. Benton,	B. L. Wall,	J. O. A. Craig,	D. A. McGregor,	W. D. Redfearn.
Ashe,	Jefferson,	W. H. Gentry,	E. E. Phillips,	M. F. Smith,	Byron Sturgill,	Byron Sturgill,	B. F. Grigsby,	George W. Bower.
Beaufort,	Washington,	Goethe Wilkins,	Dr. W. J. Bullock,	O. K. Sibley,	R. T. Hodges,	R. T. Hodges,	O. H. P. Tankard,	Rev. Nat. Harding.
Bertie,	Windsor,	W. L. Lyon,	J. B. Stokes,	Solomon Cherry,	T. C. Bond,	T. C. Bond,	R. W. Askew,	D. E. Taylor.
Bladen,	Elizabethtown,	G. F. Melvin,	P. P. Park,	J. D. Gilliam,	W. S. Clark,	W. H. G. Lucas,	W. H. G. Lucas,	Wm. M. Brunt.
Brunswick,	Southport,	S. P. Tharp,	M. C. Guthrie,	S. S. Drew,	J. A. Brookshier,	C. W. Durant,	A. F. Summery,	George Leonard.
Buncombe,	Asheville,	J. L. Cathey,	J. E. Rankin,	J. H. Cooper,	W. A. Rourk,	H. E. Courtney,	W. E. Abernethy,	W. Storms.
Burke,	Morganton,	J. W. Happoldt,	G. F. Erwin,	H. K. Patterson,	T. M. Webb,	S. C. Kirby,	D. J. Little,	J. A. Gilmer.
Cabarrus,	Concord,	James C. Gibson,	I. Dove,	W. F. F. Palmer,	L. M. Morrison,	John A. Cline,	J. N. Baird,	J. P. Cook.
Caldwell,	Lenoir,	M. F. Shell,	O. D. Coffey,	W. R. Dozier,	James V. McCall,	A. H. Courtney,	M. N. Sawyer,	G. D. Sherrill.
Camden C. H.,	Camden C. H.,	P. G. Morrisett,	M. S. Morrisett,	James C. Davis,	M. Cartwright,	G. H. Jacobs,	James H. Mason,	T. B. Bonshall.
Carteret,	Beaufort,	John D. Davis,	Wm. L. Arendell,	Frank Person,	M. A. Hill,	G. H. W. Overby,	H. S. Brandon,	W. W. Taylor.
Caswell,	Yanceyville,	J. F. Herman,	W. R. Whitener,	Geo. W. Cochran,	M. J. Rowe,	R. M. Smith,	Rev. J. A. Foil,	Rev. R. A. Yoder.
Catawba,	Newton,	S. M. Holt,	J. R. Whitener,	John T. Paschal,	Joseph J. Jenkins,	L. L. Hatch,	W. F. Fowsher,	A. H. Merritt.
Chatham,	Pittsboro,	A. S. Hill,	W. H. Hatch,	T. C. McDonald,	S. W. Davidson,	H. W. Rogers,	M. Fain,	M. C. King.
Cherokee,	Murphy,	H. C. Prevatt,	J. M. Richardson,	T. D. Byrum,	L. W. Parker,	C. S. Vann,	E. J. Burk,	B. M. Martin.
Chowan,	Edenton,	G. W. Sanderson,	W. B. Sheppard,	G. M. Fleming,	John O. Scroggs,	W. H. Hogsed,	B. M. Martin,	I. A. Sentell.
Clay,	Hayesville,	T. D. Lattimore,	J. M. Crawford,	J. F. Williams,	M. N. Hamrick,	J. S. Wray,	J. S. Carter,	I. A. Anthony.
Cleveland,	Shelby,	F. C. Williams,	I. W. Garrett,	J. A. Alderdice,	Neil McPhaul,	David Powell,	J. W. Gidney,	W. G. Birchhead.
Columbus,	Whiteville,	W. M. Watson,	Jas. M. Shipman,	J. W. Biddle,	Wm. A. Lane,	Thomas Daniels,	Rev. J. A. Smith,	John S. Long.
Craven,	Newbern,	C. G. Cain,	James A. Bryan,	H. L. Hall,	J. B. Smith,	J. B. Troy,	John S. Long,	N. A. Sinclair.
Cumberland,	Fayetteville,	H. B. Ansell,	W. S. Cook,	G. W. Williams,	Edward Tillett,	Dr. W. H. Cowell,	Wm. Alderman,	Dr. V. L. Pitts.
Currituck C. H.,	Currituck C. H.,	J. W. Evans,	Wm. H. Bray,	C. I. Daugh,	R. W. Smith,	S. E. Mann,	P. N. Neay,	A. W. Jones.
Dare,	Manteo,	H. T. Phillips,	A. W. Jones,	S. W. Finch,	C. M. Griffith,	J. W. McKary,	E. R. Biggs,	P. L. Ledford.
Davidson,	Lexington,	A. T. Grant,	C. J. Wheeler,	G. W. Sleek,	W. F. Williams,	Dr. James McGuire,	Thos. F. Carrick,	I. T. Alderman.
Davie,	Mocksville,	John A. Gavin,	H. B. Robertson,	Luther B. Carr,	J. G. Kenan,	John Wells,	E. E. Hunt,	A. W. Jones.
Duplin,	Kenansville,	C. B. Green,	Frank Keesley,	P. Lunsford,	F. D. Markham,	John W. Pope,	S. M. Grady,	W. M. Shaw.
Durham,	Durham,	E. E. Pennington,	A. H. Stokes,	J. J. Pittman,	W. T. Knight,	S. S. Nash,	G. A. Barbee,	W. G. Vickers.
Edgecombe,	Tarboro,	W. B. Stafford,	Green Williams,	W. K. Martin, Jr.,	R. M. M. Arthur,	John F. Griffith,	H. K. Nash,	F. S. Wilkinson.
Forsyth,	Winston,	B. B. Massenburg,	Thomas Collier,	J. O. Rankin,	H. C. Kearney,	Mathew S. Davis,	K. N. Gulley,	A. I. Butner.
Franklin,	Louisburg,	F. L. Wilson,	A. E. Conrad,	Lycurgus Hoffer,	W. T. Knight,	S. E. Foy,	J. Kiser,	L. M. Hoffman.
Gaston,	Dallas,	W. T. Cross,	S. M. Wilson,	W. F. Mauney,	W. S. Coxart,	J. F. Bond,	L. L. Smith,	J. R. Walton.
Gates,	Gatesville,	O. T. Williams,	S. I. Harrell,	J. A. Norwood,	K. S. Hooper,	S. B. Rose,	D. A. Taylor,	John A. Hyde.
Graham,	Robbinsville,	W. A. Robbitt,	D. K. Blanton,	C. A. Lassiter,	J. J. Egleston,	A. S. Peace,	F. P. Hobgood,	W. H. P. Jenkins.
Granville,	Oxford,	John W. Blomit,	W. B. Waller,	J. A. Kirkman,	B. W. Edwards,	John Sapp,	Dr. N. Mendenhall,	James R. Williams.
Greene,	Snow Hill,	John J. Nelson,	W. E. Best,	F. F. Brinkley,	John W. Cook,	John W. Wharton,	Dr. J. A. Collins,	W. R. Wharton.
Guilford,	Greensboro,	J. T. Gregory,	J. R. Mills,	H. B. Moore,	C. M. Haynes,	W. F. Parker,	D. B. Parker,	W. A. Daniels.
Halifax,	Halifax,	—,	Richd W. Brown,	A. S. Freeman,	C. McArtan,	M. M. Sexton,	E. A. Darden,	I. A. Campbell.
Harnett,	Lillington,	George E. Prince,	E. H. Howell,	G. A. Brown,	J. G. Grant,	R. A. L. Hyatt,	D. B. Parker,	R. A. Sentell.
Haywood,	Waynesville,	L. K. Boone,	A. Cannon,			P. J. Hart,	C. J. Edney,	R. L. Morgan.
Henderson,	Hendersonville,	C. M. Pace,	W. T. Brown,		C. M. Haynes,			
Hertford,	Winton,	T. D. Boone,		G. A. Brown,	T. S. Mitchell,	T. S. Mitchell,	W. S. Shaw,	George V. Gowan.

County	Town					
Hyde	Swan Quarter					
Iredell	Statesville	J. H. Hill,	A. F. Shepherd,	T. M. C. Davidson,	T. J. Allison,	J. C. Turner,
Jackson	Webster	J. W. Fisher,	S. H. Bryson,	W. H. H. Hughes,	E. E. McLain,	John H. Moody,
Johnston	Smithfield	W. S. Stevens,	D. P. Honeycutt,	J. U. Oliver,	J. F. Ellington,	J. Simmons,
Jones	Trenton	James F. White,	G. H. Bell,	Aug. Hoskins,	Delia hunt,	John H. Dawson,
Lenoir	Kinston	E. W. Bizzell,	B. W. Canady,	E. S. Pittman,	J. D. Sutton,	J. T. Wilkie,
Lincoln	Lincolnton	C. E. Childs,	T. H. Hoke,	B. C. Wood,	J. R. Cline,	None,
Macon	Franklin	S. L. Rogers,	John Aumans,	J. S. Sloss,	C. T. Roane,	B. Tillery,
Madison	Marshall	M. A. Chandley,	N. S. Peel,	R. F. Fox,	James H. White,	S. R. Bigrs,
Martin	Williamston	W. T. Crawford,	J. A. Teel,	J. A. Teel,	J. R. Lanier,	George H. Gardin.
McDowell	Marion	B. B. Price,	John Carson,	J. C. Brown,	George H. Garden,	J. H. McClintock,
Mecklenburg	Charlotte	J. M. Morrow,	B. H. Moore,	R. M. Cobb,	Z. T. Smith,	S. J. Black,
Mitchell	Bakersville	W. S. Hyams,	J. K. Irby,	J. C. Brown,	R. B. McKinney,	J. P. Leach,
Montgomery	Troy	B. B. Harris,	Sandy Leach,	G. N. Scarboro,	J. J. Curric,	W. A. Wadsworth,
Moore	Carthage	D. A. McDonald,	Jr. John Shaw,	Daniel S. Ray,	A. H. Kicks,	W. T. Griffin,
Nash	Nashville	Stephen E. Pane,	Thomas Westray,	Capt. J. H. Nixon,	F. H. Swedman,	H. A. Bagg,
New Hanover	Wilmington	John D. Taylor,	H. A. Fagg,	John Harr,	M F Stancell,	Rev. Wm. Grant,
Northampton	Jackson	C. Garnock,	J. G. L. Crocker,	W. Fleetwood,	F. W. Harget,	E. W. Ward,
Onslow	Jacksonville	C. Garnock,	J. W. Nfik,	J. C. Morton,	F. W. Hargec,	F. Cox,
Orange	Hillsboro	S. M. Gattis,	D. H. Hamilton,	John Laws,	J. K. Hoedge,	John Thompson,
Pamlico	Bayboro	F. Miller,	Chas. H. Fowler,	T. D. Perkins,	Thomas Campen,	D. M. Laws,
Pasquotank	Elizabeth City	J. P. Overman,	George M. Scott,	M. B. Colpepper,	T. F. Wilcox,	J. T Cooper,
Pender	Burgaw	B. Mone,	J. T. Foy,	J. V. Stringfield,	R. F. Powers,	J. E. Sawyer,
Perquimans	Hertford	D. W. Bradsher,	J. M. Whidbee,	Thos. D. Woody,	A. F. Riddick,	George W. Ward,
Person	Roxboro	Q. A. Wood,	F. H. Street,	Henry Harding,	R. W. King,	K. M. Johnson,
Pitt	Greenville	S. A. Alaze,	L. D. Morris,	N. F. Hampton,	O J. Nelson,	James H. White,
Polk	Columbus	J. P. Artege,	L. F. Walker,	W. Barkhead,	S. K. Ross,	John Flanagan,
Randolph	Asheboro	Z. F. Long,	W. T. Covington,	W. D. McRae,	J. M. Smith,	H. H. Gibbs,
Richmond	Rockingham	C. B. Townsend,	F. F. McRae,	H. H. Morrison,	H. McEachran,	W. F. Wood,
Robeson	Lumberton	J. T. Pannill,	A. J. Ellington,	W. M. Crafton,	Thos. F. Kankin,	A. M. McLean,
Rockingham	Wentworth	Wm. G. Watson,	W. L. Klutz,	H. N. Woodson,	James M. Monroe,	Thomas F Rankin,
Rowan	Salisbury	F. Flack,	C. M. Lynch,	Z. A. Edwards,	Edward Deans,	J. S. McCubbins,
Rutherford	Rutherfordton	L. Bizzell,	C. Patrick,	John A. Beaman,	J. M. Spell,	George Bingersaul,
Sampson	Clinton	S. H. Million,	J. P. Efird,	W. T. Huckabee,	J. M. Spell,	J. M. Spell,
Stanly	Albemarle	N. O. Petree,	J. P. Brown,	D. V. Carroll,	J. W. Savage,	G. D. Palmer,
Stokes	Danbury	R. S. Folger,	F. Miller,	C. H. Haynes,	Joel H. Fuller,	Joel H. Fuller,
Surry	Dobson	J. R. Snow,	D. W. Kerr,	N. B. Thompson,	G. B. McCracken,	J. A. Adams,
Swain	Bryson City	T. H. Galloway,	C. L. Osborn,	W. P. Whitmire,	W. B. Moon,	D. G. Fisher,
Transylvania	Brevard	T. L. Wolfe,	J. G. Brickhouse,	D. O. Newberry,	A. W. Owen,	Thomas W. Swain,
Tyrrell	Columbia	F. H. Wolfe,	W. H. Phifer,	J. W. Bivens,	J. P. Horn,	James McNeely,
Union	Monroe	Harry Perry,	R. W. Kearney,	R. S. Eaton,	E. A. Powell,	George Houghtling,
Vance	Henderson	J. W. Thompson,	W. C. Stroneath,	Millard Mial,	M. A. Page,	L. O. Longee,
Wake	Raleigh	W. A. White,	M. J. Hawkins,	M. F. Thornton,	H. B. Hunter,	John M. Riggan,
Warren	Warrenton	T. J. Marriner,	Jos. Skittletharpe,	J. P. Hilliard,	Levi Blount,	W. F. Green,
Washington	Plymouth	C. F. Todd,	J. F. Finley,	C. J. Cottrell,	D. F. Baird,	W. E. Green,
Watauga	Boone	C. E. Herring,	W. F. Koragray,	A. J. Brown,	J. H. Grant,	J. T. Dees,
Wayne	Goldsboro	M. McNeill,	W. M. Ausher,	D. R. Edwards,	A. M. Yannoy,	A. M. Yannoy,
Wilkes	Wilkesboro	A. B. Deans,	Wells,	J. T. Smitherman, Sr.	W. L. Kelly,	W. P. Farmer,
Wilson	Wilson	R. E. Holton,	Dr. L. G. Hunt,	J. T. Smitherman,	S. M. Warren, Sr.	A. P. Woodruff,
Yadkin	Yadkinville	W. B. Banks,	E. M. Honeycutt,	S. Riddle,	J. M. Woody,	C. H. Byrd,
Yancey	Burnsville					

TRINITY COLLEGE.

JOHN F. CROWELL, PRESIDENT, DURHAM, N. C.

" TRINITY COLLEGE INN—TRINITY PARK."

The buildings are the finest and best adapted in the State. The Staff of Instructors is chosen for its merit in and devotion to the work of educating students. Terms begin Sept. I and Jan. 4. Rooms may be secured and interesting information given by application to JOHN F. CROWELL, PRESIDENT, Durham, N. C.

FOR 1893-4 THE FOLLOWING DEPARTMENTS ARE OPEN FOR INSTRUCTION:

1. Philosophical and Literary (for A. B. candidates). 2. History, Political and Social Science (for Ph. B. candidates). 3. Scientific (for B. S. candidates). 4. Technological (for B. E. candidates). 5. Law School (Summer Term opens July 14). 6. Theological (for ministerial candidates). 7. Commercial (courses preparatory for business pursuits).

Besides these there are three special schools with courses of a more practical or professional character :

1. The Normal School for Teachers; 10 courses of professional instruction for one year.
2. School of Journalism, Prof. John L. Weber, Director; full courses of instruction in English, Economics, Civics, Political Science, History, Sociology and daily practice in newspaper work required.
3. School of Finance, Economics and Administration. Two years' courses in the higher studies related to public interests.

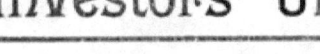

THE ELECTROPOISE.

The ELECTROPOISE cannot now be ignored.   It is an established *fact*.   Oxygen is the great life feeder. We cannot live without Oxygen.   Nature supplies the oxygen needed through the lungs.   When the lungs are diseased the supply is largely cut off, or when the man is weak and breathes slowly and feebly the needed oxygen is not supplied to the blood.

The *Electropoise* supplies the oxygen directly to the blood without any effort on the part of the patient.

It is the simplest of all treatments.

It is bound to come quickly into universal use. One answers for a whole family, and will last for many years.   You buy no more drugs, and hence the *Electropoise* will quickly pay for itself.

I know of many families now using the *Electropoise*, and not one is willing to give it up, or let it go out of the house.

Last summer I bought one for an invalid member of my family.   The effect has been truly a benediction.   The *Electropoise* is now the favorite of the whole family.   We could not let it go out of the house. Providence, in mercy, sent it along this way.

I can sell you one for $25 cash down, regular price. Or I can rent you one *three months* for $10 cash.   You can then return it or keep it by paying $17.50 additional.

I am authorized to receive orders by mail.

REV. LEVI BRANSON,
Exclusive Agent for Randolph and Rockingham Counties,
RALEIGH, N. C.

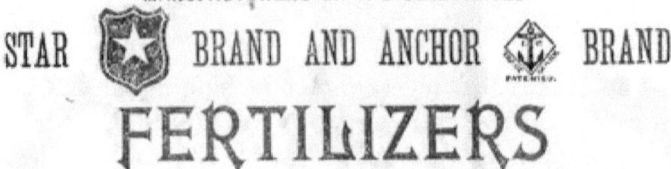

BRANSON'S SHORT CALENDAR FOR 1894.

JANUARY.

S	M	T	W	T	F	S
	1	2	3	4	5	6
7	8	9	10	11	12	13
14	15	16	17	18	19	20
21	22	23	24	25	26	27
28	29	30	31			

FEBRUARY.

S	M	T	W	T	F	S
				1	2	3
4	5	6	7	8	9	10
11	12	13	14	15	16	17
18	19	20	21	22	23	24
25	26	27	28			

MARCH.

S	M	T	W	T	F	S
				1	2	3
4	5	6	7	8	9	10
11	12	13	14	15	16	17
18	19	20	21	22	23	24
25	26	27	28	29	30	31

APRIL.

S	M	T	W	T	F	S
1	2	3	4	5	6	7
8	9	10	11	12	13	14
15	16	17	18	19	20	21
22	23	24	25	26	27	28
29	30					

MAY.

S	M	T	W	T	F	S
		1	2	3	4	5
6	7	8	9	10	11	12
13	14	15	16	17	18	19
20	21	22	23	24	25	26
27	28	29	30	31		

JUNE.

S	M	T	W	T	F	S
					1	2
3	4	5	6	7	8	9
10	11	12	13	14	15	16
17	18	19	20	21	22	23
24	25	26	27	28	29	30

JULY.

S	M	T	W	T	F	S
1	2	3	4	5	6	7
8	9	10	11	12	13	14
15	16	17	18	19	20	21
22	23	24	25	26	27	28
29	30	31				

AUGUST.

S	M	T	W	T	F	S
			1	2	3	4
5	6	7	8	9	10	11
12	13	14	15	16	17	18
19	20	21	22	23	24	25
26	27	28	29	30	31	

SEPTEMBER.

S	M	T	W	T	F	S
						1
2	3	4	5	6	7	8
9	10	11	12	13	14	15
16	17	18	19	20	21	22
23	24	25	26	27	28	29
30						

OCTOBER.

S	M	T	W	T	F	S
	1	2	3	4	5	6
7	8	9	10	11	12	13
14	15	16	17	18	19	20
21	22	23	24	25	26	27
28	29	30	31			

NOVEMBER.

S	M	T	W	T	F	S
				1	2	3
4	5	6	7	8	9	10
11	12	13	14	15	16	17
18	19	20	21	22	23	24
25	26	27	28	29	30	

DECEMBER.

S	M	T	W	T	F	S
						1
2	3	4	5	6	7	8
9	10	11	12	13	14	15
16	17	18	19	20	21	22
23	24	25	26	27	28	29
30	31					

Best Calendar!
Most Select Matter! } Safest Almanac!

PRICE, 10 CENTS.

Vol. 3.]   28th YEAR OF PUBLICATION.   [No. 8.

BRANSON'S
AGRICULTURAL
ALMANAC

FOR THE YEAR OF OUR LORD
1895,

And until the 4th of July, the 119th year of American Independence.

Carefully Calculated for the Latitude and Longitude of Raleigh, by

LEVI BRANSON, A. M., D. D.

LEVI BRANSON, Publisher, Raleigh, N. C.

COPYRIGHT, 1895, BY LEVI BRANSON.

GET THE BEST AND STICK TO IT—NO OTHER LIKE IT.

TIME.

The calculations of this Almanac are made in mean solar or clock time, which is indicated by a well regulated clock or watch, and does not correspond with the sun precisely, except on four days of the year.

Apparent time is that which makes the Sun come to the meridian at 12 o'clock. No good clock will run with the Sun; if set with the Sun on the 2d of January, the clock will seem to be one minute too fast on the 3d of January.

To adapt the calculations of this Almanac to apparent time, use the minutes in the column marked "Sun slow" or "Sun fast;" add them when fast, subtract them when slow.

The calculations are made for the Latitude and Longitude of Raleigh, N. C., but the times, phases, &c., will vary only a few minutes for any part of North Carolina, South Carolina, Georgia, Tennessee or Virginia.

RISING AND SETTING OF THE SUN.

The Almanacs generally used have made the rising and setting of the Sun together equal twelve hours. This is incorrect. During some portions of the year the Sun changes so rapidly in Right Ascension and Declination that it makes a material change in the Diurnal Arc during the day. The times here given have been rigorously calculated and compared with the authority, and are true to the nearest whole minute.

TWELVE SIGNS OF THE ZODIAC.

The Head and Face sign. ♈ Aries the Ram......Ar.

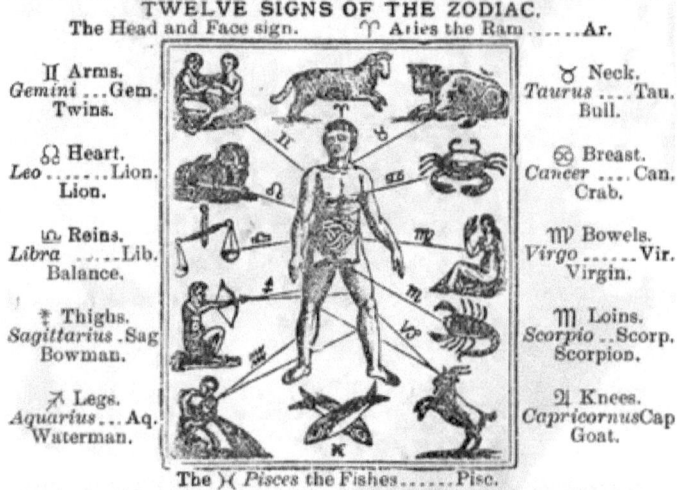

♊ Arms. *Gemini* ...Gem. Twins.

♉ Neck. *Taurus* ....Tau. Bull.

♌ Heart. *Leo* ....Lion. Lion.

♋ Breast. *Cancer* ....Can. Crab.

♎ Reins. *Libra* ......Lib. Balance.

♍ Bowels. *Virgo* ......Vir. Virgin.

♐ Thighs. *Sagittarius* .Sag Bowman.

♏ Loins. *Scorpio* ..Scorp. Scorpion.

♒ Legs. *Aquarius*... Aq. Waterman.

♑ Knees. *Capricornus*Cap Goat.

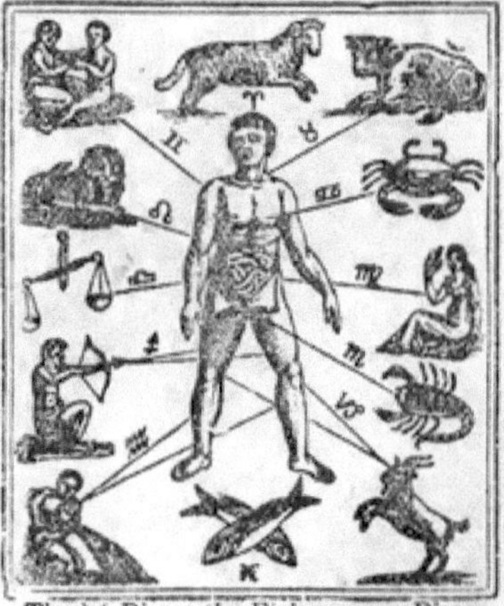

The ♓ *Pisces* the Fishes......Pisc.

To know where the sign is, find the day of the month, and against the day in the column marked Moon's Signs you have the sign or place of the Moon, and then find the sign; it will give you the part of the body it is supposed to govern.

SIGNS.

Spring Signs.	Aries, or Ram. Taurus, or Bull. Gemini, or Twins.	*Autumn Signs.*	Libra, or Balance. Scorpio, or Scorpion. Sagittarius, or Bowman
Summer Signs.	Cancer, or Crab-fish. Leo, or Lion. Virgo, or Virgin.	*Winter Signs.*	Capricornus, or Goat. Aquarius, or Waterman Pisces, or Fishes.

SIGNS OF THE PLANETS.

✳ Sun.	Moon.	♀ Venus.	♂ Mars.
♃ Jupiter.	♄ Saturn.	☌ In conjunction.	□ Quadrature.
☿ Mercury.	♅ Uranus.	♆ Neptune.	☊ Ascending Node.

MOON'S PHASES.

New Moon. ☽ First Quarter. Full Moon. ☾ Last Quarter.

ELECTROPOISE—See page 43.

CHRONOLOGICAL CYCLES AND ERAS.

Dominical Letter	F	Julian Period	6608
Epact	4	Jewish Era	5655
Golden Number	15	Era of Nabonassa	2642
Solar Cycle	28	Olympiads	2671
Roman Indiction	8	Mohammedan Era	1312

MOVABLE FEASTS OF THE CHURCH.

Epiphany	Jan. 6	Palm Sunday	March 18
Septuagesima Sunday	Jan. 21	Easter Sunday	April 14
Sexagesima Sunday	Jan. 28	Whit Sunday	May 13
Quinquagesima Sunday	Feb. 4	Trinity Sunday	May 20
Shrove Tuesday	Feb. 6	First Sunday in Advent	Dec. 2
Ash Wednesday, or Lent	Feb. 7	Ascension Day	May 3
St. Patrick's Day	March 17		

THE FOUR SEASONS.

	D.	H
Spring commences	March 20,	4 P. M.
Summer commences	June 21,	12 M.
Autumn commences	September 23,	2 A. M.
Winter commences	December 21,	3 P. M.

MORNING STARS.

Mercury will be Morning Star about....March 24, July 22, and Nov. 10.
Venus will be Morning Star from........September 19 to December 31.
Jupiter will be Morning Star from.............July 10 to December 31.

EVENING STARS.

Mercury will be Evening Star about....February 9, June 4, and Oct. 1.
Venus will be Evening Star till ....September 19.
Jupiter will be Evening Star till ....July 10.

ECLIPSES.

In the year 1895 there will be five Eclipses—three of the Sun and two of the Moon.

I. A total Eclipse of the Moon March 10 and 11, visible all over North and South America. Moon enters Penumbra 7h. 37m. p. m., and leaves Penumbra 1h. 21m. a. m., on the 11th. Middle of Eclipse 10:39 p. m. the 10th of March

II. A partial Eclipse of the Sun March 26, not visible in the United States.

III. A partial Eclipse of the Sun August 20, not visible in America.

IV. A total Eclipse of the Moon September 3 and 4, visible to North and South America. Moon enters Penumbra 9h. 48m. p. m. 3d, and leaves Penumbra 4h. 6m. a. m. 4th September. Total Eclipse on the 4th from 6m. a. m., to 1.47 a. m.

V. A partial Eclipse of the Sun September 19, invisible to America.

TIDES.

The time of tide can readily be found for the following places by adding the hours and minutes opposite the names to the time when the Moon is South on the day to which the tide is sought. The time when the Moon is South is given in the Calendar for every day. The next tide can be found very nearly by adding 12 hours and 29 minutes to the time of the one previous.

The tides are given in local time—add 12 minutes for Eastern Standard.

	H. M.		H. M.
Boston	11 12	New York	8 13
Sandy Hook	7 29	Old Point	8 17
Baltimore	6 33	Washington City	7 44
Richmond	4 32	Hatteras Inlet	7 04
Beaufort	7 26	Bald Head	7 26
Southport	7 19	Wilmington	9 06
Charleston	7 26	Savannah	9 33

Dr. Branson takes care to have all the Courts both full and accurate.—Evening Visitor.

HERSCHEL'S WEATHER PROGNOSTICATOR

For Foretelling the Weather Through all the Lunations of the Year.

This table and the accompanying remarks are the result of many years
actual observation, the whole being constructed on a due consideration
of the attractions of the Sun and Moon, in their several positions respecting the Earth, and, by simple inspection, it shows the observer what
kind of weather will most probably follow the entrance of the Moon into
any of its quarters, and that so near the truth as to be seldom or never
found to fail.

If the new moon, first quarter, full moon, or last quarter, happen—	IN SUMMER.	IN WINTER.
Between midnight and 2 in the morning	Fair	Hoar frost unless the wind be S. or S. W.
Between 2 and 4 morning	Cold, with frequent showers	Snow and stormy.
Between 4 and 6, morning	Rain	Rain.
Between 6 and 8, morning	Wind and rain	Stormy.
Between 8 and 10 morning	Changeable	Cold rain if wind be W.; snow if E.
Between 10 and 12, morning	Frequent showers	Cold and high wind.
Between 12 o'clock at noon and 2 in afternoon	Very rainy	Rain and snow.
Between 2 and 4, afternoon	Changeable	Fair and mild.
Between 4 and 6, afternoon	Fair	Fair.
Between 6 and 8, aftern'n	Fair if wind N. W.; rainy if S. or S. W.	Fair and frosty wind N. or N. E.; rain or snow if S. or S. W.
Between 8 and 10, afternoon	Ditto	Ditto.
Between 10 and midnight	Fair	Fair and frosty.

OBSERVATIONS.—1. The nearer the time for the Moon's change, first
quarter, full and last quarter are to midnight, the fairer will be the
weather during the next seven days.

2. The space for this calculation occupies from 10 at night until 2 next
morning.

3. The nearer to midday or noon the phase of the Moon happens, the
more foul or wet weather may be expected during the next seven days.

4. The space for this calculation occupies from 10 in the forenoon until
2 in the afternoon. These observations refer principally to the Summer,
though they effect Spring and Autumn nearly in the same ratio.

5. The Moon's change, first quarter, full and last quarter, happening
during six of the afternoon hours, i. e., from 4 to 10, may be followed
by fair weather, but this is mostly dependent on the wind, as is noted in
the table.

6. Though the weather, from a variety of irregular causes, is more
uncertain in the latter part of Autumn, the whole of Winter and beginning of Spring. yet, in the main, the above observations will apply to
those periods also.

7. To prognosticate correctly, especially in those cases where the wind
is concerned, the observer should be in sight of a good vane, where the
four cardinal points of the heavens are correctly placed.

Branson's Almanac is a household word.—Truth.

BRANSON MAXIMS.

BRANSON MOTTO: "CONVICTION OF DUTY, FOLLOW."

1. All men have faith in something, hence they work expecting results.—*Branson.*

2. Some men have faith in the laws governing mind; obeying those laws they attain to mental power.—*Branson.*

3. Some men have faith in the laws of health, and hence by obeying those laws they secure physical health and happiness.—*Branson.*

4. The man who has faith in the laws governing the spirit life, can realize that "the law of the Lord is perfect, converting the soul."—*Branson.*

5. The Christian religion leads a man towards the highest cultivation of all his best capabilities.—*Branson.*

6. The man who has *full faith* in *all* God's laws, and renders a perfect obedience, has peace flowing as a river, and a joy that is complete.—*Branson.*

7. To give advice unsolicited is so delightful; it magnifies our self-esteem. To receive advice unsolicited is so humiliating; it minifies our self-esteem.—*Branson.*

8. A man in whose mind his own country is not *first*, is a man who himself is not *worthy* to be first in another country.—*Branson.*

9. Our State is a diamond; let us polish it well.—*Branson.*

10. The *mind crop* is the greatest crop that can be raised on any farm or in any State.—*Branson.*

11. The *mind crop* in North Carolina is better than ever before.—*Branson.*

12. The *mind crop* should be planted early and cultivated better than cotton or tobacco.—*Branson.*

13. The stronger the *homes*, the stronger the *country* in which the homes are found.—*Branson.*

14. The greatest possibilities of a man are on his native heath; if he is great on another heath, he is still less than a native ought to have been.—*Branson.*

15. It is strange how freely we *give away* our *own* knowledge, and how freely we *pay high prices* for the knowledge we obtain from others.—*Branson.*

16. Living in obedience to spiritual *laws* brings spiritual *blessings.*—*Branson.*

17. *Do* your duty, then *wait.*—*Branson.*

18. Work for your *country*, and God will work for *you.*—*Branson.*

19. Much of our best work is unsuspected by *ourselves*, and even by the *recipients.*—*Branson.*

20. Individual comfort, State wealth, make a happy people.—*Branson.*

21. Never keep people unnecessarily waiting.—*Mrs. Branson.*

22. Be happy; life is short.—*Branson.*

23. To *sleep sweetly*, recline a few moments on your *left* side; then turn *slowly* onto your right side. Try it.—*Branson.*

24. Live with happy people, and you are likely *to be* happy.—*Branson.*

25. Do not keep a *burr* in your *throat*, nor a bit of *malice* in your *heart.*—*Branson.*

26. If you are *good* this world is *good enough* for you; if you are *mean*, then it is *too good* for you.—*Branson.*

27. Never allow your energies to slacken or your faith to weaken.—*Branson.*

28. To the end of life, do your very best.—*Branson.*

29. The more you imitate God and good people the greater you are likely to be.—*Branson.*

30. Reduce the number of your enemies, increase the number of your friends.—*Branson.*

31. In old age, you will be likely to need vast stores of friendship.—*Branson.*

A valuable household friend to every North Carolinian.—**Wil. Messenger**'

1st Month. **JANUARY, 1895.** *31 Days.*

Moon's Phases.

	D. H. M.		D. H. M.
First Quarter,	4 24 44 a. m.	Last Quarter,	17 5 47 p. m.
Full Moon,	11 1 41 a. m.	New Moon,	25 4 17 p. m.

Day of Month.	Day of Week.	Sun rises.	Sun sets.	Sun slow.	Sun's decline south.	ASPECTS OF PLANETS AND OTHER MISCELLANEOUS MATTER.	Moon's place.	Moon rises or sets.	Moon south.
1	Tue	7 10	4 58	4 22 59		NEW YEAR'S DAY. Emanci. '63.		10 11	eve.
2	We	7 10	5 0	4 22 54		⊕ in Peri. Bat. Trenton 1777.		11 9	4 58
3	Thu	7 10	5 1	5 22 48		Battle of Princeton 1777.		morn	5 38
4	Fri	7 10	5 1	5 22 42		Vanderbilt died 1877.		0 9	6 20
5	Sat	7 10	5 2	6 22 35		♂ ♂ ☽. Richmond bomb. 1781.		1 13	7 6

1. Epiphany Sunday.   Day's length 9 hours 53 minutes.

6	F.	7 10	5 3	6 22 28		EPIPHANY. OLD CHRISTMAS.		2 20	7 56
7	Mon	7 9	5 4	7 22 21		♀ in Aph. Fillmore born 1800.		3 32	8 52
8	Tue	7 9	5 5	7 22 13		♂ ♅ ☽. Bat. New Orleans 1815.		4 46	9 55
9	We	7 9	5 6	7 22 4		♂ ♃ ☽. ♂ ☿ ☉ superior.		5 57	11 0
10	Thu	7 9	5 6	8 21 56		Stamp Act passed 1765.		7 3	morn
11	Fri	7 9	5 7	8 21 46		Riot in Philadelphia 1843.		rises	0 7
12	Sat	7 9	5 8	9 21 36		Vicksburg fortified 1861.		6 49	1 11

2. First Sunday after Epiphany.   Day's length 10 hours 0 minutes.

13	F.	7 9	5 9	9 21 26		George Fox died 1690.		8 7	2 10
14	Mon	7 9	5 10	9 21 16		Commodore Maury born 1806.		9 23	3 3
15	Tue	7 9	5 11	10 21 5		Gen. Jackson born 1767.		10 35	3 53
16	We	7 9	5 12	10 20 54		Spencer died 1599.		11 45	4 40
17	Thu	7 8	5 13	10 20 42		President Tyler died 1862.		morn	5 27
18	Fri	7 8	5 14	11 20 30		☿ gr. Hel. Lat. S. ♂ ♄ ☽.		0 53	6 14
19	Sat	7 8	5 15	11 20 17		♂ ♀ ☽. Gen. R. E. Lee b. 1807.		2 1	7 1

3. Second Sunday after Epiphany   Day's length 10 hours 5 minutes.

20	F.	7 8	5 15	11 20 4		John Howard died 1790.		3 8	7 52
21	Mon	7 7	5 16	12 19 51		Stonewall Jackson born 1824.		4 12	8 44
22	Tue	7 7	5 17	12 19 37		Lord Bacon born 1651.		5 11	9 37
23	We	7 6	5 18	12 19 23		Wm. Gaston died 1844.		6 2	10 30
24	Thu	7 6	5 19	12 19 9		Pres. Johnson imp'ch'd 1868		6 47	11 21
25	Fri	7 5	5 20	13 18 54		Robert Burns born 1749.		sets	eve
26	Sat	7 4	5 21	13 18 39		♂ ☿ ☽.		6 2	6 54

4. Third Sunday after Epiphany.   Day's length 10 hours 19 minutes.

27	F.	7 3	5 22	13 18 23		Peter the Great died 1725.		7 3	1 37
28	Mon	7 2	5 23	13 18 8		Battle of Tunnel Hill 1864.		8 2	2 17
29	Tue	7 2	5 23	13 17 52		George the 4th reigns 1820.		9 2	2 57
30	We	7 2	5 24	14 17 35		♀ gr. Hel. Lat. S.		10 2	3 36
31	Thu	7 2	5 25	14 17 19		Great Eastern launched 1858.		11 3	4 17

WEATHER CONJECTURES.—JANUARY—1, 2, 3, rain or snow if wind S. or S. W.; 4, 5, 6, 7, 8, 9, 10, snow and storm; 11, 12, 13, 14, 15, 16, frost; 17, 18, 19, 20, 21, 22, 23, 24, expect fair; 25, 26, 27, 28, 29, 30, 31, fair.

DREAMIN' OF HOME.

I can't jest tell what's come to her, an' yet, I think it's clear
That somethin's goin' wrong o' late—to see her sittin' there,
A dreamin' in the doorway, with that look into her eyes,
As if they still was restin' on the old-time fields and skies.

She's always dreamin', dreamin' of the life we left behind—
The cozy little cottage where the mornin' glories twined ;
The roses in the garden—the yellow sunflowers tall ;
The violets—but she herself the sweetest flower of all.

You see, she use to sit there in the mornin's—so content ;
The sunflowers follerin' the sun, no matter where he went ;
The brown bees sippin' honey an' abuzzin' round the place ;
The roses climbin' up to her an' smilin' in her face !

An' now, she can't forget it ; when I tell her : "Little wife,
There ain't no use in grievin' for that simple country life,"
She twines her arms aroun' my neck, an' smilin' sweet to see,
She whispers : " We're so far away from where we use to be !"

There ain't no use in chidin', or in sayin' words o' cheer :
There's nothin' in this city life like she was use to there,
Where preachin' come but once a month, an' street cars didn't run,
An' folks they told the time o' day by lookin' at the sun.

An' larks got up at peep o' day an' made the medders ring !
I tell you, folks, when one's brought up to jes' that kind of thing,
It's hard to git away from it—old feelin's bound to rise
An' make a runnin' over in a woman's tender eyes !

So there she sits a dreamin', till I git to dreamin', too ;
An' when her head droops on my breast and sleep falls like the dew
An' closes them bright eyes of hers, once more we seem to be
In the old home where we'll rest some day together—her an' me !

EUROPEAN SOVEREIGNS.

Many Past Seventy, Yet Still Ruling With the Power of Youth.

The *Almanach de Gotha* for 1894 has buried in its numerous finely-printed pages some interesting facts as to the ages of European sovereigns. The oldest of all is the Pope, who is in his eighty-fourth year. Next comes the Grand Duke of little Luxemburg, who is 76. The king of Denmark and the Grand Duke of Saxe-Weimar are 75 ; Queen Victoria and the Grand Duke of Mecklenburg-Strelitz, 74. There are six other sovereigns who are older than 70 ; eleven who are between 60 and 70, and five who are between 50 and 60. Eleven are between 40 and 50, two between 30 and 40, and two more between 20 and 30. The youngest three sovereigns are King Alexander of Servia, 17 ; Queen Wilhelmina of the Netherlands, 13, and Alfonzo XIII of Spain, 7½.

Queen Victoria has had the longest reign—56½ years. Emperor Franz Josef has reigned 45 years : the Grand Duke of Baden, 41 years ; the Grand Dukes of Oldenberg, of Saxe-Weimar-Eisenach and of Saxe-Altenburg, 40 years each. Fourteen of the sovereigns of Europe have reigned fewer than 10 years. During 1893 three new sovereigns ascended the throne. They are Prince George of Schaumburg-Lippe, Prince Frederick of Waldeck, and Duke Alfred of Coburg, better known as the Duke of Edinburgh.

It has carried knowledge, science and fun into thousands of happy N. C. homes.—Orange Co. Observer.

2d Month. **FEBRUARY, 1895.** *28 Days.*

Moon's Phases.

	D.	H.	M.			D.	H.	M.	
☽ First Quarter,	2	7	7	p. m.	☾ Last Quarter,	16	8	0	a. m.
○ Full Moon,	9	0	14	p. m.	● New Moon,	24	11	35	a. m.

Day of Month.	Day of Week.	Sun rises.	Sun sets.	Sun slow.	Sun's decline south.	ASPECTS OF PLANETS AND OTHER MISCELLANEOUS MATTER.	Moon's place.	Moon rises or sets.	Moon south.
1	Fri	7 1	5 27	14	17 2	☽ Washington first elec. 1779	♈	morn	eve
2	Sat	7 1	5 28	14	16 44	Wash. Hand died 1867.	♈	0 6	5 47
5.	Fourth Sunday after Epiphany.					Day's length 10 hours 29 minutes.			
3	*F.*	7 0	5 29	14	16 27	Horace Greeley born 1811.	♈	1 13	6 38
4	Mon	6 59	5 30	14	16 9	☌ ♆ ☽. First Confed. Cong. 1861	♈	2 24	7 36
5	Tue	6 58	5 31	14	15 51	□ ♂ ☉. Bat. Hatcher's Run '65.	♈	3 34	8 38
6	We	6 58	5 32	14	15 32	☿ in ☊. Ft. Henry cap. 1862.	♉	4 42	9 43
7	Thu	6 57	5 33	14	15 13	Georgia settled 1733.	♉	5 42	10 48
8	Fri	6 56	5 34	14	14 54	○ □ ♅ ☉. Gov. Geary d. 1873	♊	6 30	11 49
9	Sat	6 55	5 35	14	14 35	☿ greatest Elon. E.	♊	rises	morn
6.	Septuagesima Sunday.					,Day's length 10 hours 40 minutes.			
10	*F.*	6 54	5 36	14	14 16	☌ ☿ ♀. ☿ in Perihelion.	♋	6 56	0 46
11	Mon	6 53	5 37	14	13 56	Canada ceded 1763.	♋	8 13	1 40
12	Tue	6 53	5 38	14	13 36	Horatio Seymour died 1886.	♌	9 25	2 30
13	We	6 52	5 39	14	13 16	Charles X of Sweden d. 1660.	♌	10 37	3 18
14	Thu	6 51	5 40	14	12 56	☌ ♄ ☽. St. Valentine's Day.	♍	11 49	4 7
15	Fri	6 50	5 41	14	12 35	☾ ☿ sta. ♄ sta. ☌ ♅ ☽.	♍	morn	4 56
16	Sat	6 49	5 42	14	12 14	Judge Battle buried 1879.	♎	0 58	5 47
7.	Sexagesima Sunday.					Day's length 10 hours 55 minutes.			
17	*F.*	6 48	5 43	14	11 53	Peace decl. with England 1815.	♎	2 4	6 40
18	Mon	6 47	5 44	14	11 32	Martin Luther died 1546.	♏	3 5	7 33
19	Tue	6 46	5 45	14	11 11	♃ sta. Florida ceded 1821.	♏	4 0	8 26
20	We	6 45	5 46	14	10 49	Battle of Olustee 1864.	♏	4 47	9 17
21	Thu	6 43	5 47	14	10 28	☿ gr. Hel. Lat. N.	♏	5 25	10 6
22	Fri	6 42	5 48	14	10 6	Washington's Birthday.	♐	5 55	10 52
23	Sat	6 41	5 48	14	9 44	Nashville captured 1862.	♐	6 23	11 36
8.	Quinquagesima Sunday.					Day's length 11 hours 8 minutes.			
24	*F.*	6 40	5 48	13	9 22	● ☌ ☿ ☽. Guttenburg d. 1648	♐	sets.	eve.
25	Mon	6 39	5 49	13	8 50	☌ ☿ ☉ inferior.	♐	6 56	0 57
26	Tue	6 38	5 50	13	8 37	☌ ♀ ☽. Napoleon esc. Elbe 1815	♑	7 54	1 36
27	We	6 37	5 51	13	8 15	First Day in Lent.	♑	8 55	2 16
28	Thu	6 36	5 52	13	7 52	Abyssinia invaded 1864.	♑	9 59	2 58

Weather Conjectures.—February—1, fair; 2, 3, 4, 5, 6, 7, 8, rain or snow if wind S. or S. W.; 9, 10, 11, 12, 13, 14, 15, rain and snow; 16, 17, 18, 19, 20, 21, 22, 23, stormy; 24, 25, 26, 27, 28, expect cold high winds.

IS GOD HERE?

The following incident is yet another instance of the power of children when used by God to bring about His purpose.

A young man of otherwise good moral character had been addicted to the use of profanity. At first it even shocked himself, but after a time he became so used to it that he ceased to notice it. He at length married a good wife and her influence over him brought about the wish that he could rid himself of the sin which had obtained such mastery over him. He tried hard, but not till his little girl had reached the age of three years did he finally throw off the habit.

One Sunday morning, as he stood before the mirror shaving, the razor slipped and inflicted a wound upon his face.

True to his old sin, he, in his impatience, spoke the name of God in anger. To his surprise, his little girl, who was near, playing with her dolly and had heard him, arose hastily and running to her father with an excited look on her face, said:

" Is God here?"

Ashamed, and not knowing what to reply, he asked:

" Why?"

"'Cause I thought he was here when I heard you speak to him."

Seeing the sad look on his face and the tears in his eyes as he looked down into her innocent face, the child lovingly patted her father on the hand and said:

" Call him again, papa, and I des he'll surely come."

At last the work was done; the hard heart broken; the voice of the beloved was heard in the simple queries of the babe. Catching the surprised little one up in his arms, the man knelt down, and for the first time in his life he prayed. In answer to that prayer forgiveness came, strength came, and the lost sheep returned to the fold.

" And a little child shall lead them."

COLLEGE LEARNING.

She was a Vassar graduate and did not know a little bit about housekeeping when she married her last beau and settled down to domestic life.

Her first order at the grocer's was a crusher, but that good man was used to all sorts of people and could interpret Vassar as easily as plain English.

" I want ten pounds of paralyzed sugar," she said with a business air.

" Yes'm. Anything else?"

" Two cans of condemned milk."

" Yes'm." He set down " pulverized sugar " and ,, condensed milk."

" Anything more, ma'am?"

" A bag of fresh salt—be sure that it is fresh."

" Yes'm. What next?"

" A pound of desecrated codfish."

" Yes'm." He wrote glibly, " desicated cod."

" Nothing more, ma'am? Here's some nice horseradish just in."

" No," she said with a sad wabble to her voice, " it would be of no use, as we don't keep a horse."

Then the grocer sat down on a kit of mackerel and fanned himself with a patent washboard. Vassar has taken the cake.—*Sel.*

A DAY OF ENJOYMENT.

MR. GABBER.—Where is Mrs. Gabber?

SERVANT.—Somebody told her an important secret this morning, and she has been out all day going from house to house visiting her friends.

3d Month. **MARCH, 1895.** **31 Days.**

Moon's Phases.

		D. H. M.		D. H. M.
☽ First Quarter,	4 7 32 a. m.	☾ Last Quarter,	18 0 23 a. m.
● Full Moon,	10 10 29 p. m.	⊕ New Moon,	26 5 16 a. m.

Day of Month.	Day of Week.	Sun rises.	Sun sets.	Sun slow.	Sun's declination, south.	ASPECTS OF PLANETS AND OTHER MISCELLANEOUS MATTER.	Moon's place.	Moon rises or sets.	Moon south.
1	Fri	6 34	5 55	12	7 29	First Spectator pub. 1711.	♈	11 4	eve.
2	Sat	6 32	5 56	12	7 6	Walpole died 1797.	♈	morn	4 32
9.	Quadragesima Sunday.					Day's length 11 hours 27 minutes.			
3	*F.*	6 30	5 57	12	6 43	☽ □ ♆ ☉. Nevada ad. 1863.	♈	0 12	5 26
4	Mon	6 28	5 58	12	6 20	Gen. Jackson inaugurt'd '29.	♈	1 21	6 25
5	Tue	6 26	6 0	12	5 57	☌ ♃ ☽. LaPlace died 1827.	♊	2 28	7 26
6	We	6 24	6 0	11	5 34	Battle of the Alamo 1836.	♊	3 28	8 29
7	Thu	6 23	6 1	11	5 11	Bible Society founded 1804.	♋	4 19	9 30
8	Fri	6 22	6 1	11	4 47	William III died 1702.	♋	5 1	10 28
9	Sat	6 20	6 2	11	4 24	☿ sta. Bat. Hampton Roads '62.	♌	5 36	11 23
10.	Second Sunday in Lent.					Day's length 11 hours 45 minutes.			
*10	*F.*	6 18	6 3	10	4 0	● ☽ ecl. visible at Washington	♌	rises	morn
11	Mon	6 17	6 4	10	3 37	Famine in Cashmere 1880.	♍	6 59	0 14
12	Tue	6 16	6 5	10	3 13	Treaty of Constantinople 1854.	♍	8 14	1 4
13	We	6 14	6 6	10	2 50	Uranus discovered 1781.	♍	9 27	1 54
14	Thu	6 13	6 6	9	2 26	☌ ♄ ☽. Klopstock died 1803.	♎	10 38	2 45
15	Fri	6 12	6 7	9	2 2	☌ ♅ ☽. Samoan disaster 1889.	♎	11 49	3 37
16	Sat	6 11	6 8	9	1 39	☿ in ♑. Mex. evac. by French '67	♏	morn	4 30
11.	Third Sunday in Lent.					Day's length 12 hours 0 minutes.			
17	*F.*	6 9	6 9	8	1 15	☾ □ ♃ ☉. St. Patrick's Day.	♏	0 54	5 25
18	Mon	6 8	6 10	8	0 51	Suez Canal completed 1869	♐	1 53	6 19
19	Tue	6 6	6 11	8	0 27	Yale College founded 1801.	♐	2 44	7 12
20	We	6 4	6 12	8	0 4	☉ enters ♈. Spring Com.	♐	3 25	8 2
21	Thu	6 3	6 12	7	north	Lucknow captured 1858.	♑	3 58	8 49
22	Fri	6 2	6 13	7	0 44	Earthquake at Quito 1859.	♒	4 26	9 33
23	Sat	6 0	6 14	7	1 7	☌ ☿ ☽. Battle Winchester 1862.	♒	4 52	10 15
12.	Fourth Sunday in Lent.					Day's length 12 hours 16 minutes.			
24	*F.*	5 59	6 15	6	1 31	☿ greatest Elong. W.	♒	5 14	10 56
25	Mon	5 58	6 16	6	1 55	☌ ♂ ♆. ☉ ecl. invis. at Wash'gt'n	♒	5 34	11 35
26	Tue	5 57	6 17	6	2 18	⊕ ☿ in Aphelion.	♓	sets.	eve.
27	We	5 55	6 18	5	2 42	Bruce crowned 1306.	♓	7 51	0 57
28	Thu	5 53	6 18	5	3 5	♀ in ♌. ♃ in ♌. ☌ ♀ ☽.	♈	8 55	1 42
29	Fri	5 51	6 19	5	3 29	Swedenborg died 1772.	♈	10 3	2 30
30	Sat	5 50	6 20	4	3 52	Calhoun died 1850.	♈	11 13	3 22
13.	Fifth Sunday in Lent.					Day's length 12 hours 33 minutes.			
31	*F.*	5 48	6 21	4	4 15	☌ ♂ ☽. Allies enter Paris 1814.	♈	morn	4 19

WEATHER CONJECTURES.—MARCH—1, 2, 3, high winds; 4, 5, 6, 7, 8, 9, stormy; 10, 11, 12, 13, 14, 15, 16, 17, fair and frosty; 18, 19, 20, 21, 22, 23, 24, 25, hoar frost unless the wind be S. or S. W.; 26, 27, 28, 29, 30, 31, expect rain.

MY SALLIE MICHAEL PIPE AN' TI-TI STEM.

The preachin' folks has just commenced a row
    Agin tobaccer usin'—say that folks
As chaw and smoke and snuff—no matter how,
    Are just as bad as straight old whiskey soaks.

But give me my old Sallie Michael pipe
    An' ti-ti stem an' good old yaller leaf
That's drunk the juice from Burke hills, rich an' ripe,
    An' then to all their preachin' I am deaf.

I love to sit an' roast my pore old shins
    That's bore the burden for some sixty years,
An' hear the green back-log when it begins
    To sing—a quaverin' like—as if in tears.

An' watch the smoke rings lazyn' towards the fire,
    Like gettin' steady for their upward flight—
A drowsin' an' a dreamin'—no desire
    Except not to be pestered of a night.

A dreamin' an' a pullin' like the deust
    When the devil gits the matter with the draw,
Believin' I'm a boy jist like I use't
    To be long years ago with Maw an' Paw.

A seein' visions through the cloud of smoke,
    Of choppin's, raisin's, quiltin's, and the like—
The swing an' sweep of scythes—the steady stroke
    Of dancin' to the tunes of "Fiddlin' Mike."

They ain't no dead folks in my smokin' dreams,
    An' Rury Ann is settin' by my side
Jist like the night I married her, it seems,
    Before the lonesome summer when she died.

I'm gittin' old, they say, my years is ripe,
    An' voices callin' from the other shore:
Jist let me keep my Sallie Michael pipe
    An' ti-ti stem an' I can ask no more.
                        —*Morganton Herald.*

THE LADY AND THE DRUGGIST.

Old Lady (to druggist)—"I want a box of canine pills."
Druggist—"What is the matter with the dog?"
Old Lady (indignantly)—"I want you to know, sir, that my husband
is a gentleman."
Druggist puts up some quinine pills in profound silence.

THE BEST GIRL.

The "girl who plays the flute,"
    To bless the world was born;
But give us still the girl with skill
    To blow the dinner horn.

I am in receipt of your most excellent Almanac.—**Clerk Superior Court
Warren Co., N. C.**

4th Month.　　　　*APRIL, 1895.*　　　　*30 Days.*

Moon's Phases.

	D. H. M.		D. H. M.
First Quarter,	2 4 19 p. m.	Last Quarter,	16 6 14 p. m.
Full Moon,	9 8 35 a. m.	New Moon,	24 8 2 p. m.

Day of Month.	Day of Week.	Sun rises.	Sun sets.	Sun slow.	Sun's decline north.	ASPECTS OF PLANETS AND OTHER MISCELLANEOUS MATTER.	Moon's place.	Moon rises or sets.	Moon south.
1	Mon	5 47	6 22	4	4 38	April Fool's Day.		3 20	eve.
2	Tue	5 46	6 23	4	5 1	Richmond, Va., evac. 1865.		1 22	6 19
3	We	5 44	6 23	3	5 24	Irving born 1781.		2 14	7 19
4	Thu	5 42	6 24	3	5 47	Gen. Harrison died 1841.		2 59	8 16
5	Fri	5 41	6 25	3	6 10	Canada discovered 1499.		3 35	9 10
6	Sat	5 39	6 26	2	6 33	Battle of Shiloh 1862.		4 5	10 1

14.　Palm Sunday.　　　　Day's length 12 hours 49 minutes.

7	F.	5 38	6 27	2	6 55	Earthquake in Mexico 1845.		4 31	10 51
8	Mon	5 36	6 28	2	7 18	Island No. 10 sur. 1862.		4 57	11 40
9	Tue	5 35	6 29	2	7 40	Gen. R. E. Lee sur. 1865.		rises	morn
10	We	5 34	6 30	1	8 2	Benton died 1858.		8 14	0 31
11	Thu	5 33	6 31	1	8 24	Chas. Reade died 1884.		9 28	1 22
12	Fri	5 31	6 31	1	8 46	Fort Sumter bombarded 1861.		10 37	2 16
13	Sat	5 30	6 32	0	9 8	Raleigh surrendered 1865		11 41	3 12

15.　Easter Sunday.　　　　Day's length 13 hours 5 minutes.

14	F.	5 28	6 33	fast	9 30	Easter Sunday. Dr. Scott d. '21		morn	4 8
15	Mon	5 27	6 34	0	9 51	Andrew Johnson Pres. 1865.		0 36	5 3
16	Tue	5 26	6 34	0	10 12	gr. Hel. Lat. S.		1 21	5 55
17	We	5 24	6 35	1	10 34	Benjamin Franklin died 1790.		1 58	6 43
18	Thu	5 23	6 36	1	10 55	Luther at Worms 1521.		2 29	7 29
19	Fri	5 22	6 37	1	11 15	Dallinger excommunicated 1871,		2 55	8 12
20	Sat	5 21	6 38	1	11 36	Charlotte Bronte born 1816.		3 17	8 52

16.　First Sunday after Easter.　　　　Day's length 13 hours 19 minutes.

21	F.	5 20	6 39	1	11 56	Santa Anna captured 1836.		3 38	9 32
22	Mon	5 18	6 40	2	12 17	Battle of Camden 1781.		3 58	10 12
23	Tue	5 17	6 41	2	12 37	Shakespeare d. 1616		4 20	10 54
24	We	5 15	6 41	2	12 57	Murelle d. 1682.		4 44	11 38
25	Thu	5 14	6 42	2	13 16	King John crown'd 1199		sets	eve
26	Fri	5 13	6 43	2	13 36	Wilkes Booth killed 1865.		9 2	1 17
27	Sat	5 12	6 43	2	13 55	Grant b. 1822.		10 12	2 13

17.　Second Sunday after Easter.　　　　Day's length 13 hours 33 minutes.

28	F.	5 11	6 44	3	14 14	Monroe born 1758.		11 16	3 13
29	Mon	5 10	6 45	3	14 32			morn	4 14
30	Tue	5 9	6 46	3	14 51	in Perihelion.		0 11	5 14

WEATHER CONJECTURES—APRIL—1, damp; 2, 3, 4, 5, 6, 7, 8, rainy; 9, 10, 11, 12, 13, 14, 15, snow if wind be East; 16, 17, 18, 19, 20, 21, 22, 23, rain or snow if wind S. or S. W.; 24, 25, 26, 27, 28, 29, 30, expect variable weather.

STATE AUDITOR'S REPORT.

Decrease in Land and Stock, but increase in Town Property.

We are indebted to State Auditor Furman for a copy of his report for the fiscal year ending November 30, 1893, from which we extract the following which is of general interest:

There are 28 236,403 acres of land for taxation, 66,916 town lots, 143,-157 horses, 108,063 mules, 634,754 head of cattle, 1,181,743 hogs and 364,-508 sheep.

The cash on hand was $4,006,000; and the solvent credits $20,210,000. The amount of net incomes listed for taxation was $162,467.

In lands there has been a decrease of $852 000; in horses and mules of $711,000; in cattle, hogs, sheep, etc., $505,000. Money on hand has shrunk $1,463,000, solvent credits have decreased $965,000, while farming utensils and other personal property show a loss of $2,272,000—a total decrease of $6,776,000.

Town property shows an increase of $856,000; stocks in incorporated companies of $964,000, and railroad property of $3,500,000—which comes within $457,000 of balancing the loss in values above stated.

The total taxes run up to $1,394,989. Of this amount the agricultural classes paid about $550,000, the remainder being paid by town property, and corporations and stock companies.

Over $750,000 of the above receipts were expended for educational purposes, and $99,000 for pensions for soldiers and their widows.

The rate of taxation has decreased until now our people pay the lowest rate on the lowest valuation of property of any State in the Union.

"LAUGH A LITTLE BIT."

BY J. EDMUND V. COOK.

Here's a motto just your fit :
" Laugh a little bit,"
When you think you're trouble hit,
" Laugh a little bit."
Look Misfortune in the face,
Brave the beldam's rude grimace;
Ten to one 'twill yield its place
If you have the grit and wit
Just to laugh a little bit.

Keep your face with sunshine lit—
" Laugh a little bit."
Gloomy shadows off will flit
If you have the wit and grit
Just to laugh a little bit.

Cherish this as sacred writ—
" Laugh a little bit."
Keep it with you, sample it—
" Laugh a little bit."
Little ills will sure betide you,
Fortune may not sit beside you,
Men may mock and fame deride you,
But you'll mind them not a bit
If you laugh a little whit.

—*St. Nicholas.*

Always carefully compiled and what it claims to be, " a valuable hand-book of information about North Carolina."—Newbern Journal.

5th Month. **MAY, 1895.** *31 Days.*

Moon's Phases.

	D.	H.	M.		D.	H.	M.
☽ First Quarter,	1	10	35 p. m.	☾ Last Quarter,	16	0	35 p. m.
◯ Full Moon,	8	6	50 p. m.	● New Moon,	24	7	38 a. m.
				☽ First Quarter,	31	3	4 a. m.

Day of Month.	Day of Week.	Sun rises.	Sun sets.	Sun fast.	Sun's decline north	ASPECTS OF PLANETS AND OTHER MISCELLANEOUS MATTER.	Moon's place.	Moon rises or sets.	Moon south.
1	We	5 8	6 47	3	15 9	MAY DAY.		0 56	eve
2	Thu	5 7	6 48	3	15 27	Stonewall Jackson wo'd'd '63		1 34	6 11
3	Fri	5 6	6 49	3	16 45	America discovered 1492.		2 7	7 55
4	Sat	5 5	6 49	3	16 2	☌ ♀ ☉ superior.		2 34	8 43
18.	Third Sunday after Easter.					Day's length 13 hours 46 minutes.			
5	*F.*	5 4	6 50	3	16 36	James L. Orr died 1873.		2 59	9 31
6	Mon	5 3	6 51	4	16 36	South Sea Act passed 1716.		3 24	10 19
7	Tue	5 2	6 51	4	16 53	☌ ♄ ☽. Gen. Worth d. 1849.		3 49	11 10
8	We	5 1	6 52	4	17 9	☍ ♅ ☉: ☌ ♅ ☽.		4 19	morn
9	Thu	5 0	6 53	4	17 25	☿ in Perihelion.		rises	0 2
10	Fri	4 59	6 54	4	17 41	CONFEDERATE MEMORIAL DAY.		9 24	0 57
11	Sat	4 58	6 54	4	17 57	F. B Reid died 1872.		10 24	1 54
19.	Fourth Sunday after Easter.					Day's length 13 hours 58 minutes.			
12	*F.*	4 57	6 55	4	18 12	Union Pacific R. R. open'd 1869		11 14	2 50
13	Mon	4 56	6 56	4	18 27	Jamestown settled 1607.		11 55	3 44
14	Tue	4 55	6 57	4	18 41	Famine in Ireland 1847.		morn	4 35
15	We	4 54	6 58	4	18 56	Cuvier died 1832.		0 28	5 22
16	Thu	4 53	6 59	4	19 9	Vendome column dest. 1871.		0 55	6 6
17	Fri	4 53	7 0	4	19 23	Lopez in Cuba 1850.		1 20	6 48
18	Sat	4 52	7 1	4	19 36	☌ ♀ ♃.		1 41	7 28
20.	Rogation Sunday.					Day's length 14 hours 9 minutes.			
19	*F.*	4 52	7 1	4	19 49	☌ ☿ ♆. French fleet cap. 1692.		2 2	8 7
20	Mon	4 51	7 2	4	20 2	MECKLENB'G INDEPEND'CE 1775.		2 23	8 48
21	Tue	4 50	7 3	4	20 14	Battle of Essling 1809.		2 45	9 31
22	We	4 49	7 3	4	20 26	♀ greatest Hel. Lat. N.		3 9	10 17
23	Thu	4 48	7 4	3	20 38	ASCENSION DAY.		3 40	11 7
24	Fri	4 48	7 5	3	20 49	Capt. Kidd executed 1701.		sets	eve
25	Sat	4 48	7 5	3	21 0	☌ ♆ ☽: ☌ ☿ ☽		9 4	1 3
21.	Sixth Sunday after Easter.					Day's length 14 hours 19 minutes.			
26	*F.*	4 47	7 6	3	21 10	☌ ♃ ☽. Bat. Ostrolinka 1831.		10 5	2 5
27	Mon	4 47	7 7	3	21 21	☌ ♅ ☽. Bat. Hanover C. H. '62		10 56	3 7
28	Tue	4 46	7 8	3	21 30	Quebec burnt 1845.		11 35	4 6
29	We	4 46	7 9	3	21 40	Gen. Putnam died 1790.		morn	5 1
30	Thu	4 45	7 10	3	21 49	FEDERAL MEMORIAL DAY.		0 9	5 52
31	Fri	4 45	7 11	3	21 57	Dr. Chalmers died 1847.		0 37	6 40

WEATHER CONJECTURES.—MAY—1, 2, 3. 4, 5, 6, 7, fair; 8, 9, 10, 11, 12, 13, 14, 15, fair and frosty if wind N. or N. E.; 16, 17, 18, 19, 20, 21, 22, 23, expect much rain; 24, 25, 26, 27, 28, 29, 30, wind and rain; 31, cold showers.

ORIGIN OF POPULAR SAYINGS.

S. T. Coleridge, 1772-1834. "A sadder and a wiser man." Bobert Southey, 1774-1843. "The march of intellect." "Agreed to differ." "Helter-skelter." "Pride that apes humility." Charles Lamb, 1775-1834. "Neat, not gaudy." Henry Clay, 1777-1852. "Sir, I would rather be right than be President." Charles Miner, 1780-1865. "Has an axe to grind." John C. Calhoun, 1782-1850. "The cohesive power of the vast surplus in the banks." (Perverted, perhaps improved, into "Cohesive power of public plunder.") Daniel Webster, 1782-1852. (Webster and Calhoun were born the same year.) "I also, am an American." "Independence now, independence forever." "The people's government, made for the people, made by the people, and answerable to the people." This was said in 1830 in the Senate (Lincoln in 1863, changed it into "the government of the people, by the people, for the people, shall not perish from the earth.") "Liberty and Union, now and forever, one and inseparable." Lord Byron, 1788-1824. "What is writ is writ." "Stranger than fiction." Thomas C. Halliburton. 1796-1865. "Upper crust." "Circumstances alter cases." Thomas Hood, 1798-1845. "Alas for the rarity of Christian charity." Sir Henry Taylor, 1800. "The world knows nothing of its greatest men." William H. Seward, 1801-1872. "A higher law." "An irrepressible conflict." Albert G. Greene, 1802-1868. "Old Grimes is dead." Mary Howitt, 1804-1888. "Will you walk into my parler? said a spider to a fly." Benjamin Disraeli, 1805-1881. "The Rupert of debate." "An organized hypocrisy." "His Christianity was muscular."

'TIS SAID THE WORLD OWES US A LIVING.

FOR THE NEWS, BY OLD FANEUIL (T. R. MAGILL).

'Tis said the world owes us a living,
    But I have not found it that way,
And if you depend on its giving
    I fear you will meet with dismay.

'Tis said the world owes us a living,
    But somehow the saying I doubt,
For you ill find it is chary in giving
    When your money and credit is out.

'Tis said the world owes us a living,
    But I feel you will die in despair
If you wait till it gives you a shilling
    That by labor you have not earned square.

'Tis said the world owes us a living,
    But the saying will lead you astray,
For the world, it is cold in its stinging,
    I care not just what they may say.

For since Adam in Eden was living,
    And Eve ate the apple you know,
We all have to do our own digging
    And live by the sweat of our brow.

Then why not be up and a doing
    And prove to the world you're a man,
And cease to be always pursuing
    A saying that's naught but a sham.

Dr Branson makes his own calculations and guarantees them to be correct.—Thomasville News.

6th Month.	*JUNE, 1895.*	*30 Days.*

Moon's Phases.

	D.	H.	M.			D.	H.	M.	
Full Moon,	7	5	51	a. m.	New Moon,	22	4	42	p. m.
Last Quarter,	15	6	19	a. m.	First Quarter,	29	8	52	a. m.

Day of Month.	Day of Week.	Sun rises.	Sun sets.	Sun fast.	Sun's decline north.	ASPECTS OF PLANETS AND OTHER MISCELLANEOUS MATTER.	Moon's place.	Moon rises or sets.	Moon south.
1	Sat	4 44	7 11	2	22 6	Battle of Cold Harbor 1864.	[illegible]	12	eve
22. Whitsun Day.						Day's length 14 hours 27 minutes.			
2	*F.*	4 44	7 11	2	22 14	Earthquake at Cairo 1754.	[illegible]	1 27	8 15
3	Mon	4 44	7 12	2	22 21	Jefferson Davis born 1808.	[illegible]	1 52	9 3
4	Tue	4 43	7 12	2	22 28	☌ ♄ ☽. ☿ greatest Elong. E.	[illegible]	2 18	9 54
5	We	4 42	7 13	2	22 35	☌ ♅ ☽ ☌ ♀ ♂. DeSoto d. 1542	[illegible]	2 50	10 47
6	Thu	4 41	7 13	2	22 41	Patrick Henry died 1799.	[illegible]	3 28	11 42
7	Fri	4 41	7 14	1	22 47	Robert Bruce died 1329.	[illegible]	rises	morn
8	Sat	4 41	7 14	1	22 53	☌ ☿ ♃. Bat. of Cross Keys 1862	[illegible]	9 4	0 39
23. Trinity Sunday.						Day's length 14 hours 34 minutes.			
9	*F.*	4 41	7 15	1	22 58	Dickens died 1870.	[illegible]	9 50	1 34
10	Mon	4 41	7 15	1	23 2	Crystal Palace opened 1851.	[illegible]	10 26	2 27
11	Tue	4 41	7 16	1	23 7	Col. Crawford burnt 1782.	[illegible]	10 55	3 16
12	We	4 41	7 16	0	23 11	☿ in ☊. Massacre in Paris 1418.	[illegible]	11 22	4 1
13	Thu	4 41	7 16	slow	23 14	Maryland charter. 1633.	[illegible]	11 44	4 43
14	Fri	4 41	7 16		23 17	First persecuti'n by Nero 64.	[illegible]	morn	5 23
15	Sat	4 41	7 17		23 20	Magna Charta 1215.	[illegible]	0 5	6 3
24. First Sunday after Trinity.						Day's length 14 hours 37 minutes.			
16	*F.*	4 41	7 18	0	23 22	Peter the Great born 1672.	[illegible]	0 24	6 42
17	Mon	4 41	7 18	1	23 24	Battle of Bunker Hill 1775.	[illegible]	0 45	7 23
18	Tue	4 41	7 19	1	23 25	☿ sta. Battle of Waterloo 1815	[illegible]	1 9	8 7
19	We	4 42	7 19	1	23 27	The Alabama sunk 1864.	[illegible]	1 37	8 55
20	Thu	4 43	7 19	1	23 27	Queen Victoria crowned 1837.	[illegible]	2 10	9 48
21	Fri	4 43	7 19	2	23 27	Sun ent. ♋. SUMMER COM.	[illegible]	2 52	10 47
22	Sat	4 43	7 19	2	23 27	☿ in Aphelion.	[illegible]	sets	11 50
25. Second Sunday after Trinity.						Day's length 14 hours 36 minutes.			
23	*F.*	4 43	7 19	2	23 26	☌ ☿ ☽: ☌ ♃ ☽.	[illegible]	8 47	eve
24	Mon	4 43	7 19	2	23 25	Labrador discovered 1497.	[illegible]	9 34	1 56
25	Tue	4 43	7 19	2	23 24	☌ ♂ ☽: ☌ ♀ ☽.	[illegible]	10 10	2 54
26	We	4 44	7 20	3	23 22	Pizarro died 1541.	[illegible]	10 40	3 48
27	Thu	4 44	7 20	3	23 20	Powers died 1876.	[illegible]	11 6	4 38
28	Fri	4 44	7 20	3	23 17	Seven day's fight begun 1862	[illegible]	11 31	5 26
29	Sat	4 45	7 20	3	23 14	St. Peter crucified 65.	[illegible]	11 56	6 13
26. Third Sunday after Trinity.						Day's length 14 hours 35 minutes.			
30	*F.*	4 45	7 20	3	23 11	☌ ♄ ☽. Montezuma d. 1530.	[illegible]	morn	7 0

WEATHER CONJECTURES.—JUNE—1, 2, 3, 4, 5, 6, cool and showery; 7, 8, 9, 10, 11, 12, 13, 14, look for rain; 15, 16, 17, 18, 19, 20, 21, wind and rain; 22, 23, 24, 25, 26, 27, 28, fair; 29, 30, changeable.

GOVERNMENT OF NORTH CAROLINA—1893-'97.

EXECUTIVE DEPARTMENT.

Elias Carr, of Edgecombe County, Governor; salary $3,000 and furnished house, fuel and lights.

R. A. Doughton, of Alleghany County, Lieut. Gov. and Speaker of the Senate.

Octavius Coke, of Wake County, Secretary of State; salary $2,000 and fees; $1,000 additional for clerical assistance.

Robert M. Furman, of Buncombe County, Auditor; salary $1,500; $1,000 additional for clerical assistance.

Samuel McD. Tate, of Burke County, Treasurer; salary $3,000.

John C. Scarborough, of Johnston County, Superintendent of Public Instruction; salary $1,500; $500 per annum additional traveling expenses.

Frank I. Osborne, of Mecklenburg County, Attorney General; salary $2,000.

R. T. Gray, Reporter to Supreme Court; salary $750.

Francis H. Cameron, of Wake County, Adjutant General; salary $600.

J. C. Ellington, of Johnston County, State Librarian; salary $1,000.

T. P. Jerman, of Warren County, Chief Clerk to Auditor; salary $1,000.

S. F. Telfair, of Beaufort County, Private Secretary to Governor; salary $1.200.

C. L. Hinton, of Wake County, Executive Clerk; salary $600.

W. P. Batchelor, of Wake County, Chief Clerk to Secretary of State; salary $1,000.

H. M. Cowan, of Chatham County, Chief Clerk to Treasurer; salary $1,500.

Ernest B. Bain, of Wake County, Teller; salary $750.

R. L. Burkhead, of Wayne County, Clerk for Charitable and Penal Institutions; salary $1,000.

C. M. Roberts, of Vance County, Superintendent of Public Buildings and Grounds; salary $850.

J. C. S. Lumsden, State Standard Keeper; salary $100.

STATE BOARD OF EDUCATION.

The Governor, Lieutenant Governor, Secretary of State, Treasurer, Auditor, Superintendent of Public Instruction and Attorney General constitute the Board.

UNIVERSITY OF NORTH CAROLINA.

(Located in Chapel Hill, Orange County, twenty-eight miles northwest of Raleigh).

Chartered in 1789, founded 1793, opened 1795. It now has 450 students and twenty-eight instructors. The equipment includes twelve large buildings, five scientific laboratories, library of 40,000 volumes, campus of fifty acres with ample athletic grounds, gymnasium, &c. Perfect sanitation, baths, closets, &c. Tuition $60 a year, total expenses $200 to $300. Scholarships and loans for the needy. Law school (seventy-five students) and medical school (thirty students.) During 1894 many students supported themse'ves by labor, the total amount earned being about $5 000. The University is non-political and non-sectarian.

FACULTY.—George Tayloe Winston, LL. D., President and Professor of Political and Social Science; Kemp Plummer Battle, LL. D., Professor of History; Francis Preston Venable, Ph. D., Professor of General and Analytical Chemistry; Joseph Austin Holmes, B. S., State Geologist and Lecturer on Geology of North Carolina; Joshua Walker Gore, C. E., Professor of Natural Philosophy; John Manning, LL. D., Professor of Law; Thomas Hume, D. D., LL. D., Professor of the English Language and Literature; Walter Dallam Toy, M. A., Professor of

Branson's Almanac—State pride compels us to admire it.—The Livingstone.

7th Month. **JULY, 1895.** ***31 Days.***

Moon's Phases.

	D. H. M.			D. H. M.
Full Moon,	6 6 20 p. m.		New Moon,	22 0 23 a. m.
Last Quarter,	14 10 22 p. m.		First Quarter,	28 3 27 p. m.

Day of Month.	Day of Week.	Sun rises.	Sun sets.	Sun slow.	Sun's decline north.	ASPECTS OF PLANETS AND OTHER MISCELLANEOUS MATTER.	Moon's place.	Moon rises or sets.	Moon south.
1	Mon	4 45	7 20	4	23 7	☌ ☿ ☉ inferior. ⊕ in Aphelion.	♍	0 23	eve
2	Tue	4 46	7 20	4	23 2	☌ ♅ ☽. Robert Peel died 1850.	♍	0 52	8 41
3	We	4 47	7 20	4	22 58	Massacre Wyoming 1778.	♎	1 27	9 35
4	Thu	4 47	7 20	4	22 53	♄ sta. INDEPENDENCE DAY.	♎	2 8	10 31
5	Fri	4 48	7 19	4	22 47	♂ in Aphelion.	♏	2 57	11 26
6	Sat	4 48	7 19	4	22 41	Battle of Carthage 1861.	♏	rises	morn

27. Fourth Sunday after Trinity. Day's length 14 hours 30 minutes.

7	***F.***	4 49	7 19	4	22 35	Gen. Quitman died 1858.	♐	8 25	0 19
8	Mon	4 50	7 19	5	22 28	Edmund Burke born 1730.	♐	8 55	1 9
9	Tue	4 50	7 19	5	22 21	Braddock's defeat 1755.	♐	9 23	1 56
10	We	4 51	7 18	5	22 14	Tobacco first in England 1586.	♑	9 46	2 39
11	Thu	4 52	7 18	5	22 6	♀ gr. Elong. E. Luke 11:9.	♑	10 8	3 20
12	Fri	4 52	7 18	5	21 58	☿ stationary. Proverbs 12:2.	♒	10 28	4 0
13	Sat	4 53	7 17	5	21 49	☿ greatest Hel. Lat. S.	♒	10 49	4 39

28. Fifth Sunday after Trinity. Day's length 14 hours 24 minutes.

14	***F.***	4 53	7 17	6	21 40	Great Chicago fire 1873.	♒	11 11	5 18
15	Mon	4 54	7 16	6	21 31	Great hail in England 1808.	♓	11 36	6 0
16	Tue	4 55	7 16	6	21 21	Flight of Mohammed 622.	♓	morn	6 45
17	We	4 55	7 15	6	21 11	Bishop White died 1836.	♈	0 5	7 35
18	Thu	4 56	7 15	6	21 0	♀ in ☊.	♈	0 42	8 30
19	Fri	4 57	7 14	6	20 50	☌ ♆ ☽. French inv. Ger. 1870.	♈	1 30	9 30
20	Sat	4 57	7 13	6	20 38	☌ ☿ ☽. Petrarch b. 1304.	♉	2 30	10 34

29. Sixth Sunday after Trinity. Day's length 14 hours 15 minutes.

21	***F.***	4 58	7 13	6	20 27	☌ ♃ ☽. Battle Bull Run '62	♉	3 41	11 38
22	Mon	4 59	7 12	6	20 15	☿ greatest Elong. W.	♊	sets	eve
23	Tue	5 0	7 12	6	20 3	□ ♄ ☉: ☌ ♂ ☽.	♋	8 39	1 36
24	We	5 1	7 11	6	19 50	♅ stationary. Bolivar b. 1783.	♋	9 7	2 30
25	Thu	5 2	7 11	6	19 38	☌ ♀ ☽. Bat. Lundy's Lane 1814	♋	9 33	3 20
26	Fri	5 3	7 10	6	19 24	First P. O. in America 1775.	♌	9 59	4 9
27	Sat	5 3	7 9	6	19 11	Portugal a monarchy 1139.	♌	10 25	4 57

30. Seventh Sunday after Trinity. Day's length 14 hours 5 minutes.

28	***F.***	5 3	7 8	6	18 57	Lord Durham died 1840.	♍	10 54	5 47
29	Mon	5 4	7 7	6	18 43	Poland dissolved 1794.	♍	11 27	6 38
30	Tue	5 5	7 6	6	18 29	William Penn died 1718.	♎	morn	7 31
31	We	5 6	7 6	6	18 14	Trinidad discovered 1498.	♎	0 6	8 26

WEATHER CONJECTURES.—**JULY—1, 2, 3, 4, 5,** variable; 6, 7, 8, 9, 10, 11, 12, 13, fair if wind N. W.; **14, 15, 16, 17,** 18, 19, 20, 21, fair; 22, 23, 24, 25, 26, 27, expect fine weather; 28, 29, 30, 31, changeable.

Modern Languages; Eben Alexander, Ph. D., LL. D., Professor of the Greek Language and Literature (on leave of absence); William Cain, C. E., Professor of Mathematics; Richard Henry Whitehead, M. D., Professor of Anatomy, Physiology and *Materia Medica;* Henry Horace Williams, A. M., B. D., Professor of Mental and Moral Science; Henry Van Peters Wilson, Ph. D., Professor of Biology; Karl Pomeroy Harrington, A. M., Professor of the Latin Language and Literature; James Shepherd, LL. D., Chief Justice of the Supreme Court of North Carolina, and Associate Professor of Common and Statute Law and Equity in Summer School; Collier Cobb, A. B., Professor of Geology and Mineralogy; Edwin Anderson Alderman, Ph. B., Professor of History and Philosophy of Education; Francis Kingsley Ball, Ph. D., Professor of Greek; Charles Baskerville, B. Sc., Instructor in Chemistry; Thomas Roswell Foust, B. E., Instructor in Mathematics; James Thomas Pugh, A. B., Instructor in Latin; Herman Howell Horne, Instructor in Modern Languages; George Stockton Wills, Ph. B.,Instructor in English; Charles Root Turner, Assistant in Physical Laboratory; Thomas Clarke, Assistant in Chemical Laboratory; Charles Robeson, George Hughes Kirby, Assistants in Biological Laboratory; George Gullett Stephens, Instructor in Physical Culture; Eugene Lewis Harris, Ph. B., Secretary and Registrar; W. T. Patterson, Bursar; Edwin Anderson Alderman, Ph. B., Librarian; Benjamin Wyche, Assistant Librarian.

UNIVERSITY CHAPLAINS.—(For conducting chapel services). Rev. John L. Carroll, A. M., D. D.; Rev. D. J. Currie, A. B.; Rev. Frederick Towers, A. B.; Rev. N. M. Watson.

PUBLIC WORKS AND INSTITUTIONS IN NORTH CAROLINA.

NORTH CAROLINA INSTITUTION FOR THE BLIND.

The North Carolina Institution for the Blind is located at Raleigh.
OFFICERS.—W. J. Young, Principal, salary $1,800; time expires 1896. Dr. Hubert Haywood, of Raleigh, Physician. salary $600; time expires 1895. John G. B. Grimes, Steward, salary $900 and board; time expires 1895. S. McD. Tate, *ex officio* Treasurer.

BOARD OF TRUSTEES.—B. F. Montague, President; time expires Jan. 1, 1897. B. F. Park, time expires Jan. 1, 1895; C. D. Heartt. time expires Jan. 1, 1899; John R. Williams, time expires Jan. 1, 1899; Dr. H. C. Herring, time expires Jan. 1, 1899; Ivan Proctor, time expires Jan. 1, 1895; Jas. A. Briggs, time expires Jan. 1, 1897.

NORTH CAROLINA SCHOOL FOR THE DEAF AND DUMB.

(Located at Morganton, N. C.)
BOARD OF DIRECTORS.—M. L. Reid, President, Biltmore; Martin H. Holt, Oak Ridge; Dr. P. L. Murphy, Morganton; N. B. Broughton, Raleigh; R. A. Grier, Charlotte; A. C. Miller, Shelby; V. V. Richardson, Whiteville.

OFFICERS.—E. McK. Goodwin, Superintendent; George L. Phifer, Steward and Treasurer; Mrs. Mary B. Malone, Matron; Mrs. C. S. Jackson, Assistant Matron; Mr. W. J. Matthews, Engineer.

TEACHERS.—Mr. D. R. Tillinghast, Mr. Z. W. Haynes, Mr. O. A. Betts, Mr. J. C. Miller, Mrs. L. A. Winston, Miss Anna C. Allen (Oral Department), Miss Eugenia Walsh (Oral Department), Miss Minnie Fleming (Oral Department), Miss Sudie Faison (Art).

We have admitted 114 children. There are over 700 deaf children of school age in North Carolina. We will accommodate 250 when completed. We have 220 acres of land and will run farm, garden and dairy in connection with the school. We will teach shoe-making, carpentry, broom and mattress making, and, later, printing.

Branson's Almanac—More information in it than any I receive.—W. R. Harris.

8th Month. ***AUGUST, 1895.*** ***31 Days.***

Moon's Phases.

	D. H. M.		D. H. M.
Full Moon,	5 8 43 a. m.	New Moon,	20 7 47 a. m.
Last Quarter,	13 0 10 p. m.	First Quarter,	27 0 35 a. m.

Day of Month.	Day of Week.	Sun rises.	Sun sets.	Sun slow.	Sun's decline north.	ASPECTS OF PLANETS AND OTHER MISCELLANEOUS MATTER.	Moon's place.	Moon rises or sets.	Moon south.
1	Thu	5 6	7 5	6	17 59	☿ in ♌. ☌ ☿ ♃.	♐	0 54	eve
2	Fri	5 7	7 4	6	17 43	South America discovered 1498.	♐	1 47	10 14
3	Sat	5 8	7 3	6	17 28	Crown Point taken 1759.	♐	2 46	11 5
31.		Eighth Sunday after Trinity.				Day's length 13 hours 53 minutes.			
4	*F.*	5 9	7 2	6	17 12	Edwin Irving born 1792.	♑	3 49	11 53
5	Mon	5 10	7 1	6	16 56	☿ in Perihelion. Math. 5:5.	♑	rises.	morn
6	Tue	5 11	7 1	6	16 39	Gen. Cromwell 1658.	♒	7 52	0 37
7	We	5 11	7 0	6	16 23	Barzelius died 1848.	♒	8 13	1 19
8	Thu	5 12	6 58	5	16 6	□ ♅ ☉. Armada dest. 1588.	♓	8 33	1 58
9	Fri	5 13	6 56	5	15 49	John Boyle O'Riley died 1890.	♓	8 54	2 37
10	Sat	5 14	6 55	5	15 31	Battle of Oak Hill 1861.	♓	9 14	3 16
32.		Ninth Sunday after Trinity.				Day's length 13 hours 40 minutes.			
11	*F.*	5 14	6 54	5	15 13	Moreau born 1763.	♈	9 37	3 57
12	Mon	5 15	6 53	5	14 55	Southey born 1774.	♈	10 3	4 40
13	Tue	5 16	6 52	5	14 37	Boulanger guilty 1889.	♈	10 36	5 26
14	We	5 17	6 51	4	14 19	Gen. Grimes assassinated 1880.	♉	11 17	6 18
15	Thu	5 18	6 50	4	14 0	☌ ♆ ☽. Napoleon born 1769.	♉	morn	7 14
16	Fri	5 19	6 49	4	13 41	☿ greatest Hel. Lat. N.	♊	0 10	8 15
17	Sat	5 19	6 48	4	13 22	☌ ☿ ☉. superior. Luke 5:23.	♊	1 16	9 17
33.		Tenth Sunday after Trinity.				Day's length 13 hours 26 minutes.			
18	*F.*	5 20	6 46	4	13 3	Cor. stone U. S. Cap. laid 1793.	♋	2 30	10 20
19	Mon	5 21	6 45	3	12 43	Sun ecl. invis. at Washingt'n	♋	3 50	11 19
20	Tue	5 21	6 44	3	12 23	☌ ☿ ☽. ♀ in Aphelion.	♌	sets	eve
21	We	5 22	6 43	3	12 3	☌ ♂ ☽. Prof. Tyndall b. 1820.	♌	7 33	1 8
22	Thu	5 23	6 42	3	11 43	☌ ♀ ☽. Dr. Gall died 1828.	♍	7 59	1 59
23	Fri	5 24	6 40	2	11 23	Cuvier born 1769.	♍	8 25	2 49
24	Sat	5 25	6 39	2	11 2	Washington City cap. 1814.	♎	8 54	3 40
34.		Eleventh Sunday after Trinity.				Day's length 13 hours 12 minutes.			
25	*F.*	5 26	6 38	2	10 42	☌ ♅ ☽. Jas. Walt died 1819.	♎	9 26	4 32
26	Mon	5 27	6 36	2	10 21	♀ sta. L. Phillipe d. 1850.	♎	10 5	5 26
27	Tue	5 27	6 35	1	10 0	Rowland died 1879.	♏	10 51	6 21
28	We	5 28	6 33	1	9 39	Battle of Centreville 1862.	♏	11 42	7 16
29	Thu	5 28	6 32	1	9 17	Battle of Groveton, 1862.	♐	morn	8 11
30	Fri	5 29	6 31	1	8 56	William Penn died 1718.	♐	0 40	9 2
31	Sat	5 30	6 30	0	8 34	Earthquake in So States 1886.	♑	1 42	9 50

WEATHER CONJECTURES.—AUGUST—1, 2, 3, 4, changeable; 5, 6, 7, 8, 9, 10, 11, 12, variable; 13, 14, 15, 16, 17, 18, 19, expect much rain; 20, 21, 22, 23, 24, 25, 26, wind and rain; 27, 28, 29, 30, 31, fair.

NORTH CAROLINA INSANE ASYLUM.

Situated in the vicinity of Raleigh, and will accommodate 300 patients.

OFFICERS.—Hon. Samuel McD. Tate, Treasurer, *ex officio*, W. T. Smith, Esq., Keeper of Records, salary $100.

RESIDENT OFFICERS.—Dr. George L. Kirby, Superintendent, salary $2,800; term 6 years from June 1, 1894. J. A. Faison, 1st Assistant Physician, salary $1,200; term 2 years from March 1, 1895. Dr. R. S. McGeachey, 2d Assistant Physician, salary $1,200; term 2 years from March 1, 1895. W. R. Crawford, Jr., Steward, salary $1,200; term 1 year from March 1, 1895. Mrs. M. A. Whitaker, Matron, salary $600; term 1 year from March 1, 1895.

BOARD OF DIRECTORS.—Major John B. Broadfoot, Cumberland County, President; Capt. J. B. Burwell, Wake County; B. F. Boykin, New Hanover County; J. D. Biggs, Martin County; Dr. George A. Foote, Warren County; R. S. Cotten, Esq., Pitt County; Dr. R. H. Speight, Edgecombe County; C. G. Latta, Wake County; J. W. Sanders, Carteret County.

The Executive Committee receive $4 per day for one day and mileage to and from their homes.

THE STATE HOSPITAL, MORGANTON.

BOARD OF DIRECTORS.—James P. Sawyer, Buncombe County, President of Board.

DIRECTORS.—I. I. Davis, Esq., Burke County; Joseph P. Caldwell, Esq., Mecklenburg County; J. G. Hall, Esq., Catawba County; Jas. P. Sawyer, Buncombe County; Jos. C. Mills, Burke County; Dr. H. T. Bahnson, Forsyth County; Dr. George H. P. Cole, Henderson County; Gen. E. R. Hampton, Jackson County; G. W. F. Harper, Caldwell County.

OFFICERS.—P. L. Murphy, M. D., Superintendent, salary $2,800; Isaac M. Taylor, M. D., Assistant Physician, salary $1,200; C. E. Ross, M. D., Assistant Physician, salary $1,200; F. M. Scroggs, Steward, salary $1,000; Mrs. C. A. Marsh, Matron, salary $550.

No member of the Board of Directors or Executive Committee receive any compensation for their work except their traveling expenses.

EASTERN HOSPITAL, GOLDSBORO.

J. F. Miller, M. D., Superintendent, salary $1,800, furnished house and board of two horses and cows; W. W. Faison, M. D., Assistant Physician, salary $900, board for self, wife, three children and nurse and board of one horse; Daniel Reid, Steward, salary $450, board of self and horse; Mrs. B. V. Smith, Matron, salary $300 and board of self and child; John W. Wilson, Engineer, salary $450, furnished house for family; Mrs. Victoria Bryan, Seamstress, salary $150 and board of self and child; John Pate, Farmer, salary $200 and house; A. A. Green, Watchman, salary $250 per annum.

BOARD OF DIRECTORS.—Dr. J. W. Vick, Chairman, Johnston County; term expires March 1, 1897. B. F. Aycock, Wayne County; term expires March 1, 1899. J. F. Southerland, Wayne County; term expires March 1, 1897. J. L. McLean, Robeson County; term expires March 1, 1897. L. H. Castex, Wayne County; term expires March 1, 1895. H. E. Dillon, Lenoir County; term expires March 1, 1895. Theophilus Edwards, Greene County; term expires March 1, 1895. W. E. Rountree, Craven County; term expires March 1, 1899. Dr. M. B. Pitt, Edgecombe County; term expires March 1, 1899.

EXECUTIVE COMMITTEE.—B. F. Aycock, L. H. Castex, J. F. Southerland. Hon. S. McD. Tate, Treasurer *ex officio*.

BUREAU OF LABOR STATISTICS.

B. R. Lacy, of Wake County, Commissioner, salary $1,500; Logan D. Terrell, Wake County, salary $900. Office in the Supreme Court Building.

Branson's Almanac—It is reliable and saves every family much valuable time.—Christian Sun.

9th Month. ***SEPTEMBER, 1895.*** ***30 Days.***

Moon's Phases.

	D.	H.	M.			D.	H.	M.	
Full Moon,	4	0	47	a. m.	New Moon,	18	3	47	p. m.
Last Quarter,	11	11	42	p. m.	First Quarter,	25	1	14	p. m.

Day of Month.	Day of Week.	Sun rises.	Sun sets.	Sun fast.	Sun's decline north.	ASPECTS OF PLANETS AND OTHER MISCELLANEOUS MATTER.	Moon's place.	Moon rises or sets.	Moon south.
35.		Twelfth Sunday after Trinity.				Day's length 12 hours 57 minutes.			
1	*F.*	5 31	6 28	0	8 12	☌ ☿ ♂. Great London fire 1666.	♑	2 45	eve
2	Mon	5 32	6 27	0	7 51	Napoleon III surrendered 1870.	♑	3 48	11 18
3	Tue	5 33	6 25	1	7 29	Moon ecl. vis. in N.&S. Amer.	♒	4 47	11 58
4	We	5 34	6 24	1	7 7	Gen. Morgan killed 1864.	♒	rises	morn
5	Thu	5 35	6 22	1	6 44	☌ ☿ ♀. Catharine Parr d. 1831.	♓	6 59	0 37
6	Fri	5 35	6 21	2	6 22	Warsaw taken 1831.	♓	7 19	1 16
7	Sat	5 36	6 19	2	6 0	Battle Borodino 1812.	♓	7 41	1 57
36.		Thirteenth Sunday after Trinity.				Day's length 12 hours 40 minutes.			
8	*F.*	5 36	6 18	2	5 37	☿ in ☋. Boston settled 1630.	♈	8 7	2 38
9	Mon	5 37	6 16	3	5 14	☌ ♀ ♂. Cal. a State 1850.	♈	8 37	3 23
10	Tue	5 38	6 15	3	4 52	□ ♆ ☉. Bastile dest. 1798.	♈	9 13	4 11
11	We	5 39	6 14	3	4 29	☌ ♆ ☽. America disc. 1492.	♈	10 0	5 5
12	Thu	5 39	6 12	4	4 6	♀ greatest Hel. Lat. S.	♈	10 58	6 2
13	Fri	5 40	6 11	4	3 43	U. S. Confederation rat. 1788.	♊	morn	7 2
14	Sat	5 41	6 10	5	3 20	Wellington died 1852.	♋	0 7	8 2
37.		Fourteenth Sunday after Trinity.				Day's length 12 hours 26 minutes.			
15	*F.*	5 42	6 8	5	2 57	New York City taken 1776.	♋	1 22	9 2
16	Mon	5 43	6 6	5	2 34	Demosthenes born 322 B. C.	♌	2 40	9 58
17	Tue	5 44	6 5	6	2 10	N. Y. Times founded 1851.	♌	4 0	10 52
18	We	5 44	6 4	6	1 47	Sun ecl. invis. in America.	♌	5 18	11 44
19	Thu	5 45	6 2	6	1 24	☌ ♀ ☉ inferior. ☌ ♂ ☽.	♍	sets	eve
20	Fri	5 45	6 1	7	1 0	☌ ☿ ☽. Battle Stillwater 1777.	♍	6 51	1 27
21	Sat	5 46	6 0	7	0 37	♆ stationary. ☌ ♄ ☽.	♎	7 23	2 20
38.		Fifteenth Sunday after Trinity.				Day's length 12 hours 11 minutes.			
22	*F.*	5 47	5 58	7	0 14	☌ ♅ ☽. Virgil died 19 B. C.	♎	8 0	3 15
23	Mon	5 48	5 56	8	south	Sun enters ♎. AUTUMN COM.	♏	8 43	4 11
24	Tue	5 49	5 54	8	0 33	King of Portugal d. 1834.	♏	9 34	5 9
25	We	5 50	5 53	8	0 57	1st Americ'n newspap'r 1690	♐	10 32	6 4
26	Thu	5 51	5 52	9	1 20	Peace Congress Lausane 1871.	♐	11 33	6 58
27	Fri	5 51	5 50	9	1 43	First R. R. in the world 1825.	♑	morn	7 47
28	Sat	5 51	5 49	9	2 7	Detroit taken 1813.	♑	0 36	8 33
39.		Sixteenth Sunday after Trinity.				Day's length 11 hours 57 minutes.			
29	*F.*	5 52	5 47	10	2 30	Gen. Nelson shot 1862.	♑	1 39	9 16
30	Mon	5 53	5 46	10	2 53	Pompey's triumph 61 B. C.	♒	2 39	9 57

WEATHER CONJECTURES.—SEPTEMBER—1, 2, 3, fair; 4, 5, 6, 7, 8, 9, 10, fair; 11, 12, 13, 14, 15, 16, 17, open weather; 18, 19, 20, 21, 22, 23, 24, changeable; 25, 26, 27, 28, 29, 30, very rainy.

N. C. BOARD OF RAILROAD COMMISSIONERS.

COMMISSIONERS.—J. W. Wilson, Burke County, Chairman, term expires April. 1899; E. C. Beddingfield, Wake County, term expires April, 1897 ; T. W. Mason, Northampton County, term expires April, 1895; salary $2,000 each; H. C. Brown, Surry County, Clerk, salary $1,500.

Special sessions of the Court are held at Raleigh. Special sessions are also held at other places, under such regulations as made by the Commission.

Offices of the Commisioners are located in the Agricultural Building.

NORTH CAROLINA GEOLOGICAL SURVEY.

Jos. A. Holmes, State Geologist; H. B. C. Nitze, Assistant State Geologist. General offices of the Survey, Raleigh, N. C.

OFFICERS N. C. STATE PENITENTIARY.

A. Leazar, Superintendent State Prison, salary $2,500; W. J. Hicks, General Supervisor, salary $1,800; J. M. Fleming, Warden, salary $900; Wm. Ledbetter. Deputy Warden, salary $500; Dr. J. W. McGee, Physician, salary $500; Jos. J. Bernard, Bookkeeper, salary $900.

BOARD OF DIRECTORS.—A. B. Young, Vice-President, Concord, N. C.; T. J. Armstrong, Rocky Point, N. C.; Frank Stronach, Raleigh, N. C.; Dr. I. E. Green, Weldon, N. C. One vacancy.

N. C. AGRICULTURAL EXPERIMENT AND FERTILIZER CONTROL STATION AND STATE WEATHER SERVICE, RALEIGH, N. C.

OFFICERS.—H. B. Battle, Ph. D., Director and State Chemist; F. E. Emery, M. S.. Agriculturist; Gerald McCarthy, B. S., Botanist and Entomologist; W. F. Massey, C. E., Horticulturist; C. F. von Hermann, Meteorologist; F. P. Williamson, D. V. S., Consulting Veterinarian; B. W. Kilgore, M. S., F. B. Carpenter, B. S., W. M. Allen and C. B. Williams, B. S., Assistant Chemists; Alex. Rhodes, Assistant Horticulturist; Roscoe Nunn, Assistant Meteorologist; A. F. Bowen, Secretary.

Offices and Laboratories in Agricultural Building, Raleigh; farm, stables and dairy at the Experiment Farm, adjoining State Fair Grounds. Visitors invited. Many interesting and valuable bulletins free on application.

N. C. COLLEGE OF AGRICULTURE AND MECHANIC ARTS.

BOARD OF TRUSTEES.—W. S. Primrose, President of the Board, Raleigh; W. F. Green, Franklinton; D. A. Tompkins, Charlotte; Henry E. Fries, Salem; N. B. Broughton, Raleigh; W. R. Williams, Falkland; J. B. Coffield, Everett's; W. R. Capehart, Avoca; W. E. Stevens, Clinton; J. H. Gilmer, Greensboro; J. F. Payne, Alma; J. R. McLelland, Mooresville; C. D. Smith, Franklin; R. W. Wharton, Washington.

EXECTIVE COMMITTEE.—W. S. Primrose, Chairman; W. F. Green, N. B. Broughton, Henry E. Fries, W. E. Stevens, J. H. Gilmer.

FINANCE COMMITTEE.—N. B. Broughton, Chairman; J. H. Gilmer, W. E. Stevens.

FACULTY AND OFFICERS.—Alexander Q. Holladay, President; W. F. Massey, C. E., Professor of Horticulture, Arboriculture and Botany; W. A. Withers, A. M., Professor of Pure and Agricultural Chemistry; D. H. Hill, A. M., Professor of English; B. Irby, M. S., Professor of Agriculture; W. C. Riddick, A. B., C. E., Professor of Mechanics and Applied Mathematics; R. E. L. Yates, A. M., Adjunct Professor of Mathematics; F. E. Emery, B. S., Assistant Professor of Agriculture; Charles M. Pritchett, B. S., Instructor in Mechanics; Charles B. Park. Instructor in Practical Mechanics; C. B. Williams, B. S., S. E Asbury, B. S., Instructors in Chemistry; Charles Pearson, B. E., Instructor in Mechanics, L. T. Yarborough, B. E., Assistant in Mechanics; B. F. Walton, B. S., Dairyman; C. D. Francks, B. E., Preparatory Department; Professor Withers, Secretary of the Faculty; Professor Hill, Bursar; Benj. S. Skinner, Superintendent of Farm and Steward; Mrs. Sue C. Carroll, Matron; J. B. Dunn, M. D., Physician.

Branson's Almanac is always welcome.—The North Carolinian

10th Month. ***OCTOBER, 1895.*** ***31 Days.***

Moon's Phases.

	D.	H.	M.			D.	H.	M.	
Full Moon,	3	5	39	p. m.	New Moon,	18	1	1	a. m.
Last Quarter,	11	9	26	a. m.	First Quarter,	25	5	56	a. m.

Day of Month.	Day of Week.	Sun rises.	Sun sets.	Sun fast.	Sun's decline south.	ASPECTS OF PLANETS AND OTHER MISCELLANEOUS MATTER.	Moon's place.	Moon rises or sets.	Moon south.
1	Tue	5 54	5 44	10	3 17	☿ greatest Elong. E.		3 40	eve
2	We	5 55	5 43	11	3 40	S. L. Riddle died 1886.		4 39	11 16
3	Thu	5 56	5 41	11	4 3	Bancroft born 1800.		5 37	11 55
4	Fri	5 57	5 40	11	4 26	R. B. Hayes born 1822.		rises	morn
5	Sat	5 58	5 39	12	4 50	A. J. Partin died 1880.		6 11	0 37
40.	Seventeenth Sunday after Trinity.					Day's length 11 hours 39 minutes.			
6	*F.*	5 59	5 38	12	5 13	May Flower sailed 1620.		6 40	1 21
7	Mon	5 59	5 36	12	5 36	Battle Saratoga 1777.		7 15	2 9
8	Tue	6 0	5 35	12	5 59	♀ stationary.		7 58	3 0
9	We	6 1	5 34	13	6 21	☌ ♆ ☽. ☿ gr. Hel. Lat. S.		8 51	3 56
10	Thu	6 2	5 32	13	6 44	Battle of Lake Erie 1813.		9 53	4 54
11	Fri	6 3	5 30	13	7 7	Battle of Brandywine 1777.		11 4	5 53
12	Sat	6 4	5 29	14	7 30	☌ ♃ ☽ Bat. Chapultepec 1847.		morn	6 50
41.	Eighteenth Sunday after Trinity.					Day's length 11 hours 23 minutes.			
13	*F.*	6 5	5 28	14	7 52	Battle Quebec 1759.		0 19	7 46
14	Mon	6 6	5 27	14	8 14	☿ stationary. Math. 13: 31.		1 35	8 39
15	Tue	6 7	5 25	14	8 37	☌ ♀ ☽. Bank of Paris 1857.		2 51	9 30
16	We	6 8	5 24	14	8 59	Napoleon at Helena 1815.		4 7	10 20
17	Thu	6 9	5 23	15	9 21	☌ ♂ ☽. Sur. Burgoyne 1777.		5 22	11 11
18	Fri	6 9	5 21	15	9 43	Morgan raid Ky. 1862.		sets	eve
19	Sat	6 10	5 19	15	10 5	☌ ☿ ☽: ♄ ☽: ♅ ☽.		5 53	0 59
42.	Nineteenth Sunday after Trinity.					Day's length 11 hours 7 minutes.			
20	*F.*	6 11	5 18	15	10 26	New York panic 1873.		6 35	1 56
21	Mon	6 12	5 17	15	10 48	Battle Ball's Bluff 1861.		7 24	2 55
22	Tue	6 13	5 16	15	11 9	Battle Marysville, Ark., 1862.		8 19	3 53
23	We	6 14	5 15	16	11 30	C. W. D. Hutchings died 1883.		9 21	4 49
24	Thu	6 15	5 14	16	11 51	Daniel Webster died 1852.		10 25	5 41
25	Fri	6 16	5 12	16	12 12	☌ ☿ ☉ inferior. ☿ in ♌.		11 28	6 21
26	Sat	6 16	5 11	16	12 32	Von Moltke born 1800.		morn	7 13
43.	Twentieth Sunday after Trinity.					Day's length 10 hours 53 minutes.			
27	*F.*	6 17	5 10	16	12 53	Battle Hatcher's Run 1864.		0 30	7 55
28	Mon	6 18	5 9	16	13 13	Dr. Milburn in Raleigh 1883.		1 30	8 35
29	Tue	6 19	5 8	16	13 33	Sir Walter Raleigh died 1618.		2 30	9 14
30	We	6 20	5 6	16	13 52	Gambetta born 1838.		3 28	9 53
31	Thu	6 21	5 5	16	14 12	□ ♃ ☉. Gen. Scott retired 1861		4 28	10 34

WEATHER CONJECTURES.—OCTOBER—1, 2, rain; 3, 4, 5, 6, 7, 8, 9, 10, fair; 11, 12, 13, 14, 15, 16, 17, changeable; 18, 19, 20, 21, 22, 23, 24, fair; 25, 26, 27, 28, 29, 30, 31, look for rain.

STATE NORMAL AND INDUSTRIAL SCHOOL.

OFFICERS AND FACULTY.—Charles D. McIver, A. B., Litt. D., President; Sue May Kirkland, Lady Principal; E. J. Forney, Bursar; Daisy E. Waite, Librarian; Mrs. W. P. Carraway, Matron; P. P. Claxton, A. M., J. Y. Joyner, Ph. B., Lucy H. Robertson, Gertrude W. Mendenhall, B. S., Dixie Lee Bryant, B. S., Joseph A. Holmes, B. S. (special Lecturer on State Geology), Mary M. Petty. B. S., Viola Boddie, L. I., Florence A. Stone, Anna M. Gove, B. S., M. D., Alice Maude Crocker, Clarence R. Brown, Mellville Vincent Fort, Edith A. McIntyre, Jennie W. Bingham, Bertha M. Lee, Fodie M. Buie.

THE MODEL HUSBAND.

Most wives will end their story with:
    "Ah, well, men are but human."
I long to tell the secret of
    A truly happy woman.

Through all the sunshine-lighted years,
    Lived now in retrospection,
My husband's words brought never tears,
    Nor caused a sad reflection.

Whate'er the burdens of the day,
    Unflinching, calm and steady,
To bear his part—the larger half—
    I always find him ready.

House-cleaning season brings no frown,
    No sarcasm pointed keenly;
Through carpets up and tacks head down
    He makes his way serenely.

Our evenings pass in converse sweet,
    Or quiet contemplation :
We never disagree, except
    To "keep up conversation."

And dewy morn of radiant June,
    Fair moonlight of September,
April, with bird and brook atune,
    Stern, pitiless December—

Each seems to my adoring eyes
    Some new grace to discover,
For he, unchanging through the years,
    Is still my tender lover.

So life no shadows hold, though we
    Have reached the side that's shady ;
My husband. Oh! a dream is he,
    And I'm a maiden lady.
        Eleanor M. Denny, in the Ladies' Home Journal.

A man's age is not to be counted by years or the ticks of the watch. The good deeds which he has done should alone measure his life, or as the poet has said:

    "We live in deeds, not years, in thoughts nor breaths,
      In feelings, not in figures on a dial.
    We should count time by heart throbs. He most lives
      Who thinks most, feels the noblest, acts the best."

Branson's Almanac—One can hardly find a 10-cent book of greater value. Alamance Gleaner.

11th Month. ***NOVEMBER, 1895.*** ***30 Days.***

Moon's Phases.

	D. H. M.		D. H. M.
Full Moon,	2 10 10 a. m.	New Moon,	16 0 3 p. m.
Last Quarter,	9 5 58 p. m.	First Quarter,	24 2 10 a. m.

Day of Month.	Day of Week.	Sun rises.	Sun sets.	Sun fast.	Sun's decline south.	ASPECTS OF PLANETS AND OTHER MISCELLANEOUS MATTER.	Moon's place.	Moon rises or sets.	Moon south.
1	Fri	6 22	5 4	16	14 31	☿ in Perihelion.	♈	5 29	11 18
2	Sat	6 23	5 4	16	14 50	☌ ♄ ☉. Jas. K. Polk b. 1795	♈	6 33	morn
44. Twenty-first Sunday after Trinity. Day's length 10 hours 39 minutes.									
3	*F.*	6 24	5 3	16	15 9	☿ stationary.	♉	rises	0 5
4	Mon	6 25	5 2	16	15 28	Geo. Peabody died 1869.	♉	5 56	0 56
5	Tue	6 26	5 1	16	15 46	☌ ♆ ☽. Kepler died 1630.	♉	6 47	1 51
6	We	6 27	5 0	16	16 4	Revolt at Montreal 1847.	♊	7 48	2 49
7	Thu	6 28	4 59	16	16 22	♀ in ♌. Bat. of Prague 1629.	♊	8 56	3 48
8	Fri	6 29	4 58	16	16 39	Warsaw taken 1794.	♋	10 3	4 45
9	Sat	6 30	4 56	16	16 57	☌ ♃ ☽. Prince of Wales b. '41	♋	11 21	5 40
45. Twenty-second Sunday after Trinity. Day's length 10 hours 25 minutes.									
10	*F.*	6 31	4 56	16	17 14	☿ greatest Elong. W.	♌	morn	6 32
11	Mon	6 32	4 55	16	17 30	Milan decree 1807.	♌	0 34	7 22
12	Tue	6 33	4 55	16	17 47	☿ greatest Hel. Lat. N.	♌	1 47	8 11
13	We	6 34	4 54	16	18 3	☌ ♀ ☽. Catherine II died 1796.	♍	3 1	9 0
14	Thu	6 35	4 53	15	18 18	Battle of Arcola 1796.	♍	4 15	9 50
15	Fri	6 36	4 53	15	18 34	☌ ☿ ☽: ☌ ♂ ☽: ♄ ☽.	♎	5 29	10 43
16	Sat	6 37	4 52	15	18 49	☌ ♅ ☽: ☌ ♄.	♎	6 45	11 39
46. Twenty-third Sunday after Trinity. Day's length 10 hours 13 minutes.									
17	*F.*	6 38	4 51	15	19 4	Queen Mary died 1558.	♏	sets	eve
18	Mon	6 39	4 51	15	19 18	☌ ♂ ♎.	♏	6 5	1 37
19	Tue	6 40	4 50	14	19 32	Tweed convicted 1873.	♐	7 5	2 35
20	We	6 41	4 50	14	19 46	☌ ☿ ♄.	♐	8 9	3 30
21	Thu	6 42	4 49	14	19 59	Voltaire died 1694.	♑	9 15	4 21
22	Fri	6 43	4 49	13	20 12	St. Domingo massacre. 1791.	♑	10 19	5 7
23	Sat	6 44	4 49	13	20 25	☌ ☿ ♂. Pres. Pierce b. 1804.	♒	11 20	5 50
47. Twenty-fourth Sunday after Trinity. Day's length 10 hours 3 minutes.									
24	*F.*	6 45	4 48	13	20 37	Ghent treaty, 1814.	♒	morn	6 31
25	Mon	6 46	4 47	13	20 49	♃ stationary.	♓	0 19	7 10
26	Tue	6 47	4 47	12	21 0	☌ ☿ ♅.	♓	1 17	7 49
27	We	6 48	4 46	12	21 11	Hoosac Tunnel opened 1873.	♓	2 16	8 29
28	Thu	6 49	4 46	12	21 22	Earthquake in N. England 1814.	♓	3 16	9 12
29	Fri	6 50	4 46	11	21 32	☌ ♂ ♅. ♀ greatest Elong. W.	♈	4 19	9 57
30	Sat	6 51	4 46	11	21 42	Polish Revolution 1830.	♈	5 23	10 47

WEATHER CONJECTURES.—NOVEMBER—1, rainy; 2, 3, 4, 5, 6, 7, 8, frequent showers; 9, 10, 11, 12, 13, 14, 15, fair and mild; 16, 17, 18, 19, 20, 21, 22, 23, very rainy; 24, 25, 26, 27, 28, 29, 30, cold with frequent showers.

EXERCISE FOR THE EYES.

Absolutely Necessary in Order That the Vision may be Preserved.

When the eyes are treated fairly, they are strengthened, not weakened, by work. Just as the arms of a blacksmith grow the stronger for his trade, so the eyes of watchmakers who work under healthy conditions are found to improve and not to deteriorate in vigor and quickness. It is the abuse of the eyes, not their use, which is to be avoided.

If a man is aware either that his eyes need no artificial correction or else have received their proper adjustment, and if his work, whether literary or mechanical, is done in a light both steady and sufficient and with a due regard as to ordinary sanitary rules, he may feel sure that he is strengthening his eyes, not weakening them, by hard work. Men of intellectual pursuits sometimes are afraid of losing their mental powers in old age because they have drawn so much upon them when young. The reverse is nearer the truth, and if they have not overtaxed their brains the fear is absolutely groundless.

The man whose intellect goes first in old age is generally some farmer or laborer who has never strengthened and invigorated it by use; not the politician, the lawyer or the man of letters. So with the eyes, those who had strengthened their eyes by using them properly keep keen sight longer than those who have never trained them. In the case of the man who has neglected to give his eyes full development they will fail in power along with his other bodily functions. When, however, the man who, born with good eyes, has kept them in constant hard work and yet never strained them, reaches old age, he may find them capable of performing their functions better than any other organ of the body.—*Philadelphia Times.*

BRANSON MAXIMS—Continued.

32. Be true to your friends and quickly.—*Branson.*
33. Don't run a man down to get his friendship.—*Father Branson.*
34. Be a man among men.—*Father Branson.*
35. I cannot afford to have an enemy more or a friend less.—*Branson.*

PROPORTIONS OF THE HUMAN FIGURE.

The proportions of the human figure are six times the length of the right foot. The face from the highest point of the forehead, where the hair begins, to the end of the chin is one-tenth of the whole stature. The hand from the wrist to the end of the middle finger is also one-tenth of the total height. From the crown to the nape of the neck is one-twelfth of the stature.—*Current Literature.*

Andrew stands for the fact that a man's success in working for Christ is not to be measured by the number of his converts. Whether this little-known apostle ever brought anyone else to Christ or not, he brought in Simon, a man who preached a single sermon that harvested three thousand souls. Mathematics cuts a small figure in spiritual results. It is not quantity, but quality.

SMALL MEN.—If you don't like the churches, go in and make them better, but do not become a grumbler. Keep yourself aloof from that class of people, for it is the easiest sort of thing to find fault. Any stupid man can do that but it takes a smart man to make things better. When a man begins to grumble and find fault, you can size him up for a light-weight right away.—*D. L. Moody.*

THE FIRST THING IN THE MORNING.—My practice since I was thirty years of age, has been to read in the Bible the first thing I do in the morning.—*John Quincy Adams.*

Branson's Almanac is one of the best of its kind.—Davidson Dispatch.

12th Month. ***DECEMBER, 1895.*** ***31 Days.***

Moon's Phases.

	D.	H.	M.			D.	H.	M.
Full Moon,	2	1	30 a. m.		New Moon,	16	1	21 a. m.
Last Quarter,	9	2	1 a. m.		First Quarter,	24	0	13 a. m.
					Full Moon,	31	8	17 p. m.

Day of Month.	Day of Week.	Sun rises.	Sun sets.	Sun fast.	Sun's decline south.	ASPECTS OF PLANETS AND OTHER MISCELLANEOUS MATTER.	Moon's place.	Moon rises or sets.	Moon south.
48.	Advent Sunday.					Day's length 9 hours 55 minutes.			
1	***F.***	6 52	4 46	11	21 51	Prince of Wales b. 1844.	♉	6 32	11 42
2	Mon	6 52	4 46	10	22 0	☌ ♆ ☽. Cortez died 1554.	♉	rises	morn
3	Tue	6 53	4 46	10	22 9	Battle Hohenlinden 1800.	♊	5 39	0 40
4	We	6 54	4 46	10	22 17	Washington's farewell 1783.	♊	6 46	1 40
5	Thu	6 55	4 46	9	22 25	☿ in ☋. VanBuren born 1782.	♋	7 59	2 39
6	Fri	6 56	4 46	9	22 32	☌ ♃ ☽.	♋	9 14	3 36
7	Sat	6 56	4 46	8	22 39	Newport taken 1776.	♌	10 27	4 29
49.	Second Sunday in Advent.					Day's length 9 hours 49 minutes.			
8	***F.***	6 57	4 46	8	22 46	☌ ♆ ☉. Dr. Bledsoe d. 1877.	♌	11 39	5 19
9	Mon	6 58	4 46	7	22 52	Milton born 1608.	♍	morn	6 8
10	Tue	6 59	4 46	7	22 57	Dr. Columbus Mills died 1882.	♍	0 50	6 55
11	We	7 0	4 46	7	23 2	♀ in Perihelion. 1 John 3: 1&2	♍	2 1	7 43
12	Thu	7 1	4 47	6	23 7	☌ ♀ ☽ Cromwell protector 1653	♎	3 13	8 34
13	Fri	7 2	4 47	6	23 11	♂ ☌ ♄ ☽: ☌ ♅ ☽. Heb. 2: 3.	♎	4 26	9 27
14	Sat	7 3	4 47	5	23 15	♂ in ☋. ♂ ☌ ☽.	♏	5 40	10 23
50.	Third Sunday in Advent.					Day's length 9 hours 44 minutes.			
15	***F.***	7 3	4 47	5	23 18	☿ in Aphelion.	♏	6 49	11 22
16	Mon	7 4	4 48	4	23 21	Boston Tea Party 1773.	♐	sets	eve
17	Tue	7 4	4 48	4	23 23	Poet Whittier born 1807.	♐	5 53	1 17
18	We	7 5	4 49	3	23 25	Sir Humphrey Davy born 1778.	♐	6 58	2 10
19	Thu	7 6	4 49	3	23 26	Rome burnt A. D. 69.	♑	8 3	2 59
20	Fri	7 7	4 49	2	23 27	☌ ☿ ☉ superior. Rom. 10: 10.	♑	9 6	3 44
21	Sat	7 7	4 50	2	23 27	Sun enters ♑. WINTER COM.	♑	10 7	4 26
51.	Fourth Sunday in Advent.					Day's length 9 hours 42 minutes.			
22	***F.***	7 8	4 50	1	23 27	☌ ♀ ♄. Dr. Winchester d. 1876.	♑	11 5	5 5
23	Mon	7 8	4 51	1	23 27	Jo. Smith born 1805.	♒	morn	5 44
24	Tue	7 9	4 51	slow	23 26	Thackeray died 1863.	♒	0 3	6 24
25	We	7 9	4 52		23 24	CHRISTMAS DAY.	♒	1 2	7 4
26	Thu	7 9	4 53	1	23 22	Stephen Girard d. 1831.	♓	2 4	7 48
27	Fri	7 10	4 53	1	23 20	Charles Lamb born 1834.	♓	3 7	8 36
28	Sat	7 10	4 54	2	23 17	☌ ♀ ☉.	♈	4 13	9 28
52.	Sunday after Christmas.					Day's length 9 hours 44 minutes.			
29	***F.***	7 10	4 54	2	23 14	Battle Stone River 1862.	♈	5 20	10 25
30	Mon	7 11	4 55	3	23 10	Battle Vicksburg 1862.	♉	6 25	11 26
31	Tue	7 11	4 56	3	23 5	Battle Murfreesboro 1862.	♊	7 25	12 27

WEATHER CONJECTURES.—DECEMBER—1, snowy; 2, 3, 4, 5, 6, 7, 8, frost; 9, 10, 11, 12, 13, 14, 15, expect snow; 16, 17, 18, 19, 20, 21, 22, 23, hoar frost; 24, 25, 26, 27, 28, 29, 30, 31, expect heavy weather.

GOT THE BLESSING.

Last Sunday there was preachin', and we all went out to hear;
The little church was crowded, for the rich and poor was there;
It was jes' a splendid sermon, an' the singin' full and free—
"Amazin grace, how sweet the sound that saved a wretch like me."

When I call the sermon splendid, I mean it was the kind
To take deep root an' bear good fruit in every sinner's mind;
It was full of consolation for weary hearts that bleed—
'Twas full of invitation to Christ and not to creed.

The text was 'bout the prodigal who spent his livin' neat,
Until he came at last to want the husks the swine did eat;
But a sweet thought gave him comfort when he hardly wished to live,
"I will go unto my father—for my father will forgive."

"I'm talkin' to you fellers," said the preacher, "here to-day,
Who spent the Master's livin' in a country far away;
You've got to go where that feller was—you can't tell why or how,
But come back to the Father—He's waitin' for you now!"

From the amen corner to the door the people gathered near,
An' "pray for us!" they shouted, an' it seemed the Lord was there;
An' such a great handshakin'! well, the precious time is past,
But the old church in the backwoods got the blessin' that'll last!

Atlanta Constitution.

AN "OUT-OF-DATE" COUPLE.

E. MATHESON.

We are "so out of date," they say—
    Ned and I;
We love in an old-fashioned way,
    Long since gone by.
He says I am his helpmate true
    In everything.
And I—well, I will own to you
    He is my king.
We met in no romantic way
    "Twixt glow and gloom;"
He woed me on a winter day,
    And in—a room;
Yet, through life's hour of stress and storm,
    When griefs befell,
Love kept our small home corner warm
    And all was well.
Ned thinks no woman like his wife—
    But let that pass;
Perhaps we view the dual life
    Through roseate glass;
Even if the prospect be not bright,
    We hold it true
That heaviest burdens may grow light
    When shared by two.
Upon the gilded scroll of fame,
    Emblazoned fair,
I cannot hope to read the name
    I proudly bear,
But happy in their even flow,
    The years glide by;
We are behind the times still now—
    Ned and I.

The Branson Maxims are well worth reading.—Gold Leaf.

SUPERIOR COURTS OF NORTH CAROLINA FOR 1895.

(Subject to changes made by the Legislature of 1895.)

JUDGES.

Name.	District.	Residence.
George H. Brown,	1	Washington.
Henry R. Bryan,	2	Newbern.
Jacob Battle,	3	Rocky Mount.
W. R. Allen,	4	Goldsboro.
Robert W. Winston,	5	Oxford.
Edward T. Boykin,	6	Clinton.
James D. McIver,	7	Carthage.
B. F. Long,	8	Statesville.
W. N. Mebane,	9	Madison.
W. B. Council,	10	Boone.
W. Alexander Hoke,	11	Lincolnton.
H. B. Carter,	12	Asheville.

SOLICITORS.

Name.	District.	Residence.
Wm. M. Bond,	1	Edenton.
W. E. Daniel,	2	Weldon.
John E. Woodard,	3	Wilson
Edward W. Pou, Jr.,	4	Smithfield.
Edward S. Parker,	5	Graham.
O. H. Allen,	6	Kinston.
N. Archie McLean,	7	Lumberton.
E. C. Roper,	8	Lexington.
W. W. Barber,	9	Wilkesboro.
W. C. Newland,	10	Lenoir.
J. L. Webb,	11	Shelby.
George A. Jones,	12	Franklin.

Time of Holding Courts.

FIRST JUDICIAL DISTRICT.

Spring—Judge Boykin.
Fall—Judge McIver.

Beaufort—†Feb. 18th (2), May 27th (2), Nov 25th (2).
Currituck—March 4th, Sept. 2d.
Camden—March 11th, Sept. 9th.
Pasquotank—March 18th, Sept. 16th.
Perquimans—March 25th, Sept. 23d.
Chowan—April 1st, Sept. 29th.
Gates—April 8th, Oct. 7th.
Hertford—April 15th, Oct. 14th.
Washington—May 6th, Nov. 4th.
Tyrrell—April 22d, Oct. 21st.
Dare—April 30th, Oct. 28th.
Hyde—May 13th, Nov. 11th.
Pamlico—May 20th, Nov. 18th.

SECOND JUDICIAL DISTRICT.

Spring—Judge McIver.
Fall—Judge Boykin.

Halifax—†March 4th (2), May 13th (2), Nov. 11th (2).
Northampton—April 1st (2), †Aug. 5th (2), Sept. 30th (2).
Bertie—Feb. 4th, April 29th (2), Oct. 28th (2).
Craven—†Feb. 11th (2), May 27th (2), Nov. 25th (2)
Warren—March 18th (2), Sept. 16th (2).
Edgecombe—April 15th (2), Oct. 14th (2)

THIRD JUDICIAL DISTRICT.

Spring—Judge Long.
Fall—Judge McIver.

Pitt—†Jan. 7th (2), March 4th (2), †April 1st (2), Sept. 16th (2), †Dec. 2d (2).
Franklin—Jan. 21st (2), April 15th (2), Oct. 21st (2).
Wilson—†Feb. 4th (2), June 3d, Oct. 28th.
Vance—Feb. 18th (2), May 20th (2), Sept. 30th (2).
Martin—March 18th (2), Sept. 2d (2).
Nash—April 29th (2), Nov. 18th (2).

FOURTH JUDICIAL DISTRICT.

Spring—Judge Mebane.
Fall—Judge Long.

Wake—*Jan. 7th (2), †Feb. 25th (2), *Mar. 25th (2), †April 22d (2), *Sept 23d (2), †Oct. 21st (3).
Wayne—Jan. 21st (2), April 15th, Sept. 9th (2), Oct. 14th.
Harnett—Feb. 4th, Aug. 5th, †Nov 25th.
Johnston—March 11th (2), Aug. 26th (2), Nov. 11th (2).

FIFTH JUDICIAL DISTRICT.

Spring—Judge Council.
Fall—Judge Mebane.

Durham—Jan. 14th (2), March 25th (2), June 3d (2), Oct. 7th (2).
Granville—Jan. 28th (2), April 22d (2), July 22d (2), Nov. 25th (2).
Chatham—Feb. 11th, May 6th, Sept. 23d (2).
Guilford—Feb. 18th (2), May 27th, Aug. 26th (2), Dec. 9th (2).
Alamance—March 11th, May 20th, Nov. 11th.
Orange—March 18th, Aug. 5th, Oct. 28th.
Caswell—April 8th, Aug. 12th, Oct. 21st (2).
Person—April 15th, Aug. 19th, Nov. 18th.

SIXTH JUDICIAL DISTRICT.

Spring—Judge Hoke.
Fall—Judge Council.

Pender—March 4th, Sept. 9th (2).
Greene—Feb. 25th, Aug. 12th, Nov. 25th.
New Hanover—†Jan 21st (2), †April 15th (2), †Sept. 23d (2)
Lenoir—May 6th (2), Nov. 11th (2).
Duplin—Feb. 18th, Aug. 5th, Dec. 2d.
Sampson—Feb. 4th (2), April 29th, Oct. 7th (2).
Carteret—March 18th, Oct. 21st.
Jones—March 25th, Oct. 28th.
Onslow—April 1st, Nov. 4th.

SEVENTH JUDICIAL DISTRICT.

Spring—Judge Carter.
Fall—Judge Hoke.

Columbus—Feb. 25th, July 15th, Nov. 4th.
Anson—*Jan. 7th, †April 29th, *Sept. 2d, †Nov. 25th.
Cumberland—Jan. 21st, †May 6th (2), July 22d, †Nov. 11th (2).
Robeson—Jan. 28th (2), *May 20th, Sept. 30th (3).
Richmond—Feb. 11th (2), June 3d, Sept. 16th (2), Dec. 2d.
Bladen—March 19th (2) (Tuesday), Oct. 22d (Tuesday.)
Brunswick—April 8th, Sept. 9th.
Moore—March 4th (2), *Aug. 12th, †Aug. 19th, *Dec. 9th, †Dec. 16th.

EIGHTH JUDICIAL DISTRICT.

Spring—Judge Brown.
Fall—Judge Carter.

Cabarrus—Jan. 21st (2), July 22d (2).
Iredell—Feb. 4th (2), May 20th (2), Aug. 5th (2), Nov. 4th (2).

SUPERIOR COURTS—Continued.

Rowan—Feb. 18th (2), May 6th (2), Aug. 19th (2), Nov. 18th (2).
Davidson—March 4th (2), Sept. 2d (2), †Dec. 2d.
Randolph—March 18th (2), Sept. 16th (2).
Montgomery—April 1st, Sept. 30th (2).
Yadkin—April 15th, Oct. 14th (2).

NINTH JUDICIAL DISTRICT.

Spring—Judge Bryan.

Fall—Judge Battle.

Alexander—Jan. 21st, July 22d.
Rockingham—Jan. 28th (2), July 29th, Nov. 4th (2).
Forsyth—Feb. 25th, May 20th (2), Aug. 5th (2), Dec. 2d (2).
Wilkes—March 4th (2), Sept. 2d (2).
Alleghany—April 1st, Sept. 16th.
Davie—April 8th (2), Sept. 23d (2).
Stokes—April 22d (2), Oct. 21st (2).
Surry—March 18th (2), Oct. 7th (2).

TENTH JUDICIAL DISTRICT.

Spring—Judge Battle.

Fall—Judge Bryan.

Catawba—Feb. 18th (2), July 22d (2).
McDowell—March 4th (2), Aug. 19th (2).
Burke—March 18th (2), Sept. 2d (2).
Caldwell—April 1st, Sept. 16th.
Ashe—April 18th, Sept. 23d (2).
Watauga—April 29th, Oct. 7th.
Mitchell—May 6th, Oct. 14th (2).
Yancey—May 12th (2), Oct. 28th (2).

ELEVENTH JUDICIAL DISTRICT.

Spring—Judge Allen.

Fall—Judge Battle.

Union—Jan. 28th (3), Aug. 19th (2).
Stanly—Feb. 18th (2), Sept. 16th (2).
Mecklenburg—†March 4th (2), †June 3d, †Sept. 2d (2), †Dec. 16th.
Gaston—March 18th (2), Sept. 30th (2).
Lincoln—April 1st (2), Oct. 14th.
Cleveland—April 15th (2), Aug. 5th (2), Oct. 21st (2).
Rutherford—April 29th (2), Nov. 4th (2).
Polk—May 13th, Nov. 18th.
Henderson—May 20th (2), Nov. 25th (2).

TWELFTH JUDICIAL DISTRICT.

Spring—Judge Winston.

Fall—Judge Allen.

Madison—Feb. 25th (2), July 29th (2).
Buncombe—†March 11th (3), †Aug. 12th (3), †Dec. 2d (2).
Transylvania—April 1st, Sept. 2d.
Haywood—April 8th (2), Sept. 9th (2).
Jackson—April 22d (2), Sept. 23d.
Macon—May 6th, Sept. 30th.
Clay—May 13th, Oct. 7th.
Cherokee—May 20th (2), Oct. 14th (2).
Graham—June 3d, Oct. 28th.
Swain—June 10th, Nov. 18th (2).

*For criminal cases.
†For civil cases alone.
‡For civil cases alone except jail cases.
(2)Means two weeks, etc.

CRIMINAL COURTS.

NEW HANOVER COUNTY.—Oliver P. Meares, Wilmington, Judge; A. M. Waddell, Wilmington, Solicitor. Court begins January 6th, March 18th, May 20th, July 15th, September 16th, November 18th.

MECKLENBURG COUNTY.—Oliver P. Meares, Judge; John E. Brown, Charlotte, Solicitor. Court begins February 11th, April 8th, August 12th, October 7th, December 2d.

BUNCOMBE COUNTY.—H. B. Carter, Asheville, Judge; Thomas A. Jones, Asheville, Solicitor. Court begins January 27th, April 22d, July 22d, October 21st.

U. S. CIRCUIT AND DISTRICT COURTS.

WESTERN DISTRICT.—R. P. Dick, Greensboro, Judge; E. B. Glenn, District Attorney; D. A. Covington, Assistant Attorney; S. L. Trogden, Clerk: *Greensboro*—Circuit and District—April 2d, October 1st. *Statesville*—Circuit and District—H. C. Cowles, Clerk; April 15th, October 14th. *Asheville*—Circuit and District—...... Patterson, Clerk: April 29th, October 28th. *Charlotte*—Circuit and District—...... Patterson, Clerk; June 10th, December 9th.

EASTERN DISTRICT.—A. S. Seymour, Judge; C. B. Aycock, Goldsboro, District Attorney; Sol. Weil, Wilmington, Assistant Attorney; W. C. Brooks, Clerk: *Elizabeth City*—District Court—April 15th, October 14th. *Newbern*—District Court—Geo. Green, Clerk; April 22d, October 21st. *Wilmington*—Circuit and District—N. J. Riddick, Clerk; V. Royster, Assistant Clerk in Raleigh; W. H. Shaw, Clerk of District and Deputy of Circuit Court at Wilmington; O. J. Carroll, Marshal; April 29th, October 29th. *Raleigh*—Circuit Court—N. J. Riddick, Clerk; V. Royster, Assistant Clerk in Raleigh; W. H. Shaw, Clerk of District and Deputy of Circuit Court at Wilmington; O. J. Carroll, Marshal; May 27th, October 5d.

SUPREME COURT.

SUPREME COURT meets first Monday in February. Examinations on Friday and Saturday before. First District, February 4th; Second District, February 11th, Third District, February 19th; Fourth District, February 26th; Fifth District, March 4th, Sixth District, March 11th; Seventh District, March 18th; Eighth District, March 25th; Ninth District, April 1st; Tenth District, April 8th; Eleventh District, April 15th; Twelfth District, April 22d. End of Docket, April 29th.

Last Monday in September. Examinations Friday and Saturday before. First District, September 23d; Second District, September 30th; Third District, October 7th; Fourth District, October 14th; Fifth District, October 21st; Sixth District, October 28th; Seventh District, November 4th; Eighth District, November 11th, Ninth District, November 18th; Tenth District, November 25th; Eleventh District, December 2d; Twelfth District, December 9th, etc.

Chief Justice—James E. Shepherd, Beaufort County. Associate Justices—Armistead Burwell, Mecklenburg County; Alphonso C. Avery, Burke County; Walter Clark, Wake County; James C. MacRae, Cumberland County. Salaries, $2,500 each. Frank I. Osborne, Attorney-General; salary, $2,000. R. T. Gray, Reporter; salary, $750. Thos. S. Kenan, Clerk; salary, $300 and fees. R. H. Bradley, Marshal; salary $800. J. L. Seawell, Office Clerk.

NANKIN'S PORCELAIN TOWER.

The city of Nankin, the capital of China, has for centuries been famous to the "barbarians" of the outer world for its porcelain tower—a relic of the splendor of its ancient days before Pekin usurped its dignity as the seat of the empire. The place is now to a great extent a city of ruins, and the city proper has shrunk to one-fourth of its former dimensions. The porcelain tower was built quite early in the fifteenth century, by the order of the Emperor Yung Loh, and as a work of filial piety. It was a monument to the memory of his mother, and he determined that its beauty should as far outshine that of any similar memorial as the transcendent virtues of the parent, in her son's eyes, surpassed those of the rest of her sex. No expense was spared in its erection, and its total cost is estimated at more than three-fourths of a million of our own money. The work was commenced at noon on a certain day in 1413, and occupied nearly twenty years in its completion. The total height of the porcelain tower was more than 200 feet, or about equal to that of the monument of London, and it was faced from top to bottom with the finest porcelain, glazed and colored. It consisted of nine stories, surmounted by a spire on the summit of which was a ball of brass, richly gilt. From this ball eight iron chains extended to as many projecting points of the roof, and from each chain was suspended a bell which hung over the face of the tower. The same arrangement was carried out in every story. The bells added much to the graceful appearance of the tower, breaking its otherwise formal and monotonous outline. Round the outer face of each story were several apertures for lanterns, and when these were all illuminated, we are told, in the magniloquent language of the Chinese historian, that "their light illuminated the entire heavens, shining into the hearts of men, and eternally removing human misery." It is not difficult to imagine, however, that the appearance of the tower on such an occasion must have been beautiful in the extreme. On the top of the tower were placed two large brazen vessels and a bowl, which together contained various costly articles in the nature of an offering and a charm to avert evil influences. Among these were several pearls of various colors, each supposed to possess miraculous properties, together with other precious stones and a quantity of gold and silver. In this connection, designed to represent the best treasures of the state, were also placed a box of tea, some pieces of silk, and copies of some ancient Chinese writings. The tower was demolished by the Taeping rebels in 1853.

PLEASE, FATHER TIME.

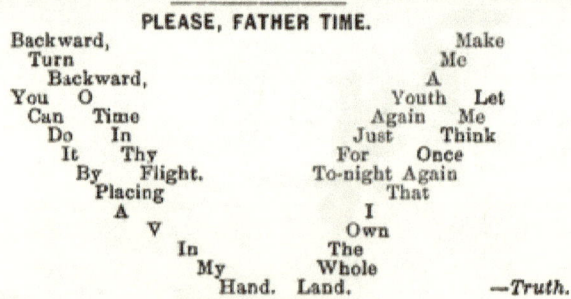

```
Backward,                                    Make
  Turn                                        Me
   Backward,                                  A
You    O                                    Youth   Let
  Can   Time                               Again   Me
    Do   In                                 Just   Think
     It    Thy                              For   Once
      By   Flight.                     To-night  Again
       Placing                              That
          A                                  I
           V                               Own
        In                          The
         My                        Whole
          Hand.   Land.                        —Truth.
```

WANTED: DEEDS.

Not words of winning note,
Not thoughts from life remote,
Not fond religious airs,
Not sweetly languid prayers,
Not love of scent and creeds.
Wanted: Deeds.

NORTH CAROLINA STATE GUARD—OFFICERS OF THE GENERAL STAFF.

Col. F. H. Cameron, Adjutant General; Col. A. L. Smith, Inspector General; Col. E. G. Harrell, Quartermaster General; Col. Julian S. Carr, Paymaster General; Col. Benehan Cameron, Inspector S. A. P.; Col. Hubert Haywood, Surgeon General; Col. Thos. W. Strong, Judge Advocate General.

STATE BOARD OF PHARMACY.

E. V. Zoeller, Tarboro, President; P. W. Vaughan, Durham; W. H. Wearn, Charlotte; O. M. Royster, Hickory; Wm. Simpson, Raleigh, Secretary and Treasurer; J. H. Bobbitt, Raleigh, President N. C. P. A.; W. R. Horn, Fayetteville, Secretary.

STATE BOARD OF MEDICAL EXAMINERS.

W. H. Whitehead, M. D., President, Rocky Mount; term expires May 1896; L. J. Picot, M. D., Secretary, Littleton; term expires May 1896; Geo. W. Long, M. D., Graham; term expires May 1896; Julian M. Baker, Tarboro; term expires May 1898; H. B. Weaver, M. D., Asheville; term expires 1898; T. S. Burbank, M. D., Wilmington; term expires 1900; J. M. Hays, M. D., Greensboro; term expires 1900.

NORTH CAROLINA BOARD OF HEALTH.

Geo. Gillett Thomas, M. D., Wilmington, President; S. Westray Battle, M. D., Asheville; Richard H. Lewis, M. D., Raleigh, Secretary and Treasurer; W. H. Harrell, M. D., Williamston; W. H. G. Lucas, M. D., White Hall; John Whitehead, M. D., Salisbury; Prof. F. P. Venable, Ph. D., Chapel Hill; J. C. Chase, Civil Engineer, Wilmington.

STATE MUSEUM.

Located in the Agricultural Building at Raleigh; contains a complete collection of geological rocks and ores of the State; also a fine collection of timbers, agricultural products, fish and aquatic birds—in fact, a complete collection of the resources of the State. G. F. Greene, Curator. Office hours from 9 to 1, and from 2 to 5 p. m. Under control of the State Board of Agriculture.

NORTH CAROLINA BOARD OF PUBLIC CHARITIES.

Charles Duffy, President, Newbern; term expires Jan. 1, 1899; C. B. Denson, Secretary, Raleigh; L. J. Haughton, Pittsboro; term expires Jan. 1, 1898; W. N. Jones, Raleigh; term expires Jan. 1, 1896; S. W. Reid, Charlotte; term expires Jan. 1, 1895; W. A. Blair, Winston; term expires Jan. 1, 1897.

EVAPORATED SWEET POTATOES.

Few people know how easily sweet potatoes can be dried, even in the sun, and how handy and useful the dried potatoes are. At best sweet potatoes are a troublesome crop to keep, but when dried or cured in an evaporator they are really no trouble to keep and are always at hand for use on the table at short notice. They should be sliced and then evaporated. Then to use them they are soaked to restore the evaporated moisture and then baked in pans as the fresh ones often are. They are an admirable article for puddings and pies. For this purpose it would be better to grind them into meal and put up in packages with directions for making puddings. Put up in this way it ought not to be much trouble to create a market for the dried sweet potatoes. If an evaporating plant would but undertake the putting up of the sweet potato meal in packages the article would sell well. Grocerymen are slow to take hold of such products in the crude evaporated state, but in such packages, with a few attractive hand-bills and a lot of receipts for making the many delicious preparations that can be made from sweet potatoes, a market could soon be made for a product that Eastern North Carolina can supply in limitless quantities. Who will start this enterprise?— *W. F. Massey, N. C. Experiment Station.*

Branson's Almanac stands the test of an intelligent public.—Gold Leaf.

SHELLS AND LIME.

"Please state the difference between shell and other lime. Are shells reduced to lime by burning?"—W. H. L., Princeton, N. C.

(Answered by H. B. Battle, Director N. C. Experiment Station.)

Shell lime is merely shells burned. Rock lime or stone lime is the crude limestone after it has been burnt. The combination in all the crude materials is carbonate of lime, which by the action of heat is changed to the oxide of lime, or caustic lime; building lime is also the caustic lime. Marl contains refuse of shells and consequently has a varying percentage of carbonate of lime.

ANECDOTE OF DR. CLOSS.

Showing the wisdom of not committing one's self too far. While a boy on his first circuit he had boasted of being a dear lover of pumpkin pie. In the eastern section of the State pumpkins were plentiful, and the "punkin" pie was standard in every family. At one place on his circuit the family happened to have but little else for breakfast, dinner and supper. But the Doctor's reputation having preceded him as a lover of this article, the good lady of the house did not hesitate to insist that Bro. Closs would eat freely of his favorite dish. Having committed himself beforehand, he felt bound to sustain his reputation, and ate heartily at every meal. But, unfortunately, this good sister had failed to cook the pumpkins as much as usual, and the result was a sick circuit rider on her hands to nurse for several days, and the preacher was ever afterwards noted for conservatism.

Wharton makes first-class Crayons, Pastels and Water Colors.

ENGLISH AS SHE IS SPOKE BY A SON OF OLD YALE.

Two Yale seniors sat on the steps of Osborne Hall one warm day last week, says a Boston paper. One of these collegians was in a confiding mood and he talked of the incidents of the morning and the evening before, which had interfered with his hours of study He said:

"Had a long grouch last night and felt rocky a plenty, so after feeding my face I blew down to Mory's with a couple of heelers. Struck Jimmy down there and he had pinched a beautiful skate. He wanted me to get in the push, but I couldn't split his wood. Sat down, though, and had some whales on toast and threw a couple of tobys under my chest. We horsed Jones to death—he is easy fruit, that man—and gave him the loud gee when he tried to get into our jeans. The good Charlie blew in and gave us the glad hand, but he was loaded for elephants, so we gave him the cold shake. They were trying to sew him up, I could see, and I wasn't going to get my leg jerked, so I cut the game, as I had a lot of grinding to do. It was such a dead smooth night that I went an easy pace and spieled along Chapel street to look at the queens. William was diked out to beat the band, and was bound for a skirt party somewhere. He is a terrible fusser, and he's full of tacks. I don't believe he cuts much ice with the girls after all. This morning I woke up with a dark brown taste in my mouth, and cut chapel and then shoved in a sick excuse at Baldy. I cut that history course whenever I can. The tutor's head is full of wheels, and he gives me a pain in the neck. Come around to my joint and feed this noon, will you? There are a couple of swipes and a greasy grind there, but you needn't wood up for them. Let's spin tops just a few. I'd flunk this recitation dead if I went, and I must make a cold rush in that course or I'll slip my trolley sure. My stand is rotten."

Dr. Branson has done the State valuable service.—Wilmington Messenger.

THE SMILE THAT AWAITS ME AT HOME

Something I own that wealth cannot buy,
  And not offered for sale on the mart;
Something for which the great often sigh
  With an unhidden void in the heart;
Something possessed by one little spot
  In a corner I know on earth's loam,
Waiting for me in a neat, cosy cot,
  'Tis a sweet loving smile in my home.

When all the world is dreary and cold,
  And the clouds darkly hang o'er the way;
Friendship and honor purchased with gold,
  And a world seems to win to betray;
Still one fond thought thro' shadows will shine,
  As I back to that humble cot roam,
Feeling as rich as a wealth-laden mine
  With a sweet, loving smile in my home.

When that bright scene shall vanish and fade
  Into visions of heaven beyond—
The earth grow dim in death's misty shade,
  With the forms so loving and fond,
Yet will remain forever in mind,
  Though afar in the heavens' broad dome,
The sweet happy-face, so loving and kind,
  With the smile that awaits me at home.

ANECDOTE OF DR. WM. CLOSS.

The Doctor was always ready for a bit of dry wit or repartee. If the joke was against him, he related it afterwards with just the same relish as if it had been in his favor.

He relates that on one occasion he walked into a barber shop in Little Washington to have his hair trimmed. He was very bald, having only a light fringe of hair that showed out behind under the rim of his hat. He said to the barber: "I want to make a bargain with you. As I do not charge you for preaching, you may trim my hair without charging." "All right," said the barber, "take a seat and let me proceed." The Doctor seated himself and removed his hat in his usual dignified manner. Whereupon the barber drew back with affected astonishment and exclaimed: "Dr. Closs, if I don't get any more preaching than I get hair off of your head, hell will be my portion, certain." Both preacher and barber laughed heartily, and were ever afterwards good, jolly friends.

THE NORTH CAROLINA
HOME INSURANCE CO.,
OF RALEIGH, N. C.

Insures Against Loss by Fire.

THIS COMPANY HAS BEEN IN SUCCESSFUL OPERATION FOR TWENTY-FIVE YEARS.

W. S. PRIMROSE, President. CHARLES ROOT, Sec. and Treas.
W. G. UPCHURCH, V.-President. P. COWPER, Adjuster.

2—BOOKS—2

THAT EVERY CITIZEN OF NORTH CAROLINA SHOULD HAVE.

TALKS ABOUT LAW,

By JUDGE R. W. WINSTON, of the Superior Court. Price Fifty and Sixty Cents.

THE N. C. MANUAL OF LAW AND FORMS,

By J. N. HOLDING. Esq. The only complete and revised to date Hand-Book to be had. Price $2.00.

Address, **EDWARDS & BROUGHTON,**
Printers and Binders, RALEIGH, N. C.

Have your old Pictures Enlarged by Wharton.

CARE OF STOCK IN WINTER.

Soon will be the time when stock-owners can make some valuable trials for themselves in testing the value of advice given for winter care of stock.

Of two or three milch cows try giving one a comfortable stall well lighted and ventilated without holes for cold drafts or rain to enter, and keep her dry and clean. Turn the others off in the usual way, and compare food eaten and milk produced, and remember that there is left in the stall a compost worth over five-sixths of all the fertilizing elements in the food, and all well preserved.

Try other stock in the same way, and it will be found to pay well in growth and compost made.—*F. E. Emery, N. C. Experiment Station.*

FIRE BLIGHT OF APPLE TREE.

I sent you specimens of apple twigs from my orchard which were attacked last spring. The disease attacks both branches and twigs. In some cases only the twigs are killed, but in other cases large branches or the whole tree is dead. What is the cause and remedy? I also send diseased or blighted pear twigs. We had a hundred dwarf pear trees, but they are dying off one by one.—J. S H.. Bowman's Bluff, N. C.

(Answered by Gerald McCarthy, Botanist, N. C. Experiment Station.)
The disease on both apple and pear trees is the same—the so-called fire blight. This is caused by a species of bacteria, micrococcus amylovorous. There is no remedy except destruction of affected parts. The disease is very contagious, and the cutting out must be promptly attended to or it will infect the whole orchard. Destroy by fire all dead branches.

The best 10-cent book the farmer can buy—no other like it.—Weekly News

ANECDOTE OF DR. CLOSS.

In the early history of the Methodist Church a frontier circuit was
formed down on the Sound in Carteret County. The Bishop sent Bro.
Closs to this then out-of-the-way circuit. The people were industrious,
good livers, and ready for any pleasant wit, of which the preacher was
always full. In those days Yeopon tea, which grows on the Sound in
great abundance, was the principal beverage, and really equal to the
best Chinese tea. On special occasions, when the preacher paid a pas-
toral visit, the good lady would go into the large chest and get out some
good old Rio coffee and prepare a strong decoction of the berry as a
compliment to the pastor's cultured, up-country taste. On one occasion
the good pastor, after a hard day's preaching, sat down to supper in a
good condition to relish strong, hot coffee. After passing his cup for
the seventh time, the landlady, evidently feeling that the supply was
likely soon to be exhausted, ventured, with a twinkle of mischief in her
eye, to suggest: "Bro. Closs, you certainly must love coffee." The
preacher kept on putting down the seventh cupful and slowly remarked:
"Sister Smith, I am certainly a very dear lover of coffee, but then, you
see, I have to drink a large amount of hot water in order to get a little
coffee." As the sister knew that her coffee, made for the honored guest,
was really strong and good, no offence was taken. All laughed heartily
and good fellowship continued to abound.

This joke has ever since been current all over Methodism, and the
memory of good Dr. Closs is kept green.

REMEDIES FOR BORER OF PEACHTREE.

Will wrapping the base of a peachtree in tarred paper keep the borer
out?—W. M., Speight's Bridge, N. C.

(Answered by Gerald McCarthy, Entomologist, N. C. Experiment
Station.)

Wrapping the base of trunk will prevent the female borer moth from
laying her eggs on the collar of the tree if the paper is wrapped suffi-
ciently tight to keep the insect from crawling down between paper and
bark. This is difficult to do, and therefore the treatment is not reliable.
Mounding, or use of washes recommended in Bulletin 92 of this Station,
are much more satisfactory.

THE DEPTH TO PLANT WHEAT.

The result of an experiment made by the N. C. Agricultural Experiment Station at Raleigh to test the best depth to plant wheat is as follows: The average yield per acre when planted at a depth of two inches was 24.5 bushels; planted three inches deep, it was 32.1 bushels per acre; four inches, 23.7 bushels per acre. It will be seen, therefore, that the decided preference lay with the three-inch planting. In this test, the seed was planted very late, on the 24th December, after turnips had been taken off the land. The depth of planting was carefully gauged by a dibble. The best stand on the following 28th March was noted on the shallow planting, and the more scattering stand on the deepest planting, though the plants on these last were almost as large and vigorous as the others. It is probable that with an earlier sowing the result of the deepest planting would have been more favorable.

FARMERS WHO READ.

There are now on the mailing lists of the N. C. Agricultural Experiment Station, which have just been revised, 13,000 names of farmers from North Carolina. The bulletins are mailed free to those who request them and show their appreciation by reading them. All the newspapers in the State receive each publication of the Station as it is issued, as well as various news notes which interest the reader. The bulletins contain matters which are of immediate interest and value to the agriculturists of the State and are written in plain language for unscientific readers. Agriculture is based on science, and accordingly scientific matters necessarily receive attention at the Station. The result of these scientific experiments are not included in the general bulletin issue, but are printed in technical bulletins, sent only to scientists, and those who especially request them. Summaries of the technical work appear in the general bulletins of the Station. Publications are sent free to all within the limits of North Carolina upon application; to others a small fee is charged.

THE ELECTROPOISE.

THE ELECTROPOISE cannot now be ignored. It is an established *fact*. Oxygen is the great feeder of life. We cannot live without Oxygen. Nature supplies the oxygen needed through the lungs. When the lungs are diseased the supply is largely cut off, or when the man is weak and breathes slowly and feebly the needed oxygen is not supplied to the blood.

The *Electropoise* supplies the oxygen directly to the blood through the pores of the skin without any effort on the part of the patient.

It is the simplest of all treatments.

It is bound to come quickly into universal use. One answers for a whole family, and will last for many years. You buy no more drugs, and hence the *Electropoise* will quickly pay for itself.

I know of many families now using the *Electropoise*, and not one willingly gives it up, or lets it go out of the house.

Last summer I bought one for an invalid member of my family. The effect has been truly a benediction. The *Electropoise* is now a favorite in the family. We like to have it always in the house. Providence, in mercy, sent it along this way.

I can sell you one for $25 cash down, regular price. Or I can rent you one *three months* for $15 cash. You can then return it or keep it by paying $12.50 additional.

I am authorized to receive orders by mail.

REV. LEVI BRANSON,
Exclusive Agent for Randolph and Rockingham Counties,
RALEIGH, N. C.

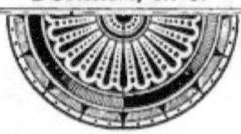

BRANSON'S SHORT CALENDAR FOR 1895.

JANUARY.

S	M	T	W	T	F	S
		1	2	3	4	5
6	7	8	9	10	11	12
13	14	15	16	17	18	19
20	21	22	23	24	25	26
27	28	29	30	31		

FEBRUARY.

S	M	T	W	T	F	S
					1	2
3	4	5	6	7	8	9
10	11	12	13	14	15	16
17	18	19	20	21	22	23
24	25	26	27	28		

MARCH.

S	M	T	W	T	F	S
					1	2
3	4	5	6	7	8	9
10	11	12	13	14	15	16
17	18	19	20	21	22	23
24	25	26	27	28	29	30
31						

APRIL.

S	M	T	W	T	F	S
	1	2	3	4	5	6
7	8	9	10	11	12	13
14	15	16	17	18	19	20
21	22	23	24	25	26	27
28	29	30				

MAY.

S	M	T	W	T	F	S
			1	2	3	4
5	6	7	8	9	10	11
12	13	14	15	16	17	18
19	20	21	22	23	24	25
26	27	28	29	30	31	

JUNE.

S	M	T	W	T	F	S
						1
2	3	4	5	6	7	8
9	10	11	12	13	14	15
16	17	18	19	20	21	22
23	24	25	26	27	28	29
30						

JULY.

S	M	T	W	T	F	S
	1	2	3	4	5	6
7	8	9	10	11	12	13
14	15	16	17	18	19	20
21	22	23	24	25	26	27
28	29	30	31			

AUGUST.

S	M	T	W	T	F	S
				1	2	3
4	5	6	7	8	9	10
11	12	13	14	15	16	17
18	19	20	21	22	23	24
25	26	27	28	29	30	31

SEPTEMBER.

S	M	T	W	T	F	S
1	2	3	4	5	6	7
8	9	10	11	12	13	14
15	16	17	18	19	20	21
22	23	24	25	26	27	28
29	30					

OCTOBER.

S	M	T	W	T	F	S
	1	2	3	4	5	
6	7	8	9	10	11	12
13	14	15	16	17	18	19
20	21	22	23	24	25	26
27	28	29	30	31		

NOVEMBER.

S	M	T	W	T	F	S
					1	2
3	4	5	6	7	8	9
10	11	12	13	14	15	16
17	18	19	20	21	22	23
24	25	26	27	28	29	30

DECEMBER.

S	M	T	W	T	F	S
1	2	3	4	5	6	7
8	9	10	11	12	13	14
15	16	17	18	19	20	21
22	23	24	25	26	27	28
29	30	31				

A VALUABLE HAND BOOK OF INFORMATION.

Best Calendar!
Most Select Matter! } Safest Almanac!

PRICE, 10 CENTS.

Vol. 3.] 29th YEAR OF PUBLICATION. [No. 9.

BRANSON'S
AGRICULTURAL
ALMANAC

FOR THE YEAR OF OUR LORD
1896,

And until the 4th of July, the 120th year of American Independence.

Carefully Calculated for the Latitude and Longitude of Raleigh, by

LEVI BRANSON, A. M., D. D.

LEVI BRANSON, Publisher, Raleigh, N. C.

GET THE BEST AND STICK TO IT—NO OTHER LIKE IT.

TIME.

The calculations of this Almanac are made in mean solar or clock time, which is indicated by a well-regulated clock or watch, and does not correspond with the Sun precisely, except on four days of the year.

Apparent time is that which makes the Sun come to the meridian at 12 o'clock. No good clock will run with the Sun; if set with the Sun on the 2d day of January, the clock will seem to be one minute too fast on the 3d of January.

To adapt the calculations of this Almanac to apparent time, use the minutes in the column marked "Sun slow" or "Sun fast;" add them when fast, substract them when slow.

The calculations are made for the Latitude and Longitude of Raleigh, N. C., but the times, phases, &c., will vary only a few minutes for any part of North Carolina, South Carolina, Georgia, Tennessee or Virginia.

RISING AND SETTING OF THE SUN.

The Almanacs generally used have made the rising and setting of the Sun together equal twelve hours This is incorrect. During some portions of the year the Sun changes so rapidly in Right Ascension and Declination that it makes a material change in the Diurnal Arc during the day. The times here given have been rigorously calculated and compared with the authority, and are true to the nearest whole minute.

TWELVE SIGNS OF THE ZODIAC.

The Head and Face sign. ♈ Aries the Ram.......Ar.

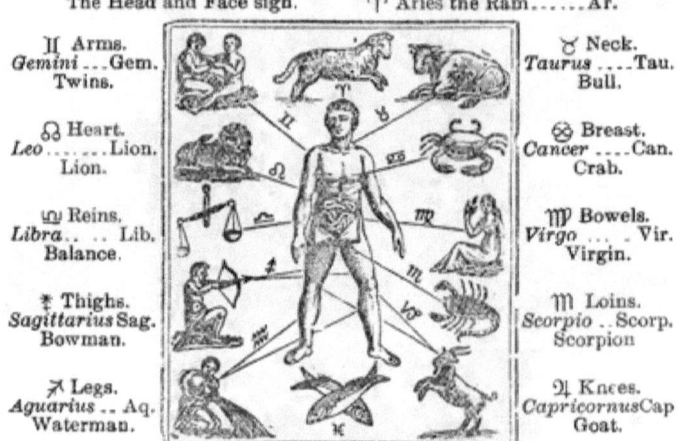

♊ Arms.
Gemini....Gem.
Twins.

♌ Heart.
Leo........Lion.
Lion.

♎ Reins.
Libra.. .. Lib.
Balance.

♐ Thighs.
Sagittarius Sag.
Bowman.

♒ Legs.
Aguarius .. Aq.
Waterman.

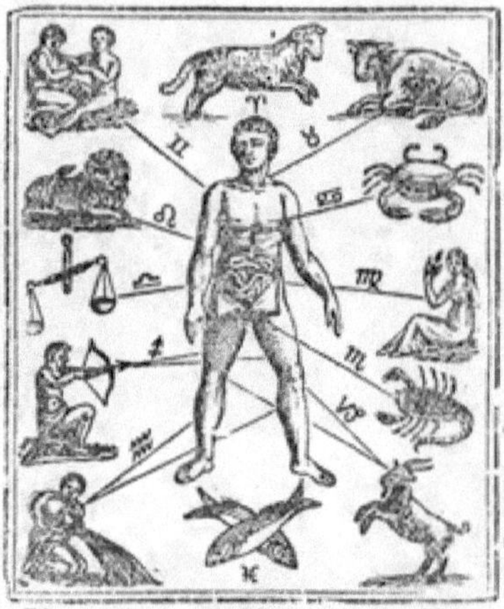

♉ Neck.
Taurus.....Tau.
Bull.

♋ Breast.
Cancer.....Can.
Crab.

♍ Bowels.
Virgo .... . Vir.
Virgin.

♏ Loins.
Scorpio .. Scorp.
Scorpion

♑ Knees.
Capricornus Cap
Goat.

The ♓ *Pisces* the Fishes........Pisc.

To know where the sign is, find the day of the month, and against the day in the column marked Moon's Signs you have the sign or place of the Moon, and then find the sign; it will give you the part of the body it is supposed to govern.

SIGNS.

SPRING SIGNS.	Aries, or Ram. Taurus, or Bull. Gemini, or Twins.	AUTNMN SIGNS.	Libra, or Balance. Scorpio, or Scorpion. Sagittarius, or Bowman.
SUMMER SIGNS.	Cancer, or Crab-fish. Leo, or Lion. Virgo, or Virgin.	WINTER SIGNS.	Capricornus, or Goat. Aquarius, or Waterman. Pisces, or Fishes.

SIGNS OF THE PLANETS.

✳ Sun.	☾ Moon.	♀ Venus.	♂ Mars.
♃ Jupiter.	♄ Saturn.	☌ In Conjunction.	□ Quadrature.
☿ Mercury.	♅ Uranus.	♆ Neptune.	☊ Ascending Node.

MOON'S PHASES.

● New Moon. ☽ First Quarter. ○ Full Moon. ☾ Last Quarter.

CHRONOLOGICAL CYCLES AND ERAS.

Dominical Letter	ED	Julian Period	6609
Epact	15	Jewish Era	5656
Golden Number	16	Era of Nabonassa	2648
Solar Cycle	1	Olympiads	2672
Roman Indication	9	Mahommedan Era	1313

MOVABLE FEASTS OF THE CHURCH.

Epiphany	Jan. 6	Palm Sunday	March 29
Septuagesima Sunday	Feb. 2	Easter Sunday	April 5
Sexagesima Sunday	Feb 9	Whit Sunday	May 24
Quinquagesima Sunday	Feb. 16	Trinity Sunday	May 31
Shrove Tuesday	Feb. 18	First Sunday in Advent	Nov. 29
Ash Wednesday, or Lent	Feb. 19	Ascension Day	May 14
St. Patrick's Day	March 17		

THE FOUR SEASONS.

		D.	H.
Spring commences	March 19,	8	P. M.
Summer commences	June 20,	4	P. M.
Autumn commences	September 22,	7	A. M.
Winter commences	December 21,	1	A. M.

MORNING STARS.

Mercury will be Morning Star about .....March 5, July 3, and Oct. 24.
Venus will be Morning Star till ...July 9.
Jupiter will be Morning Star..Jan. 24, and from Aug. 11 to end of year.

EVENING STARS.

Mercury will be Evening Star about ....Jan. 23, May 16, Sept. 13.
Venus will be Evening Star from............July 9 to end of the year.
Jupiter will be Evening Star till................August 11.

ECLIPSES.

During the year 1896 there will be four eclipses—two of the Sun and two of the Moon.

I. Feb. 13—*An annular eclipse of the Sun*, invisible to North America.
II. Feb. 28—*A partial eclipse of the Moon*, invisible to North America.
III. Aug. 9—*A total eclipse of the Sun*, invisible to North America, exclusive of Alaska. Visible in the Arctic regions. The line of totality running through Nova Zembla and Yesso, Japan.
IV. Aug. 22-23—*A partial eclipse of the Moon*, visible entire to North and South America. The Moon enters Penumbra 10h. 7m., P. M.; the Moon leaves Penumbra 23d, 3h. 48m., A. M.; middle of eclipse, 23d, 0h. 58m., A. M.

TIDES.

The time of tide can readily be found for the following places by adding the hours and minutes opposite the names to the time when the Moon is South on the day to which the tide is sought. The time when the Moon is South is given in the Calendar for every day. The next tide can be found very nearly by adding 12 hours and 29 minutes to the time of the one previous.

The tides are given in local time—add 12 minutes for Eastern Standard:

	H. M.		H. M.
Boston	11 12	New York	8 13
Sandy Hook	7 29	Old Point	8 17
Baltimore	6 33	Washington City	7 44
Richmond	4 32	Hatteras Inlet	7 04
Beaufort	7 26	Bald Head	7 26
Southport	7 19	Wilmington	9 06
Charleston	7 26	Savannah	9 33

Dr. Branson takes care to have all the Courts both full and accurate.—Evening Visitor.

HERSCHEL'S WEATHER PROGNOSTICATOR

For Foretelling the Weather Through all the Lunations of the Year.

This table and the accompanying remarks are the result of many years actual observation, the whole being constructed on a due consideration of the attractions of the Sun and Moon, in their several positions respecting the Earth, and, by simple inspection, it shows the observer what kind of weather will most probably follow the entrance of the Moon into any of its quarters, and that so near the truth as to be seldom or never found to fail.

If the new moon, first quarter, full moon, or last quarter, happen—	IN SUMMER.	IN WINTER.
Between midnight and 2 in the morning	Fair	Hoar frost unless the wind is S. or S. W.
Between 2 and 4, morning	Cold, with frequent showers	Snow and stormy.
Between 4 and 6, morning	Rain	Rain.
Between 6 and 8, morning	Wind and rain	Stormy.
Between 8 and 10, morning	Changeable	Cold rain if wind be W.; snow if E.
Between 10 and 12, morning	Frequent showers	Cold and high wind.
Between 12 o'clock at noon and 2 in afternoon	Very rainy	Rain and snow.
Between 2 and 4, afternoon	Changeable	Fair and mild.
Between 4 and 6, afternoon	Fair	Fair.
Between 6 and 8, aftern'n	Fair if wind N. W.; rainy if S. or S. W.	Fair and frosty wind N. or N.E.; rain or snow if S. or S. W.
Between 8 and 10, afternoon	Ditto	Ditto.
Between 10 and midnight	Fair	Fair and frosty.

OBSERVATIONS.—1. The nearer the time for the Moon's change, first quarter, full and last quarter are to midnight, the fairer will be the weather during the next seven days.

2. The space for this calculation occupies from 10 at night until 2 next morning.

3. The nearer to midday or noon the phase of the Moon happens, the more foul or wet weather may be expected during the next seven days.

4. The space for this calculation occupies from 10 in the forenoon until 2 in the afternoon. These observations refer principally to the Summer, though they affect Spring and Autumn nearly in the same ratio.

5. The Moon's change, first quarter, full and last quarter happening during six of the afternoon hours, i. e., from 4 to 10, may be followed by fair weather, but this is mostly dependent on the wind, as is noted in the table.

6. Though the weather, from a variety of irregular causes, is more uncertain in the latter part of Autumn, the whole of Winter and beginning of Spring, yet, in the main, the above observations will apply to these periods also.

7. To prognosticate correctly, especially in those cases where the wind is concerned, the observer should be in sight of a good vane, where the four cardinal points of the heavens are correctly placed.

Branson's Almanac is a household word.—Truth.

GOVERNMENT OF NORTH CAROLINA—1893-'97.

EXECUTIVE DEPARTMENT.

Elias Carr, of Edgecombe County, Governor; salary $3,000, and furnished house, fuel and lights.

R. A. Doughton, of Alleghany County, Lieut. Gov. and Speaker of the Senate.

Chas. M. Cooke, of Franklin County, Secretary of State; salary $2,000 and fees; $1,000 additional for clerical assistance.

Robert M. Furman, of Buncombe County, Auditor; salary $1,500; $1,000 additional for clerical assistance.

William H. Worth, of Lenoir County, Treasurer; salary $3,000.

John C. Scarborough, of Johnston County, Superintendent of Public Instruction; salary $1,500; $500 per annum additional traveling expenses.

Frank I. Osborne, of Mecklenburg County, Attorney General; salary $2,000.

R. T. Gray, Reporter to Supreme Court; salary $750.

Francis H. Cameron, of Wake County, Adjutant General; salary $600.

J. C. Ellington, of Johnston County, State Librarian; salary $1,000.

T. P. Jerman, Jr., of Warren County, Chief Clerk to Auditor; salary $1,000.

S. F. Telfair, of Beaufort County, Private Secretary to Governor; salary $1,200.

C. L. Hinton, of Wake County, Executive Clerk; salary $600.

W. P. Batchelor, of Wake County, Chief Clerk to Secretary of State; salary $1,000.

J. W. Denmark, of Wake County, Chief Clerk to Treasurer; salary $1,500.

Jos. Potts, of Guilford County, Teller; salary $750.

W. H. Worth, Treasurer *ex officio*, and Wm. H. Martin, of Wake County, Clerk for Charitable and Penal Institutions; salary $1,000.

C. M. Roberts, of Vance County, Superintendent of Public Buildings and Grounds; salary $850.

J. C. S. Lumsden, State Standard Keeper; salary $100.

STATE BOARD OF EDUCATION.

The Governor, Lieutenant Governor, Secretary of State, Treasurer, Auditor, Superintendent of Public Instruction and Attorney General constitute the Board.

A FABLE FOR LICENSE MEN.

There was once a donkey that fed in a grassy meadow, wherein were many fresh-water ponds greatly infested by leeches. When the donkey went into the water to drink, or to cool himself, the leeches would fasten upon him and greatly deplete the blood supply. At last the donkey resolved to do something to get rid of the leeches. First, he shook his long ears at them, and said it was a shame. Next, he got on a platform and brayed at them. Then he went to the ponds and kicked at them, but all to no purpose; the leeches stuck to him as tenaciously as ever. At last, an idea came like a sudden inspiration. "I have it," said the donkey; "as I can't prevent the leeches from sucking my blood, I'll regulate the business by giving them a license to do it, on condition that they give me back a small portion of the blood as a license fee." And so he did. It was a brilliant idea, and eminently worthy of an ass.

MORAL.—If you are an ass, license the saloon leech to prey on your blood.

Branson's Almanac—State pride compels us to admire it.—The Livingstone.

1st Month. JANUARY, 1896. 31 Days.

Moon's Phases.

	D. H. M.		D. H. M.
Last Quarter,	7 10 16 a. m.	First Quarter,	22 9 34 p. m.
New Moon	14 5 11 p. m.	Full Moon,	30 3 47 p. m.

Day of Month.	Day of Week.	Sun rises.	Sun sets.	Sun slow.	Sun's decline south.	ASPECTS OF PLANETS AND OTHER MISCELLANEOUS MATTER.	Moon's place.	Moon rises or sets.	Moon south.	High tides.
1	We	7 10	4 58	4	23 0	NEW YEAR'S DAY.		5 43	mo'n	m'rn
2	Thu	7 10	5 0	4	22 55	Battle of Trenton 1777.		6 59	1 27	8 53
3	Fri	7 10	5 1	5	22 50			8 14	2 23	9 49
4	Sat	7 10	5 1	5	22 44	☿ gr. Hel. Lat. E.		9 28	3 15	11 4
1.	Epiphany Sunday.					Day's length 9 hours 52 minutes.				
5	*E.*	7 10	5 2	6	22 37	Richmond bomb. 1781.		10 41	4 5	10 53
6	Mon	7 9	5 3	6	22 30	EPIPHANY. Old Chr.		11 53	4 53	11 17
7	Tue	7 9	5 4	6	22 23	1st St. House b. 1791		mo'n	5 41	0 8
8	We	7 9	5 5	7	22 15	Forsyth Co. f'm'd 1848.		1 4	6 30	1 2
9	Thu	7 9	5 6	7	22 6	Populist Leg. met 1895.		2 16	7 22	2 1
10	Fri	7 9	5 6	8	21 58	☌ ♄ ☽ ♅. Vic. Em. d. 1824		3 28	8 16	4 5
11	Sat	7 9	5 7	8	21 48	First Gov. of N. C. 1664.		4 37	9 12	4 9
2.	First Sunday after Epiphany.					Day's length 10 hours 1 minute.				
12	*E.*	7 9	5 8	9	21 39	Gaston Co. f'm'd 1846.		5 41	10 10	5 12
13	Mon	7 9	5 9	9	21 29	Geo. Fox died 1681.		6 36	11 7	6 8
14	Tue	7 9	5 10	9	21 18	G. Burrington q. 1724		sets	eve	6 55
15	We	7 9	5 11	10	21 7	British Museum op. 1759		5 50	0 51	7 40
16	Thu	7 8	5 12	10	20 56	☌ ☿ ☽. Pitt Co. f'md 1760		6 54	1 38	8 24
17	Fri	7 8	5 13	10	20 45	Siamese Twins died 1874		7 56	2 21	9 1
18	Sat	7 8	5 14	11	20 32	Gov. Jarvis born 1836.		8 55	3 1	9 36
3.	Second Sunday after Epiphany.					Day's length 10 hours 7 minutes.				
19	*E.*	7 8	5 15	11	20 20	GEN. LEE'S BIRTHD. 1807		9 54	3 40	10 10
20	Mo	7 7	5 15	11	20 7	Northampt'n Co. f'd 1741		10 52	4 19	10 48
21	Tue	7 7	5 16	12	19 54	Gov. Bragg d. 1872.		11 50	4 59	11 25
22	We	7 6	5 17	12	19 40	Halifax Co. f'd 1758.		mo'n	5 41	0 1
23	Thu	7 6	5 18	12	19 26	☿ gr. Elon. E.		0 50	6 26	0 34
24	Fri	7 5	5 19	12	19 12	☿ in ♌. ☍ ♃ ☉.		1 54	7 15	1 26
25	Sat	7 4	5 20	13	18 57	Fayetteville settled 1749.		3 1	8 9	2 25
4.	Third Sunday after Epiphany.					Day's length 10 hours 18 minutes.				
26	*E.*	7 3	5 21	13	18 42	Royal Acad. char. 1765.		4 6	9 7	3 29
27	Mo	7 2	5 22	13	18 27	Dr. Caldwell died 1838.		5 7	10 8	4 36
28	Tue	7 2	5 23	13	18 11	☿ in Perihelion.		6 3	11 9	5 39
29	We	7 2	5 23	13	17 55	Nap. 3d mar. 1853.		6 50	mo'n	6 34
30	Thu	7 2	5 24	14	17 39	☿ stationary.		rises.	0 7	7 22
31	Fri	7 2	5 25	14	17 23	Mrs. E. B Englehard d. '95		7 9	1 3	8 13

WEATHER CONJECTURES.—JANUARY—1, 2, 3, 4, 5, cold rain; 6, 7, snow; 8, 9, 10, 11, 12, 13, 14, expect heavy weather; 15, 16, 17, 18, fair; 19, 20, 21, 22, variable; 23, 24, 25, 26, look for rain or snow; 27, 28, 29, 30, 31, expect frost.

BRANSON MAXIMS.

BRANSON MOTTO: "CONVICTION OF DUTY, FOLLOW."

1. All men have faith in something, hence they work expecting results.—*Branson.*

2. Some men have faith in the laws governing mind; obeying those laws they attain to mental power.—*Branson.*

3. Some men have faith in the laws of health, and hence by obeying those laws they secure physical health and happiness.—*Branson.*

4. The man who has faith in the laws governing the spirit life, can realize that "the law of the Lord is perfect, converting the soul,"—*Branson.*

5. The Christian religion leads a man towards the highest cultivation of all his best capabilities.—*Branson.*

6. The man who has *full faith in all* God's laws, and renders a perfect obedience, has peace flowing as a river, and a joy that is complete.—*Branson.*

7. To give advice unsolicited is delightful ; it so magnifies our self-esteem.   To receive advice unsolicited is humiliating; it so minifies our self-esteem.—*Branson.*

8. A man in whose mind his own country is not *first*, is a man who himself is not *worthy* to be first in another country.—*Branson.*

9. Our State is a diamond; let us polish it well.—*Branson.*

10. The *mind crop* is the greatest crop that can be raised on any farm or in any State.—*Branson.*

11. The *mind crop* in North Carolina is better than ever before.—*Branson.*

12. The *mind crop* should be planted early and cultivated better than cotton or tobacco.—*Branson.*

13. The stronger the *homes*, the stronger the *country* in which the homes are found.—*Branson.*

14. The greatest possibilities of a man are on his native heath; if he is great on another heath, he is still less than a native ought to have been.—*Branson.*

15. It is strange how freely we *give away* our *own* knowledge, and how freely we *pay high prices* for the knowledge we obtain from others.—*Branson.*

16. Living in obedience to spiritual *laws* brings spiritual *blessings.*—*Branson.*

17. *Do* your duty, then *wait.*—*Branson.*

18. Work for your *country*, and God will work for *you.*—*Branson.*

19. Much of our best work is unsuspected by *ourselves*, and even by the *recipients.*—*Branson.*

20. Individual comfort, State wealth, make a happy people.—*Branson.*

21. Never keep people unneccessarily waiting.—*Mrs. Branson.*

22. Be happy; life is short.—*Branson.*

23. To *sleep sweetly*, recline a few moments on your *left* side ; then turn *slowly* onto your right side.   Try it.—*Branson.*

24. Live with happy people, and you are likely *to be* happy.—*Branson.*

25. Do not keep a *burr* in your *throat*, nor a bit of *malice* in your *heart.*—*Branson.*

26. If you are *good*, this world is *good enough* for you; if you are *mean*, then it is *too good* for you.—*Branson.*

27. Never allow your energies to slacken, or your faith to weaken.—*Branson.*

28. To the end of life, do your very best.—*Branson.*

29. The more you imitate God and good people, the greater you are likely to be.—*Branson.*

30. Reduce the number of your enemies; increase the number of your friends.—*Branson.*

31. In old age, you will be likely to need vast stores of friendship.—*Branson.*

32. Be true to your friends, and quickly.—*Branson.*

33. Don't run a man down to get his friendship.—*Father Branson.*

34. Be a man among men.—*Father Branson.*

Mr. F. S. Royster, Tarboro, N. C.:

Dear Sir—My net yield from my Tobacco crop, when I used your Orinoco Guano, was $400 per acre. I use 1,000 pounds per acre.

J. O. BRYAN, Battleboro, N. C.

2d Month.   FEBRUARY, 1896.   29 Days.

Moon's Phases.

	D. H. M.		D. H. M.
Last Quarter,	5 7 29 p.m.	First Quarter, 21	4 6 p.m.
New Moon,	13 11 4 a.m.	Full Moon, 28	2 43 p.m.

Day of Month.	Day of Week.	Sun rises.	Sun sets.	Sun slow.	Sun's decline south.	ASPECTS OF PLANETS AND OTHER MISCELLANEOUS MATTER.	Moon's place.	Moon rises or sets.	Moon south.	High Tides.
1	Sat	7 1	5 29	14	17 6	Col.Shaw k.by Fed. 1863		8 25	mo'n	mo'n

5.   Septuagesima Sunday.   Day's length 10 hours 29 minutes.

2	E.	7 1	5 30	14	16 48	Peace Conference 1865.		9 40	2 47	9 40
3	Mo	7 0	5 31	14	16 31	Gen. R.Barringer d.1895		10 53	3 36	10 24
4	Tue	6 59	5 32	14	16 13	Guiteau sent'c'd 1882		mo'n	4 26	11 8
5	We	6 58	5 33	14	15 55	BRANSON'S BIRTHD.		0 7	5 18	11 52
6	Thu	6 58	5 34	14	15 37	♂♄☽☊.J.J.Daniel d.'48		1 20	6 12	0 38
7	Fri	6 57	5 34	14	15 18	Pope Pius IX d, '78.		2 35	7 8	1 43
8	Sat	6 56	5 35	14	14 59	♀ gr. Hel. Lat. N.		3 35	8 5	2 51

6.   Sexagesima Sunday.   Day's length 10 hours 41 minutes.

9	E.	6 55	5 36	14	14 40	Gen. Hancock died 1886		4 32	9 1	3 58
10	Mo	6 54	5 37	14	14 20	Treaty of Paais 1763.		5 21	9 56	4 59
11	Tue	6 53	5 38	14	14 1	E. B.Englehardt bu. 1896		6 0	10 47	5 52
12	We	6 53	5 39	14	13 41	Seymour died 1886.		6 32	11 34	6 35
13	Thu	6 52	5 40	14	13 21	SUN ECLIPSED, INV.		sets.	eve.	7 13
14	Fri	6 51	5 41	14	13 1	Gibbon died 1794.		6 45	0 59	7 52
15	Sat	6 50	5 42	14	12 40	Gr. fire in Durham 1881.		7 44	1 38	8 27

7.   Shrove Sunday.   Day's length 10 hours 54 minutes.

16	E.	6 49	5 46	14	12 19	Judge Battle buried 1879		8 42	2 17	9 0
17	Mo	6 48	5 44	14	11 58	Mrs. Cuninggim d. 1895.		9 40	2 56	9 31
18	Tue	6 47	5 45	14	11 37	FIRST DAY OF LENT.		10 39	3 37	10 5
19	We	6 46	5 46	14	11 16	ASH WEDNESDAY.		11 42	4 20	10 46
20	Thu	6 45	5 47	14	10 54	♀ sta. Douglass d '95		mo'n	5 7	11 27
21	Fri	6 43	5 48	14	10 33	Gov. Clark d. 1874.		0 46	5 57	0 8
22	Sat	6 42	5 48	14	10 21	WASHINGTON'S BIRTHD.		1 45	6 52	0 52

8.   First Sunday in Lent.   Day's length 11 hours 7 minutes.

23	E.	6 41	5 48	14	9 49	Mrs.M.E.Speight d. 1895		2 51	7 50	1 57
24	Mo	6 40	5 49	13	9 27	♅ stationary.		3 48	8 49	3 7
25	Tue	6 39	5 50	13	9 5	Fayetteville settled 1749		4 38	9 48	4 15
26	We	6 38	5 51	13	8 42	Napoleon escaped 1815.		5 21	10 45	5 19
27	Thu	6 37	5 52	13	8 20	♄ sta. ☿ sta.		5 55	11 40	6 13
28	Fri	6 36	5 53	13	7 57	☽ p'tly ecl.inv.at W		rises.	mo'n	6 59
29	Sat	6 35	5 54	13	7 34	This day only ev. 4 years		7 15	0 32	7 46

WEATHER CONJECTURES.—FEBRUARY—1, 2, 3, 4, 5, fair and mild ; 6, 7, 8, 9, 10, rain or snow; 11, 12, 13, expect snow; 14, 15, 16, 17, cold; 18, 19, 20, 21, cold wind; 22, 23, 24, 25, 26, 27, 28, expect open weather; 29, mild.

THE HEAVENLY VOYAGE.

REV. D. A. CROCKER.

When for eternal worlds we steer.
And seas are calm, and skies are clear,
And faith in lively exercise
The distant hills of Canaan rise—
The soul, with all her sails unfurled,
Waves back this tempting, fleeting world
    A last adieu.

As o'er the glassy sea she glides,
Urged on by the favoring winds and tides;
Or tossed upon the stormy deep,
Where billows over billows leap,
With cheerful hope she spreads her way,
And sings a joyful, happy lay—
    I'm homeward bound.

To siren song no ear she lends;
With steady form her course she bends;
Or calm or storm alike defies
While her great Chief the helm applies;
And through the night and all the day
She sings her joyful, happy lay—
    I'm homeward bound.

And as she nears the blissful shore,
Her raptured eyes its scenes explore;
While spring breezes trip her sails,
And odors sweet her sense regales.
And now for joy she sings again.
A nobler, softer, a sweeter strain—
    I'm almost home.

With all her canvass widely spread,
And all her banners overhead,
Into the port she swiftly glides,
And casting anchor, safely rides;
While angels make all Heaven ring.
As with united voice they sing,
    Home, sweet home.

FOUL AIR IN WELLS.

A good extemporized apparatus for removing carbonic acid gas from wells, is simply an opened-out umbrella let down and rapidly hauled up a number of times in succession. The person who made and reports this experiment, stated that the effect was to remove the gas in a few minutes from a well so soul as to instantly extinguish a candle previous to the use of the umbrella.

THE RUINS of the Tower of Babel are within the walls of Babylon, in Asia Minor.

IT IS stated that the Chinese high officials have been instructed to travel henceforeh in gunboats, on account of the frequent disasters to merchant steamers.

THE INTERESTING old house in Kersington Gore. London, which has been successively inhabited by Guizot, Cavour, Kinglake, Grote, Macaulay and Thackeray, is soon to be pulled down.

A YOUNG New Yorker has gone into the business of devising "catchy" titles for articles and stories sent him in manuscript. He is an adept at it, and he may succeed in creating a new literary business.

3d Month. MARCH, 1896. 31 Days.

Moon's Phases.

	D.	H.	M.		D.	H.	M.
☾ Last Quarter,	6	6	20 a.m.	☽ First Quarter,	22	6	48 a.m.
● New Moon,	14	5	39 a.m.	○ Full Moon,	29	0	13 a.m.

Day of Month.	Day of Week.	Sun rises.	Sun sets.	Sun slow.	Sun's decline south.	ASPECTS OF PLANETS AND OTHER MISCELLANEOUS MATTER.	Moon's place.	Moon rises or sets.	Moon south	High Tides.
9.	Fifth Sunday before Easter.					Day's length 11 hours 21 minutes.				
1	*D.*	6 34	5 55	12	7 12	Spectator pub. 1711.	♍	8 31	mo'n	mo'n
2	Mo	6 32	5 56	12	6 49	Walpole died 1797.	♍	9 42	2 16	9 15
3	Tue	6 30	5 57	12	6 26	Nevada admitted 1863.	♎	11 4	3 9	9 59
4	We	6 28	5 58	12	6 3	Gen. Jackson Pres. 1829	♎	mo'n	4 4	10 52
5	Thu	6 26	6 0	12	5 39	☾ □♆☉. ☿ gr. Elon. W	♏	0 19	5 1	11 40
6	Fri	6 24	6 0	11	5 16	Bat. of Alomo 1836.	♏	1 28	5 59	0 21
7	Sat	6 23	6 1	11	4 53	Bible Society f'nd'd 1804	♐	2 28	6 57	1 28
10.	Fourth Sunday before Easter.					Day's length 11 hours 39 minutes.				
8	*D.*	6 22	6 1	11	4 29	William III died 1702.	♐	3 20	7 52	2 37
9	Mo	6 20	6 2	10	4 6	Rev. Wm. Grant d. 1895	♑	4 2	8 44	3 39
10	Tue	6 18	6 3	10	3 42	☌ ♂ ☽.	♑	4 35	9 32	4 37
11	We	6 17	6 4	10	3 19	☌ ♀ ☿ ☽.	♒	5 3	10 16	5 25
12	Thu	6 16	6 5	10	2 55	☿ in Aphelion.	♒	5 27	10 58	6 6
13	Fri	6 14	6 6	9	2 31	● Pop. Leg. adj. 1895,	♒	5 49	11 38	6 41
14	Sat	6 13	6 6	9	2 8	☌♀ capricorni.	♓	sets.	eve.	7 14
11.	Third Sunday before Easter,					Day's length 11 hours 55 minntes.				
15	*D.*	6 12	6 7	9	1 44	Samoan disaster 1889.	♓	7 33	0 56	7 50
16	Mo	6 11	6 8	9	1 20	Mexico evac. by Fr'ch '67	♓	8 32	1 36	8 24
17	Tue	6 9	6 9	8	0 57	ST. PATRICK'S DAY.	♈	9 33	2 18	8 58
18	We	6 8	6 10	8	0 33	Suez Canal compl. 1869.	♈	10 35	3 3	9 34
19	Thu	6 6	6 11	8	0 9	☉ ent. ♈. SPRING COM.	♉	11 39	3 51	10 16
20	Fri	6 4	6 12	7	n'rth		♉	mo'n	4 44	10 58
21	Sat	6 3	6 12	7	0 38	Lucknow fell 1858.	♉	0 40	5 39	11 50
12.	Second Sunday before Easter.					Day's length 12 hours 11 minutes.				
22	*D.*	6 2	6 13	7	1 2	☽ Earthq. at Quito 1859	♊	1 38	6 36	0 32
23	Mo	6 0	6 13	6	1 26	Bat. Winchester '62.	♊	2 29	7 33	1 38
24	Tue	5 59	6 14	6	1 49	♃ stationary.	♋	3 13	8 29	2 47
25	We	5 58	6 15	6	2 13	Thames Tunnel op. 1843.	♋	3 50	9 23	3 52
26	Thu	5 57	6 16	6	2 36	Mrs. E. B. Moore d. 1895.	♌	4 22	10 16	4 52
27	Fri	5 55	6 17	6	3 0	Bruce crowned 1306.	♌	4 52	11 7	5 46
28	Sat	5 53	6 18	5	3 23	Davidson Col. op. 1837.	♍	5 17	11 59	6 33
13.	Palm Sunday.					Day's length 12 hours 27 minutes.				
29	*D.*	5 51	6 18	5	3 46	○ Swedenborg d. 1772.	♍	rises.	mo'n	7 15
30	Mo	5 50	6 19	4	4 10	Calhoun died 1850.	♎	8 39	0 53	0 5
31	Tue	5 48	6 20	4	4 33	Sam'l M. Parish d. 1895.	♎	9 56	1 49	8 53

WEATHER CONJECTURES.—MARCH—1, 2, 3, 4, 5, 6, mild; 7, 8, 9, 10, stormy; 11, 12, 13, expect wind and rain; 14, 15, 16, 17. 18, 19, 20, 21, rainy; 22, 23, 24, 25, high winds; 26, 27, 28, 29, stormy; 30, 31, expect snow.

THE MAN THAT IS WANTED.

One of the most frequent requests I get, week after week, is for a "first-class energetic man." There are hundreds of first class men with whom I am acquainted. I mean they rank first, and are no second-rate characters in anything that goes to make the morality and religion of a man; but many of them are very much depraved in all that makes up an energetic man. Some one has said that the original sin consists largely of laziness, and the man without energy is closely related to the man who is lazy. There is a laziness of the mind, which is more to be despised than laziness of the body. An energetic mind is never associated with a lazy body.

Most of these requests are made for young men who are wanted to fill places as teachers or principals in schools. But everybody wants a first-class man. In many such cases the intention is to put him in a fourth-class school house; but the first-class man has many more offers than this one, and can therefore choose between the better and the worse positions that are offered to him.

It is very much to be regretted that there is such a scarcity of first-class men. But what is a first-class man? A first-class man is one who has done his best where he has last been, who has helped others when their needs have come in his way, who attends religious services, and is in sympathy with the religious and moral efforts of the community. One of the most important things that a first-class man has to do is to make himself kind and agreeable to everybody; the next thing he must do is to manage his business as he thinks will be best, and not try to please everybody just for the sake of their favor, but at the same time he must have a polite regard for the opinions and wishes of others, even though he cannot conform to them.

An energetic young man is one who goes to bed and gets up regularly, eats moderately, thinks earnestly, and fills up his time with faithfulness to his duties. Energy means saving what we have, to use it in effort. Unused energy does not exist. He must regard time as an investment, and must make the most of it. If he finds himself diverted from his business, let him make out a programme of things to be done each day, and stick to that until he gets in the way of making out a plan in his own mind, and working it to completion. Do not let people tell you what to do when you are attending to your own business, but at the same time do not forget that you have a public as well as a private duty. An energetic young man is not afraid of facts and figures, as a means of guiding him in the pursuit of his business. He must not be afraid of details, nor of drudgery; otherwise, his energy will be of about as much service as that of a ram butting its head against a wall. Energy and system are to each other as the steam and the engine are to each other.—*John F. Crowell.*

HOT WATER AS A REMEDY.

BY EMMET DENSMORE, M. D.

While in attendance upon lectures in New York University Medical College, I often heard Professor Loomis—a very skilful physician, and the leading spirit and pride of the college—say to his classes that if he were reduced to a single remedy, he would select opium. As the result of an extensive practice, and also of a very thorough study of all the prominent systems of current medical practice, I am free to say that if I were reduced to a single remedy, I would choose hot water. Of course, if hot water was taken as a single remedy, it would give the physician the privilege of useing it hot or cold. Thanks to Preissnitz, an unlettered German peasant, and to the water-cure agitation that followed upon his discoveries, the most conservative of the self-styled regular physicians of the present day have learned the very great value of ice water in the reduction of temperature in dangerous fevers. From the same source, the modern physician has been made aware of the very great value as a curative agent of the application of either hot cloths or hot bags applied to any region of great pain. But of the great value of hot water as an

4th Month. APRIL, 1896. 30 Days.

Moon's Phases.

	D.	H.	M.			D.	H.	M.	
☾ Last Quarter,	4	7	15	p.m.	☽ First Quarter,	20	5	38	p.m.
● New Moon,	12	11	16	p.m.	○ Full Moon,	27	8	39	a.m.

Day of Month.	Day of Week.	Sun rises.	Sun sets.	Sun slow.	Sun's decline north.	ASPECTS OF PLANETS AND OTHER MISCELLANEOUS MATTER.	Moon's place.	Moon rises or sets.	Moon south.	High Tides.
1	We	5 47	6 22	4	4 56	APRIL FOOL'S DAY.		11 11	mo'n	mo'n
2	Thu	5 46	6 23	3	5 19	☿ gr. Hel. Lat. S.		mo'n	3 47	10 35
3	Fri	5 44	6 23	3	5 42	☾ GOOD FRIDAY.		0 17	4 47	11 25
4	Sat	5 42	6 24	3	6 5			1 14	5 45	0 7
14.	Easter Sunday.					Day's length 12 hours 48 minutes.				
5	*D.*	5 41	6 25	2	6 27	Jefferson born 1743.		2 0	6 39	1 11
6	Mo	5 39	6 26	2	6 50	Richard I. died 1199.		2 37	7 29	2 13
7	Tue	5 38	6 27	2	7 12	Socrates d. 333 B. C.		3 7	8 15	3 10
8	We	5 36	6 28	2	7 35	☌ ♂ ☽. DeMedice d. 1492		3 31	8 57	4 1
9	Thu	5 35	6 29	1	7 57	Lee surrendered 1865.		3 54	9 37	4 46
10	Fri	5 34	6 30	1	8 19	☌ ♀ ☽.		4 15	10 16	5 27
11	Sat	5 33	6 31	1	8 41	Benj. West died 1820.		4 35	10 35	6 4
15.	Low Sunday.					Day's length 13 hours 0 minutes.				
12	*D.*	5 31	6 31	1	9 3	● Dr. Young d. 1765.		4 55	11 35	6 39
13	Mo	5 30	6 32	0	9 25	Raleigh surr'd 1865.		sets.	eve.	7 13
14	Tue	5 28	6 33	0	9 46	Lincoln assassin'td 1865.		8 27	1 1	7 52
15	We	5 27	6 34	fast	10 7			9 33	1 49	8 32
16	Thu	5 26	6 34		10 21	Mathew Arnold d. 1865.		10 34	2 40	9 13
17	Fri	5 24	6 35	1	10 50	☌ ♆ ☽.		11 32	3 34	9 57
18	Sat	5 23	6 36	1	11 11	☿ ☌ ⊙. Conklin d. 1888.		mo'n	4 29	10 49
16.	Second Sunday after Easter.					Day's length 13 hours 15 minutes.				
19	*D.*	5 22	6 37	1	11 31	☽ DeIsraeli d. 1704.		0 25	5 25	11 41
20	Mo	5 21	6 38	1	11 52	1st newspa. U.S. 1704		1 10	6 20	0 17
21	Tue	5 20	6 39	1	12 12	☿ in ♌.		1 43	7 13	1 19
22	We	5 18	6 40	2	12 32	Oklahoma opened 1889.		2 20	8 4	2 23
23	Thu	5 17	6 41	2	12 52	Cervantes died 1616.		2 49	8 54	3 23
24	Fri	5 15	6 41	2	13 12	♀ gr. Hel. Lat. S.		3 17	9 44	4 21
25	Sat	5 14	6 41	2	13 31	☿ in Perihelion.		3 44	10 36	5 14
17.	Third Sunday after Easter.					Day's length 13 hours 30 minutes.				
26	*D.*	5 13	6 43	2	13 50	○ Gen. Johnson sur. '65		4 11	11 30	6 5
27	Mo	5 12	6 43	3	14 9	Gen. Grant born '22		rises.	mo'n	6 51
28	Tue	5 11	6 44	3	14 28	☌ ♅ ☽. Monroe born 1758		8 45	0 28	7 42
29	We	5 10	6 45	3	14 46	Capitol disas. Richm'd '70		9 58	1 29	8 35
30	Thu	5 9	6 46	3	15 5	Washington inaug. 1789		11 0	2 31	9 27

WEATHER CONJECTURES.—APRIL—1, 2, 3, look for snow ; 4, 5, 6, 7, 8, 9, 10, 11, rain or snow, if wind S. or S. W.; 12, 13, 14, 15, 16, 17, 18, 19, 20, fair and frosty ; 21, 22, 23, 24, fair, if the wind N. or N. E.; 25, 26, 27, fair ; 28, 29, 30, expect cold rain.

HOT WATER AS A REMEDY.—Continued.

internal remedy, the profession are about as ignorant as they were thirty years ago of the value of water, both hot and cold, applied externally.

In a great majority of cases where a patient is taken with severe pains in any of the vital organs, and especially in the region of the stomach and bowels, a persistent administration of large amounts of hot water will quell such pains quite as effectually, although not as quickly, as a hypodermic injection of morphine; and there are not only no injurious after effects, as is the case of opium, but a decided benefit to the system even after the pain has been quelled. Let it be understood that it must be hot, not warm water. The water ought not to be made so hot that the patient is obliged to sip it slowly; it ought to be at such a temperature that a half pint of it may be taken continuously; but the hotter the better. Hot water passes rapidly through the walls of the stomach, and enters at once into the circulation. For this reason, the patient can drink a much larger quantity of water than is generally supposed. Whenever a person is taken with severe pains, he or she ought to take a half pint of very hot water every five minutes until two or three quarts have been consumed. In a majority of cases, the pain will have been greatly modified by that time. Continue, after that, taking the half pint every five, or ten, or fifteen minutes, until the pain is all gone. There is no tendency to nausea in taking very hot water, as is the case with warm water; but if taking very hot water should cause vomiting, it will be seen to be helpful, and all the patient has to do is to continue drinking it At the same time the patient ought to have hot-water bags, or jugs filled with boiling water, applied to the feet, and also hot bags or bottles applied to the seat of pain, whether in the stomach or bowels, or elsewhere.

A person unaccustomed to this treatment is quite likely to find that he cannot swallow the hot water, and will tell you that his stomach is full, and that it is impossible. This is the result of ignorance. All the physician has to do is to insist that his patient follow these directions, taking the half pint every five or ten minutes, to see that there is great improvement in the next thirty or sixty minutes.

So far, I have touched upon the value of hot water in an emergency, and when the patient is suffering from an acute attack of pain. Dr. J. Milner Fothergill, a famous London physician, recently deceased, earnestly strove to teach the profession the value of drinking large quantities of water in all dyspeptic and weak conditions of the digestive system. He explained that drinking large quantities of water has the effect of throwing off impurities from the system, that it stimulates the action of the kidneys and bowels, and is a very important therapeutic agent. While this is true, it will be found by experiment that a much greater advantage will accrue from the use of hot water. All persons suffering from constipation, a weak stomach, a bad taste in the mouth, bad breath, or any similar derangement, will find great benefit by taking a half pint or a pint of very hot water fifteen or thirty minutes previous to each meal, and then again just before going to bed. An important fact, which is not generally known, but which can be readily verified by any one, is that hot water will more readily quench thirst than cold; and so, while all persons of a dyspeptic tendency should take the hot water before meals and before retiring without reference to thirst, they ought also to drink hot water at any other time if there is thirst.

The simple truth is that water is the only rightful drink for man. It is quite true that all persons in robust health do not need hot water; it is also true that persons living on a diet of meat and fruits and nuts, or meat and milk and fruit without the use of salt and other stimulants, will experience very little thirst. But all persons taking the usual diet of civilization, will be found to suffer more or less from thirst, and hot water, taken as above directed, will be found the best remedy to overcome it.

If the above simple directions were resolutely followed in every case of illness, it would be seen that in a large majority of instances there is no need of calling a physician.

5th Month.   MAY, 1896.   31 Days.

Moon's Phases.

	D. H. M.		D. H. M.
C Last Quarter,	4 10 17 a.m.	First Quarter, 20	1 12 a.m.
New Moon.	12 2 38 a.m.	Full Moon, 26	4 48 p.m.

Day of Month.	Day of Week.	Sun rises.	Sun sets.	Sun slow.	Sun's decline north.	ASPECTS OF PLANETS AND OTHER MISCELLANEOUS MATTER.	Moon's place.	Moon rises or sets.	Moon south.	High Tides.
1	Fri	5 8	6 47	3 15	23	Apian Way. Cont. 312 BC	♐	11 53	mo'n	mo'n
2	Sat	5 7	6 48	3 15	41	S. H. Young d. 1882.	♐	mo'n	4 29	11 20

18. Fourth Sunday after Easter.   Day's length 13 hours 43 minutes.

3	D.	5 6	6 49	3 15	58	☾ ☌ ♀ Piscium.	♒	0 34	5 22	0 1
4	Mo	5 5	6 49	3 16	15	Dr. W.G. Hill d. 1877	♒	1 7	6 10	0 40
5	Tue	5 4	6 50	4 16	32	♂ ♄ ☉.	♓	1 33	6 55	1 34
6	We	5 3	6 51	4 16	49	☿ gr. Hel. Lat. N.	♓	1 57	7 36	2 26
7	Thu	5 2	6 51	4 17	5	☌ ☉ ☽. M.C. Doub d. 1876	♒	2 19	8 15	3 13
8	Fri	5 1	6 52	4 17	22	Battle Palo Alto 1846.	♒	2 40	8 54	3 59
9	Sat	5 0	6 53	4 17	37	Bat. Spotsylv'nia C. H. '64	♈	3 0	9 33	4 43

19. Regation Sunday.   Day's length 13 hours 55 minutes.

10	D.	4 59	6 54	4 17	53	CONFED. MEMORIAL DAY	♈	3 22	10 15	5 25
11	Mo	4 58	6 54	4 18	8	☉ Queen Mary d. 1694.	♈	3 48	10 58	6 5
12	Tue	4 57	6 55	4 18	23	● Bat. Raymond 1863.	♉	4 16	11 45	6 44
13	We	4 56	6 56	4 18	38	Bat. Brazos, Texas, 1865	♉	sets.	eve.	7 25
14	Thu	4 55	6 57	4 18	52	ASCEN. DAY—HOLY THU	♉	9 26	1 29	8 11
15	Fri	4 54	6 58	4 19	6	Dan. O'Connell d. 1847.	♊	10 22	2 25	8 58
16	Sat	4 53	6 59	4 19	20	☿ gr. Elon. E.	♊	11 8	3 21	9 46

20. Sixth Sunday after Easter.   Day's length 14 hours 7 minutes.

17	D.	4 53	7 0	4 19	33	John Penn born 1741.	♋	11 47	4 16	10 36
18	Mo	4 52	7 1	4 19	46	☌ ♃ ☽ Matamoras fel '46	♋	mo'n	5 9	11 26
19	Tue	4 52	7 1	4 19	59	☽ ♂ gr. Hel. Lat. S.	♌	0 21	5 59	0 6
20	We	4 51	7 2	4 20	11	☽ MECK. DEC. DAY.)	♌	0 50	6 48	0 54
21	Thu	4 50	7 3	4 20	23	Conf. Mon. unv. May 20 ⟩	♌	1 18	7 36	1 53
22	Fri	4 49	7 3	3 20	35	Buchanan born 1791.	♍	1 44	8 25	2 50
23	Sat	4 48	7 4	3 20	46	Eivingstone died 1886.	♍	2 11	9 17	3 48

21. Pentecost—Whit Sunday   Day's length 14 hours 19 minutes.

24	D.	4 48	7 5	3 20	57		♎	2 40	10 11	4 46
25	Mo	4 48	7 5	3 21	8	☉ Col. Tucker d. 1882.	♎	3 13	11 10	5 42
26	Tue	4 47	7 6	3 21	18	● John Calvin d. 1564.	♏	3 53	mo'n	6 35
27	We	4 47	7 7	3 21	28	W. Q. Gresham d. 1895.	♏	rises.	0 11	7 26
28	Thu	4 46	7 8	3 21	37	Noah Webster d. 1843.	♐	9 41	1 14	8 23
29	Fri	4 46	7 9	3 21	47	☿ sta. and then ℞.	♐	10 27	2 14	9 13
30	Sat	4 45	7 10	3 21	55	FEDERAL DECORA. DAY.	♑	11 4	3 11	10 1

22. Trinity Sunday.   Day's length 14 hours 27 minutes.

| 31 | D. | 4 45 | 7 11 | 2 22 | 4 | Johnstown disas. 1889. | ♑ | 11 35 | 4 2 | 10 50 |

WEATHER CONJECTURES.—MAY—1, 2, 3, cold ; 4, 5, 6, 7, 8, 9, 10, 11,
frequent showers ; 12, 13, 14, 15, changeable ; 16, 17, 18, 19, rainy; 20,
21, 22, 23, 24, 25, fair ; 26, 27, 28, 29, 30, 31, look for fair and open weather.

THAT WONDERFUL TOP DRAWER.

If anything is *lost*, from cellar to garret,
    Needed by master or even wood sawer,
Very likely you'll find it, most surely you'll find it,
    In the *top drawer*, that HANDY *top drawer*.

If anything is *wanted*, in cellar or garret,
    To mend the door latch, or dress the hall floor,
Go look for it quickly—yes, quickly look for it—
    In the *top drawer*, that SHALLOW *top drawer*.

If anything is *shaky*, in cellar or garret,
    And needs tying up to make it last more,
Go find a good string—yes, also a stringlet—
    Right in the *top drawer*, that STRINGY *top drawer*.

If anything is *broken*, in cellar or garret,
    And needs to be mended to look like of yore,
You'll find scraps of glue, also a gimlet,
    Down in the *top drawer*, that LOVELY *top drawer*.

If anything is *found*, from cellar to garret,
    Not needed at once, nor yet for an hour,
Where will you put it?—say, where would you put it?
    Surely in the *top drawer*, that WONDERFUL *top drawer*.

WHEN EASTER COMES.

A friend of the *Boston Transcript*, "E. M. H.," writes: "I was attracted by the suggestion in your paper to-day to compose a rhyme which would give the reasons for the movable nature of the Easter feast." The following clever rhymes are added. They should be taught in the primary schools:

"Thirty days hath September,"
    Every person can remember;
But to know when Easters come,
    Puzzles even scholars some.

When March the twenty-first is past,
    Just watch the silvery moon,
And when you see it full and round,
    Know Easter'll be here soon.

After the moon has reached its full,
    Then Easter will be here,
The very Sunday after,
    In each and every year.

And if it hap on Sunday
    The moon should reach its height,
The Sunday following this event
    Will be the Easter bright.

THE WALTZ had its beginning in Germany.

FROM Poland came the stately polonaise, or polacca and mazourka.

THE Congo River, in Africa, is fifteen miles wide in some places. Steamers often pass each other, but out of sight.

AT Crown Point, N. Y., there is a handsome granite monument which was erected to the memory of a horse. The horse was "Old Pink," and the monument was erected by General John Hammond, who rode the old war-horse during the Civil War.

6th Month. JUNE, 1896. 30 Days.

Moon's Phases.

	D. H. M.		D. H. M.
☾ Last Quarter,	3 2 54 a.m.	☽ First Quarter,	18 6 32 a.m.
● New Moon,	11 3 34 a.m.	○ Full Moon,	25 1 46 a.m.

Day of month.	Day of Week.	Sun rises.	Sun sets.	Sun fast.	Sun's decline north.	Aspects of Planets and other Miscellaneous Matter.	Moon's place.	Moon rises or sets.	Moon south.	High Tides.
1	Mo	4 44	7 11	2	22 12	Pres. Buchanan d. 1868.	♒	mo'n	mo'n	mo'n
2	Tue	4 44	7 12	2	22 17	☾ N. M. Alston d. 1850	♓	0 0	5 32	0 1
3	We	4 43	7 12	2	22 26	Jeff. Davis born 1808	♓	0 22	6 12	0 46
4	Thu	4 42	7 13	2	22 33	Corpus Christi.	♈	0 43	6 51	1 32
5	Fri	4 41	7 13	2	22 40	Telegraph in China 1871	♈	1 4	7 31	2 20
6	Sat	4 41	7 14	1	22 46	Patrick Henry d. 1799.	♈	1 26	8 11	3 7
23.	First Sunday after Trinity.					Day's length, 14 hours 33 minutes.				
7	*D.*	4 41	7 14	1	22 51	First Amer. Cong. 1765.	♉	1 49	8 53	3 55
8	Mo	4 41	7 15	1	22 57	☿ in Aphelion.	♉	2 16	9 39	4 44
9	Tue	4 41	7 15	1	23 1	Dickens died 1870.	♉	2 50	10 29	5 34
10	We	4 41	7 16	1	23 6	● ☌ ☿ ☉ sup. ♀ with ☽	♉	3 29	11 22	6 22
11	Thu	4 41	7 16	slow	23 10	☌ ♅ ☽.	♊	sets.	eve.	7 9
12	Fri	4 41	7 16		23 13	♂ in Perihelion.	♊	9 6	1 15	7 58
13	Sat	4 41	7 16		23 17	Gen. Scott born 1786.	♊	9 49	2 11	8 47
24.	Second Sunday after Trinity.					Day's length 14 hours 36 minutes.				
14	*D.*	4 41	7 17	0	23 19	U. S. Flag adopted 1777.	♋	10 23	3 5	9 33
15	Mo	4 41	7 18	0	23 22	Magna Charta 1215.	♋	10 54	3 57	10 20
16	Tue	4 41	7 18	1	23 24	Luther excom. 1520.	♌	11 22	4 46	
17	We	4 41	7 19	1	23 25	☽ Addison died 1719.	♌	11 48	5 33	11 50
18	Thu	4 41	7 19	1	23 26	Bat. Waterloo 1815.	♍	mo'n	6 21	0 25
19	Fri	4 42	7 19	1	23 27	Council of Nice 325.	♍	0 13	7 10	1 20
20	Sat	4 43	7 19	1	23 27	☉ ent. ♋. Sum. Com.	♎	0 41	8 2	2 19
25.	Third Sunday after Trinity.					Day's length 14 hours 36 minutes.				
21	*D.*	4 43	7 19	2	23 27	Black Hole Trag. 1756.	♎	1 12	8 58	3 21
22	Mo	4 43	7 19	2	23 27	☌ ♅ ☽. ☿ sta.	♏	1 50	9 56	4 26
23	Tue	4 43	7 19	2	23 26	R. S. Pullen died 1895.	♏	2 34	10 58	5 27
24	We	4 43	7 19	2	23 24	○ St. John Baptist.	♐	3 28	11 59	6 25
25	Thu	4 43	7 20	3	23 23	L. Bonaparte d. 1846	♐	rises.	mo'n	7 15
26	Fri	4 44	7 20	3	23 20	Thos. Bashford d. 1881.	♑	9 0	0 37	8 8
27	Sat	4 44	7 20	3	23 28	Hiram Powers d. 1873.	♒	9 33	1 51	8 54
26.	Fourth Sunday after Trinity.					Day's length 14 hours 36 minutes.				
28	*D.*	4 44	7 20	3	23 15	Seven days fight beg. '62	♒	10 0	2 40	9 34
29	Mo	4 45	7 20	3	23 11	☿ gr. Hel. Lat. S.	♓	10 24	3 25	10 13
30	Tue	4 45	7 20	4	23 8	☌ ♀ ♆ Montezuma d. 1530	♓	10 46	4 7	10 55

Weather Conjectures.—June—1, 2, fair; 3, 4, 5, 6, 7, 8, 9, 10, cool with frequent showers; 11, 12, 13, 14, 15, 16, 17, 18, expect cool wet weather; 19, 20, 21, 22, windy; 23, 24, rainy; 25, 26, 27, 28, 29, 30, expect fair weather.

The Criminal Court of Hertford County.—Two terms held per year when ordered by the Justices of the Peace. B. B. WINBORNE, Judge.

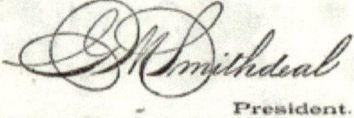

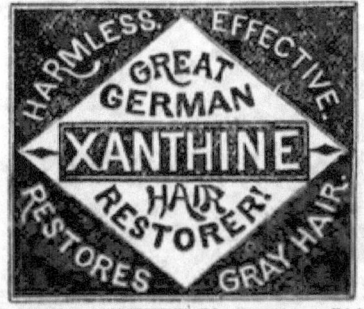

HYGIENE OF THE BED.

The bed is a place where we spend about one-third of our lives. A woman who has reached sixty has spent twenty years in bed. Many bad habits and bad positions are formed during sleep. Some girls assume an attitude which cramps the chest so that respiration is not full and complete. This does their health much harm. The shoulders should not be drawn forward then, nor the arms folded tightly over the chest. A narrow bed is preferable for girls, so they will not have room to sprawl over a large space, nor be able to assume a dozen grotesque shapes. The pillow should be small and hard. A large soft pillow should not be tolerated by any girl who desires to have her head well set on her shoulders. The bed clothing should be light, but warm, and allow the air to pass through it freely. If the air in a bed, which soon becomes saturated with the prespiration from our bodies, does not pass off, it makes us uneasy and restless, and sound sleep is impossible. Some women say they can sleep only on one side. If so, there must be something wrong with them. One side is probably not evenly developed with the other. A healthy woman or girl can sleep, and should sleep, on one side and then on the other, even changing unconsciously in the night. Some women twist and contort their faces during sleep into bad shapes and thus form wrinkles which continue during their waking hours. The reasons for this are various. Indigestible food in the stomach is one cause. Going to bed in a depressed state of mind causes the corners of the mouth to be drawn down, and gives a sad expression. In going to sleep think of pleasant things, of your many blessings, the goodness of the great Spirit, of the joys of life, the blessings of home, friends, parents or children. Under no circumstances let the sun go down on your wrath, or on any other evil thought. If you have enemies, forgive them—even love them. Love is the great beautifier of the faces of women, and hate and evil thoughts act contrariwise.—*Journal of Hygiene.*

MARKET PHRASES.

BULLS—Traders who believe prices will advance.

BEARS—Traders who believe prices will decline.

LONGS—Those who have bought for future delivery.

SHORTS—Those who have sold for future delivery.

COVERING—Closing out trades.

OPEN ORDER—An order that is intended to stand open until it is executed, or until the customer countermands it.

STOP ORDER—Limit of price given by the customer at which to close his trade in case the market reaches that limit.

MARGIN—The deposit of a customer with his broker.

PUTS—An agreement to buy wheat or corn at a specified price at the close of the following market session.

CALLS—An agreement to sell wheat or corn at a specified price at the close of the following market session.

FUTURE DELIVERY—To buy or sell grain, provisions or other commodities for "Future Delivery" is to make a contract between buyer and seller, the seller agreeing to deliver a certain commodity at a stipulated price in some future stated month; the buyer agreeing to receive the commodity at the stipulated price at any time during the stated month. The time of the month in which delivery may be made is always optional with the seller.

32. Don't lose faith in your fellow-men; for then you are near to rebellion against your maker.—BRANSON.

33. There are many things worse than poverty.—BRANSON.

2

18 BRANSON'S NORTH CAROLINA ALMANAC.

7th Month. JULY, 1896. 31 Days.

Moon's Phases.

	D. H. M.		D. H. M.
Last Quarter,	2 8 15 p.m.	First Quarter,	17 10 56 a.m.
New Moon,	10 2 26 p.m.	Full Moon,	24 0 36 p.m.

Day of Month.	Day of Week.	Sun rises.	Sun sets.	Sun slow.	Sun's decline north.	ASPECTS OF PLANETS AND OTHER MISCELLANEOUS MATTER.	Moon's place.	Moon rises or sets.	Moon south.	High Tides.
1	We	4 45	7 20	4 23	3	Bat. Malvern Hill '62		11 6	m'rn	m'rn
2	Thu	4 46	7 20	4 22	59	Garfield assass. 1881		11 28	5 27	0 15
3	Fri	4 47	7 20	4 22	54	in Aphelion.		11 51	6 6	0 40
4	Sat	4 47	7 20	4 22	48	INDEPENDENCE DAY.		m'rn	6 48	1 27

27. Fifth Sunday after Trinity. Day's length 14 hours 31 minutes.

5	D.	4 48	7 19	4 22	43	Monroe died 1831.		0 16	7 32	2 19
6	Mo	4 48	7 19	5 22	36	Hamlin died 1891.		0 47	8 20	3 13
7	Tue	4 49	7 19	5 22	30	Sheridan died 1816.		1 24	9 11	4 11
8	We	4 50	7 19	5 22	23	Port Hudson sur. 1863.		2 9	10 6	5 9
9	Thu	4 50	7 19	5 22	15	♂ ♀ ☉ superior.		3 5	11 4	6 4
10	Fri	4 51	7 18	5 22	8			sets	eve.	6 54
11	Sat	4 52	7 18	5 21	59	J. Q. Adams born 1767.		8 23	0 58	7 44

28. Sixth Sunday after Trinity. Day's length 14 hours 26 minutes.

12	D.	4 52	7 18	5 21	51	♂ ♃ ☽		8 55	1 51	8 32
13	Mo	4 53	7 17	6 21	42	♂ ♀ Gem. Fremont d.'90		9 25	2 42	9 15
14	Tue	4 53	7 17	6 21	33	Peace Cong. in London'90		9 52	3 31	9 57
15	We	4 54	7 16	6 21	23	Flight of Mohammed 622		10 17	4 19	10 42
16	Thu	4 55	7 16	6 21	13	♄ stationary.		10 43	5 8	11 27
17	Fri	4 55	7 15	6 21	3	Compere cap. '57.		11 13	5 58	0 13
18	Sat	4 56	7 15	6 20	52	☿ in ♌.		11 47	6 52	0 53

29. Seventh Sunday after Trinity Day's length 14 hours 17 minutes.

19	D.	4 57	7 14	6 20	41	E. P. Roe died 1888.		m'rn	7 48	1 57
20	Mo	4 57	7 13	6 20	30	Bat. Winchester, Va., '64		0 29	8 47	3 5
21	Tue	4 58	7 13	6 20	18	Battle Bull Run 1862.		1 18	9 48	4 14
22	We	4 59	7 12	6 20	6	☿ in Perihelion.		2 18	10 46	5 19
23	Thu	5 0	7 12	6 19	53	♀ in Perihelion.		3 22	11 41	6 14
24	Fri	5 1	7 11	6 19	41	Bolivar born 1783.		rises	m'rn	7 0
25	Sat	5 2	7 11	6 19	28	Bat. Lundy's Lane 1814.		8 0	1 19	7 46

30. Eighth Sunday after Trinity. Day's length 14 hours 7 minutes.

26	D.	5 3	7 10	6 19	14	Argentine Rev. 1890.		8 26	1 19	8 27
27	Mo	5 3	7 9	6 19	1	Princess Louisa mar.'89		8 49	2 2	9 4
28	Tue	5 3	7 8	6 18	46	☿ stationary.		9 9	2 43	9 37
29	We	5 4	7 7	6 18	32	Burke died 1797.		9 31	3 23	10 12
30	Thu	5 5	7 6	6 18	17	Wm. Penn died 1718.		9 53	4 2	10 50
31	Fri	5 5	7 6	6 18	3	♂ ☿ ☉ superior.		10 17	4 43	11 28

WEATHER CONJECTURES.—JULY—1, 2, open weather; 3, 4, 5, 6, 7, 8.
9, fair if wind N. W., rain if S. or S. W.; 10, 11, 12, 13, 14, 15, 16, changeable; 17, 18, 19, 20, 21, 22, 23, look for frequent showers; 24, 25, 26, 27,
28, 29, 30, 31, expect much rain.

BUREAU OF STATISTICS OF N. C., (Denominational).

LEVI BRANSON, Secretary.

DENOMINATIONS.	Number Ministers.	Number Churches.	Number Members.
White.			
Methodist Episcopal Church South................	723	1,520	127,483
Methodist Episcopal Church.......................	65	115	8,941
Wesleyan Methodist Church.......................	7	7	141
Methodist Protestant Church	63	199	14,351
Christian (Followers of Jas. O'Kelly).............	60	101	9,000
Evangelical Lutheran.............................	73	130	12,872
Presbyterian	149	336	30,278
Universalists	3	3	255
Protestant Episcopal	96	184	9,025
Missionary Baptist	700	1,487	153,648
Primitive Baptist	150	317	11,914
Seventh Day Adventist...........................	5	5	83
Free Will Baptist	160	168	10,224
Baptist Church of Christ	16	16	659
Old Two-Seed Baptist	9	9	183
Disciples of Christ (Campbellites)...............	93	186	12,437
Seventh Day Baptist	1	1	10
Reformed Church of U. S	17	40	3,140
Church of Jesus Christ of Latter Day Saints......	24	1	136
Friends	52	52	5,328
Dunkards	9	9	510
Moravians	11	6	2,513
Waldenses	1	1	215
Roman Catholics................................	24	24	2,640
Hebrews	4	4	386
Salvation Army	2	2	59
Advent Christian Church........................	18	18	1,549
Associate Reformed	20	20	2,109
Colored.			
Missionary Baptists	500	1,198	136,856
African M. E. Zion Church......................	150	526	121,154
African M. E. Church...........................	240	147	16,156
Colored M. E. Church in America...............	25	26	2,786
Methodist Episcopal	2	2	130
Protestant Episcopal	6	10	1,200
Congregational	20	20	1,002
Christians	50	53	3,746
Free Will Baptist	10	25	1,640
Primitive Baptist	15	20	1,000
Presbyterian North.............................	173	306	17,851

Subject to annual revision.

THE WORLD'S SEVEN WONDERS.

The seven wonders of the world are : The Pyramids, the Colossus of Rhodes, Diana's Temple at Ephesus; the Pharos of Alexandria, the Hanging Garden at Babylon, the Statue of the Olympian Jove, and the Mausoleum by Artemisia at Halicarnassus.

8th Month. AUGUST, 1896. 31 Days.

Moon's Phases.

	D. H. M.		D. H. M.
Last Quarter,	1 1 26 p.m.	First Quarter,	15 3 54 p.m
New Moon,	8 11 53 p.m.	Full Moon,	23 1 56 a.m
		Last Quarter,	31 3 47 a.m

Day of Month.	Day of Week.	Sun rises.	Sun sets.	Sun slow.	Sun's decline north.	ASPECTS OF PLANETS AND OTHER MISCELLANEOUS MATTER.	Moon's place.	Moon rises or sets.	Moon south.	High Tides.
1	Sat	5 6	7 5	6	17 47	Dogdaystill lastAug		10 44	m'rn	m'rn
31. Ninth Sunday after Trinity. Day's length 13 hours 57 minutes.										
2	*D.*	5 7	7 4	6	17 32	☿ gr. Hel. Lat. N.		11 18	6 11	0 41
3	Mo	5 8	7 3	6	17 16	Crown Point taken 1759		m'rn	7 0	1 37
4	Tue	5 9	7 2	6	17 0	□ ♄ ⊙. Tilden d. 1886.		0 0	7 53	2 39
5	We	5 10	7 1	6	16 43	☌ ♃ ☿. Sheridan d. 1888.		0 51	8 49	3 43
6	Thu	5 11	7 1	6	16 27	Kemler ex. by electri. '90		1 50	9 47	4 47
7	Fri	5 11	7 0	5	16 10	Barzelius d. 1848.		2 58	10 44	5 47
8	Sat	5 12	6 58	5	15 53	Sun eclip. Invisible		4 12	11 40	6 36
32. Tenth Sunday after Trinity. Day's length 13 hours 43 minutes.										
9	*D.*	5 13	6 56	5	15 35	☌ ♃ ☽. O'Riley d. 1890.		sets	eve.	7 23
10	Mo	5 14	6 55	5	15 18	Battle Oak Hill 1861.		7 53	1 23	8 9
11	Tue	5 14	6 54	5	15 0	Cardinal Newman d. '90		8 20	2 14	8 52
12	We	5 15	6 53	5	14 41	☌ ♃ ☽. □ ♅ ⊙.		8 46	3 3	9 33
13	Thu	5 16	6 52	5	14 23	Boulanger convicted '89		9 15	3 54	10 17
14	Fri	5 17	6 51	4	14 4	♀ gr. Hel. Lat. N.		9 48	4 48	11 1
15	Sat	5 18	6 50	4	13 46	Napoleon born 1769.		10 27	5 44	
33. Eleventh Sunday after Trinity. Day's length 13 hours 30 minutes.										
16	*D.*	5 19	6 49	4	13 27	Senator Hill died 1832.		11 14	6 42	0 37
17	Mo	5 19	6 48	4	13 7	Battle of Preston 1648.		m'rn	7 41	1 45
18	Tue	5 20	6 46	4	12 48	Cor. stone U.S.Cap. 1793		0 10	8 40	2 56
19	We	5 21	6 45	3	12 28	Bat. of Gravelotte 1870.		1 13	9 35	4 5
20	Thu	5 21	6 44	3	12 8	Benj. Harrison b. 1833.		2 19	10 27	5 5
21	Fri	5 22	6 43	3	11 48	Prof. Tyndall b. 1820.		3 26	11 14	5 57
22	Sat	5 23	6 42	3	11 28	Moon p'tly ecl.inv.at W.		4 32	10 58	6 38
34. Twelfth Sunday after Trinity. Day's length 13 hours 16 minutes.										
23	*D.*	5 24	6 40	2	11 7	Com. Perry d. 1820.		rises	m'rn	7 14
24	Mo	5 25	6 39	2	10 47	Bat. Gladenburg 1814		7 14	0 40	7 53
25	Tue	5 26	6 38	2	10 26	☿ in ☊. J. Turner im.' 70		7 35	1 20	8 28
26	We	5 27	6 36	1	10 5	Battle of Dresden 1813.		7 56	1 59	9 1
27	Thu	5 27	6 35	1	9 44	Sir Rowland Hill d. '79.		8 20	2 39	9 33
28	Fri	5 28	6 33	1	9 23	First Cable mess. 1858.		8 46	3 21	10 10
29	Sat	5 28	6 32	1	9 1	Battle of Groveton 1862.		9 16	4 5	11 53
35. Thirteenth Sunday after Trinity. Day's length 13 hours 2 minutes.										
30	*D.*	5 29	6 31	0	8 40	Wm. Penn d. 1718.		9 53	4 52	11 36
31	Mo	5 30	6 30	0	8 18	Charleston earth. '86		10 29	5 43	0 8

WEATHER CONJECTURES.—AUGUST—1, rainy; 2, 3, 4, 5, 6, 7, very rainy; 8, 9, 10, 11, 12, 13, 14, fair; 15, 16, 17, 18, changeable; 19, 20, 21, 22, variable weather; 23, 24, 25, 26, fair; 27, 28, 29, 30, fair; 31, expect rain.

IF YOU WANT A KISS.

There's a jolly fresh proverb
   That is pretty much like this:
That a man is half in heaven
   When he has a woman's kiss.
But there's danger in delaying,
   And the sweetness may forsake it;
So I tell you, bashful lover,
   If you want a kiss, why, take it.

Never let another fellow
   Steal a march on you in this;
Never let a laughing maiden
   See you spoiling for a kiss.
There's a royal way to kissing,
   And the jolly ones who make it
Have a motto that is winning—
   If you want a kiss, why, take it.

Any fool may face a cannon,
   Anybody wear a crown,
But a man must win a woman
   If he'd have her for his own.
Would you have the golden apple,
   You must find the tree and shake it,
If the thing is worth the having,
   And you want a kiss, why, take it.

Who would burn upon a desert,
   With a forest smiling by?
Who would give this sunny weather
   For a black and wintry sky?
Oh, I tell you, there is magic,
   And you cannot, cannot break it,
For the sweetest part of loving
   Is to want a kiss and take it.—*Boston Globe.*

ZEB. VANCE AS A CANDIDATE.

Vance said: "I was first a candidate for the Legislature when I was barely twenty one years old. I got on my horse and rode up to Asheville to make a start. I tied up my pony and walked up to the Court House, where I found about two dozen old farmers sitting out on the benches in front of the building, whittling sticks and talking politics, as usual, on Saturdays especially. I was a little bashful then—you would hardly suppose it now—so I gathered the first man I came to warmly by the hand and looking around at the sturdy crowd, I said, just *imagine*, boys, that I have shaken hands all round and it will be *all right*. Whereupon one old farmer, looking out quisically from under the broad brim of his old wool hat, remarked, 'See here, Zeb! You just *imagine* that we have all voted for you next November, and *that* will *be all right, too.*' He had the laugh and I had the lesson. So I at once proceeded to shake the boys all round, and I have been shaking ever since."—*Branson.*

WEIGHT OF A MILLION DOLLARS.

The United States gold dollar contains 25 8 troy grains. A troy pound contains 5,760 troy grains. Therefore, $1,000,000 in United States gold coin weigh 3,686.4 pounds avoirdupois. A United States standard silver dollar weighs 412.5 troy grains, and $1,000,000 in United States silver coin of the present standard weight 56,931 pounds avoirdupois, or nearly 281¼ tons.

9th Month. SEPTEMBER, 1896. 30 Days.

Moon's Phases.

	D. H. M.		D. H. M.
☉ New Moon,	7 8 35 a.m.	☉ Full Moon,	21 5 41 p.m.
☽ First Quarter,	13 11 1 p.m.	☾ Last Quarter,	29 8 50 p.m.

Day of Month.	Day of Week.	Sun rises.	Sun sets.	Sun fast.	Sun's decline north.	ASPECTS OF PLANETS AND OTHER MISCELLANEOUS MATTER.	Moon's place.	Moon rises or sets.	Moon south.	High Tides.
1	Tue	5 31	6 28	fast	7 56	Arringt'n Com. in Ral. '95	♉	11 34	m'rn	m'rn
2	We	5 32	6 27		7 34	Atlanta captured 1864.	♊	m'rn	7 32	2 11
3	Thu	5 33	6 25	1	7 12	Elizabeth Glenn d. 1894.	♊	0 38	8 29	3 19
4	Fri	5 34	6 24	1	6 50	☿ in Aphelion.	♋	1 49	9 24	4 23
5	Sat	5 35	6 22	2	6 27	Confederates inv. Md '62	♌	3 2	10 18	5 21
36. **Fourteenth Sunday after Trinity.**						**Day's length 12 hours 46 min.**				
6	*D.*	5 35	6 21	2	6 5	☌ ♃ ☽.	♌	4 17	11 11	6 13
7	Mo	5 36	6 19	2	5 42	LABOR DAY.	♌	sets	eve.	6 57
8	Tue	5 36	6 18	3	5 20	Jews leave Poland 1870.	♍	6 48	0 2	7 41
9	We	5 37	6 16	3	4 57	☌ ☿ ☽. Sebastapol fell '55	♍	7 15	1 45	8 27
10	Thu	5 38	6 15	3	4 34	S. S. Cox died 1889.	♎	7 47	2 39	9 10
11	Fri	5 39	6 14	4	4 11	☌ ♄ ☾ America disc. 1492	♎	8 25	3 36	9 58
12	Sat	5 39	6 12	4	3 48	□ ♆ ⊙. R. A. Proctor d. '88	♏	9 11	4 35	10 53
37. **Fifteenth Sunday after Trinity.**						**Day's length 12 hours 21 minutes.**				
13	*D.*	5 40	6 11	4	3 25	☿ gr. Elong. E.	♏	10 6	5 35	11 48
14	Mo	5 41	6 10	5	3 2	Dr. F. T. Fuller d. '94	♐	11 6	6 35	0 29
15	Tue	5 42	6 8	5	2 39	Gen. Scott took Mex. '47.	♐	m'rn	7 31	1 37
16	We	5 43	6 6	5	2 16	Farenheit died 1736.	♑	0 11	8 24	2 44
17	Thu	5 44	6 5	6	1 53	Mt. Cenis Tunnel op. '71	♑	1 18	9 12	3 46
18	Fri	5 44	6 4	6	1 29	Fugitive slave act 1850.	♑	2 24	9 56	4 41
19	Sat	5 45	6 2	7	1 6	☌ ♃ Leonis.	♒	3 27	10 38	5 27
38. **Sixteenth Sunday after Trinity.**						**Day's length 12 hours 6 minutes.**				
20	*D.*	5 45	6 1	7	0 43	Arthur inaug. '81.	♒	4 28	11 18	6 7
21	Mo	5 46	6 0	7	0 19	Nicaraugua ind. '21.	♓	5 27	11 58	6 41
22	Tue	5 47	5 58	8	s'uth	⊙ ent. ♎. AUTUMN COM.	♓	rises.	m'rn	7 14
23	We	5 48	5 56	8	0 27	Russian fleet sunk '54.	♓	6 25	0 38	7 51
24	Thu	5 49	5 54	8	0 51	Gen. D. H. Hill d. '89.	♈	6 49	1 19	8 27
25	Fri	5 50	5 53	9	1 14	☿ gr. Hel. Lat. S.	♉	7 17	2 2	9 4
26	Sat	5 51	5 52	9	1 38	☿ stationary.	♉	7 51	2 48	9 41
39. **Seventeenth Sunday after Trinity.**						**Day's length 11 hours 59 min.**				
27	*D.*	5 51	5 50	9	2 1	Strasburg sur. 1870.	♉	8 33	3 36	10 25
28	Mo	5 51	5 49	10	2 24	Bish. Randall d. '73.	♊	9 24	4 28	11 9
29	Tue	5 52	5 47	10	2 48	MICHAELMAS DAY.	♊	10 22	5 22	11 53
30	We	5 53	5 46	10	3 11	Whitfield died 1770.	♊	11 27	6 17	0 43

WEATHER CONJECTURES.—SEPTEMBER—1, 2, 3, 4, 5, 6, look for rain; 7, 8, 9, 10, 11, 12, changeable weather; 13, 14, 15, 16, 17, 18, 19, 20, generally fair; 21, 22, 23, 24, 25, 26, 27, 28, fair; 29, 30, fair.

The Mechanics and Investor's Union of Raleigh has proved quite a success. Have you stock in it?

BRANSON'S NORTH CAROLINA ALMANAC. 23

SUPERIOR COURTS OF NORTH CAROLINA FOR 1896.

(Taken from the Calendar of Smith & Andrews. Revised by F. H. Busbee.)

JUDGES.			SOLICITORS.		
Name.	District.	Residence.	Name.	District.	Residence.
George H. Brown,	1	Washington.	W. J. Leary,	1	Eliz'b'th City.
Henry R. Bryan,	2	Newbern.j	W. E. Daniel,	2	Weldon.
E. W. Timberlake,	3	Louisburg.	C. M. Bernard,	3	Greenville.
W. S. O'B. Robinson,	4	Goldsboro.	Edward W. Pou, Jr.,	4	Smithfield.
Aug. W. Graham,	5	Oxford.	W. P. Bynum, Jr.,	5	Greensboro.
Edward T. Boykin,	6	Clinton.	Milton C. Richardson,	6	Clinton.
James D. McIver,	7	Carthage.	H. F. Seawell,	7	Carthage.
Albert L. Coble,	8	Statesville.	J. Q. Holton,	8	Yadkinville.
Henry R. Starbuck,	9	Winston.	M. L. Mott,	9	Wilkesboro.
Leander L. Green,	10	Boone.	J. F Spainhour,	10	Lenoir.
W. Alexander Hoke,	11	Lincolnton.	J. L. Webb,	11	Shelby.
W. L. Norwood,	12	Waynesville.	George A. Jones,	12	Franklin.

Time of Holding Courts.

FIRST JUDICIAL DISTRICT.

Spring—Judge Robinson.

    Fall—Judge Timberlake.

Beaufort—†Feb. 17th (2), May 25th (2), Nov. 30th (2).
Currituck—March 2d, Sept. 7th.
Camden—March 9th, Sept. 14th.
Pasquotank—March 16th, Sept. 21st.
Perquimans—March 23d, Sept. 28th.
Chowan—March 30th, October 5th.
Gates—April 6th, Oct. 12th.
Hertford—April 13th, Oct. 19th.
Washington—May 30th, June 8th, Oct. 26th.
Tyrrell—April 27th, Nov. 2d.
Dare—May 4th, Nov. 9th.
Hyde—May 11th, Nov. 16th.
Pamlico—May 18th, Nov. 23d.

SECOND JUDICIAL DISTRICT.

Spring—Judge Graham.

    Fall—Judge Robinson.

Halifax—†March 2d (2). May 28th (2), Nov. 23d (2).
Northampton..March 30th (2), †Aug. 3d (2), Oct. 26th (2).
Bertie—†Feb. 17th, April, 27th (2). Sept. 14th (2), Nov. 9th.
Craven—†Feb. 3d (2), May 4th (2), Nov. 30th (2).
Warren—March 16th (2), Sept. 21st (2).
Edgecombe—April 10th (2), †June 8th, Oct. 12th (2).

THIRD JUDICIAL DISTRICT.

Spring—Judge Boykin.

    Fall—Judge Graham.

Pitt—Jan. 6th (2), †March 2d (2), March 30th, †April 1st (2), Sept. 21st (2), †Dec. 7th (2).
Franklin—Jan. 20th (2), April 10th (2), Oct. 21st.
Wilson—†Feb. 3d (2), June 21st, Nov. 2d (2).
Vance—Feb. 17th (2), May 18th (2), Oct. 5th (2).
Martin—March 16th (2), Sept. 7th (2).
Nash—April 27th (2), Nov. 23d (2).

FOURTH JUDICIAL DISTRICT.

Spring—Judge McIver.

    Fall—Judge Boykin.

Wake—*Jan. 6th (2), †Feb. 24th (2), *Mar. 23d (2), †April 19th (2), *July 13th (2), *Sept. 28th (2), †Oct. 20th (3).

Wayne—Jan. 20th (2), April 13th, Sept. 14th (2), Oct. 19th.
Harnett—Feb. 17th, Sept. 17th, †Nov. 30th.
Johnston—March 9th (2), Aug. 31st, Nov. 16th (2).

FIFTH JUDICIAL DISTRICT.

Spring—Judge Coble.

    Fall—Judge McIver.

Durham—Jan. 13th (2), †March 23d (2), *May 11th, *Sept. 14th, †Oct. 12th (2).
Granville—Jan. 25th (2), April 20th (2), July 17th (2), Nov. 30 (2).
Chatham—Feb. 10th, May 4th. Sept. 28th (2).
Guilford—Feb. 17th (2), May 25th, Aug. 31st (2), Dec. 14th (2).
Alamance—March 9th, May 18th, Nov. 16th.
Orange—March 16th, Aug. 10th, Nov. 2.
Caswell—April 6th, Aug. 17th, Oct. 21st.
Person—April 17th, Aug. 24th, Nov. 23d.

SIXTH JUDICIAL DISTRICT.

Spring—Judge Starbuck.

    Fall—Judge Coble'

Pender—March 2d, Sept. 14th (2).
Greene—Feb. 24th, Aug. 19th, Nov. 30th.
New Hanover—†Jan. 20th (2), †April 13th (2), †Sept. 28th (2).
Lenoir—May 4th (2), Nov. 16th (2).
Duplin—Feb. 17th, Aug. 10th, Dec. 7th.
Sampson—Feb. 3d (2), April 27th, Oct. 12th (2).
Carteret—March 16th, Oct. 26th.
Jones—March 26th, Nov. 2d.
Onslow—March 30th, Nov. 9th.

SEVENTH JUDICIAL DISTRICT.

Spring—Judge Green.

    Fall—Judge Starbuck.

Columbus—Feb. 24th, July 20th, Nov. 9th.
Anson—*Jan. 6th, †April 27th, *Sept. 7th, †Nov. 30th.
Cumberland—*Jan. 20th, †April 20th (2), †May 11th. July 27th, †Nov. 16th (2).
Robeson—Jan. 27th (2), May 18th, Sept. 30th (3), Oct. 5th (2).
Richmond—*Feb. 10th (2), †April 13th, June 1st, †Aug. 3d (2), *†Sept. 21st, Dec. 7th.
Bladen—March 16th (2) (Tuesday), Oct. 26th (Tuesday), (1).
Brunswick—April 6th, Sept. 14th.
Moore—†January 13th, †March 2d (2), *†Aug. 17th (3), *Dec. 14th.

24   BRANSON'S NORTH CAROLINA ALMANAC.

10th Month.   OCTOBER, 1896.   31 Days.

Moon's Phases.

	D. H. M.		D. H. M.
New Moon,	6 5 10 p. m.	Full Moon,	21 11 9 a. m.
First Quarter,	13 9 39 a.m.	Last Quarter,	29 10 12 a.m.

Day of Month.	Day of Week.	Sun rises.	Sun sets.	Sun fast.	Sun's decline south.	ASPECTS OF PLANETS AND OTHER MISCELLANEOUS MATTER.	Moon's place.	Moon rises or sets.	Moon south.	High Tides.
1	Thu	5 54	5 44	11	3 34	Pres. sig'd McKinly b. '90		m'rn	m'rn	m'rn
2	Fri	5 55	5 43	11	3 58	Gen. As. at Edenton 1722.		0 38	8 4	2 52
3	Sat	5 56	5 41	11	4 21	♂ ♃ ☽. Black Hawk d. '38		1 51	8 56	3 54
40.						**Eighteenth Sunday after Trinity. Day's length 11 hours 43 min.**				
4	**D.**	5 57	5 40	12	4 44	Bat. Germantown 1777.		3 5	9 47	4 51
5	Mo	5 58	5 36	12	5 7	A. J. Partin d. 1880		4 20	10 37	5 44
6	Tue	5 59	5 35	12	5 30	Judge Dick b. '23.		5 35	11 29	6 28
7	We	5 59	5 34	12	5 53	☿ ☽ Bat. Saratoga 1777		sets	eve.	7 14
8	Thu	6 0	5 32	13	6 16	♂ ☿ ☉ superior.		6 20	1 21	8 4
9	Fri	6 1	5 30	13	6 39	♂ ♄ ☽. ♀ in ☊.		7 4	2 22	8 54
10	Sat	6 2	5 29	13	7 2	Stuart raided Pa. 1862.		7 56	3 24	9 46
41.						**Nineteenth Sunday after Trinity. Day's length 11 hours 25 min.**				
11	**D.**	6 3	5 28	13	7 24	Samuel Wesley d. 1737.		8 56	4 26	10 42
12	Mo	6 4	5 27	14	7 47	Gen. R. E. Lee d. '70		10 2	5 25	11 38
13	Tue	6 5	5 25	14	8 9	♂ in ☊.		11 10	6 20	0 17
14	We	6 6	5 24	14	8 31	☿ in ☊.		m'rn	7 10	1 19
15	Thu	6 7	5 23	14	8 54	☿ ♀ ♄. B'k of Paris 1857		0 16	7 55	2 18
16	Fri	6 8	5 21	15	9 16	Napoleon at Helena 1815		1 20	8 38	3 13
17	Sat	6 9	5 19	15	9 37	☿ stationary.		2 21	9 18	4 3
42.						**Twentieth Sunday after Trinity. Day's length 11 hours 9 minutes.**				
18	**D.**	6 9	5 18	15	9 59	Judge E. G. Reade d. '94		3 22	9 58	4 47
19	Mo	6 10	5 17	15	10 21	Bat. Hatcher's Run '64.		4 20	10 37	5 29
20	Tue	6 11	5 16	15	10 42	Grace Darling d. '42		5 18	11 18	6 6
21	We	6 12	5 15	15	11 4	Bat. Ball's Bluff '61.		6 17	m'rn	6 41
22	Thu	6 13	5 14	16	11 25	Bat. Marysville, Ark. '62		rises.	0 0	7 16
23	Fri	6 14	5 12	16	11 46	Wm. Hooper d. 1790.		5 54	0 45	7 58
24	Sat	6 15	5 11	16	12 7	☿ gr. Elong. W.		6 33	1 33	8 39
43.						**Twenty-first Sunday after Trinity. Day's length 10 hours 54 min.**				
25	**D.**	6 16	5 10	16	12 27	♂ ♃ ☽. Newbern set. 1712		7 10	2 24	9 21
26	Mo	6 16	5 9	16	12 48	Salisbury laid off 1753.		8 15	3 17	10 6
27	Tue	6 17	5 8	16	13 8	Dr. Carradine in Ral. '94		9 16	4 10	10 58
28	We	6 18	5 7	16	13 28	☿ gr. Hel. Lat. N.		10 22	5 3	11 45
29	Thu	6 19	5 6	16	13 48	Sir W. Raleigh d. 1618		11 32	5 55	0 21
30	Fri	6 20	5 5	16	14 7	Gambetta born 1838.		m'rn	6 46	1 19
31	Sat	6 21	5 5	16	14 27	Gen. Scott retired 1861.		0 43	7 35	2 20

WEATHER CONJECTURES.—OCTOBER—1, 2, 3, 4, 5, fair if wind N. W.,
rainy if S. or S. W.; 6, 7, 8, 9, 10, 11, 12, expect mostly fair weather; 13,
14, 15, 16, changeable; 17, 18, 19, 20, not steady; 21, 22, 23, 24, 25, 26, 27,
28, look for frequent showers; 29, 30, 31, much the same.

The South Atlantic Life and Endowment Company was chartered by the last Legislature.

BRANSON'S NORTH CAROLINA ALMANAC. 25

SUPERIOR COURTS—Continued.

EIGHTH JUDICIAL DISTRICT.

Spring—Judge Hoke.

Fall—Judge Green.

Cabarrus—Jan. 20th (2), July 27th (2).
Iredell—Feb. 2d (2), May 18th (2), Aug. 10th (2), Nov. 9th.
Rowan—Feb. 17th (2), May 11th, Aug. 24th (2), Nov. 22d (2).
Davidson—March 2d (2), Sept. 7th (2).
Randolph—March 16th (2), July 13th (2).
Montgomery—March 30th, Oct. 5th (2).
Yadkin—May 4th. Oct. 26th (2).

NINTH JUDICIAL DISTRICT.

Spring—Judge Norwood.

Fall—Judge Hoke.

Alexander—Jan. 20th, July 27th.
Rockingham—Jan. 27th (2), Aug. 3d, Nov. 9th (2).
Forsyth—Feb. 17th (2), May 11th (2), Aug. 10th (2), Dec. 7th (2).
Wilkes—March 2d (2), Sept. 7th (2).
Alleghany—March 30th, Sept. 21st.
Davie—April 16th (2), Sept. 28th (2).
Stokes—April 20th (2), Oct. 20th (2).
Surry—March 16th (2), Oct. 12th (2).

TENTH JUDICIAL DISTRICT.

Spring—Judge Brown.

Fall—Judge Norwood.

Catawba—Feb. 17th (2), Aug. 3d (2).
McDowell—March 2d (2), Aug. 17th (2).
Burke—March 16th (2), Aug. 31st (2).
Caldwell—March 30th (2), Sept. 14th (2).
Ashe—April 13th, Sept. 28th (2).

Watauga—April 27th, Oct. 12th.
Mitchell—May 4th, Oct. 19th (2).
Yancey—May 18th, Nov. 2d (2).

ELEVENTH JUDICIAL DISTRICT.

Spring—Judge Bryan.

Fall—Judge Brown.

Union—*Jan. 27th† (3), Aug. 24th (2)*†.
Stanly—March 2d (2), Sept. 7th (2).
Mecklenburg—†Jan. 20th, March 16th† (2), †June 1st, †Oct. 5th (2), †Dec. 16th.
Gaston—Feb. 17th†, Sept. 21st (2).
Lincoln—March 30th (2), Oct. 19th.
Cleveland—April 13th (2), Oct. 21st (2).
Rutherford—April 27th (2), Nov. 9th (2).
Polk—May 11th, Nov. 2th.
Henderson—May 18th† (2),†Nov. 30th (2)

TWELFTH JUDICIAL DISTRICT.

Spring—Judge Timberlake.

Fall—Judge Bryan.

Madison—†Feb. 24th (2), Aug. 3d† (2).
Buncombe—†March 9th (3), †Aug. 17th (3), †Dec. 7th (2).
Transylvania—March 30th, Sept 7th.
Haywood—†April 6th (2), Sept. 12th (2).†
Jackson—April 20th (2), Sept. 28th.
Macon—May 4th, Oct. 5th.
Clay—May 11th, Oct. 12th.
Cherokee—May 18th*† (2),Oct. 19th*† (2).
Graham—June 1st, Nov. 9th (2).
Swain—June 8th (2), Nov. 23d (2).

*For criminal cases.
†For civil cases alone.
‡For civil cases alone except jail cases.
(2)Means two weeks, etc.

CRIMINAL COURTS.

EASTERN DISTRICT.

Judge—Oliver P. Mears, Wilmington.
New Hanover—Jan. 6th, March 9th, Oct. 12th.
Warren—Jan. 20th. July 13th.
Vance—Jan. 27th, Sept. 14th.
Edgecombe—Feb. 10th, Nov. 2d.
Craven—Feb. 17th, Oct. 5th.
Halifax—Feb. 24th, Dec. 7th.
Mecklenburg—April 15th, Sept. 7th.
Robeson—April 20th.

WESTERN DISTRICT.

Buncombe, Haywood, Madison and Henderson, Judge. Hamilton G. Ewart, Hendersonville; Solicitor, Robert S. Mc-Call, Asheville; Clerk, W. H. Wilson.
Haywood—Jan. 13th, April 27th.
Buncombe—Jan. 27th, July 27th, Oct. 26th.
Madison—Feb. 10th, June 8th, Nov. 9th.
Henderson—April 13th, June 22, Oct. 12.

U. S. CIRCUIT AND DISTRICT COURTS.

Charles H. Simonton, Charleston, S. C., Judge of Fourth Circuit of U. S. Courts.
Nathan Goff, West Virginia, Judge of U. S. Circuit Court of Appeals for Fourth District.

WESTERN DISTRICT.—R. P. Dick, Greensboro, Judge; R. B. Glenn, District Attorney; D. A. Covington, Assistant Attorney; S. L. Trogden, Clerk. *Greensboro*—Circuit and District—April 6th, October 6th. *Statesville*—Circuit and District—H. C. Cowles, Clerk; April 10th, October 19th. *Asheville*—Circuit and District—R. O. Patterson, Clerk; May 4th, November 3d. *Charlotte*—Circuit and District—H. C. Cowles, Clerk ; June 8th. December 14th.

EASTERN DISTRICT.—A. S. Seymour, Judge; C. B. Aycock, Goldsboro, District Attorney ; Sol C. Weil, Wilmington, Assistant Attorney; W. C. Brooks, Clerk. *Elizabeth City*, District Court—April 20th, October 19th. *Newbern*—District Court—Geo. Green, Clerk; April 27th, October 26th. *Wilmington*—Circuit and District—N. J. Riddick, Clerk ; V Royster, Assistant Clerk in Raleigh ; W. H. Shaw, Clerk of District and Deputy of Circuit Court at Wilmington ; O. J. Carroll, Marshal ; May 4th, November 2d. *Raleigh*—Circuit Court—N. J. Riddick, Clerk; V. Royster, Assistant Clerk in Raleigh, W. H. Shaw; Clerk of District and Deputy of Circuit Court at Wilmington ; O. J. Carroll, Marshal ; May 20th, December 7th.

SUPREME COURT.

SUPREME COURT meets first Monday in February. Examinations on Monday. First District, February 4th ; Second District, February 11th ; Third District, February 18th ; Fourth District, February 25th ; Fifth District, March 3d; Sixth District, March 10th ; Seventh District, March 17th ; Eighth District, March 24th; Ninth District, March 31st ; Tenth District, April 7th ; Eleventh District, April 14th; Twelfth District, April 2ad. End of Docket, April 28th.

11th Month. NOVEMBER, 1896. 30 Days.

Moon's Phases.

	D. H. M.		D. H. M.
New Moon,	5 2 18 a.m.	Full Moon,	20 5 16 a.m.
First Quarter.	12 0 32 a.m.	Last Quarter,	27 9 35 p.m.

Day of Month.	Day of Week.	Sun rises.	Sun sets.	Sun fast.	Sun's decline south.	ASPECTS OF PLANETS AND OTHER MISCELLANEOUS MATTER.	Moon's place.	Moon rises or sets.	Moon south.	High Tides.
44. Twenty-second Sunday after Trinity. Day's length 10 hours 41m.										
1	*D.*	6 22	5 3	16	14 46	Gen. McLellan in com. '61		1 55	m'rn	m'rn
2	Mo	6 23	5 2	16	15 5	♂ stationary.		3 8	9 14	4 15
3	Tue	6 24	5 1	16	15 23	Bat. Hohenlinden 1800.		4 22	10 6	5 10
4	We	6 25	5 0	16	15 42	☌ ☿ ☽ Peabody d. '69		5 41	11 1	6 3
5	Thu	6 26	5 59	16	16 0	☌ ♄ ☽		sets	eve.	6 52
6	Fri	6 27	5 58	16	16 18	Lincoln elected 1860.		5 41	1 4	7 45
7	Sat	6 28	4 56	16	16 35	☌ ♀ ☽. Dr. Draven d. '82.		6 40	2 8	8 41
45. Twenty-third Sunday after Trinity Day's length 10 hours 27 min.										
8	*D.*	6 29	4 56	16	16 53	Milton died 1694.		7 47	3 11	9 34
9	Mo	6 30	4 55	16	17 10	Prince of Wales born '41		8 57	4 10	10 29
10	Tue	6 31	4 55	16	17 26	Martin Luther born 1483		10 5	5 3	11 24
11	We	6 32	4 54	16	17 43	Wm. E. Pell d. 1870.		11 11	5 51	0 1
12	Thu	6 33	4 53	16	17 59	♀ in Aphelion.		m'rn	6 36	0 45
13	Fri	6 34	4 53	15	18 15	Fall of Meteors 1833		0 13	7 17	1 38
14	Sat	6 35	4 52	15	18 30	Herschel born 1738.		1 14	7 57	2 27
46. Twenty-fourth Sunday after Trinity. Day's length 10 hours 12 min.										
15	*D.*	6 36	4 51	15	18 45	Bat. Campbell's Sta. '63.		2 12	8 36	3 15
16	Mo	6 37	4 51	15	19 0	Sherman's march 1864.		3 11	9 16	4 0
17	Tue	6 38	4 50	15	19 15	Suez Canal op. 1869.		4 9	9 58	4 45
18	We	6 39	4 50	15	19 29	Leg. at Fayetteville 1786		5 9	10 42	5 29
19	Thu	6 40	4 49	14	19 43	Gen. Ass. Newbern 1771		6 11	11 30	6 11
20	Fri	6 41	4 49	14	19 56	☌ ☿ ☉.		rises.	m'rn	6 51
21	Sat	6 42	4 49	14	20 9	☿ in ☊.		5 17	0 20	7 35
47. Twenty-fifth Sunday after Trinity. Day's length 10 hours 5 min.										
22	*D.*	6 43	4 48	13	20 22	Gen. Jos. Graham d. '36		6 11	1 13	8 22
23	Mo	6 44	4 47	13	20 34	Gov. Ellis born 1820.		7 11	2 6	9 7
24	Tue	6 45	4 47	13	20 46	Aunt Abbey House d. '81		8 16	3 0	9 51
25	We	6 46	4 46	13	20 58	Isaac Watts d. 1748.		9 24	3 52	10 40
26	Thu	6 47	4 46	12	21 9	Bish. Marvin d. 1875.		10 32	4 41	11 29
27	Fri	6 48	4 46	12	21 19	J. H. Wheeler d. '94.		11 41	5 30	0 2
28	Sat	6 49	4 46	12	21 30	☌ ♃ ☽ and ☌ ☿ ☉ sup.		m'rn	6 17	0 48
48. First Sunday in Advent. Day's length 9 hours 56 minutes.										
29	*D.*	6 50	4 46	11	21 40	Savannah taken 1778.		0 50	7 4	1 43
30	Mo	6 51	4 46	11	21 49	SAINT ANDREW.		2 2	8 45	2 41

WEATHER CONJECTURES.—NOVEMBER—1, 2, 3, 4, showery; 5, 6, 7, 8, 9, 10, 11, showery and stormy; 12, 13, 14, 15, 16, 17, 18, 19, frost, unless the wind be S. or S. W.; 20, 21, 22, 23, rain; 24, 25, 26, expect cloudy weather; 27, 28, 29, 30, fair and frosty if wind N. or N. E., rain or snow if S. or S. W.

SUPREME COURT—Continued.

Last Monday in September. Examinations on Monday. First District, September 29th; Second District, October 6th; Third District, October 13th; Fourth District, October 20th; Fifth District, October 27th; Sixth District, November 3d; Seventh District, November 10th; Eighth District, November 17th; Ninth District, November 24th; Tenth District, December 1st; Eleventh District, December 8th; Twelfth District, December 15th, etc.

Chief Justice—Wm. Turner Faircloth, Wayne County. Associate Justices—Alphonso C. Avery, Burke County; Walter Clark, Wake County; David M. Furches, Iredell County,; Walter A. Montgomery, Wake County. Salaries $2,750 each. Frank I.Osborne, Attorney General; salary $2,000. R. T. Gray, Reporter; salary $750. Thos. S. Kenan, Clerk; salary $300 and fees. R. H. Bradley, Marshal; salary $800. J. L. Seawell, Office Clerk.

UNIVERSITY OF NORTH CAROLINA.

(Located in Chapel Hill, Orange County, twenty-eight miles northwest of Raleigh.)

Chartered in 1789, founded 1793, opened 1795. It now has 471 students and 35 instructors. The equipment includes twelve large buildings, five scientific laboratories, library of 40,000 volumes, campus of fifty acres with ample athletic grounds, gymnasium, &c. Perfect sanitation, baths, closets, &c. Tuition $60 a year, total expenses $200 to $300. Scholarships and loans for the needy. Law school (seventy five students) and medical school (thirty students.). A summer school for teachers is conducted each July. It enrolled 140 teachers in 1895.. The Faculty enrolled 19 Professors. During 1894 and 1895, many students supported themselves by labor, the total amount earned being about $5,000. The University is non-political and non-sectarian.

FACULTY.—George Tayloe Winston LL. D., President and Professor of Political and Social Science; Kemp Plummer Battle, LL D., Professor of History; Francis Preston Venable. Ph. D., Professor of General and Analytical Chemistry; Joseph Austin Holmes, B. S., State Geologist and Lecturer on Geology of North Carolina; Joshua Walker Gore, C. E., Professor of Natural Philosophy; John Manning, LL. D., Professor of Law; Thomas Hume. D. D., LL. D., Professor of the English Languages and Literature; Walter Dallam Toy, M. A., Professor of Modern Languages; Eben Alexander. Ph D., LL. D., Professsr of the Greek Language and Literature (on leave of absence); William Cain, C. E., Professor of Mathematics; Richard Henry Whitehead, M. D., Professor of Anatomy, Physiology and *Materia Medica*; Henry Horace Williams, A. M., B. D., Professor of Mental and Moral Science; Henry Van Peters Wilson. Ph. D., Professor of Biology; Karl Pomeroy Harrington. A. M., Professor of the Latin Languages and Literature; James Shepherd. LL. D., Ex-Chief Justice of the Supreme Court of North Carolina, and Associate Professor of Common and Statute Law and Equity in Summer School; Collier Cobb, A. B., Professor of Geology and Mineralogy; Edwin Anderson Alderman. Ph. B., Professor of The History and Philosophy of Education; Francis Kingsley Ball. Ph. D., Professor of Greek; Charles Baskerville. B. Sc., Assistant Professor of Chemistry; H. P. Butler, B. E., Instructor in Mathematics; Fredrick Louis Carr, B. E., Instructor in Latin; Herman Howell Horne. A. M., Instructor in Modern Languages; George Stockton Wills.Ph.B., Instructor in English. William R. Kenan, Jr., Sc. B., Assistant in Physical Laboratory; Thomas Clarke. Assistant in Chemical Laboratory; Charles Robeson, George Hughes Kirby, Assistants in Biological Laboratory; George Gullett Stephens, Instructor in Physical Culture; Eugene Lewis Harris, Ph. B., Secretary and Registrar; W T. Patterson, Bursar; Edwin Anderson Alderman. Ph. B., Librarian; Benjamin Wyche, Assistant Librarian.

36. Do the very best you can to-day, and hope to do still better to-morrow.—BRANSON.

12th Month.   DECEMBER, 1896.   ,   31 Days.

Moon's Phases.

	D. H. M.		D. H. M.
New Moon,	4 0 42 p.m.	Full Moon,	19 10 57 p.m.
First Quarter,	11 7 21 p.m.	Last Quarter,	27 7 0 a.m.

Day of Month.	Day of Week.	Sun rises.	Sun sets.	Sun fast.	Sun's decline south.	ASPECTS OF PLANETS AND OTHER MISCELLANEOUS MATTER.	Moon's place.	Moon rises or sets.	Moon south.	High Tides.
1	Tue	6 51	4 46	10	21 58	☿ in Perihelion.		3 15	m'rn	m'rn
2	We	6 52	4 46	10	22 7	51st Cong. 2d sess. op. '90		4 33	9 41	4 41
3	Thu	6 53	4 46	10	22 15	☾ ☌ ♄ ☾.		5 52	10 42	5 41
4	Fri	6 54	4 46	9	22 23			sets	11 46	6 38
5	Sat	6 55	4 46	9	22 31	Bush. Wilson in Ral. '94.		5 24	eve.	7 32

49.   Second Sunday in Advent.   Day's length 9 hours 50 minutes.

Day of Month.	Day of Week.	Sun rises.	Sun sets.	Sun fast.	Sun's decline south.	ASPECTS	Moon's place.	Moon rises or sets.	Moon south.	High Tides.
6	D.	6 56	4 46	8	22 38	Jefferson Davis d. 1889.		6 35	1 53	8 30
7	Mo	6 56	4 46	8	22 44	Inst. D.&D.&B. est. 1847		7 46	2 50	9 20
8	Tue	6 57	4 46	8	22 50	Eli Whitney born 1765.		8 55	3 42	10 7
9	We	6 58	4 46	7	22 56	Milton born 1608.		10 1	4 29	10 54
10	Thu	6 59	4 46	7	23 1	☽ Dumas died 1870.		11 4	5 13	11 41
11	Fri	7 0	4 46	6	23 6	☿ ☌ ☉.		m'rn	5 54	0 3
12	Sat	7 1	4 47	6	23 10	Cromwell Protector 1653		0 3	6 33	0 48

50   Third Sunday in Advent.   Day's length 9 hours 45 minutes.

Day of Month.	Day of Week.	Sun rises.	Sun sets.	Sun fast.	Sun's decline south.	ASPECTS	Moon's place.	Moon rises or sets.	Moon south.	High Tides.
13	D.	7 2	4 47	5	23 14	Robert Tombs d. 1885.		1 2	7 13	1 35
14	Mo	7 3	4 47	5	23 17	Washington died 1799.		2 1	7 54	2 23
15	Tue	7 3	4 47	4	23 20	Sitting Bull killed 1890.		3 1	8 38	3 13
16	We	7 4	4 48	4	23 22	Boston Tea Party 1773.		4 2	9 24	4 3
17	Thu	7 4	4 48	3	23 24	Poet Whittier b. 1807.		5 2	10 14	4 53
18	Fri	7 4	4 49	3	23 26	Sir H. Davy b. 1779.		6 3	11 6	5 45
19	Sat	7 6	4 49	2	23 27	☉ ☌ ☽		7 1	m'rn	6 32

51.   Sunday before Christmas.   Day's length 9 hours 42 minutes.

Day of Month.	Day of Week.	Sun rises.	Sun sets.	Sun fast.	Sun's decline south.	ASPECTS	Moon's place.	Moon rises or sets.	Moon south.	High Tides.
20	D.	7 7	4 49	2	23 27	South Carolina sec. 1860.		rises	0 0	7 16
21	Mo	7 7	4 50	1	23 27	☉ ent. ♑. WINTER COM.		6 9	0 55	8 7
22	Tue	7 8	4 50	1	23 27	☿ gr. Hel. Lat. S.		7 16	3 48	8 51
23	We	7 8	4 51	slow	23 26	Henry W. Grady d. '89.		8 25	2 39	9 33
24	Thu	7 9	4 51	slow	23 25	Dr. Wm. Little d. 1879.		9 33	3 28	10 16
25	Fri	7 9	4 52	slow	23 23	CHRISTMAS DAY.		10 41	4 15	10 59
26	Sat	7 9	4 53	1	23 20	John J. Ormond d. '94.		11 50	5 1	11 42

52.   Sunday after Christmas.   Day's length 9 hours 43 minutes.

Day of Month.	Day of Week.	Sun rises.	Sun sets.	Sun fast.	Sun's decline south.	ASPECTS	Moon's place.	Moon rises or sets.	Moon south.	High Tides.
27	D.	7 10	4 53	2	23 18	☾ St. John Evan. Day.		m'rn	5 49	0 16
28	Mo	7 10	4 54	2	23 14	☿ ☌ ☾.		1 1	6 38	1 11
29	Tue	7 10	4 54	3	23 11	W. E. Gladstone b. 1809		2 15	7 30	2 11
30	We	7 11	4 55	3	23 6	Battle Vicksburg 1862.		3 31	8 27	3 16
31	Thu	7 11	4 56	4	23 2	⊕ in Perihelion.		4 45	9 27	4 24

WEATHER CONJECTURES.—DECEMBER—1, 2, 3, look for snow; 4, 5, 6, 7, 8, 9, 10, fair; 11, 12, 13, 14, fair and frosty; 15, 16, 17, 18, expect rain or snow; 19, 20, 21, 22, fair and frosty; 23, 24, 25, 26, expect frost; 27, 28, 29, 30, 31, fair and frosty if wind N. or N. E.

CURIOUS DATE FIGURING.

A gentleman was showing a curious thing in the State House this noon—showing how to tell the day of the week of any date. He gave the following formula, which can be tried by any one : Take the last two figures of the year, add a quarter of this, disregarding the fraction; add the figure in the following list, one figure standing for each month, 8 6 6 2 4 0 2 5 1 3 6 1. Divide the sum by seven and the remainder will give the number of the day in the week, and when there is no remainder the day will be Saturday. As an example, take today, March 19th, 1890. Take 90, add 22. add 19, and 6. This gives 137, which divided by 7 leaves a remainder of 4, which is the number of the day, or Wednesday.—*Providence Telegram.*

THE OLD SILVER DOLLAR.

The following from the Chenoa (Ill.) Gazette, will be read with interest for its excellent sentiment if not the poetic inspiration it breathes.

"How dear to our hearts is the old silver dollar, when some kind subscriber presents it to view; the liberty bust without necktie or collar, and all the strange things that to us seem so new; the wide spreading eagle, the arrows below it, the stars and the words with the strange things they tell; the coin of our fathers, we're glad that we know it, for some time or other 'twill come in right well—the spread eagle dollar, the old silver dollar, that we all love so well."

JUDGE CALDWELL.

In the earlier days of our State there were some rough characters about the court assemblings, so that even Judges had their troubles. On one occasion, at Gatesville Court, perhaps, one stalwart fisherman stalked into the court room throwing his arms akimbo, and remarked in corn whiskey style. *I'm a horse! I'm a horse!!* Whereupon Judge Caldwell said, "Sheriff! take that horse and put him in the stable." The Court went on as if nothing had happened, and perfect order prevailed, as was usual at all of the good old Judge's courts.

The Monroe Doctrine was announced in a message to Congress, December 2, 1823. The following words contain the principle involved: "We owe it to candor and to the amicable relations existing between the United States and the European powers to declare that we should consider any attempt on their part to extend their system to any portion of this hemisphere as dangerous to our peace and safety." This, with the accompanying reasons for the position taken, was a statement of the doctrine that "America is for Americans," and exemplified the policy of Washington—"No entangling alliances." Congress deemed the position necessary, but did not enforce it.

ZEB VANCE AS A PRISONER.

Zeb was our great war Governor, but on approach of Sherman's army 13th of April, 1865, as a matter of prudence, Zeb went away on a short tour up the country. But Sherman came; and having politely requested, Zeb., he returned to Raleigh and made himself as agreeable as could have been expected. He even escorted some of the officers on to Washington City. While walking down Pennsylvania Avenue, he met some old friends (Zeb. was in Congress when the war broke out) who at once besought him to tell some of his good jokes. Zeb touched off a few in a moderate way and excused himself from further talk, saying, "I am saving my best jokes for *hanging day.* Of course the crowd laughed, and no one thought Zeb. likely to hang soon.

COUNTY OFFICERS—Corrected as Changes Occur.

	County	County Town	Clerk Superior Court.	Chairm'n County Commissioners.	Register of Deeds.	Sheriff.	Treasurer.	County Examiner.
1	Alamance	Graham	G. D. Vincent	S. H. Webb	P. A. Mitchell	R. T. Kernodle	R. C. Dickey	Rev. P. H. Fleming
2	Alexander	Taylorsville	J. B. Pool	A. A. Hill	Thos. A. Hudson	J. W. Watts	J. M. Watts	Wm. M. Smith
3	Alleghany	Sparta	W. K. Cox	Allen Jones	J. N. Edwards	Levi J. Jaines	Levi J. Joiner	T. J. Fender
4	Anson	Wadesboro	J. C. McLauchlin	H. W. Ledbetter	S. A. Benton	Benj. L. Wall	D. L. Saylor	W. D. Redfearn
5	Ashe	Jefferson	P. Blevin	E. E. Phillips	M. L. Smith	Byron Stmrgill	B. Sturgill	J. W. Jones
6	Beaufort	Washington	G. W. Guilford	Dr. W. J. Bullock	O. K. Stilley	R. T. Hodges	R. T. Hodges	Dr. B. Stilley
7	Bertie	Windsor	W. L. Lyon	T. S. Norfleet	Sol. Cherry	T. C. Bond	T. C. Bond	R. W. Askew
8	Bladen	Elizabethtown	W. J. Sutton	C. P. Farmer	Jas. R. Mulford	S. G. Wooten	S. M. Robbins	J. R. Dunham
9	Brunswick	Southport	S. P. Tharp	S. J. Stanly	J. W. Brooks	D. R. Walker	S. M. Robbins	George Leonard
10	Buncombe	Asheville	J. L. Cathey	J. L. Rankin	J. J. Mackey	J. A. Brookshire	J. H. Courtney	C. B. Wray
11	Burke	Morganton	P. W. Patton	G. P. Erwin	John H. Cooper	Thos. M. Webb	J. H. Courtney	Rev. R. L. Patton
12	Cabarrus	Concord	James C. Gibson	Jacob Dove	W. M. Weddington	John A. Sims	G. Ed. Keatler	James P. Cook
13	Caldwell	Lenoir	Jas. V. McCall	John M. Downs	W. R. Dozier	A. H. Boyd	A. H. Courtney	C. D. Sherrill
14	Camden	Camden C. H.	R. L. Forbes	G. H. Riggs	W. F. F. Palmer	D. S. Bartlett	G. H. Jacobs	C. H. Spencer
15	Carteret	Beaufort	L. A. Garner	W. L. Arendall	F. A. Pierson	D. R. Pierce	N. W. Taylor	Jasper Pigott
16	Caswell	Yanceyville	Spencer B. Adams	F. A. Hoyte	F. A. Carrow	John F. Durwhe	T. H. Harrison	A. E. Henderson
17	Catawba	Newton	John W. Rockett	C. R. Scott	John F. Herman	Theo. L. Bandy	Noah Barringer	J. W. Rowe
18	Chatham	Pittsboro	R. H. Dixon	A. H. Sudderth	L. T. Paschal	J. J. Jenkins	Thomas Payne	A. H. Merritt
19	Cherokee	Murphy	D. L. Watts	E. G. Smith	T. C. McDonald	J. J. Jenkins	J. J. Jenkins	James Lovinggood
20	Chowan	Edenton	H. C. Privitt	L. W. Garrett	L. D. Byrum	S. W. Davidson	C. S. Vann	Rev. J. E. White
21	Clay	Hayesville	T. H. Hancock	Frank Wood	G. M. Fleming	Geo. M. Johnson	R. G. Ketron	I. H. Chambers
22	Cleveland	Shelby	T. D. Lattimore	S. N. Forney	J. F. Williams	F. S. Fortenberry	J. B. Byers	J. A. Anthony
23	Columbus	Whiteville	A. H. Lennon	Jas. A. Bryan	D. B. F. Nance	Mathew J. Ward	J. K. Gore	L. W. Stanly
24	Craven	Newbern	W. M. Watson	J. M. Lamb	J. M. Biddle	W. B. Lane	Thos. Daniels	John S. Long
25	Cumberland	Fayetteville	Cyrus Murphy	B. J. Daniels	Alex. McNeill	McD. Geddie	J. B. Troy	H. B. King
26	Currituck	Currituck C. H.	E. W. Ansell	J. W. Lee	G. W. Williams	Edward Tillett	Ed. Tillett	V. L. Pitts
27	Dare	Manteo	L. E. Hunt	N. A. Peebles	C. J. Daugh	R. M. Smith	S. E. Mann	A. W. Jones
28	Davidson	Lexington	J. T. Grant	J. W. Lee	Wfl. Harris	P. J. Leonard	P. J. Leonard	Allen Cash
29	Davie	Mocksville	J. A. Gavin	I. F. Hill	G. W. Sheek	W. T. Williams	Dr. James McGuire	Leon Cash
30	Duplin	Kenansville	W. J. Christian	C. B. Green	Thaddeus Jones	Daniel Moore	Daniel Moore	R. W. Millard
31	Durham	Durham	R. L. Pennington	Orren Williams	W. W. Woods	I. V. Riggsbee	T. J. Holloway	Rev. Geo J. Dowell
32	Edgecombe	Tarboro	N. S. Wilson	M. D. Bailey	B. F. Lawson	W. T. Knight	S. J. Nash	F. S. Wilkinson
33	Forsyth	Winston	Rufus R. Harris	T. S. Collie	J. F. Miller	R. M. McArthur	B. F. Wilder	Dr. A. P. Davis
34	Franklin	Louisburg	G. H. Davis	George Patrick	W. K. Martin	R. M. Kearney	Lee R. Stowe	N. Y. Gulley
35	Gaston	Dallas	W. T. Cross	S. I. Harrell	J. J. Ormand	A. F. Loftin	H. S. Cross	A. A. Wilson
36	Gates	Gatesville	T. A. Carpenter	T. D. Waller	L. Hofler	R. O. Riddick	S. B. Rose	John R. Walton
37	Graham	Robbinsville	J. M. Sikes	T. O. Crisp	W. F. Mauney	John A. Ammons	B. H. Cozart	J. A. Hyde
38	Granville	Oxford	John W. Blount	W. F. Best	Chas. F. Crews	Wiley S. Cozart	John Sugg	W. H. P. Jenkins
39	Greene	Snow Hill	E. L. Ragan	J. H. Mills	Chas. A. Lassiter	Benj. W. Edwards	Jona A. Hodgin	E. A. Darden
40	Guilford	Greensboro	S. M. Gary	R. W. Brown	A. G. Kirkman	J. R. Hoskins	John Sugg	Simeon A. Hodgin
41	Halifax	Halifax C. H.	Felix M. McKay	John M. Hodges	F. P. Brinkley	Samuel Clark	George D. Spence	Aaron Prescott
42	Harnett	Lillington	J. K. Boone	A. Cannon	J. McK. Byrd	W. J. Haynes	W. C. Hannah	L. B. Chapin
43	Haywood	Waynesville	C. M. Pace	J. A. Tate	H. B. Moore	John H. Pope	W. J. Davis	A. J. Garner
44	Henderson	Hendersonville	Thos. D. Boone	Wm. T. Brown	John B. Arlidge	H. B. Arlidge	J. G. Grant	C. J. Edney
45	Hertford	Winton			Geo. A. Brown	Wm. E. Cullens	W. E. Cullens	S. M. Aunack

A roster table (names listed by county and town):

No.	County	Town					
46	Hyde,	Swan Quarter,	Jas. H. Wahab,	J. B. Watson,	L. H. Lindell,	R. D. Harris,	C. P. Benson,	J. M. Watson,
47	Iredell,	Statesville,	H. V. Forches,	J. A. Cooper,	M. F. Ramsey,	M. A. White,	W. A. V. Wright,	R. V. Tharpe.
48	Jackson,	Webster,	H. C. Cowan,	S. H. Bryson,	J. K. Long,	J. E. McLain,	A. V. F. Bryson,	John N. Wilson.
49	Johnston,	Smithfield,	W. S. Stevens,	F. H. C. Dupree,	Aug. Haskins,	J. J. T. Ellington,	T. R. Hood,	Ira T. Turlington.
50	Jones,	Trenton,	S. E. Koonce,	J. A. Smith,	C. S. Pittman,	H. Bell,	Lewis King,	T. J. Whitaker.
51	Lenoir,	Kinston,	R. F. Churchill,	Henry Tull,	J. F. Killian,	J. D. Sutton,	J. H. Dawson,	E. G. Tisdal.
52	Lincoln,	Lincolnton,	G. A. Barkley,	H. E. Ramsaur,	J. S. Sloan,	C. H. Rhodes,	D. L. Yount,	L. A. Abernethy.
53	Macon,	Franklin,	Lee Crawford,	Jos. B. Colfield,	R. F. Fox,	C. T. Roane,	C. T. Roane,	L. H. Garland.
54	Madison,	Marshall,	M. A. Chandley,	Jasper Ebbs,	Jas. A. Teel,	James H. White,	Enoch Rector,	W. P. Jervis.
55	Martin,	Williamston,	N. S. Peel,	John Carson,	J. C. Brown,	N. J. Hardison,	S. R. Biggs,	Dr. N. H. Harrell.
56	McDowell,	Marion,	B. B. Price,	Thos. Grier,	J. W. Cobb,	G. H. Gardin,	G. H. Gardin,	Frank Wilson.
57	Mecklenburg,	Charlotte,	J. M. Morrow,	J. T. Wade,	R. M. Davis,	Z. T. Smith,	E. H. Walker,	Hugh A. Gray.
58	Mitchell,	Bakersville,	C. Bowman,	John Shaw,	G. S. Beaman,	George K. Pritchard,	W. S. Daniels,	J. J. Britt.
59	Montgomery,	Troy,	J. S. Lewis,	A. A. Wiseman,	D. S. Ray,	D. E. Ewing,	D. A. Ewing,	W. H. McNeill.
60	Moore,	Carthage,	D. A. McDonald,	T. E. Westray,	J. H. T. Baker,	J. L. Currie,	Dr. K. M. Ferguson,	J. A. Bridges.
61	Nash,	Nashville,	M. B. Williford,	Horace A. Bagg,	M. F. Stancell,	J. P. Arrington,	E. J. Braswell,	M. C. S. Noble.
62	New Hanover,	Wilmington,	J. D. Taylor,	C. L. Crocker,	C. C. Martin,	Elijah Hewlett,	S. Van Amringe,	A. J. Conner.
63	Northampton,	Jackson,	J. T. Flythe,	D. J. Sanders,	John Lane,	W. H. Buffaloe,	Alveston Burgwynn,	E. M. Koonce.
64	Onslow,	Jacksonville,	Charles Gerock,	D. H. Hamilton,	Alexander Lee,	F. W. Hargett,	J. F. Cox,	H. C. Thompson.
65	Orange,	Hillsboro,	L. F. Crawford,	C. H. Fowler,	M. B. Calpepper,	John K. Hughes,	W. F. Jackson,	T. A. Mazingo.
66	Pamlico,	Bayboro,	Festus Miller,	G. W. Scott,	J. P. Stringfield,	W. J. Parker,	John T. Cooper,	Gaston Pool.
67	Pasquotank,	Elizabeth City,	J. T. Overman,	J. T. Foy,	W. O. White,	T. P. Wilcox,	J. S. Morris,	J. T. Bland.
68	Pender,	Burgaw,	W. W. Larkins,	C. W. Wood,	H. J. Whitt,	W. W. Alderman,	Jacob H. Parker,	W. G. Gaither.
69	Perquimans,	Hertford,	L. A. Moye,	T. H. Street,	W. M. King,	A. F. Riddick,	J. C. Pass,	W. E. Webb.
70	Person,	Roxboro,	E. A. Moye,	Council Dawson,	J. T. Newman,	J. A. Carver,	James L. Little,	W. H. Ragsdale.
71	Pitt,	Greenville,	N. B. Hampton,	C. W. Pearson,	J. T. Winslow,	R. W. King,	J. K. Gibbs,	A. L. McNorry.
72	Polk,	Columbus,	J. M. Millikin,	J. E. Walker,	C. Dockery,	W. C. Robertson,	J. L. Swain,	N. B. English.
73	Randolph,	Asheboro,	C. B. Townsend,	N. T. Covington,	J. H. Morrison,	G. G. Hendrix,	A. M. McLean,	W. B. McIver.
74	Richmond,	Rockingham,	T. S. Malloy,	E. F. McRae,	R. L. Sneed,	J. M. Smith,	J. S. McCubbins,	J. A. McAlister.
75	Robeson,	Lumberton,	W. G. Watson,	John M. Galloway,	W. J. Mode,	Geo. R. McLoud,	W. O. Baber,	N. S. Smith.
76	Rockingham,	Wentworth,	T. C. Smith,	W. L. Kluttz,	A. F. Herring,	W. B. Wray,	J. M. Marshburn,	R. G. Kizer.
77	Rowan,	Salisbury,	W. A. Pigford,	J. F. Flack,	W. T. Huckabee,	J. S. McCubbins,	George D. Palmer,	H. W. Howe.
78	Rutherford,	Rutherfordton,	A. Hobbs,	I. P. Efird,	D. V. Carroll,	W. O. Baber,	Joel H. Fulton,	Geo. E. Butler.
79	Sampson,	Clinton,	S. R. Milton,	Dr. John W. Neal,	C. H. Haynes,	J. M. Marshburn,	D. G. Fisher,	R. A. Crowell.
80	Stanley,	Albemarle,	N. O. Petree,	J. A. Park,	N. B. Thompson,	George D. Palmer,	Vance Galloway,	M. T. Chilton.
81	Stokes,	Danbury,	W. W. Hampton,	A. H. Hayes,	E. S. English,	Joel H. Fulton,	J. C. Meekins, Sr.	J. B. Sparger.
82	Surry,	Dobson,	T. H. Hampton,	G. W. Wilson,	S. C. Newberry,	J. A. Adams,	James McNeely,	J. Lamar.
83	Swain,	Charleston,	T. D. Holmes,	R. S. Hassell,	J. W. Bivens,	J. F. Teague,	H. P. Hicks,	M. L. Shepperson.
84	Transylvania,	Brevard,	F. H. Wolfe,	W. L. Howie,	T. S. Eaton,	V. B. McGaha,	H. H. Knight,	Arthur Spruill.
85	Tyrrell,	Columbia,	D. H. Gill,	Jas. K. Young,	J. J. Rogers,	A. W. Owens,	Nathan M. Palmer,	T. D. McConley.
86	Union,	Monroe,	Dan. H. Young,	W. C. Stronach,	W. F. Thornton,	J. P. Horn,	Thomas J. Bazingh,	J. T. Jenkins.
87	Vance,	Henderson,	W. A. White,	M. J. Hawkins,	W. H. Stubbs,	W. H. Smith,	A. A. Green,	J. H. Goodwin.
88	Wake,	Raleigh,	Thos. J. Mariner,	Io. Skittletharpe,	John W. Hodges,	M. W. Page,	Clarence Call,	J. R. Rodwell.
89	Warren,	Warrenton,	N. B. Blackburn,	W. C. Coffey,	G. G. Scarcegay,	H. Allen,		H. S. Ward.
90	Washington,	Plymouth,	C. F. Herring,	I. E. Peterson,	D. R. Edwards,	Levi Blount,		W. M. Francum.
91	Watauga,	Boone,	A. M. Vannoy,	W. M. Absher,	W. A. Hall,	B. F. Scott,	W. T. Farmer,	E. T. Atkinson.
92	Wayne,	Goldsboro,	J. D. Hardin,	W. W. Farmer,	A. B. Silver,	Clarence Call,	A. P. Woodruff,	Rev. R. W. Barber.
93	Wilkes,	Wilkesboro,	R. F. Holton,	J. M. Jones,		J. W. Crowell,	C. H. Byrd,	J. W. Hayes.
94	Wilson,	Wilson,	W. B. Banks,	A. J. Bennett,		J. M. Woody,		J. C. Pinnix.
95	Yadkin,	Yadkinville,						Jas. L. Hyatt.
96	Yancey,	Burnsville,						

PUBLIC WORKS AND INSTITUTIONS IN NORTH CAROLINA.

NORTH CAROLINA COLLEGE OF AGRICULTURE AND MECHANIC ARTS.

Located at Raleigh, and managed by the

STATE BOARD OF AGRICULTURE.—Col. W. F. Green, Chairman, 4th District; J. B. Coffield, 1st District; Dr. W. R. Capehart 2d District; H. E. King, 3d District; J. H. Gilmer, 5th District; D. A. Tompkins, 6th District; Dr. J. R. McLelland, 7th District; H. E. Fries, 8th District; E. A. Aiken, 9th District. *State at Large*—W. S. Primrose, R. W. Wharton, N. B. Broughton, J. L. Nelson, Frank Wood. And *ex-officio*—Dr. Cyrus Thompson, President State Farmers' Alliance.

EXECUTIVE COMMITTEE OF BOARD.—Col. W. F. Green, Dr. W. R. Capehart, Col. R. W. Wharton, J. L. Nelson.

FINANCE COMMITTEE OF BOARD.—J. B. Coffield, J. H. Gilmer, E. A. Aiken.

OFFICERS OF BOARD.—S. L. Patterson, Commissioner; T. K. Bruner, Secretary; H. B. Battle, Ph. D., Chemist and Director of the Experiment Station.

EXECUTIVE COMMITTEE OF THE COLLEGE.—W. S. Primrose, H. E. Fries, J. R. McLelland, D. A. Tompkins.

FINANCE COMMITTEE OF THE COLLEGE.—N. B. Broughton, H. E. King, Frank Wood.

FACULTY AND OFFICERS.—Alexander Q. Holladay, President; W. F. Massey, C. E., Professor of Horticulture, Arboriculture and Botany; W. A. Withers, A. M., Professor of Pure and Agricultural Chemistry; D. H. Hill, A. M., Professor of English; B. Irby, M. S., Professor of Agriculture; W. C. Riddick, A. B., C. E., Professor of Mechanics and Civil Engineering; R. Henderson, Lieut. U. S. Navy, Professor Physics; N. R. Craighill, M. E., Professor of Mechanics; R. E. L. Yates, A. M., Adjunct Professor of Mathematics; F. E. Emery, B. S., Assistant Professor of Agriculture; Charles M. Pritchett, B. S., Instructor in Mechanics; Charles B. Park, Superintendent Shops; J. A. Bizzell, B. S., S. E. Asbury, B. S., Instructors in Chemistry; Charles Pearson, B. E., Instructor in Mechanics; David Clark, B. E., Assistant in Mechanics; W. A. Bullock, B. S., Dairyman; A. A. Wilson, Preparatory Department; Professor Withers, Secretary of the Faculty; Professor Hill, Bursar; Benj. S. Skinner, Superintendent of Farm and Steward; Mrs. Sue C. Carroll, Matron; J. B. Dunn, M. D., Physician.

THE STATE HOSPITAL, MORGANTON.

OFFICERS.—P. L. Murphy, M. D., Superintendent, salary $2,800; Isaac M. Taylor, M. D., Assistant Physician, salary, $1,200; C. E. Ross, M. D., Assistant Physician salary, $1,200; F. M. Scroggs, Steward, salary $1,000; Mrs. C. A. Marsh, Matron, salary $550.

BOARD OF DIRECTORS.—James P. Sawyer, Buncombe County, President; I. I. Davis, Esq., Burke County; Joseph P. Caldwell, Esq., Mecklenburg County; J. G. Hall, Esq., Catawba County; Jas. P. Sawyer, Buncombe County; Jos. C. Mills, Burke County; G. W. F. Harper, Caldwell County; J. R. Love, Jackson County; R. L. Whitener, Catawba County; S. A. White, Alamance County.

No member of the Board of Directors or Executive Committee receive any compensation for their work, except their traveling expenses.

BUREAU OF LABOR STATISTICS.

B. R. Lacy, of Wake County, Commissioner, salary $1,500; Logan D. Terrell, Wake County, salary $900. Office in the Supreme Court Building.

NORTH CAROLINA INSANE ASYLUM.

Situated in the vicinity of Raleigh, and will accommodate 300 patients.

OFFICERS.—Hon. W. H. Worth, Treasurer, *ex officio*; W. H. Martin, Clerk to Treasurer, *ex officio*; W. T. Smith, Esq., Keeper of Records, salary $100.

RESIDENT OFFICERS.—Dr. George L Kirby, Superintendent, salary $2,800; term 6 years from June 1, 1894. J. A Faison. 1st Assistant Physician, salary $1,200; term 2 years from March 1, 1895. D. R. S. McGeachey, 2d Assistant Physician, salary $1,200; term 2 years from March 1, 1895. W. R. Crawford, Jr., Steward, salary $1,200; term 1 year from March 1, 1895. Mrs. M. E. Whitaker, Matron, salary $600; term 1 year from March 1, 1895.

BOARD OF DIRECTORS—Major John B. Broadfoot, Cumberland County, President; J. R Smith, Wayne County; B. F. Boykin, New Hanover County; J. D. Biggs, Martin County; Geo. B. Curtis, Halifax County; R. S. Cotten, Esq., Pitt County; Dr. R. H. Speight, Edgecombe County; Jas. D. Bellamy, Nash County; J. W. Sanders, Carteret County.

NORTH CAROLINA INSTITUTION FOR THE DEAF, DUMB AND THE BLIND.

The North Carolina Institution for the Blind is located at Raleigh.

OFFICERS.—W. J. Young. Principal, salary $1,800; time expires 1896. Dr. Hubert Haywood, of Raleigh, Physician, salary $500; time expires 1897. Wm. H. Rand, Steward, salary $750 and board; time expires 1895. W. H. Worth, *ex officio* Treasurer.

BOARD OF TRUSTEES.—B. F. Montague, President; time expires Jan. 1, 1897. I. M. Proctor; time expires Jan. 1, 1901. Hugh Morson; time expires Jan. 1, 1899. John R. Williams; time expires Jan. 1, 1899. Dr. H. C. Herring; time expires Jan. 1, 1899. Jas. A. Briggs; time expires Jan. 1, 1897.

OFFICERS N. C. STATE PENITENTIARY.

A. Leazar, General Manager, salary $2,500; J. M. Fleming, Warden, salary $900; Wm. Ledbetter, Deputy Warden, salary $780; Dr. J W. McGee, Physician, salary $500; Jos. J. Bernard, Bookkeeper, salary $900;

BOARD OF DIRECTORS.—A. B. Young, Vice President, Concord, N, C.; T. J. Armstrong, Rocky Point, N. C.; D N. Bennett, Norwood, N. C.; Dr. I. E. Green, Weldon, N. C. One vacancy.

STATE MUSEUM.

Located in the Agricultural Building at Raleigh; contains a complete collection os geological rocks and ores of the State; also a fine collection of timbers, agricultural products, fish and aquatic birds—in fact a complete collection of the resources of the State. H. H. Brimley, Curator. Office hours from 9 to 1, and from 2 to 5 p. m. Under control of the State Board of Agriculture.

NORTH CAROLINA BOARD OF PUBLIC CHARITIES.

Charles Duffy, President, Newbern, term expires Jan. 1, 1899; C. B. Denson, Secretary, Raleigh; L. J Haughton, Pittsboro, term expires Jan. 1, 1898; W. N. Jones, Raleigh, term expires Jan. 1, 1896; S. W. Reid, Charlotte, term expires Jan. 1, 1895; W. A. Blair, Winston, term expires Jan. 1, 1897.

STATE BOARD OF PHARMACY.

E. V. Zoeller, Tarboro, President; W. H. Wearn, Charlotte; O. M. Royster, Hickory; Wm. Simpson, Raleigh, Secretary and Treasurer, P. W. Vaughan, Durham.

JAMES A. ARNOLD. Raleigh, N. C. Market House. Beef, Fresh Meats and Sausage.

3

STATE NORMAL AND INDUSTRIAL SCHOOL.

Located at Greensboro, N. C.

This school was chartered by the General Assembly of North Carolina, 1891. The first class of girls was graduated in 1803.

The school has ten Direct rs and an Executive Board of five—J. C. Scarborough, *ex officio* President of the Board.

Charles D. McIvr. A. B. Lit. D President (University of N. C.), is assisted by the following teachers and helpers, viz.: P P. Claxton, A. M., J. Y. Joyner, Ph. B , Lucy H Robertson, Gertrude W. Underhill, B. S., Dixie Lee Bryant. B. S., Joseph A. Holmes, B. S., Mary M. Petty, B. S., Viola Baddie. L. I., Florence A. Stone. Annie M Grove, M. D., Alice Maude Crocker, Clarence R. Brown. Melville Vincent Fort. Edith A. McIntyre, Bertha M. Lee, Sue May Kirkland, E J. Forney, Jennie W. Bingham, Fodie M. Buie, Ettie Spier, Grace Smallbones, Margaret Perry, Kate Moore, Daisy B Wait, Gertrude Royster, Eliza N. Williams, Margaret Gorman, Mrs. W. P. Carraway.

N. C. AGRICULTURAL EXPERIMENT AND FERTILIZER CONTROL STATION AND STATE WEATHER SERVICE, RALEIGH. N. C.

OFFICERS.—H B. Battle, Ph. D., Director and State Chemist; F. E. Emery. M. S , Agriculturist; Gerald McCarthy, B. S , Botanist and Entomologist; W. F. Massey, C. E., Horticulturist; C. F. von Hermann, Meteorologist; F. P. Williamson, D. V. S., Consulting Veterinarian; B. W. Kilg re, M. S , F. B. Carpenter, B. S., W. M. Allen and C. B. Williams, B. S., Assistant Chemists; Alex. Rhodea, Assistant Horticulturist; Roscoe Nunn. Assistant Meteorologist; A. F. Bowen, Secretary.

Offices and Laboratories in Agricultural Building. Raleigh; farm, stables and dairy at the Experiment Farm. adjoining State Fair Grounds. Visitors invited. Many interesting and valuable bulletins free on application.

EASTERN HOSPITAL, GOLDSBORO.

OFFICERS.—J. F. Miller, M. D. Superintendent. salary $1,800, furnished house and board of two horses and cows; W. W. Faison, M D., Assistant Physician. salary $900. board for self. wife, three children and nurse and board of one horse; Daniel Reid, Steward, salary $450. board of self and horse; Mrs. B. V. Smith. Matron, Salary $300 and board of self and child; John W. Wilson, Engineer, salary $450, furnished house for family; Mrs Victoria Bryan. Seamstress, salary $150 and board of self and child; John Pate. Farmer. salary $200 and house; A. A. Green, Watchman, salary $250 per annum. Hon. W. H. Worth, Treasurer, *ex officio.*

BOARD OF DIRECTORS. —Dr. J. W. Vick, President, Johnson County; B F. Aycock, Wayne County; J. F. Southerland, Wayne County; T. B. Parker, Wayne County; W. F. Rountree, Craven County; J. L. McLean, Robeson County; Dr M B. Pitt, Edgecombe County; Major Joshua B. Hill, Wake County; Henry I. Faison, Duplin County

EXECUTIVE COMMITTEE.—B. F. Aycock, J. F. Southerland, Thos. B. Parker

N. C. BOARD OF RAILROAD COMMISSIONERS.

COMMISSIONERS.—J. W. Wilson, Burke County, Chairman, term expires April, 1899; E. C. Beddingfield, Wake County, term expires April, 1897; S. Otho Wilson. Wake County. term expires April. 1901; salary $2,000 each; H C. Brown, Surry County. Clerk. salary $1,200.

Special sessions of the Court are held at Raleigh. Special sessions are also held at other places, under such regulations as made by the Commission.

Offices of the Commissioners are located in the Agricultural Building.

NORTH CAROLINA GEOLOGICAL SURVEY.

Jos. A. Holmes, State Geologist; H. B. C. Nitze, Assistant State Geologist. General offices of the Survey, Raleigh, N. C.

JAMES A. ARNOLD, Raleigh, N. C. Market House. Beef, Fresh Meats and Sausage.

MILITARY SCHOOLS.

A. & M. College (Military feature).....................................Raleigh
Bingham School...Asheville
Cape Fear Academy...Wilmington
Davis School...Winston
Horner School..Oxford
Quackenbosh Academy..Laurinburg
Rutherfordton Academy......................................Rutherfordton
Thompson School..Siler City
Turlington Institute...Smithfield

ORPHAN SCHOOLS.

Home and Industrial School (Independent)...................Asheville
Orphanage (Friends)..Archdale
Orphan's Home (Presbyterian).........................Barium Springs
Orphanage (colored—State aid)......................................Oxford
Oxford Orphan Asylum (Masons—State aid)...................Oxford
Orphan Home (Odd Fellows)...................................Goldsboro
Orphanage (Baptist)...Thomasville
Thompson Orphanage (Episcopal).............................Charlotte

JAMES A. ARNOLD, Raleigh, N. C. Market House. Beef, Fresh Meats and Sausage.

NORTH CAROLINA COLLEGES, AND OTHER GRADUATING SCHOOLS.

(Names, character and location.)

Asheville Female College (Methodist) ....Asheville
Chowan Female Institute (Baptist)......................... Murfreesboro
Claremont Female College (Reformed Church of U. S.) ....Hickory
Catawba College (Reformed Church of U. S).................:.Newton
Concordia College (Lutheran) ....Conover
Davenport Female College (Methodist) ....Lenoir
Davidson College (Presbyterian).. ....Davidson College
Elon College (Christian) ....Elon College
Greensboro Female College (Methodist).....................Greensboro
Gaston College (Lutheran)............... ....Dallas
Guilford College (Friends) ....Guilford College
Hayesville College (Independent) ....Hayesville
Judson College (Methodist) ....Hendersonville
Kinston College (Independent) .... Kinston
Louisburg Female College (Methodist)......................Louisburg
Littleton Female College (Methodist)........................Littleton
Mt. Amoena Seminary (Lutheran) ....Mt. Pleasant
Mt. St. Joseph Academy (Catholic).........................Asheville
North Carolina College (Lutheran).......................Mt. Pleasant
North Carolina Agricultural and Mechanical College (State) ....Raleigh
Oxford Female Seminary (Baptist) .... Oxford
Oak Ridge Institute (Independent)..................... ....Oak Ridge
Peace Institute (Independent)...........................Raleigh
Rutherford College, Burke Co. (Independent) ....Rutherford College
St. Mary's College (Catholic)..........................Belmont
Shelby Female College (Independent)........................Shelby
St. Mary's School (Episcopal) ....Raleigh
Salem Academy (Moravian) .... Salem
St. Paul's Seminary (Lutheran Theological) ....Hickory
State Normal and Industrial School (State) ....Greensboro
Trinity College (Methodist)..........................Durham
University of North Carolina (State) ....Chapel Hill
Weaverville College (Methodist) .. .. Weaverville
Wake Forest College (Baptist)......... ....Wake Forest

COLORED SCHOOLS—Graduating.

Agricultural and Mechanical College (State).................Greensboro
Bennett Seminary (Methodist)..............................Greensboro
Biddle University (Presbyterian)..........................Charlotte
Building and Trade's College (Independent)............Southern Pines
Christian Institute (Christian).............................Franklinton
Livingstone College (Methodist)..............................Salisbury
Normal and Industrial College (Methodist)...................Kittrell
Normal School (State) .... Elizabeth City
Normal School (State) ....Goldsboro
Normal School (State) .... Salisbury
Normal School (State)...........................Franklinton
Normal School (State)................. ....Plymouth
Normal School (State)..............................Fayetteville
Shaw University (Baptist)...... ....Raleigh
St. Augustine Normal College (Episcopal).......................Raleigh
Scotia Female Seminary (Presbyterian).....................Concord
Slater Industrial and Normal School (Independent)........... Winston

LEVI BRANSON, Publisher,
RALEIGH, N. C.

NORTH CAROLINA STATE GUARD—OFFICERS OF THE GENERAL STAFF.

Gen. F. H. Cameron, Adjutant General; Col. A. L. Smith, Inspector General; Col. E. G. Harrell, Quartermaster General; Col. Julian S. Carr, Paymaster General; Col. Benehan Cameron, Inspector S. A. P.; Colonel Hubert Haywood, Surgeon General; Col. Wm. Gaston Lewis, Chief of Engineers; Col. Thos. W. Strange, Judge Advocate General.

RALEIGH CHAMBER OF COMMERCE AND INDUSTRY.

OFFICERS—J. E. Pogue, President; R. B. Raney, Vice-President; Frank Stronach, Second Vice-President; Frank T. Ward, Treasurer; George Allen, Secretary; A. R. D. Johnson, Assistant Secretary.

N. C. PHARMACEUTICAL ASSOCIATION.

P. W. Vaughan, Durham, President; H. K. Horn, Fayetteville, Secretary; A. J. Cooke, Fayetteville, Treasurer.

STATE BOARD OF MEDICAL EXAMINERS.

W. H. Whitehead, M. D President, Rocky Mount; term expires May 1896; L. J. Picot, M. D., Secretary, Littleton ; term expires May, 1896; Geo. W. Long, M. D., Graham; term expires May, 1896; Julian M. Baker, Tarboro; term expires May, 1898; H. B. Weaver, M. D., Asheville; term expires 1898; T. S. Burbank, M. D., Wilmington; term expires 1900; J. M. Hays, M. D., Greensboro; term expires 1900.

NORTH CAROLINA BOARD OF HEALTH.

Geo. Gillett Thomas, M. D., Wilmington, President; S. Westray Battle, M. D., Asheville; Richard H. Lewis, M. D., Raleigh, Secretary and Treasurer; W. H. Harrell, M. D., Williamston; W. H. G. Lucas, M. D., White Hall; John Whitehead, M. D., Salisbury; Prof. F. P. Venable, Ph. D., Chapel Hill; J. C. Chase, Civil Engineer, Wilmington.

DR. CLOSS vs. DR. BURTON.

. Two finer debaters were rarely seen on the floor of the N. C. Conference. At the Goldsboro Conference in Dec., 1857, the two good Doctors were pitted on opposite side of some exciting question. In the first speech Dr. Closs had taken strong ground, causing much feeling. Dr. Burton replied in a long, strong speech, making a many good hits. In his introduction he had referred to his birth place on the "classic Roanoke," his military education, etc.; he also illustrated some salient point, by relating the incident of the turkey gobler that, being made drunk on brandy cherries had all his feathers picked off before he became sober enough to say quit.

In the rejoinder, Dr. Closs (who was not classically educated) said: Mr. Speaker, I am proud to say that *I was born* on the bank of the classic "Jumping Run." Then proceeding slowly and with great deliberation, as was his manner, he said, "as to Bro. Burton's turkey story, I cannot see the application, unless he means to say that he, Burton, was the *turkey* and that I, (Dr. Closs), picked him.

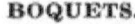

The Spirit of the Age says " BRANSON'S ALMANAC has carried knowledge, science and fun into thousands of North Carolina homes."

If the subscribers of this ALMANAC profit by reading the selected advertisements which appear therein, they will know that the old reliable

J. A. JONES.   A. M. POWELL.

JONES & POWELL,

Retailers and Jobbers of

Horse and Cow Feed,

COAL, ICE,

WOOD, LUMBER, LATHS, SAWED AND SHAVED PINE AND CYPRESS SHINGLES.

———

SHIPPED DIRECT TO ANY DEPOT.

———

Warehouse on railroad track, where cars are unloaded and reloaded, avoiding drayage and waste.

Crystal Ice Factory similarly located.

Coal, Wood and Lumber Yards on both railroad systems.

Uptown Office—107 Fayetteville Street.

Coal Yards—West end of Park Avenue; South end of West Street.

Postoffice—Lock Box 216.

Telephones—Fayetteville Street Office, No. 41; Coal Yard Office, No. 71; Ice Factory Office, No. 146.

(See Page 40.)

Remember, that WHARTON'S is the leading Photographic Gallery in Central North Carolina.

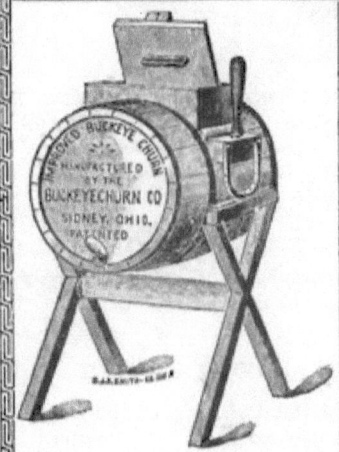

BRANSON'S SHORT CALENDAR FOR 1896.

JANUARY.

S	M	T	W	T	F	S
			1	2	3	4
5	6	7	8	9	10	11
12	13	14	15	16	17	18
19	20	21	22	23	24	25
26	27	28	29	30	31	

FEBRUARY.

S	M	T	W	T	F	S
						1
2	3	4	5	6	7	8
9	10	11	12	13	14	15
16	17	18	19	20	21	22
23	24	25	26	27	28	29

MARCH.

S	M	T	W	T	F	S
1	2	3	4	5	6	7
8	9	10	11	12	13	14
15	16	17	18	19	20	21
22	23	24	25	26	27	28
29	30	31				

APRIL.

S	M	T	W	T	F	S
			1	2	3	4
5	6	7	8	9	10	11
12	13	14	15	16	17	18
19	20	21	22	23	24	25
26	27	28	29	30		

MAY

S	M	T	W	T	F	S
					1	2
3	4	5	6	7	8	9
10	11	12	13	14	15	16
17	18	19	20	21	22	23
24	25	26	27	28	29	30
31						

JUNE.

S	M	T	W	T	F	S
1	2	3	4	5	6	
7	8	9	10	11	12	13
14	15	16	17	18	19	20
21	22	23	24	25	26	27
28	29	30				

JULY.

S	M	T	W	T	F	S
			1	2	3	4
5	6	7	8	9	10	11
12	13	14	15	16	17	18
19	20	21	22	23	24	25
26	27	28	29	30	31	

AUGUST.

S	M	T	W	T	F	S
						1
2	3	4	5	6	7	8
9	10	11	12	13	14	15
16	17	18	19	20	21	22
23	24	25	26	27	28	29
30	31					

SEPTEMBER.

S	M	T	W	T	F	S
	1	2	3	4	5	
6	7	8	9	10	11	12
13	14	15	16	17	18	19
20	21	22	23	24	25	26
27	28	29	30			

OCTOBER.

S	M	T	W	T	F	S
				1	2	3
4	5	6	7	8	9	10
11	12	13	14	15	16	17
18	19	20	21	22	23	24
25	26	27	28	29	30	31

NOVEMBER.

S	M	T	W	T	F	S
1	2	3	4	5	6	7
8	9	10	11	12	13	14
15	16	17	18	19	20	21
22	23	24	25	26	27	28
29	30					

DECEMBER.

S	M	T	W	T	F	S
	1	2	3	4	5	
6	7	8	9	10	11	12
13	14	15	16	17	18	19
20	21	22	23	24	25	26
27	28	29	30	31		

Vol. 3.] 30th YEAR OF PUBLICATION. [No. 10.

BRANSON'S
AGRICULTURAL
ALMANAC

FOR THE YEAR OF OUR LORD

1897,

And until the 4th of July, the 121st year of American Independence.

Carefully Calculated for the Latitude and Longitude of Raleigh, by

LEVI BRANSON, A. M., D. D.

LEVI BRANSON, Publisher, Raleigh, N. C.

POSTMASTERS ARE AUTHORIZED AGENTS FOR THIS ALMANAC.

1. All men have faith in something, hence they work expecting results.—*Branson*.

2   BRANSON'S NORTH CAROLINA ALMANAC.

TIME.

The calculations of this Almanac are made in mean solar or clock time, which is indicated by a well regulated watch or clock, and does not correspond with the Sun precisely, except on four days of the year.

Apparent time is that which makes the Sun come to the meridian at 12 o'clock. No good clock will run with the Sun; if set with the Sun on the 2d day of January, the clock will seem to be one minute too fast on the 3d of January.

To adapt the calculations of this Almanac to apparent time, use the minutes in the column marked "Sun slow" or "Sun fast;" add them when fast, substract them when slow.

The calculations are made for the Latitude and Longitude of Raleigh, N. C., but the times, phases, &c., will vary only a few minutes for any part of North Carolina, South Carolina, Georgia, Tennessee or Virginia.

TWELVE SIGNS OF THE ZODIAC.

The Head and Face sign.   ♈ Aries the Ram......Ar.

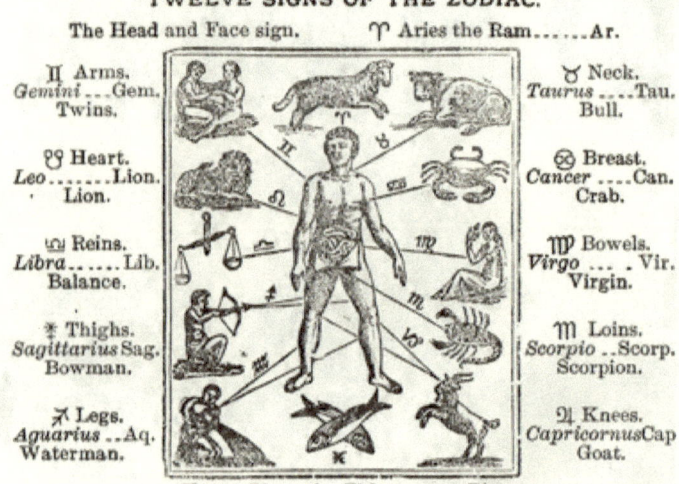

♊ Arms.
Gemini ...Gem.
Twins.

♋ Heart.
Leo........Lion.
Lion.

♎ Reins.
Libra......Lib.
Balance.

♐ Thighs.
Sagittarius Sag.
Bowman.

♒ Legs.
Aquarius ..Aq.
Waterman.

♉ Neck.
Taurus ....Tau.
Bull.

♋ Breast.
Cancer .....Can.
Crab.

♍ Bowels.
Virgo ... . Vir.
Virgin.

♏ Loins.
Scorpio ..Scorp.
Scorpion.

♑ Knees.
*Capricornus*Cap
Goat.

The ♓ *Pisces* the Fishes........Pisc.

To know where the sign is, find the day of the month, and against the day in the column marked Moon's Signs you have the sign or place of the Moon, and then find the sign; it will give you the part of the body it is supposed to govern.

SIGNS.

SPRING SIGNS. { Aries or Ram. / Taurus, or Bull. / Gemini, or Twins.

SUMMER SIGNS. { Cancer, or Crab-fish. / Leo, or Lion. / Virgo, or Virgin.

AUTMMN SIGNS. { Libra, or Balance. / Scorpio, or Scorpion. / Sagittarius, or Bowman.

WINTER SIGNS. { Capricornus, or Goat. / Aquarius, or Waterman. / Pisces, or Fishes.

SIGNS OF THE PLANETS.

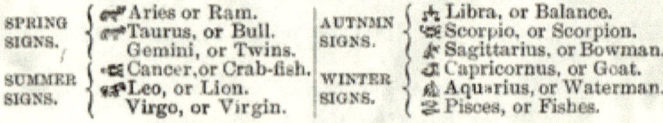

☀ Sun.   ☽ Moon.   ♀ Venus.   ♂ Mars.
♃ Jupiter.   ♄ Saturn.   ☌ In Conjunction.   ☐ Quadrature.
☿ Mercury.   ♅ Uranus.   ♆ Neptune.   ☊ Ascending Node.

MOON'S PHASES.

● New Moon.   ☽ First Quarter.   ● Full Moon.   ☾ Last Quarter.

CHRONOLOGICAL CYCLES AND ERAS.

Dominical Letter	C	Julian Pepiod	6610
Epact	26	Jewish Era	5657
Golden Number	17	Era of Nabonassa	2644
Solar Cycle	2	Olympiads	2673
Roman Indication	10	Mahommedan Era	1314

MOVABLE FEASTS OF THE CHURCH.

Epiphany	Jan. 6	Palm Sunday	April 11
Septuagesima Sunday	Feb. 14	Easter Sunday	April 18
Sexagesima Sunday	Feb. 21	Whit Sunday	June 6
Quinquagesima Sunday	Feb. 28	Trinity Sunday	June 13
Shrove Tuesday	March 2	First Sunday in Advent	Nov. 28
Ash Wednesday, or Lent	March 3	Ancension Day	May 27
St. Patrick Day	March 17		

THE FOUR SEASONS.

	D.	H.	
Spring commences	March 20,	3	A. M.
Summer commences	June 20,	11	P. M.
Autumn commences	September 22,	2	P. M.
Winter commences	December 21,	8	A. M.

MORNING STARS.

Mercury will be Morning Star about.......Feb. 15, June 15, and Oct. 9.
Venus will be Morning Star from..........April 28 to end of the year.
Jupiter will be Morning Star..Feb. 23, and from Sept. 13 to end of year.

EVENING STARS.

Mercury will be Evening Star about..Jan. 6, April 28, Aug. 26, Dec. 20.
Venns will be Evening Star till from ....Jan. 1 to April 28.
Jupiter will be Evening Star from.........February 23 to September 13.

ECLIPSES.

During the year 1897 there will be two eclipses—both of the Sun.

I. *An annular eclipse of the Sun* February 1, visible in the eastern and southern part of the United States, to Mexico and Central America, the western part of South America, and the South Pacific Ocean. Visible here as a partial eclipse towards sunset, as follows: Eclipse begins 1h. 17m. P. M.; middle of eclipse 2h. 58m. P. M.; eclipse ends 4h. 56m. P. M.

II. *An annular eclipse of the Sun* July 29, visible to the greater portions of North and South America, a small part of the Pacific Ocean, the greater part of the Atlantic Ocean, and the extreme western part of Africa. Visible here as a partial eclipse, as follows: Eclipse begins 8h. 56m. A. M.; middle of eclipse 10h. 51m. A. M.; eclipse ends 0h. 41m. P. M.

TIDES.

The time of tide can readily be found for the following places by adding the hours and minutes opposite the names to the time when the Moon is South on the day to which the tide is sought. The time when the Moon is South is given in the Calendar for every day. The next tide can be found very nearly by adding 12 hours and 29 minutes to the time of the one previous.

The tides are given in local time—add 12 minutes for Eastern Standard:

	H. M.		H. M.
Boston	11 12	New York	8 13
Sandy Hook	7 29	Old Point	8 17
Baltimore	6 33	Washington City	7 44
Richmond	4 32	Hatteras Inlet	7 04
Beaufort	7 26	Bald Head	7 26
Southport	7 19	Wilmington	9 06
Charleston	7 26	Savannah	9 33

Dr. Branson takes care to have all the Courts both full and accurate. *Evening Visitor.*

3. Some men have faith in the laws of health, and hence by obeying those laws they secure physical health and happiness.—*Branson.*

HERSCHEL'S WEATHER PROGNOSTICATOR

For Foretelling the Weather Through all the Lunations of the Year.

This table and the accompanying remarks are the result of many years actual observation, the whole being constructed on a due consideration of the attractions of the Sun and Moon, in their several positions respecting the Earth, and, by simple inspection, it shows the observer what kind of weather will most probably follow the entrance of the Moon into any of its quarters, and that so near the truth as to be seldom or never found to fail.

If the new moon, first quarter, full moon, or last quarter, happen—	IN SUMMER.	IN WINTER.
Between midnight and 2 in the morning	Fair	Hoar frost unless the wind is S. or S. W.
Between 2 and 4, morning	Cold, with frequent showers	Snow and stormy.
Between 4 and 6, morning	Rain	Rain.
Between 6 and 8, morning	Wind and rain	Stormy.
Between 8 and 10, morning	Changeable	Cold rain if wind be W.; snow if E.
Between 10 and 12, morning	Frequent showers	Cold and high wind.
Between 12 o'clock at noon and 2 in afternoon	Very rainy	Rain and snow.
Between 2 and 4, afternoon	Changeable	Fair and mild.
Between 4 and 6, afternoon	Fair	Fair.
Between 6 and 8, aftern'n	Fair if wind N. W.; rainy if S. or S. W.	Fair and frosty wind N. or N.E.; rain or snow if S. or S. W.
Between 8 and 10, afternoon	Ditto	Ditto.
Between 10 and midnight	Fair	Fair and frosty.

OBSERVATIONS.—1. The nearer the time for the Moon's change, first quarter, full and last quarter are to midnight, the fairer will be the weather during the next seven days

2. The space for this calculation occupies from 10 at night until 2 next morning.

3. The nearer to midday or noon the phase of the Moon happens, the more foul or wet weather may be expected during the next seven days.

4. The space for this calculation occupies from 10 in the forenoon until 2 in the afternoon. These observations refer principally to the Summer, though they affect Spring and Autumn nearly in the same ratio.

5. The Moon's change, first quarter, full and last quarter happening during six of the afternoon hours, i. e., from 4 to 10, may be followed by fair weather, but this is mostly dependent on the wind, as is noted in the table.

6. Though the weather, from a variety of irregular causes, is more uncertain in the latter part of Autumn, the whole of Winter and beginning of Spring, yet, in the main, the above observations will apply to those periods also.

7. To prognosticate correctly, especially in those cases where the wind is concerned, the observer should be in sight of a good vane, where the four cardinal points of the heavens are correctly placed.

Branson's Almanac is a household word—*Truth.*

4. The man who has faith in the laws governing the spirit of life, can
realize that the law of the Lord is perfect, converting the soul.—*Branson*.

TENDER AND TRUE.

Tender and true! Tender and true!
   Ah, Love, the sweet refrain,
Is set to music and my heart
   Repeats it o'er and o'er again.

Repeats it o'er and o'er again,
   With heart beats counting out the time;
And every hope and thought and wish
   Finds echo in its silvery chime.

Tender and true, tender and true,
   O Heart of sterling gold!
There is no richer gift in life
   Than what those two words hold.

Only be true and tender
   And I'll yield without one fear,
My heart into your keeping
   My future to your care.
          —*Rebecca Cameron, Hillsboro, N. C.*

ABOUT THE EYE.

SOME FACTS THAT EVERY ONE MAY NOT KNOW.

The upturned eye is typical of devotion.
Wide open eyes are indicative of rashness.
The eye is really a self adjustable telescope.
Cretia Borgia had prominent half-closed eyes.
Side-glancing eyes are always to be distrusted.
Brown eyes are said by oculists to be the strongest.
The eyes should not be used in weakness or sickness.
Small eyes are commonly supposed to indicate cunning.
Near-sighted people almost always have prominent eyes.
The proper distance between the eyes is the width of one eye.
There are from four to six grains of aqueous humor in the eye.
The downcast eye has in all ages been typical of modesty.
Many eyes supposed to be black are only a deep orange brown.
Eyes in rapid and constant motion betoken anxiety, fear or care.
People of melancholic temperament rarely have clear blue eyes.
The eyes of birds and fish are round, with no angles at the corners.
The chameleon is almost the only reptile provided with an eyelid.
The deer really weeps, its eyes being provided with larchymal glands.
Whenever blue occurs in the iris it is generally the predominant color.
Eyes with long, sharp corners indicate great discernment and penetration.
In all nocturnal animals the eyes are placed to look forward, as in the case of man.
The eye of the octopus is said to be black, large and as vicious as that of a snake.
In mythology, Pluto and the malevolent deities were represented with small eyes.

CAUSE OF HOG CHOLERA.

It comes from using impure water; so says Alfred Forbes, of Greenville, N. C. Every *wet* summer there is very little hog cholera, because there is plenty of fresh water on top of the ground for them to drink. Every *dry* summer we have much cholera, for example: this year. However, the dry years are much better for the health of man, because the water is deeper in the ground and purer.

MORAL.—Be certain to give your hogs plenty of good pure water.

5. The Christian religion leads a man towards the highest cultivation of all his best capabilities.—*Branson*.

1st Month.   JANUARY, 1897.   31 Days.

Moon's Phases.

	D. H. M.		D. H. M.
New Moon,	3 0 55 a. m.	Full Moon,	18 3 8 p. m.
First Quarter,	10 4 37 p. m.	Last Quarter,	25 3 0 p. m.

Day of Month.	Day of Week.	Sun rises.	Sun sets.	Sun slow.	Sun's decline south.	ASPECTS OF PLANETS AND OTHER MISCELLANEOUS MATTER.	Moon's place.	Moon rises or sets.	Moon south.	High tides.
1	Fri	7 10	4 58	4 22	57	NEW YEAR'S DAY.		5 52	m'rn	morn
2	Sat	7 10	5 0	4 22	52	Battle of Trenton 1777.		6 55	11 33	6 37
1.	*Second Sunday after Christmas.*							*Day's length 9 hours 51 min.*		
3	*C.*	7 10	5 1	5 22	46	Bat. Princeton 1777.		sets.	0 33	7 27
4	Mo	7 10	5 1	5 22	39	Vanderbilt d. 1877.		6 55	1 28	8 16
5	Tue	7 10	5 2	6 22	32	Bomb'dm't Richm'd 1781		7 42	2 18	9 2
6	We	7 9	5 3	6 22	25	☿ gr. Elon. E. EPIPHA.		8 48	3 4	9 47
7	Thu	7 9	5 4	7 22	17	1st S'. House burnt 1791		9 52	3 47	10 30
8	Fri	7 9	5 5	7 22	9	Forsyth Co. form'd 1848		10 48	4 28	11 1
9	Sat	7 9	5 6	8 22	0	Legislature met 1895.		11 47	5 8	11 58
2.	*First Sunday after Epiphany.*							*Day's length 9 hours 57 minutes.*		
10	*C.*	7 9	5 6	8 21	51	Stampact pas'd 1765		m'rn	5 49	0 37
11	Mo	7 9	5 7	8 21	42	First Gov. N.C. 1664.		0 46	6 32	1 28
12	Tue	7 9	5 8	9 21	32	Gaston Co. formed 1846.		1 46	7 16	2 21
13	We	7 9	5 9	9 21	22	☿ sta. Fox died 1681.		2 45	8 4	3 14
14	Thu	7 9	5 10	9 21	11	⊕ in Perihelion.		3 43	8 55	4 3
15	Fri	7 9	5 11	10 21	0	Andrew Jackson b. 1767		4 40	9 49	4 51
16	Sat	7 8	5 12	10 20	48	Gibbon d. 1794.		5 36	10 44	5 36
3.	*Second Sunday after Epiphany.*							*Day's length 10 hours 5 min.*		
17	*C.*	7 8	5 13	10 20	36	Dr. Franklin b. 1706		6 25	11 39	6 20
18	Mo	7 8	5 14	11 20	24	Gov. Jarvis b. 1836.		rises.	m'rn	7 1
19	Tue	7 8	5 15	11 20	11	GEN. LEE'S BIRTHDAY.		6 14	0 31	7 41
20	We	7 7	5 15	11 19	58	John Howard d. 1790.		7 23	1 22	8 23
21	Thu	7 7	5 16	12 19	44	♂ ♉ ☾ Gov. Bragg d, 1872		8 33	2 11	9 6
22	Fri	6 57	5 17	12 19	31	♂ ♉ sup. Bacon b.1561		9 40	2 59	9 49
23	Sat	7 6	5 18	12 19	16	Wm. Gaston d. 1844.		10 48	3 46	10 36
4.	*Third Sunday after Epiphany.*							*Day's length 10 hours 14 minutes.*		
24	*C.*	7 5	5 19	12 19	2	☾ gr. Hel. Lat. N.		m'rn	4 35	11 26
25	Mo	7 4	5 20	13 18	47	Fayette'v'le set. 1749		0 2	5 26	0 11
26	Tue	7 3	5 21	13 18	32	Battle of Newbern 1864.		1 16	6 20	1 20
27	We	7 2	5 22	13 18	16	Dr. Caldwell d. 1838.		2 29	7 18	2 21
28	Thu	7 2	5 23	13 18	0	Tripple Alliance 1867.		3 39	8 18	3 28
29	Fri	7 2	5 23	13 17	44	Kansas admitted 1861.		4 43	9 20	4 31
30	Sat	7 2	5 24	14 17	27	Charles I beheaded 1647.		5 38	10 20	5 29
5.	*Fourth Sunday after Epiphany.*							*Day's length 10 hours 23 minutes.*		
31	*C.*	7 2	5 25	14 17	10	Mrs. E. B. Englehard d. 1895.		6 23	11 16	6 22

WEATHER CONJECTURES—JANUARY—1, 2, fair and frosty; 3, 4, 5, 6, 7, 8, 9, frost unless wind be S. or S. W.; 10, 11, 12, 13, 14, 15, 16, 17, fair; 18, 19, 20, 21, 22, 23, 24, fair and mild; 25, 26, 27, 28, 29, 30, 31, generally fair and moderate weather.

5. The man who has *full faith in all* God's laws, and renders a perfect obedience, has peace flowing as a river, and a joy that is complete-*Branson*

BRANSON'S NORTH CAROLINA ALMANAC.   7

FARM AND GARDEN WORK FOR JANUARY.—Plant peas, beans, beets, onions, Irish potatoes, horse radish; sow turnips, spinach, lettuce, radish, parsley, carrots, salsify. Plant early peas; artichokes must now be dressed, also asparagus beds; this is the proper time to sow early spring tomatoes, etc.

Prepare land for the next crop, if not done. In the low country, if mud marsh or rushes are used, this is a good time to haul out and spread in the alleys, and throw upon it a light listing. Repair fences, plow, ditch, drain and manure. You can sow oats for a first crop.

THE LITTLE PATCHED TROUSERS.

How dear to my heart are the pants of my childhood,
  When fond recollection presents to view,
The pants that I wore in the deep tangled wild wood,
  And likewise the groves where the crab apple grew;
The wide-spreading seat with its little square patches,
  The pockets that bulged with my luncheon for noon,
And also with marbles and fish-worms and matches
  And gumdrops and kite strings from March until June—
The little patched trousers, the made-over trousers,
  The high-water trousers that fit me too soon.

No pantaloons ever performed greater service
  In filling the hearts of us youngsters with joy;
They made the descent from Adolphus to Jarvis,
  Right down through a family of ten little boys,
Though no fault of mine, known to me or to others,
  I'm the tenderest branch on our big family tree;
And having done service for nine older brothers,
  They came down to me slightly bagged at the knee—
The little patched trousers, the second-hand trousers,
  The old family trousers that bagged at the knee.
                                    —*Hon. Z. B. Vance.*

PLATONIC PHILOSOPHY.

Believe in Platonics? Why, no; not exactly:
  You see, it's right hard to define
Between the strong real, and purely ideal,
  A clear yet intangible line.

The theory's pretty; and very convenient!
  But, where distinctions are so very "thin."
It's sometimes quite vexing, as well as perplexing
  To settle just which it has been.

You swore in Platonics, and meant to be honest,
  It silenced all scruples the same.
Some day you discover the "friend" is a lover!
  The difference lies just in the name!

It is fatally baited for those who are mated
  With not over-dear husbands or wives,
For before it is over, this love under cover
  Makes shipwreck of one or more lives.

It is best to eschew what you'll certainly rue;
  If you make love, why call it love making,
To play with edged tools is the pastime of fools
  And ends always in tears or heart breaking.
                          —*Rebecca Cameron, Hillsboro, N. C.*

7. To give advice unsolicited is delightful; it so magnifies our self-esteem.—*Branson*.

8   BRANSON'S NORTH CAROLINA ALMANAC.

| 2d Month. | FEBRUARY, 1897. | 28 Days. |

Moon's Phases.

	D. H. M.		D. H. M.
New Moon,	1 3 5 p.m.	Full Moon,	17 5 3 a.m.
First Quarter,	9 2 17 p.m.	Last Quarter,	23 10 35 p.m

Day of Month	Day of Week	Sun sets	Sun sets	Sun slow	Sun's decline south	ASPECTS OF PLANETS AND OTHER MISCELLANEOUS MATTER.	Moon's Place	Moon rises or sets	Moon south	High tides
1	Mo	7 1	5 29	14	16 53	AN. ECLIPSE OF SUN		sets.	eve.	m'rn
2	Tue	7 1	5 30	14	16 36	3 sta. Pe'ce Conf '65		6 30	0 55	7 58
3	We	7 0	5 31	14	16 18	Gen. R. Barringer d.1895.		7 36	1 40	8 41
4	Thu	6 59	5 32	14	16 0	Galvani died 1770.		8 34	2 22	9 21
5	Fri	6 58	5 33	14	15 42	BRANSON'S BIRTHDAY'32		9 34	3 3	10 0
6	Sat	6 58	5 34	14	15 23	J. J, Daniel d. 1848.		10 34	3 44	10 36

6. Fifth Sunday after Trinity   Day's length 10 hours 37 minutes.

7	C.	6 57	5 34	14	15 4	Suez Canal com. 1867.		11 34	4 26	11 11
8	Mo	6 56	5 35	14	14 45	Bat. Roanoke Isla'd'1862		m'rn	5 9	11 48
9	Tue	6 55	5 36	14	14 26	Gen. Hancock d. '86.		0 33	5 56	0 29
10	We	6 54	5 37	14	14 6	Treaty of Paris 1763		1 31	6 45	1 31
11	Thu	6 53	5 38	14	13 46	Thos. A. Eddison b. 1847.		2 28	7 37	2 28
12	Fri	6 53	5 39	14	13 26	H. Seymour d. 1896.		3 24	8 31	3 24
13	Sat	6 52	5 40	14	13 6	Fernanno Wood d. 1881.		4 15	9 25	4 17

7. Septuagesima Sunday.   Day's length 10 hours 50 minutes.

14	C.	6 51	5 41	14	12 46	ST. VALENTINE'S DAY.		5 2	10 19	5 6
15	Mo	6 50	5 42	14	12 25	♀ gr. Elon. W.		5 43	11 11	5 52
16	Tue	6 49	5 43	14	12 4	Judge Battle buried 1879		rises.	m'rn	6 36
17	We	6 48	5 44	14	11 43	♀ in ☍.		6 15	0 . 2	7 18
18	Thu	6 47	5 45	14	11 22	☋ ♄ ⊙. Luth'r d.1546		7 28	0 51	8 0
19	Fri	6 46	5 46	15	11 0	♂♂♅. H.Vaughan d.'86		8 35	1 40	8 43
20	Sat	6 45.	5 47	14	10 39	Bat. of Olista, Fla., 1864		9 49.	2 30	9 26

8, Sexagesima Sunday.   Day's length 11 hours 5 minutes.

21	C.	6 43	5 48	14	10 17	Gov. Clark d. 1874.		11 5	3 21	10 13
22	Mo	6 42	5 48	14	9 55	WASHINGTON'S		m'rn	4 16	11 3
23	Tue	6 41	5 48	13	9 33	[BIRTHDAY 1732.		0 20	5 13	0 1
24	We	6 40	5 49	13	9 11	Monterey surrend'd 1846		1 31	6 13	0 53
25	Thu	6 39	5 50	13	8 49	Battle of Montreal 1775.		2 36	7 13	2 0
26	Fri	6 38	5 51	13	8 26	Bonaparte esc.Elba 1815		3 33	8 13	3 9
27	Sat	6 37	5 52	13	8 3	♀ in Aphelion.		4 20	9 9	4 13

9. Quinquagesima Sunday.   Day's length 11 hours 17 minutes.

| 28 | C. | 6 36 | 5 53 | 13 | 7 41 | Dr. Wingate d. 1879. | | 4 58 | 10 1 | 5 13 |

WEATHER CONJECTURES—FEBRUARY—1, 2, 3, 4, 5, 6, 7, 8, fair and mild; 9, 10, 11, 12, 13, 14, 15, 16, expect moderate and pleasant weather; 17, 18, 19, 20, 21, 22, look for rain ; 23, 24, 25, 26, 27, 28, fair and frosty.

8. A man in whose mind his own country is not *first*, is a man who himself is not *worthy* to be first in another country.—*Branson.*

FARM AND GARDEN WORK FOR FEBRUARY —Continue to sow peas, and such vegetables as were omitted in January. Plant pole beans, first crop (in the low country); full crop Irish potatoes, beets and carrots; dress artichokes and asparagus. Tomatoes, peppers and cucumbers sow in hot beds; put out mangoes.

This is considered the opening month of the planter's year. Continue preparing as in January. Sow oats for a full crop in the low country; plant Irish potatoes; make up sprout beds for sweet potatoes. Plant root crop of sweet potatoes.

BUREAU OF STATISTICS OF N. C. (Denominational).

LEVI BRANSON, Secretary.

DENOMINATIONS.	Number Ministers.	Number Churches.	Number Members.
White.			
Methodist Episcopal Church South	661	1,520	128,691
Methodist Episcopal Church	65	115	8,941
Wesleyan Methodist Church	7	7	141
Methodist Protestant Church	64	208	16,416
Christian (Followers of James O'Kelly)	60	101	9,000
Evangelical Lutheran	73	130	12,872
Presbyterian	149	336	30,278
Universalists	3	3	255
Protestant Episcopal	96	184	9,025
Missionary Baptist	*722	1,538	148,693
Primitive Baptist	150	317	11,914
Seventh Day Adventist	5	5	83
Free Will Baptist	160	168	10,224
Baptist Church of Christ	16	16	659
Old Two-Seed Baptist	9	9	183
Deciples of Christ (Campbellites)	98	186	12,437
Seventh Day Baptist	1	1	10
Reformed Church of U. S.	17	40	3,140
Church of Jesus Christ of Latter Day Saints	24	1	136
Friends	52	52	5,328
Dunkards	9	9	510
Moravians	7	19	3,548
Waldenses	1	1	215
Roman Catholics	24	24	2,640
Hebrews	4	4	386
Salvation Army	2	2	59
Advent Christian Church	18	18	1,549
Associate Reformed	20	20	2,109
Colored.			
Missionary Baptists	*572	1,131	109,871
African M. E. Zion Church	150	526	121,154
African M. E. Church	240	147	16,156
Colored M. E. Church in America	25	26	2,786
Methodist Episcopal	2	2	130
Protestant Episcopal	6	10	1,200
Congregational	20	20	1,002
Christians	50	53	3,746
Free Will Baptist	10	25	1,640
Primitive Baptist	15	20	1,000
Presbyterian North	173	306	17,851

*Quoted from Minutes Baptist State Convention, December 1895.

9. Our State is a diamond; let us polish it well.—*Branson*.

10   BRANSON'S NORTH CAROLINA ALMANAC.

3d Month.   **MARCH, 1897.**   **31 Days.**

Moon's Phases.

	D. H. M.		D. H. M.
☽ New Moon,	3 6 43 a.m.	☽ Full Moon,	18 4 19 p.m.
☽ First Quarter,	11 10 20 a.m.	☾ Last Quarter,	25 6 51 a.m.

Day of Month,	Day of Week.	Sun rises.	Sun sets.	Sun slow.	Sun's decline south.	ASPECTS OF PLANETS AND OTHER MISCELLANEOUS MATTER.	Moon's place.	Moon rises or sets.	Moon south.	High tides.
1	Mo	6 34	5 55	12	7 18	Bishop Andrews d. 1871	♋	5 30	m'rn	m'rn
2	Tue	6 32	5 56	12	6 55	☽ SHROVE TUESDAY.	♋	5 57	11 35	6 53
3	We	6 30	5 57	12	6 32	☽ ASH WEDNESDAY.	♌	sets.	0 17	7 37
4	Thu	6 28	5 58	12	6 9	♀ in Perihelion.	♌	7 20	0 58	8 16
5	Fri	6 26	6 0	12	5 46	Addison born 1750.	♒	8 21	1 39	8 52
6	Sat	6 24	6 0	11	5 22	Bat. of the Alamo 1836.	♒	9 21	2 21	9 25

10. First Sunday in Lent.   Day's length 11 hours 38 minutes.

7	*C.*	6 23	6 1	11	4 59	Bib. Society found'd 1804	♐	10 21	3 4	9 56
8	Mo	6 22	6 1	11	4 36	William III d. 1703.	♐	11 20	3 49	10 27
9	Tue	6 20	6 2	11	4 12	Battle Vera Cruz 1847.	♐	m'rn	4 37	11 0
10	We	6 18	6 3	10	3 49	☽ Bat. Manas. Junc. '62	♒	0 17	5 27	11 43
11	Thu	6 17	6 4	10	3 25	☽ Wm. Barringer d. '82	♒	1 13	6 19	0 46
12	Fri	6 16	6 5	10	3 1	First Parliam't Ass. 1683.	♓	2 5	7 12	1 43
13	Sat	6 14	6 6	9	2 38	Pocahontas d. 1616.	♓	2 52	8 5	2 44

11. Second Sunday in Lent.   Day's length 11 hours 53 minutes.

14	*C.*	6 13	6 6	9	2 14	West Point estab. 1802.	♈	3 35	8 58	3 41
15	Mo	6 12	6 7	9	1 50	Ex.sess. Leg. conv'd 1880	♈	4 12	9 48	4 35
16	Tue	6 11	6 8	9	1 27	♂ ☽ . Monroe b. 1751.	♉	4 45	10 38	5 23
17	We	6 9	6 9	8	1 3	☽ ST. PATRICK'S DAY.	♉	5 13	11 28	6 8
18	Thu	6 8	6 10	8	0 39	Suez Canal comp.'69	♊	rises	m'rn	6 53
19	Fri	6 6	6 11	8	0 16	☿ gr. Hel. Lat. S.	♊	7 28	0 18	7 36
20	Sat	6 4	6 12	7	no'th	☉ ent. ♈ . SPRING BEG.	♋	8 56	1 10	8 20

12. Third Sunday in Lent.   Day's length 12 hours 9 minutes.

21	*C.*	6 3	6 12	7	0 33	Lucknow fell 1858.	♌	10 4	2 5	9 6
22	Mo	6 2	6 13	7	0 57	♂ ♄ ☽ . Stamp Act 1765.	♌	11 19	3 4	9 53
23	Tue	6 0	6 13	7	1 20	Battle Winchester 1862.	♍	m'rn	4 5	10 47
24	We	5 59	6 14	6	1 44	☾ Queen Eliz'th d. 1603	♍	0 28	5 7	11 48
25	Thu	5 58	6 15	6	2 8	☾ Thames Tun. op. 1843	♎	1 28	6 8	0 31
26	Fri	5 57	6 16	6	2 31	♀ gr. Hel. Lat. N.	♎	2 19	7 5	1 39
27	Sat	5 55	6 17	5	2 55	Bruce crowned 1306.	♏	3 0	7 59	2 48

13. Fourth Sunday in Lent.   Day's length 12 hours 25 minutes.

28	*C.*	5 53	6 18	5	3 18	Davidson Coll. op'd 1857	♏	3 32	8 47	3 53
29	Mo	5 51	6 18	5	3 41	Brit. Museum fn'd 1753.	♏	4 0	9 33	4 51
30	Tue	5 50	6 19	4	4 5	Bat. Somerville, Ky. 1863	♐	4 24	10 15	5 43
31	We	5 48	6 20	4	4 28	S. M. Parish d. 1895.	♐	4 44	10 56	6 28

WEATHER CONJECTURES—MARCH—1, 2, 3, fair and frosty; 3, 4. 5, 6, 7. 8. 9, 10. expect storms; 11. 12, 13, 14, 15, 16, 17, look for cold and high winds; 18. 19, 20, 21, 22, 23, 24, fair; 25, 26, 27, 28, 29, 30, 31. stormy weather.

10. The *mind crop* is the greatest crop that can be raised on any farm or in any State.—*Branson.*

FARM AND GARDEN WORK FOR MARCH.—Plant bush squash, pumpkins, water and muskmelons, okra, Guinea squash or egg-plant, sugar beets, carrots, beans, peas. radishes, lettuce, corn, celery (first crop), tanyah and mangoes in the low country and elsewhere as soon as danger from frost is over.

This is the first planting month for cotton, corn and rice. Plant your high lands first; leave the low lands for April. Plant rice about the 20th of the month.

THE SWEETEST PART OF LIFE.

You may talk about a feller
  When he's in his courtin' days,
And I know he's mighty mellor
  And has awful catfish ways,
But that feller then's a livin'
  'Way ahead of you or I—
Not a sixpence is he givin'
  What's a comin' by and by.

And the future has no shadder
  For a feller in his state:
He's a climbin' Cupid's ladder,
  Not for fame but for a mate;
And he has no thought of stoppin'
  Till the proper one he's found,
And the question he's a poppin'
  As he goes from 'round to 'round.

He's not doin' much at savin'
  Of the little that he makes—
There are other things he's cravin'
  More than large and bulky stakes;
Plenty of love within a cottage
  Will do them to begin—
Not knowin', on sich pottage
  He will grow uncommon thin.

But let's not disturb his dreamin',
  It's the sweetest part of life.
When you're hustlin' and a schemin'
  For to try and get a wife—
And you're mighty shore to find her
  If you'll keep on lookin' 'round,
For there's plenty of them kinder
  Jest a waitin' to be found.

And my advice to ev'ry feller
  Of the single harness kind
Is to find one and to tell her
  What's a weighin' on his mind,
And my all's agin a shillin'
  That he'll always bless the day
When she told him she was willin'
  To be his'n right away.
          —*Sam Bean in Charlotte Observer.*

Little Dick: "Papa, didn't you tell mamma we must economize?" 'Papa: "I did my son." Little Dick: "Well, I was thinkin' that mebbe if you'd get me a pony, I wouldn't wear out so many shoes."—*Good News.*

11. 'The *mind crop* in North Carolina is better than ever before.— *Branson*.

4th Month.	APRIL, 1897.	30 Days.

Moon's Phases.

	D. M. H.		D. M. H.
New Moon,	1 11 15p.m	Full Moon,	17 1 17a.m.
First Quarter,	10 3 18a.m.	Last Quarter,	23 4 39p.m.

Day of Month.	Day of Week.	Sun rises.	Sun sets.	Sun slow.	Sun's decline north.	ASPECTS OF PLANETS AND OTHER MISCELLANEOUS MATTER.	Moon's place.	Moon rises or sets.	Moon south.	High tides.
1	Thu	5 47	6 22	4	4 51	ALL FOOLS DAY.	≈	5, 12	eve.	m'rn
2	Fri	5 46	6 23	3	5 14	Richmond sur 1865	≈	sets.	0 18	7 47
3	Sat	5 44	6 23	3	5 37	and evacuated 1865.	≈	8 12	1 1	8 20

14. Fifth Sunday in Lent.   Day's length 12 hours 42 minutes.

4	C.	5 42	6 24	3	6 0	Gen. Harrison d. 1871.	♐	9 11	1 45	8 51
5	Mo	5 41	6 25	3	6 23	Jefferson born 1743.	♐	10 9	2 32	9 20
6	Tue	5 39	6 26	2	6 45	Battle of Shiloh 1862.	♐	11 5	3 21	9 50
7	We	5 38	6 27	2	7 8	Socrates died 333 B. C.	♑	11 58	4 12	10 25
8	Thu	5 36	6 28	2	7 30	☿ in ☋. DeMedici d.1492	♑	m'rn	5 4	11 12
9	Fri	5 35	6 29	1	7 52	Lee sur. '65.	♑	0 46	5 56	0 5
10	Sat	5 34	6 30	1	8 14	A, T. Stuart d. 1876.	♑	1 30	6 47	1 2

15. Palm Sunday.   Day's length 12 hours 58 minutes.

11	C.	5 33	6 31	1	8 36	Benj. West died 1820.	♒	2 9	7 37	2 3
12	Mo	5 31	6 31	1	8 58	☿ in Perihelion.	♒	2 42	8 25	3 3
13	Tue	5 30	6 32	0	9 20	Raf'n sur. to Sherman '65	♓	3 10	9 14	4 0
14	We	5 28	6 33	fast	9 42	Lincoln assassinated '65.	♓	3 37	10 3	4 52
15	Thu	5 27	6 34	1	10 3	Andrew Johnson Pres.'65	♈	4 8	10 54	5 40
16	Fri	5 26	6 34	1	10 24	GOOD FRIDAY.	♈	4 37	11 48	6 28
17	Sat	5 24	6 35	1	10 45	Dr. Franklin d. 1790	♈	rises.	m'rn	7 16

16. Easter Sunday.   Day's length 13 hours 13 minutes.

18	C.	5 23	6 36	1	11 6	Luther at Worms 1521.	♉	8 57	0 47	8 2
19	Mo	5 22	6 37	1	11 27	David S. Reid b. 1813.	♉	10 12	1 49	8 50
20	Tue	5 21	6 38	1	11 47	Napoleon 3d born 1808.	♉	11 19	2 53	9 42
21	We	5 20	6 39	1	12 8	Santa Anna cap. 1836.	♊	m'rn	3 57	10 38
22	Thu	5 18	6 40	2	12 28	☿ gr. Het. Lat. N.	♊	0 14	4 58	11 35
23	Fri	5 17	6 41	2	12 48	Cervantes d. 1616.	♋	0 59	5 54	0 12
24	Sat	5 15	6 41	2	13 7	Dr. McKee died 1875.	♋	1 35	6 45	1 16

17. Low Sunday.   Day's length 13 hours 27 minutes.

25	C.	5 14	6 41	2	13 27	Dr. A. Smedes d. 1877.	♋	2 3	7 31	2 23
26	Mo	5 13	6 43	2	13 46	♃ sta. Johnson sur. '65.	♌	2 28	8 15	3 26
27	Tue	5 12	6 43	3	14 5	Emerson died 1882.	♌	2 50	8 56	4 23
28	We	5 11	6 44	3	14 24	☿ gr. Elon. E.	♍	3 16	9 36	5 16
29	Thu	5 10	6 45	3	14 43	La. ceded to U. S. 1803.	♍	3 38	10 17	6 1
30	Fri	5 9	6 46	3	15 1	Washington inaug. 1789	♍	4 2	10 59	6 43

WEATHER CONJECTURES—APRIL—1, 2, 3, 4, 5, 6, 7, 8, 9, fair and frosty; 10, 11, 12, 13, 14, 15, 16, snow and stormy; 17, 18, 19, 20, 21, 22, frost, unless the wind be S or S. W ; 23, 24, 25, 26, 27, 28, 29, 30, look for fair weather.

12. The *mind crop* should be planted early and cultivated better than cotton or tobacco.—*Branson.*

FARM AND GARDEN WORK FOR APRIL.—Whatever has been omitted in March, do not neglect any longer. Sow green glazed cabbage, pickling cabbage, full crop of cauliflower and brocoli, okra, tomatoes, peppers, beets, carrots, leeks, melons, cucumbers, celery.

Full crops of corn, cotton and rice should be put in during this month. Plant your lowland corn. Commence early to hoe your young cotton, and thin out to stand. Plant pumpkins for a field crop.

A COUNTRY CHRISTMAS.

Hear the fiddles hummin'—
  Holly hangin' high;
(Knowed it was a-comin'
  Fourth o' last July—
Christmas!) How the fire
  Blazes—red an' blue!
Take your place, Maria!
  (Who's been kissin' you?)

It's Christmas in the country,
  And Christmas in the sky;
Mistletoe is temptin'
  An' the holly hangin' high!

Banjos—fiddles playin';
  Almost shake the shed!
(Moll, what's Dick been sayin',
  Makes your cheeks so red?)
Now the dancers rally—
  Liveliest set in town!
Tip it light, Miss Sally!
  Come in, Betsy Brown!

For it's Christmas in the country,
  An' there's kissin' on the sly;
Mistletoe is temptin'
  An' the holly's hangin' high.

Music's goin' steady;
  Now the figures call:
Ladies! are you ready?
  Swing your partners all!
Lively now! Miss Molly—
  Come in with the girls!
(Dick's been kissin' Polly—
  Rumpled all her curls!)

For it's Christmas in the country—
  Music in your feet;
An' the mistletoe is tempting',
  An' kissin's mighty sweet!

Now the dancin' is over—
  Fiddles stopped their fuss,
Talk 'bout folks in clover—
  Take a look at us!
Hick'ry nuts a crackin'—
  Eggnog—apple pie;
Pretty lips a-smackin'—
  Heaven on the sly!

For it's Christmas in the country,
  An' it's Christmas in the sky,
An' the mistletoe is temptin',
  An' the holly's hangin' high!

14   BRANSON'S NORTH CAROLINA ALMANAC.

5th Month.   MAY, 1897.   31 Days.

Moon's Phases.

	D. H. M.		D. H. M.
New Moon,	1 3 38 p.m.	Full Moon,	16 8 46 a.m.
First Quarter,	9 4 28 p.m.	Last Quarter,	23 4 26 a.m.
		New Moon,	31 7 17 a.m.

Day of Month	Day of Week	Sun rises	Sun sets	Sun fast	Sun's decline north	ASPECTS OF PLANETS AND OTHER MISCELLANEOUS MATTER.	Moon's place	Moon rises or sets	Moon south	High tides
1	Sat	5 8	6 47	3	15 19	QUEEN OF MAY.		4 31	eve.	m'rn

18. Second Sunday after Easter.   Day's length 13 hours 41 minutes.

2	C.	5 7	6 48	3	15 37	S. H. Young died 1882.		sets.	0 29	7 50
3	Mo	5 6	6 49	3	15 54	Gov. Tryon met Ass. 1765		8 58	1 17	8 19
4	Tue	5 5	6 49	3	16 12	Dr. Wm. G. Hill d. 1777		9 53	2 8	8 49
5	We	5 4	6 50	3	16 29	Bat. Williamsburg 1862.		10 43	2 59	9 21
6	Thu	5 3	6 51	4	16 46	Bat. Wilderness, Va., '64		11 29	3 51	10 3
7	Fri	5 2	6 51	4	17 2	. M. C. Doub d. 1876		m'rn	4 41	10 52
8	Sat	5 1	6 52	4	17 18	Battle of Palo Alto 1846.		.0 8	5 30	11 51

19. Third Sunday after Easter.   Day's length 13 hours 53 minutes.

9	C.	5 0	6 53	4	17 34	Bat. Spots'lva CH '64		0 41	6 18	0 25
10	Mo	4 59	6 54	4	17 50	8 sta. CONFED. DEC.		1 10	7 4	1 23
11	Tue	4 58	6 54	4	18 5	Queen Mary d. 1699.		1 37	7 52	2 24
12	We	4 57	6 55	4	18 20	Battle Raymond 1863.		2 4	8 40	3 23
13	Thu	4 56	6 56	4	18 35	Bat. Brazos, Texas, 1865.		2 35	9 31	4 20
14	Fri	4 55	6 57	4	18 49	Battle Resaca, Ga, 1864.		3 2	10 27	5 15
15	Sat	4 54	6 58	4	19 3	Gov. Colquit Met. Hall '86		3 33	11 27	6 8

20. Fourth Sunday after Easter.   Day's length 14 hours 6 minutes.

16	C.	4 53	6 59	4	19 17	8 in .		rises.	m'rn	7 0
17	Mo	4 53	7 0	4	19 31	John Penn b. 1741.		9 0	0 32	7 50
18	Tue	4 52	7 1	4	19 44	h ⊙. Matam'ras fell '46		10 1	1 38	8 42
19	We	4 52	7 1	4	19 57	Vicksburg defended '63.		10 53	2 42	9 34
20	Thu	4 51	7 2	4	20 9	MECKL. DEC. INDEP. 1775		11 33	3 43	10 28
21	Fri	4 50	7 3	4	20 21	♂ 8 ⊙ Inf N.C. sec. 1861		m'rn	4 38	11 26
22	Sat	4 49	7 3	4	20 33	♂ in Aphelion.		0 7	5 27	0 1

21. Rogation Sunday.   Day's length 14 hours 16 minutes.

23	C.	4 48	7 4	3	20 44	Livingston d. 1886.		0 31	6 12	0 31
24	Mo	4 48	7 5	3	20 55	Qu. Victoria b. 1819.		0 55	6 55	1 49
25	Tue	4 48	7 5	3	21 6	Bat. Winchester, Va., '62		1 18	7 36	2 49
26	We	4 47	7 6	3	21 16	8 in Aph. Calvin d. 1564		1 43	8 16	3 48
27	Thu	4 47	7 7	3	21 26	ASCENSION DAY.		2 6	8 58	4 41
28	Fri	4 46	7 8	3	21 36	Noah Webster d. 1843.		2 33	9 41	5 30
29	Sat	4 46	7 9	3	21 45	Rhode Island adm. 1790.		3 3	10 26	6 11

22. Sunday after Ascension.   Day's length 14 hours 25 minutes.

| 30 | C. | 4 45 | 7 10 | 3 | 21 54 | FED. DEC. DAY. | | 3 40 | 11 14 | 6 47 |
| 31 | Mo | 4 45 | 7 11 | 3 | 22 2 | Bat. Fair Oaks 1862. | | sets. | eve. 4 | 7 18 |

WEATHER CONJECTURES—MAY—1, 2, 3, 4, 5, 6, 7, 8, changeable; 9, 10, 11, 12, 13, 14, 15, fair; 16, 17, 18, 19, 20, 21, 22, changeable; 23, 24, 25, 26, 27, 28, 29, 30, expect rain; 31, wind and rain.

14. The greatest possibilities of a man are on his native heath; if he is great on another heath, he is still less than a native ought to have been.—*Branson*

BRANSON'S NORTH CAROLINA ALMANAC.   15

FARM AND GARDEN WORK FOR MAY.—Plant snap beans and squashes. Sow cabbages for winter use, cauliflower, brocoli, celery, beets, carrots, salsify. Plant cucumbers, melons and pumpkins for late crop. Gather herbs for drying; always dry gently in the shade.

Look well to your hoeings and plowings. Continue to plant corn in low lands. Sow first crop of early cow peas. Rice planting is generally postponed until June, as the birds are very bad in May, and the May bird is exceedingly destructive.

INCOGNITO.

(A LEAP YEAR LYRIC.)

If, hiding now my face from thee,
  I should reveal my heart,
And thou therein couldst only see
  How dear to me thou art,
Thou wouldst not wantonly disdain
  A sanctuary where
Thine image must enthroned remain
  The sovereign idol there:
Then howsoever high thy state,—
  Mine howsoever low,
I would not murmer at my fate,
  Nor weary of its woe;
For I would know thy heart had seen
  No heart so leal as mine,
And wert thou worshipped as a queen,
  Less royalty were thine!

I would not quench this passion fraught
  With tenderness so sweet,
Though I may only lay in thought
  Its treasures at thy feet;
For if—concealing from thy sight
  The altar and its flame,
I pass again into the night
  As lonely as I came:—
Unseen—thy sorrows still to weep—
  Unknown, thy joy to share,
One hope would yet survive to keep
  My spirit from despair:
Mayhap a fairer day will dawn,
  And I may live to see
Thy heart from lighter loves withdrawn—
  Then—thou wilt come to me!

—*Theo. H. Hill.*

DOMINICAL LETTER.

I am often asked the meaning of "Dominical Letter." Dominical is derived from the Latin word *dominus*, which means master or lord. The first seven letters of the alphabet are used in turn to represent the Lord's day or Sunday in the Almanacs. The letter so used is called the Dominical or governing letter.   LEVI BRANSON.

The lecturer inquired dramatically, "Can any one in this room tell me of a perfect man?" There was a dead silence. "Has any one," he continued, "heard of a perfect woman?" Then a patient-looking little woman in a black dress rose up at the back of the auditorium and answered: "There was one. I've often heard of her, but she's dead now. She was my husband's first wife."

15. It is strange how freely we *give away* our *own* knowledge, and how freely we *pay high prices* for the knowledge we obtain from others.—*Branson.*

6th Month. JUNE, 1897. 30 Days.

Moon's Phases.

	D.	H.	M.		D.	H.	M.
First Quarter,	8	1	54 a.m.	Last Quarter,	21	6	15 p.m.
Full Moon,	14	3	53 p.m.	New Moon,	29	9	47 p.m.

Day of Month.	Day of Week.	Sun rises.	Sun sets.	Sun fast.	Sun's decline north.	Aspects of Planets and Other Miscellaneous Matter.	Moon's place.	Moon rises or sets.	Moon south.	High tides.
1	Tue	4 44	7 11	2	22 10	Battle Cold Harbor 1864.		8 41	eve.	m'rn
2	We	4 44	7 12	2	22 18	☿ sta. Marietta taken '64		9 26	1 47	8 23
3	Thu	4 43	7 12	2	22 25	Jeff. Davis born 1808.		10 6	2 38	9 1
4	Fri	4 42	7 13	2	22 32	George I born 1738.		10 42	3 27	9 43
5	Sat	4 41	7 13	2	22 39	Telegraph in China 1871.		11 13	4 15	10 34
23.	Pentecost—Whit Sunday.					Day's length 13 hours 33 minutes.				
6	*C.*	4 41	7 14	2	22 45	Patrick Henry d. 1799.		11 40	5 1	11 30
7	Mo	4 41	7 14	1	22 51	Rob't Bruce d. 1329.		m'rn	5 46	0 1
8	Tue	4 41	7 15	1	22 56	Bat. Cross Keys 1862		0 4	6 33	0 47
9	We	4 41	7 15	1	23 1	Georgia chartered 1732.		0 34	7 21	1 46
10	Thu	4 41	7 16	1	23 5	☌ ♆ ☉. Dickens d. 1870		1 1	8 12	2 48
11	Fri	4 41	7 16	1	23 9	Sherman at Kennesaw '64		1 31	9 9	2 52
12	Sat	4 41	7 16	0	23 13	☌ ♅ ♄ ☽. Bryant d. 1878.		2 11	10 10	4 55
24.	Trinity Sunday.					Day's length 14 hours 35 minutes.				
13	*C.*	4 41	7 16		23 16	Gen. Scott b. 1786.		2 57	11 15	5 55
14	Mo	4 41	7 17	slow	23 19	1st pros. by Nero 64.		rises.	m'rn	6 49
15	Tue	4 41	7 18		23 22	☿ gr. Elon. W.		8 40	0 21	7 42
16	We	4 41	7 18	0	23 24	☿ gr. Hel. Lat. S.		9 26	1 25	8 33
17	Thu	4 41	7 19	1	23 25	Addison died 1719.		10 2	2 24	9 23
18	Fri	4 41	7 19	1	23 27	☌ ♄ ♅ Bat. Waterloo 1815		10 33	3 17	10 15
19	Sat	4 42	7 19	1	23 27	Council of Nice 325		10 57	4 6	11 5
25.	First Sunday after Trinity.					Day's length 14 hours 36 minutes.				
20	*C.*	4 43	7 19	1	23 28	☉ ent. ♋. SUM. BEG		11 21	4 50	11 59
21	Mo	4 43	7 19	2	23 28	The Bl'k Hole tr. 1756		11 47	5 33	0 16
22	Tue	4 43	7 19	2	23 27	Bat. Ramseur's Mills 1780		m'rn	6 14	1 10
23	We	4 43	7 19	2	23 27	Bat. of Chickahominy '62		0 9	6 55	2 6
24	Thu	4 43	7 19	2	23 25	ST. JOHN BAPTIST.		0 35	7 38	3 5
25	Fri	4 43	7 20	2	23 24	♀ in Aphelion.		1 5	8 23	4 2
26	Sat	4 44	7 20	3	23 22	☌ ♀ ☽. L. Bonaparte d. '46		1 39	9 10	4 50
26.	Second Sunday after Trinity.					Day's length 14 hours 36 minutes.				
27	*C.*	4 44	7 20	3	23 19	Big fire in Raleigh 1883.		2 20	9 59	5 36
28	Mo	4 44	7 20	3	23 16	Vicksburg bomb. '62		3 5	10 50	6 13
29	Tue	4 45	7 20	3	23 13	Henry Clay d. 1852.		3 58	11 43	6 49
30	We	4 45	7 20	3	23 9	Montezuma d. 1530.		sets.	0 34	7 24

WEATHER CONJECTURES—JUNE—1, 2, 3, 4, 5, 6, 7, wind and rain; 8, 9, 10, 11, 12, 13, fair; 14, 15, 16, 17, 18, 19, 20, changeable; 21, 22, 23, 24, 25, 26, 27, 28, fair if wind N. W., rainy if S. or S. W.; 29, 30, fair.

FARM AND GARDEN WORK FOR JUNE.—Sow full crops of cabbages for
fall and winter use. Cauliflower and brocoli may yet be sown, also a
few carrots. Continue to sow tomatoes, okra, radishes, snap beans.
Transplant leeks: pull and dry onions, garlic and eschalots. A few
cucumbers and melons plant for a late crop, and a few ruta baga turnips.

Keep constantly at the plow and hoe; this is the most important grass
month! If the vines from your sweet potato sprout-bed are fit you can
draw and plant out first good rain. Sow cow-peas between your corn
hills and rows. The end of this month is a good time to put in the first
crop of standing field peas.

A LITTLE HEROINE.

"Nannie, dear, I want you to hem those napkins this afternoon without fail. Can I trust you to do it? I must go out for the whole afternoon,
and cannot remind you of them," said Mrs. Barton to her little girl.

"Yes mother, dear, I will. You can trust me," said Nannie.

Now Nannie did not like to hem napkins any better than you do; but
she went at once to her work basket, took out her needle and thread
and thimble, and began work. Pretty soon she heard the sound of
music. It came nearer, and at last it sounded right in front of the house.
She dropped her sewing to run to the window, and then she stopped.

"No; I promised mother, and she trusted me," said Nannie to herself; and she sat down again and went to sewing. Soon the door burst
open, and in rushed several little girls.

"Nannie! Nannie! where are you? There's a monkey out here and a
trained dog, and they're playing lovely tricks! Come on!"

"I can't. I promised mother, and she trusted me," she answered.

They coaxed and scolded, but all to no purpose. So they left her.

Just as she finished the last napkin, her mother came in. "My little
heroine!" she said, as she kissed Nannie.

"Why, mother, I didn't save anybody's life or do anything brave; I
only kept my promise," answered Nannie, wonderingly.

"It is sometimes harder to keep a promise and do one's duty than to
save a life. You did a brave, noble thing, and I thank God for you, my
dear," said Mrs. Barton.—*Our Little Ones.*

TWELVE CONUNDRUMS.

What is that which increases the more you take from it?—A hole.

Why are coals in London like towns given up to plunder?—Because
they are sacked and burnt.

Why is a gatepost like a potato? Because they are both put into the
ground to propagate.

What word may be pronounced quicker by adding a syllable to it?
Quick.

What is that which Adam never saw, never possed, and yet gave two
to each of his children? Parents.

What is that which we often see made, but never see after it is made?
A noise.

What is that which no one wishes to have and no one wishes to lose?
A bald head.

What is the difference between a sailor and a beer drinker? One puts
his sail up and the other puts his ale down.

What is that which is above all human imperfections, and yet shelters
and protects the weakest and wickedest as well as the wisest and best of
mankind? A hat.

What is that which is often brought to the table, always cut, and
never eaten? A pack of cards.

7th Month.   JULY, 1897.   31 Days.

Moon's Phases.

	D. H. M.		D. H. M.
☽ First Quarter,	7 8 24 a.m.	☾ Last Quarter,	21 10 0 a.m
● Full Moon,	13 11 44 p.m.	● New Moon,	29 10 49 a.m

Day of Month.	Day of Week.	Sun rises.	Sun sets.	Sun slow.	Sun's decline north.	ASPECTS OF PLANETS AND OTHER MISCELLANEOUS MATTER.	Moon's place.	Moon rises or sets.	Moon south.	High Tides.
1	Thu	4 45	7 20	4 23	5	⊕ in Aphelion.		8 43	eve.	m'rn
2	Fri	4 46	7 20	4 23	1	Garfield assassin't'd 1881		9 16	2 13	8 42
3	Sat	4 47	7 20	4 22	56	♂♂☽. Prov. 12:2.		9 43	2 59	9 26
27.			**Third Sunday after Trinity.**			**Day's length 14 hours 33 minutes.**				
4	*C.*	4 47	7 20	4 22	50	♂☽☽. INDE. DAY 1776.		10 8	3 45	10 14
5	Mo	4 48	7 19	4 22	45	☿ in ☾. Monroe d. 1881.		10 36	4 30	11 4
6	Tue	4 48	7 19	5 22	38	Hamlin d. 1891.		11 5	5 17	11 59
7	We	4 49	7 19	5 22	32	♀ gr. Elon. W.		11 32	6 6	0 15
8	Thu	4 50	7 19	5 22	25	Vicksburg cap. 1863.		m'rn	6 58	1 13
9	Fri	4 50	7 19	5 22	18	☿ in Perihelion.		0 6	7 56	2 20
10	Sat	4 51	7 18	5 22	10	♂ ♄ ☽.		0 49	8 57	3 32
28.			**Fourth Sunday after Trinity.**			**Day's length 14 hours 26 minutes.**				
11	*C.*	4 52	7 18	5 22	2	J. Q. Adams b. 1767.		3 39	10 2	4 40
12	Mo	4 52	7 18	5 21	54	Bat. of Bayou 1690.		2 41	11 6	5 43
13	Tue	4 53	7 17	6 21	45	Gen. Fremont d. 1890		rises.	m'rn	6 40
14	We	4 53	7 17	6 21	36	Peace Cong. London 1890		7 57	0 7	7 32
15	Thu	4 54	7 16	6 21	26	♂ ☿ ⊙ superior.		8 32	1 3	8 21
16	Fri	4 55	7 16	6 21	16	Mrs. Lincoln d. 1882 .		8 57	1 55	9 7
17	Sat	4 55	7 15	6 21	6	Cownpore cap. 1857.		9 21	2 42	9 53
29.			**Fifth Sunday after Trinity.**			**Day's length 14 hours 19 minutes.**				
18	*C.*	4 56	7 15	6 20	55	Kirk in Yanceyville '70.		9 50	3 26	10 38
19	Mo	4 57	7 14	6 20	44	☿ gr. Hel. Lat. N.		10 12	4 9	11 20
20	Tue	4 57	7 13	6 20	33	Bat. Winchester Va. '64.		10 36	4 51	11 59
21	We	4 58	7 13	6 20	21	Bat. Bull Run 1862.		11 7	5 33	0 20
22	Thu	4 59	7 12	6 20	9	Electricity 1850.		11 38	6 18	1 13
23	Fri	5 0	7 12	6 19	57	Read Branson Maxims.		m'rn	7 4	2 13
24	Sat	5 1	7 11	6 19	44	Bolivar b. 1783.		0 15	7 52	3 15
30.			**Sixth Sunday after Trinity.**			**Day's length 14 hours 9 minutes.**				
25	*C.*	5 2	7 11	6 19	31	Bat. Lundy's Lane 1814.		1 0	8 43	4 11
26	Mo	5 3	7 10	6 19	18	Argentine Revolu. 1890.		1 49	9 35	4 58
27	Tue	5 3	7 9	6 19	4	Cab strike in London '58.		2 46	10 27	5 42
28	We	5 3	7 8	6 18	50	♄ stationary.		3 47	11 19	6 21
29	Thu	5 4	7 7	6 18	36	An. ecl. of sun, visibl.		sets.	ev 8	7 0
30	Fri	5 5	7 6	6 18	22	♂ ☿ ☽. Wm. Penn d. 1718		7 47	0 56	7 39
31	Sat	5 6	7 6	6 18	7	Diving bell invent. 1538.		8 13	1 43	8 20

WEATHER CONJECTURES—JULY—1, 2, 3, 4, 5, 6, fair; 7, 8, 9, 10, 11, 12, changeable; 13, 14, 15, 16, 17, 18, 19, 20, fair; 21, 22, 23, 24, changeable; 25, 26, 27, 28, frequent showers; 29, 30, 31, look for showers.

FARM AND GARDEN WORK FOR JULY.—Sow cabbages, but protect from hot sun when young. Water at night. Plant snap beans and a few Irish potatoes. Continue to sow radishes, lettuce, endive, cresses, mustard and small salading. The early Dutch turnip is the best to sow for the first crop; follow with the yellow Swedish or ruta-baga.

Now do not omit to sow full crops of standing cow-peas. Sow a few turnips, carrots and beets as field crops, though the hot suns are apt to destroy them; should they escape they will be fine; the next month is the best for these crops.

SEEING THE POINT.

A boy returned from school one day with the report that his scholarship had fallen below the usual average.

"Son," said his father, "you've fallen behind this month, haven't you?"

"Yes, sir."

"How did that happen?"

"Don't know, sir."

The father knew, if the son did not. He had observed a number of dime novels scattered about the house; but had not thought it worth while to say anything until a fitting opportunity should offer itself. A basket of apples stood upon the floor, and he said:

"Empty those apples, and take the basket and bring it to me half full of chips."

Suspecting nothing, the boy obeyed.

"And now," he continued, "put those apples back into the basket."

When half the apples were replaced, the boy said:

"Father, they roll off. I can't put any more in."

"Put them in, I tell you."

"But, father, I can't put them in."

"Put them in? No, of course you can't put them in. You said you didn't know why you fell behind at school, and I will tell you why. Your mind is like that basket. It will not hold more than so much. And here you've been the past month filling it up with chip dirt—dime novels."

The boy turned on his heel, whistled, and said: "Whew! I see the point." Not a dime novel has been seen in the house from that day to this.

TELL ME SO.

If you love me tell me so,
Wait not 'till the summer glow
Fades in autumn's changeful light,
Amber clouds and purple night;
Wait not 'till the winter hours
Heap with snow drifts all the flowers,
Till the tide of life runs low—
If you love me tell me so.

If you love me tell me so,
While the river's dreamy flow
Holds the love-enchanted hours,
Steeped in music, crowned with flowers,
Ere the summer's vibrant days
Vanish in the opal haze;
Ere is hushed the music flow—
If you love me tell me so.

If you love me tell me so,
Let me hear the sweet words low;
Let me know, while life is fair
While in womanhood's first bloom,
Ere shall come dark days of gloom,
In the first fresh dawning glow—
If you love me tell me so.   —*Lillian Whiting.*

19. Much of our best work is unsuspected by *ourselves*, and even by the *recipients*.—*Branson.*

8th Month. AUGUST, 1897. 31 Days.

Moon's Phases.

	D.	H.	M.		D.	H.	M.
☽ First Quarter,	5	1	16p.m.	☾ Last Quarter,	20	3	21a.m.
Full Moon,	12	9	14a.m.	New Moon,	27	10	21p.m.

Day of Month.	Day of Week.	Sun rises.	Sun sets.	Sun slow.	Sun's decline north.	ASPECTS OF PLANETS AND OTHER MISCELLANEOUS MATTER.	Moon's place.	Moon rises or sets.	Moon south.	High Tides.
31. Seventh Sunday after Trinity. Day's length 13 hours 59 minutes.										
1	*C.*	5 6	7 5	6	17 52	☌♃☽. George II cr. 1714.		8 41	eve.	m'rn
2	Mo	5 7	7 4	6	17 36	☍ sta. Bat. Pleeva 1877		9 9	3 15	9 53
3	Tue	5 8	7 3	6	17 20	Columbus left Spain 1492		9 35	4 3	10 43
4	We	5 9	7 2	6	17 4	Tilden d. 1886.		10 7	4 54	11 25
5	Thu	5 10	7 1	6	16 48	Battle Athens 1861.		10 46	5 49	0 1
6	Fri	5 11	7 1	6	16 31	☌♄☽. Ft Gains sur. 1864		11 33	6 48	1 0
7	Sat	5 11	7 0	6	16 15	Barzelius d. 1848.		m'rn	7 50	2 0
32. Eighth Sunday after Trinity. Day's length 13 hours 46 minutes.										
8	*C.*	5 12	6 58	5	15 57	Sp'nish Armada des. 1588		0 29	8 52	3 16
9	Mo	5 13	6 56	5	15 40	Gov. Graham d. 1875.		1 33	9 53	4 28
10	Tue	5 14	6 55	5	15 22	Battle Oak Hill 1861.		2 43	10 50	5 31
11	We	5 14	6 54	5	15 5	Card. Newman d. '90		3 55	11 43	6 27
12	Thu	5 15	6 53	5	14 47	☿ in ☋. R E. Lee d. '70		rises.	m'rn	7 16
13	Fri	5 16	6 52	5	14 28	☌☿♃. Conova d. 1822.		7 23	0 32	8 0
14	Sat	5 17	6 51	4	14 10	Battle of Hastings 1066.		7 50	1 18	8 43
33. Ninth Sunday after Trinity. Day's length 13 hours 32 minutes.										
15	*C.*	5 18	6 50	4	13 51	Napoleon b. 1769.		8 16	2 2	9 25
16	Mo	5 19	6 49	4	13 32	Napoleon at Helena 1815		8 38	2 45	10 7
17	Tue	5 19	6 48	4	13 13	Snr. of Burgoyne 1777.		9 4	3 27	10 49
18	We	5 20	6 46	4	12 53	Cor. Stone U.S. Cap 1793		9 36	4 11	11 20
19	Thu	5 21	6 45	3	12 34	☾ Bat. Hatch'r's Rue '66		10 12	4 57	11 58
20	Fri	5 21	6 44	3	12 14	Benj. Harrison b. '33		10 53	5 45	0 23
21	Sat	5 22	6 43	3	11 54	Bat. of Ball's Bluff 1861.		11 41	6 34	1 8
34. Tenth Sunday after Trinity. Day's length 13 hours 19 minutes.										
22	*C.*	5 23	6 42	3	11 33	☿ in Aphe. Gough b. '17		m'rn	7 26	2 18
23	Mo	5 24	6 40	2	11 13	Com. Perry d. 1820.		0 34	8 18	3 23
24	Tue	5 25	6 39	2	10 52	☌♀☽ D. Webster d. '52		1 32	9 9	4 19
25	We	5 26	6 38	2	10 32	Josiah Turner in Ral. '70		2 35	10 0	5 9
26	Thu	5 27	6 36	2	10 11	☿ gr. Elon. E.		3 39	10 49	5 51
27	Fri	5 27	6 35	1	9 50	Bish'p Doggett d. '80		4 45	11 36	6 33
28	Sat	5 28	6 33	1	9 28	☌♃☽. 1st Cable Mes. 1858		sets.	0 24	7 17
35. Eleventh Sunday after Trinity, Day's length 13 hours 4 minutes.										
29	*C.*	5 28	6 32	1	9 7	Brigham Young d. 1877.		7 13	1 11	8 0
30	Mo	5 29	6 31	0	8 45	☌☿☽. Wm. Penn d. 1718.		7 40	2 0	8 44
31	Tue	5 30	6 30	0	8 24	Earthquake 1886		8 10	2 51	9 32

WEATHER CONJECTURES—AUGUST—1, 2. 3, 4, frequent showers; 5, 6, 7, 8, 9, 10, 11, fair; 12, 13, 14, 15, 16, 17, 18, 19, changeable; 20, 21, 22, 23, 24, 25, 26, cool with frequent showers; 27, 28, 29, 30, 31, expect fair weather

20. Individual comfort, State wealth, make a happy people.—*Branson*.

BRANSON'S NORTH CAROLINA ALMANAC. 21

FARM AND GARDEN WORK FOR AUGUST.—Transplant all kinds of cabbage, cauliflower and celery. Sow carrots and beets, turnips of all kinds, spinach, lettuce, radish and onions.

Now sow full crops of field turnips, carrots and beets, and such other crops as were omitted last month: strip fodder. Early rice will be fit to cut the last of this month. Look to it. This is a good time to plant vines of the first slips, in order to procure seed potatoes for the next year's crops.

NORTH CAROLINA COLLEGES, AND OTHER GRADUATING SCHOOLS.

(Names, character and location.)

Asheville Female College (Methodist)......................Asheville
Chowan Female Institute (Baptist)....................Murfreesboro
Claremont Female College (Reformed Church of U. S.)........Hickory
Catawba College (Reformed Church of U. S.)................Newton
Concordia College (Lutheran)....................Conover
Davenport Female College (Methodist)........................Lenoir
Davidson College (Presbyterian)........................Davidson College
Elon College (Christian).....................................Elon College
Greensboro Female College (Methodist).....................Greensboro
Gaston College (Lutheran).................................Dallas
Guilford College (Friends)......................Guilford College
Hayesville College (Independent)......................Hayesville
Judson College (Methodist)........................Hendersonville
Kinston College (Independent)...........................Kinston
Louisburg Female College (Methodist)......................Louisburg
Littleton Female College (Methodist)......................Littleton
Mt. Amoena Seminary (Lutheran)................Mt. Pleasant
Mt. St. Joseph Academy (Catholic)..................Asheville
North Carolina College (Lutheran)................Mt. Pleasant
North Carolina Agricultural and Mechanical College (State)....Raleigh
Oxford Female Seminary (Baptist)........................Oxford
Oak Ridge Institute (Independent)......................Oak Ridge
Peace Institute (Independent)..........................Raleigh
Rutherford College, Burke Co. (Independent).......Rutherford College
St. Mary's College (Catholic)........................Belmont
Shelby Female College (Independent)......................Shelby
St. Mary's School (Episcopal)........................Raleigh
Salem Academy (Moravian)..........................Salem
St. Paul's Seminary (Lutheran Theological)................Hickory
State Normal and Industrial School (State).........Greensboro
Trinity College (Methodist)........................Durham
University of North Carolina (State)................Chapel Hill
Weaverville College (Methodist)......................Weaverville
Wake Forest College (Baptist)........................Wake Forest

COLORED SCHOOLS—Graduating.

Agricultural and Mechanical College (State)..............Greensboro
Bennett Seminary (Methodist)........................Greensboro
Biddle University (Presbyterian)........................Charlotte
Building and Trade's College (Independent)...........Southern Pines
Franklinton Christian College (Christian)..............Franklinton
Livingstone College (Methodist)........................Salisbury
Normal and Industrial College (Methodist)............Kittrell
Normal School (State)........................Elizabeth City
Normal School (State)........................Goldsboro
Normal School (State)........................Salisbury
Normal School (State)........................Franklinton
Normal School (State)........................Plymouth
Normal School (State)........................Fayetteville
Shaw University (Baptist)........................Raleigh
St. Augustine Normal College (Episcopal).............Raleigh
Scotia Female Seminary (Presbyterian)..............Concord
Slater Industrial Academy and Normal School (State).........Winston

9th Month.   SEPTEMBER, 1897.   30 Days.

Moon's Phases.

	D.	H.	M.			D.	H.	M.
First Quarter,	3	6	5p.m.		Last Quarter,	18	9	42p.m.
Full Moon,	10	9	3p.m.		New Moon,	26	8	38a.m.

Day of Month.	Day of Week.	Sun rises.	Sun sets.	Sun fast.	Sun's decline north.	ASPECTS OF PLANETS AND OTHER MISCELLANEOUS MATTER.	Moon's place.	Moon rises or sets.	Moon south.	High Tides.
1	We	5 31	6 28	8	2	Battle of Ox Hill 1862.		8 47	eve.	m'rn
2	Thu	5 32	6 27		7 40	Atlanta cap. 1864.		9 31	4 43	11 10
3	Fri	5 33	6 25		7 18	Eliz. Glenn d. 1894.		10 23	5 43	11 57
4	Sat	5 34	6 24	1	6 56	Gen. Morgan k. 1864.		11 25	6 45	0 30

36. Twelfth Sunday after Trinity.   Day's length 12 hours 47 minutes.

5	C.	5 35	6 22	2	6 33	Confed. invade Md. '62.		m'rn	7 45	1 48
6	Mo	5 35	6 21	2	6 11	LABOR DAY.		0 31	8 43	3 5
7	Tue	5 36	6 19	2	5 28	Castelor inaug. 1873.		1 42	9 36	4 15
8	We	5 36	6 18	3	5 26	☿ sta. Jewsle. Poland 187		2 51	10 25	5 14
9	Thu	5 37	6 16	3	5 3	California admitted 1850		4 0	11 12	6 7
10	Fri	5 38	6 15	3	4 40	S. S. Cox d. 1889.		5 8	11 56	6 53
11	Sat	5 39	6 14	4	4 18	☿ gr. Hel. Lat. S.		rises.	m'rn	7 36

37. Thirteenth Sunday after Trinity.   Day's length 12 hours 33 min.

12	C.	5 39	6 12	4	3 55	Bat. of Chapultepec 1847		6 41	0 39	8 16
13	Mo	5 40	6 11	4	3 32	♂♃⊙. Bat. Quebec1750.		7 6	1 22	8 55
14	Tue	5 41	6 10	5	3 9	☿♇⊙. Dr. Fuller d. '88.		7 35	2 5	9 33
15	We	5 42	6 8	5	2 45	Gen. Scott took Mex.1847		8 9	2 50	10 13
16	Thu	5 43	6 6	5	2 22	Farenheit d. 1737.		8 48	3 37	10 50
17	Fri	5 44	6 5	6	1 59	Mt. Cenis Tun. op. '71.		9 33	4 26	11 35
18	Sat	5 44	6 4	6	1 36	Fug. slave act 1850.		10 23	5 17	0 2

38. Fourteenth Sunday after Trinity.   Day's length 12 hours 17 min.

19	C.	5 45	6 2	6	1 12	Garfield d. 1881.		11 19	6 8	0 30
20	Mo	5 45	6 1	7	0 49	Arthur inaugurat'd 1881		m'rn	6 59	1 25
21	Tue	5 46	6 0	7	0 26	Bat. of Fisher's Hill 1864		0 18	7 49	2 40
22	We	5 47	5 58	7	0 2	⊙ ent. ♎ AUTUMN BEG.		1 21	8 38	3 41
23	Thu	5 48	5 56	8	so'th	Russian fleet sank 1854.		2 26	9 26	4 34
24	Fri	5 49	5 54	8	0 46	Gen. D. H. Hill d. 1889.		3 34	10 13	5 21
25	Sat	5 50	5 53	8	1 9	♂ ☿ ☽. Bat. Montreal1775		4 43	11 1	6 8

39. Fifteenth Sunday after Trinity.   Day's length 12 hours 1 minute.

26	C.	5 51	5 52	9	1 33	Proverbs 22: 1.		5 48	11 50	6 53
27	Mo	5 51	5 50	9	1 56	Steam. Arctic lost '54		sets.	ev 42	7 39
28	Tue	5 51	5 49	9	2 19	Bishop Randall d. 1873		6 44	1 36	8 25
29	We	5 52	5 47	10	2 43	Read Branson's Maxims		7 28	2 35	9 13
30	Thu	5 53	5 46	10	3 6	☿ in ♌ Whitfield d.1770		8 18	3 36	10 3

WEATHER CONJECTURES—SEPTEMBER—1, 2, fair; 3, 4, 5, 6, 7, 8, 9, wind and rain; 10, 11, 12, 13, 14. 15, 16, 17, fair if wind N. W., rain if S. or S· W.; 18, 19, 20, 21, 22, 23, 24, 25, fair if wind N. W., rain if S. or S. W.; 26, 27, 28, 29, 30, changeable.

FARM AND GARDEN WORK FOR SEPTEMBER.—Now sow full crops of all kinds—turnips, onions, carrots, beets, cabbage, lettuce, cresses. Look after your mushroom beds. Hoe and thin your turnips.

Continue to sow ffeld turnips, carrots and beets. Southern seed is always better than the imported; those from the latter are apt to run to seed early in the spring, unless it be English seed. Prepare land for sowing rye in October. Pick cotton; harvest corn.

UNIVERSITY OF NORTH CAROLINA.

(Located in Chapel Hill, Orange County, twenty-eight miles northwest of Raleigh.)

Chartered in 1789, founded 1793, opened 1795. It now has in all departments 539 students and 35 instructors. The equipment includes twelve large buildings, five scientific laboratories, library of 40,000 volumes, campus of fifty acres with ample athletic grounds, gymnasium, &c. Perfect sanitation, baths, closets, &c. Tuition $60 a year, total expenses $200 to $300. Scholarships and loans for the needy. Law school and medical school. A summer school for teachers is conducted each July. It enrolled 153 teachers in 1896. The Faculty enrolled 19 Professors. During 1895 and 1896 many students supported themselves by labor, the total amount earned being about $5,000. The University is non-political and non-sectarian.

FACULTY.—Edwin Anderson Alderman, D. C L., President and Professor of Political and Social Science; Kemp Plummer Battle, LL. D., Professor of History; Francis Preston Venable, Ph. D., Professor of General and Analytical Chemistry; Joseph Austin Holmes, B. S., State Geologist and Lecturer on Geology of North Carolina; Joshua Walker Gore, C. E., Professor of Natural Philosophy; John Manning, LL. D., Professor of Law; Thomas Hume, D. D., LL. D., Professor of the English Languages and Literature; Walter Dallam Toy, M. A., Professor of Modern Languages; Eben Alexander, Ph. D., LL. D., Professor of the Greek Language and Literature (on leave of absence); William Cain, C. E., Professor of Mathematics; Richard Henry Whitehead, M. D., Professor of Anatomy and Pathology; Henry Horace Williams, A. M., B. D., Professor of Mental and Moral Science; Henry Van Peters Wilson, Ph. D., Professor of Biology; Karl Pomeroy Harrington, A. M., Professor of the Latin Languages and Literature; James Shepherd, LL. D., Ex-Chief Justice of the Supreme Court of North Carolina, and Associate Professor of Common and Statute Law and Equity in Summer School; Collier Cobb, A. M., Professor of Geology, Francis Kingsley Ball, Ph. D., Professor of Greek; Charles Baskerville, Ph. D., Assistant Professor of Chemistry; Charles Staples Mangum, A. B., Professor of Physiology and Materia Medica; —— ——, Professor of Pedagogy; George Phineas Butler, B. E., Instructor in Mathematics; Samuel May, A. B., Instructor in Modern Languages; Henry Farrar Linscott, A. B., Instructor in Latin; William Robert Webb, Jr., A. B., Instructor in English; William Cunningham Smith, Ph. B., Instructor in Pedagogies; Harry Ellsworth Mechling, Director of Gymnasium; Robert Ervin Coke, S B., Assistant in Biology; George Hughes Kirby, S B., Assistant in Biology; Arthur Williams Belden, Assistant in Chemistry; John Gilchrist McCormick, Assistant in Geology; Arch Turner Allen, Assistant in Physics; Stanford Hunter Harris, Assistant in Chemistry; Collier Cobb, A. M., Secretary of Faculty; Francis Kingsley Ball, Ph. D., Supervisor of Library; Benjamin Wyche, Litt. B., Librarian; Eugene Lewis Harris, Ph. B., Registrar; Willie Thomas Patterson, Bursar.

A boy jumped into the water, and by his quickness and the help of a life-preserver, saved a man from drowning. To reward him, the man took sixpence from his pocket and handed it to his preserver. The boy looked at it for a minute and then exclaimed: "Well, I am overpaid for this job, at least."—*Selected.*

23. To *sleep sweetly*, recline a few moments on your *left* side; then turn *slowly* onto your right side. Try it.—*Branson.*

24   BRANSON'S NORTH CAROLINA ALMANAC.

10th Month.	OCTOBER, 1897.	31 Days.

Moon's Phases.

	D. H. M		D. H. M.
☽First Quarter,	3 0 23a.m.	☾Last Quarter,	18 4 0p.m.
●Full Moon,	10 11 33a m.	○New Moon,	25 6 20p.m·

Day of Month.	Day of Week.	Sun rises.	Sun sets.	Sun fast.	Sun's decline north.	ASPECTS OF PLANETS AND OTHER MISCELLANEOUS MATTER.	Moon's place.	Moon rises or sets.	Moon south.	High Tides.
1	Fri	5 54	5 44	10	3 29		♋	9 18	eve.	m'rn
2	Sat	5 55	5 43	11	3 53	Gen. Ass. at Edenton 1722	♌	10 25	5 40	11 58

40. Sixteenth Sunday after Trinity.   Day's length 11 hours 45 min.

3	C.	5 56	5 41	11	4 16	☽Black Hawk d.1838.	♌	11 34	6 38	0 21
4	Mo	5 57	5 40	11	4 39	☽Bat Germ't'wn 1777	♌	m'rn	7 32	1 37
5	Tue	5 58	5 37	12	5 2	☿ in Perihelion.	♌	0 42	8 22	2 52
6	We	5 59	5 35	12	5 25	☿♃Judge Dick b.1823	♍	1 51	9 8	3 56
7	Thu	5 59	5 34	12	5 48	☿ gr. Elon. W.	♍	2 57	9 52	4 52
8	Fri	6 0	5 32	13	6 11	Bat. Fort Pickens 1861.	♎	4 1	10 35	5 42
9	Sat	6 1	5 30	13	6 34	Gr. Fire in Chicago 1871	♎	4 59	11 18	6 27

41. Seventeenth Sunday after Trinity.   Day's length 11 hours 27 min.

10	C.	6 2	5 29	13	6 57	●Stuart raid, Pa. 1862	♏	rises.	m'rn	7 9
11	Mo	6 3	5 28	13	7 19	●Rev.W.E. Pell d. '70.	♏	5 36	0 1	7 48
12	Tue	6 4	5 27	14	7 42	Gen. R. E Lee d. 1870.	♐	6 9	0 45	8 26
13	We	6 5	5 25	14	8 4	Canova d. 1822.	♐	6 46	1 32	9 3
14	Thu	6 6	5 24	14	8 27	Bat. of Hastings 1066.	♐	7 29	2 20	9 40
15	Fri	6 7	5 23	14	8 49	☿ gr. Hel. Lat. N.	♒	8 16	3 10	10 19
16	Sat	6 8	5 21	14	9 11	Napoleon at Helena 1815	♒	9 10	4 0	11 2

42. Eighteenth Sunday after Trinity.   Day's length 11 hours 10 min.

17	C.	6 9	5 19	15	9 33	☾Sur. Burgoyne 1777.	♒	10 6	4 51	11 50
18	Mo	6 9	5 18	15	9 55	☾Judge Reade d. 1894	♒	11 6	5 40	0 10
19	Tue	6 10	5 17	15	10 16	Bat. Cedar Creek 1866.	♓	m'rn	6 29	0 59
20	We	6 11	5 16	15	10 38	Grace Darling d. 1842.	♓	0 8	7 16	2 8
21	Thu	6 12	5 15	15	10 59	Bat. of Ball's Bluff 1861	♈	1 13	8 2	3 9
22	Fri	6 13	5 14	15	11 20	Hon. Thos. Kenan d. 1843	♈	2 22	8 49	4 5
23	Sat	6 14	5 12	16	11 41	Wm. Hooper d. 1790.	♈	3 25	9 37	4 56

43. Nineteenth Sunday after Trinity.   Day's length 10 hours 56 min.

24	C.	6 15	5 11	16	12 2	Water Mills invent. 555.	♉	4 38	10 27	5 45
25	Mo	6 16	5 10	16	12 23	●Newbern set 1712.	♉	5 55	11 21	6 33
26	Tue	6 16	5 9	16	12 43	●Salisb'ry l'id off 1753	♋	sets.	0 19	7 19
27	We	6 17	5 8	16	13 4	Dr.Caradine in Ral. 1894	♋	6 8	1 21	8 8
28	Thu	6 18	5 7	16	13 24	Proverbs 28: 1.	♌	7 6	2 26	8 57
29	Fri	6 19	5 6	16	13 44	Walter Ral'gh d.1618	♌	8 12	3 30	9 48
30	Sat	6 20	5 5	16	14 3	Gambetta b. 1838.	♌	9 23	4 31	10 42

44. Twentieth Sunday after Trinity.   Day's length 10 hours 44 min.

| 31 | C. | 6 21 | 5 5 | 16 | 14 23 | ♂ in ☋.Gen.Scott ret.'61 | ♌ | 10 35 | 5 28 | 11 40 |

WEATHER CONJECTURES—OCTOBER—1, 2, changeabl 3, 4, 5, 6, 7, 8, 9, fair; 10, 11, 12, 13, 14, 15, 16, 17, rainy weather; 18, 19, 20, 21, changeable; 22, 23, 24, fair; 25, 26, 27, 28, 29, 30, 31, fair if wind N., or rainy if wind S. or S. W

24.—Live with happy people, and you are likely *to be* happy.—*Branson*.

BRANSON'S NORTH CAROLINA ALMANAC. 25

FARM AND GARDEN WORK FOR OCTOBER.—You may make two sowings of cabbage this month, and, if of English seed, they will not "run" in the spring. Sow lettuce; hoe turnips and thin; put out leeks and onions; sow principal crop of spinach; earth up celery.

Continue picking your cotton as it blows. Sow early rye, wheat and barley. Dig your sweet potatoes when the weather becomes cool and you expect frost.

PUBLIC WORKS AND INSTITUTIONS IN NORTH CAROLINA.

N. C. STATE BOARD OF AGRICULTURE.

S. L. Patterson, Commissioner; T. K. Bruner, Secretary; H. B. Battle, Ph. D., Chemist and Director Experiment Station.

EXECUTIVE COMMITTEE.—Col. W. F. Green, H. E. Fries, Dr. W. R. Capehart, Col. R. W. Wharton, J. L. Nelson.

Col. W. F. Green, Chairman Board of Directors.

NORTH CAROLINA COLLEGE OF AGRICULTURE AND MECHANIC ARTS.

Located at Raleigh.

FACULTY AND OFFICERS.—Alexander Q. Holladay, LL.D., President and Professor of History; W. F. Massey, C. E., Professor of Horticulture, Arboriculture and Botany; W. A. Withers, A. M., Professor of Pure and Agricultural Chemistry, and Secretary; D. H. Hill, A. M., Professor of English; B. Irby, M. S., Professor of Agriculture; W. C. Riddick, A. B., C. E., Professor of Civil Engineering and Mathematics; Nathaniel R. Craighill, S. B., Professor of Mechanical Engineering; Nathan Hale Barnes, A. M., Ph. D., Lieutenant (retired) U. S Navy, Professor of Physics and Elec. Eng. and of Military Science and Tactics; R. E. L. Yates, A. M., Adjunct Professor of Mathematics; Frank E. Emery, M. S., Assistant Professor of Agriculture; Charles M. Pritchett, B. S., M. E., C. E., Instructor in Drawing and Snop Work; Charles B. Park, Superintendent of Shops; B. S. Skinner, Assistant in Farm Practice, and Farm Superintendent; F. P. Williams n, D. V. S., Instructor in Veterinary Science; J. A. Bizzell, B. S., Assistant in Chemistry; W. K. Davis, Jr., B. E., Assistant in Physics; David Clark, M. E., Assistant in Drawing and Shops; A. H. Prince, B. S., Assistant in Dairying; S. E Asbury, Assistant in Mathematics and English; J. I. Blount, B. E., Tutor of Sub-Freshman Class; Mrs. Sue C. Carroll, Matron; James R. Rogers, M. D., Physician.

EXECUTIVE COMMITTEE.—W. S. Primrose, Chairman; H. E. Fries, D. A. Tompkins, Dr. J. R. McLelland, Dr. Cyrus Thompson.

FINANCE COMMITTEE.—N. B. Broughton, Chairman; H. E. King, Frank Wood.

THE STATE HOSPITAL, MORGANTON.

OFFICERS.—P. L. Murphy, M. D., Superintendent, salary $2 800; Isaac M. Taylor, M. D., Assistant Physician, salary $1,200; C. E. Ross, M. D., Assistant Physician, salary $1,200; T. W. S Mott, M. D., Assistant Physician, salary $1,200; F. M. Scroggs, Steward, salary $1,000; Mrs. C. A. Marsh, Matron, salary $350.

BOARD OF DIRECTORS.—James P. Sawyer, Buncombe County, President; I. I. Davis, Esq., Burke County; Joseph P. Caldwell, Esq., Mecklenburg County; J. G. Hall, Esq., Catawba County; Joseph C. Mills, Burke County; G. W. F. Harper, Caldwell County; J. R. Love, Jackson County; L R. Whitener, Catawba County; S. A. White, Alamance County.

No member of the Board of Directors or Executive Committee receive any compensation for their work, except their traveling expenses.

25. Do not keep a *burr* in your *throat*, nor a bit of *malice* in your *heart*.—*Branson*.

11th Month. NOVEMBER, 1897. 30 Days.

Moon's Phases.

	D.	H.	M.		D.	H.	M.
☽First Quarter,	1	9	28a.m.	☾Last Quarter,	17	8	54a.m.
Full Moon,	9	4	42a.m.	New Moon,	24	4	11a.m.
				☽First Quarter,	30	10	6p.m.

Day of Month.	Day of Week.	Sun rises.	Sun sets.	Sun fast.	Sun's decline south.	ASPECTS OF PLANETS AND OTHER MISCELLANEOUS MATTER.	Moon's place.	Moon rises or sets.	Moon south.	High Tides.
1	Mo	6 22	5 3	16	14 42	McLellan in com. '61		11 43	eve.	m'rn
2	Tue	6 23	5 2	16	15 1	Proverbs 26 : 4, 5.		m'rn	7 7	1 21
3	We	6 24	5 1	16	15 20	Bat. of Hohenlinden 1800		1 50	7 51	2 23
4	Thu	6 25	5 0	16	15 38	Geo. Peabody d. 1869.		1 54	8 34	3 30
5	Fri	6 26	4 59	16	15 56	Gen. Grant's 2d elec. 1870		2 54	9 16	4 25
6	Sat	6 27	4 58	16	16 14	♀ gr. Hel. Lat· N.		3 54	9 59	5 41
45. Twenty-first Sunday after Trinity. Day's length 10 hours 28 min.										
7	*C.*	6 28	4 56	16	16 32	Dr. B. Craven d. 1882.		4 55	10 42	5 59
8	Mo	6 29	4 56	16	16 49	☌ ☿ ☽ superior.		5 53	11 28	6 40
9	Tue	6 30	4 55	16	17 6	Dr. L. Pierce d. 1879.		rises.	m'rn	7 20
10	We	6 31	4 55	16	17 23	Martin Luther b. 1483.		5 26	0 15	7 58
11	Thu	6 32	4 54	16	17 39	Washington admit. 1889		6 12	1 5	8 34
12	Fri	6 33	4 53	16	17 56	☌ ☿ ♂.		7 3	1 55	9 11
13	Sat	6 34	4 53	16	18 12	Fall of Meteors 1833.		7 58	2 45	9 49
46. Twenty-second Sunday after Trinity. Day's length 10 hours 17m.										
14	*C.*	6 35	4 52	15	18 27	Herschel b. 1738.		8 56	3 35	10 29
15	Mo	6 36	4 51	15	18 42	Bat. Campbell Sta. 1863.		9 56	4 23	11 13
16	Tue	6 37	4 51	15	18 57	Sherman's mar. '64.		10 58	5 9	11 59
17	We	6 38	4 50	15	19 12	Suez Canal op. 1869.		m'rn	5 55	0 31
18	Thu	6 39	4 50	15	19 26	☿ in Aphelion.		0 2	6 39	1 35
19	Fri	6 40	4 49	14	19 40	Gen. Ass. at Newb'rn 1771		1 9	7 25	2 36
20	Sat	6 41	4 49	14	19 53	Erup. of Mt Vesuvius 57.		2 12	8 12	3 36
47. Twenty third Sunday after Trinity. Day's length 10 hours 7 min.										
21	*C.*	6 42	4 49	14	20 7	☌ ♂ ☉.		3 26	9 3	4 29
22	Mo	6 43	4 48	14	20 19	Gen. Jos. Graham d. 1836		4 40	9 58	5 22
23	Tue	6 44	4 47	13	20 32	Gov. Ellis b. 1820.		6 0	10 59	6 13
24	We	6 45	4 47	13	20 44	☌ ☿ ☽.!		sets.	0 3	7 3
25	Thu	6 46	4 46	13	20 55	☌ ♄ ☉. Isa'c Watts d. 1748		5 51	1 10	7 53
26	Fri	6 47	4 46	12	21 7	Bishop Marvin d. 1875.		7 4	2 16	8 43
27	Sat	6 48	4 46	12	21 18	☌ ♂ ♄. J.H. Whe'ler d. '94		8 18	3 17	9 34
48. First Sunday in Advent. Day's length 9 hours 57 minutes.										
28	*C.*	6 49	4 46	12	21 28	Irving d. 1859.		9 29	4 12	10 26
29	Mo	6 50	4 46	11	21 38	Savannah taken 1778		10 40	5 3	11 20
30	Tue	6 51	4 46	11	21 48	Fire at Durham 1880		11 47	5 49	0 1

WEATHER CONJECTURES—NOVEMBER—1, 2, 3, 4, 5, 6. 7, 8, cold rain if wind be West, snow if East; 9, 10, 11, 12, 13, 14. 15, 16, rain; 17, 18, 19, 20, 21, 22, 23, cold rain if wind be W., snow if E.; 24, 25, 26. 27, 28, 29, rain; 30, fair and frosty.

26. If you are *good*, this world is *good enough* for you; if you are *mean*, then it is *too good* for you.—*Branson*.

BRANSON'S NORTH CAROLINA ALMANAC. 27

FARM AND GARDEN WORK FOR NOVEMBER.—Sow your first crop of peas and a few turnips. Plant out onions raised from seed in August and September. Plant Windsor and long-pod beans. Dress asparagus and artichokes.

Sow full crops of rye, barley, wheat and other small grains. Harvest your sweet potatoes.

NORTH CAROLINA INSTITUTION FOR THE DEAF, DUMB AND THE BLIND.

The North Carolina Institution for the Blind is located at Raleigh.

OFFICERS.—John E. Ray, Principal, salary $2,000; time expires 1899. W. J. Young, Assistant Principal. Dr. Hubert Haywood, of Raleigh, Physician, salary $500; time expires 1898. Wm. H. Rand, Steward, salary $750 and board; time expires 1897. W. H. Worth, *ex officio* Treasurer.

BOARD OF TRUSTEES.—B. F. Montague, President; time expires Jan. 1, 1897. 1 M. Proctor; time expires Jan. 1, 1901. Hugh Morson; time expires Jan. 1, 1899. John R. Williams; time expires Jan. 1, 1899. Dr. H. C. Herring; time expires Jan. 1, 1899. Jas. A. Briggs; time expires Jan. 1, 1897.

STATE MUSEUM.

Located in the Agricultural Building at Raleigh; contains a complete collection of geological rocks and ores of the State; also a fine collection of timbers, agricultural products, native birds, animals and fishes—in fact, a complete collection of the resources of the State, pictorially as well as in kind. H. H. Brimley, Curator. Office hours from 9 to 1, and from 2 to 5 p. m. Under control of the State Board of Agriculture. Visited annually by 20,000 people.

STATE NORMAL AND INDUSTRIAL SCHOOL.

Located at Greensboro, N. C.

This school was chartered by the General Assembly of North Carolina, 1891. The first class of girls was graduated in 1893.

OFFICERS AND FACULTY.—Chas. D. McIver, A. B., Litt. D., President; P. P. Claxton, A. M., J. Y. Joyner, Ph. B., Lucy H. Robertson, Gertrude W. Mendenhall, B. S., Dixie Lee Bryant, B. S., Joseph A. Holmes, B. S., Mary M. Petty, B. S., Viola Boddie, L. I., Jennie W. Bingham, Caroline Hetrick, M. D., Mrs. B. C. Sharpe, Clarence R. Brown, Melville Vincent Fort, Fanny H. Massey, Minnie Jamison, Bertha M. Lee, Sue May Kirkland, Lady Principal, E. J. Forney, Fodie M. Buie, Minnie Haliburton, Annie Wiley, Nettie Allen, Mary Sanders, Laura Coit, E. J. Forney, Bursar, Annie F. Petty, Eliza N. Williams, Mrs. W. P. Carraway, Matron.

N. C. AGRICULTURAL EXPERIMENT AND FERTILIZER CONTROL STATION, RALEIGH, N. C.

OFFICERS.—H. B. Battle, Ph. D., Director and State Chemist; F. E. Emery, M. S., Agriculturist; Gerald McCarthy, B. S., Botanist and Entomologist; W. F. Massey, C. E., Horticulturist; F. P. Williamson, D. V. S., Consulting Veterinarian; T. E. Hege, Poultry Manager; B. W. Kilgore, M. S., W. M. Allen, and H. K. Miller, M. S., Assistant Chemists; Alex. Rhodes, Assistant Horticulturist; A. F. Bowen, Secretary.

Offices and Laboratories in Agricultural Building, Raleigh; farm, stables and dairy at the Experiment Farm, adjoining State Fair Grounds. Visitors invited. Many interesting and valuable bulletins free on application.

BUREAU OF LABOR STATISTICS.

B. R. Lacy, of Wake County, Commissioner, salary $1,500; W. E. Faison, Wake County, salary $900. Office in the Supreme Court Building.

27. Never allow your energies to slacken, or your faith to weaken.—
Branson.

12th Month.   DECEMBER, 1897.   31 Days.

Moon's Phases·

	D. H. M.		D. H. M.
Full Moon,	8 11 26p.m.	New Moon,'	23 2 47p.m
Last Quarter, 16 11 13p m.		First Quarter, 30	2 18p.m

Day of Month.	Day of Week.	Sun rises.	Sun sets.	Sun fast.	Sun's decline south.	ASPECTS OF PLANETS AND OTHER MISCELLANEOUS MATTER.	Moon's place.	Moon rises or sets.	Moon south.	High Tides.
1	We	6 51	4 46	11	21 57	Bat. of Austerlitz 1805.		m'rn	eve.	m'rn
2	Thu	6 52	4 46	10	22 6	John Brown hung 1859.		0 45	7 15	2 0
3	Fri	6 53	4 46	10	22 14	Bat. Hohenlinden 1800.		1 46	7 57	3 0
4	Sat	6 54	4 46	9	22 22	Alabama admit. 1818.		2 48	8 41	3 55

49. Second Sunday in Advent.   Day's length 9 hours 51 minutes.

5	*C.*	6 55	4 46	9	22 g0	Bishop Wison in Ral.'94.		3 49	9 25	4 45
6	Mo	6 56	4 46	9	22 37	Jefferson Davis d. 1889.		4 48	10 12	5 30
7	Tue	6 56	4 46	8	22 43	Ed. Badger d. 1878.		5 46	11 1	6 13
8	We	6 67	4 46	8	22 49	gr. Hel. Lat. S.		6 41	11 51	6 52
9	Thu	6 58	4 46	7	22 55	Milton b. 1608.		rises.	m'rn	7 30
10	Fri	6 59	4 46	7	23 0	Dumas d. 1870.		5 53	0 41	8 7
11	Sat	7 0	4 46	6	23 5	Indiana admitted 1816.		6 51	1 31	8 44

50. Third Sunday in Advent.   Day's length 9 hours 46 minutes.

12	*C.*	7 1	4 47	6	23 10	⊙.Browning d. 1889		7 50	2 20	9 20
13	Mo	7 2	4 47	5	23 13	Robt. Tombs d. 1884.		8 51	3 7	9 58
14	Tue	7 3	4 47	5	23 17	HALCYON DAYS.		9 53	3 52	10 39
15	We	7 3	4 47	4	23 20	S ting Bull k. 1890.		10 58	4 36	11 25
16	Thu	7 4	4 48	4	23 22	Bost. Tea Barty 1773		11 59	5 20	0 3
17	Fri	7 4	4 48	3	23 24	Poet Whitier b. 1807.		m'rn	6 4	1 3
18	Sat	7 5	4 49	3	23 26	Humphrey Davy b. 1779		0 5	6 52	2 5

51. Fourth Sunday in Advent.   Day's length 9 hours 43 minutes.

19	*C.*	7 6	4 49	2	23 27	Henry the 11th cr. 1154.		2 17	7 43	3 7
20	Mo	7 7	4 49	2	23 28	gr. Eton. E.		3 30	8 38	4 6
21	Tue	7 7	4 50	1	23 28	⊙ ent. WINTER BEG.		4 49	9 40	5 2
22	We	7 8	4 50		23 28			6 2	10 45	5 57
23	Thu	7 8	4 51	slow	23 27	H. W. Grady'd. 1889.		7 11	11 52	6 49
24	Fri	7 9	4 51		23 26	Thackary d. 1863		sets.	ev 56	7 40
25	Sat	7 9	4 52	1	23 24	CHRISTMAS DAY.		7 5	1 56	8 29

52. First Sunday after Christmas.   Day's length 9 hours 44 minutes.

26	*C.*	7 9	4 53	1	23 22	Girard d. 1831.		8 18	2 51	9 18
27	Mo	7 10	4 53	2	23 19	in ꭥ. St. John Evan.		9 30	3 41	10 8
28	Tue	7 10	4 54	2	23 16	stationery.		10 37	4 27	10 58
29	We	7 10	4 54	2	23 12	W. E. Gladstone b. 1809.		11 35	5 11	11 49
30	Thu	7 11	4 55	3	23 8			m'rn	5 55	0 27
31	Fri	7 11	4 56	3	23 4	Bat. Murfreesb'ro '62		0 40	6 38	1 25

WEATHER CONJECTURES—DECEMBER—1. 2, 3, 4, 5, 6, 7, fair and frosty;
8, 9, 10, 11, 12, 13, 14. 15, look for frost; 16, 17. 18, 19, 20, 21, 22, fair and
frosty; 23, 24, 25, 26, 27, 28, 29, fair and mild; 30, 31, fair good weather.

FARM AND GARDEN WORK FOR DECEMBER.—Plant peas of all kinds; set out onions, garlic, eschalots and cabbage. Sow a few lettuce, spinach, carrots and radishes. You may try a few Irish potatoes.

Finish picking cotton; get out crops of rice and prepare for market. Commence plowing, ditching, draining and manuring as early as possible for next year's crop.

STATE BOARD OF PHARMACY.

E. V. Zoeller, Tarboro, President; W. H. Wearn, Charlotte; N. D. Fetzer, Concord; Wm. Simpson, Raleigh, Secretary and Treasurer; P. W. Vaughan, Durham.

EASTERN HOSPITAL, GOLDSBORO.

OFFICERS.—J. F. Miller, M. D., Superintendent, salary $2 000, furnished house and board of two horses and cows; W. W. Faison, M. D., Assistant Physician, salary $900, board for self, wife three children and nurse and board of one horse; Daniel Reid, Steward, salary $450, board of self and horse; Mrs. B. V. Smith, Matron, salary $300 and board of self and child; John W. Wilson, Engineer, salary $400, furnished house for family; Mrs. Victoria Bryan, Seamstress, salary $150, and board of self and child; John Davis, Farmer, salary $200 and house; A. A. Green, Watchman, salary $250 per annum. Hon. W. H. Worth, Treasurer *ex officio.*

BOARD OF DIRECTORS.—Dr. J. W. Vick, President, Johnston County; B. F. Aycock, Wayne County; J. F. Southerland, Wayne County; T. B. Parker, Wayne County; W. F. Rountree, Craven County; J. L. McLean, Robeson County; Dr. M. B Pitt, Edgecombe County; Major Joshua B. Hill, Wake County; Henry I. Faison, Duplin County.

EXECUTIVE COMMITTEE.—B. F. Aycock, J. F. Southerland, Thomas B. Parker.

N. C. BOARD OF RAILROAD COMMISSIONERS.

COMMISSIONERS.—J. W. Wilson, Burke County, Chairman; term expires April, 1899. E. C. Beddingfield, Wake County; term expires April, 1897. S. Otho Wilson, Wake County; term expires April, 1901. Salary $2,000 each. H. C. Brown, Surry County, Clerk, salary $1,200.

Special sessions of the Court are held at Raleigh. Special sessions are also held at other places, under such regulations as made by the Commission.

Offices of the Commissioners are located in the Agricultural Building.

NORTH CAROLINA GEOLOGICAL SURVEY.

Jos. A. Holmes, State Geologist; H. B. C. Nitze, Assistant State Geologist. General offices of the Survey, Raleigh, N. C.

NORTH CAROLINA STATE GUARD—OFFICERS OF THE GENERAL STAFF.

Gen. F. H. Cameron, Adjutant General; Col. A. L. Smith, Inspector General; Col. E. G. Harrell, Quartermaster General; Col. Julian S. Carr, Paymaster General; Col. Benehan Cameron. Inspector S. A. P.; Colonel Hubert Haywood, Surgeon General; Col. Wm. Gaston Lewis, Chief of Engineers; Col. Thos. W. Strange, Judge Advocate General.

RALEIGH CHAMBER OF COMMERCE AND INDUSTRY.

OFFICERS—J. E. Pogue, President; R. B. Raney, Vice-President; W. H. Williamson, Second Vice-President; Frank T. Ward, Treasurer; Geo. Allen, Secretary.

N. C. PHARMACEUTICAL ASSOCIATION.

Julian M. Baker, President, Tarboro; term expires May, 1898; H. B. Weaver, M. D., Asheville; term expires 1898; T. S. Burbank, M. D., Wilmington; term expires 1900; J. M. Hays, M. D., Greensboro; term expires 1900; David T. Tayloe, Washington; Richard H. Whitehead, Chapel Hill; Thos. E. Anderson, Statesville.

29. The more you imitate God and good people, the greater you are likely to be.—*Branson.*

SUPERIOR COURTS OF NORTH CAROLINA FOR 1897.

JUDGES.			SOLICITORS.		
Name.	*District.*	*Residence.*	*Name.*	*District.*	*Residence.*
George H. Brown,	1	Washington.	W. J. Leary,	1	Eliz'b'th City.
Henry R. Bryan,	2	Newbern.¹	W. E. Daniel,	2	Weldon.
E. W. Timberlake,	3	Louisburg.	C. M. Bernard,	3	Greenville.
W. S. O'B. Robinson,	4	Goldsboro.	Edward W. Pou, Jr.,	4	Smithfield.
Aug. W. Graham,	5	Oxford.	W. P. Bynum, Jr.,	5	Greensboro.
Edward T. Boykin,	6	Clinton.	Milton C. Richardson,	6	Clinton.
James D. McIver,	7	Carthage.	H. F. Seawell,	7	Carthage.
Albert L. Coble,	8	Statesville.	J. Q. Holton,	8	Yadkinville.
Henry R. Starbuck,	9	Winston.	M. L. Mott,	9	Wilkesboro.
Leander L. Green,	10	Boone.	J. F. Spainhour,	10	Lenoir.
W. Alexander Hoke,	11	Lincolnton.	J. L. Webb,	11	Shelby.
W. L. Norwood,	12	Waynesville.	George A. Jones,	12	Franklin.

Time of Holding Courts.

FIRST JUDICIAL DISTRICT.

Spring—Judge Bryan.

Fall—Judge Brown.

Beaufort—‡Feb. 15th (2), May 24th (2), Nov. 29th (2).
Currituck—March 1st, Sept. 6th.
Camden—March 8th, Sept. 13th.
Pasquotank—March 15th, Sept. 20th.
Perquimans—March 22d, Sept. 27th.
Chowan—March 29th, October 4th.
Gates—April 5th, Oct. 11th.
Hertford—April 12th, Oct. 18th.
Washington—April 19th, June 7th, Oct. 25th.
Tyrrell—April 26th, Nov. 1st.
Dare—May 3d, Nov. 8th.
Hyde—May 10th, Nov. 15th.
Pamlico—May 17th, Nov. 22d,

SECOND JUDICIAL DISTRICT.

Spring—Judge Timberlake.

Fall—Judge Bryan.

Halifax—March 1st (2). May 24th (2), Nov. 22d (2).
Northampton—March 29th (2), †Aug. 23d (2), Oct. 25th (2).
Bertie—‡Feb. 15th, April, 26th ‡Sept. 13th (2), Nov. 8th.
Craven—‡Feb. 1st (2), May 3d (2), Dec. 6th (2).
Warren—March 15th (2), Sept. 20th (2).
Edgecombe—April 12th (2), †June 16th (2), Oct. 11th (2).

THIRD JUDICIAL DISTRICT.

Spring—Judge Robinson.

Fall—Judge Timberlake.

Pitt—Jan. 4th (2), †March 1st (2), March 29th, (2), †April 1st (2), Sept. 20th (2), †Dec. 6th (2).
Franklin—Jan. 18th (2), April 12th (2), Oct. 26th.
Wilson—‡Feb. 1st (2), May 31st (2), June 21st, Nov. 1st (2).
Vance—Feb. 15th (2), May 17th (2), Oct. 4th (2).
Martin—March 15th (2), Sept. 6th (2).
Nash—April 26th (2), Nov. 22d (2).

FOURTH JUDICIAL DISTRICT.

Spring—Judge Graham.

Fall—Judge Robinson.

Wake—*Jan. 4th (2), †Feb. 22d (2), *Mar. 22d (2), †April 19th (2), *July 12th (2), *Sept. 20th (2), †Oct. 25th (3).

Wayne—Jan. 18th (2), April 12th, Sept. 13th (2), Oct. 18th.
Harnett—Feb. 15th, Sept. 6th, ‡Nov. 29th.
Johnston—March 8th (2), Aug. 30th, Nov. 16th (2).

FIFTH JUDICIAL DISTRICT.

Spring—Judge Boykin.

Fall—Judge Graham.

Durham—Jan. 11th (2), †March 22d (2), *May 10th, *Sept. 13th, †Oct. 11th (2).
Granville—Jan. 25th (2), April 19th (2), July 26th (2), Nov. 29 (2).
Chatham—Feb. 8th, May 3d. Sept. 27th (2).
Guilford—Feb. 15th (2), May 24th, Aug. 30th (2), Dec. 13th (2).
Alamance—March 8th, May 17th, Nov. 15th.
Orange—March 15th, Aug. 9th, Nov. 1.
Caswell—April 5th, Aug. 16th, Oct. 25th.
Person—April 12th, Aug. 23d, Nov. 22d.

SIXTH JUDICIAL DISTRICT.

Spring—Judge McIver.

Fall—Judge Boykin.

Pender—March 1st, Sept. 13th (2).
Greene—Feb. 22d, Aug. 16th, Nov. 29th.
New Hanover—‡Jan. 18th (2). †April 12th (2), †Sept. 27th (2).
Lenoir—May 3d (2), Nov. 15th (2).
Duplin—Feb. 15th, Aug. 9th, Dec. 6th.
Sampson—Feb. 1st (2), April 26th, Oct. 11th (2).
Carteret—March 15th, Oct. 25th.
Jones—March 22d, Nov. 1st.
Onslow—March 29th, Nov. 8th.

SEVENTH JUDICIAL DISTRICT.

Spring—Judge Coble.

Fall—Judge McIver.

Columbus—†Feb. 22d, July 19th, Nov. 8th.
Anson—*Jan. 4th, †April 26th, *Sept. 6th, †Nov. 29th.
Cumberland—*Jan. 18th, †April 19th (2), †May 10th, *July 25th, †Nov. 15th (2).
Robeson—Jan. 25th (2), May 17th, †Aug. 2d (3), Oct. 4th (2).
Richmond—*Feb. 8th (2), †April 12th, May 31st, †Aug. 3d, *†Sept. 20th, Nov. 1st, Dec. 6th.
Bladen—March 15th (2), Oct. 25th.
Brunswick—April 5th, *Sept. 13th.
Moore—†Jan. 11th, March 1st (2), *†Aug. 16th (3), *Dec. 13th.

30. Reduce the number of your enemies; increase the number of your friends.—*Branson.*

SUPERIOR COURTS—Continued.

EIGHTH JUDICIAL DISTRICT.

Spring—Judge Starbuck.

Fall—Judge Coble.

Cabarrus—Jan. 18th (2), July 26th (2).
Iredell—Feb. 1st (2), May 17th (2), Aug. 9th (2), Nov. 8th.
Rowan—Feb. 15th (2), May 10th, Aug. 23d (2), Nov. 22d (2).
Davidson—March 1st (2), Sept. 6th (2).
Randolph—March 15th (2), July 12th (2), Nov. 15th.
Montgomery—March 29th, Oct. 4th (2).
Yadkin—May 3d. Oct. 25th (2).

NINTH JUDICIAL DISTRICT.

Spring—Judge Green.

Fall—Judge Starbuck.

Alexander—Jan. 18th, July 26th.
Rockingham—Jan. 25th (2), Aug. 2d. Nov. 8th (2).
Forsyth—Feb. 15th (2), May 10th (2), Aug. 9th (2), Dec. 6th (2).
Wilkes—March 1st (2), Sept. 6th (2).
Alleghany—March 29th, Sept. 20th.
Davie—April 5th (2), Sept. 27th (2).
Stokes—April 12th (2), Oct. 25th (2).
Surry—March 15th (2), Oct. 11th (2).

TENTH JUDICIAL DISTRICT.

Spring—Judge Hoke.

Fall—Judge Green.

Catawba—Feb. 15th (2), Aug. 2d (2).
McDowell—March 1ts (2), Aug. 16th (2).
Burke—March 15th (2), Aug. 30th (2).
Caldwell—March 29th (2), Sept. 13th (2).
Ashe—April 12th, Sept. 27th (2).

Watauga—April 26th, Oct. 11th.
Mitchell—May 3d (2), Oct. 18th (2).
Yancey—May 17th, Nov. 1st (2).

ELEVENTH JUDICIAL DISTRICT.

Spring—Judge Norwood.

Fall—Judge Hoke.

Union—*†Jan. 25th *†Aug. 23d (2).
Stanly—March 1st (2), Sept. 6th (2).
Mecklenburg—†Jan. 18th, †March 15th (2), †May 31st, †Oct. 4th (2), †Dec. 16th.
Gaston—†Feb. 15th, Sept. 20th (2).
Lincoln—March 29th (2), Oct. 18th.
Cleveland—April 12th (2), Oct. 25th (2).
Rutherford—April 26th (2), Nov. 8th (2).
Polk—May 10th, Nov. 22d.
Henderson—†May 17th (2),†Nov. 29th (2)

TWELFTH JUDICIAL DISTRICT.

Spring—Judge Brown.

Fall—Judge Norwood.

Madison—†Feb. 22d (2), †Aug. 2d (2).
Buncombe—†March 8th (3), †Aug. 16th (3), †Dec. 6th (2).
Transylvania—March 29th, Sept. 6th.
Haywood—†April 5th (2), †Sept. 13th (2).
Jackson—April 19th (2), Sept. 27th.
Macon—May 3d, Oct. 4th.
Clay—May 10th, Oct. 11th.
Cherokee—*†May 17th (2),*†Oct. 18th (2).
Graham—May 31st, Nov. 8th (2).
Swain—June 7th (2), Nov. 22d (2).

*For criminal cases.
†For civil cases alone.
‡For civil cases alone except jail cases.
(2)Means two weeks, etc.

CRIMINAL COURTS.

EASTERN DISTRICT.

Judge—Oliver P. Mears, Wilmington.
New Hanover—*Jan. 4th, March 8th, Oct. 13th.
Warren—Jan. 18th, July 12th.
Vance—Jan. 25th, Sept. 13th.
Edgecombe—Feb. 8th, Nov. 1st.
Craven—Feb. 15th, Oct. 4th.
Halifax—Feb. 22d, Dec. 6th.
Mecklenburg—April 12th, Sept. 6th.
Robeson—April 19th.

WESTERN DISTRICT.

Buncombe, Haywood, Madison and Henderson, Judge, Hamilton G. Ewart, Hendersonville ; Solicitor, Robert S. McCall, Asheville ; Clerk, W. H. Wilson.
Haywood—Jan. 11th, June 21st.
Buncombe—Jan. 25th, April 26th. July 26th, Oct. 25th.
Madison—Feb. 8th, June 4th, Nov. 8th.
Henderson—April 12th, June 22, Oct. 1 .

U. S. CIRCUIT AND DISTRICT COURTS.

Charles H Simonton, Charleston, S. C., Judge of Fourth Circuit of U. S. Courts.
Nathan Goff, West Virginia, Judge of U. S. Circuit Court of Appeals for Fourth District.

WESTERN DISTRICT.—R. P. Dick, Greensboro, Judge ; R. B. Glenn, District Attorney; D. A. Covington, Assistant Attorney ; S. L. Trogden, Clerk. *Greensboro*—Circuit and District—April 5th, October 4th. *Statesville*—Circuit and District—H. C. Cowles, Clerk; April 19th, October 18th. *Asheville*—Circuit and District—R. O. Patterson, Clerk ; May 3d, November 1st. *Charlotte*—Circuit and District—H. C. Cowles, Clerk ; June 14th, December 13th.

EASTERN DISTRICT—A. S. Seymour, Judge ; C. B. Aycock, Goldsboro, District Attorney ; Sol. C. Weil, Wilmington, Assistant Attorney ; W. C. Brooks, Clerk. *Elizabeth City*—District Court—April 19th, October 25th. *Newbern*—District Court—Geo. Green, Clerk ; April 26th, November 1st. *Wilmington*—Circuit and District—N. J. Riddick, Clerk ; V. Royster, Assistant Clerk in Raleigh ; W. H. Shaw, Clerk of District and Deputy of Circuit Court at Wilmington ; O. J. Carroll, Marshal ; May 3d, November 3d. *Raleigh*—Circuit Court—N. J. Riddick, Clerk ; V. Royster, Assistant Clerk in Raleigh ; W. H. Shaw, Clerk of District and Deputy of Circuit Court at Wilmington ; O. J. Carroll, Marshal ; May 31st, December 6th.

31. In old age you will be likely to need vast stores of friendship.—*Branson*.

32   BRANSON'S NORTH CAROLINA ALMANAC.

SUPREME COURT.

SUPREME COURT meets first Monday in February. Examinations on Monday. First District, February 1st; Second District, February 8th; Third District, February 15th, Fourth District, February 22d; Fifth District, March 1st; Sixth District, March 8th; Seventh District, March 15th; Eighth District, March 22d; Ninth District, March 29th; Tenth District, April 5th; Eleventh District, April 12th; Twelfth District, April 19th.

Last Monday in September. Examinations on Monday. First District, September 27th; Second District, October 4th; Third District, October 11th; Fourth District, October 18th; Fifth District, October 25th; Sixth District, November 1st; Seventh District, November 8th; Eighth District, November 15th; Ninth District, November 22d; Tenth District, November 29th; Eleventh District, December 6th; Twelfth District, December 13th.

Chief Justice—Wm. Turner Faircloth, Wayne County. Associate Justices—R. M. Douglass, Guilford County; Walter Clark, Wake County; David M. Furches, Iredell County; Walter A. Montgomery, Wake County. Salaries $2,750 each. Zeb. V. Walser, Attorney General; salary $2,000. R. T. Gray, Reporter; salary $750. Thos. S. Kenan, Clerk; salary $300 and fees. R. H. Bradley, Marshal; salary $800. J. L. Seawell, Office Clerk.

GOVERNMENT OF NORTH CAROLINA—1897-1901.

EXECUTIVE DEPARTMENT.

Daniel L. Russell, of New Hanover County, Governor; salary $3,000, and furnished house, fuel and lights.

James A. Reynolds, of Forsyth County, Lieutenant Governor and Speaker of the Senate.

Cyrus Thompson, of Onslow County, Secretary of State; salary $2,000 and fees; $1,000 additional assistance.

Hal W. Ayer, of Wake County, Auditor; salary $1,500; $1,000 additional for clerical assistance.

William H. Worth, of Wake County, Treasurer; salary $3,000.

Charles H. Mebane, of Catawba County, Superintendent of Public Instruction; salary $1,500; $500 per annum additional traveling expenses.

Zebulon Vance Walser, of Davidson County, Attorney General; salary $2,000.

R. T. Gray, Reporter to Supreme Court; salary $750.

Francis H. Cameron, of Wake County, Adjutant General; salary $600.

J. C. Ellington, of Johnston County, State Librarian; salary $1,000.

—— ——, County, Chief Clerk to Auditor; salary $1,000.

—— ——, County, Private Secretary to Governor; salary $1,200.

—— ——, County, Executive Clerk; salary $600.

W. P. Batchelor, of Wake County, Chief Clerk to Secretary of State; salary $1,000.

J. W. Denmark, of Wake County, Chief Clerk to Treasurer; salary $1,500.

S. L. Crowder, of Warren County, Teller; salary $750.

W. H. Worth, Treasurer *ex officio*, and Wm. H. Martin, of Wake County, Clerk for Charitable and Penal Institutions, salary $1,000.

C. M. Roberts, of Vance County, Superintendent of Public Buildings and Grounds; salary $850.

J. C. S. Lumsden, State Standard Keeper; salary $100.

STATE BOARD OF EDUCATION.

The Governor, Lieutenant Governor, Secretary of State, Treasurer, Auditor, Superintendent of Public Instruction and Attorney General constitute the Board.

A sporting-looking character in Birmingham, who rather apes the "Johnny," being at the same time an extraordinary looking individual, reminding one of the gorilla species, deigned to notice a newspaper boy who was watching him attentively. "Awh, Tommy," remarked the sporting character, "what are you staring at?" "Can't say, sir; but I'll go and look you up in my natural history book."—*Exchange*.

MEMBERS OF THE GENERAL ASSEMBLY OF NORTH CAROLINA, 1897-'98.

SENATE.

First District—Currituck, Camden, Pasquotank, Hertford, Gates, Chowan and Perquimans counties, J L. Whidby, r., and J. F. Newsome, p.

Second District—Tyrrell, Washington, Martin, Dare, Beaufort, Hyde and Pamlico, McCaskie, p., and —— Yeager, r.

Third District—Bertie and Northampton, J. M. Early, p.

Fourth District—Halifax, E. T. Clark, p.

Fifth District—Edgecombe, Lee Person, r.

Sixth District—Pitt. — Moye, p.

Seventh District—Wilson, Nash and Franklin, J. F. Mitchell, p.; J. T. Sharp, r.

Eighth District—Craven, Jones, Carteret, Lenoir, Greene and Onslow, G. L. Hardison, p.; and —— McCarthy, r.

Ninth District—Duplin, Wayne and Pender, H. L. Grant, r., and R. G. Maxwell, p.

Tenth District—New Hanover and Brunswick, Geo. H. Cannon, p.

Eleventh District—Vance and Warren, W. B. Henderson, r.

Twelfth District—Wake; C. H. Utley, p.

Thirteenth District—Johnston, E. S. Abell, d.

Fourteenth District—Sampson, Harnett and Bladen, Geo. Butler, p., and E. N. Roberson, p.

Fifteenth District — Columbus and Robeson, Angus Shaw, p., and J. D. Maultsby, r.

Sixteenth District—Cumberland, —— Geddy, p.

Seventeenth District—Granville and Person, Dr. Wm. Merritt, p.

Eighteenth District — Caswell, Alamance. Orange and Durham, Capt. E. S. Parker, d., and J. E. Lyon, p.

Nineteenth District — Chatham, Jno. W. Atwater, p.

Twentieth District — Rockingham, J. A. Walker, p.

Twenty-first District—Guilford, Alf. Scales, d.

Twenty-second District — Randolph and Moore, D. Reid Parker, p.

Twenty-third District — Richmond, Montgomery, Anson and Union, W. H. Adams, p., and Daniel Patterson, r.

Twenty-fourth District—Cabarrus and Stanly, C. D. Barringer, d.

Twenty-fifth District—Mecklenburg, Dr. J. B. Alexander, p.

Twenty-six District—Rowan, Davidson and Forsyth, S. Earnhardt, p., and Jno. A. Ramsey, r.

Twenty-seventh District — Iredell, Davie and Yadkin, —— Shore and —— Sharp, r.

Twenty-eighth District—Stokes and Surry, —— r.

Twenty-ninth District—Catawba, Lincoln, Wilkes and Alexander, R. H. W. Barker, p., and —— r.

Thirtieth District — Alleghany, Ashe and Wautauga, Thos. Sutherland, d.

Thirty-first District — Caldwell, Burke, Mitchell, McDowell and Yancey, E. F. Wakefield, p., and —— r.

Thirty-second District—Gaston, Cleveland, Rutherford and Polk, M. H. Justice, d., J. A. Anthony, d.

Thirty-third District—Buncombe, Madison and Haywood, Geo. H. Smathers, r.; and W. W. Rollins, r.

Thirty-fourth District—Henderson, Transylvania, Jackson and Swain, H. S. Anderson, r.

Thirty-fifth District — Macon, Clay, Cherokee and Graham, J. Frank Ray, p.

The representation would stand: Populists, 24; Democrats, 9; Republicans, 17.

HOUSE.

Alexander—J. W. Watts, d.
Alamance—S. A. White, r.
Alleghany—M. F. Jones, d.
Anson—T. C. Leak, d.
Ashe—Spencer Blackburn, r.
Beaufort—H. E. Hodges, p.
Bertie—H. W. White, r.
Bladen—Sidney Meares, r.
Brunswick—W. W. Drew, p.
Buncombe—V. S. Lusk, r.; W. G. Candler, r.
Burke—John H. Pearson, d.
Cabarrus—A. F. Hileman, p.
Caldwell—J. L. Nelson, d.
Camden— — r.
Carteret—E. C. Duncan, r.
Caswell—C. J. Yarborough, p.
Catawba—L. R. Whitener, p.
Camden—J. E. Burgess, r., and J. E. Bryan, p.
Cherokee—D. W. Deweese, d.
Chowan—Richard Elliott, r.
Clay—Wm. Plott, d.
Cleveland—Dr. B. F. Dixon, d.
Columbus—J. B. Schulken, p.
Craven—Robt. Hancock, r.
Cumberland—Thos. H. Sutton, r., and W. P. Weymiss, r.
Currituck—W. H. Gallop, d.
Dare—George C. Daniels, r.
Davidson—J. W. McCreary, r.
Davie—W. A. Bailey, r.
Duplin—Maury Ward, p.
Durham—John W. Umstead, d.
Edgecombe—Jordan Dancy, r., and E. E. Bryan, r.
Forsyth—J. L. Grubbs, r., and W. P. Ormsley, r.
Franklin—Carter Barrow, p.
Gaston— — White, d.
Gates—J. J. Gatling, d.
Graham—John Dayton, r.
Granville—John King, p.; W. H. Crews, r.
Guilford—J. T. Burch, d.; B. G. Chilcutt, r.
Greene—W. R. Dixon, p.
Halifax—J. H. Arrington, r.; Scott Harris, p.
Harnett— — Chapin, r.
Haywood—J. W. Ferguson, d.
Henderson—J. B. Freeman, r.
Hertford—Stark Hare, r.
Hyde—Jno. G. Harris, p.
Iredell—J. R. McLelland, d., and J. A. Hartness, d.
Jackson—Walter E. Moore, d.
Johnston—Claude M. Smith, d., and Chas. M. Creech, d.
Jones— — Brown, p.

Lenoir—E. P. Hauser, p.
Lincoln—L. A. Abernethy, p.
Macon— — Lyle, d.
Madison—J. W. Roberson, r.
Martin— — Fagan, d.
McDowell—W. A. Conley, d.
Mecklenburg—Sol. Reid, d.; R. P. Craven, p.
Mitchell—L. A. Green, r.
Montgomery—J. A. Reynolds, p.
Moore—W. H. H. Lawhorn, d.
Nash—V. B. Carter, p.
New Hanover—Jno. T. Horne, r.; D. D. Sutton, r.
Northampton—N. R. Rawls, r.
Onslow—R. Duffy, d.
Orange—A. R. Holmes, d..
Pamlico—C. M. Babbitt, p.
Pasquotank—Wm. G. Pool, r.
Perquimans—J. D. Parker, p.
Pender—Gibson James, d.
Person—Jno. S. Cunningham, d.
Pitt—E. V. Cox, r., and Slade Chapman, p.
Polk—Grayson Alredge, r.
Randolph—J. J. White, p., and J. M. Allen, r.
Richmond—Claude Dockery, r., and Y. C. Morton, p.
Robeson—Duncan McBride, p., and W. J. Curry, r.
Rockingham—A. E. Walters, d.; T. B. Foster, p.
Rowan—J. H. McKenzie, d., and Walter Murphy, d.
Rutherford—Lindsey Pergason, r.
Sampson—C. H. Johnson, p., and R. W. Crumpler, p.
Stanly—E. T. Eddins, d.
Stokes—R. J Petree, r.
Surry—J. M. Brower, r.
Swain—J. H. Cathey, d.
Transylvania—E. A. Aiken, r.
Tyrell—Dr. Abe Alexander, r.
Union—J. N. Price, p.
Vance—W. M Peace, r.
Wake—Jas. H. Young, r.; J. P. H. Adams, r., and James Ferrell, p.
Warren—C. A. Cook, r.
Washington—L. N. C. Spruill, r.
Wautauga—Thos. Bingham, r.
Wayne—T. B. Parker, d.; J. E. Person, p.
Wilkes—J. Q. A. Adams, r.; C. H. Summers, r.
Wilson—Dr. B. T. Person, p.
Yadkin—J. C. Pinnix, r.
Yancey— —, d.

This will give the several parties representation as follows: Republicans, 49; Democrats, 35; Populists, 34; doubtful, 2.

GOVERNORS OF NORTH CAROLINA—1585 TO 1776.

1. Ralph Lane, Governor of First Colony, 1585. Residence Roanoke Island, one year.

2. John White, commissioned by Sir Walter Raleigh, as Governor of Raleigh, 1587. He was father of Eleanor, mother of Virginia Dare. Residence Roanoke Island. There were sixteen proprietary governors 1663–1734.

1. William Drummond, 1663, appointed by Sir William Berkeley, one of the Lord's proprietors and Governor of Virginia. Drummond was afterward beheaded by this same Berkeley in 1667 for participating in the Bacon Rebellion.

2. Stephens, 1667. First assembly that made laws for Carolina, assembled in the fall of 1669. Population about 4,000. Bancroft says here, "Are there any who doubt man's capacity for self-government, let them study the history of North Carolina." Their first objects were freedom of conscience and security from taxation, except by their own consent. But the proprietors now tried to introduce "The fundamental constitution of Carolina," drawn up by Locke.

3. Carteret, chosen to succeed Stephens, 1764, returned to England.

4. Eastchurch, appointed 1675; Miller usurped authority, aided by Culpepper; John Harvey governed, 1680, succeeded by Jenkins, and he by Wilkinson, 1681.

5. Seth Sothel, one of the proprietors 1683, who had purchased the rights of Lord Clarendon, Williamson says: "During the six years that he misruled the people of North Carolina, the dark shades of his character were not relieved by a single ray of virtue." He was condemned by the Assembly and exiled from the province.

6. Philip Ludwell, 1693; Alexander Lillington, Deputy Governor, 1693; Thomas Harvey, 1695.

7. Thomas Smith, appointed 1695. He advised proprietors to send out one who could harmonize affairs, and they sent out.

8. John Archibald, a follower of Fox, 1695, "whose administration was wise and salutary, cultivation of Rice and introduced by Thomas Smith. Thomas Harvey, Deputy Governor, 1696.

9. Henderson Walker, 1699–1704. A period of peace, content and growth. We find on his tombstone: "Henderson Walker, President of the Council and Commander-in-Chief of North Carolina, during whose administration the province enjoyed that tranquility which is to be wished it may never want."

10. Robert Daniel, appointed by Sir Nat. Johnston, 1709. First church built in North Carolina, in Chowan County, in 1705. "Boston News Letter," the first American newspaper. In 1704, by intrigue, was passed a law disfranchising all Dissenters, Quakers, etc., the majority of the population. Governor and people together opposed and petitioned Parliament. House of Lords declared the act repugnant to the laws of England, and contrary to the charter of the proprietors, etc." Thus was North Carolina advanced as to the principle of "divorce of church and State."

11. Thomas Cary, appointed by Sir Nat. Johnston, 1705, disapproved by Lords, Proprietors. Glover chosen by the Council. Great dissension and anarchy.

12. Edward Hyde receives appointment, but peace was not restored, and he was in office until 1712. He died of yellow fever scourge, 1712. Now had commenced the trouble with the Indians and the Tuscaxona wars.

13. George Pollock, 1712. The first issue of paper money in North Carolina was to pay the heavy debts of the Indian wars.

14. Charles Eden, 1713. During his government were committed the piratical ravages of Edward Teach or "Black Beard," as he was known. Some in authority were accused of sharing in his booty. He was captured and beheaded. Eden resided at Chowan Court House, now called

35. Do the very best you can to-day, and hope to do still better to-morrow.—*Branson*.

BRANSON'S NORTH CAROLINA ALMANAC. 37

for him Edenton. His home was Eden House. He was buried in Bertie county.

15. Thomas Pollock, 1722.

16. George Burrington, 1724. Last of the Proprietory Government. Royal Governors, five, 1729, 1776. In 1729 the Lords Proprietors surrendered their charter under Charles II and thus ended their government of sixty-six years, and their last Governor was by the King George IV appointed to rule again five years

1. George Burrington, 1729. He had not proven himself before, yet they endured his tyranical and vitcious conduct till he was forced to flee in 1734. Afterwards murdered in England. Nathaniel Rice qualified in Edenton, April, 1734.

2. Gabriel Johnston appointed; arrived October, 1734. Was qualified in Brunswick. Under his prudent administration the colony revived, and from this period increased in population, wealth and resources. In 1738 commissioners ran the line between North and South Carolina. France declared war against England and Ft. Johnston is built 1745. A printing press imported by James Davis, 1749. Boundary between Virginia and North Carolina extended, 1749. The computation of time altered by Parliament, 1750. Eleven days omitted—Johnston died in 1752 and government was administered by Matthew Rowan, until a successor was appointed. Troops sent to Virginia 1754. Rowan qualified at Brunswick. Parkham says: "North Carolina was thus the first to respond to the call for help against the Indians and French."

3. Arthur Dobbs, 1754, 1765—Printing encouraged; "Fort Dobbs" built on the Yadkin; Col. Hugh Waddell commissioned to treat with the Catawbas and Cherokees.

4. William Tryon, 1765-'71; who governed in the turbulous but interesting term of the Stamp Act of the Regulators.

5. Josiah Martin, 1771-'76; who was true to his King, but there was no longer any King for America, as shown May 20th, 1775. In 1776 he went to South Carolina, but was with Cornwallis at Guilford Court House.

THE MONTH OF APRIL, 1865.

This month was probably the most eventful of any one month known to the American people.

2d of April General Lee evacuated Richmond, Va.

9th. Gen. Lee surrendered at Appomattox Court House. The last charge was said to have been made by N. C. troops.

11th. Battle of Bentonville, Johnston, county, of this State.

13th. Raleigh surrendered to General W. T. Sherman.

14th. President Lincoln was assassinated by Booth at Ford's Theatre, in Washington City.

15th. President Andrew Johnson was sworn into office.

26th. Gen. Jo. Johnson surrendered to Gen. Sherman, near Durham, N. C.

These events all occurred in the month of April, 1865, and were all of National importance.

It is also remarkable that so many of these things took place on our soil, and nearly all were largely participated in by North Carolina people.

LEVI BRANSON.

---

*The draft horse is the best for the farmer for several reasons. He works more satisfactorily and at less expense and worry; he sells more readily and at better prices than any other; it costs less to raise and break him and get him ready for market because of his docility; he will pay his keep after two years old, and is fully broken when matured.

A USEFUL POULTRY HOUSE.

[Extract from Bulletin 130 of the N. C. Agr. Experiment Station.]

The farmer can no more expect to realize a profit on his hens, when
they are not properly housed, than he would from his cattle allowed to
remain out in all manner of weather. In housing the poultry, it is not
necessary to build elaborate, expensive structures, but simply have them
warm, dry, and in the right location. The houses should always face
south or a little southeast, that they may have the benefit of the morning sun in winter. The warmer the hens are in winter the more eggs
they will lay. A good, cheap, substantial house for use in our State is
shown in the accompanying illustration.

A USEFUL POULTRY HOUSE.—The house herewith described (Fig. 1)
is about the correct size for eight or ten hens and a cock, and is of the
style we have built for general use in the yards of the Experiment Station. Should more than this number of fowls be kept, the length can
be correspondingly increased. Ground plan, 6 x 8 ft.; height, front 10
ft., back 7 ft. The house should face south. The north, west, and east
ends should be planked up and down with rough pine plank one inch
thick; let the bottom extend down into the ground four or six inches,
then pile dirt well in around it, so as to exclude water and air. The
joints all around should be tightly broken with three-inch strips.

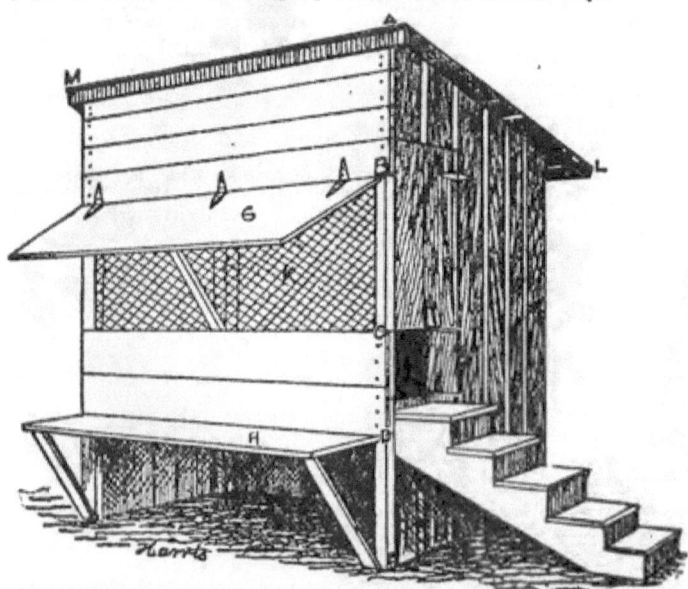

Fig, 1—A convenient poultry house.   Such as is used at the Experiment Station.

The cost of such a house, with rough lumber at 75 cents per 100, would
be about $8.00.   The lumber required to build such a house is as follows:

Rough pine plank, 10 in. wide, 1 in. thick ....200 feet.
     "   "   studding, 2x4 in.........................100 feet.
     "   "   strips for breaking joints, 1x3............ 49 feet.
Shingling laths.......................................100 lineal feet.
Tongue and groove flooring............................. 50 square feet.
Shingles 500

The floor should be of tongue-and-grooved stuff. Place the floor 2½ feet above the ground, then underneath the house the fowls have good dry quarters in case of rain, snow, or high winds. The front underneath should be open.

Place a large door (F) 2 ft. x 5½ ft. in east end; at lower left hand corner of F make a small door, size 7 x 9 inches, to allow the fowls to come and go without opening the large door. The steps should be rather flat; a rise of six inches will answer very well. The front should be made as follows: Place plank lengthwise from A to B 3 ft., then from B to C a piece of woven fence wire (K) 3 ft. wide, 2 inch mesh, C to D 1½ ft. of plank, D to E 2½ ft. and open. G represents a shutter hung over the wire for use in cold weather. It may be lowered or raised. It also serves to keep out rain or snow. H is a 12-inch plank placed immediately in front of the floor to serve as a protection against rain beating underneath the house.

Two roosts should be placed lengthwise, ten inches from the floor and near the back of the house. They can be made from strips two inches square, with both top edges rounded.

The roof should be of tarred paper or good shingles, and should project over on all sides at least 10 inches.

NEST BOXES.—The subject of nest boxes is a much discussed one, opinions differing greatly. We prefer single boxes outside the roosting house, because where hens lay and sit, lice naturally congregate, and where the nests are built in the house the whole affair is soon full of them.

Make boxes 15 inches wide, 18 inches long, 14 inches high in front, 9 inches high at back. Make a good, tight, removable top. Cut a door 6x8 inches in one corner of front end. No bottom is needed; scoop out a shallow hole where box is to sit, and put in plenty of clean hay or straw. When the straw becomes soiled, place the box with the contents a sufficient distance away from the house and burn the straw while in the box This way all lice will be killed. Before adding new nest material, give the inside of box a good coat of whitewash, or kerosene emulsion.

ORPHAN SCHOOLS.

Home and Industrial School (Independent) .... Asheville
Orphanage (Friends) .... Archdale
Orphan's Home (Presbyterian) .... Barium Springs
Orphanage (colored—State aid) .... Oxford
Orphanage Home (Odd Fellows) .... Goldsboro
Orphanage (Baptist) .... Thomasville
Thompson Orphanage (Episcopal) .... Charlotte

CLEVELAND SPRINGS,

SHELBY, N. C.

LEE & MILLER, Proprietors.   F. W. ELDREDGE, Manager.

....Attractions....

White and red sulphur and iron springs; hot and cold sulphur baths; unsurpassed summer climate; Piedmont region, one thousand feet above sea level; cool nights; no mosquitos; charming walks and drives; good roads; excellent livery facilities at reasonable rates; mountain views; music, dancing, bowling, tennis, croquet; pleasant company; and, not least, the near-by town of Shelby, with its beautiful homes and churches and attractive stores.

COUNTY OFFICERS—Corrected as Changes Occur.

#	County	County Town	Clerk Superior Court	Chair'n County Commissioners	Register of Deeds	Sheriff	Treasurer	County Examiner
1	Alamance,	Graham,	C. D. Vincent,	S. H. Webb,	P. A. Mitchell,	R. T. Kernodie,	R. C. Dickey,	Rev. P. H. Fleming.
2	Alexander,	Taylorsville,	J. B. Pool,	A. A. Hill,	Thos. A. Hudson,	J. W. Watts,	J. M. Watts,	William M. Smith.
3	Alleghany,	Sparta,	M. F. Cox,	Allen Jones,	J. N. Edwards,	W. F. Thompson,	Levi J. Jones,	T. J. Fender.
4	Anson,	Wadesboro,	J. C. McLauchlin,	H. W. Ledbetter,	S. A. Denton,	Benjamin L. Wall,	J. O. Craig,	W. D. Redfearn.
5	Ashe,	Jefferson,	P. Blevin,	E. H. Phillips,	M. L. Smith,	Byron Sturgill,	B. Sturgill,	J. W. Jones.
6	Beaufort,	Washington,	G. W. Guilford,	Dr. W. J. Bullock,	O. K. Silliey,	R. T. Hodges,	R. T. Hodges,	Dr. B. Stilley.
7	Bertie,	Windsor,	W. L. Lyon,	J. R. Stokes,	Sol. Cherry,	T. C. Bond,	T. C. Bond,	R. W. Askew.
8	Bladen,	Elizabethtown,	W. J. Sutton,	C. P. Parham,	Jas. R. Mulford,	S. G. Wooten,	R. L. Bridges,	J. R. Dunham.
9	Brunswick,	Southport,	S. P. Tharp,	S. J. Stanly,	J. W. Brooks,	D. R. Walker,	S. M. Robbins,	George Leonard.
10	Buncombe,	Asheville,	J. L. Cathey,	J. P. Erwin,	John H. Cooper,	Thomas M. Webb,	J. H. Courtuey,	J. H. Feimot.
11	Burke,	Morganton,	P. W. Patton,	G. P. Erwin,	W. M. Weddington,	John A. Sims,	Waters,	Rev. R. L. Patton.
12	Cabarrus,	Concord,	James C. Gibson,	Jacob Dove,	W. F. F. Palmer,	A. H. Boyd,	G. Ed. Kestler,	J. F. Shinn.
13	Caldwell,	Lenoir,	Jas. W. McCall,	John M. Downs,	W. K. Dozier,	W. S. Bartlett,	A. H. Courtney,	C. D. Sherrill.
14	Camden,	Camden C. H.,	L. A. Garner,	G. H. Riggs,	N. L. Carrow,	M. A. Hill,	G. H. Jacobs,	C. H. Speacer.
15	Carteret,	Beaufort,	L. A. Forbes,	W. L. Arendell,	F. A. Pierson,	T. T. Donoho,	N. W. Taylor,	Jasper Pigott.
16	Caswell,	Yanceyville,	Spencer B Adams,	J. W. Corbett,	John F. Herman,	Theo. L. Bandy,	T. H. Harrison,	A. E. Henderson.
17	Catawba,	Newton,	John W. Rockett,	P. A. Hoyle,	T. C. McDonald,	J. J. Jenkins,	Noah Barringer,	J. W. Rowe.
18	Chatham,	Pittsboro,	R. H. Dixon,	W. A. Lineberry,	L. D. Byrum,	W. Davidson,	I. J. Jenkins,	R. B. Lineberry.
19	Cherokee,	Murphy,	D. L. Watts,	A. H. Sudderth,	I. F. Williams,	L. W. Parker,	Thomas Payne,	James Lovingood.
20	Chowan,	Edenton,	T. H. Hancock,	Frank Wood,	D. B. F. Nance,	George M. Johnson,	C. S. Vann,	Rev. J. E. White.
21	'lay,	Hayesville,	H. C. Privatt,	E. G. Smith,	I. M. Biddle,	A. B. Suttle,	R. G. Ketron,	I. H. Chambers.
22	Cleveland,	Shelby,	T. D. Lattimore,	I. W. Garrett,	Alex. McNeill,	Mathew J. Ward,	J. B. Byers,	J. A. Anthony.
23	Columbus,	Whiteville,	A. H. Lennon,	S. N. Forney,	C. J. Daugh,	W. B. Lane,	J. K. Gore,	L. W. Stanly.
24	Craven,	Newbern,	W. M. Watson,	Jas. A. Bryan,	Wil. Harris,	McD Geddie,	Thomas Daniels,	John S. Long.
25	Cumberland,	Fayetteville,	Cyrus Murphy,	J. M. Lamb,	G. W. Williams,	Edward Tillett,	J. B. Troy,	H. E. King.
26	Currituck,	Currituck C. H.,	E. W. Ansell,	A. M. Willcy,	G. W. Williams,	R. M. Smith,	Ed. Tillett,	V. L. Pitts.
27	Dare,	Manteo,	J. B Jennett,	B. L. Daniels,	G. W. Sheek,	F. J. Leonard,	S. E. Mann,	D. E. P. Gates.
28	Davidson,	Lexington,	George E Hunt,	J. W. Lee,	Thadeus Jones,	W. T. Williams,	Dr. James McGuire,	Allen Jones.
29	Davie,	Mocksville,	A. T. Grant,	N. A. Peebles,	W. W. Woods,	Daniel Moore,	Daniel Moore,	Leon Cash.
30	Duplin,	Kenansville,	A. J. Christian,	I. F. Hill,	B. F. Lawson,	J. W. Riggsbee,	T. J. Holloway,	R. W. Millard.
31	Durham,	Durham,	E. J. Pennington,	C. B Green,	J. F. Miller,	W. T. Knight,	S. S. Nash,	— Blalock.
32	Edgecombe,	Tarboro,	S. Wilson,	Orren Williams,	W. K. Martin,	Kapp.	J. F. Griffith,	F. S. Wilkinson.
33	Forsyth,	Winston,	Rufus R. Harris,	M. D. Bailey,	J. J. Ormond,	H. C. Kearney,	B. F. Wilder,	Dr. A. P. Davis.
34	Franklin,	Louisburg,	G. H. Davis,	T. S. Collie,	J. Holler,	A. F. Loftin,	Lee R. Stowe,	N. Y. Gulley.
35	Gaston,	Dallas,	W. T. Cross,	George Patrick,	W. F. Manney,	R. O. Riddick,	H. B. Cross,	L. G. Cathey.
36	Gates,	Gatesville,	J. M. Sikes,	S. J. Harrell,	Dr. L. C. Taylor,	John A. Ammons,	S. B. Rose,	John R. Wilton.
37	Graham,	Robbinsville,	John W. Blount,	W. D. Crisp,	Chas. A. Lassiter,	Wiley S. Coaart,	A. S. Peace,	J. A. Hyde.
38	Granville,	Oxford,	E. L. Ragan,	J. A. Bullock,	A. G. Kirkman,	Benj. W. Edwards,	John Sugg,	Alex. Baker.
39	Greene,	Snow Hill,	S. M. Gary,	W. E. Best,	J. F. Brinkley,	Samuel Clark,	John A. Hodgin,	E. A. Darden.
40	Guilford,	Greensboro,		J. H. Mills,	J. McK. Byrd,	John H. Pope,	W. F. Parker,	Simeon A. Hodgin.
41	Halifax,	Halifax C. H.,		W. M. Brown,	H. B. Moore,	W. J. Haynes,	George D. Speace,	Aaron Prescott.
42	Harnett,	Lillington,	Felix M. McKay,	John M. Hodges,	John B. Aridge,	John G. Grant,	W. C. Hannah,	L. B. Chapin.
43	Haywood,	Waynesville,	C. M. Pace,	J. M. Tate,	Geo. A. Brown,	William E. Cullens,	W. J. Davis,	A. J. Garner.
44	Henderson,	Hendersonville,		A. Cannon,			W. E. Cullens,	C. J. Edney.
45	Hertford,	Winton,	Thos. D. Boone,	Wm. T. Brown,				S. M. Aumack.

No.	County	Seat						
46	Hyde	Swan Quarter	Jas. H. Wahab,	J. D. Watson,	L. H. Swindell,	R. D. Harris,	C. L. Benson,	L. N. Watson.
47	Iredell	Statesville	H. V. Furches,	J. A. Cooper,	M. E. Ramsey,	M. A. White,	W. A. Wright,	R. V. Tharpe.
48	Jackson	Webster	H. C. Cowan,	S. H. Bryson,	J. R. Long,	J. E. McLain,	A. V. P. Bryson,	John N. Wilson.
49	Johnston	Smithfield	W. S. Stevens,	P. H. C. Dupree,	A. K. Smith,	J. T. Ellington,	T. R. Hood,	Ira T. Turlington.
50	Jones	Trenton	S. E. Koonce,	J. A. Smith,	Ang. Haskins,	J. H. Bell,	Lewis King,	T. J. Whitaker.
51	Lenoir	Kinston	S. H. Bright,	Henry Tull,	C. S. Pittman,	T. R. Hodges,	J. H. Dawson,	E. G. Tindall.
52	Lincoln	Lincolnton	G. A. Barkley,	H. E. Ramsaur,	J. F. Killian,	C. H. Rhodes,	D. L. Yount,	L. A. Abernethy.
53	Macon	Franklin	Lee Crawford,	John Ammons,	J. S. Sloan,	C. T. Roane,	C. T. Roane,	L. H. Garland.
54	Madison	Marshall	M. A. Chandley,	Jasper Ebbs,	R. F. Fox,	James H. White,	Enoch Rector,	W. P. Jervis.
55	Martin	Williamston	N. S. Peel,	Jos. B. Coffield,	Jas. A. Teel,	N. J. Hardison,	S. R. Biggs,	Dr. N. H. Harrell.
56	McDowell	Marion	B. B. Price,	J. C. Conley,	J. C. Brown,	R. J. Nichols,	G. H. Gardin,	J. Frank Wilson.
57	Mecklenburg	Charlotte	J. M. Morrow,	Jno. R. Erwin,	J. W. Cobb,	Z. T. Smith,	R. H. Walker,	M. A. Gray.
58	Mitchell	Bakersville	J. C. Bowman,	A. A. Wiseman,	G. S. Beaman,	George K. Pritchard,	W. S. Daniels,	J. J. Britt.
59	Montgomery	Troy	J. S. Lewis,	J. T. Wade,	D. S. Ray,	D. E. Ewing,	D. A. Ewing,	Joseph W. Dixon.
60	Moore	Carthage	D. A. McDonald,	John Shaw,	J. H. T. Baker,	J. L. Currie,	Dr. K. M. Ferguson,	W. H. McNeill.
61	Nash	Nashville	M. B. Williford,	T. E. Westray,	John Haar,	I. P. Arrington,	E. J. Braswell,	Maj. M. L. Conyers.
62	New Hanover	Wilmington	J. T. Flythe,	W. P. Vick,	M. F. Stancell,	Elijah Hewlett,	S. Van Amringe,	M. C. S. Noble.
63	Northampton	Jackson	J. D. Taylor,	Horace A. Bagg,	C. C. Martin,	W. H. Buffaloe,	Alveston Burgwynn,	A. J. Conner.
64	Onslow	Jacksonville	Charles Gecock,	D. J. Sanders,	John Lane,	F. W. Hargett,	J. F. Cox,	E. M. Koonce.
65	Orange	Hillsboro	D. F. Crawford,	D. H. Hamilton,	Alexander Lee,	John K. Hughes,	W. F. Jackson,	H. C. Thompson.
66	Pamlico	Bayboro	Festus Miller,	G. W. Scott,	M. B. Culpepper,	T. J. Parker,	John C. Cooper,	T. A. Mazingo.
67	Pasquotank	Elizabeth City	W. T. Overman,	J. J. Fay,	L. P. O. Stringfield,	T. P. Wilcox,	J. S. Morris,	Gaston Pool.
68	Pender	Burgaw	W. W. Larkins,	C. T. Wood,	W. O. White,	W. W. Alderman,	W. W. Alderman,	J. T. Bland.
69	Perquimans	Hertford	J. O. A. Wood,	T. H. Street,	H. J. White,	A. F. Riddick,	Jacob H. Parker,	W. E. Webb.
70	Person	Roxboro	L. W. Bradsher,	Council Dawson,	J. A. Carver,	J. A. Carver,	C. Pass,	W. H. Ragsdale.
71	Pitt	Greenville	R. A. Moye,	C. W. Pearson,	J. W. King,	J. K. King,	J. Johnson,	A. L. McNowry.
72	Polk	Columbus	N. B. Hampton,	J. E. Walker,	J. T. Winslow,	W. C. Robertson,	L. Swaim,	N. C. English.
73	Randolph	Asheboro	J. M. Miltikin,	W. T. Covington,	C. Dockery,	G. G. Hendrix,	E. G. Johnson,	M. I. McIver.
74	Richmond	Rockingham	Z. P. Lon...,	Jno. M. Galloway,	A. S. Thompson,	J. M. Smith,	W. B. Wray,	W. R. Searls.
75	Robeson	Lumberton	T. S. Malloy,	C. W. Pearson,	R. I. Sneed,	George B. McLoud,	W. B. Wray,	N. S. Smith.
76	Rockingham	Wentworth	W. C. Watson,	W. I. Kinttt,	H. N. Woodson,	James M. Monroe,	J. S. McCubbins,	R. G. Kizer.
77	Rowan	Salisbury	W. A. Pigford,	J. W. Biggerstaff,	J. W. Mode,	J. V. McFarland,	C. L. Miller,	H. W. Howe.
78	Rutherford	Rutherfordton	S. H. Milton,	A. Hobbs,	A. F. Herring,	J. N. Marshburn,	J. M. Marshburn,	George E. Butler.
79	Sampson	Clinton	S. O. Petree,	I. P. Efird,	W. T. Huckabee,	George R. McCain,	George D. Palmer,	R. A. Crowell.
80	Stanley	Albemarle	W. W. Hampton,	Dr. John W. Neal,	D. V. Carroll,	Joel H. Fulton,	Joel H. Fulton,	M. T. Chilton.
81	Stokes	Danbury	J. B. Snow,	J. A. Park,	J. A. Haynes,	J. A. Adams,	J. A. Adams,	Lee Marr.
82	Surry	Dobson	V. H. Hampton,	A. H. Hayes,	N. B. Thompson,	J. F. Teague,	B. G. Fisher,	J. B. Sparger.
83	Swain	Charleston	F. H. Holmes,	C. L. Osborne,	E. S. English,	V. R. McGaha,	Vance Galloway,	Judson Corn.
84	Transylvania	Brevard	F. D. Wolfe,	R. S. Hassell,	A. W. Owens,	A. W. Owens,	J. C. Meekins Sr.,	Arthur Spruill.
85	Tyrrell	Columbia	D. H. Gill,	James A. Monk,	P. P. Plyler,	B. A. Horu,	James McNeely,	Lee Marr.
86	Union	Monroe	Dan. H. Young,	Jas. Young,	T. S. Eaton,	A. W. Owens,	H. P. Hicks,	C. E. Fuller.
87	Vance	Henderson	W. A. White,	Jas. Hill,	J. J. Rogers,	W. H. Smith,	H. H. Knight,	J. H. Boyte.
88	Wake	Raleigh	Thos. J. Marriner,	M. J. Hawkins,	W. F. Thornton,	Hambleton T. Jones,	Nathan M. Palmer,	J. R. Rodwell.
89	Warren	Warrenton	M. B. Blackburn,	W. C. Sikerthorpe,	W. H. Stubbs,	W. E. Davis,	Thomas J. Basinght,	H. S. Ward.
90	Washington	Plymouth	A. M. Vannoy,	J. E. Peterson,	John W. Hodges,	Levi Mount,	L. A. Greca,	W. M. Francum.
91	Watauga	Boone	J. D. Bardin,	W. C. Coffey,	G. C. Kornegay,	W. P. Scott,	Clarence Call,	E. T. Atkinson.
92	Wayne	Goldsboro	A. F. Herring,	I. E. Edwards,	D. G. Edwards,	Clarence Call,	Clarence Call,	Rev. R. W. Barber.
93	Wilkes	Wilkesboro	R. E. Holton,	J. M. Jones,	W. M. Willis,	W. L. Crowell,	A. F. Woodruff,	R. W. Hayes.
94	Wilson	Wilson	W. B. Baaks,	A. J. Bennett,	A. B. Silver,	J. S. Huskins,	C. M. Byrd,	J. C. Pismix.
95	Yadkin	Yadkinville						
96	Yancey	Burnsville						James L. Wyatt, Jr.

COL. AVERY'S BODY FOUND.

It was about the finding of the long lost grave of the late Col. Isaac E. Avery.

He was in the front in the charge at Gettysburg.

He was shot in the forehead and killed.

A reporter of the *News and Observer* happened to be telling Major J. W. Wilson, of Morganton, who sat in his office, about the finding of the body, a brief account of which appeared in the Baltimore *Sun.* A negro happened to be digging in Riverview Cemetery in Williamsport, Md., and upon examining the body found charcoal in the coffin, that had been put there by friends. This was known, and the body was thus identified as well as by the Confederate uniform which was still recognizable. Judge A. C. Avery and Mr. McPherson, of Fayetteville, had last June vainly sought for the remains, but the story went on to say that they would now be reburied at Gettysburg, and a monument be put over the spot.

The reporter had quite finished his story, when Major Wilson said quietly, in a tone that seemed to be weighted in memories: "I put that charcoal there."

So there sat the man, who, besides an old negro still living, is the only one who saw laid to rest that knight of North Carolina.

"The old negro," said the Major, "his name is Lije; he is still living up in Morganton; he was the body-servant of Col. Avery. When Judge Avery went last June to try to find his brother's body, I gave him a diagram to aid him, and turning to Lige, who was near, I said, 'Lije, do you reckon you would know that spot now?' 'I mought not know how to git to dat part ob de country,' he replied, 'but ef you put me in dat cemetery, I could find de place.' When Col. Avery was killed, Lije and I and Sergeant Brown, from McDowell County (he died last year), took the body up and put it in a wagon, and Lije drove on ahead in the wagon. When I got up to Williamsport on the retreat, I had the body carried to a barn, and I got some rough oak boards and made the best coffin we could, and I got some charcoal from an old blacksmith shop in the corner, and put it all around the body. I hoped to preserve it until we could get it across the river to Virginia soil. Col. Avery was killed, I think, July 2d, and I overtook Lije at Williamsport, near a little graveyard, between the town and the river. We dug the grave ourselves the best we could, and laid the body away with the head to a little cedar, which I notched with a hatchet, and on which I cut his name. There was a little pine tree there, too. I remember the pine and the cedar," the Major continued, with his eyes seeming to be looking through the years. "This was on July 5th."

The Major talked more of Col. Avery, of his magnificent physique and quiet, almost silent courage. He was only 33 years of age, handsome, strong, made of war stuff.

Will it be that, when his body is taken to its second resting place, the Major and Lije will be there? Even if they are not, the face of his master will come to Lije, and the soul of his comrade will come to the Major only as they beheld them that July morning—silent except for the sigh of the little cedar and the burial hymn of the river.

Jennie was learning to read and spell, but it was very hard for her to remember what her teacher had told her about pronouncing a double letter when she came to one. She would say "a a," or "e e," or "t t," instead of "double a," or "double e," etc. Her teacher had one day drilled her considerably on this matter in spelling. Shortly afterward Jennie was called on to read. The paragraph began, "Up, up, Lucy," and Jennie read it triumphantly, "Double up, Lucy !"

How easy it is for a lazy man to prove that luck is against him.

NORFOLK & SOUTHERN RAILROAD

—THE—

... DIRECT RAIL LINE TO ALL POINTS IN EASTERN NORTH CAROLINA...... ...

Double daily trains between NORFOLK, ELIZABETH CITY, HERTFORD, SNOWDEN, EDENTON, MACKEY'S FERRY, ROPER, PANTEGO, BELHAVEN, etc. Connects at Elizabeth City with the Sound Line Steamers for NEWBERNE, ROANOKE ISLAND, KINSTON, GOLDSBORO, MOREHEAD CITY, WILMINGTON, and all points on the Atlantic & North Carolina R. R. and Wilmington, New Berne & Norfolk R. R. Connects at Edenton with N. & S. R. R. Co.'s Steamers for Plymouth, Windsor and all landings on the Roanoke, Cashie, Chowan and Scuppernong Rivers and Salmon Creek. Connects at Belhaven with Old Dominion Steamer for Aurora, South Creek, Washington, N. C., and landings on Pungo and Pamlico Rivers. This Company, with its annex steamboat service on the rivers and sounds of Eastern North Carolina, affords to shippers quick and reliable transportation at low rates.

——HOME-SEEKERS——

Should not fail to visit the section traversed by the Norfolk & Southern. It offers many advantages to those seeking homes in a mild climate and productive country. Lands can be bought at reasonable figures and on easy terms, which are especially adapted to the cultivation of early vegetables and truck, corn, cotton, rice, peanuts, etc. Large and extensive saw mills for the manufacture of Lumber are located on the line of the Norfolk & Southern Railroad, which supply North Carolina Pine Lumber to all sections reached l rail, at favorable through rates. Connecting with the various transportation lines at Norfolk, quick dispatch of Truck, Fish and Perishable Freight is given daily to all Northern markets. Special rates for land buyers and prospectors will be given upon application to the General Office of the Norfolk & Southern Railroad Co., Norfolk, Va.

M. K. KING,
General Manager.

H. C. HUDGINS,
General Freight and Passenger Agent.

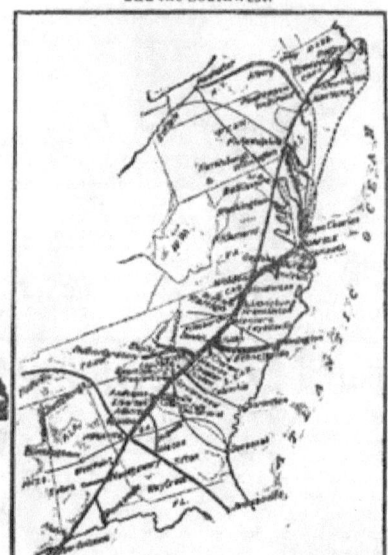

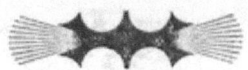

BRANSON'S SHORT CALENDAR FOR 1897.

JANUARY.

S	M	T	W	T	F	S
					1	2
3	4	5	6	7	8	9
10	11	12	13	14	15	16
17	18	19	20	21	22	23
24	25	26	27	28	29	30
31						

FEBRUARY.

S	M	T	W	T	F	S
	1	2	3	4	5	6
7	8	9	10	11	12	13
14	15	16	17	18	19	20
21	22	23	24	25	26	27
28						

MARCH.

S	M	T	W	T	F	S
	1	2	3	4	5	6
7	8	9	10	11	12	13
14	15	16	17	18	19	20
21	22	23	24	25	26	27
28	29	30	31			

APRIL.

S	M	T	W	T	F	S
				1	2	3
4	5	6	7	8	9	10
11	12	13	14	15	16	17
18	19	20	21	22	23	24
25	26	27	28	29	30	

MAY.

S	M	T	W	T	F	S
						1
2	3	4	5	6	7	8
9	10	11	12	13	14	15
16	17	18	19	20	21	22
23	24	25	26	27	28	29
30	31					

JUNE.

S	M	T	W	T	F	S
	1	2	3	4	5	
6	7	8	9	10	11	12
13	14	15	16	17	18	19
20	21	22	23	24	25	26
27	28	29	30			

JULY.

S	M	T	W	T	F	S
				1	2	3
4	5	6	7	8	9	10
11	12	13	14	15	16	17
18	19	20	21	22	23	24
25	26	27	28	29	30	31

AUGUST.

S	M	T	W	T	F	S
1	2	3	4	5	6	17
8	9	10	11	12	13	24
15	16	17	18	19	20	21
22	23	24	25	26	27	8
29	30	31				

SEPTEMBER.

S	M	T	W	T	F	S
			1	2	3	4
5	6	7	8	9	10	11
12	13	14	15	16	17	18
19	20	21	22	23	24	25
26	27	28	29	30		

OCTOBER.

S	M	T	W	T	F	S
					1	2
3	4	5	6	7	8	9
10	11	12	13	14	15	16
17	18	19	20	21	22	23
24	25	26	27	28	29	30
31						

NOVEMBER.

S	M	T	W	T	F	S
	1	2	3	4	5	6
7	8	9	10	11	12	13
14	15	16	17	18	19	20
21	22	23	24	25	26	27
28	29	30				

DECEMBER.

S	M	T	W	T	F	S
			1	2	3	4
5	6	7	8	9	10	11
12	13	14	15	16	17	18
19	20	21	22	23	24	25
26	27	28	29	30	31	

Vol. 4.]   31st YEAR OF PUBLICATION.   [No. 1.

BRANSON'S

AGRICULTURAL

ALMANAC

FOR THE YEAR OF OUR LORD

1898,

And until the 4th of July, the 122d year of American Independence.

Carefully Calculated for the Latitude and Longitude of Raleigh, by

LEVI BRANSON, A. M., D. D.

LEVI BRANSON, Publisher, Raleigh, N. C.

1. All men have faith in something, hence they work expecting results.—*Branson.*

TIME.

The calculations of this Almanac are made in mean solar or clock time, which is indicated by a well regulated watch or clock, and does not correspond with the Sun precisely, except on four days of the year.

Apparent time is that which makes the Sun come to the meridian at 12 o'clock. No good clock will run with the Sun; if set with the Sun on the 2d day of January, the clock will seem to te one minute too fast on the 3d of January.

To adapt the calculations of this Almanac to apparent time, use the minutes in the column marked "Sun slow" or "Sun fast;" add them when fast, substract them when slow.

The calculations are made for the Latitude and Longitude of Raleigh, N. C., but the times phases &c., will vary only a few minutes for any part of North Carolina, South Carolina, Georgia, Tennessee or Virginia.

TWELVE SIGNS OF THE ZODIAC.

The Head and Face sign.   ♈ Aries the Ram......Ar.

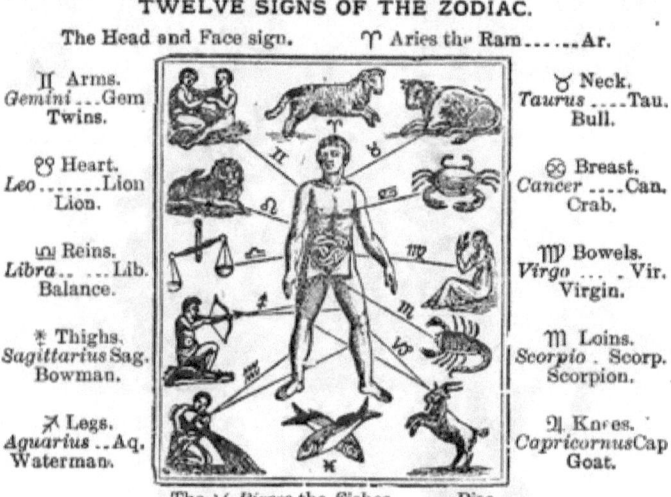

♊ Arms.
Gemini ...Gem
Twins.

♌ Heart.
Leo.......Lion
Lion.

♎ Reins.
Libra.. ...Lib.
Balance.

♐ Thighs.
Sagittarius Sag.
Bowman.

♒ Legs.
Aquarius ...Aq.
Waterman.

♉ Neck.
Taurus ....Tau.
Bull.

♋ Breast.
Cancer ....Can.
Crab.

♍ Bowels.
Virgo ... . Vir.
Virgin.

♏ Loins.
Scorpio . Scorp.
Scorpion.

♑ Knees.
Capricornus Cap
Goat.

The ♓ *Pisces* the Fishes .. ...Pisc.

To know where the sign is, find the day of the month, and against the day in the column marked Moon's Signs you have the sign or place of the Moon, and then find the sign; it will give you the part of the body it is supposed to govern

SIGNS.

SPRING SIGNS.
- Aries or Ram.
- Taurus, or Bull.
- Gemini, or Twins

SUMMER SIGNS.
- Cancer, or Crab-fish.
- Leo, or Lion.
- Virgo, or Virgin.

AUTMNN SIGNS.
- Libra, or Balance.
- Scorpio, or Scorpion.
- Sagittarius, or Bowman.

WINTER SIGNS.
- Capricornus, or Goat.
- Aquarius, or Waterman.
- Pisces, or Fishes.

SIGNS OF THE PLANETS.

☀ Sun.	☽ Moon.	♀ Venus.	♂ Mars.
♃ Jupiter.	♄ Saturn.	☌ In Conjunction.	▢ Quadrature.
☿ Mercury.	♅ Uranus.	♆ Neptune.	☊ Ascending Node.

MOON'S PHASES.

● New Moon.   ☽ First Quarter.   ● Full Moon.   ☾ Last Quarter.

LUMSDEN & SONS, Shovels, Hoes, Rakes, Pitchforks, Garden Tools,
Fayetteville Street, opposite Market, Raleigh, N. C.

2. Some men have faith in the laws governing mind; obeying those
laws they attain to mental power.—*Branson.*

BRANSON'S NORTH CAROLINA ALMANAC.   3

CHRONOLOGICAL CYCLES AND ERAS.

Dominical Letter	B	Julian Period	6611
Epact	7	Jewish Era	5658
Golden Number	18	Era of Nabonassa	2645
Solar Cycle	3	Olympiads	2674
Roman Indication	11	Mahommedan Era	1315

MOVABLE FEASTS OF THE CHURCH.

Epiphany	Jan. 6	Palm Sunday	April 3
Septuagesima Sunday	Feb. 6	Easter Sunday	April 10
Sexagesima Sunday	Feb. 13	Whit Sunday	May 29
Quinquagesima Sunday	Feb. 20	Trinity Sunday	June 5
Shrove Tuesday	Feb. 22	First Sunday in Advent	Nov. 28
Ash Wednesday, or Lent	Feb. 23	Ancension Day	May 19
St. Patrick's Day	March 17	First Sunday in Lent	Feb. 27

THE FOUR SEASONS.

		D. H.
Spring commences	March 20,	8 A. M.
Summer commences	June 21,	4 A. M.
Autumn commences	September 22,	7 P. M.
Winter commences	December 21,	1 P. M.

MORNING STARS.

Mercury will be Morning Star about......Jan. 29, May 28, and Sept. 21
Venus will be Morning Star till..Feb. 15 and from Dec. 1 to end of year
Jupiter will be Morning Star..Mar. 25. then from Oct. 13 to end of year

EVENING STARS.

Mercury will be Evening Star about ....April 10, Aug. 8, Dec. 8
Venus will be Evening Star from ....Feb. 15 to Dec. 1
Jupiter will be Evening Star from..............March 25 to October 13

ECLIPSES.

In the year 1898 there will be six Eclipses—three of the *Sun* and three
of the *Moon.*

I. *A partial Eclipse of the Moon* January 7th, visible over a large part
of the world, begin about 5 47 p. m., and end about 7 11 p. m. Shows
about one-sixth dark surface.

II. *A total Eclipse of the Sun* January 22, invisible in North America.

III. *A partial Eclipse of the Moon* July 3, invisible in North America.

IV. *An Annular of the Sun* July 18 invisible in North America.

V. *A partial Eclipse of the Sun* Dec. 13, invisible in America.

VI. *A total Eclipse of the Moon* December 27, visible to all the Continents of the world, except Australia. Total begins at 4 57 p. m., and
ends at 6 27 p. m.

TIDES.

The time of tide can readily be found for the following places by adding the hours and minutes opposite the names to the time when the
Moon is South on the day to which the tide is sought. The time when
the Moon is South is given in the Calendar for every day. The next tide
can be found very nearly by adding 12 hours and 29 minutes to the time
of the one previous.

The tides are given in local time—add 12 minutes for Eastern Standard:

	H. M.		H. M.
Boston	11 12	New York	8 13
Sandy Hook	7 29	Old Point	8 17
Baltimore	6 33	Washington City	7 44
Richmond	4 32	Hatteras Inlet	7 04
Beaufort	7 26	Bald Head	7 26
Southport	7 19	Wilmington	9 06
Charleston	7 26	Savannah	9 33

3. Some men have faith in the laws of health, and hence by obeying those laws they secure physical health and happiness.—*Branson*.

HERSCHEL'S WEATHER PROGNOSTICATOR

For Foretelling the Weather Through all the Lunations of the Year.

This table and the accompanying remarks are the result of many years actual observation, the whole being constructed on a due consideration of the attractions of the Sun and Moon, in their several positions respecting the Earth, and, by simple inspection, it shows the observer what kind of weather will most probably follow the entrance of the Moon into any of its quarters, and that so near the truth as to be seldom or never found to fail.

If the new moon, first quarter, full moon, or last quarter, happen—	IN SUMMER.	IN WINTER.
Between midnight and 2 in the morning	Fair	Hoar frost unless the wind is S. or S. W.
Between 2 and 4, morning	Cold, with frequent showers	Snow and stormy.
Between 4 and 6, morning	Rain	Rain.
Between 6 and 8, morning	Wind and rain	Stormy.
Between 8 and 10, morning	Changeable	Cold rain if wind be W.; snow if E.
Between 10 and 12, morning	Frequent showers	Cold and high wind.
Between 12 o'clock at noon and 2 in afternoon	Very rainy	Rain and snow.
Between 2 and 4, afternoon	Changeable	Fair and mild.
Between 4 and 6, afternoon	Fair	Fair.
Between 6 and 8, aftern'n	Fair if wind N. W.; rainy if S. or S.W.	Fair and frosty wind N. or N.E.; rain or snow if S. or S.W.
Between 8 and 10, afternoon	Ditto	Ditto.
Between 10 and midnight	Fair	Fair and frosty.

OBSERVATIONS.—1. The nearer the time for the Moon's change, first quarter, full and last quarter are to midnight, the fairer will be the weather during the next seven days

2. The space for this calculation occupies from 10 at night until 2 next morning.

3. The nearer to midday or noon the phase of the Moon happens, the more foul or wet weather may be expected during the next seven days.

4. The space for this calculation occupies from 10 in the forenoon until 2 in the afternoon. These observations refer principally to the Summer, though they affect Spring and Autumn nearly in the same ratio.

5. The Moon's change, first quarter, full and last quarter happening during six of the afternoon hours, i. e., from 4 to 10, may be followed by fair weather, but this is mostly dependent on the wind, as is noted in the table.

6. Though the weather, from a variety of irregular causes, is more uncertain in the latter part of Autumn, the whole of Winter and beginning of Spring, yet, in the main, the above observations will apply to those periods also.

7. To prognosticate correctly, especially in those cases where the wind is concerned, the observer should be in sight of a good vane, where the four cardinal points of the heavens are correctly placed.

Branson's Almanac is a household word—*Truth*.

4. The man who has faith in the laws governing spiritual life, can realize that the law of the Lord is perfect, converting the soul.—*Branson*.

STATISTICS OF LIBRARIES IN NORTH CAROLINA, 1897.

Through the untiring efforts of our efficient State Librarian, Mr. R. A. Cobb, we are enabled to give correctly the great progress that has been made in our State in the last few years towards placing within the reach of the great masses of our people, useful information that has heretofore been beyond the reach of the common class of our citizens, by establishing public Libraries, accessible to all who are in search of useful knowledge.

NAMES OF LIBRARIES.	Where Located.	When Established.	No. of Vols.	Money Used Each Year.	Librarian.
State Library	Raleigh	1841	50,000	$ 500	R. A. Cobb.
Female College	Asheville		1,000		
Asheville Library	Asheville		2,389	675	Miss H. A. Champion.
Bishop Atkinson Lib	Asheville		2,400		Rev. A. H. Stubbs.
St. Mary's College	Belmont	1885	10 000		F. Bernard.
N. C. University	Chapel Hill	1790	35,000	1,000	R. H. Graves.
Biddle Univ'r'ty (col)	Charlotte		8,000		
Buckhorn Academy	Como		2,000		
Scotia Seminary	Concord	1870	1,000		
Davidson College Lib	Davidson	1887	12,000		F. F. Rowe.
Public School Libra'y	Durham	1884	2,400		C. W. Toms.
Trinity College Lib	W. Durham	1887	13,000		Geo. B Pegram.
Elon College Library	Elon	1890	1,285		W. P. Lorance.
Cross Creek, I. O.O.F.	Fayetteville	1845	1,000		
Christian College Lib	Franklinton	1882	1,000		N. D. McReynolds.
Female College	Greensboro	1895	5,000		Dred Peacock.
State Normal College	Greensboro		3,000		
Guilford College Lib	Guilford Col	1837	4,000		Miss M. E. Mendenhall
Shortia School	Highlands	1888	1,500		
Good Will Free Lib	Ledger	1888	6,000		C. H. Wing.
Pioneer Library	Lenoir	1875	1,500		I. F. W. Harper.
N. C. College	Mt. Pleasant	1858	2,800		H. T J. Ludwig.
Bap. Female Instit'e.	Murfr'esb'ro		1,000		
Collegiate Institute	Newbern		1,000		
Catawba College	Newton		2,500		
Oak Ridge Institute	Oak Ridge	1852	2,000	200	J. E. Holt.
A. & M. College	Raleigh	1890	3,300	200	A. Q. Holladay.
D. & D. Kelly Lib'ry	Raleigh	1877	2,500		
St. Mary's School	Raleigh		3,000		
Shaw University	Raleigh	1865	1,500		
Supreme Court Lib	Raleigh		11,000		R. H. Bradley.
Rutherford Col. Lib.	R. College	1853	600		W. E. Abernethy.
Female College	Salem	1802	4,000		J H. Clewell
Livingston College	Salisbury		3,000		
Wake F. College Lib	Wake For'st	1833	15,000	485	W L. Poteat.
Rab Library	Waynesville	1891	1,000	62	L. B. Lewis.
Wayne School	Waynesville	1886	3,000		T. G. Harbison.
Classical School	Wilmingt'n		2,000		
Library Association	Wilmington	1855	5,000	249	T. C. Diggs.
City School Library	Winston	1896	3,000	290	J. J. Blair.
College Library	Lenoir	1800	400		J. D. Minick.
A. & M. College (col)	Greensboro	1894	2,600		J H. M. Butler.
Hickory Library	Hickory	1893	1,000		E. McComb.
Durham Library	Durham	1897	900		H. A. Forshee.
Morganton Library	Morganton	1878	1,000		Miss A. L. Avery

45 libraries in all. 240,000 volumes of good books.

SUNDAY.

Like a great river Thy love flows,
  Let not it run to waste,
I'll dip my hand, so near it goes,
  Sure I thereof may taste.   —*Ingelow.*

We need all our strength and all the grace God can give us for to-day's burden's and to-day's battle. To-morrow belongs to our Heavenly Father.—*Theodore Cuyler, D. D.*

5. The Christian religion leads a man towards the highest cultivation of all his best capabilities.—*Branson.*

1st Month. JANUARY, 1898. 31 Days.

Moon's Phases.

	D.	H.	M.		D.	H.	M.
☺ Full Moon,	7	7	16 p.m.	☻ New Moon,	22	2	16 a.m
☾ Last Quarter,	15	10	33 a.m.	☽ First Quarter,	29	9	24 a.m

Day of Month.	Day of Week.	Sun rises.	Sun sets.	Sun slow.	Sun's decline south.	ASPECTS OF PLANETS AND OTHER MISCELLANEOUS MATTER.	Moon's place.	Moon rises or sets.	Moon south.	High tides at Beaufort.
1	Sat	7 10	4 50	4	23 57	♀ in ☊. ⊕ in Peri.	♈	sets.	7 22	mo'n
1.	Sunday after Christmas.					Day's length 9 hours 48 minutes.				
2	*B.*	7 10	4 58	4	22 52	Battle of Trenton 1777.	♈	2 43	8 9	3 23
3	Mo	7 10	4 59	5	22 46	Bat. of Princeton 1777.	♉	3 43	8 57	4 3
4	Tue	7 10	5 0	5	22 39	Vanderbilt died 1877.	♉	4 41	9 47	5 13
5	We	7 10	5 1	6	22 32	☌ ☿ ⊙ inferior.	♉	5 35	10 37	6 13
6	Thu	7 9	5 2	6	22 25	☺ EPIPHANY. [ington.	♊	6 25	11 28	6 54
7	Fri	7 9	5 3	7	22 17	Moon ecl. vis. at Was	♊	rises.	m'rn	7 20
8	Sat	7 9	5 4	7	22 9	Forsyth Co. form'd 1848	♋	5 42	0 17	7 43
2.	First Sunday after Epiphany.					Day's length 9 hours 56 minutes.				
9	*B.*	7 9	5 5	8	22 0	N. C. Legisl. met 1895.	♋	6 44	1 5	8 31
10	Mo	7 9	5 6	8	21 51	Stamp Act passed 1765.	♌	7 47	1 51	9 17
11	Tue	7 9	5 7	8	21 42	☿ gr. Hel. Lat. N.	♌	8 50	2 35	10 00
12	We	7 9	5 8	9	21 32	Gaston Co. formed 1846.	♌	9 55	3 19	10 45
13	Thu	7 9	5 9	9	21 22	☌ ☿ ♂. Fox died 1681.	♍	11 0	4 3	11 29
14	Fri	7 9	5 10	9	21 11	☾ Com. Maury b. 1806.	♍	m'rn	4 48	0 14
15	Sat	7 9	5 11	10	21 0	And. Jackson b. 1767	♍	0 7	5 36	1 1
3.	Second Sunday after Epiphany.					Day's length 10 hours 2 minutes.				
16	*B.*	7 8	5 12	10	20 48	Gibbon died 1794.	♍	1 17	6 28	1 54
17	Mo	7 8	5 13	10	20 36	☿ sta. Dr. Franklin b. 1706	♎	2 29	7 25	2 51
18	Tue	7 8	5 14	11	20 24	☌ ♄ ☾. Jarvis b. 1836.	♏	3 43	8 26	3 52
19	We	7 8	5 15	11	20 11	Gen. Rob't E. Lee's birthd	♐	4 51	9 30	4 56
20	Thu	7 7	5 15	11	19 58	☌ ♂ ☾ Howard d. 1790	♐	5 52	10 35	6 00
21	Fri	7 7	5 16	12	19 44	☻ Sun ecl. inv. at Wash	♑	6 42	11 37	7 3
22	Sat	7 6	5 17	12	19 31	Bacon b. 1561 [ingt'n	♑	sets.	eve.	7 58
4.	Third Sunday after Epiphany.					Day's length 10 hours 12 minutes.				
23	*B.*	7 6	5 18	12	19 16	Wm. Gaston d. 1844.	♑	7 5	1 28	8 54
24	Mo	7 5	5 19	12	19 2	♃ stationary.	♑	8 17	2 17	9 43
25	Tue	7 4	5 20	13	18 47	Fayetteville settl'd. 1749	♒	9 23	3 3	10 29
26	We	7 3	5 21	13	18 32	Battle of Newbern 1864.	♒	10 28	3 48	11 14
27	Thu	7 2	5 22	13	18 16	Dr. Caldwell died 1838.	♒	11 30	4 32	11 58
28	Fri	7 2	5 23	13	18 0	☽ Tripple Allian'e 1667	♈	m'rn	5 17	0 43
29	Sat	7 2	5 23	13	17 44	☿ gr. Elong W.	♈	0 32	6 3	1 29
5.	Fourth Sunday after Epiphany.					Day's length 10 hours 22 minutes.				
30	*B.*	7 2	5 24	14	17 27	Charles I beheaded 1647	♈	1 33	6 51	2 17
31	Mo	7 2	5 25	14	17 10	Mrs. E. B Engleh'rd d. '95	♈	2 32	7 40	3 17

WEATHER CONJECTURES—JANUARY—1, 2, 3, 4, 5, 6, generally good weather; 7, 8, 9, 10, 11, 12, 13, expect storms; 14, 15, 16, 17, 18, 19, cold high winds; 20, 21, 22, 23, expect snow and stormy weather; 24, 25, 26, 27, 28, snow; 29, 30, 31, cold rain if wind be West, snow if East.

5. The man who has *full faith in all* God's laws, and renders a perfect obedience, has peace flowing as a river, and a joy that is complete—*Branson*

BRANSON'S NORTH CAROLINA ALMANAC.　　7

FARM AND GARDEN WORK FOR JANUARY.—Plant peas, beans, beets, onions, Irish potatoes, horse radish; sow turnips, spinach, lettuce, radish, parsley, carrots, salsify. Plant early peas; artichokes must now be dressed, also asparagus beds; this is the proper time to sow early spring tomatoes, etc.

Prepare land for the next crop, if not done. In the low country, if mud marsh or rushes are used, this is a good time to haul out and spread in the alleys, and throw upon it a light listing. Repair fences, plow, ditch, drain and manure. You can sow oats for a first crop.

MONEY IN WALNUT TREES.

The editor of the *Press and Carolinian* recently sold a walnut tree for $75. He gives this advice:

Plant some walnut, brother, plant walnuts. You can plant 160 trees on an acre and never interfere with farming. In twenty years' time the trees will be worth $75 apiece. You can get one years' growth by placing the walnuts in single layer on smooth ground and covering with thin layer of dirt, then when they have had about two freezes they will crack open; then the first warm spell plant them in squares in an old field, 160 to the acre.

The walnut enriches the soil and soon you will have a fine field fit for cultivating and growing crops, and your walnuts will also be increasing in value at the rate of ten cents per tree each year to a certain period, when it is augmented in almost geometrical proportion. Finest business in the world. "Savie?" A big field of walnuts planted now will be of more value to your boy when you die than a big bank account. North Carolina is the home of the walnut.

EMANCIPATION.—On the 22d of September, 1862, Mr. Lincoln issued his first emancipation proclamation, liberating the slaves of all secessionists who failed to return to their allegiance by the close of the year, On the 1st of January, 1863, Mr. Lincoln performed the great act of his life (as considered by his friends) the issuing of his proclamation of emancipation for all the slaves in the country. The measure was quite unanimously supported by the Republicans, but more or less censured by the Democrats.

Rev. Levi Branson has commenced work preparatory to his fourth volume of North Carolina Sermons. The last volume contains thirty first class sermons by thirty ministers from various denominations in our State. One of them, "The Rich Fool," is by our townsman, Rev. J. F. Butt. The work contains over 300 pages, and sells in cloth binding for $1, and paper binding for 50 cents.—*Newbern Journal, Aug. 19. 1893.*

I refer to your State Directory more frequently than to any other Directory, and feel that it is indispensable in my business.—Hugh W. Harris, Attorney at Law, Charlotte, N. C.

MONDAY.

I have learned to seek my happiness by limiting my desires, rather than in attempting to satisfy them.—*John Stuart Mill.*

A small circle of useful as is not to be despised. A light that doesn't shine beautifully around the family table at home is not fit to take a long way off to do a great service somewhere else.—*J. Hudson Taylor.*

7. To give advice unsolicited is delightful; it so magnifies our self-esteem.—*Branson.*

2d Month. FEBRUARY, 1898. 28 Days.

Moon's Phases.

	D.	H.	M.			D.	H.	M.	
Full Moon,	6	1	16	p.m.	New Moon,	20	2	32	p.m.
Last Quarter.	13	7	20	p.m.	First Quarter,	28	6	5	p.m.

Day of Month.	Day of Week.	Sun rises.	Sun sets.	Sun slow.	Sun's decl'ine south.	ASPECTS OF PLANETS AND OTHER MISCELLANEOUS MATTER.	Moon's place.	Moon rises or sets.	Moon south.	High tides at Beaufort.
1	Tue	7 1	5 27	14	16 53	Washington el. Pres. 1789	♉	m'rn	eve.	m'rn
2	We	7 1	5 29	14	16 36	Peace Conference 1865.	♉	4 20	2 21	4 47
3	Thu	7 0	5 31	14	16 18	Gen. R. Barringer d. 1895	♊	5 6	10 11	5 57
4	Fri	6 59	5 32	14	16 0	☿ in ☋. ♀ in Aphelion.	♊	5 45	10 59	6 24
5	Sat	6 58	5 33	14	15 42	Branson's birthday.	♋	6 20	11 47	7 13
6. Septuagesima Sunday.						**Day's length 10 hours 36 minutes.**				
6	*B.*	6 58	5 34	14	15 23		♌	ris-s.	m'rn	7 36
7	Mo	6 57	5 34	14	15 4	Suez Canal Com. '67	♌	6 42	0 33	7 59
8	Tue	6 56	5 35	14	14 45	Bat. Roanoke Isl'nd 1862	♌	7 46	1 17	8 43
9	We	6 55	5 36	14	14 26	Gen. Hancock d. 1886.	♍	8 51	2 2	9 28
10	Thu	6 54	5 37	14	14 6	Treaty of Paris 1763.	♍	9 59	2 47	10 13
11	Fri	6 53	5 38	14	13 46	Thos. A. Eddison b. 1847	♍	11 8	3 34	11 00
12	Sat	6 53	5 39	14	13 26	H. Seymour d. 1886.	♍	m'rn	4 25	11 51
7. Sexagesima Sunday.						**Day's length 10 hours 48 minutes.**				
13	*B.*	6 52	5 40	14	13 6		♎	0 19	5 19	0 45
14	Mo	6 51	5 41	14	12 46	ST. VALENTINE DAY	♏	1 30	6 17	1 43
15	Tue	6 50	5 42	14	12 25	☌ ♀ ☉ superior.	♏	2 39	7 18	2 44
16	We	6 49	5 43	14	12 4	Judge Battle buried 1879	♐	3 41	8 20	3 46
17	Thu	6 48	5 44	14	11 43	Moliere died 1673.	♐	4 34	9 22	4 48
18	Fri	6 47	5 45	14	11 22	☌ ♂ ☾. Luther d. 1546.	♑	5 19	10 20	5 46
19	Sat	6 46	5 46	14	11 0	☌ ☿ ☾.	♑	5 55	11 14	6 40
8. Quinquagesima—Shrove Sunday,						**Day's length 11 hours 2 minutes.**				
20	*B.*	6 45	5 47	14	10 39		♑	sets.	eve.	7 12
21	Mo	6 43	5 48	14	10 17	Bat of Olisto, Fla. '64	♒	7 2	0 52	8 28
22	Tue	6 42	5 48	14	9 55	WASHINGTONS BIRTHD'Y	♒	8 8	1 38	9 4
23	We	6 41	5 48	13	9 33	ASH WEDNESDAY.	♒	9 13	2 24	10 10
24	Thu	6 40	5 49	13	9 11	Monterey surrend. 1846.	♒	10 16	3 9	10 35
25	Fri	6 39	5 50	13	8 49	Battle of Montreal 1775.	♓	11 19	3 56	11 22
26	Sat	6 38	5 51	13	8 26	♀ gr. Hel. Lat. S.	♓	m'rn	4 43	0 9
9. First Sunday in Lent.						**Day's length 11 hours 14 minutes.**				
27	*B.*	6 37	5 52	13	8 3	Longfellow b. 1807.	♈	0 20	5 32	0 58
28	Mo	6 36	5 53	13	7 41	Dr. Wingate d. 1879	♈	1 18	6 22	1 48

WEATHER CONJECTURES—FEBRUARY—1, 2, 3, 4, 5, snow if wind from the West; 6, 7, 8, 9, 10, 11, 12, rain and snow; 13, 14, 15, 16, 17, 18, 19, fair and frosty; 20, 21, 22, 23, 24, 25, 26, 27, fair and mild; 28, stormy.

8. A man in whose mind his own country is not *first*, is a man who himself is not *worthy* to be first in another country.—*Branson.*

FARM AND GARDEN WORK FOR FEBRUARY.—Continue to sow peas, and such vegetable as were omitted in January. Plant pole beans, first crop (in the low country); full crop Irish potatoes, beets and carrots; dress artichokes and asparagus. Tomatoes, peppers and cucumbers sow in hot beds; put out mangoes.

This is considered the opening month of the planter's year. Continue preparing as in January. Sow oats for a full crop in the low country; plant Irish potatoes; make up sprout beds for sweet potatoes. Plant root crop of sweet potatoes

BUREAU OF STATISTICS OF N. C. (Denominational.)
LEVI BRANSON, Secretary.

DENOMINATIONS.	Number Ministers.	Number Churches	Number Members.
White.			
Methodist Episcopal Church South	574	1,302	130,276
Methodist Episcopal Church.	65	115	8.941
Wesleyan Methodist Church	7	7	141
Methodist Protestant Church	64	208	16.416
Christians (followers of James O'Kelly)	60	101	9.000
Evangelical Lutheran	73	130	12,872
Presbyterian	150	350	32 482
Universalists	3	3	255
Protestant Episcopal	96	190	14 239
Missionary Baptist	840	1,566	150.274
Primitive Baptist	150	317	11.914
Seventh Day Adventist	5	5	83
Free Will Baptist	160	168	10.224
Baptist Church of Christ	16	16	659
Old Two Seed Baptist	9	9	183
Disciples of Christ	54	125	12,437
Seventh Day Baptist	1	1	10
Reformed Church of U. S	22	43	3,317
Church of Jesus Christ of Latter Day Saints	24	1	136
Friends	52	52	5.328
Dunkards	9	9	510
Moravians	7	19	3 548
Waldenses	1	1	215
Roman Catholics	24	24	2,640
Hebrews	4	4	386
Salvation Army	2	2	59
Advent Christian Church	18	18	1,549
Associate Reformed	20	20	2,109
Congregationalist	8	8	368
Colored.			
Missionary Baptists	572	1,131	109,871
African M. E. Church	150	526	121,154
African M. E. Zion Church	240	147	16,156
Colored M. E. Church in America	25	26	2,786
Methodist Episcopal	2	2	130
Protestant Episcopal	6	10	1,200
Congregational	20	38	1.752
Christians	50	53	3,746
Disciples of Christ	10	61	1,000
Free Will Baptist	10	25	1,640
Primitive Baptist	15	20	1.000
Presbyterian North	173	306	17.851

3d Month.   MARCH, 1898.   31 Days.

Moon's Phases.

	D. H. M.		D. H. M.
Full Moon,	8 4 20a.m.	New Moon,	22 3 28a.m.
Last Quarter,	15 2 39a.m.	First Quarter,	30 2 32a.m.

Day of Month.	Day of Week.	Sun rises.	Sun sets.	Sun slow.	Sun's decline south.	ASPECTS OF PLANETS AND OTHER MISCELLANEOUS MATTER.	Moon's place.	Moon rises or sets	Moon south.	High tides at Beaufort.
1	Tue	6 34	5 55	12	7 18	Bishop Andrews d. 1871		m'rn	m'rn	m'rn
2	We	6 32	5 56	12	6 55	John Wesley d. 1791.		2 58	8 3	3 29
3	Thu	6 30	5 57	12	6 32	Serfdom abol.in Rus. '63		3 41	8 52	4 28
4	Fri	6 28	5 58	12	6 9	Cong. first met N.Y.1789		4 17	9 39	5 5
5	Sat	6 26	6 0	12	5 46	Addison born 1750.		4 50	10 26	5 52

10. Second Sunday in Lent.   Day's length 11 hours 36 minutes.

6	B.	6 24	6 0	11	5 22	♂ gr. Hel. Lat. S.		5 19	11 11	6 37
7	Mo	6 23	6 1	11	4 59	Bible Soc.fo'n'd 1804		5 44	11 57	7 23
8	Tue	6 22	6 1	11	4 36	William III d. 1703.		m'rn	eve.	7 45
9	We	6 20	6 2	11	4 12	♂ ☽ C. Bat.VeraCruz '47		7 46	0 42	8 8
10	Thu	6 18	6 3	10	3 49	Bat. Manassas Junc.1862		8 57	1 30	8 56
11	Fri	6 17	6 4	10	2 25	Rev. W. Barringer d. '82		10 9	2 21	9 47
12	Sat	6 16	6 5	10	3 1	First Parliament as. 1683		11 21	3 14	10 40

11. Third Sunday in Lent.   Day's length 12 hours 8 minutes.

13	B.	6 14	6 6	9	2 38	Pocahontas d. 1616.		m'rn	4 12	11 33
14	Mo	6 13	6 6	9	2 14	West Point est.1802.		0 30	5 12	0 38
15	Tue	6 12	6 7	9	1 50	Ext.ses. Leg.con. '80		1 35	6 14	1 40
16	We	6 11	6 8	9	1 27	♂ ☿ ☉ superior.		2 29	7 14	2 40
17	Thu	6 9	6 9	8	1 3	St. Patrick's Day.		3 15	8 12	3 38
18	Fri	6 8	6 10	8	0 39	Suez Canal compl. 1869.		3 54	9 6	4 32
19	Sat	6 6	6 11	8	0 16	Dr. Livingston b. 1813.		4 26	9 56	5 22

12. Fourth Sunday in Lent.   Day's length 12 hours 8 minutes.

20	B.	6 4	6 12	7	no'th	☉ ent. ♈. SPRING COM		4 54	10 44	6 10
21	Mo	6 3	6 12	7	0 33	Lucknow fell 1858		5 22	eve.	6 55
22	Tue	6 2	6 13	7	0 57	♄ sta. Sta. Act.1765		sets.	0 16	7 42
23	We	6 0	6 13	7	1 20	Battle Winchester 1862.		8 0	1 1	8 27
24	Thu	5 59	6 14	6	1 44	Queen Elizabeth d. 1603		9 3	1 47	9 13
25	Fri	5 58	6 15	6	2 28	Thames Tunnel op. 1843		10 6	2 35	10 1
26	Fri	5 57	6 16	6	2 31	Earthquake in Cal. 1872		11 5	3 24	10 50

13. Fifth Sunday in Lent.   Day's length 12 hours 22 minutes.

27	B.	5 55	6 17	5	2 55	Bruce crowned 1306.		m'rn	4 14	11 40
28	Mo	5 53	6 18	5	3 18	Davidson Col. op'd 1837		0 0	5 4	0 30
29	Tue	5 51	6 18	5	3 41	Brit.Muse'm f'd1753		0 50	5 54	1 21
30	We	5 50	6 19	4	4 5	☿ in Perihelion.		1 35	6 43	2 9
31	Thu	5 48	6 20	4	4 28	S. M. Parrish d. 1895.		2 14	7 31	2 57

WEATHER CONJECTURES—MARCH—1, 2, 3, 4, 5, 6, 7, stormy; 8, 9, 10, 11, 12, 13, 14, rain; 15, 16, 17, 18, 19, 20, 21, snow and stormy; 22, 23, 24, 25, 26, 27, 28, 29, look for snow; 30, 31, expect more snow or sleet.

Farmers should use "NATIONAL" Fertilizer for Tobacco; and "BEEF, BLOOD and BONE" brand for Cotton, Corn and Wheat. Strictly reliable. Ask your Fertilizer Merchant for them. Carefully prepared by

(See top 3d cover page.) *S. W. TRAVERS & CO., Branch, Richmond, Va.*

10. The *mind crop* is the greatest crop that can be raised on any farm or in any State.—*Branson.*

FARM AND GARDEN WORK FOR MARCH.—Plant bush squash, pumpkins, water and muskmelons, okra, Guinea squash or egg-p ant, sugar beets, carrots, beans, peas, radishes, lettuce, corn, celery (first crop) tanyah and mangoes in the low country and elsewhere as soon as danger from frost is over.

This is the first planting month for cotton, corn and rice. Plant your high lands first; leave the low lands for April. Plant rice about the 20th of the month.

ADVERTISE.

HIS MISTAKE.

He seems to think, since at the fair,
   He took the highest prize,
There is no further call for him
   His goods to advertise.
But this is where to make mistakes
   The fellow has begun,
For, since he doesn't advertise,
   Why, no one knows he won.
           —*Detroit Free Press.*

LITTLE DROPS.

Little drops of printer's ink,
   A little type displayed.
Make our merchant princes
   And all their big parade.
Little bills of stinginess.
   Disregarding printer's ink,
Bursts the man of business
   And sees his credit sink.
           Allentown (Pa.) Leader.

THERE WAS A WAY.

Great Richard, who, in direct need,
Offered his kingdom for a steed,
And Alexander, shedding tears,
Because no world defied his spears,
Had writ success on history's page
If they had calmed despair and rage
   And advertised.

HE ADVERTISED.

Diogenes returned to earth,
   Wisely philosophized;
Of honest men he found no dearth—
   He advertised.

THE FORTY-FIFTH STATE.

Do you know how many States there are in the Union? No, of course not. No one knows except school children and Congressmen and flag-makers. Every four years the political arithmeticians learn the number in the process of figuring up the Presidential election returns, but they forget again almost immediately.

Next year's United States flag will have forty-five stars, the latest being for Utah, which became a State on the Fourth of July. Utah will get into the flag six months or more before she gets into the Union. She is to be represented in the new sets of regimental colors that Secretary Lamont has ordered for the army. Her star in the official flag goes to the right of the fourth row from the top.—*Harper's Weekly.*

11. The *mind crop* in North Carolina is better than ever before.—
Branson.

4th Month.   APRIL, 1898.   30 Days.

Moon's Phases.

	D. H. M.		D. H. M.
Full Moon,	6 4 11p.m	New Moon,	20 5 12p.m
Last Quarter,	13 9 20a.m.	First Quarter,	28 8 56p.m

Day of Month.	Day of Week.	Sun rises.	Sun sets.	Sun slow.	Sun's decline north.	ASPECTS OF PLANETS AND OTHER MISCELLANEOUS MATTER.	Moon's place.	Moon rises or sets.	Moon south.	High tides at Beaufort.
1	Fri	5 47	6 22	4	4 56	ALL FOOLS DAY.		m'rn	eve.	m'rn
2	Sat	5 46	6 28	3	5 19	Gen. Lee evac. Rich'd '64		3 17	9 2	4 28

14. Palm Sunday.   Day's length 12 hours 39 minutes.

Day of Month.	Day of Week.	Sun rises.	Sun sets.	Sun slow.	Sun's decline north.	ASPECTS OF PLANETS AND OTHER MISCELLANEOUS MATTER.	Moon's place.	Moon rises or sets.	Moon south.	High tides at Beaufort.
3	*B.*	5 44	6 23	3	5 42	Peter Cooper d. 1883.		3 44	9 48	5 14
4	Mo	5 42	6 24	3	6 5	Gen. Harrison d. 1871.		4 11	10 33	5 59
5	Tue	5 41	6 25	2	6 27	Jefferson b. 1743.		4 36	11 21	6 47
6	We	5 39	6 26	2	6 50	♂ gr. Hel. Lat. S.		rises.	m'rn	7 11
7	Thu	5 38	6 27	2	7 12	Socrates d. 333 B. C.		7 50	1 11	7 37
8	Fri	5 36	6 28	2	7 35	GOOD FRIDAY.		9 5	1 5	8 31
9	Sat	5 35	6 29	1	7 57	☿ gr. Hel. Lat. N.		10 18	2 3	9 29

15. Easter Sunday.   Day's length 12 hours 56 minutes.

Day of Month.	Day of Week.	Sun rises.	Sun sets.	Sun slow.	Sun's decline north.	ASPECTS OF PLANETS AND OTHER MISCELLANEOUS MATTER.	Moon's place.	Moon rises or sets.	Moon south.	High tides at Beaufort.
10	*B.*	5 34	6 30	1	8 19	☿ gr. Elon E. EASTER		11 26	3	4 10 30
11	Mo	5 33	6 31	1	8 41	Benjamin West d. 1870.		m'rn	4	7 11 33
12	Tue	5 31	6 31	1	9 3	Benton d. 1858 ['65		0 26	5	9 0 35
13	We	5 30	6 32	0	9 25	Ral. sur. to Sherman		1 14	6	8 1 34
14	Thu	5 28	6 33	0	9 46	Prest. Lincoln assass. '65		1 54	7	2 2 28
15	Fri	5 27	6 34	0	10 7	A. Johnson Pres't 1865.		2 28	7 53	3 19
16	Sat	5 26	6 34	fast.	11 21	French evac. Mexico '67		2 57	8 41	4 7

16. Low Sunday.   Day's length 13 hours 11 minutes.

Day of Month.	Day of Week.	Sun rises.	Sun sets.	Sun slow.	Sun's decline north.	ASPECTS OF PLANETS AND OTHER MISCELLANEOUS MATTER.	Moon's place.	Moon rises or sets.	Moon south.	High tides at Beaufort.
17	*B.*	5 24	6 35	1	10 50	♂ ♂ ☾.		3 24	9 26	4 52
18	Mo	5 23	6 36	1	11 11	Luther at Worms 1521.		3 49	10 11	5 37
19	Tue	5 22	6 37	1	11 31	David S. Reid b. 1813		4 15	10 56	6 22
20	We	5 21	6 38	1	11 52	☿ sta. Nap. 3d b. 1808		4 41	eve.	7 7
21	Thu	5 20	6 39	1	12 12	Santa Ana cap. 1836.		sets.	0 28	7 54
22	Fri	5 18	6 40	2	12 32	Battle of Camden 1782.		8 54	1 17	8 44
23	Sat	5 17	6 41	2	12 52	Cervantes d'ed 1616.		9 51	2 6	9 32

17. Second Sunday after Easter.   Day's length 13 hours 26 minutes.

Day of Month.	Day of Week.	Sun rises.	Sun sets.	Sun slow.	Sun's decline north.	ASPECTS OF PLANETS AND OTHER MISCELLANEOUS MATTER.	Moon's place.	Moon rises or sets.	Moon south.	High tides at Beaufort.
24	*B.*	5 15	6 41	2	13 12	☿ ☽ ☿ ☾.		10 43	2 57	9 83
25	Mo	5 14	6 41	2	13 31	Dr. A. Smedes d. 1877.		11 30	3 47	11 13
26	Tue	5 13	6 43	2	13 50	Gen. Jos. Johnson at Dur		m'rn	4 36	0 2
27	We	5 12	6 43	3	14 9	Emerson d. 1882.		0 10	5 24	0 50
28	Thu	5 11	6 44	3	14 28	Jas. Monroe b. 1759.		0 45	6 10	1 36
29	Fri	5 10	6 45	3	14 46	La. ceded to U. S. 1803.		1 17	6 54	2 20
30	Sat	5 9	6 46	3	15 5	♂ in Perihelion.		1 44	7 39	3 5

WEATHER CONJECTURES—APRIL—1, 2, 3, 4, 5, expect sleet; 6, 7, 8, 9,
10, 11, 12, fair; 13, 14, 15, 16, 17, 18, 19, cold rain if wind be West, snow
if East; 20, 21, 22, 23, 24, 25, 26, 27, fair; 28, 29, 30, fair and frosty if
wind N. or N. E.; rain or snow if S. or S. W.

12. The *mind crop* should be planted early and cultivated better than cotton or tobacco.—*Branson*.

FARM AND GARDEN WORK FOR APRIL.—Whatever has been omitted in March, do not neglect any longer. Sow green glazed cabbage, pickling cabbage, full crop of cauliflower and broccoli, okra, tomatoes, peppers, beets, carrots, leeks, melons, cucumbers, celery.

Full crops of corn, cotton and rice should be put in during this month. Plant your lowland corn. Commence early to hoe your young cotton, and thin out to stand. Plant pumpkins for a field crop.

THE COMING DAY.

A better time is coming girls,
    Just wait a little longer,
Its morning breeze now sweeps the trees,
    Its light is growing stronger.
The car of progress rushes on,
    Fresh spoils of conquest bringing,
And on the higher planes of life
    The birds of hope are singing.

Hark! on the zephyrs of the west
    A strong new sound is swelling!
Of equal rights and juster laws
    Its stirring notes are telling.
Blind prejudice and hoary wrongs
    Are swiftly disappearing,
And woman, pleading for her own,
    Commands respectful hearing.

Wyoming, in her mountain home,
    Her lesson still repeating,
To Colorada, newly won,
    Displays her star in greeting.
And both, in gold and silver decked,
    Like queens of ancient history,
Now watch and wait, while Kansas comes
    To join them in their glory.

Across the states the spirit spreads,
    Back to its primal sources,
Where woman's rights, in modern sénse,
    First mustered in their forces.
Where Lucy Stone and Susan B,
    Led kindred souls to battle
For woman's higher hopes and needs
    And raised her from a chattel.

Through storms of ridicule and scorn
    They bore their cause undaunted,
Till through the land, from shore to shore,
    Its burning truths are planted.
Their light is shining brightly, girls—
    Each year 'tis growing stronger—
Truth must prevail and error fail,
    Just wait a little longer!   —*Exchange*.

TUESDAY.

Oh, fear not, in a world like this,
    And thou shalt know ere long,
Know how sublime a thing it is
    To suffer and be strong.   —*Longfellow*.

13. The stronger the *homes*, the stronger the *country* in which the homes are found.—*Branson.*

5th Month. MAY, 1898. 31 Days.

Moon's Phases.

	D.	H.	M.		D.	H.	M.
Full Moon,	6	1	25 a.m.	New Moon,	20	7	50 a.m
Last Quarter,	12	4	26 p.m.	First Quarter,	28	0	5 p.m

Day of Month.	Day of Week.	Sun rises.	Sun sets.	Sun slow.	Sun's decline north.	ASPECTS OF PLANETS AND OTHER MISCELLANEOUS MATTER.	Moon's place.	Moon rises or sets.	Moon south.	High tides at Beaufort.
18.	Third Sunday after Easter.					Day's length 13 hours 39 minutes.				
1	*B.*	5 8	6 47	3	15 23	☌ ☿ ☉ inf. Queen of May		m'rn	eve.	m'rn
2	Mo	5 7	6 48	3	15 41	S H. Young d. 1882.		2 35	9 9	4 35
3	Tue	5 6	6 49	3	15 58	☌ ♃ ☾. ☿ in ☊.		3 3	9 58	5 24
4	We	5 5	6 49	3	16 15	Dr. Wm G. Hill d. 1877		3 32	10 50	6 16
5	Thu	5 4	6 50	4	16 32	Bat of Williamsb'g 1862		4 6	11 47	7 13
6	Fri	5 3	6 51	4	16 49	Bat. of Wildern'ss '64		rises.	m'rn	7 48
7	Sat	5 2	6 51	4	17 5	☌ ♅ ☾. ☌ ♄ ☾.		9 10	0 48	8 24
19.	Fourth Sunday after Easter.					Day's length 13 hours 51 minutes.				
8	*B.*	5 1	6 52	4	17 22	Bat. of Palo Alto 1846		10 16	1 53	9 19
9	Mo	5 0	6 53	4	17 37	Bat. Spottsylv'a C.H '64		11 9	2 58	10 24
10	Tue	4 59	6 54	4	17 53	CONFED. MEMORIAL DAY		11 52	4 0	11 26
11	We	4 58	6 54	4	18 8	Queen Mary d. 1699		m'rn	4 57	0 23
12	Thu	4 57	6 55	4	18 23	Bat. of Raymond '63		0 29	5 50	1 16
13	Fri	4 56	6 56	4	18 38	☿ stationary.		1 1	6 39	2 5
14	Sat	4 55	6 57	4	18 52	Battle Resaca, Ga. 1864.		1 28	7 25	2 51
20.	Rogation Sunday.					Day's length 14 hours 4 minutes.				
15	*B.*	4 54	6 58	4	19 6	Gov. Colquit sp. in Ral. '86		1 53	8 10	3 36
16	Mo	4 53	6 59	4	19 20	☌ ♂ ☾.		2 17	8 54	4 22
17	Tue	4 53	7 0	4	19 33	John Penn born 1741.		2 43	9 38	5 4
18	We	4 52	7 1	4	19 46	Matamoras fell 1846.		3 13	10 24	5 50
19	Thu	4 52	7 1	4	19 59	ASCENSION DAY.		3 48	11 12	6 38
20	Fri	4 51	7 2	4	20 11	Meckl'b'g Inde. 1775		sets.	eve.	6 58
21	Sat	4 50	7 3	4	20 23	N. C. seceded 1861.		8 37	0 51	8 17
21.	Sunday after Ascension.					Day's length 13 hours 52 minutes.				
22	*B.*	4 49	7 3	3	20 35	☌ ♆ ☾. ☍ ♅ ☉ ☌ ♀ ☾		9 2	1 42	8 68
23	Mo	4 48	7 4	3	20 46	Dr. Livingston d. 1886.		10 8	2 31	9 57
24	Tue	4 48	7 5	3	20 57	Queen Victoria b. 1819		10 43	3 19	10 45
25	We	4 48	7 5	3	21 8	Battle Winchester 1862.		11 15	4 5	11 31
26	Thu	4 47	7 6	3	21 18	John Calvin d. 1564.		11 44	4 50	0 16
27	Fri	4 47	7 7	3	21 28	♃ sta.		m'rn	5 33	0 59
28	Sat	4 46	7 8	3	21 37	♀ in Peri.		0 11	6 16	1 42
22.	Pentecost—Whit Sunday.					Day's length 14 hours 23 minutes.				
29	*B.*	4 46	7 9	3	21 47	Rhode Island adm. 1790		0 36	7 0	2 26
30	Mo	4 45	7 10	3	21 55	☌ ♃ ☾. FEDERAL MEM.		1 0	7 46	3 12
31	Tue	4 45	7 11	2	22 4	Bat. of Fair Oaks 1862		1 27	8 35	4 1

WEATHER CONJECTURES—MAY—1, 2 3, 4 5, fair if wind N. W.; rainy if S. or S. W.; 6, 7, 8 9 10, 11, fair; 12, 13, 14, 15, 16, 17, 18, 19, fair; 20, 21, 22, 23, 24, 25, 26, 27, expect wind and rain; 28, 29, 30, 31, very rainy.

14. The greatest possibilities of a man are on his native heath; if he is great on another heath, he is still less than a native ought to have been.—*Branson*

FARM AND GARDEN WORK FOR MAY.—Plant snap beans and squashes. Sow cabbages for winter use, cauliflower, broccoli, celery, beets, carrots, salsify. Plant cucumbers, melons and pumpkins for late crops. Gather herbs for drying; always dry gently in the shade.

Look well to your hoeings and plowings. Continue to plant corn in low lands. Sow first crop of early cow peas. Rice planting is generally postponed until June, as the birds are very bad in May, and the May bird is exceedingly destructive.

This page is prepared by Dr. D. REID PARKER, Director of Farmer's Institutes, Trinity, N. C.

Carolina! Carolina! heaven's blessings attend her!
While we live, we will cherish, protect and defend her!

*   *   *   *

True development begins with the *germ*—primogeniture, environment and training. If these be neglected or misdirected, disastrous failure will be the consequence.

*   *   *   *

There is a young woman in Dakota who is successfully working a one hundred and sixty acre farm, and she declares that she could work one twice as large if the men who want to marry her would stop bothering her.

*   *   *   *   *

Whoever does his duty faithfully and well, whatever that duty may be, is the honorable man. Whoever shirks his duty or uses his talent in dishonest efforts to promote his own interest at the expense of his fellow-citizen, is the dishonorable man.

*   *   *   *

The whole system of education in this country tends to vain expectations, and is full of disappointments and failures. The country needs useful men and women, well taught in lessons of patience, contentment, industry and love of country. The country is given, year after year, an army full of useless men and women, full of foolish aspirations, silly ambitions, impatience, discontent and love of themselves. They are equipped by their parents and teachers and sent forth to shoot at the moon. They fail, and become a burden to themselves and to others.

*   *   *   *

CONDENSE—BOIL DOWN—BE BRIEF.

When you've got a thing to say,
Say it! Don't take half a day.
When your tale's got little in it,
Crowd the whole thing in a minute!
Life is short—a fleeting vapor—
Don't fill an eight paged paper
With a tale which at a pinch,
Could be cornered in an inch!
Boil her down until she simmers!
Polish her until she glimmers,
When you've got a thing to say,
Say it! Don't take half a day.

*   *   *   *

If there is anything going wrong about your cow, your milk or butter, that you cannot understand, write to Prof. F. E. Emery, Raleigh, N. C. He will gladly and freely assist you.

*   *   *   *

If there should be a Farmer's Institute anywhere near you during the year, be sure to attend. It will do you and your entire community good.

*   *   *   *

If you should have any trouble with your poultry, write to Mr. Frank E. Hege, Raleigh, N. C.

(See page 17.)

15. It is strange how freely we *give away* our own knowledge, and how freely we *pay high prices* for the knowledge we obtain from others —*Branson.*

6th Month.	JUNE, 1898.	30 Days.

Moon's Phases.

	D. H. M.		D. H. M.
Full Moon,	4 9 3a.m.	New Moon,	18 11 11p.m
Last Quarter, 11	3 35a.m.	First Quarter, 26	11 45p.m

Day of Month.	Day of Week.	Sun rises.	Sun sets.	Sun slow.	Sun's decline North.	ASPECTS OF PLANETS AND OTHER MISCELLANEOUS MATTER.	Moon's place.	Moon rises or sets.	Moon south.	High tides at Beaufort.
1	We	4 44	7 11	2 22	12	Battle Cold Harbor 1864		1 57	eve.	m'rn
2	Thu	4 44	7 12	2 22	17	☿ gr. Hel. Lat. S.		2 35	10 28	5 54
3	Fri	4 43	7 12	2 22	26	Jeff. Davis b. 1808.		3 20	11 32	6 58
4	Sat	4 42	7 13	2 22	33	George I b. 1738.		rises.	m'rn	7 30

23.   Trinity Sunday.   Day's length 14 hours 32 minutes.

5	B.	4 41	7 13	2 22	40	Telegraph in China 1871		8 55	0 38	8 4
6	Mo	4 41	7 14	1 22	46	Patrick Henry d. 1799.		9 43	1 43	9 9
7	Tue	4 41	7 14	1 22	51	Robert Bruce d. 1329.		10 27	2 45	10 11
8	We	4 41	7 15	1 22	57	Battle Cross Keys 1862.		11 1	3 42	11 8
9	Thu	4 41	7 15	1 23	1	CORPUS CHRISTI.		11 31	4 34	12 0
10	Fri	4 41	7 16	1 23	6	Dickens d. 1870.		11 57	5 22	0 48
11	Sat	4 41	7 16	1 23	10	Sherman at Ken. '64		m'rn	6 8	1 34

24.   First Sunday after Trinity.   Day's length 14 hours 35 minutes.

12	B.	4 41	7 16		23	13	Bryant d. 1878.		0 33	6 53	2 19
13	Mo	4 41	7 16	slow	23	17	♂♆☉. Gen.Scott b.1786		0 49	7 37	3 3
14	Tue	4 41	7 17		23	19	First persecu. by Nero 64		1 17	8 22	3 48
15	We	4 41	7 18	0	23	22	Sun and clock together.		1 47	9 9	4 35
16	Thu	4 41	7 18	1	23	24	Winthrop born 1682.		2 23	9 58	5 24
17	Fri	4 41	7 19	1	23	25	Addison born 1718.		3 5	10 47	6 13
18	Sat	4 41	7 19	1	23	26	Bat. Waterloo 1815.		3 52	11 38	7 4

25.   Second Sunday after Trinity.   Day's length 14 hours 37 minutes.

19	B.	4 42	7 19	1	23	27	♀ gr. Hel. Lat. N.		sets.	eve.	7 53
20	Mo	4 43	7 19	1	23	27			8 45	1 16	8 42
21	Tue	4 43	7 19	2	23	27	☉ ent. ♋. SUMMER BEG		9 19	2 3	9 29
22	We	4 43	7 19	2	23	27	♃☉. ♂☿☉.		9 48	2 48	10 14
23	Thu	4 43	7 19	2	23	26	Bat. Chickahominy 1862		10 14	3 31	10 57
24	Fri	4 43	7 19	2	23	24	ST. JOHN THE BAPTIST.		10 38	4 13	11 39
25	Sat	4 43	7 20	3	23	23	Custer defeated 1876.		11 2	4 56	0 22

26.   Third Sunday after Trinity.   Day's length 14 hours 36 minutes.

26	B.	4 44	7 20	3	23	20	☿ in Peri. ♂♃☾.		11 29	5 40	1 6
27	Mo	4 44	7 20	3	23	28	♃ in Aphelion.		11 57	6 26	1 52
28	Tue	4 44	7 20	3	23	15	Vicksburg bomb. 1862.		m'rn	7 16	2 42
29	We	4 45	7 20	3	23	11	Henry Clay died 1852.		0 30	8 10	3 36
30	Thu	4 45	7 20	4	23	8	♂☿☉ superior.		1 9	9 10	4 36

WEATHER CONJECTURES—JUNE—1, 2, 3, expect much rain; 4, 5, 6, 7, 8, 9, 10, changeable; 11, 12, 13, 14, 15, 16, 17, fair; 18, 19, 20, 21, 22, 23, 24, 25, very rainy; 26, 27, 28, 29, 30, fair.

Farmers should use ''NATIONAL'' Fertilizer for Tobacco; and ''BEEF, BLOOD and BONE '' brand for Cotton, Corn and Wheat. Strictly reliable. Ask your Fertilizer Merchant for them. Carefully prepared by

(See top 3d cover page:)   *S. W. TRAVERS & CO., Branch, Richmond, Va.*

FARM AND GARDEN WORK FOR JUNE.—Sow full crops of cabbages for fall and winter use. Cauliflower and broccoli may yet be sown, also a few carrots. Continue to sow tomatoes, okra, radishes, snap beans. Transplant leeks; pull and dry onions, garlic and eshcalots. A few cucumbers and melons plant for a late crop, and a few ruta baga turnips.

Keep constantly at the plow and hoe; this is the most important grass month! If the vines from your sweet potato sprout bed are fit you can draw and plant out first good rain. Sow cow-peas between your corn hills and rows. The end of this month is a good time to put in the first crop of standing field peas.

(Continued from page 15.)
THE FARMER.

" Swing inward, O gates of the future,
   Swing outward ye doors of the past ;
A giant is waking from slumber,
   And rending his fetters at last,
From the dust where his proud tyrants found him,
   Unhonored and scorned and betrayed ;
He shall rise with the sunlight around him,
   And rule in the realm he has made."

It is every boy's ambition to be a successful man. How many stop to think that the successful men were once successful boys—the boys who did thoroughly whatever work they had to do?

The *American Agriculturist* says: " How rapidly the months and years come and go! We cannot stand still. The farmer has to deal with the matter that is ever changing. And an accurate knowledge of these changes is essential to the highest success."

This is agricultural science, pure and simple. The farmer must study these changes, and then apply his knowledge to the daily duties of the farm. We freely and fully admit the importance of good government, of cheap and rapid transportation, of mechanical inventions, and of manufactures, trades, and of commerce ; but, at the same time, we know that farming is the basis of our material prosperity.

*   *   *   *   *

If there is anything the matter with your fruit trees or grape vines, write to the director of the Experiment Station, Raleigh, N. C.

*   *   *   *   *

It takes a sensible well informed man to make a good farmer. The farmer comes in contact at every turn in his daily work with the elements of great power for or against him. Sunshine, air, water, heat and cold, and their combined action upon soils, growing plants and animal life—these mysterious forces are ever present with him and would hasten to do his bidding, if intelligently directed. May-be-so's will not do, guess work will not do, moon vagaries and luck signs will not avail—nothing short of *the truth* will take the prize. How many farmers are there in North Carolina to day who are patiently and persistently investigating the foundation principles of a successful agriculture?

*   *   *   *   *

Every farmer in North Carolina who takes any pride in his calling, ought to take a good agricultural paper. *Try it one year*, any how.

THURSDAY.

What's hallowed ground? 'Tis what gives birth
To sacred thoughts in souls of worth!—
Peace! Independence! Truth! go forth
      Earth's compass round ;
And your high-priesthood shall make earth
      All hallowed ground.   —*Thomas Campbell.*

2

7th Month. JULY, 1898 31 Days.

Moon's Phases.

	D. H. M.		D. H. M.
Full Moon,	3 4 3p.m.	New Moon,	18 2 39p.m.
Last Quarter,	10 11 34a.m.	First Quarter,	26 8 31a.m.

Day of Month.	Day of Week.	Sun rises.	Sun sets.	Sun slow.	Sun's decline north.	ASPECTS OF PLANETS AND OTHER MISCELLANEOUS MATTER.	Moon's place.	Moon rises or sets.	Moon south.	High tides at Beaufort.
1	Fri	4 45	7 20	4	23 3	Bat. of Gettysburg 1863	[illegible]	1 58	eve.	m'rn
2	Sat	4 46	7 20	4	22 59	Garfield assassinat'd '81	[illegible]	2 57	11 21	6 47
27.	F u th Sunday after Trinity.					Day's length 14 hours 33 minutes.				
3	*B.*	4 47	7 20	4	22 54	Moon ecl. inv. Wash.	[illegible]	rises.	m'rn	7 20
4	Mo	4 47	7 20	4	22 48	INDEPEND DAY 1776	[illegible]	8 20	1 26	8 52
5	Tue	4 48	7 19	4	22 43	Monroe d. 1881.	[illegible]	8 58	2 22	9 48
6	We	4 48	7 19	5	22 36	☿ gr. Hel. Lat N.	[illegible]	9 30	3 14	10 40
7	Thu	4 49	7 19	5	22 30	Dem. Conv. Chicago 1896	[illegible]	9 59	4 2	11 28
8	Fri	4 50	7 19	5	22 23	Vicksburg cap. 1863.	[illegible]	10 25	4 48	0 14
9	Sat	4 50	7 19	5	22 15	Braddock's defeat 1755.	[illegible]	10 50	5 34	1 0
28.	Fifth Sunday after Trinity.					Day's length 14 hours 27 minutes.				
10	*B.*	4 51	7 18	5	22 8	Calvin b. 1509.	[illegible]	11 18	6 20	1 46
11	Mo	4 52	7 18	5	21 59	J. Q. Adams b. 1767.	[illegible]	11 49	7 6	2 32
12	Tue	4 52	7 18	5	21 51	Battle of B you 1690.	[illegible]	m'rn	7 54	3 20
13	We	4 53	7 17	6	21 42	Gen. Fremont d. 1860.	[illegible]	0 22	8 44	4 10
14	Thu	4 53	7 17	6	21 33	Peace Cong. London 1890	[illegible]	1 3	9 34	5 0
15	Fri	4 54	7 16	6	21 23	☌ ♆ ☾.	[illegible]	1 48	10 24	5 50
16	Sat	4 55	7 16	6	21 13	Mrs. Lincoln d. 1882.	[illegible]	2 38	11 13	6 39
29.	Sixth Sunday after Trinity.					Day's length 14 hours 20 minutes.				
17	*B.*	4 55	7 15	6	21 3	GRADU'TN DAY 1856	[illegible]	3 34	eve.	7 2
18	Mo	4 56	7 15	6	20 52	Sun ecl. inv. Wash.	[illegible]	sets.	0 0	7 26
19	Tue	4 57	7 14	6	20 41	French revol. began 1789	[illegible]	7 52	0 46	7 72
20	We	4 57	7 13	6	20 30	Battle Winchester 1864.	[illegible]	8 18	1 30	8 56
21	Thu	4 58	7 13	6	20 18	Battle Bull Run 1862.	[illegible]	8 48	2 13	9 39
22	Fri	4 59	7 12	6	20 6	Read "Branson's Max."	[illegible]	9 8	2 55	10 21
23	Sat	5 0	7 12	6	19 53	Gibraltar taken 1704.	[illegible]	9 33	3 38	11 4
30.	Seventh Sunday after Trinity.					Day's length 14 hours 10 minutes.				
24	*B.*	5 1	7 11	6	19 41	☌ ♃ ☾. Boliver b. 1783	[illegible]	10 0	4 22	11 48
25	Mo	5 2	7 11	6	19 28	Bat Lundy's Lane '14	[illegible]	10 29	5 10	0 36
26	Tue	5 3	7 10	6	1[illegible] 14	Argentine Rev. 1890	[illegible]	11 3	6 1	1 27
27	We	5 3	7 9	6	19 [illegible]	☌ ☿ with Leonis	[illegible]	11 46	6 57	2 23
28	Thu	5 3	7 8	6	18 46	☌ ♂ ☾. ☌ ♄ ☾.	[illegible]	m'rn	7 57	3 33
27	Fri	5 4	7 7	6	18 32	Hiram Powers b. 1805	[illegible]	0 39	9 1	4 27
30	Sat	5 5	7 6	6	18 17	☿ in ♉ Wm. Penn b. 1718	[illegible]	1 42	10 5	5 31
31	Eighth Sunday after Trinity.					Day's length 14 hours 0 minutes.				
31	*B.*	5 6	7 6	6	18 3	Diving bell inv. 1538.	[illegible]	2 54	11 7	6 33

WEATHER CONJECTURES—JULY—1, 2, fair; 3, 4, 5. 6. 7, 8, 9 fair; 10, 11. 12, 13, 14, 15. 16, 17. expect frequent showers; 18. 19, 20, 21, 22, 23, 24. 25. changeable; 26, 27. 28, 29. 30, 31. unsteady weather.

FARM AND GARDEN WORK FOR JULY.—S w cabbages, but protect from hot sun when young. Water at night. Plant snap beans and a few Irish potatoes. Continue to sow radishes, lettuce, endive, cresses, mustard and small sa'ading. The early Dutch turnip is the best to sow for the first crop; follow with the yellow Swedish or ruta bags.

Now do not omit to sow full crops of stand ng cow-peas. Sow a few turnips, carrots and beets as fi-ld crops, th ugh the hot suns are apt to destroy them; should they escape they will be fine; the next month is the best for these crops.

TO-DAY.

Rise! for the day is passing,
And you lie dreaming on—
And others have buckled their armor,
And forth to the fight have gone.
A place in the ranks awaits you,
Each man has some part to play;
The past and the future are nothing,
In the face of the stern to day.

Rise from your dreams of the future,
Of gaining some hard fought field,
Of storming some airy fortress,
Or bidding some giant yield.
Your future has deeds o' glory,
Of honor (God grant it may!)
But your arm will never be stronger,
Or the need so great as to day!

Rise! If the past detains you,
H r sunshine and storms forget;
No chains so unwor hy to hold you
As those of a vain regret.
Sad or bright, she is lifeless forever;
Cast her phantom arms away,
Nor look back save to learn the lesson
Of a nobler strife to-day.

Rise! for the day is passing;
The low sounds that you scarcely hear,
Is the enemy marching to battle;
Arise! for the foe is near!
Stay not to sharpen your weapons,
Or the hour will strike at last,
When, from dreams of a coming battle,
You may find it past!
—Household Magazine.

FRIDAY.

A man that is young in years may be old in hours, if he have lost no time, which happeneth rarely.—*Bacon.*

SATURDAY.

O Lord, thy heavenly grace impart,
And fix my f ail, inconstant heart,
Henceforth my chief desire shall be
To dedicate myself to Thee. *—Oberlin.*

8th Month.   AUGUST, 1898.   31 Days.

Moon's Phases.

	D. H. M.		D. H. M.
Full Moon,	1 11 20p.m.	New Moon,	17 5 25a.m.
Last Quarter,	9 1 4a.m.	First Quarter,	24 3 23p. m
		Full Moon,	31 7 42a.m.

Day of Month.	Day of Week.	Sun rises.	Sun sets.	Sun slow.	Sun's decline north.	ASPECTS OF PLANETS AND OTHER MISCELLANEOUS MATTER.	Moon's place.	Moon rises or sets.	Moon south.	High Tides at Beaufort.
1	Mo	5 6	7 5	6	17 47	Geo. II crown'd 1714		4 11	m'rn	m'rn
2	Tue	5 7	7 4	6	17 32	Bat. of Plevna 1877.		rises.	0 6	7 32
3	We	5 8	7 3	6	17 16	Columbus left 1492.		7 57	1 0	8 26
4	Thu	5 9	7 2	6	17 0	Tilden died 1886.		8 25	2 0	9 26
5	Fri	5 10	7 1	6	16 43	Battle of Athens 1861.		8 52	2 40	10 6
6	Sat	5 11	7 1	6	16 27	Fort Gaines sur. 1864.		9 20	3 27	10 53

32.   Ninth Sunday after Trinity.   Day's length 13 hours 49 minutes.

7	*B.*	5 11	7 0	5	16 10	sta. Barzihous d. 1848		9 49	4 14	11 40
8	Mo	5 12	6 58	5	15 53	Span. Arma. des 1588		10 23	5 1	0 27
9	Tue	5 13	6 56	5	15 35	gr. Elon. E. sta.		11 1	5 49	1 15
10	We	5 14	6 55	5	15 18	Battle Oak Hill 1861.		11 44	6 39	2 5
11	Thu	5 14	6 54	5	15 0	Card. Newman d. 1890		m'rn	7 29	2 55
12	Fri	5 15	6 53	5	14 41	Robert E. Lee d. 1870.		0 33	8 19	3 45
13	Sat	5 16	6 52	5	14 23	Conova d. 1822.		1 26	9 8	4 34

33.   Tenth Sunday after Trinity.   Day's length 13 hours 34 minutes.

14	*B.*	5 17	6 51	4	14 4	in . Bat. Hasting 1066		2 24	9 57	5 23
15	Mo	5 18	6 50	4	13 46	Napoleon b. 1769.		3 23	10 43	6 9
16	Tue	5 19	6 49	4	13 27	Napol. at St. Hel 1815		4 24	11 28	6 54
17	We	5 19	6 48	4	13 7	Burgoyne sur. 1777.		sets.	eve.	7 15
18	Thu	5 20	6 46	4	12 48	Cor. Stone U.S. Cap. 1793		7 14	0 54	8 20
19	Fri	5 21	6 45	3	12 28			7 37	1 7	9 3
20	Sat	5 21	6 44	3	12 8	Benj. Harrison b 1833.		8 4	2 22	9 48

34.   Eleventh Sunday after Trinity.   Day's length 13 hours 21 min.

21	*B.*	5 22	6 43	3	11 48	Capt. T. A. Branson k. '64		8 32	3 8	10 34
22	Mo	5 23	6 42	3	11 28	sta.		9 5	3 57	11 23
23	Tue	5 24	6 40	2	11 7	Com. Perry d. 1820.		9 45	4 51	0 17
24	We	5 25	6 39	2	10 47			10 32	5 48	1 14
25	Thu	5 26	6 38	2	10 26	Turner in Raleigh 1870.		11 29	6 48	2 14
26	Fri	5 27	6 36	1	10 5	Battle of Dresden 1813.		m'rn	7 50	3 16
27	Sat	5 27	6 35	1	9 44	Bishop Daggett d. 1880.		0 37	8 52	4 18

35.   Twelfth Sunday after Trinity.   Day's length 13 hours 5 minutes.

28	*B.*	5 28	6 33	1	9 23	First Cable mes. sent '58		1 49	9 50	5 16
29	Mo	5 28	6 32	1	9 1	. . Lat. S.		3 4	10 46	6 12
30	Tue	5 29	6 31	0	8 40	Wm. Penn d. 1718.		4 19	11 38	7 14
31	We	5 30	6 30	0	8 18	in .		rises.	m'rn	8 13

WEATHER CONJECTURES—AUGUST—1, 2, 3, 4, 5, 6, 7, 8, fair; 9, 10, 11, 12, 13, 14, 15, 16, fair; 17, 18, 19, 20, 21, 22, 23, rain; 24, 25, 26, 27, 28, 29, 30, changeable; 31, unsettled weather.

LUMSDEN & SONS, Wood and Willow Ware, Iron Hollow Ware, Fayetteville Street, opposite Market, Raleigh, N. C.

BRANSON'S NORTH CAROLINA ALMANAC. 21

⋈ FARM AND GARDEN WORK FOR AUGUST.—Transplant all kinds of cabbage, cauliflower and celery. Sow carrots and beets, turnips of all
kinds, spinach, lettuce, radish and onions.

Now sow full crops of field turnips, carrots and beets, and such other
crops as were omitted last month; strip fodder. Early rice will be fit to
cut the last of this month. Look to it. This is a good time to plant
vines of the first slips, in order to procure seed potatoes for the next
year's crops.

NORTH CAROLINA COLLEGES, AND OTHER GRADUATING SCHOOLS.
(Names, character and location.)

Asheville Female College (Methodist)..........................Asheville
Chowan Female Institute (Baptist)......................Murfreesboro
Claremont Female College (Reformed Church of U. S.)........Hickory
Catawba College (Reformed Church of U. S.)..................Newton
Concordia College (Lutheran)................................Conover
Davenport Female College (Methodist)........................Lenoir
Davidson College (Presbyterian).............. ....Davidson College
Elon College (Christian).................................Elon College
Greensboro Female College (Methodist)...................Greensboro
Gaston College (Lutheran)....................................Dallas
Guilford College (Friends)........................Guilford College
Hayesville College (Independent).........................Hayesville
Tudson College (Methodist)..........................Hendersonville
Kinston College (Independent)...............................Kinston
Louisburg Female College (Methodist).....................Louisburg
Littleton Female College (Methodist).....................Littleton
Mt. Amoena Seminary (Lutheran)........................Mt. Pleasant
Mt. St. Joseph Academy (Catholic).........................Asheville
North Carolina College (Lutheran).....................Mt. Pleasant
North Carolina Agricultural and Mechanical College (State).....Raleigh
Oxford Female Seminary (Baptist).............................Oxford
Oak Ridge Institute (Independent).........................Oak Ridge
Peace Institute (Independent)...............................Raleigh
Rutherford College, Burke Co. (Independent).......Rutherford College
St. Mary's College (Catholic)..............................Belmont
Shelby Female College (Independent)..........................Shelby
St. Mary's School (Episcopal)...............................Raleigh
Salem Academy (Moravian).....................................Salem
St. Paul's Seminary (Lutheran Theological)..................Hickory
State Normal and Industrial School (State)...............Greensboro
Trinity College (Methodist) ....Durham
University of North Carolina (State)....................Chapel Hill
Weaverville College (Methodist).........................Weaverville
Wake Forest College (Baptist)...........................Wake Forest
Business University..Raleigh

COLORED SCHOOLS—Graduating.

Agricultural and Mechanical College (State).............Greensboro
Bennett Seminary (Methodist) ....Greensboro
Biddle University (Presbyterian)..........................Charlotte
Building and Trade's College (Independent).........Southern Pines
Franklinton Christian College (Christian)..............Franklinton
Livingstone College (Methodist) ....Salisbury
Normal and Industrial College (Methodist)................ Kittrell
Normal School (State)................................Elizabeth City
Normal School (State)....................................Goldsboro
Normal School (State)....................................Salisbury
Normal School (State)..................................Franklinton
Normal School (State).....................................Plymouth
Normal School (State)..................................Fayetteville
Shaw University (Baptist)..................................Raleigh
St. Augustine Normal College (Episcopal)..................Raleigh
Scotia Female Seminary (Presbyterian) ....Concord
Slater Industrial Academy and Normal School (State).........Winston

9th Month. SEPTEMBER, 1898. 30 Days.

Moon's Phases.

	D.	H.	M.		D.	H.	M.
☾ Last Quarter,	7	5	42p.m.	☽ First Quarter,	22	9	31p.m.
New Moon,	15	7	2 a.m.	Full Moon,	29	6	2p.m.

Day of Month.	Day of Week.	Sun rises.	Sun sets.	Sun fast.	Sun's decline north.	ASPECTS OF PLANETS AND OTHER MISCELLANEOUS MATTER.	Moon's place.	Moon rises or sets.	Moon south.	High Tides at Beaufort.
1	Thu	5 31	6 28	fast	7 56	Battle of Ox Hill 1862.	♓	rises.	m'rn	m'rn
2	Fri	5 32	6 27		7 34	Atlanta captured 1864	♓	7 19	1 16	8 42
3	Sat	5 33	6 25	1	7 12	Elizabeth Glenn d 1894.	♓	7 50	2 4	9 30
36. Thirteenth Sunday after Trinity.						Day's length 12 hours 50 min.				
4	*B.*	5 34	6 24	1	6 50	Gen. Morgan k. 1864.	♈	8 22	2 52	10 18
5	Mo	5 35	6 22	2	6 27	☌ ☿ ☉ superior.	♈	8 58	3 41	11 7
6	Tue	5 35	6 21	2	6 5	LABOR DAY 1ST MON	♈	9 39	4 31	11 57
7	We	5 36	6 19	2	5 42	Castelar inaug. 1873	♈	10 26	5 22	0 48
8	Thu	5 36	6 18	3	5 20	Destruc. Jerusalem 70.	♈	11 18	6 12	1 38
9	Fri	5 37	7 16	3	4 57	California admit. 1850.	♊	m'rn	7 2	2 28
10	Sat	5 38	7 15	3	4 34	S. S. Cox. died 1889.	♊	0 13	7 51	3 17
37. Fourteenth Sunday after Trinity.						Day's length 12 hours 35 min.				
11	*B.*	5 39	6 14	4	4 11	Battle Brandywine 1777	♋	1 13	8 38	4 4
12	Mo	5 39	6 12	4	3 48	Bat. of Chapultepec 1847	♋	2 14	9 28	4 49
13	Tue	5 40	6 11	4	3 25	Battle of Quebec 1750	♋	3 14	10 7	5 33
14	We	5 41	6 10	5	3 2	☿ sta. ☌ ☿ ☾. ['47	♋	4 16	10 51	6 17
15	Thu	5 42	6 8	5	2 39	Gen. Scott to'k Mex.	♍	5 19	11 34	7 00
16	Fri	5 43	6 6	5	2 16	Farenheit died 1737.	♍	sets.	eve.	7 45
17	Sat	5 44	6 5	6	1 53	♀ in Aphe. ☌ ♃ ☾.	♍	6 36	1 5	8 31
38. Fifteenth Sunday after Trinity.						Day's length 12 hours 20 min.				
18	*B.*	5 44	6 4	6	1 29	☽ i ♌.	♎	7 8	1 54	9 20
19	Mo	5 45	6 2	7	1 6	☌ ♀ ☾. Garfield d. 1881	♎	7 44	2 47	10 13
20	Tue	5 45	6 1	7	0 43	☌ ♆ ☾. Arthur inaug.'81	♎	8 31	3 43	11 9
21	We	5 46	6 0	7	0 19	☿ gr. Elon. W.	♏	9 25	4 43	11 9
22	Thu	5 47	5 58	8	south	♀ gr. Elon. E. ☿ in	♏	10 28	5 43	1 9
23	Fri	5 48	5 56	8	0 27	Peri. ☉ ent ♎. AUT. COM	♐	11 36	6 43	2 9
24	Sat	5 49	5 54	8	0 51	Gen. D. H. Hill d. 1889	♐	m'rn	7 41	3 7
39. Sixteenth Sunday after Trinity.						Day's length 12 hours 3 minntes.				
25	*B.*	5 50	5 53	9	1 14	Battle Montreal 1775.	♑	0 48	8 36	4 2
26	Mo	5 51	5 52	9	1 38	Daniel Boone d. 1820.	♑	2 0	9 28	4 54
27	Tue	5 51	5 50	9	2 1	♆ sta. Str. Arctic lost '55	♑	3 13	10 17	5 43
28	We	5 51	5 49	10	2 24	Bish Randall d 1873	♓	4 23	11 6	6 34
29	Thu	5 52	5 47	10	2 48	MICHALMAS DAY.	♓	5 30	11 53	7 19
30	Fri	5 53	5 46	10	3 11	Whitfield d 1770	♓	rises.	m'rn	8 4

WEATHER CONJECTURES—SEPTEMBER—1, 2, 3, 4. 5. 6. wind and rain; 7, 8, 9, 10, 11, 12, 13. 14. fair; 15, 13, 17, 18, 19 20, 21, fair if wind be from N. W.; rainy if S or S. W.; 22, 23, 24, 25 26, 27. 28, about the same sort of weather; 29, 30, look for rain if wind S. or S. W.

FARM AND GARDEN WORK FOR SEPTEMBER.—Now sow full crops of all kinds—turnips, onions, carrots, beets, cabbage, lettuce, cresses. Look after your mushroom beds. Hoe and thin your turnips.

Continue to sow field turnips, carrots and beets. Southern seed is always better than the imported; those from the latter are apt to run to seed early in the spring, unless it be English seed. Prepare land for sowing rye in October. Pick cotton; harvest corn.

THE UNIVERSITY OF NORTH CAROLINA.

(Located in Chapel Hill, Orange County, twenty-eight miles north-west of Raleigh.)

Chartered in 1789. founded in 1793, opened 1795. It now has 467 students and 25 instructors. The equipment includes twelve large buildings, six scientific laboratories, library of 40 000 volumes, campus of fifty acres with ample athletic grounds, gymnasium, &c. Perfect sanitation, baths, closets, &c. Tuition $60 a year, total expenses $200 to $300. Scholarships and loans for the needy. Law school 164, medical school thirty-nine, pharmacy fourteen. A summer school for teachers is conducted each July. It enrolled 185 teachers in 1895. The Faculty enrolled nineteen Professors. During 1896 and 1897, many students supported themselves by labor, the total amount earned being about $5,000. The University is non political and non sectarian.

FACULTY.—Edwin Anderson Alderman, D. C. L., President of the University, and Professor of Political and Social Science; Kemp Plummer Battle, LL.D , Alumni Professor of History; Francis Preston Venable, Ph.D , Smith Professor of General and Analytical Chemistry; Joseph Austin Holmes, S. B., (State Geologist), Lecturer on the Geology of North Carolina; Joshua Walker Gore, C. E., Professor of Physics; John Manning, LL.D., Professor of Law; Thomas Hume, D.D., LL.D., Professor of the English Language and Literature; Walter Dallam Toy. M. A., Professor of Modern Languages; Eben Alexander, Ph.D., LL.D., Professor of Greek Language and Literature; William Cain. C. E., Professor of Mathematics; Richard Henry Whitehead, M.D., Professor of Anatomy and Pathology; Henry Horace Williams, A.M. B.D., Professor of Philosophy; Henry Van Peters Wilson, Ph.D., Professor of Biology; Karl Pomeroy Harrington, M.A., Professor of Latin Language and Literature; Collier Cobb, A.M., Professor of Geology, Charles Baskerville, Ph.D., Assistant Professor of Chemistry; Charles Staples Mangum, M.D., Professor of Physiology and *Materia Medica*; Edward Vernon Howell, A.B , Ph G., Professor of Pharmacy; Henry Farrar Linscott, Ph.D., Associate Professor of Classical Philology; Ernest Taylor Bynum, Ph D., Adjunct Professor of History and Political Science;———Professor of Pedagogy.

INSTRUCTORS.—George Phineas Butler, B.E., Instructor in Mathematics; Samuel May, A.B., Instructor in Modern Languages; William Cunningham Smith. Ph.B., Instructor in English; Harry Ellsworth Mechling, Director of Gymnasium.

ASSISTANTS IN LABORATORIES.—Arthur William Belden, Litt. B:, Assistant in Chemistry; John Gilchrist McCormick, Assistant in Geology; Edward Emmett Sams. Assistant in Physics; Albert Franklin Williams, Jr., A. B , Assistant in Biology; Edward Jenner Wood, Assistant in Biology; George Edgar Newby, Assistant in Biology.

OFFICERS.—Collier Cobb, A M , Secretary of the Faculty; Eben Alexander, Ph.D., LL.D , Supervisor of the Library; Ralph Henry Graves, A. B , Librarian; Eugene Lewis Harris, Ph.B., Registrar; Willie Thomas Patterson, Bursar.

WEDNESDAY.

They are never alone that are accompanied with noble thoughts.—*Sir Philip Sidney.*

10th Month. OCTOBER, 1898. 31 Days.

Moon's Phases.

	D.	H.	M.		D.	H.	M.
☾ Last Quarter,	7	0	56p.m.	☽ First Quarter,	22	4	1a.m.
New Moon,	15	7	29a.m.	Full Moon,	29	7	10a.m.

Day of Month.	Day of Week.	Sun rises.	Sun sets.	Sun fast.	Sun's decline south.	ASPECTS OF PLANETS AND OTHER MISCELLANEOUS MATTER.	Moon's place.	Moon rises or sets.	Moon south.	High Tides at Beaufort.
1	Sat	5 54	5 44	11	3 34			rises.	m'rn	m'rn
40. Seventeenth Sunday after Trinity. Day's length 11 hours 50 min.										
2	*B.*	5 53	5 43	11	3 58	♀ gr. Hel. Lat. N.		6 55	1 31	8 57
3	Mo	5 56	5 41	11	4 21	Black Hawk d. 1838.		7 34	2 21	9 57
4	Tue	5 57	5 40	12	4 44	Bat. Germantown 1777.		8 19	3 12	10 38
5	We	5 58	5 36	12	5 7	Jon'th'n Edwards b 1703		9 9	4 3	11 29
6	Thu	5 59	5 35	12	5 30	☾ Judge Dick b. 1823.		10 5	4 54	0 21
7	Fri	5 59	5 34	12	5 53	Edgar A. Poe d. 1849		11 2	5 43	1 9
8	Sat	6 0	5 32	13	6 16	Bat. Fort Pickens 1861.		m'rn	6 31	1 57
41. Eighteenth Sunday after Trinity. Day's length 11 hours 29 min.										
9	*B.*	6 1	5 30	13	6 39	Grt. fire in Chicago 1871		0 1	7 16	2 42
10	Mo	6 2	5 29	13	7 2	♀ gr. Hel Lat. S. ☌ ♀ ♅		1 1	8 1	3 27
11	Tue	6 3	5 28	13	7 24	Rev. W. E. Pell d. 1870.		2 2	8 44	4 10
12	We	6 4	5 27	14	7 47	Gen. R. E. Lee d. 1870.		3 3	9 27	4 53
13	Thu	6 5	5 25	14	8 9	☌ ♃ ⊙. Conova d. 1822.		4 6	10 12	5 38
14	Fri	6 6	5 24	14	8 31	Bat. Hastings 1066.		5 12	10 58	6 24
15	Sat	6 7	5 23	14	8 54	☌ ☿ ☾. ☌ ♃ ☾.		sets.	11 47	7 13
42. Nineteenth Sunday after Trinity. Day's length 11 hours 13 min.										
16	*B.*	6 8	5 21	15	9 16	Noah Webster b. 1758.		5 44	eve.	8 2
17	Mo	6 9	5 19	15	9 37	Earthq. in Asia Minor 83		6 28	1 36	9 2
18	Tue	6 9	5 18	15	9 59	☌ ♅ ♀ ☾. ☌ ♄ ☾.		7 20	2 36	10 4
19	We	6 10	5 17	15	10 21	☌ ☿ ⊙ inferior.		8 21	3 37	11 3
20	Thu	6 11	5 16	15	10 42	Grace Darling d. 1812.		9 29	4 38	0 4
21	Fri	6 12	5 15	15	11 4	☽ Bat. Ball's Bluff 1861		10 40	5 37	1 3
23	Sat	6 13	5 14	16	11 25	☌ ♀ ♄.		11 52	6 32	1 58
43. Twentieth Sunday after Trinity. Day's length 10 hours 58 min.										
23	*B.*	6 14	5 12	16	11 46	Wm. Hooper d. 1790.		m'rn	7 23	2 49
24	Mo	6 15	5 11	16	12 7	Water mills inven. 555.		1 2	8 12	3 38
25	Tue	6 16	5 10	16	12 27	Newbern settled 1712.		2 11	9 0	4 26
26	We	6 16	5 9	16	12 48	☿ in ☊. Hogarth d. 1764		3 18	9 47	5 13
27	Thu	6 17	5 8	16	13 8	♀ greatest brilliancy.		4 25	10 34	6 0
28	Fri	6 18	5 7	16	13 28	Proverbs 28: 1.		5 30	11 22	6 48
29	Sat	6 19	5 6	16	13 48	Sir Walt. Ral. d. 1618		rises.	m'rn	7 38
44. Twenty first Sunday after Trinity. Day's length 10 hours 45 min.										
30	*B*	6 20	5 5	16	14 7	Gambetta born 1838.		5 30	0 12	8 3
31	Mo	6 21	5 5	16	14 27	Gen. Scott retired 1861.		6 13	1 3	8 29

WEATHER CONJECTURES—OCTOBER—1, 2, 3, 4, 5, 6, fair if wind N. or N. W.; rain if S. or S. W; 7, 8, 9, 10, 11, 12, 13, 14, very rainy; 15, 16, 17, 18, 19, 20, 21, wind and rain; 22, 23, 24, 25, 26, 27, 28, rain; 29, 30, 31, expect wind and rain.

℃ 24.—Live with happy people, and you are likely *to be* happy.—*Branson*.

BLANSON'S NORTH CAROLINA ALMANAC. 25

FARM AND GARDEN WORK FOR OCTOBER.—You may make two sowings of cabbage this month, and, if of English seed, they will not "run" in the spring. Sow lettuce; hoe turnips and thin; put out leeks and onions; sow principal crop of spinach; earth up celery.

᛭ Continue picking your cotton as it blows. Sow early rye, wheat and barley. Dig your sweet potatoes when the weather becomes cool and you expect frost.

PUBLIC WORKS AND INSTITUTIONS IN NORTH CAROLINA.

THE NORTH CAROLINA COLLEGE OF AGRICULTURE AND MECHANIC ARTS.

Located on the Hillsboro road, one and one-half miles west of the capitol. Opened October 3d, 1889.

BOARD OF TRUSTEES.—Hon. J. C. L. Harris, President, Raleigh; Col. L. C. Edwards, Oxford; J. W. Harden, Jr., Raleigh; Judge H G. Connor, Wilson; Dr. Matt Moore, Warsaw; J Z Waller, Burlington; H. E. Bonitz, Wilmington; Dr. B. F. Dixon, King's Mountain; Prof. J J. Britt, Bakersville; Dr. Alex. Q. Holladay, Raleigh; Prof. J. R. Chamberlain, Raleigh; S. L. Crowder, Halifax.

EXECUTIVE COMMITTEE.—Hon. J. C. L. Harris, Chairman; J. Z Waller. Dr. Alex. Q. Holladay. Prof. J. R. Chamberlain, S. L. Crowder.

FINANCE COMMITTEE.—Jno. W. Harden, Jr., Chairman; L. C. Edwards, B. F. Dixon.

FACULTY AND OFFICERS.—Alex. Q. Holladay, LL. D., President and Professor of History; W. F. Massey, C. E., Professor of Horticulture, Arboriculture and Botany; W. A. Withers, A. M., Professor of Pure and Agricultural Chemistry; D. H. Hill, A. M., Professor of English; W. C. Riddick, A. B., C. E., Professor of Civil Engineering and Mathematics; F. E. Emery, M. S., Professor of Agriculture; Jno. C. Gresham, Capt. U. S. A., Professor of Military Science and Tactics; John C. Gresham, Professor of Modern Languages; F. A. Weiche, Ph. D., Professor of Physics and Electrical Engineering; C. W. Scribner, A. B., M. E., Professor of Mechanical Engineering; E. G. Butler, Assistant Professor of English, and Bursar; C. M. Pritchett, B. S., C. E., M. E., Instructor in Drawing; C. B. Park, Superintendent of Shops; C. W. Hyams, Instructor in Botany; J. M. Johnson, M S., Instructor in Agriculture; T. L. Wright, Ph. B., Instructor in Mathematics; J. A. B'zzell, B. S., Assistant in Chemistry; C. D. Francks, B. E., Assistant in Mathematics; L. R. Whitted, B. S., Assistant in Physics and Electricity; J. W. Carroll, B. S., Assistant in Dairying; W. A. G. Clark, B. S., Assistant in Civil Engineering; Lea Watson, B. S., Assistant in Shop Work; H. W. Primrose, B. S., Assistant in Chemistry; B. S. Skinner, Superintendent of Farm; Mrs. Sue C. Carroll, Matron; James R. Rogers, M. D., Physician.

CENTRAL HOSPITAL, GEO. L. KIRBY, SUPERINTENDENT, RALEIGH, N. C.

Hon. W. H. Worth, Treasurer *ex officio*; W. H. Martin, Clerk to Treasurer *ex officio*; J. B. Bellamy, Keeper of Records.

RESIDENT OFFICERS.—Dr. George L. Kirby, Superintendent, salary $2,800; term, six years from March 1, 1894. Dr. T. S. W. Mott, First Assistant Physician, salary $1,200; term, two years from March 1, 1897. Dr. Geo. Davis, salary $1.000; term, two years from March 1, 1897. W. R. Crawford, Jr., Steward, salary $1,200; term, one year from March 1, 1897. Mrs. M. E. Whitaker, Matron, salary $600; term, one year from March 1, 1897.

BOARD OF DIRECTORS.—Capt. J. D. Biggs, President; Jno. R. Smith, Wayne County; Dr. R. H. Speight, Edgecombe County; Dr. J. W. Saunders, Carteret County; J. R. Rogers, Wake County; Geo. B. Curtis, Halifax County; J. B. Bellamy, Nash County; J. W. Williams, Wake County; J. G. Ball, Wake County.

25. Do not keep a *burr* in you *throat*, nor a bit of *malice* in your *heart*. *Branson.*

11th Month. NOVEMBER, 1898. 30 Days.

Moon's Phases.

	D.	H.	M.		D.	H.	M.
☾ Last Quarter,	6	9	19 a.m.	☽ First Quarter,	20	16	56 a.m.
● New Moon,	13	7	12 p.m.	○ Full Moon,	27	11	31 p.m.

Day of Month.	Day of Week.	Sun rises.	Sun sets.	Sun fast.	Sun's decline south.	ASPECTS OF PLANETS AND OTHER MISCELLANEOUS MATTER.	Moon's place.	Moon rises or sets.	Moon south.	High Tides at Beaufort.
1	Tue	6 22	5 3	16	14 46	America discov. 1492.	♑	rises.	m'rn	m'rn
2	We	6 23	5 2	16	15 5	Jenny Lind died 1887.	♒	7 55	2 45	9 71
3	Thu	6 24	5 1	16	15 23	Bat. Hohenlinden 1800.	♒	8 52	3 36	10 62
4	Fri	6 25	5 0	16	15 42	Geo. Peabody d. 1869.	♒	9 50	4 24	11 50
5	Sat	6 26	4 59	16	16 0	☿ in Aphe. ☌ ♂ ☾	♓	10 50	5 10	0 36
45.	Twenty-second Sunday after Trinity.					Day's length 10 hours 31m.				
6	*B.*	6 27	4 58	16	16 18	☾ Lincoln elect. 1860	♈	11 49	5 54	1 20
7	Mo	6 28	4 56	16	16 35	Dr. B. Craven d. 1882	♈	m'rn	6 37	2 3
8	Tue	6 29	4 56	16	16 53	Milton died 1674.	♈	0 49	7 20	2 46
9	We	6 30	4 55	16	17 10	Dr. Lovic Pierce d. 1879.	♉	1 49	8 3	3 29
10	Thu	6 31	4 55	16	17 26	Martin Luther b. 1483.	♉	2 53	8 47	4 13
11	Fri	6 32	4 54	16	17 43	♀ sta. ☌ ☿ ♅ sta.	♉	3 58	9 35	5 1
12	Sat	6 33	4 53	16	17 59	☌ ♃ ☾	♉	5 7	10 26	5 52
46.	Twenty third Sunday after Trinity.					Day's length 10 hours 19 m.				
13	*B.*	6 34	4 53	15	18 15	● Fall of meteors 1833	♊	6 19	11 22	6 48
14	Mo	6 35	4 52	15	18 30	Merrimon d. 1892.	♋	sets	eve.	7 49
15	Tue	6 36	4 51	15	18 45	☌ ♄ ☾. ☌ ♀ ☾.	♋	6 8	1 25	8 51
16	We	6 37	4 51	15	19 0	Sherman's march 1864.	♌	7 17	2 28	9 54
17	Thu	6 38	4 50	15	19 15	Suez Canal op'd 1869	♌	8 29	3 29	10 55
18	Fri	6 39	4 50	1[illegible]	19 29	Eruption Mt. Etna 1832.	♍	9 42	4 27	11 53
19	Sat	6 40	4 49	14	19 43	Gen. As. met N'wb'n 1771	♍	10 55	5 20	0 46
47.	Twenty fourth Sunday after Trinity.					Day's length 10 hours 8 m.				
20	*B.*	6 41	4 49	14	19 56	☽ Erup. Mt. Vesuv. 57	♎	m'rn	6 10	1 36
21	Mo	6 42	4 49	14	20 9	Berlin decree 1806.	♏	0 3	6 58	2 24
22	Tue	6 43	4 48	13	20 22	Gen. Jos. Graham d 1836	♏	1 10	7 44	3 10
23	We	6 44	4 47	13	20 34	Gov. Ellis born 1820.	♏	2 16	8 30	3 56
24	Thu	6 45	4 47	13	20 46	Bat. Lookout M't'n 1863.	♏	3 22	9 17	4 43
25	Fri	6 46	4 46	13	20 58	☌ ♅ ☉. ☿ gr. H. l. Lat. S.	♑	4 27	10 6	5 32
26	Sat	6 47	4 46	12	21 9	Bishop Marvin d. 1875.	♑	5 29	10 55	6 21
48.	First Sunday in Advent.					Day's length 9 hours 58 minutes.				
27	*B.*	6 48	4 46	12	21 19	○ Rev. J H. Wheeler d.	♑	6 30	11 46	7 12
28	Mo	6 49	4 46	12	21 30	Irving d. '59. ['94.	♑	rises.	m'rn	7 37
29	Tue	6 50	4 46	11	21 40	Savannah taken 1778.	♒	5 47	0 38	8 4
30	We	6 51	4 46	11	21 49	SAINT ANDREW.	♒	6 42	1 28	8 54

WEATHER CONJECTURES—NOVEMBER—1, 2, 3, 4, 5, stormy; 6, 7, 8, 9, 10, 11, 12, cold rain if wind be West; snow if East; 13 14, 15 16 17, 18, 19, fair and frosty if wind N. or N. E.; rain or snow if S. or S. W.; 20, 21, 22, 23, 24, 25, 26, cold high wind; 27, 28, 29, 30, fair and frosty.

LUMSDEN & SONS, Chattanooga Cane Mills and Evaporators, Fayetteville Street, opposite Market, Raleigh, N. C.

BRANSON'S NORTH CAROLINA ALMANAC. 27

FARM AND GARDEN WORK FOR NOVEMBER.—Sow your first crop of peas and a few turnips. Plant out onions raised from seed in August and September. Plant Windsor and long pod beans. Dress asparagus and artichokes.

Sow full crops of rye, barley, wheat and other small grains. Harvest your sweet potatoes.

THE N. C. AGRICULTURAL EXPERIMENT STATION.

Founded April, 1877. A department of the N. C. College of Agriculture and Mechanic Arts. and governed by its Board of Trustees.

STATION COUNCIL.—Alex. Q Holladay. LL. D, President of the College, Chairman; W. A. Withers, A. M., Professor of Chemistry; F. E. Emery, M. S., Professor of Agriculture; W. F. Massey, C. E., Professor of Horticulture.

STATION STAFF.—W. A. Withers, A. M., State Chemist and Acting Director; F. E. Emery, M. S., Agriculturist; W. F. Massey, C. E. Horticulturist; C. B. Williams, M. S.. First Assistant Chemist; H. K. Miller, M. S., Assistant Chemist; C. D. Harris, B. S. Assistant Chemist; A. W. Blair, A. M., Assistant Chemist; J. D. Hufham. Jr., A. B., Assistant Chemist; J. A. Bizzell. B. S., Assistant Chemist; Alex. Rhodes. Assistant Horticulturist; C. W. Hyams, Assistant Botanist; J. M. Johnson, M. S., Assistant Agriculturist; F. E Hege. Poultry Manager; R. S. Skinner, Superintendent of the Farm; J. M. Fix. Secretary; H. E King, Chief Clerk; F G. Kelly and S. B. Moore, Clerks; Miss M. S. Birdsong, stenographer.

The Director's office is in the main building of the N. C. College of Agriculture and Mechanic Arts, Raleigh. The farm is on the Hillsboro road, about half a mile west of the College; the chemical laboratory is in the Agricultural Building. just north of the capital, and the greenhouses are on the College grounds. Bulletins are sent free to all who apply for them.

THE STATE HOSPITAL, MORGANTON.

OFFICERS —P. L. Murphy. M. D., Superintendent. salary $2,800; Isaac M. Taylor. M. D., Assistant Physician. salary $1,200; C. E. Ross, M. D., Assistant Physician. salary $1 200; F. M. Scroggs, Steward, salary $1 000; Mrs. C. A. Marsh, Matron. salary $550.

BOARD OF DIRECTORS —James P. Sawyer, Buncombe County, President; I I Davis, Esq.. Burke County; Joseph P. Caldwell Esq., Mecklenburg County; J. G. Hall, Esq., Catawba County; Joseph C. Mills, Burke County; G. W. F. Harper, Caldwell County; J R. Love, Jackson County; L. R. Whitener, Catawba County; S. A. White, Alamance County.

No member of the Board of Directors or Executive Committee receive any compensation for their work. except their traveling expenses.

EASTERN HOSPITAL. GOLDSBORO.

OFFICERS.—J. F. Miller, M. D., Superintendent. salary $2.000, furnished house and board of two horses and cows; W. W. Faison, M. D., Assistant Physician. salary $900, board for self. wife three children and nurse and board of one horse; 21 Assistant Physician, Dr. Clara E. Jones, salary $700 and board; Daniel Reid, Steward. salary $450. board of self and horse; Mrs. B. V. Smith. Matron, salary $300 and board of self and child; W J. Mathews, Engineer, salary $600 and board; Mrs. Victoria Bryan, Seamstress. salary $150, and head of self and child; John Davis, Farmer, salary $200 and house; A. A. Green, Watchman. salary $250 per annum. Hon. W. H. Worth, Treasurer ex officio.

BOARD OF DIRECTORS —Dr. J. W. Vick. President, Johnston County; B. F. Aycock, Wayne County; J E Peterson, Warren County; C. S. Wharton, Lenoir County; W. F. Rountree. Craven County; J. L. McLean, Robeson County; Dr. M B. Pitt, Edgecombe County; Major Joshua B Hill, Wake County; Henry I Faison, Duplin County.

EXECUTIVE COMMITTEE.—B. E. Aycock, J. F. Southerland, Thomas B. Parker.

27. Never allow your energies to slacken, or your faith to weaken.—*Branson.*

12th Month. DECEMBER, 1898. 31 Days.

Moon's Phases.

	D.	H. M.		D.	H. M.
☾ Last Quarter,	6	4 57 a.m.	☽ First Quarter,	19	10 13 p.m.
● New Moon,	13	6 25 a.m.	○ Full Moon,	27	6 31 p.m.

Day of Month.	Day of Week.	Sun rises.	Sun sets.	Sun fast.	Sun's decline south.	ASPECTS OF PLANETS AND OTHER MISCELLANEOUS MATTER.	Moon's place.	Moon rises or sets.	Moon south.	High Tides at Beaufort.
1	Thu	6 51	4 46	10	21 58	☌ ♀ ☉ inf. HOME STR'CH		rises.	m'rn	m'rn
2	Fri	6 52	4 46	10	22 7	Monroe doc. ann. 1823.		8 40	3 4	10 30
3	Sat	6 53	4 46	10	22 15	☌ ♂ ☾. ☿ gr. Elon. E.		9 38	3 49	11 15
49. Second Sunday in Advent.						Day's length 9 hours 52 minutes.				
4	*B.*	6 54	4 46	9	22 23	Alabama admit. 1818.		10 34	4 32	11 58
5	Mo	6 55	4 46	9	22 31	☾ ♀ in ♌.		11 36	5 14	0 40
6	Tue	9 56	4 46	8	22 38	Jeff. Davis d. 1889.		m'rn	5 56	1 22
7	We	6 56	4 46	8	22 44	Ed. Badger died 1878.		0 36	6 38	2 4
8	Thu	6 57	4 46	8	22 50			1 38	7 23	2 59
9	Fri	6 58	4 46	7	22 56	Milton born 1608.		2 44	8 11	3 37
10	Sat	6 59	4 46	7	23 1	☌ ♃ ☾. ♂ sta. ☌ ♀ ♅.		3 54	9 4	4 30
50. Third Sunday in Advent.						Day's length 9 hours 46 minutes.				
11	*B.*	7 0	4 46	6	23 6	Indiana admitted 1816.		5 4	10 2	5 28
12	M.	7 1	4 47	7	23 10	● ☉ ecl. invis. in N. C		6 16	11 4	6 30
13	Tue	7 2	4 47	5	23 14	Robt. Tombs d. 1884		sets.	eve.	7 33
14	We	7 3	4 47	5	23 17	☿ in ♌. HALCION DAYS		6 8	1 13	8 39
15	Thu	7 3	4 47	4	23 20	Sitting Bull k. 1890.		7 23	2 15	9 41
16	Fri	7 4	4 48	4	23 22	Boston Tea Party 1773.		8 39	3 12	10 38
17	Sat	7 4	4 48	3	23 24	Poet Whittier b. 1807.		9 51	4 5	11 31
51. Fourth Sunday in Advent.						Day's length 9 hours 44 minutes.				
18	*B.*	7 5	4 49	3	23 26	☽ Sir H. Davy b. 1779.		11 1	4 55	0 21
19	Mo	7 6	4 49	2	23 27	☿ in Peri.		m'rn	5 42	1 8
20	Tue	7 7	4 49	2	23 27	South Carolina sec. 1860		0 9	6 29	1 55
21	We	7 7	4 50	1	23 27	♀ sta. ☉ ent. ♑. WIN. BE		1 15	7 15	2 41
22	Thu	7 8	4 50	1	23 27	Dr. Winchester d. 1876		2 19	8 3	3 29
23	Fri	7 8	4 51	slow	23 26	Henry W. Grady d. 1889		3 22	8 52	4 18
24	Sat	7 9	4 51		23 25	Thackery d. 1863.		4 23	9 42	5 8
52. Fifth Sunday in Advent.						Day's length 9 hours 43 minutes.				
25	*B.*	7 9	4 52	0	23 23	CHRISTMAS DAY.		5 22	10 33	5 59
26	Mo	7 9	4 53	1	23 20	○ ☌ ♆ ☾. [ington.		6 16	11 23	5 49
27	Tue	7 10	4 53	2	23 18	Moon ecl. inv. Wash-		rises	m'rn	6 39
28	We	7 10	4 54	2	23 14	McCaulay died 1859.		5 33	0 13	7 39
29	Thu	7 10	4 54	3	23 11	☿ gr. Hel. Lat. N.		6 32	1 1	8 27
30	Fri	7 11	4 55	3	23 6	☌ ♂ ☾.		7 30	1 46	9 12
31	Sat	7 11	4 56	4	23 2	⊕ eart in Perihelion.		8 29	2 30	9 56

WEATHER CONJECTURES—DECEMBER—1, 2, 3, 4, 5, fair and frosty; 6, 7, 8, 9, 10, 11, 12, rain; 13, 14, 15, 16, 17, 18, stormy; 19, 20, 21, 22, 23, 24, 25, 26, fair and frosty; 27, 28, 29, 30, 31, about the same.

FARM AND GARDEN WORK FOR DECEMBER.—Plant peas of all kinds; set out onions, garlic, eschalots and cabbage. Sow a few lettuce, spinach, carrots and radishes. You may try a few Irish potatoes.

Finish picking cotton; get out crops of rice and prepare for market. Commence plowing, ditching, draining and manuring as early as possible for next year's crop.

STATE BOARD OF PHARMACY.

E. V. Zoeller, Tarboro, President; W. H. Wearn, Charlotte; N. D. Fetzer, Concord; Wm. Simpson, Raleigh, Secretary and Treasurer; P. W. Vaughan, Durham.

NORTH CAROLINA PHARMACEUTICAL ASSOCIATION.

J. P. Stedman, Oxford, President; W. M. Yearby, Durham. J. B. Smith, Lexington; J. I. Johnson, Raleigh, Vice President; H. R. Horne, Fayetteville, Secretary; A. J. Cook, Fayetteville, Treasurer; J. H. Bobbitt, Chairman of Executive Committee, Raleigh.

SUPERIOR COURTS OF NORTH CAROLINA FOR 1898.

Compiled by FAB. H. BUSBEE, Attorney.

JUDGES.

Name.	District.	Residence.
Geo. H. Brown,	1	Washington.
Henry R. Bryan,	2	Newbern.
E W. Timberlake,	3	Louisburg.
W. S. O'B. Robinson,	4	Goldsboro.
S. B. Adams,	5	Roxboro.
O. H. Allen,	6	Kinston.
James D. McIver,	7	Carthage.
A. L. Coble,	8	Statesville.
Henry R. Starbuck,	9	Winston.
Leander L. Greene,	10	Boone.
W. Alexander Hoke,	11	Lincolnton.
W. L. Norwood,	12	Waynesville.

SOLICITORS.

Name.	District.	Residence.
W. J. Leary,	1	Edenton.
W. E. Daniel,	2	Weldon.
C. M. Bernard,	3	Greenville.
Edward W Pou, Jr.,	4	Smithfield.
W. P. Byrum, Jr.,	5	Greensboro.
M. C. Richardson,	6	Clinton.
H. F. Seawell,	7	Carthage.
J. Q. Holton,	8	Yadkinville.
M. L. Mott,	9	Wilkesboro.
J. F. Spainhour,	10	Lenoir.
J. L. Webb,	11	Shelby.
George A. Jones,	12	Franklin.

Time of Holding Courts.

FIRST JUDICIAL DISTRICT.

Spring—Judge Norwood.
Fall—Judge Hoke.
Beaufort—‡Feb. 14th (2), May 30th (2), Nov. 28th (2).
Currituck—March 7th, Sept. 5th.
Camden—March 14th, Sept. 12th.
Pasquotank—March 21st, Sept. 19th.
Chowan—April 4th, Oct. 3d.
Perquimans—March 28th, Sept. 26th.
Gates—April 11th Oct. 10th.
Hertford—April 18th, Oct. 17th.
Washington—April 25th, Oct. 24th.
Tyrrell—May 2d, Oct. 31st.
Dare—May 9th, Nov. 7th.
Hyde—May 16th, Nov. 14th.
Pamlico—May 23d, Nov. 21st.

SECOND JUDICIAL DISTRICT

Spring—Judge Brown.
Fall—Judge Norwood.
Halifax—March 7th (2), †May 30th (2), †Nov. 21st (2)
Northampton—April 4th (2), ‡Aug. 1st (2), Oct 24th (2).
Bertie —‡Feb. 21st, May 2d, Sept. 12th (2), Nov. 7th.
Craven—‡Feb. 7th (2), May 9th (2), †Nov. 28th (2).
Warren—†March 21st (2),†Sept. 19th (2).
Edgecombe—†April 18th (2),†June 13th (2), †Oct. 10th (2).

THIRD JUDICIAL DISTRICT.

Spring—Judge Bryan.
Fall—Judge Brown.
Pitt—Jan. 10th (2) †March 7th (2), April 4th (2), Sept. 19th (2), †Dec. 5th (2).
Franklin—Jan. 24th (2), April 18th (2), Oct. 24th.
Wilson—†Feb. 7th (2), ‡June 6th (2), Oct. 31st (2).
Vance—Feb. 21st (2), May 23d (2), Oct. 3d (2).
Martin—March 21st (2), Sept. 5th (2).
Nash—†May 2d (2), Nov. 21st (2).

FOURTH JUDICIAL DISTRICT.

Spring—Judge Timberlake.
Fall—Judge Bryan.
Wake—*Jan. 10th (2), †Feb. 28th (2), *March 28th (2) †April 25th ( ), July 11th (2), *Sept. 26th (2), †Oct. 24th (2).
Wayne—Jan. 24th (2), April 18th, Sept. 12th (2), Oct. 17th)
Harnett—Feb. 21st, Sept. 5th, ‡Nov. 28th (2).
Johnston—March 14th (2), Aug. 29th, Nov. 14th (2),

FIFTH JUDICIAL DISTRICT.

Spring—Judge Robinson.
Fall—Judge Timberlake.
Durham—Jan. 17th (2), †March 28th (2), *May 16th, *Aug. 5th, *Sept. 5th, †Oct. 3d (2).
Granville—Jan. 31st (2), April 25th (2), July 25th (2), Nov. 21st (2).
Chatham—Feb. 14th, May 9th, Sept. 19th (2).
Guilford—Feb. 21st (2), June 6th (3), Aug. 22d (2), Dec. 5th (2).
Alamance—March 14th, May 23d, †Sept. 12th, Nov. 7th.
Orange—March 21st, †May 30th, Aug. 8th, Oct. 31st.
Caswell—April 11th, Aug. 22d, Oct. 17th.
Person—April 18th, Aug. 15th, Nov. 14th

SIXTH JUDICIAL DISTRICT.

Spring—Judge Adams.
Fall—Judge Robinson.
Pender—March 7th, Sept. 12th (2).
Greene—Feb. 28th, Aug 8th, Nov 28th.
New Hanover—†Jan. 24th (2), †April 18th (2), †Sept. 26th (2).
Lenoir—May 9th (2), Nov. 14th (2).
Duplin—Feb. 21st, Aug. 1st, Dec. 5th.
Sampson—Feb. 7th (2), May 2d, Oct. 10th (2)
Carteret—March 21st, Oct. 24th).
Jones—March 28th, Oct. 31st.
Onslow—April 4th, Nov. 7th.

SEVENTH JUDICIAL DISTRICT.

Spring—Judge Allen.
Fall—Judge Adams.
Columbus—March 14th, Aug. 15th, Nov 8th, Oct 24th.
Anson—*Jan. 10th, †April 18th, *Sept. 5th, †Oct 31st.
Cumberland—†March 28th, †April —, (2), †May 9th (2), *July 25th, †Nov. 14th (2).
Robeson—†Feb. 14th, †May 2d, †Mar. 28th (3), †Dec. 5th (2).
Richmond—*Jan. 17th (Tuesday) (2), April 25th, *May 23d, *Sept. 12th (2), Nov. 7th.
Bladen—March 7th (Tuesday), Oct. 3d (Tuesday). (2)
Brunswick—March 21st, Oct. 17th.
Moore—†Jan. 31st (2), *April 4th (2), *Aug. 22d (2), Nov. 28th.

EIGHTH JUDICIAL DISTRICT.

Spring—Judge McIver.
Fall—Judge Allen.
Cabarrus—Jan. 24th (2), July 25th (2).

SUPERIOR COURTS—Continued.

Iredell—Feb. 7th (2), May 23d (2), Aug. 8th (2), Nov. 7th.

Rowan—Feb. 21st (2), May 9th (2), Aug. 22d (2), Nov. 28th.

Davidson—March 7th (2), Sept. 5th (2).

Randolph—March 21st (2), July 11th (2), Nov. 21st.

Montgomery—Jan. 3d (2), April 18th, Oct. 3d (2).

Yadkin—May 2d, Oct. 24th (2).

NINTH JUDICIAL DISTRICT.

Spring—Judge Allen.
Fall—Judge McIver.

Alexander—Jan. 24th, July 18th.

Rockingham—Jan. 31st (2), July 28th, Oct. 31st (2).

Forsyth—Feb. 21st (2), May 16th (2), Aug. 1st (2), Nov 28th (2).

Wilkes—March 7th (2), Aug. 29th.

Alleghany—April 4th, Sept. 12th.

Davie—April 11th (2), Sept. 19th (2).

Stokes—April 25th (2), Oct. 17th (2).

Surry—March 21st (2), Oct. 3d (2).

TENTH JUDICIAL DISTRICT.

Spring—Judge Starbuck.
Fall—Judge Coble.

Catawba—Feb. 21st (2), July 4th, Oct. 31st (2).

McDowell—†March 7 (2), †Sept. 19 (2).

Burke—March 21st (2), Oct 3d (2).

Caldwell—April 4th (2), Oct. 17 h (2).

Ashe—April 25th, ‡July 25th (2), Nov. 14th.

Watauga—May 2d, ‡Aug. 8th, Nov. 21.

Mitchell—May 9th (2), Aug. 22d (2), Nov. 28th.

Yancey—May 23d, Sept. 5th (2).

ELEVENTH JUDICIAL DISTRICT.

Spring—Judge Greene.
Fall—Judge Starbuck.

Union—*†Jan. 31st (3), *†Aug. 22d (2).

Stanly—March 7th (2), Sept. 5th (2).

Mecklenburg—†Jan 24th, †March 21st (2), †Oct. 3d (2), †June 6th, †Dec. 16th.

Gaston—†Feb. 21st (2), Sept. 19th (2).

Lincoln—April 4th (2), Oct. 17th.

Cleveland—April 18th (2), Oct. 24th (2).

Rutherford—May 2d (2), Nov. 7th (2).

Polk—May 16th, Nov 21st.

Henderson—†May 2d (2), †Nov. 28 (2).

TWELFTH JUDICIAL DISTRICT.

Spring—Judge Hoke.
Fall—Judge Greene.

Madison †Feb. 28th (2). †Aug. 1st (2).

Buncombe—†March 14th (3),†Aug.15th (3), †Dec. 5th (2).

Transylvania—April 4th, Sept. 5th.

Haywood—†April 11 (2), †Sept. 12 (2).

Jackson—April 25th (2), Sept. 26th.

Macon—March 9th, Oct. 3d.

Clay—May 16th, Oct. 10th.

Cherokee—†May 23d (2),*†Oct. 17th (2).

Graham—June 6th, Nov. 7th (2).

Swain—June 13th (3), Nov. 21st (2).

*For criminal cases.

†For civil cases alone.

‡For civil cases alone, except jail cases

(2) Means two weeks, etc.

CRIMINAL COURTS.

EASTERN DISTRICT.

Judge—Sutton, of Fayetteville.

New Hanover—*Jan. 3d, March 14th, Oct. 10th.

Warren—*Jan. 17th, July 11th.

Vance—*Feb. 14th.

Edgecombe—*Feb. 14th, *Nov. 7th.

Craven—*Feb. 21st, Oct. 3d.

Halifax—*Feb. 28th, *Dec. 5th.

Mecklenburg—*April 11th, *Sept. 5th.

Robeson—April 18th, *Oct 17th.

Cumberland—*Feb 7th *Sept. 19th.

Wilson—*May 28th,*Oct 17th, Aug.22.

Nash—*Jan 23, Sept. 12th.

WESTERN DISTRICT.

Judge—Hamilton G. Ewart, of Hendersonville.

Solicitor—Robt. S. McCall Asheville.

Haywood—*Jan. 10th, *July 4th.

Buncombe—*Jan. 24th, *April 25th, *July 25th, *O t. 24th.

Madison—*Feb. 21st, *Jan. 13th, Nov. 14th.

Henderson—†Sept. 12th, April 11th.

McDowell—*July 11th, *Dec. 12th.

U. S. CIRCUIT AND DISTRICT COURTS.

Charles H. Simonton, Charleston, S. C , Judge of Fourth Circuit of U. S. Courts. Nathan Goff, West Virginia, Judge of U. S Circuit Court of Appeals for Fourth District.

WESTERN DISTRICT.—R. P. Dick, Greensboro, Judge; R. B. Glenn, District Attorney; D. A. Covington, Assistant Attorney; S. L. Trogden, Clerk. *Greensboro*—Circuit and District—April 4th, Oct ber 3d. *Statesville*—Circuit and District—H. C. Cowles, Clerk; April 18th, October 14th. *Asheville*—Circuit and District—R. O. Patterson, Clerk; May 24, November 7th. *Charlotte*—Circuit and District—H. C. Cowles, Clerk; June 13th, December 11th.

EASTERN DISTRICT.—T. R Purnell, Judge; C. B Aycock, Goldsboro, District Attorney; Sol. C. Weil, Wilmington, Assistant Attorney; W. C. Knooks Clerk. *Elizabeth City*—District Court—April 13th, October 17th *Newbern*—District Court—Geo. Green, Clerk; April 25th, October 24th. *Wilmington*—Circuit and District—N J Riddick, Clerk; V. Royster, Assistant Clerk in Raleigh; W. H. Shaw, Clerk of District and Deputy of Circuit Court at Wilmington; O. J. Carroll, Marshall; May 2d. October 31st. *Raleigh*—Circuit Court—N. J. Riddick, Clerk; V. Royster, Assistant Clerk in Raleigh; W. H. Shaw, Clerk of District and Deputy of Circuit Court at Wilmington; O. J. Carroll, Marshall; May 30th, December 5th.

31. In old age you will be likely to need vast stores of friendship.—
Branson.

SUPREME COURT.

SUPREME COURT meets first Monday in February   Examinations on Monday.
First District, February 7th; Second District, February 14th; Third District, February 21st; Fourth District, February 28th; Fifth District, March 7th; Sixth District, March 14th; Seventh District, March 21st; Eighth District, March 28th; Ninth District, April 4th; Tenth District, April 11th; Eleventh District, April 18th; Twelfth District, April 25th; end of Docket May 2d.

Last Monday in September. Examinations on Monday. First District, September 26th; Second District, October 3d; Third District, October 10th; Fourth District, October 17th; Fifth District, October 24th; Sixth District, October 31st; Seventh District, November 7th; Eighth District, November 14th; Ninth District, November 21st; Tenth District, November 28th; Eleventh District, December 5th; Twelfth District, December 12th.

Chief Justice—Wm Turner Faircloth, Wayne County. Associate Justices—R. M. Douglass, Guilford County; Walter Clark, Wake County; David M. Furches, Iredell County; Walter A. Montgomery, Wake County. Salaries $2,750 each. Zeb. V. Walser, Attorney General; salary $2,000. R. T. Gray, Reporter; salary $750. Thos. S. Kenan, Clerk; salary $900 and fees. R. H. Bradley, Marshal; salary $800. J. L. Seawell, Office Clerk.

GOVERNMENT OF NORTH CAROLINA—1897-1901.

EXECUTIVE DEPARTMENT.

Daniel L. Russell, of New Hanover County, Governor; salary $3,000, and furnished house, fuel and lights.

Charles A. Reynolds, of Forsyth County, Lieutenant Governor and Speaker of the Senate.

Cyrus Thompson, of Onslow County, Secretary of State; salary $2,000 and fees; $1,000 additional assistance.

D. H. Senter, Clerk in Secretary of State's office.

Hal W. Ayer, of Wake County, Auditor; salary $1,500; $1,000 additional for clerical assistance.

William H. Worth, of Wake County, Treasurer; salary $3,000.

C. Cole, Clerk in Treasurer's office.

Charles H. Mebane, of Catawba County, Superintendent of Public Instruction; salary $1,500; $500 per annum additional traveling expenses.

Zebulon Vance Walser, of Davidson County, Attorney General; salary $2,000

R. T. Gray, Reporter to Supreme Court; salary $1,250.

A. D. Cowles, of Iredell County, Adjutant General; salary $400.

R. A. Cobb, of Burke County, State Librarian: Salary $1,000.

John A. Sims, Cabarrus County, Chief Clerk to Auditor; salary $1,000.

J. E. Alexander, Tyrrell County, Private Secretary to Governor; salary $1,200.

L. V. Darby, New Hanover County, Executive Clerk; salary $600.

A. D. K. Wallace, Rutherford County, Chief Clerk to Secretary of State; salary $1,000.

J. W. Denmark, of Wake County, Chief Clerk to Treasurer; salary $1,500.

S. L. Crowder, of Warren County, Teller; salary $750.

W. H. Worth, Treasurer *ex officio*, and Wm. H. Martin, of Wake County, Clerk for Charitable and Penal Institutions, salary $1,000.

J. L. Burns, of Martin County, Superintendent of Public Buildings and Grounds; salary $850.

Albert Johnson, of Wake County, State Standard Keeper; salary $100.

STATE BOARD OF EDUCATION.

The Governor, Lieutenant Governor, Secretary of State, Treasurer, Auditor, Superintendent of Public Instruction and Attorney General constitute the Board.

Discontent is the want of self-reliance: it is the infirmity of will.—
Emerson.

Splendid Estate...

~FOR SALE~

FINE CHANCE FOR PAYING INVESTMENT.

FINE Grain and Stock Farm in **Amelia County, Va.,** twenty miles west from **Petersburg,** four miles of **N. & W. R. W.,** contains 2,357 acres of rich creek-bottom, fine for grasses. Upland gently undulating—no steep hills or swamps. Healthy as any place in the State. About one-third cleared land in cultivation, 1,000 acres or more in young tall pines, the increase of which will pay well to hold for, being on good soil and vigorous. Two 'residences on the place—one with 11 rooms, several halls, closets, &c. The other, one and a-half miles away, has 6 rooms, nice grove and out-houses.

This is considered about the best farm in the section, and can be had at a great bargain.

J. A. JONES,
RALEIGH, N. C.

Russell Creek Coal

**KINDLES QUICKLY
BURNS BRIGHTLY
LASTS LONG
MAKES HOT FIRES
BURNS UP CLEAN
IS VERY HARD
HAS LITTLE SLACK**

For holding or keeping fire it has no superior, and is therefore a very economical fuel.

SAVE MONEY BY USING IT.

Refer to the following parties, who have given us testimonials as to the merits of our Coal:

H. W. HINES, Reidsville, N. C.; Rev. JOHN H. CLEWELL, Principal Salem (N. C.) Female College; J. W. CANNON, Concord, N. C.; R. R. PINKSTON, Henderson, N. C.; J. H. CRAWFORD, Raleigh, N. C.; J. C. PITTMAN, Raleigh, N. C.; E. C. EDMUNDS, Winston, N. C.

This justly celebrated coal is sold by the principal dealers in all cities and towns that can be reached. If your dealer does not handle it, write direct to

RUSSELL CREEK COAL CO.,
Virginia City, Va.,

Or to JONES & POWELL, at RALEIGH,
for price of car-loads, delivered at any depot.

LUMSDEN & SONS, Tobacco Flues, Engine Stacks, etc., Fayetteville Street, opposite Market, Raleigh, N. C.

BRANSON'S NORTH CAROLINA ALMANAC. 33

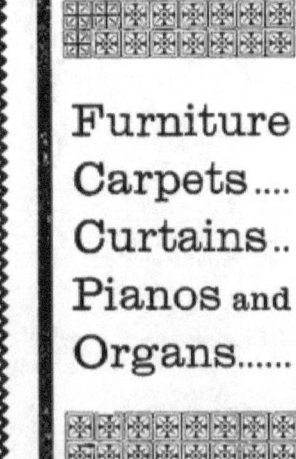

LUMSDEN & SONS, Stoves and Hardware, Fayetteville Street, opposite
Market, Raleigh, N. C.

BRANSON'S NORTH CAROLINA ALMANAC. 39

COUNTY OFFICERS FROM ELECTION OF NOVEMBER, 1896.—CORRECTED ANNUALLY.

	COUNTIES.	COUNTY TOWN.	CLERKS.	REGISTERS.	SHERIFF.	TREASURER.	SUPERVISORS OF SCHOOLS.
1	Alamance,	Graham,	G. D. Vincent,	A. Mitchell,	R. T. Kernodle,	R. C. Dickey,	Rev. P. H. Fleming.
2	Alexander,	Taylorsville,	J. B. Fool,	V. W. Teague,	J. G. Williams,	J. M. Watts,	A. F. Tharpe.
3	Alleghany,	Sparta,	W. E. Cox,	J. N. Edwards,	Levi Joines,	Levi J. Jones,	S. W. Brown.
4	Anson,	Wadesboro,	J. G. McLaughlin,	S. A. Benton,	Joel F. Gaddy,	J. O. Craig,	W. D. Redfearn.
5	Ashe,	Jefferson,	F Blevins,	David A. Osborn,	Byron Sturgill,	Byron Sturgill,	B. Silley.
6	Beaufort,	Washington,	Geo. W. Guilford,	J. W. Chapin,	R. T. Hodges,	R. T. Hodges,	B. Silley.
7	Bertie,	Windsor,	W. L. Lyon,	W. L. King,	Wm. G. Burden,	T. C. Bond,	W. B. Askew.
8	Bladen,	Elizabethtown,	J. P. Sutton,	J. R. Dunham,	S. G. Wooten,	R. L. Bridges,	R. S. Cromartie.
9	Brunswick,	Southport,	S. P. Tharp,	John W. Brooks,	D. R. Walker,	S. M. Robbins,	Isaac Jeannette.
10	Buncombe,	Asheville,	J. L. Cathey,	W. J. Beachboard,	W. M. Wooley,	J. H. Courtney,	D. L. Ellis.
11	Burke,	Morganton,	T. W. Patton,	W. F. Hallyburton,	T. M. Webb,	Waters,	R. L. Patton.
12	Cabarrus,	Concord,	Jas. C. Gibson,	W. M. Weddington,	M. L. Buchanan,	G. Ed. Kestler,	H. T. J. Ludwig.
13	Caldwell,	Lenoir,	J. V. McCall,	W. R. Dozier,	A. H. Boyd,	A. H. Courtney,	E. B. Phillips.
14	Camden,	Camden C. H.,	R. L. Forbes,	N. L. Carrow,	W. S. Bartlette,	G. H. Jacobs,	C. B. Garrett.
15	Carteret,	Beaufort,	L. A. Garner,	J. T. Graves,	M. A. Hill,	N. W. Taylor,	Jasper Pigott.
16	Caswell,	Yanceyville,	N. M. Richardson,	J. F. Herman,	J. T. Donaho,	T. H. Harrison,	A. R. Henderson.
17	Catawba,	Newton,	J. W. Rockett,	J. T. Paschal,	A. C. Hilderbrand,	Noah Barringer,	J. D. Rowe.
18	Chatham,	Pittsboro,	R. H Dixon,	M. A. Hughes,	S. W. Davidson,	J. J. Jenkins,	R. B. Lineberry.
19	Cherokee,	Murphy,	D. L. C Privatt,	M. M. Burch,	A. Q. Elliott,	Thos. Payne,	D W. Deweese.
20	Chowan,	Edenton,	H. C Privatt,	J. P. R. Williams,	J. O. Scroggs,	C. S. Vann,	W. F. Watson.
21	Clay,	Hayesville,	T. H. Hancock,	D. B. F. Nance,	A. B. Sattle,	R. G. Ketron,	W. J. Winchester.
22	Cleveland,	Shelby,	T. D. Lattimore,	J. B. Willis,	M. J. Ward,	I. K. Gore,	J. A. Anthony.
23	Columbus,	Whiteville,	A. A. Lennon,	A. L. McCaskill,	J. J. Hahn,	Thos. Daniels,	W. H. Sellers.
24	Craven,	Newbern,	W. M. Watson,	W. H Bray,	M. D. Geddie,	I. B. Troy,	John S. Long.
25	Cumberland,	Fayetteville,	Cyrus Murphy,	C. J Dough,	Edward Tillett,	Ed Tillett,	H. E. King.
26	Currituck,	Currituck C. H.,	E. W. Ansell,	C. J Dough,	L. Cudworth,	S. E. Mann,	V. L. Pitts.
27	Dare,	Manteo,	J. B. Jennett,	J. C. Harris,	J. J. Leonard,	J. W. McCrary,	L. Bassight.
28	Davidson,	Lexington,	Geo. E. Hunt,	Geo W. Sheets,	E. R Vogler,	Dr. Jas. McGuire,	E. F. Mendenhall.
29	Davie,	Mocksville,	A. T. Grant,	Thad. Jones, Jr.,	Daniel Moore,	Daniel Moore,	C. M. Sheets.
30	Duplin,	Kenansville,	I. A. Gavin,	W. R. Woods,	F. D. Markham,	T. J. Holloway,	B W. Millard.
31	Durham,	Durham,	W. J. Christian,	B. J. Keech,	W. L. Stallings,	S. S. Nash,	Geo. J. Dowell.
32	Edgecombe,	Tarboro,	Ed. Fennington,	J. F. Miller,	E. T. Kapps,	J. F. Griffith,	R. M. Davies.
33	Forsyth,	Winston,	N. S. Wilson,	John T. Clifton,	H. C Kearney,	D F. Wilder,	Dr. A. F. Davis.
34	Franklin,	Louisburg,	R. H. Harris,	J. J. Ormand,	R. O. Riddicks,	Lee R. Stowe,	B. S. Mitchell.
35	Gaston,	Dallas,	G. H. Davis,	Lycurgus Hofler,	R. O. Riddicks,	H. B. Cross,	L. M. Hoffman.
36	Gates,	Gatesville,	T. A. Cross,	J. A. Hyde,	J. A. Ammons,	S. B. Rose,	J. R. Walton.
37	Graham,	Robbinsville,	T. A. Carpenter,	L. C. Taylor,	J. A. Ammons,	A. S. Peace,	J. N. Moody.
38	Granville,	Oxford,	J. M. Sikes,	W. E. Murphy,	W. S. Cozart,	John Sugg,	Alex. Baker.
39	Greene,	Snow Hill,	J. W. Blount,	A. G. Kirkman,	R. D. S. Dixon,	W. A. Hodgin,	Fred L. Carr.
40	Guilford,	Greensboro,	Ed. L. Lyon,	McM. Furgerson,	J. A Hoskins,	W. F. Parker,	J. A. Wharton.
41	Halifax,	Halifax C. H.,	S. M. Gary,	I. McK. Byrd,	J. T. Dawson,	Geo. D. Spence,	Aaron Prescott.
42	Harnett,	Lillington,	F. M. McKay,	H. B. Moore,	J. H. Pope,	Geo. D. Hannah,	Rev. J. A. Campbell.
43	Haywood,	Waynesville,	K. Boone,	W. A. Hood,	W. J. Haynes,	H. J. Davis,	H. J. Garner.
44	Henderson,	Hendersonville,	C. M. Pace,	E. E. Marsh,	John Williams,	W. J. Davis,	C. J. Edney.
45	Hertford,	Winton,	Thos. D. Boone,	E. E. Marsh,	J. S. Mitchell,	W. E. Cullens,	P. E. Shaw.

Town					
Swan Quarter,	J. H. Wafab,	L. H. Swindell,	T. C. Mann,	C. L. Benson,	H. L. McGowan.
Statesville,	H. V. Furche,	Wm. W. Turner,	J. H. Wycoff,	W. A. Wright,	J. A. Butler.
Webster,	H. C. Cowan,	J. R. Long,	W. A. Henson,	A. V. F. Bryson,	J. H. Painter.
Smithfield,	W. S. Stevens,	W. H. Cox,	J. H. Harrison,	T. R. Hood,	Ira T. Turlington.
Trenton,	S. E. Koonce,	B. L. Taylor,	Benj. Sutten,	Lewis King,	W. H. Hammond.
Kinston,	S. H. Bright,	J. F. Killian,	C. H. Rhodes,	J. H. Dawson,	E. A. Simkins.
Lincolnton,	G. A. Barkley,	H. D. Dean,	C. T. Roane,	D L. Yount,	J. E. Hoover.
Franklin,	Lee Crawford,	Van B. Davis,	J. M. Ramsey,	Enoch Rector,	J. R. Pendergrass.
Marshall,	M. A. Chandley,	W. H. Willson,	J. D. Biggs,	S. R. Biggs,	R. J. Jervis.
Williamston,	N. S. Peel,	Jas. C. Brown,	R. L. Nichols,	G. H. Gardin,	W. P. Jervis.
Marion,	B. B. Price,	W. M. Key,	Z. T. Smith,	E. H. Walker,	R. J. Peel.
Charlotte,	J. M. Morrow,	G. S. Beaman,	Geo. K. Pritchard,	W. S. Daniels,	W. F. Wood.
Bakersville,	J. C. Bowman,	W. H. Battley,	D. A. Ewing,	D. A. Ewing,	H. A. Gray.
Troy,	J. S. Lewis,	J. H. T. Baker,	S. M. Jones,	Dr. K. M Ferguson,	J. J Britt.
Carthage,	D. A. McDonald,	C. W. Norwood (d),	J. H. Wheeler,	E. J. Braswell,	G. M. Deaton.
Nashville,	M. B. Williford,	H. R. Deloach,	Elijah Hewlett,	S Van Amringe,	E. M. Cole.
Wilmington,	P. Cummings,	C. C. Morton,	W. H Buffaloe,	A. Burgwynn,	M. L. Conyers.
Jackson,	J. T. Flythe,	John Laws,	F. W. Hargett,	I. F. Cox,	M. C. S. Noble.
Jacksonville,	Chas. Gerock,	Alex Lee,	John K. Hughes,	W. F. Jackson,	Paul J. Long.
Hillsboro,	D. F. Crawford,	N. B. Culpeper,	John W. Aldridge,	John J. Cooper,	A. W. Cooper
Bayboro,	F. Miller,	W. P. Stringfield,	F. P. Wilcox,	J. S. Morris,	John Thompson.
Elizabeth City,	J. P. Overman,	Wm. R. White,	A. W. Alderman,	W. W. Alderman,	W W Cole.
Burgaw,	W. W. Larkins,	Henry J. White,	A. F. Riddick,	Jacob H. Parker,	J. M. Millikin.
Hertford,	J. O. A. Wood,	J. I. Perkins,	John R. Sims,	J. C. Pass,	T. H. W. McIntyre.
Roxboro,	D. W. Brasher,	J. W. Newman,	W. C. Robertson,	James L. Little,	Francis Pickard.
Greenville,	E. A. Moye,	J. T. Winslow,	W. F. Redding,	J. K. Gibbs,	G. F. Holloway.
Columbus,	N. B. Hampton,	R. J. Pence,	J. M. Smith,	J. L. Swain,	J. R. Lengle.
Asheboro,	J. M. Millikan,	Jas. A. Scales,	J. W. Hall,	J M. Smith,	J. K. Gibbs.
Rockingham,	Z. F. Long,	A. S. Thompson,	Wm. B. Wray,	E. G. Johnson,	N. C. English.
Lumberton,	S. A. Edmund,	H. N. Woodson,	Jas. M. Monroe,	Wm. B. Wray,	M. N. McIver.
Wentworth,	Thos. S. Malloy,	W. J. Mode,	J. V. McParland,	S. McCubbins,	W. R. Searles.
Salisbury,	W. G. Watson,	D. F. Herring,	J. M. Marshburn,	J. M. Marshburn,	E. P. Ellington.
Rutherfordton,	T. C. Smith,	W. T. Huckabee,	Geo. R. McCain,	G. D. Palmer,	R. G. Kizer.
Clinton,	W. K. Pigford,	Isaac M. Gordon,	R. J. Joyce,	J. H. Fulton,	C. C. Gettys.
Albemarle,	S. H. Milton,	Thos. W. Davis,	J. M. Davis,	J. A. Adams,	Street Brewer.
Danbury,	N. G. Petree,	A. J. DeHart,	Jas. F. Teague,	D. G. Fisher,	J. F. Bivens.
Dobson,	W. W. Hampton,	E. S English,	V. B. McCaha,	Vance Galloway,	M. T. Chilton.
Bryson City,	J. R. Snow,	D. Q. Newberry,	F. L. W. Caloon,	J. C. Meekins, Sr.,	J. B. Sparger.
Brevard,	T. H. Hampton,	P. P. W. Pigler,	B. A. Horn,	Jas. McNeely,	J. U. Gibbs.
Columbia,	D. T. Holmes,	Thos. S. Eaton,	Wm. H. Smith,	H P. Hicks,	Judson Corn.
Monroe,	F. H. Wolfe,	J. J. Rogers,	Ham T. Jones,	H. H Knight,	Plummer Stewart.
Henderson,	D. H. Gill,	M. F. Thornton,	J. B. W. Jones,	N. M. Palmer,	A. M. Matics.
Raleigh (State Cap.)	D. H. Young,	W. H. Stubbs,	L. A. Gray,	Thos. J. Bassnight,	H. W. Norris.
Warrenton,	Wm. A. White,	J. W. Hodges,	W. H. Caloway,	L. A. Green,	Jas. R. Rodwell.
Plymouth,	T. J. Mariner,	G. C. Kornegay,	W. F. Scott,	A. T. Uzzell,	P. S. Swain.
Boone,	M. B. Blackburn,	E. M. Blackburn,	Clarence Call,	Clarence Call,	J. B. Johnson, Sr.
Goldsboro,	C. F. Herring,	Geo H. Griffin,	John W. Cherry,	W. T. Farmer,	E. T. Atkins.
Wilkesboro,	G. C. Kornegay,	W. A. Hall,	A. P. Woodruff,	A. F. Woodruff,	Jas. H. Foote.
Wilson,	J. D. Bardin,	A. B. Silver,	J. S. Huskin,	C. M. Blankenship,	Jas. W. Hayes.
Yadkinville,	R. E. Hotton,				J. H. Peterson.
Burnsville,	R. E. Banks,				W. M. Peterson.

Life Insurance, do not fail to see what the SUN LIFE of Canada can do for you.

J. R. JOHNSTON. State Manager, Raleigh, N. C.

LUMSDEN & SONS, Tin, Sheet Iron. and Copper Ware, Fayetteville Street, opposite Market, Raleigh. N. C.

42   BRANSON'S NORTH CAROLINA ALMANAC.

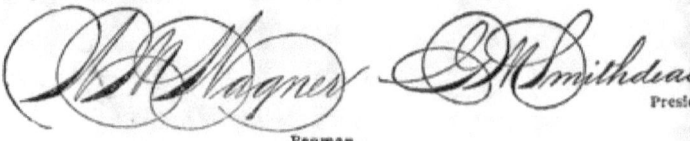

LUMSDEN & SONS, House Furnishing Goods, Fayetteville Street, opposite Market, Raleigh, N. C.

BRANSON'S NORTH CAROLINA ALMANAC. 45

MILITARY SCHOOLS.

A. & M. College (Military feature)..............................Raleigh
Bingham School ....Asheville
Cape Fear Academy...Wilmington
Davis School ....Winston
Horner School ....Oxford
Quackenbosh Academy ....Laurinburg
Rutherfordton Academy ....Rutherfordton
Thompson School ....Siler City
Turlington Institute...Smithfield

ORPHAN SCHOOLS.

Home and Industrial School (Independent) ....Asheville
Orphanage (Friends)...Archdale
Orphan's Home (Presbyterian) ....Barium Springs
Orphanage (colored—State aid) ....Oxford
Oxford Orphan Asylum (Masons—State aid).....................Oxford
Orphan Home (Odd Fellows)................................. Goldsboro
Orphanage (Baptist) ....Thomasville
Thompson Orphanage (Episcopal)...........................Charlotte

The North Carolina College of Agriculture and Mechanic Arts

BRANSON'S SHORT CALENDAR FOR 1898.

JANUARY.

S	M	T	W	T	F	S
						1
2	3	4	5	6	7	8
9	10	11	12	13	14	15
16	17	18	19	20	21	22
23	24	25	26	27	28	29
30	31					

FEBRUARY.

S	M	T	W	T	F	S
		1	2	3	4	5
6	7	8	9	10	11	12
13	14	15	16	17	18	19
20	21	22	23	24	25	26
27	28					

MARCH.

S	M	T	W	T	F	S
		1	2	3	4	5
6	7	8	9	10	11	12
13	14	15	16	17	18	19
20	21	22	23	24	25	26
27	28	29	30	31		

APRIL.

S	M	T	W	T	F	S
					1	2
3	4	5	6	7	8	9
10	11	12	13	14	15	16
17	18	19	20	21	22	23
24	25	26	27	28	29	30

MAY.

S	M	T	W	T	F	S
1	2	3	4	5	6	7
8	9	10	11	12	13	14
15	16	17	18	19	20	21
22	23	24	25	26	27	28
29	30	31				

JUNE.

S	M	T	W	T	F	S
			1	2	3	4
5	6	7	8	9	10	11
12	13	14	15	16	17	18
19	20	21	22	23	24	25
26	27	28	29	30		

JULY.

S	M	T	W	T	F	S
					1	2
3	4	5	6	7	8	9
10	11	12	13	14	15	16
17	18	19	20	21	22	23
24	25	26	27	28	29	30
31						

AUGUST.

S	M	T	W	T	F	S
1	2	3	4	5	6	
7	8	9	10	11	12	13
14	15	16	17	18	19	20
21	22	23	24	25	26	27
28	29	30	31			

SEPTEMBER.

S	M	T	W	T	F	S
				1	2	3
4	5	6	7	8	9	10
11	12	13	14	15	16	17
18	19	20	21	22	23	24
25	26	27	28	29	30	

OCTOBER.

S	M	T	W	T	F	S
						1
2	3	4	5	6	7	8
9	10	11	12	13	14	15
16	17	18	19	20	21	22
23	24	25	26	27	28	29
30	31					

NOVEMBER.

S	M	T	W	T	F	S
		1	2	3	4	5
6	7	8	9	10	11	12
13	14	15	16	17	18	19
20	21	22	23	24	25	26
27	28	29	30			

DECEMBER.

S	M	T	W	T	F	S
				1	2	3
4	5	6	7	8	9	10
11	12	13	14	15	16	17
18	19	20	21	22	23	24
25	26	27	28	29	30	31

PRICE LIST.

1 Almanac, per mail	$ 10
1 dozen Almanacs, sent per mail	75
20 copies sent per mail	1 00
½ gross Almanacs, sent per Express (card on back)	3 50
1 gross Almanacs, sent per Express (card on back)	6 00
500 Almanacs, sent per freight	20 00
1,000 Almanacs, sent per freight	35 00

☞ Order one-half gross or more and I will print your business card on this blank space free of cost to you.

Unsold copies (if reported to me by first of June), will be replaced by new ones next year, so that you run no risk whatever.

Order at once of

LEVI BRANSON,
RALEIGH, N. C.

Vol. 4.]   32 YEAR OF PUBLICATION.   No. 2.]

BRANSON'S
AGRICULTURAL
ALMANAC

PRICE, 10 CENTS

FOR THE YEAR OF OUR LORD

1899,

And until the 4th of July, the 123d year of American Independence.

Carefully Calculated for the Latitude and Longitude of Raleigh, by

LEVI BRANSON, A. M., D. D.

LEVI BRANSON, Publisher, Raleigh, N. C.

GET THE BEST AND STICK TO IT—NO OTHER LIKE IT.

1 All men have faith in something, hence they work expecting results.—*Branson*.

2 BRANSON'S NORTH CAROLINA ALMANAC.

TIME.

The calculations of this Almanac are made in mean solar or clock time, which is indicated by a well regulated watch or clock, and does not correspond with the Sun precisely, except on four days of the year.

Apparent time is that which makes the Sun come to the meridian at 12 o'clock. No good clock will run with the Sun; if set with the Sun on the 2d day of January, the clock will seem to be one minute too fast on the 3d of January.

To adapt the calculations of this Almanac to apparent time, use the minutes in the column marked " Sun slow " or " Sun fast ;" add them when fast, substract them when slow.

The calculations are made for the Latitude and Longitude of Raleigh, N. C., but the times phases &c., will vary only a few minutes for any part of North Carolina, South Carolina, Georgia, Tennessee or Virginia.

TWELVE SIGNS OF THE ZODIAC.

The Head and Face sign.　　Aries the Ram......Ar.

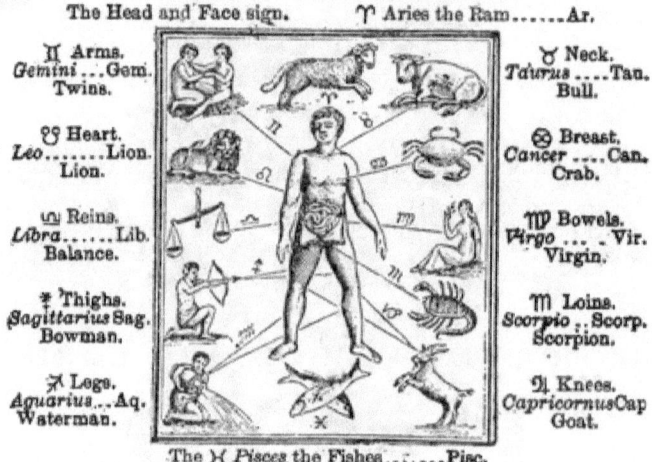

Arms. Gemini...Gem. Twins.	Neck. Taurus....Tau. Bull.
Heart. Leo.......Lion. Lion.	Breast. Cancer.....Can. Crab.
Reins. Libra......Lib. Balance.	Bowels. Virgo ... .Vir. Virgin.
Thighs. Sagittarius Sag. Bowman.	Loins. Scorpio ..Scorp. Scorpion.
Legs. Aquarius...Aq. Waterman.	Knees. CapricornusCap Goat.

The Pisces the Fishes,......Pisc.

To know where the sign is, find the day of the month, and against the day in the column marked Moon's Signs you have the sign or place of the Moon, and then find the sign ; it will give you the part of the body it is supposed to govern.

SIGNS.

SPRING SIGNS.	Arises or Ram. Taurus, or Bull. Gemini, or Twins.	AUTNMN SIGNS.	Libra, or Balance. Scorpio, or Scorpion. Sagittarius, or Bowman.
SUMEER SIGNS.	Cancer, or Crab-fish. Leo, or Lion. Virgo, or Virgin.	WINTER SIGNS.	Capricornus, or Goat. Aquarius, or Waterman. Pices, or Fishes.

SIGNS OF THE PLANETS.

Sun.　　Moon.　　Venus.　　Mars.
Jupiter.　　Saturn.　　In Conjunction.　　Quadrature.
Mercury.　　Uranus.　　Neptune.　　Ascending Node.

MOON'S PHASES.

New Moon.　　First Quarter.　　Full Moon.　　Last Quarter.

CHRONOLOGICAL CYCLES AND ERAS.

Dominical Letter	A	Julian Pepiod	6612
Epact	18	Jewish Era	5659
Golden Number	19	Era of Nabonassa	2646
Solar Cycle	4	Olympiads	2675
Roman Indication	12	Mahommedan Era	1316

MOVABLE FEASTS OF THE CHURCH.

Epiphany	Jan. 6	Palm Sunday .... March 26
Septuagesima Sunday	Jan. 29	Easter Sunday .... April 2
Sexagesima Sunday	Feb. 13	Whit Sunday .... May 21
Quinquagesima Sunday	Feb. 12	Trinity Sunday .... May 28
Shrove Tuesday	Feb. 22	First Sunday in Advent ..... Dec 3
Ash Wednesday, or Lent	Feb. 15	Ancension Day .... May 21
St. Patrick's Day	March 17	
Good Friday	March 31	First Sunday in Lent .... Feb 19

MORNING STARS.

Mercury will be Morning Star about Jan. 11. Venus will be Morning Star till Sept. 15. Jupiter will be Morning Star till April 25, then from Nov. 12 to end of year.

EVENING STARS.

Mercury will be Evening Star about..... March 24, July 22, and Nov. 16
Venus will be Evening Star from................September 15
Jupiter will be Evening Star from...................April 25, till Nov. 12

ECLIPSES.

In the year 1899 there will be *five Eclipses*—three of the *Sun* and two of the *Moon*.

I. *A partial Eclipse of the Sun*, January 11th, not visible in North Carolina.

II. *A partial Eclipse of the Sun*, June 7-8, visible in Alaska, Greenland and the North-polar Sea, also in northern Europe and Asia.

III. *A total Eclipse of the Moon*, June 23-24, visible on northern coast of North America and the Pacific Ocean.

IV. *An Annular Eclipse of the Sun*, Dec. 2-3, not visible in the United States, but visible at the South Pole.

V. *A partial Eclipse of the Moon*, Dec. 16, visible more or less to North and South America, occurring as follows in North Carolina :

Moon enters Shadow	Dec. 16,	5:45 P. M.
Middle of Eclipse	Dec. 16,	7:26 P. M.
Moon leaves Shadow	Dec. 16,	9:07 P. M.

This Eclipse is 0.996 one thousandths of the Moon's diameter.

TIDES.

The time of tide can readily be found for the following places by adding the hours and minutes opposite the names to the time when the Moon is South on the day to when the tide is sought. The time when the Moon is South is given in the Calendar for every day. The next tide can be found very nearly by adding 12 hours and 29 minutes to the time of the one previous.

The tides are given in local time—add 12 minutes for Eastern Standard:

	H. M.		H. M.
Boston	11 12	New York	8 13
Sandy Hook	7 29	Old Point	8 17
Baltimore	6 33	Washington City	7 44
Richmond	4 32	Hatteras Inlet	7 04
Beaufort	7 26	Bald Head	7 26
Southport	7 19	Wilmington	9 06
Charleston	7 26	Savannah	9 33

THE FOUR SEASONS.

Spring commences..................................March 20, 1 P. M.
Summer commences.................................June 21, 9 A. M.
Autumn commences ....September 23, 0 A. M.
Winter commences ....December 21, 6 P. M.

HERSCHEL'S WEATHER PROGNOSTICATOR.

For Foretelling the Weather Through all the Lunations of the year.

This table and the accompanying remarks are the result of many years
actual observation, the whole being constructed on a due consideration
of the attractions of the Sun and Moon, in their several positions respecting the Earth, and, by simple inspection, it shows the observer what
kind of weather will most probably follow the entrance of the Moon into
any of its quarters, and that so near the truth as to be seldom or never
found to fail.

If the new moon, first quarter, full moon, or last quarter, happen—	IN SUMMER.	IN WINTER.
Between midnight and 2 in the morning.............	Fair	Hoar frost unless the wind is S. or S. W.
Between 2 and 4, morning	Cold, with frequent showers.........	Snow and stormy.
Between 4 and 6, morning..	Rain...............	Rain.
Between 6 and 8, morning..	Wind and rain.......	Stormy.
Between 8 and 10, morning	Changeable	Cold rain if wind be W.; snow if E.
Between 10 and 12 morning	Frequent showers...	Cold and high wind.
Between 12 o'clock at noon and 2 in afternoon	Very rainy.........	Rain and snow.
Between 2 and 4, afternoon	Changeable	Fair and mild.
Between 4 and 6, afternoon	Fair	Fair.
Between 6 and 8, aftern'n	Fair if wind N. W.; rainy if S. or S. W.	Fair and frosty wind N. or N.E.; rain or snow if S. or S. W.
Between 8 and 10, afternoon	Ditto	Ditto
Between 10 and midnight....	Fair	Fair and frosty.

OBSERVATIONS.—1. The nearer the time for the Moon's change, first
quarter, full and last quarter are to midnight, the fairer will be the
weather during the next seven days.

2. The space for this calculation occupies from 10 at night until 2 next
morning.

3. The nearer to midday or noon the phase of the Moon happens, the
more foul or wet weather may be expected during the next seven days.

4. The space for this calculations occupies from 10 in the forenoon until
2 in the afternoon. These observations refer principally to the Summer,
though they affect Spring and Autumn nearly in the same ratio.

5. The Moon's change, first quarter, full and last quarter happening
during six of the afternoon hours, *i. e.*. from 4 to 10, may be followed
by fair weather, but this is mostly depeudent on the wind, as is noted in
the table.

6. Though the weather, from a variety of irregular causes, is more
uncertain in the latter part of Autumn, the whole of Winter and beginning of Spring, yet, in the main, the above observations will apply to
those periods also.

7. To prognosticate correctly, especially in those cases where the wind
is concerned, the observer should be in sight of a good vane, where the
four cardinal points of the heavens are correctly placed.

STATISTICS OF LIBRARIES IN NORTH CAROLINA, 1898.

Through the untiring efforts of our efficient State Librarian, Mr. R. A. Cobb, we are enabled to give correctly the great progress that has been made in our State in the last few years towards placing within the reach of the great masses of our people, useful information that has heretofore been beyond the reach of the common class of our citizens, by establishing public Libraries, accessible to all who are in search of useful knowledge.

NAMES OF LIBRARIES.	Where Located.	When Established*	No. of Vols.	Money Used Each Year.	Librarian
State Library	Raleigh	1841	50,500	$ 500	. A. Cobb.
Female College	Asheville		1,000		
Asheville Library	Asheville		3,000	675	Miss H. A. Champion
Bishop Atkinson Lib.	Asheville		2,400		Rev. A. H. Stubbs.
St. Mary's College	Belmont	1885	10,000		F. Bernard
N. C. University	Chapel Hill	1790	36,000	1,000	R. H. Graves.
Biddle Univ'rty (col)	Charlotte		8,000		
Buckhorn Academy	Como		2,000		
Scotia Seminary	Concord	1870	1,000		
Davidson College Lib	Davidson	1887	12,000		F. F. Rowe.
Public School Libra'y	Durham	1884	2,400		C. W. Toms.
Trinity College Lib.	W. Durham	1887	13,000		Geo. B. Pegram.
Elon College Library	Elon	1890	1,285		W. P. Lorance.
Cross Creek, I. O. O. F.	Fayetteville	1845	1,000		
Christian College Lib	Franklinton	1882	1,000		N. D. McReynolds.
Female College	Greensboro	1895	6,000		Dred Peacock.
State Normal College	Greensboro		3,000		
Guilford College Lib.	Guilford Col	1837	4,000		Miss M. E. Mendenhall
Shortia School	Highlands	1888	1,500		
Good Will Free Lib.	Ledger	1888	6,000		C. H. Wing.
Pioneer Library.	Lenoir	1875	1,500		I. F. W. Harper.
N. C. College	Mt. Pleasant	1858	2,600		H. T. J. Ludwig.
Bap. Female Institute	Murfr'esb'ro		1,000		
Collegiate Institute	Newbern		1,000		
Catawba College	Newton		2,500		
Oak Ridge Institute	Oak Ridge	1852	2,700	200	J. E. Holt.
A. & M. College	Raleigh	1890	3,300	200	A. Q. Holladay.
D. & D. Kelly Lib'ry	Raleigh	1877	2,500		
St. Mary's School	Raleigh		3,000		
Shaw University	Raleigh	1865	1,500		
Supreme Court Lib.	Raleigh		11,000		R. H. Bradley.
Rutherford Col. Lib.	R.' College	1853	600		W. E. Abernethy.
Female College	Salem	1802	4,000		J. H. Clewell.
Livingston College	Salisbury		3,000		
Wake F. College Lib.	Wake Forest	1833	15,500	485	W. L. Poteat.
Rab. Library	Waynesville	1891	1,100	62	L. B. Lewis.
Wayne School	Waynesville	1886	3,000		T. G. Harbison.
Classical School	Wilmington		2,000		
Library Association	Wilmington	1855	5,250	249	T. C. Diggs.
City School Library	Winston	1896	3,300	290	J. J. Blair.
College Library	Lenoir	1860	400		J. D. Minick.
A. & M. College (col)	Greensboro	1894	2,600		J. H. M. Butler.
Hickory Library	Hickory	1893	1,000		E. McComb.
Durham Library	Durham	1897	900		H. A. Forshee.
Morganton Library	Morganton	1878	1,000		Miss A. L. Avery.

45 libraries in all. 246,350 volumes of good books.

THE E. C. BROOKS CO., Portsmouth, Va.

Established half a century ago.

1st Month.   JANUARY, 1899.   31 Days.

Moon's Phases.

	D. H. M.		D. H. M.
● New Moon,	11 5 41 p.m.	◐ Full Moon,	26 2 25 p.m.
☽ First Quarter,	18 11 27 p.m.	☾ Last Quarter,	4 10 13 p.m.

Day of Month.	Day of Week.	Sun rises.	Sun sets.	Sun Slow.	Sun's decline south.	ASPECTS OF PLANETS AND OTHER MISCELLANEOUS MATTER.	Moon's place.	Moon rises or sets.	Moon south.	High tides at Beaufort.
1.						**Sunday after Christmas.** Day's length 9 hours 48 minutes.				
1	A	7 10	4 50	4	22 59	*New Year's—Legal Hd*		9 27	2 15	morn
2	Mo	7 10	4 52	4	22 54	Battle of Trenton 1777.		10 26	3 15	9 41
3	Tue	7 10	4 59	5	22 48	Battle of Princeton 1777		11 25	4 34	10 41
4	We	7 10	5 0	5	22 42	☽ ♂ ♀ ♂. Vand'r.d.'77		morn	5 17	eve
5	Thu	7 10	5 1	6	22 35	☽ Gr. Brilliancy.		0 27	6 2	1 28
6	Fri	7 9	5 2	6	22 27	*Epiphany.* [1791.		1 33	6 51	2 17
7	Sat	7 9	5 3	7	22 20	♀ in Per. 1st St'te H. C.		2 41	7 44	3 10
2						**First Sunday after Epiphany.** Day's length 9 hours 56 minutes.				
8	A	7 9	5 4	7	22 12	♂ ♂ ☽. Frsyth co est.'48		3 51	8 42	4 8
9	Mo	7 9	5 5	8	22 04	♄ b ☽. Leg. Met. 1895.		4 59	9 45	5 11
10	Tue	7 9	5 6	8	21 55	Stamp Act Passed 1765.		6 1	10 49	6 15
11	We	7 9	5 7	8	21 46	☽ Ecl in vin N. C.		sets	11 53	7 19
12	Thu	7 9	5 8	9	21 36	☽ Gaston co est 1846.		6 13	eve	7 50
13	Fri	7 9	5 9	9	21 26	Fox died 1681.		7 30	0 51	8 17
14	Sat	7 9	5 10	9	21 15	Com. Maurey b. 1806.		8 44	2 44	10 10
3						**Second Sunday after Epiphany.** Day's length 10 hours 2 minutes.				
15	A	7 9	5 11	10	21 04	Andrew Jackson b 1767.		9 54	3 45	11 11
16	Mo	7 8	5 12	10	20 53	Gibbon died 1794.		11 3	4 23	11 49
17	Tue	7 8	5 13	10	20 41	Dr. Franklin b 1706.		morn	5 11	morn
18	We	7 8	5 14	11	20 29	♂ ♂ ☀ Jarvis b.' 36.		0 9	6 0	0 37
19	Thu	7 8	5 15	11	20 16	☽ Gen. R.E.Lee's b'd.		1 13	6 49	1 26
20	Fri	7 7	5 15	11	20 3	Howard died 1790.		2 16	7 38	2 15
21	Sat	7 7	5 16	12	19 50	♀ in ☊ Gov. Bragg d '72		3 17	8 29	3 4
4						**Third Sunday after Epiphany.** Day's length 10 hours 12 minutes				
22	A	7 6	5 17	12	19 36	♂ ☽ ☽. Bacon b 1571.		4 12	9 20	3 55
23	Mo	7 6	5 18	12	19 22	Wm. Gaston d 1844.		5 1	10 9	4 46
24	Tue	7 5	5 19	12	19 8	Swedenborg b 1688.		5 45	10 57	5 35
25	We	7 4	5 20	13	18 53	♂ ♀ ♄ Fayette. set. 1749		6 22	11 44	6 23
26	Thu	7 3	5 21	13	18 38	◐ Bat. of Newb'n '64.		rises	morn	7 20
27	Fri	7 2	5 22	13	18 23	☽ Dr. Caldwell d. '38.		6 22	0 28	7 54
28	Sat	7 2	5 23	13	18 7	Tripple Alliance 1667.		7 20	1 11	8 37
5						**Fourth Sunday after Epiphany.** Day's length 10 hours 22 minutes.				
29	A	7 2	5 23	13	17 51	♂ ♃ ☀. Paine b 1739		8 20	1 52	9 18
30	Mo	7 2	5 24	14	17 34	Charles I beheaded 1647		9 19	2 34	10 00
31	Tue	7 2	5 25	14	17 18	☿. in Aphelion.		10 20	3 16	10 42

WEATHER CONJECTURES—January—1, 2, 3, 4, fair and frosty: 5, 6, 7, 8, 9, 10, 11, fair and frosty; 12, 13, 14, 15, 16, 17, 18, fair; 19, 20, 21, 22, 23, 24, 25, 26, look for cold high wind; 27, 28, 29; 30, 31, fair and mild.

FARM AND GARDEN WORK FOR JANUARY.—Plant peas, beans, beets, onions, Irish potatoes, horse radish; sow turnips, spinach, lettucs, radish, parsley, carrots, srlsify. Plant early peas; artichokes must now be dressed, also asparagus beds; this is the proper time to soft early spring tomatoes, etc.

NORTH CAROLINA COLLEGES, AND OTHER GRADUATING SCHOOLS.
(Names, character and location.)

Asheville Female College (Methodist)............................Asheville
Chowan Female Institute (Baptist)....................Murfreesboro
Claremont Female College (Reformed Church of U. S.)..........Hickory
Catawba College (Reformed Church of U. S.)..................Newton
Concordia College (Lutheran)...............................Conover
Davenport Female College (Methodist)........................Lenoir
Davidson College (Presbyterian)....................Davidson College
Elon College (Christian)........................Elon College
Greensboro Female College (Methodist)...................Greensboro
Gaston College (Lutheran)..............................Dallas
Guilford College (Friends)....................Guilford College
Hayesville College (Independent)........................Hayesville
Judson College (Methodist)....................Hendersonville
Kinston College (Independent)............................Kinston
Louisburg Female College (Methodist)....................Louisburg
Littleton Female College (Methodist)....................Littleton
Mt. Amoena Seminary (Lutheran)....................Mt. Pleasant
Mt. St. Joseph Academy (Catholic)........................Asheville
North Carolina College (Lutheran)....................Mt. Pleasant
North Carolina Agricultural and Mechanical College (State)....Raleigh
Oxford Female Seminary (Baptist)........................Oxford
Oak Ridge Institute (Independent)....................Oak Ridge
Peace Institute (Independent)..........................Raleigh
Rutherford College, Burke Co. (Independent).......Rutherford College
St. Mary's College (Catholic)..........................Belmont
Shelby Female College (Independent)....................Snelby
St. Mary's School (Episcopal)..........................Raleigh
Salem Academy (Moravian)..............................Salem
St. Pauls Seminary (Lutheran Theological)..............Hickory
State Normal and Industrial College (State)...........Greenboro
Trinity College (Methodist...........................Durham
University of North Carolina (State)................Chapel Hill
Weaverville College (Methodist)....................Weaverville
Wake Forest College (Baptist)....................Wake Forest
Elizabeth College (Lutheran)..........................Charlotte
Presbyterian College (Presbyterian)....................Charlotte
Whitsett Institute [Independendent]....................Whitsett

COLORED SCHOOLS—Graduating.

Agricultural and Mechanical College (State)...............Greensboro
Bennett Seminary (Methodist)..........................Greensboro
Biddle University (Presbyterian)........................Charlotte
Building and Trade's College (Independent)...........Southern Pines
Franklintou Christian College (Christian)..............Franklinton
Kittrell College [A. M. E. C.]..........................Kittrell
Livingstone College (Methodist)........................Salisbury
Normal and Industrial College (Methodist)..............Kittrell
Normal School (State)..............................Elizabeth City
Normal School (State)..............................Goldsboro
Normal School (State)..............................Salisbury
Normal School [State]..............................Plymouth
Normal School [State].............................Fayetteville
Normal School [State]..............................Franklinton
Shaw University [Baptist]..........................Raleigh
St. Augustine Normal College [Episcopal]..............Raleigh
Scotia Female Seminary [Presbyterian]..................Concord
Slater Industrial Academy and Normal School [State].........Winston

1. The *mind crop* is the greatest crop that can be raised on any farm or in any State.—*Branson.*

2d Month.   FEBRUARY, 1899.   28 Days.

Moon's Phases.

	D. H. M.		D. H. M.
Last Quarter,	3 0 16 p.m.	First Quart'r	17 3 43 a.m.
New Moon,	10 4 25 a.m.	Full moon	25 9 7 a.m.

THE E. C. BROOKS CO., Portsmouth, Va.

WANTED.—Black-eye Pease and Dried Fruits.

Day of Month.	Day of Week.	Sun rises.	Sun sets.	Sun slow.	Sun's decline south.	ASPECTS OF PLANETS AND OTHER MISCELLANEOUS MATTER	Moon's place.	Moon rises or sets	Moon South.	High tides at Beaufort
1	We	7 1	5 27	14	17 1	Washingt'n el. Pres. 1789		11 23	morn	11 24
2	Thu	7 1	5 29	14	16 43	Peace Conf'r'nce '65		morn	4 45	eve
3	Fri	7 0	5 31	14	16 26	♂ ♃ ☾ Barringer '95		0 27	5 35	1 1
4	Sat	6 59	5 32	14	16 8	Battle of Moorefield '64		1 33	6 29	1 55
6						Sexagesima Sunday. Day's length 10 hours 36 minutes.				
5	A	6 58	5 33	14	15 50	*Branson Nativity 1832.*		2 39	7 27	2 53
6	Mo	6 58	5 34	14	15 31	♂ ♀ ☾ Aaron Burr b 1756		3 43	8 29	3 54
7	Tue	6 57	5 34	14	15 12	Suez Canal Com. '67.		4 41	9 31	4 57
8	We	6 56	5 35	14	14 53	B. Roanoke Island '62.		5 30	10 33	5 59
9	Thu	6 55	5 36	14	14 34	♂ ♀ ☾ Gen. Hanc'k d '86.		6 12	11 32	6 58
10	Fri	6 54	5 37	14	14 15	Gr'at'st Elong W.		sets	eve	7 56
11	Sat	6 53	5 38	14	13 55	Thos A. Edison b '47.		7 29	1 21	8 47
7						Quinquagesima or Shrove Sunday. Day's length 10 hours 48 minutes.				
12	A	6 53	5 39	14	13 35	H. Seymore d. '86.		8 42	2 12	9 38
13	Mo	6 52	5 40	14	13 15	Brit'h E. A'g'sta Ga 1779		9 52	3 2	10 28
14	Tue	6 51	5 41	14	12 55	*St. Valentine's Day.*		10 59	3 52	11 18
15	We	6 40	5 42	14	12 34	*Ashe Wednesday.*		morn	4 42	morn
16	Thu	6 49	5 43	14	12 13	Judge Battle buried '79.		0 4	5 33	0 8
17	Fri	6 48	5 44	14	11 52	Molaire d. 1673.		1 6	6 24	0 59
18	Sat	6 57	5 45	14	11 31	Luther d. 1546.		1 4	7 15	1 50
8						First Sunday in Lent. Day's length 11 hours 2 minutes.				
19	A	6 46	5 46	14	11 10	♂ ♅ ☾.		2 56	8 5	2 41
20	Mo	6 45	5 47	14	10 48	Beauregard d. '93.		3 42	8 54	3 31
21	Tue	6 43	5 48	14	10 26	♂ ♂ ☾; ♀ Gr Hel Lat. S.		4 22	9 41	4 20
22	We	6 42	5 48	14	10 5	*Washington's Birthday.*		4 56	10 25	5 17
23	Thu	6 41	5 48	13	9 43	Wm. Gaston d. '44		5 26	11 9	5 51
24	Fri	6 40	5 49	13	9 21	♃. Sta.		5 54	11 51	6 35
25	Sat	6 39	5 50	13	8 58	Bat. of Montreal 1775		rises	morn	7 17
9						Second Sunday in Lent. Day's length 11 hours 14 minutes.				
26	A	6 38	5 51	13	8 36	⌊ ☌ ☀ Thos. Moore d '52		7 12	0 33	7 59
27	Mo	6 37	5 52	13	8 13	♂ ♀ ☀ Superior.		8 14	1 15	8 41
28	Tue	6 36	5 53	43	7 51	Dr. Wingate d. '79.		9 17	1 58	9 24

WEATHER CONJECTURES—February—1, 2, 3, look for fair weather; 4, 5, 6. 7, 8, 9, 10, snow and stormy; 11, 12, 13, 14, 15, 16, 17, expect rain; 18, 19, 20, 21, 22, 23, 24, 25, snow and stomy; 26, 27, 28, cold rain if wind be West, snow if East.

Farmers should use "NATIONAL" Fertilizer for Tobacco; and "BEEF, BLOOD and BONE" brand for Cotton, Corn and Wheat. Strictly reliable. Ask your Fertilizer Merchant for them. Carefully prepared by S. W. TRAVERS & CO., Branch, Richmond, Va.

[See top 3d cover page.]

Farm and Garden Work for February.—Continue to sow peas, and such vegetable as were omitted in January. Plant pole beans, first crop [in the low country]; full crop Irish Potatoes, beets and carrots; dress artichokes and asparagus. Tomatoes, peppers and cucumbers sow in hot beds; put out mangoes.

This is considered the opening month of the planter's year. Continue preparing as in January. Sow oats for a full crop in the low country; plant Irish potatoes; make up sprout beds for sweet potatoes. Plant root crop of sweet potatoes.

BUREAU OF STATISTICS OF N. C. [Denominational.]
Levi Branson, Secretary.

DENOMINATIONS.	Number Ministers.	Number Churches	Number Members
White.			
Methodist Episcopal Church South	605	636	140,869
Methodist Episcopal Church	65	115	8,941
Wesleyan Methodist Church	7	7	141
Methodist Protestant Church	64	208	16,416
Christians, followers of James O'Kelly	60	101	9,000
Evangelical Lutheran	73	130	12,872
Presbyterian	150	350	32,482
Universalists	3	3	255
Protestant Episcopals	96	190	15,439
Missionary Baptist	840	1,628	158,892
Primitive Baptist	150	317	11,914
Seventh Day Adventist	5	5	83
Free Will Baptist	160	168	10,224
Baptist Church of Christ	16	16	659
Old Two Seed Baptist	9	9	183
Disciples of Christ	54	125	12,437
Seventh Day Baptist	1	1	10
Reformed Church of U. S	23	43	3,317
Church of Jesus Christ of Latter Day Saints	24	1	136
Friends	52	52	5,328
Dunkards	9	9	510
Moravians	7	19	3,548
Waldenses	1	1	215
Roman Catholics	24	24	2,640
Hebrews	4	4	386
Salvation Army	2	2	59
Advent Christian Church	18	18	1,549
Associate Reformed	20	20	2,109
Congregationalist	4	4	106
Colored			
Missionary Baptists	765	1,190	129,265
African M. E. Church	182	216	25,218
African M. E. Zion Church	240	526	121,154
Colored M. E. Church in America	25	26	2,786
Methodist Episcopal	2	2	130
Protestant Episcopal	6	10	1,200
Congregational	21	39	2,087
Christians	50	53	3,746
Disciples of Christ	10	61	1,000
Free Will Baptist	10	25	1,640
Primitive Baptist	15	20	1,000
Presbyterian North	173	306	17,851

3d Month. MARCH, 1899. 31 Days.

Moon's Phases.

	D. H. M.			D. H. M.
☾ Last Quarter,	4 10 58 p.m.		☽ First Quarter,	18 10 15 p.m.
🌑 New Moon,	11 2 44 p.m.		🌕 Full Moon,	27 1 10 a.m.

Day of Month.	Day of Week.	Sun rises.	Sun sets.	Sun slow.	Sun's decline south.	ASPECTS OF PLANETS AND OTHER MISCELLANEOUS MATTER.	Moon's place.	Moon rises or sets.	Moon south.	High tides at Beaufort.
1	We	6 34	5 55	12	7 28	Bishop Andrews d 1871		10 19	2 44	10 10
2	Thu	6 32	5 56	12	7 5	☌♃☾. J. Wesley d 1791		11 24	3 32	10 58
3	Fri	6 30	5 57	12	6 42	♆ Sta. [in N.Y. 1789		Morn	4 24	11 50
4	Sat	6 28	5 58	12	6 19	☌♅☾ Cong. 1st met		0 30	5 20	Eve
10.	Third Sunday in Lent.					Days length 11 hours 36 minutes.				
5	A	6 26	6 0	12	5 50	☌♄☾ Addison b 1750.		1 33	6 18	1 44
6	Mo	6 24	6 0	11	5 33	Gould railw'y strike '86.		2 30	7 18	2 44
7	Tue	6 23	6 1	11	5 9	Bible soci'ty found'd '04		3 21	8 18	3 44
8	We	6 22	6 1	11	4 46	☌♀☾ William 3rd 1703.		4 5	9 16	4 42
9	Thu	6 20	6 2	11	4 22	Battle of Vera Cruz 1847		4 44	10 11	5 37
10	Fri	6 18	6 3	10	5 59	Bat. Man'ss's Jc. '62		5 18	11 5	6 31
11	Sat	6 17	6 4	10	3 35	Wm. Barringer'd '82		Sets	11 57	7 23
11.	Fourth Sundy in Lent.					Days length 12 hours 8 minutes.				
12	A	6 16	6 5	10	3 12	□♆✶: ☿ in ♉.		7 27	Eve	8 13
13	Mo	6 14	6 6	9	2 48	□♄✶ Pocah'nt's d 1616		8 37	1 39	9 5
14	Tue	6 13	6 6	9	2 24	West Point Est. 1802.		9 45	2 30	9 56
15	We	6 12	6 7	9	2 1	Extra ses. Leg. con. '80		10 51	3 22	10 48
16	Thu	6 11	6 8	9	2 37	Moore b 1751. [in peri		11 53	4 14	11 40
17	Fri	6 9	6 9	8	1 13	St. Patrick's day ☿		Morn	5 7	Morn
18	Sat	6 8	6 10	8	0 50	☌♆Su'zC'n'lc'm'69		0 48	5 58	0 33
12.	Fifth Sunday in Lent.					Days length 12 hours 8 minutes.				
19	A	6 6	6 11	8	0 26	Dr. Livingston b. '13.		1 37	6 48	1 24
20	Mo	6 4	6 12	7	0 2	*Sun Enters aries.Spring*		2 19	7 36	2 14
21	Tue	6 3	6 12	7	0 21	Lucknow fell '58. [*Com.*		2 56	8 21	3 2
22	We	6 2	6 13	7	N'r'h	Stamp act passed 1765.		3 29	9 5	3 47
23	Thu	6 0	6 13	7	1 8	Battle of Winchester '62		3 58	9 48	4 31
24	Fri	6 59	6 14	6	1 32	☿. Greatest Elong. E.		4 24	10 30	5 14
25	Sat	5 58	6 15	6	1 55	Thames Tunnel op. '48.		4 49	11 12	5 56
13.	Palm Sunday.					Days length 12 hours 32 minutes.				
26	A	5 57	6 16	6	2 19	♀ in ♉ EarthqCal '72		5 14	11 55	6 38
27	Mo	5 55	6 17	5	2 42	☿ Gr. Hel. Lat. N.		Rises	Morn	7 21
28	Tue	5 53	6 18	5	3 6	Davidson Col. op'd '37.		8 10	0 41	7 44
29	We	5 57	6 18	5	3 29	☌♃☾Sw'd'nbo'o d 1772		9 16	1 30	8 7
30	Thu	5 50	6 19	4	3 52	S. M. Parish d. 1895.		10 22	2 21	8 56
31	Fri	5 48	6 20	4	4 16	Good Friday.		11 26	3 15	9 47

WEATHER CONJECTURS—March—1, 2, 3. 4, snow if wind be East; 5, 6, 7, 8, 9, 10, 11, fair and frosty; 12, 13, 14, 15, 16, 17, 18, fair and mild. 19, 20, 21, 22, 23, 24, 25, 26, 27. fair; 28, 29, 30, 31, fair and moderate.

[See top 3d cover page.]

3. Some men have faith in the laws of health, and hence by obeying those laws they secure physical health and happiness.—*Branson.*

FARM AND GARDEN WORK FOR MARCH.—Plant bush squash, pumpkins, water and muskmelons, okra, Guinea squash or egg-plant, sugar beets, carrots, beans, peas, radishes, lettuce, corn, celery [first crop] tanyah and mangoes in the low country and elsewhere as soon as danger from frost is over.

This is the first planting month for cotton, corn and rice. Plant your high lands first; leave the low land for April. Plant rice about the 20th of the mouth.

THE UNIVERSITY OF NORTH CAROLINA.

(Located in Chapel Hill, Orange County, twenty-eight miles northwest of Raleigh.

Charted in 1798, founded in 1793, opened 1795. It now has 450 students and 25 instructors. The equipment includes twelve large buildings six scientific laboratories, library of 40,000 volumes, campus of fifty acres with ample athletic grounds, gymnasium, &c. Perfect sanitation baths, closets, &c. Tuition $60 a year, total expenses $200 to $300. Scholarships and loans for the needy. Law school 64, medical school 34, pharmacy 18. A summer school for teachers is conducted each July. It enrolled 147 teachers in 1898. The Faculty includes 21 Professors. During 1897 and 1898, many students supported themselves by labor, the total amount earned being about $5,000. The University is non political and non sectarian.

FACULTY.—Edwin Anderson Alderman, D. C. L., President of the University, and Professor of Aolitical and Social Science; Kemp Plummer Battle, LL.D., Alumni Professor of History; Frances Preston Venable, Ph. H., Smith Professor of General and Analytical Chemistry; Joseph Austin Holmes, S. B., State Geologist, Lecturer an the Geology of North Carolina; Joshua Walker Gore, C. E., Professor of Physics; John Manning, LL.D., Professor of Laws; Thomas Hume, D.D., LL.D., Professor of Greek Language and Literature; William Cain, C. E., Professor of Mathematics; Richard Henry Whitehead, M. D., Professor of Anatomy and Pathology; Henr Hoyrace Williams, A. M., B D., Professor of Philosophy; Henry Van Peters Wilson, Ph. D., Professor of Biology; Darl Pomeroy Harrington, M. A., Professor of Latin Language and Litterature; Collier Cobb, A. M. Professor of Geology; Charles Baskerville, Ph. D., Assistant Professor of Chemistry; Charles Staples Mangum, M.D., Professor of Physiology and *Materia Medica*; Edward Vernon Howell, A.B., Ph. G., Professor of Pharmacy; Henry Farrar Lincsott, Ph. D., Associate Professor of Classical Philology; M. C. S. Noble, Professor of Pedagogy; J. C. Biggs, Ph. B., Assistant Professor of Law.

INSTRUCTORS.—Archibald Henderson, A. B. Instructor in Mathematics; Samuel May, A, B., Instructor in Modern Languages. William Cunningham Smith, Ph. B., Instructor in English; James W. Calder, Director of Gymnasium.

ASSISTANTS IN LABORATORIES.—T. C. Clarke, Ph. D., Assistant in Chemistry; H. M. Londen, Assistants in Geology; J. K. Dozier and W. E. Cox, Assistants in Physics; A. F. Williams, Jr. A.B , Assistant in Biology; Edward James Word, Assistant in Biology.

OFFICERS.—Walter D. Toy, M. A., Secretary of the Faculty; Eben Alexander, Ph.D., LL. D., Supervisor of the Library; Ralph Henry Graves, A. M., Librarian; Eugene Lewis Harris, Ph. B. Registrar; Willie Thomas Patterson, Bursar.

2. A man in whose mind his own country is not *first*, is a man who himself is not *worthy* to be first in another country.—*Branson.*

4th Month. APRIL, 1899. 30 Days.

Moon's Phases.

	D. H. M.		D. H. M.
☾ Last Quarter,	3 6 47 a.m.	☽ First Quarter,	17 5 34 p.m.
● New Moon	10 1 12 a.m.	○ Full Moon,	25 2 13 p.m.

Day of Month.	Day of Week.	Sun rises.	Sun sets.	Sun slow.	Sun's decline north.	ASPECTS OF PLANETS AND OTHER MISCELLANEOUS MATTER.	Moon's place.	Moon rises or sets.	Moon south.	High tides at Beaufort.
1	Sat	5 47	6 21	4	4 39	*April Fool's Day.*	♓	morn	morn	10 38
14		Easter Sunday.				Day's length 12 hours 39 minutes.				
2	A	5 46	6 22	3	5 2	☾ ☿ Stationery; ♄ S ta.	♓	0 24	5 12	eve.
3	Mo	5 44	6 23	3	5 25	Peter Cooper d. '88.	♈	1 16	6 11	1 37
4	Tue	5 42	6 24	3	5 48	Gen. Harrison d. '71.	♈	2 1	7 7	2 33
5	We	5 41	6 25	2	6 11	Jefferson b. 1743.	♉	2 41	8 2	3 28
6	Thu	5 39	6 26	2	6 33	Battle Shiloh '62.	♉	3 16	8 55	4 21
7	Fri	5 38	6 27	2	6 56	♂ ♀ ☾ Socrates d 333 B.C.	♊	3 47	9 46	5 12
8	Sat	5 36	6 28	2	7 18	♂ . in Alph.	♊	4 17	10 36	6 2
15		Low Sunday.				Day's length 12 hours 56 minutes.				
9	A	5 35	6 29	1	7 41	Gen. Robt. E. Lee Sur. '65	♋	4 46	11 26	6 52
10	Mo	5 34	6 30	1	8 3	♂ ☿ ☾ C. Ft. Pulaski	♋	Sets	eve.	7 43
11	Tue	5 33	6 31	1	8 25	B West d '70 [Sur '62	♌	8 32	1 9	8 35
12	We	5 31	6 31	1	8 47	♂ ☿ ✶. Inferior.	♌	9 37	2 2	9 28
13	Thu	5 30	6 32	0	9 9	Ral. N.C. Sur. to Sh'rman	♌	10 36	2 55	10 21
14	Fri	5 28	6 33	0 Fast	9 30	♂ ☿ ☾ Li'c'l'n Ass'65 ['65	♍	11 28	3 48	11 14
15	Sat	5 27	6 34	0	9 52	A Johnson Inaug't'd '65	♍	morn	4 39	morn
16		Second Sunday after Easter.				Day's length 13 hours 11 minutes.				
16	A	5 26	6 34	0	10 13	Fren. evac. Mex. '67	♎	0 13	5 28	0 5
17	Mo	5 24	6 35	1	10 34	♂ ♂ ☾ Dr Frank'n d.	♎	0 51	6 15	0 54
18	Tue	5 23	6 36	1	10 55	Luther at Worms [1790.	♏	1 25	7 0	1 41
19	We	5 22	6 37	1	11 16	David S Reid b. 1813 [1523	♏	1 57	7 42	2 26
20	Thu	5 21	6 38	1	11 37	☿ in ♒. Nap. 3d b. '08.	♐	2 25	8 24	3 8
21	Fri	5 20	6 39	1	11 57	P McK'ly or. sqd to Cu'98	♐	2 50	9 6	3 50
22	Sat	5 18	6 40	2	12 17	N. A. sqd leaves K. W.	♑	3 15	9 49	4 32
17		Third Sunday after Easter.				Day's length 13 hours 26 minutes.				
23	A	5 17	6 41	2	12 37	☐ ♂ ✶. [Vol. called for]	♑	3 41	10 34	5 15
24	Mo	5 15	6 41	2	12 57	☿ Spain de. war with	♒	4 8	11 22	6 0
25	Tue	5 14	6 41	2	13 17	♃ ☽ ☾ . [U.S.	♒	rises	morn	6 48
26	We	5 13	6 42	2	13 36	Jos. Johnson at Dur. '62	♓	8 9	0 13	7 13
27	Thu	5 12	6 43	3	13 55	♂ ☽ ☾ [Matanzas Bomb.	♓	9 16	1 8	7 39
28	Fri	5 11	6 44	3	14 14	Cianfuegos Bombarded.	♈	10 18	2 6	8 34
29	Sat	5 10	6 45	3	14 33	♂ ☾ ☾ C.dis. R. Va. '70	♈	11 13	3 6	9 32
18		Fourth Sunday after Easter.				Day's length 13 hours 39 minutes.				
30	A	5 9	6 46	3	14 51	☿ in Aph. Cabanas bomb	♉	morn	4 5	10 32

WEATHER CONJECTURES—April—1, 2, 3, open weather; 4, 5, 6, 7, 8, 9, 10, wind and rain; 11, 12, 13, 14, 15, 16, 17, fair; 18, 19, 20, 21, 22, 23, 24, 25, expect fair weather; 26, 27, 28, 29, 30, changeable.

FARM AND GARDEN WORK FOR APRIL.—Whatever has been omitted in March, do not neglect any longer. Sow green glazed cabbage, pickling cabbage, full crop of cauliflower and broccoli, okra, tomatoes, peppers, beets, carrots, leeks, melons, cucumbers, celery.

Full crops of corn, cotton and rice should be put in during this month. Plant your lowland corn. Commence early to hoe your young cotton, and thin out to stand. Plant pumpkins for a field crop.

1898.   CARDENAS BAY.   1948.

BY GEO. I. NOWITZKY.

Prologue.—On the eleventh day of May, 1948, a Veteran of the War with Spain was seated in the family arm-chair.—About him were gathered his grand-children, who urged him to tell them a war story. Upon recalling that it was the fiftieth Anniversary of the fight on Cardenas Bay—in which young Bagley was the first American to loose his life—the old Sea Fighter wiped the rapidly falling tears from his eyes and said:—

Yes, children, come and gather this way,
And I'll tell you of the fight at Cardenas Bay,
Which occured just fifty years ago to-day.
'Twas at the beginning of our war with Spain—
The fight in which young Bagley was slain—
Just fifty years ago this very day.
On the blood-stained waters of Cadenas Bay.

We were blockading the Cuban Coast,
And holding in check the Spanish host ;
Each of our ships at their proper post.
One gunboat, one tug and a little craft
As unprotected as an open raft ;
With these we were holdtng the right of way,
To the land-locked waters of Cardenas Bay.

On the eleventh day of fragrant May,
On a shimmering sea, neath a tropic ray,
Came the order to heave and sail away,
And attack the Spaniard right and left,
On hill, valley and protected cleft,
And silence every fort that blocked the way
To the open waters of Cardenas Bay.

Led by the Winslow—a hundred tons,
We steamed forward under their very guns,
And bid defiance to the hostile "Dons."
They met our fleet with shot and shell,
But we served our guns so quick and well
That not a Spaniard by night would stay
In the battered forts of Cardenas Bay.

The deck of the boat, which so bravely led,
Was changed in hue to a mournful red,
Dyed by the blood of our heroic dead.
And in that shower of shot and shell,
Brave Bagley was the first that fell;
And no braver fell to the closing day
Than this Ensign hero of Cardenas Bay.

In the Capitol City of the great North State,
Tower many Monuments to the good and great,
But none carry more historic weight
Than the one that tells of the eventful strife,
In which this young Ensign lost his life,
On that terrible day in fragrant May,
On the blood-stained waters of Cardenas Bay.

5th Month.   MAY, 1899.   31 Days.

Moon's Phases.

D. H. M		D. H. M.
☾ Last Quarter, 2 0 38 p.m.	☽ First Quarter, 17 0 4 p.m.	
● New Moon, 9 0 30 p.m.	● Full Moon, 25 0 40 a.m.	
	☾ Last Quarter, 31 5 46 p.m.	

(Left margin, vertical text:) For quick sales and prompt returns ship your Produce to the THE E. C. BROOKS CO., Portsmouth, Va.

Day of Month.	Day of Week.	Sun rises.	Sun sets.	Sun fast.	Sun's decline north.	ASPECTS OF PLANETS AND OTHER MISCELLANEOUS MATTER.	Moon's place.	Moon rises or sets.	Moon south.	High tides at Beaufort
1	Mo	5 8	6 47	3	15 9	Spaish Fl't at M'lla des.		0 0	5 3	11 31
2	Tue	5 7	6 48	3	15 27	☾ S. H. Young d 1882.		0 41	5 58	eve.
3	We	5 6	6 49	3	15 45	Col. dis. Jamaica 1494		1 16	6 51	2 17
4	Thu	5 5	6 59	3	16 2	Dr. Wm. G. Hill d 1877		1 47	7 41	3 7
5	Fri	5 4	6 50	4	16 20	Bat. of Williamsburg '62		2 17	8 30	3 56
6	Sat	5 3	6 51	4	16 37	Bat. of Wilderness 1864		2 46	9 18	3 44

19   Regation Sunday.   Day's length 13 hours 51 minutes.

7	A	5 2	6 51	4	16 53	♂ ♀ ☾ Matanzas Ft.Sh'll		3 18	10 8	5 34
8	Mo	5 1	6 52	4	17 10	Bat.of Palo.Alto.'46		3 51	10 59	6 25
9	Tue	5 0	6 53	4	17 26	☿ Gre. Elong W.		sets	11 51	7 17
10	We	4 59	6 54	4	17 41	Con. Memorial Day.		8 22	eve.	8 9
11	Thu	4 58	6 54	4	17 57	Ascen. Day—Holy Thu.		9 18	1 38	9 4
12	Fri	4 57	6 55	4	18 12	♂ ♥ ☾ En. W. Bagley k'll		10 7	2 30	9 56
13	Sat	4 56	6 56	4	18 27	Fly Sqd lv Hamp R'ds.		10 48	3 20	10 46

20   Sunday after Assension.   Day's length 14 hours 4 minutes.

14	A	4 55	6 57	4	18 41	Bat. of Reseca, Ga. '64.		11 24	4 8	11 34
15	Mo	4 54	6 58	4	18 56	Colquit sp. in Ral. '86.		11 56	4 54	morn
16	Tue	4 53	6 59	4	19 10	♂ ☾ 1st.Ste'er c.oc.'19		morn	5 37	0 20
17	We	4 53	7 00	4	19 23	John Penn b. 1741.		0 24	6 19	1 3
18	Thu	4 52	7	1	19 36	Sqd.ar.at Key West		0 50	7 0	1 45
19	Fri	4 52	7	1	19 49	Cervera's sqd. atSant.hb		1 15	7 42	2 26
20	Sat	4 51	7	2	20 2	Mecklenburg Ind. 1775.		1 41	8 26	3 8

21   Pentecost—White Sunday.   Day's length 13 hours 52 minutes.

21	A	4 50	7	3	20 14	N. C. Seceded 1861.		2 8	9 12	3 52
22	Mo	4 49	7	3	20 26	☿ Gen. Hel. Lat. South		2 38	10 1	4 38
23	Tue	4 48	7	4	20 38	David Livington d 1886		3 12	10 55	5 27
24	We	4 48	7	5	20 49	Queen Victoria b '19.		3 53	11 53	6 21
25	Thu	4 48	7	5	21 0	● ♂ ☾ [75.000 men		risis	morn	7 19
26	Fri	4 47	7	6	21 10	♄ ♭ ☾ Calvin d 1564		9 5	0 54	8 20
27	Sat	4 47	7	7	21 20	♂ ♂ ✳ St. Louis Cyc.'96		9 56	1 55	9 21

22   Trenty Sunday.   Day's length 14 hours 23 minutes.

28	A	4 46	7	8	21 30	Noah Webster d 1843.		10 40	2 56	10 22
29	Mo	4 46	7	9	21 40	Reode Island ad. 1790.		11 18	3 53	11 19
30	Tue	4 45	7	10	21 49	*Federal Memorial Day.*		11 51	4 47	eve.
31	We	4 45	7	11	21 57	Santiago Fort bom'd'98		morn	5 38	1 4

WEATHER CONJECTURES—May—1, 2, changeable; 3, 4, 5, 6, 7, 8, 9, very rainy; 10, 11, 12, 13, 14 15, 16, 17, fair; 18, 19, 20, 21, 22, 23, 24, 25, expect much rain; 26, 27, 28, 29, 30, 31, fair.

FARM AND GARDEN WORK FOR MAY.—Plant snaps beans and squashes. Sow cabbages for winter use, cauliflower, broccoli, celery, beets, carrots, salsify. Plant cucumbers, melons and pumpkins for late crops. Gather herbs for drying; always dry gently in the shade.

Look well to your hoeing and plowings. Continue to plant corn in low lands. Sow first crop of early cow peas. Rice planting is generally postponed until June, as the birds are very bad in May, and the May bird is exceedingly destructive.

This page is prepared by Dr. D. REID PARKER, Director of Farmer's Institutes, Trinity, N. C.

Agriculture is the most healthful, most useful, and most noble employment of man.—*Washington.*

* * * *

Until quite recent years the farmer was left to grope his weary and uncertain way as best he could. Although he had to deal with the most wonderful and the most important forces and elements of all created nature, he had no special training for his life work, he had no scientific investigations whatever to guide and encourage him in his toilsome and uncertain labors. The farmer is most surely the most important factor in all the make up of a great people.

All other trades and callings are directly or indirectly dependent upon him for their very existence. Without the patient toil of the farmer in planting and tilling the fields, what would become of the learned professions, so called? The pursuits of the fine arts and sciences, of business and trafic of every kind?

It would no longer be a question of volume of business and profits; it would simply be a question of animal existence, and if these conditions were long continued, civilization itself would disappear from the face of of the earth.

* * * *

Farmers' Institutes are doing a great and lasting work for the State without one dollar being appropriated by the State for this purpose. Let the farmer have all the helps he possibly can get, as he richly deserves the very best efforts the State and National Governments can afford in his behalf.

* * * *

God bless the man that sows the wheat,
That finds us milk and fruit and meat,
May his pocket be heavy, his heart be light,
His cattle and corn and all go right.
God bless the seed his hand lets fall,
For the farmer, he must feed us all.

* * * *

If there should be a Farmer's Institute anywhere near you during the year, be sure to attend. It will do you and your entire community good.

* * * *

They also have erred through wine, and through strong drink are out of the way, Isa. xxviii-7.

* * * *

In passing a farm house you can always tell what sort a fellow lives there. If everything is dirty or dingy and dogish—old plunder and rubbish scattered in wreckless profusion in the yard, on the fences, in the lanes and out in the public road, you may know at a glance that a shabby sort of a fellow stays there. He cannot deny it as the evidences are too apparent to everyone who may chance to pass that way. Oh, how a little cleaning up would help all such places. Even a lowly cabin by the wayside with neat surroundings looks inviting and restful. The house work is lighter and easier where everything is neat, orderly and convenient. The lamp gives a better light. The children are brighter and better. The The mother is more patient and contented. The husband and father

[See page 17.]

6th Month.   **JUNE, 1899.**   **30 Days.**

Moon's Phases.

	D. H. M.		D. H. M.
New Moon,	8 1 12 a.m.	Full Moon,	23 9 11 a.m.
First Quarter,	16 4 38 a.m.	Last Quarter,	29 11 36 p.m.

Day of Month.	Day of Week.	Sun rises.	Sun sets.	Sun slow.	Sun's decline north.	ASPECTS OF PLANETS AND OTHER MISCELLANEOUS MATTER.	Moon's place.	Moon rises or sets.	Moon south.	High tides at Beaufort.
1	Thu	4 44	7 11	2 22	6	Corpus Christi.		0 21	6 28	1 54
2	Fri	4 44	7 12	2 22	13	Battle Cold Harbor '64.		0 51	7 16	2 42
3	Sat	4 43	7 12	2 22	21	Hobson Sinks Merrimac		1 20	8 4	3 30
23.			First Sunday after Trininty.			Days length 14 hours 32 minutes.				
4	A	4 42	7 13	2 22	28	Geo. I b. 1738.		1 51	8 54	4 20
5	Mo	4 41	7 13	2 22	35	♂ ♀ ℂ Tel. in China '71.		2 26	9 44	5 10
6	Tue	4 41	7 14	1 22	41	Santiago Forts Bomb.		3 06	10 36	6 2
7	We	4 41	7 14	1 22	47	☉ ♂ ☿ ℂ✳. Eclipsed		3 51	11 29	6 55
8	Thu	4 41	7 15	1 22	52	♂ ♅ ℂ; ☿ in ♋ In'is		Sets	Eve	7 50
9	Fri	4 41	7 15	1 22	57	Marines land at Guan.		8 43	1 13	8 39
10	Sat	4 41	7 16	1 23	02	Dickens d. '70.		9 22	2 2	9 28
24			Second Sunday after Trinity.			Days length 14 hours 35 minutes.				
11	A	4 41	7 16	1 23	6	♂ ♄ ✳ J.Q.Adams b.1767		9 57	2 48	10 14
12	Mo	4 41	7 16	1 23	10	Bryant d. '78.		10 27	3 32	10 58
13	Tue	4 41	7 16	1 23	14	♀ in Perihelion.		10 53	4 15	11 41
14	We	4 41	7 17	1 23	17	♂ ♀ ✳. Superior. ['36		11 18	4 56	Morn
15	Thu	4 41	7 18	1 23	19	☽ ♂ ♀ ♅ ✳ Ark, a Sta.		11 42	5 37	0 22
16	Fri	4 41	7 18	1 23	22	☽ Fort Caimanera.		Morn	6 19	1 3
17	Sat	4 41	7 19	1 23	24	Addison b. 1718. [demol.		0 7	7 3	1 45
25			Third Sunday after Trinity.			Days length 14 hours 37 minutes.				
18	A	4 41	7 19	1 23	25	Battle of Waterloo 1815		0 35	7 50	2 29
19	Mo	4 42	7 19	1 23	26	♂ ♃ ℂ. Shafter at Baiqui		1 6	8 41	3 16
20	Tue	4 43	7 19	1 23	27	Cornwallis at Rd. 1781		1 43	9 36	4 7
21	We	4 43	7 19	2 23	27	Sun ent's Can sum. com.		2 29	10 36	5 2
22	Thu	4 43	7 19	2 23	27	Moon eclip.inv.at Wash.		3 25	11 38	6 2
23	Fri	4 43	7 19	2 23	26	☉ ☿ Gen. Hel. Lat. N.		Rises	Morn	7 4
24	Sat	4 43	7 19	2 23	25	St. John Baptist.		8 34	0 40	8 6
26			Fourth Sunday after Trinity.			Day's length 14 hours 36 miuutes.				
25	A	4 43	7 20	3 23	23	Custer defeated c '76.		9 16	1 41	9 7
26	Mo	4 44	7 20	3 23	22	Cadiz Fleet at Port Said.		9 52	2 39	10 5
27	Tue	4 44	7 20	3 23	19	♃. Stationery.		10 34	3 23	10 59
28	We	4 44	7 20	3 23	17	ℂ 3d. Manilla ex. sail.		10 53	4 24	11 50
29	Thu	4 45	7 20	3 23	13	ℂ 1st. ex. ar. at Man'l		11 23	5 13	eve
30	Fri	4 45	7 20	4 23	10	Caney eva. by the Sp'd.		11 55	6 18	1 44

WEATHER CONJECTURES—June—1, 2, 3, 4, 5, 6, 7, 8, generally fair; 9, 10, 11, 12, 13, 14, 15, 16, fair and mild; 17, 18 19, 20, 21, 22, 23, expect rain; 24, 25, 26, 27, 28, 29, changeable; 30, fair.

FARM AND GARDEN WORK FOR JUNE.—Sow full crops of cabbages for fall and winter use. Cauliflower and broccoli may yet be sown, also a few carrots. Continue to sow tomatoes, okra, radishes, snap beans. Transplant leeks; pull and dry onions, garlic and ashcalots. A few cucumbers and melons plant for a late crop, and a few ruta baga turnips.

Keep constantly at the plow and hoe; this is the most important grass month! If the vines from your sweet potato sprout bed are fit you can draw and plant out first good rain. Sow cow-peas between your corn hills and rows. The end of this month is a good time to put in the first crop of standing field peas.

[Continued from page 15.]

wears a genial face and is gentle and kind. Even the cattle and horses the chickens and dogs tell of this better life in the house. Any and all of us may do better and have these desirable surroundings if we will try. Clean up! Clean up!!

    *   *   *   *

Give fools their gold and Knaves their power;
Let fortune,s bubble rise and fall,
Who sows a field or trains a flower,
Or plants a tree is more than all.

For he who blesses most, is blest ;
And God and man shall own his worth
Who tails to leave as his bequest,
An added beauty to the earth.

And soon or late to all that sow,
The time of harvest shall be given,
The flower shall bloom, the fruit shall grow,
If not on earth, at least in heaven.

STATE BOARD OF EDUCATION.

Gov. D. L. Russell, President, ex-officio; Cyrus Thompson, Secretary of State; W. H. Worth, State Treasurer; Hal. W. Ayer, State Auditor; Z. V. Walser, Attorney General; C. H. Mebane, Superintendent Public Instruction, Secretary ex-officio.

STATE BOARD OF EXAMINERS.

C. H. Mebane, Chairman ex-officio; W. L. Poteat, Wake Forest College; L. L. Hobbs, Guilford College; M. C. S. Noble, University of N. C.

PUBLIC FUND SPENT FOR PUBLIC SCHOOLS DURING THE YEAR 1898.

Total, $986,514.85; total census of children of school age for 1898, 628,-480; total enrollment for 1898, 399,375; average length of term for whites in 1898, 71 days; for colored, 64 days; average salaries paid teachers—white males, $24.66; average salaries paid teachers—colored males, $21.64; average salaries paid teachers—white females, $22.96; average salaries paid teachers—colored females, $19.85.

THE E. C. BROOKS CO., Portsmouth, Va.

We can sell anything you ship.

7th Month.   JULY, 1899.   31 Days.

Moon's Phases.

	D. H. M.		D. H. M.
New Moon,	7 3 23 p.m.	Full Moon,	22 4 33 p.m.
First Quarter, 15	6 50 p.m.	Last Quarter, 29	7 34 a.m.

Day of Month.	Day of Week.	Sun rises.	Sun sets.	Sun Slow.	Sun's decline north.	ASPECTS OF PLANETS AND OTHER MISCELLANEOUS MATTER.	Moon's place.	Moon rises or sets.	Moon south.	High tides at Beaufort.
1	Sat	4 45	7 20	4 23	6	Works at Santiago taken		morn	6 51	2 17
27		Fifth Sunday after Trinity.				Day's length 14 hours 33 minutes.				
2	A	4 46	7 20	4 23	2	San Juan tkn & Cervera		0 29	7 41	3 7
3	Mo	4 47	7 20	4 22	57	⊕ in Aphelion [fleet des		1 6	8 32	3 58
4	Tue	4 47	7 20	4 22	52	Independence Day		1 49	9 24	4 50
5	We	4 48	7 19	4 22	46	♂ ♀ ☾ ♈ ☾ Monroe d'31		2 37	10 17	5 43
6	Thu	4 48	7 19	5 22	40	♂ ♀ Ψ Alphonso XII des		3 29	11 18	6 44
7	Fri	4 49	7 19	5 22	34	Dew'y c. Is. Gra'de		sets	11 57	7 23
8	Sat	4 50	7 19	5 22	27	Camara fl't ret to Sp		-7 59	eve	8 5
28		Sixth Sunday after Trinity				Day's length 14 hours 27 minutes.				
9	A	4 50	7 19	5 22	20	♂ ♀ ☾ Brad'ck deft 1755		8 29	1 29	8 55
10	Mo	4 51	7 18	5 22	13	Bombard Santiago res		8 56	2 12	9 38
11	Tue	4 52	7 18	5 22	5	J Q Adams b 1767		9 21	2 54	10 20
12	We	4 52	7 18	5 21	57	♂ ♂ ☾ Battle Bayou 1690		9 45	3 34	11 00
13	Thu	4 53	7 17	6 21	48	Truce asked by Linares		10 10	4 15	11 41
14	Fri	4 53	7 17	6 21	39	Santiago sur. 1898		10 36	4 58	morn
15	Sat	4 54	7 16	6 21	30	☾ Mar. law dec in Sp'in		11 5	5 42	0 24
29		Seventh Sunday after Trinity.				Day's length 14 hours 20 minutes.				
16	A	4 55	7 16	6 21	20	♂ ♃ ☾ Toral sur Sant'go		11 59	6 30	1 8
17	Mo	4 55	7 15	6 21	10	☿ in ♍ ♀ in ♎ Am flg San		morn	7 22	1 56
18	Tue	4 56	7 15	6 20	59	♂ ☋ ☾ Porto Rico invad		0 19	8 18	2 48
19	We	4 57	7 14	6 20	49	♂ ♄ ☾ Frch rev beg 1789		1 7	9 18	3 44
20	Thu	4 57	7 13	6 20	37	Span cab sue for peace		2 6	10 20	4 44
21	Fri	4 58	7 13	6 20	26	Garcia l'ves Shafter		3 13	11 22	5 46
22	Sat	4 59	7 12	6 20	14	☿ Gre Elon East		sets	morn	6 48
30		Eigth Sunday after Trinity.				Day's length 14 hours 10 minutes.				
23	A	5	7 12	6 20	2	Spaniards cont'ue to sur		7 49	0 22	7 48
24	Mo	5 1	7 11	6 19	50	☐ ♃ ☀ Shafter active		8 21	1 20	8 46
25	Tue	5 2	7 11	6 13	37	Miles lands at Guanica		8 54	2 14	9 40
26	We	5 3	7 10	6 19	23	Spain for sues for peace		9 25	3 6	10 32
27	Thu	5 3	7 9	6 19	10	☿ in Aphelion [Po Rico		9 57	3 57	11 23
28	Fri	5 3	7 8	6 18	56	☾ Miles raises Am flag		10 39	4 47	eve
29	Sat	5 4	7 7	6 18	42	☾ Pres rep peace o'tus		11 7	5 38	1 4
31		Ninth Sunday after Trinity.				Day's length 14 hours 0 minutes.				
30	A	5 5	7 6	6 18	28	Wm Penn b 1718		11 49	6 29	1 55
31	Mo	5 6	7 6	6 18	13	Dining bell invent 1583		morn	7 21	2 47

WEATHER CONJECTURES—July—1, 2, 3, 4, 5, 6, 7, generally fair; 8, 9, 10, 11, 12, 13, 14, 15, fair; 16, 17, 18, 19, 20, 21, 22, fair if W. rain if S. or S. W.; 23, 24, 25, 26, 27, 28, 29 fair; 30, 31, wind and rain.

FARM AND GARDEN WORK FOR JULY.—Sow cabbages, but protect from hot sun when young. Water at night. Plant snap beans and a few Irish potatoes. Continue to sow radishes, lettuce, endive, cresses, mustard and small salading. The early Dutch turnip is the best to sow for the first crop; follow with the yellow Swedish or ruta baga.

Now do not omit to sow full crops of standing cow-peas. Sow a few turnips, carrots and beets as field crops, though the hot suns are apt to destroy them; should they escape they will be fine; the next month is the best for these crops.

VALUE OF PUBLIC SCHOOL PROPERTY FOR 1898, $930,214.00.

1898, total number of schools taught, 6,339. The State tax is 18c on the hundred dollars valuation of property, and 54c on the poll. Eleven townships voted a special tax upon themselves at the August election, 1897. Rev. C. H. Wiley was the first Superintendent of Common Schools, as they were called, he came into office in 1852 and served most faithfully and heroicly for 13 years.

The following persons have filled the office since its establishment, Rev. S. S. Ashly, Alex McIver, Elder Jas. Reid, elected but died before being installed into office. Gov. Holden appointed Hon. Kemp P. Battle, but the Courts retained McIver on account of his successor, Reid having died, before being qualified.   STEPHEN D. POOL, JOHN POOL, JOHN C. SCARBOROUGH, S. M. FINGER, C. H. McIVER.

OFFICERS OF STATE MEDICAL SOCIETY.

Dr. L. V. Pecot, Littleton, President; Dr. Geo. W. Pressley, Charlotte, Secretary. Meeting in Asheville 1899.

STATE BOARD OF MEDICAL EXAMINERS.

Dr. D. T. Tayloe, Washington, President; Dr. Thos. E. Anderson, Statesville, Secretary; Dr. Herbert Anderson, Wilson; Dr. W. H. H. Cobb, Goldsboro; Dr. J. H. Way, Waynesville; Dr. Kemp. P. Battle, Raleigh; Dr. E. C. Register, Charlotte.

Traveling expenses and $4.00 per day during session.

8th Month. AUGUST, 1899. 31 Days.

Moon's Phases.

	D. H. M.		D. H. M.
New Moon	6 6 39 a.m.	Full Moon,	20 11 38 p.m.
First Quarter,	14 6 45 r.m.	Last Quarter,	27 6 48 a.m.

Day of Month.	Day of Week	Sun rises.	Sun sets.	Sun slow.	Sun's decline north.	ASPECTS OF PLANETS AND OTHER MISCELLANEOUS MATTER.	Moon's place.	Moon rises or sets.	Moon south.	High tides at Beaufort.
1	Tue	5 6	7 5	6	17 58	Geo. II crowned 1714.		0 34	8 13	3 39
2	We	5 7	7 4	6	17 43	♂♀☽ Bat. Pleana 1877		1 26	9 4	4 30
3	Thu	5 8	7 3	6	17 27			2 20	9 54	5 40
4	Fri	5 9	7 2	6	17 11	☿ Station'y; Tild'n d'86		3 18	10 42	6 8
5	Sat	5 10	7 1	6	16 55	♂♀☿ Bat. Athens '61		4 17	11 27	6 53

32 Tenth Sunday after Trinity. Day's length 13 hours 49 minutes.

6	A	5 11	7 1	6	16 38	Fort Gaines sur '64		sets	eve	7 36
7	Mo	5 12	7 0	5	16 22	♂♀☽ Barillios d '48		7 27	0 53	8 19
8	Tue	5 12	6 58	5	16 5	Sp'ish Armada des. 1588		7 50	1 34	9 0
9	We	5 13	6 56	5	15 47	Dryden b. 1681.		8 14	2 15	9 41
10	Thu	5 14	6 55	5	15 30	♂♂☽ Bat. Oak Hill '61		8 40	2 56	19 22
11	Fri	5 14	6 54	5	15 12	Pres. signs *peace protocol*		9 8	3 39	11 5
12	Sat	5 15	6 54	5	14 54	☉ sta. R E Lee d. '70		9 38	4 25	11 51

33 Eleventh Sunday after Trinity. Day's length 13 hours 34 minutes.

13	A	5 16	6 52	5	14 36	♂♃☽ Conova d. '22		10 14	5 14	morn
14	Mo	5 17	6 51	4	14 18	Bat. Hastings 1066		10 58	6 6	0 40
15	Tue	5 18	6 50	4	13 59	♂♂☽ Nap. b. 1769		11 50	7 3	1 32
16	We	5 19	6 49	4	13 40	♀ Gre. Hel. Lat. S.		morn	8 2	2 29
17	Thu	5 19	6 48	4	13 21	Burgoyne sur. 1777.		0 52	9 3	3 28
18	Fri	5 20	6 46	3	13 1	Cor. stone U.S. cap.1793		2 1	10 2	4 29
19	Sat	5 21	6 45	3	12 42	♂☿※ Inferior.		3 15	11 2	5 29

34 Twelfth Sunday after Trinity. Day's length 13 hours 21 minutes.

20	A	5 21	6 44	3	12 22	♀ Per, Har'son b '33		4 33	11 58	6 28
21	Mo	5 22	6 43	3	12 2	♄ sta. Branson k 64		rises	morn	7 24
22	Tue	5 23	6 42	3	11 42	♂☿♀ Gough b. 1817.		7 23	0 52	8 18
23	We	5 24	6 41	2	11 22	Com. Perry d. 1820.		7 55	1 45	9 11
24	Thu	5 25	6 40	2	11 1	Daniel Webster d 1852		8 29	2 37	10 3
25	Fri	5 26	6 38	2	10 41	Turner in Raleigh 1870		9 6	3 29	10 55
26	Sat	5 27	6 36	1	10 20	Battle of Dresden 1813		9 47	4 22	11 48

35 Thirteenth Sunday after Trinity. Days length 13 hours 5 minutes.

27	A	5 27	6 35	1	9 59	☽□♂※Mad'n b 1751		10 32	5 15	eve
28	Mo	5 28	6 33	1	9 38	☿ sta 1st cab mes '58		11 21	6 8	1 34
29	Tue	5 28	6 32	1	9 16	♂♀☽		morn	7 0	2 26
30	We	5 29	6 31	1	8 55	Wm Penn d 1718		0 15	7 51	3 17
31	Thu	5 30	6 30	0	8 33	Charleston earthq'ke 86		1 12	8 39	4 5

WEATHER CONJECTURES—August—1, 2, 3, 4, 5, 6, wind and rain; 7, 8, 9, 10, 11, 12, 13, 14, more wind and rain; 15, 16, 17, 18, 19, 20, changeable; 21, 22, 23, 24, 25, 26, 27, fair; 28, 29, 30, 31, wind and rain.

You can't do better than to send your Poultry and Eggs to the E. C. BROOKS CO., Portsmouth, Va.

FARM AND GARDEN WORK FOR AUGUST.—Transplant all kinds of cabbage, cauliflower and celery. Sow carrots and beets, turnips of all kinds, spinach, lettuce, radish and onions.

Now sow full crops of field turnips, carrots and beets, and such other crops as were omitted last month; strip fodder. Early rice will be fit to cut the last of this month. Look to it. This is a good time to plant vines of the first slips, in order to procure seed potatoes for the next year's crops.

LEGISLATURE OF NORTH CAROLINA FOR 1899 AND 1900.

SENATE.

First District (Camden, Chowan, Currituck, Gates, Pasquotank, Perquimans, Hertford)—T G Skinner, d., Hertford; George Cowper, d., Winton.

Second District (Dare, Hyde, Tyrrell, Washington, Pamlico, Martin, Beaufort)—H S Ward, d., Plymouth; G W Miller, d., Bayboro.

Third District (Northampton and Bertie)—W E Harris, P., Seaboard.

Fourth District (Halifax)—E L Travis, d., Halifax.

Fifth District (Edecombe)—Dr R H Speight, d., Wrendale.

Sixth District (Pitt)—F G James, d., Greenville.

Seventh District (Wilson, Nash and Franklin)—R A P Cooley, d., Nashville; T S Coolie, D., Louisburg.

Eigth District (Craven, Carteret, Jones, Onslow, Lenoir and Greene)—James a Bryan, d., Newbern; J Q Jackson, D., Kinston.

Nineth District (Wayne Duplin and Pender—Frank A Daniels, D., Goldsboro; I F Hill, d., Faison.

Tenth District (New Hanover and Brunswick)—William J Davis, d., Winnabow.

Eleventh District (Warren and Vance—T O Fuller, r., Warrenton.

Twelfth District (Wake)—Fabius A Whitaker, d., Raleigh.

Thirteenth District (Johnston)—Elder J A Jones, d., Gully's Mill.

Fourteenth District (Sampson, Harnett and Bladen)—F M White, r., and J M Robinson, d

Fifteenth District (Robeson and Columbus)—Stephen McIntyre, d., Lumberton; Jos. A Brown, d., Chadbourn.

Sixteenth District (Cumberland)—W L Williams, d., Little River Academy.

Seventeenth District (Granville and Person)—A A Hicks, d., Oxford.

Eighteenth District (Caswell, Alamance, Orange and Durham)—T M Cheek, d., Mebane, J M Satterfield, d., Estelle.

Nineteenth District (Chatham)—J A Goodwin, r., Pittsboro.

Twentieth District (Rockingham)—William Lindsay, d., Reidsville.

Twenty-first District (Guilford)—John N Wilson, d., Greensboro.

Twenty-second District (Randolph and Moore)—J C Black, d., Carthage.

Twenty-third District (Richmond, Montgomery, Anson and Union)—T J Jerome, d., Monroe, Charles Stanback, d., Mt. Gilead.

Twenty-fourth District (Cabarrus and Stanly)—R L Smith, d , Norwood.

Twenty-fifth District (Mecklenburg)—Frank I Osborne, d., Charlotte.

Twenty-sixth District (Rowan, Davidson and Forsyth)—R B Glenn. d., Winston; J C Thomas, d., Midway.

Twenty-seventh District (Iredell, Yadkin and Davie)—James A Butler, d., Statesville; F C Hairston, d., Fork Church.

Twenty-eighth District (Stokes and Surry)—J C Newsome, R., Kings.

Twenty-nineth District (Alexander, Wilkes, Lincoln, and Catawba)—D A Lowe, d., Lincolnton; H T Campbell, R., Vashti.

Thirtieth District (Alleghany, Ashe and Watauga)—W C Fields, d., Sparta.

Thirty-first District (Caldwell, Burke, McDowell, Mitchell and Yancey) Commodore Keeley, P., Morganton; W J Souther, R.

Thrity-second District Gaston, Cleveland, Rutherford and Polk)—M H Justice, d., Rutherfordton; O F Mason, d., Dallas.

Thirty-third District (Buncombe, Madison and Haywood) W J Cocke, d., Asheville; Thos J Murray, d., Marshal.

9th Month. SEPTEMBER, 1899. 30 Days.

Moon's Phases.

	D. H. M.		D. H. M.
New Moon,	4 10 24 p.m.	Full moon	19 7 23 a.m.
First Quart'r	12 4 40 p.m.	Last Quarter,	26 9 54 a.m.

(left margin, vertical) We sell Fruits and Produce. THE E. C. BROOKS CO., Portsmouth, Va.

Day of Month.	Day of Week.	Sun rises.	Sun sets.	Sun fast.	Sun's decline north.	ASPECTS OF PLANETS AND OTHER MISCELLANEOUS MATTER	Moon's place.	Moon rises or sets	Moon South.	High tides at Beaufort
1	Fri	5 31	6 28	1	8 12	Battle Ox Hill 1862		2 10	9 25	4 51
2	Sat	5 32	6 27	1	7 50	Atlanta captured 1864		3 9	10 10	5 36

36 Fourteenth Sunday after Trinity. Days length 12 hours 50 minutes.

3	A	5 33	6 25	2	7 28	♂ ☾ Eliz Glenn d 1894		4 7	10 52	6 18
4	Mo	5 34	6 24	2	7 5	☿ in ♌: ♂ ☽ ☽		5 11	33	6 59
5	Tue	5 35	6 22	2	6 43	☿ Gre Elong W		sets	eve	7 49
6	We	5 35	6 21	2	6 31	Lafayette born 1757		6 46	0 56	8 22
7	Thu	5 36	6 19	2	5 58	Whittier died 1892		7 12	1 38	9 4
8	Fri	5 36	6 18	3	5 36	♂ ☾ Des Jerusalem 70		7 43	2 23	9 49
9	Sat	5 37	6 16	3	5 13	☿ in Peri. : ♂ ♃ ☾		8 18	3 11	10 37

37 Fifteenth Sunday after Trinity. Day's length 12 hours 35 minutes.

10	A	5 38	6 15	3	4 50	☐ ♄ ✶ S S Cox d 1889		8 57	4 1	11 27
11	Mo	5 39	6 14	4	4 28	♃ Gr Hel Lat N		9 44	4 55	morn
12	Tue	5 39	6 12	4	4 5	☽ ♂ ♄ ☾ Bat Chapulpc		10 40	5 52	0 21
13	We	5 40	6 11	4	3 42	☽ Bat Quebec 1750		11 45	6 50	1 18
14	Thu	5 41	6 10	5	3 19	Humboldt b 1769		morn	7 48	2 16
15	Fri	5 42	6 8	5	2 56	Scott took Mexico 1847		0 54	8 45	3 14
16	Sat	5 43	6 6	5	2 32	♂ ♀ ✶ Superior		2 5	9 41	4 11

38 Sixteenth Sunday after Trinity. Day's length 12 hours 20 minutes.

17	A	5 44	6 5	6	2 9	Bat Sharpsburg 1862		3 32	10 36	5 7
18	Mo	5 44	6 4	6	1 46	☉ ♂ in ♍		4 38	11 29	6 2
19	Tue	5 45	6 2	7	1 23	☿ Gra Hel Lat N		rises	morn	6 55
20	We	5 45	6 1	7	0 59	☐ ♅ ✶ Arthur inaug '81		6 23	0 22	7 48
21	Thu	5 46	6 0	7	0 36	Bat Fisher's Hill 1864		7 0	1 15	8 41
22	Fri	5 47	5 58	8	S	*Sun ents Libra, Au com*		7 40	2 10	9 36
23	Sat	5 48	5 56	8	0 10	Nepturn discov 1846		8 26	3 4	10 30

39 Seventeenth Sunday after Trinity. Days length 12 hours 3 minutes.

24	A	5 49	5 54	8	0 33	Gen D H Hill died 1889		9 15	3 59	11 25
25	Mo	5 50	5 53	9	0 57	♂ ♀ ☾ Bat Montre'l 1775		10 8	4 53	eve
26	Tue	5 51	5 52	9	1 20	☾ Dan'l Boone d 1820		11 4	5 45	1 11
27	We	5 51	5 50	9	1 44	☾ Str Arctic lost 1855		morn	6 35	2 1
28	Thu	5 51	5 49	10	2 7	Bishop Randall d 1873		0 2	7 22	2 48
29	Fri	5 52	5 47	10	2 30	MICHAELMAS DAY		1 0	8 7	3 33
30	Sat	5 53	5 46	10	2 54	St Andrew. ♅ sta		1 58	8 50	4 16

WEATHER CONJECTURES—September—1, 2, 3, 4, rainy; expect open weather; 5, 6, 7, 8, 9, 10, 11, 12, fair; 13, 14, 15, 16, 17, 18, 19, more open weather; 20, 21, 22, 23, 24, 25, 26, wind and rain; 27, 28, 29, 30, changeable.

FARM AND GARDEN WORK FOR SEPTEMBER.—Now sow full crops of all kinds—turnips, onions, carrots, beets, cabbage, lettuce, cresses. Look after your mushroom beds. Hoe and thin your turnips.

Continue to sow field turnips, carrots and beets. Southern seed is always better from the imported; those from the latter aae apt to run to seed early in the spring, unless it be English seed. Prepare land for sowing rye in October. Pick cotton; harvest corn.

Thirty-fourth District (Henderson, Transylvania, Jackson and Swain)—Josh Franks, R., Bryson City.

Thirty-fifth District (Macon, Cherokee, Clay and Graham)—J L Crisp, R., Murphy.

Democrats.. 40
Fusionists 10
                                                                    ——
    Total... 50

HOUSE OF REPRESENTATIVES.

Alamance—W H Carroll, d., Burlington.
Alexander—A C McIntosh, d., Taylorsville.
Alleghany—J M Gambrill, d., Amelia.
Anson—Jas A Leak, d., Wadesboro.
Ashe—Dr E B Reeves, d., Lamar.
Beaufort—Dr B B Nicholson, d., Washington.
Bertie—F D Winston, d., Windsor.
Bladen—George H Currie, d., Elizabethtown.
Brunswick—Dr McNeill, d., Southport.
Buncombe—Locke Craig, D., J C Curtis, d., Asheville.
Burke—J H Hoffman, d., Morganton.
Cabarrus—L T Hartsell, d., Concord.
Caldwell—S L Patterson, d., Yadkin Valley.
Camden—J K Abbott, d., Camden.
Carteret—J B Russell, d., Beaufort.
Caswell—C J Yarboro, r., Locust Hill.
Catawba—A C Boggs, d., Claremont.
Chatham—L L Wrenn, r., Siler City; R J H Giles, r., Pittsboro.
Cherokee—W E Mauny, d., Murphy.
Chowan—W Welsh, d., Gliden.
Clay—Wm Sanderson, d., Hayesville.
Cleveland—C R Hoey, d., Shelby.
Columbus—D C Allen, d., Armour.
Craven—Isaac Smith, r., Newbern.
Cumberland—H McD Robinson, d., Fayetteville; D J Ray, d., Endon.
Currituck—S M Beasley, d., Poplar Branch.
Dare—Williams, d., Manteo.
Davidson—C M Thompson, d , Lexington.
Davie—White, r , Mocksville.
Duplin—J O Carr, d., Kenansville.
Durham—H A Foushee, d., Durham.
Edgecombe—H A Gilliam, d., Tarboro; S L Hardy, d., Heartsease.
Forsyth—W A Lowry, r., Kernersville; J K P Carter, r., White Road.
Franklin—P A Davis, d., Laurel.
Gaston—L H J Houser, d., Cherryville.
Gates—John M Trotman, d., Trotville.
Graham—O P Williams, d., Yellow Creek.
Granville—C W Bryan, d.; A A Lyon, d., Lyon.
Greene—J E W Sugg, d., Snow Hill.
Guilford—J C Kennett, d., Pleasant Garden; J C Bunch, d., Oak Ridge.
Halifax—H S Harrison, d., Halifax; W P White, d , Halifax.
Harnett—D H McLean, d., Dunn.
Haywood—Joseph S Davis, d , Iron Duff.
Henderson—M S Justice, r., Hendersonville.
Hertford—J F Snipes, r., Menola.
Hyde—Claude W Davis, d., Englehard.

10th Month.　OCTOBER, 1899　31 Days.

Moon's Phases.

	D. H. M.		D. H. M.
New Moon,	4 2 5 p.m.	Full Moon,	18 4 56 p.m.
First Quarter,	12 1 1 a.m.	Last Quarter,	26 4 31 a.m.

(left margin, vertical): Wanted—Cord-wood and Cedar Posts.　THE E. C. BROOKS CO., Portsmouth, Va.

Day of Month	Day of Week	Sun rises	Sun sets	Sun fast	Sun's decline north	ASPECTS OF PLANETS AND OTHER MISCELLANEOUS MATTER.	Moon's place	Moon rises or sets	Moon south	High tides at Beaufort
40						Eighteenth Sunday after Trinity.　Day's length 11 hours 50 minutes.				
1	A	5 54	5 44	11	3 17			2 55	9 31	4 57
2	Mo	5 55	5 43	11	3 40	Renan died 1892		3 53	10 12	5 38
3	Tue	5 56	5 41	11	4 4	Black Hawk died 1838		4 52	10 54	6 20
4	We	5 57	5 40	12	4 27	Bat Ger'town 1777		5 50	eve	7 2
5	Thu	5 58	5 38	12	4 50	♂ ♅ ℂ; ♂ ♀ ℂ		sets	0 21	7 47
6	Fri	5 59	5 36	12	5 13	Judge Dick born 1823		6 19	1 8	8 34
7	Sat	5 59	5 34	12	5 36	♂ ♂ ℂ; ♂ ♃ ℂ		6 58	1 59	9 25
41						Nineteenth Sunday after Trinty.　Day's length 11 hours 29 minutes.				
8	A	6 0	5 32	13	5 59	♂ ☌ ℂ Bat FtPickens '61		7 43	2 52	10 18
9	Mo	6 1	5 30	13	6 22	♂ ♄ ℂ Big fire Chi'go '71		8 35	3 47	11 13
10	Tue	6 2	5 29	13	6 45	♀ Stuard raid Pa '62		9 36	4 44	morn
11	We	6 3	5 28	13	7 7	♂ ♂ ♃ RevWm Pell d '70		10 42	5 41	0 10
12	Thu	6 4	5 27	14	7 30	R E Lee died 1870		11 52	6 37	1 7
13	Fri	6 5	5 25	14	7 52	☿ in ♍; Conova d '22		morn	7 31	2 3
14	Sat	6 6	5 24	14	8 15	Bat of Hastings 1066		1 4	8 24	2 57
42						Twentieth Sunday after Trinity.　Day's length 11 hours 13 minutes.				
15	A	6 7	5 23	14	8 37	Koskiusko d 1817		2 16	9 16	3 50
16	Mo	6 8	5 21	15	8 59	Noah Webster d 1758		3 28	10 8	4 42
17	Tue	6 9	5 19	15	9 21	Earthqke Asia Minor '83		4 40	11 0	5 34
18	We	6 9	5 18	15	9 43	Judge Reade d '94		5 53	11 54	6 26
19	Thu	6 10	5 17	15	10 5	Bat Ced Crk Va '64		rises	morn	7 20
20	Fri	6 11	5 16	15	10 26	Grace Darling d 1812		6 16	0 49	8 15
21	Sat	6 12	5 15	15	10 48	Bat Ball's Bluff '61		7 5	1 45	9 11
43						Twenty-first Sunday after Trinity.　Day's length 10 hours 58 minutes.				
22	A	6 13	5 14	44	11 9	Liszt born 1811		7 58	2 40	10 6
23	Mo	6 14	5 12	11	11 30	♂ ♅ ℂ; ☿ in Aphe		8 54	3 35	11 1
24	Tue	6 15	5 11	11	11 51	Water mills inv A D 555		9 52	4 26	11 52
25	We	6 16	5 10	10	12 12	♂ ☿ ♃ Newbern set 1712		10 51	5 15	eve
26	Thu	6 16	5 9	9	12 32	♀ ♂; a Librae		11 49	6 2	1 28
27	Fri	6 17	5 8	9	12 53	Bat Hatchrs Run'64		morn	6 45	2 11
28	Sat	6 18	5 7	7	13 13			0 47	7 27	2 53
44						Twenty-sec'd Sunday after Trinity.　Day's length 10 hours 45 minutes.				
29	A	6 19	5 6	6	13 33	♂ ♀ ♃; Raleigh d 1618		1 44	8 9	3 35
30	Mo	6 20	5 5	5	13 53	Gambetta born 1838		2 41	8 50	4 16
31	Tue	6 21	5 5	5	14 12	Span seiz Virginius '73		3 40	9 32	4 58

WEATHER CONJECTURES—October—1, 2, 3, 4, changeable; 5, 6, 7, 8, 9, 10, 11, 12, changeable; 13, 14, 15, 16, 17, 18, fair; 19, 20, 21, 22, 23, 24, 25, 26, expect more fair weather; 27, 28, 29, 30, 31, rain.

FARM AND GARDEN WORK FOR OCTOBER.—You may make two sowings of cabbage this month, and, if of English seed, they will not "run" in the spring. Sow lettuce; hoe turnips and thin; put out leeks and onions; sow principal crop of spinach; earth up celery.

Continue picking your cotton as it blows. Sow early rye, wheat and barley. Dig your sweet potatoes when the weather becomes cool and you expect frost.

Iredell—John B Holman, d., Cool Spring; Thomas J Williams, d., Mooresville.
Jackson—Walter E Moore, d., Webster.
Johnston—J F Brown, d., Earpsboro; D G Johnson, d., Rome.
Jones—G G Noble, d., Tuckahoe.
Lincoln—J F Reinhart, d., Reinhart.
Lenoir—W W Carraway, d., Kinston.
Macon—J Frank Ray, d., Franklin.
Madison—A P Bryan, r., Mars Hill.
Martin—W H Stubbs, d., Williamston.
McDowell—E J Justice, d., Marion.
Mecklenburg—Heriot Clarkson, d., Charlotte; R M Ransom, d.; J E Henderson, d.
Mitchell—J R Pritchard, r., Bakersville.
Montgomery—Wm. Cochran, d., Mt Gilead.
Moore—John L Currie, d., Carthage.
Nash—Cicero Ellen, d., Nashville.
New Hanover—George Rountree, d., M S Willard, d., Wilmington.
Northampton—W C Courts, r., Jackson.
Onslow—Frank Thompson, d., Jacksonville.
Orange—S M Gattis, d., Hillsboro.
Pamlico—Williams, r.
Pasquotank—J A Leigh, d., Elizabeth City.
Pender—Gibson James, d., Maple Hill.
Perquimans—F H Nicholson, r., Hertford.
Person—C W Whitfield, d., Yancey.
Pitt—W J Nichols, d., Greenville; T H Barnhill, d., Bethel.
Polk—J W McFarland, r., Poor's Ford.
Randolph—T J Redding, d., Asheboro; J M Barrow, r., Carraway.
Richmond—H C Wall, d., Rockingham; Hector McLean, d., Laurinburg.
Robinson—G B Pattison, d., Maxton; J S Oliver, d., Lumberton.
Rockingham—Joseph H Lane, d., Leaksville; J R Garrett, d., Thompsonville.
Rowan—Lee S Overman, d., Salisbury; D R Julian, d., Salisbury.
Rutherford—J F Alexander, d., Rutherfordton.
Sampson—Allen Daughtry, r., Clinton; L L Mathis, p., Clinton.
Stanly—J M Brown, d., Albemarle.
Stokes—R J Peatree, r., Germanton.
Surry—W W Hampton, r., Dobson.
Swain—R L Leatherwood, d., Bryson City.
Transylvania—G W Wilson, d., Brevard.
Tyrrell—d., Columbia.
Union—R L Stevens, d., Waxhaw.
Vance—J Z Eaton, r., Henderson.
Wake—J D Boushall, d.; Gaston Powell, d., W H Holland, d., Raleigh.
Warren—J H Wright, r., Warrenton.
Washington—T L Tarkinton, r., Mackey's Ferry.
Watauga—W B Councill, Jr d., Boone.
Wayne—W R Allen, d., Goldsboro; J M Wood, d., Goldsbor.
Wilkes—E B Hendrin, r., W A Thorp, r., Wilkesboro.
Wilson—H G Connor, d., Wilson.
Yadkin—H S Williams, r., East Bend.
Yancey W M Austin, d., Boonville.

Democrats.. 94
Fusionists 26

Total.. 120

11th Month. NOVEMBER, 1899. 30 Days.

Moon's Phases.

	D. H. M.		D. H. M.
New Moon,	3 5 18 a.m.	Full Moon,	17 5 10 a.m.
First Quarter,	10 8 26 a.m.	Last Quarter,	25 1 26 a.m.

Day of Month.	Day of Week.	Sun rises.	Sun sets.	Sun fast.	Sun's decline south.	ASPECTS OF PLANETS AND OTHER MISCELLANEOUS MATTER.	Moon's place.	Moon rises or sets.	Moon south.	High tides at Beaufort
1	We	6 22	5 3	16	14 31	America discov 1492		4 41	10 16	5 42
2	Thu	6 23	5 2	16	14 50	Jenny Lind died 1887		5 42	11 3	6 29
3	Fri	6 24	5 1	16	15 9	☌ ♃ ☾ Dak amit '89		sets	11 53	7 19
4	Sat	6 25	5 0	16	15 28	☌ ☿ ♂; ☌ ♀ ☾		5 40	eve	8 9
45	Twenty-third Sunday after Trinity.					Day's length 10 hours 31 m				
5	A	6 26	4 59	16	15 46	☌ ♅ ☾ Guy Fawkes day		6 32	1 42	9 8
6	Mo	6 27	4 58	16	16 4	☌ ♄ ☾; ♀ in ☊. [in Eng		7 31	2 39	10 5
7	Tue	6 28	4 56	16	16 22	Dr Braxt'n Craven d '82		8 36	3 36	11 2
8	We	6 29	4 56	16	16 40	☌ ☿ ♅ Milton d 1674		9 44	4 32	11 58
9	Thu	6 30	4 55	16	16 57	Dr Lovic Pierce d 1879		10 54	5 27	morn
10	Fri	6 31	4 55	16	17 14	Mart. Luther b 1483		morn	6 19	0 53
11	Sat	6 32	4 54	16	17 30	Washington ad '89		0 4	7 9	1 45
46	Twenty-fourth Sunday after Trinity.					Day's length 10 hours 19 m.				
12	A	6 33	4 53	16	17 47	☿ Gre Hel Lat S		1 14	7 59	2 35
13	Mo	6 34	4 53	15	18 3	☌ ♃ ✳ Fall meteors 1833		2 24	8 50	3 25
14	Tue	6 35	4 52	15	18 18	☌ ♀ ♅ Merriman d 1892		3 34	9 42	4 26
15	We	6 36	4 51	15	18 34	Dom Pedro dethron '89		4 44	10 35	5 8
16	Thu	6 37	4 51	15	18 49	☿ Gre Elong E		5 53	11 30	6 1
17	Fri	6 38	4 50	15	19 4	Suez canal op '69		rises	morn	6 56
18	Sat	6 39	4 50	15	19 18	Suez aanal op '69		5 44	0 26	7 52
47	Twenty-fifth Sunday after Trinity.					Day's length 10 hours 8 m.				
19	A	6 40	4 49	14	19 32	☌ ♆ ☾ Leg mt N'brn 1771		6 41	1 21	8 47
20	Mo	6 41	4 49	14	19 46	Grt erup Mt Vesuv 1857		7 39	2 15	9 41
21	Tue	6 42	4 49	14	19 59	Berlin decree 1806		8 38	3 6	10 32
22	We	6 43	4 48	13	20 12	Gen Jos Graham d 1836		9 38	3 54	11 20
23	Thu	6 44	4 47	13	20 25	Gov Ellis b 1820		10 36	4 39	eve
24	Fri	6 45	4 47	13	20 37	Bat Lookout mt '63		11 33	5 22	0 48
25	Sat	6 46	4 46	13	20 49	Bat Mis Ridge '63		morn	6 4	1 30
48	Twenty-sixth Sunday after Trinity.					Day's length 9 hours 58 m.				
26	A	6 47	4 46	12	21 0	☿ sta. Bish Marvin d '75		0 30	6 44	2 10
27	Mo	6 48	4 46	12	21 11	☌ ♀ ♄ J H Wheeler d '94		1 26	7 26	2 52
28	Tue	6 49	4 46	12	21 22	Irving died 1859		2 25	8 9	3 35
29	We	6 50	4 46	11	21 32	☌ ♅ ✳ Sav'nah tak 1778		3 25	8 54	4 20
30	Thu	6 51	4 46	11	21 42	Saint Andrew		4 28	9 42	5 8

WEATHER CONJECTURES—November—1, 2, 3, rainy; 4, 5, 6, 7, 8, 9, 10, rain; 11, 12, 13, 14, 15, 16, 17, changeable; 18 19, 20, 21, 22, 23, 24, 25, rainy; 26, 27, 28, 29, 30, fair.

FARM AND GARDEN WORK FOR NOVEMBER.—Sow your first crop of peas and a few turnips. Plant out onions raised from seed in August and September. Plant Windsor and long pod beans. Dress asparagus and artichokes.

Sow full crops of rye, barley, wheat and other small grains. Harvest your sweet potatoes.

SUPERIOR COURTS OF NORTH CAROLINA FOR 1899.

Compiled by FAB. H. BUSBEE, Attorney.

JUDGES.			SOLICITORS.		
NAMES.	DISTRICT.	RESIDENCE.	NAMES.	DISTRICT.	RESIDENCE.
Geo. H. Brown,	1	Washington.	Geo. W. Ward,	1	Elizabeth City
Henry R. Bryan,	2	New Bern.	W. E. Daniel,	2	Weldon.
E. W. Timberlake,	3	Louisburg.	Larry I. Moore.	3	Greenville.
W. S. O'B. Robinson,	4	Goldsboro.	Edward W. Pou.	4	Smithfield.
Thos. J. Shaw,	5	Greensboro.	A. L. Brooks,	5	Greensboro.
O. H. Allen,	6	Kinston.	Rodolph Duffy,	6	Jacksonville.
Thos. A. McNeill,	7	Lumberton.	C. M. McLean,	7	Elizabethtown
A. L. Coble,	8	Statesville.	Wiley Rush,	8	Asheboro.
Henry R. Starbuck,	9	Winston.	M. L. Mott,	9	Wilkesboro.
Jacob W. Bowman,	10	Bakersville.	J. F. Spainhour,	10	Lenoir.
W. Alexander Hoke,	11	Lincolnton.	J. L. Webb,	11	Shelby.
Fred. Moore,	12	Asheville.	Jas. W. Ferguson,	12	Waynesville.

Time of Holding Courts.

FIRST JUDICAL DISTRICT.

Spring—Judge Brown.
Fall—Starbuck.
Beaufort—‡Feb 20 2 May 29th 2 Nov 28th 2.
Currituck—March 9th Sept 11th.
Camden—March 13th Sept 11th.
Pasquotank—March 20th Sept 18
Chowan—April 3d Oct 2d.
Perqnimans—March 2d Sept 25.
Gates—April 10th Oct 9th.
Hertford—April 17th Oct 10th.
Washington—April 24th Oct 24th
Tyrrell—May 1st Oct 30th.
Dare—May 3d Nov 6th.
Hyde—May 15th Nov 13th.
Pamlico—May 22d Nov 20th

SECOND JUDICAL DISTRICT.

Spring—Hoke.
Fall—Judge Brown.
Halifax—March 6th 2 †May 29th 2 †Nov 20th 2.
Northampton—April 3d 2 ‡July 31st 2 Oct 23d 2.
Bertie—‡Feb 20th May 1st Sept 11th 2 Nov 6th.
Craven—‡Feb 6th 2 †May 8th 2 †Nov 27th 2.
Warren—†March 20th 2 †Sept 18th 2.
Edgecombe—†April 17th 2 †June 12th 2 ⅔Oct 9th 2.

THIRD JUDICIAL DISTRICT.

Spring—Judge Moore.
Fall—Judge Hoke.
Pitt—Jan 9th 2 ⅔Mch 6th 2 April 3d 2 Sept 8th 2 Dec 4th 2.

Franklin—Jan 23d 2 April 17th 2 Oct 23d.
Wilson—⅔Feb 6th 2 ⅔June 5th 2 Oct 30th 2.
Vance—Feb 20th 2 May 22 2 Oct 2d 2.
Martin—March 20th 2 Sept 4th 2.
Nash—†May 1st 2 Nov 29th 2.

FOURTH JUDICAL DISTRICT.

Spring—Judge Brown.
Fall—Judge Moore.
Wake—*Jan 9th 2 †Feb 27th 2. *March 27th 2 †April 24th July 10 2 *Sept 25th †Oct 23.
Wayne—Jan 23th 2 April 17th Sept 11th 2 Oct 16.
Harnett—Feb 20th Sept 4th ‡Nov 27th 2.
Johnston—March 13th 2 Aug 20. Nov 13th 2.

FIFTH JUDICAL DISTRICT.

Spring—Judge Bryan.
Fall—Judge Brown.
Durham—Jan 10th 2 †March 27th 2 *May 10th *Sept 4th †Oct 2d 2.
Granville—Jan 30th 2 April 24th 2 July 24th 2 Nov. 20th 2.
Chatham—Feb 13th May 8th Sept 18th 2.
Guilford—Feb 20th 2 June 5th 3 Aug 21st 2 Dec 4th 2.
Alamance—March 13th May 22d ⅔Sept 11th Nov 6th.
Orange—March 20th ⅔May 29th Aug 7th Oct 30th.
Caswell—April 10th Aug 22d Oct 16th.

12th Month. DECEMBER, 1899. 31 Days.

Moon's Phases.

	D. H. M.		D. H. M.
New Moon,	2 7 39 p.m.	Full Moon,	16 8 22 p.m.
First Quarter,	9 3 54 p.m.	Last Quarter,	24 16 49 p.m.

(left margin, vertical:) THE E. C. BROOKS CO., Portsmouth, Va. Correspondence Solicited. Quotations furnished.

Day of Month.	Day of Week.	Sun rises.	Sun sets.	Sun fast.	Sun's decline south.	ASPECTS OF PLANETS AND OTHER MISCELLANEOUS MATTER.	Moon's place.	Moon rises or sets.	Moon south.	High tides at Beaufort.
1	Fri	6 52	4 46	10	21 51	☿ in ♎; ♂ ♃ ☾		5 32	10 35	6 1
2	Sat	6 53	4 46	10	22 0	♂ ☌ ☾ *Sun eclip inv*		6 35	11 30	6 56

49 First Sunday in Advent. Day's length 9 hours 52 minutes.

3	A	6 54	4 46	10	22 9	♂ ☿ ☾; ♂ ☌ ☾; ♂ ♄ ☾		sets	eve	7 50
4	Mo	6 55	4 46	9	22 17	♂ ♀ ☾ Tyndall d 1893		6 25	1 28	8 54
5	Tue	6 56	4 46	9	22 25	♂ ☿ ✳ Inferior		7 35	2 26	9 52
6	We	6 57	4 46	8	22 32	☿ in peri. J Davis d '89		8 46	3 22	10 48
7	Thu	6 58	4 46	8	22 39	Ed Badger d 1878		9 56	4 16	11 42
8	Fri	6 59	4 46	8	22 45	Zola died 1895		11 6	5 7	morn
9	Sat	7 0	4 46	7	22 51	Milton born 1608		morn	5 57	0 33

50 Second Sunday in Advent. Day's length 9 hours 46 minutes.

10	A	7 1	4 46	7	22 57	♂ ☿ ☽ Miss admitted '17		0 15	6 46	1 23
11	Mo	7 2	4 47	6	23 2	Indiana admitted 1816		1 25	7 36	2 12
12	Tue	7 2	4 47	6	23 6	Browning d 1889		2 34	8 28	3 2
13	We	7 3	4 47	5	23 10	Robt Tombs d 1884		3 41	9 21	3 54
14	Thu	7 3	4 47	5	23 14	*Halcion Days.*		4 46	10 15	4 47
15	Fri	7 4	4 47	4	23 17	☿ sta. Sit Bull k '90		5 48	11 10	5 41
16	Sat	7 4	4 48	4	23 20	☿ Gre Hel Lat N		6 48	morn	6 36

51 Third Sunday in Advent. Day's length 9 hours 44 minutes.

17	A	7 4	4 48	3	23 22	♂ ♅ ✳. Whittier b 1807		rises	0 4	7 30
18	Mo	7 5	4 49	3	23 24	♂ ♄ ✳ Sir H Davy b 1779		6 25	0 56	8 22
19	Tue	7 6	4 49	2	23 25	Harry 11th crncfd 1154		7 25	1 46	9 12
20	We	7 7	4 49	2	23 26	S Carolina seceded '60		8 23	2 33	9 59
21	Thu	7 7	4 50	1	23 27	*Sun ent. cap; winter com*		9 21	3 18	10 44
22	Fri	7 8	4 50	½	n'rth	Dr Winchester d '76		10 18	3 59	11 25
23	Sat	7 8	4 51	½	23 26	♂ ☿ ☽ Grady d '89		11 15	4 40	eve

52 Fourth Sunday in Advent. Day's length 9 hours 43 minutes.

24	A	7 9	4 51	0	23 25	☾ Thackary d '63		morn	5 20	0 46
25	Mo	7 9	4 52	1	23 24	☾ CHRISMAS DAY		0 2	6 2	1 28
26	Tue	7 9	4 53	1	23 22	Stephen Girard d '31		1 11	6 45	2 11
27	We	7 10	4 53	2	23 19	*St. John, Evangelist*		2 11	7 31	2 57
28	Thu	7 10	4 54	2	23 16	McCaulay d 1859		3 13	8 21	3 47
29	Fri	7 10	4 54	3	23 13	♂ ♃ ☾ Gladstone b 1809		4 16	9 14	4 40
30	Sat	7 11	4 55	3	23 9	♂ ♄ ☾; ♂ ☿ ☾		5 19	10 12	5 38

53 First Sunday after Christmas. Day's length 9 hours 44 minutes.

| 31 | A | 7 11 | 4 56 | 4 | 23 5 | Johnson b 1808 | | 6 10 | 11 11 | 6 37 |

WEATHER CONJECTURES—December—1, 2, fair; 3, 4, 5, 6, 7, 8, 9, fair if wind N. W.; rainy if S. or S. W.; 10, 11, 12, 13, 14, 15, 16, changeable; 17, 18, 19, 20, 21, 22, 23, 24, changeable; 25, 26, 27, 28, 29, 30, 31, fair.

FARM AND GARDEN WORK FOR DECEMBER.—Plant peas of all kinds; set out onions, garlic, eschalots and cabbage. Sow a few lettuce, spinach, carrots and radishes. You may try a few Irish potatoes.

Finish picking cotton; get out crops of rice and prepare for market. Commence plowing, ditching, draining and manuring as early as possible for next year's crop.

Person—April 17th Aug 14th Nov 15th.

SIXTH JUDICAL DISTRICT.

Spring—Judge Timberlake.
Fall—Judge Bryan.
Pender—March 6th Sept 11th 2.
Greene—Feb 27th Aug 7th Nov 27th.
New Hanover—§Jan 23d 2 §April 17th 2 §Sept 25th 2.
Lenoir—May 8th 2 Nov 13th 2.
Duplin—Fec 20th July 31st Dec 4th.
Sampson—Feb 6th 2 May 1st Oct 9th 2.
Carteret—March 20th Oct 23d.
Jones—27th Oct 30th.
Onslow—April 3d Nov 6th.

SEVENTH JUDICIAL DISTRICT.

Spring—Judge Robinson.
Fall—Judge Timberlake.
Columbus—March 13thAug 14th. Nov 8th Oct 23d.
Anson—*Jan 9th §April 17th, Sept 4th §Oct 30th.
Cumberland—§March27th §April 2 §May 8th 2 *July 25th §Nov 13th 2.
Robeson—§Feb 13th §May 1st §Dec 4th 2.
Richmond—*Jan 16th Tuesday 2 April 24th *May 23d * ept 4th 2 Nov 6th.
Bladen—March 6th Tuesday Oct 2d Tuesday 2.
Brunswick—March 20th Oct 16th
Moore—§Jan 30th 2 §April 3d 2 §Aug 21st 2 Nov 27th.

EIGHTH JUDICIAL DISTRICT.

Spring—Judge Shaw.
Fall—Judge Robinson.
Cabarrus—Jan 23d 2 July 24th 2.
Iredell—Feb 6th 2 May 22 2 Aug 17th Nov 6th.
Rowan—Feb 20th 2 May 8th 2 Aug 21st 2 Nov 27th.
Davidson—March 6th 2 Sep 4th 2.
Randolph—March 20th 2 July 11th 2 Nov 20th.
Montgomery—Jan 2d 2 April 17th Oct 3d 2.
Yadkin—May 1st Oct 23d 2.

NINTH JUDICAL DISTRICT.

Spring—Judge Allen.
Fall—Judge Shaw.
Alexander—Jan 23d July 17th.
Rockingham—Jan 30th 2 July 28 Oct 30th 2.
Forsyth—Feb 20th 2 May 15th 2 July 31 2 Nov 27th 2.
Wilkes—March 6th 2 Aug 28th.
Alleghany—April 3d Sep 11th.
Davie—April 10th 2 Sep 18th 2.
Stokes—April 24th 2 Oct 16 2.
Surry—March 20th 2 Oct 2nd 2.

TENTH JUDICIAL DISTRICV.

Spring—Judge McNeill.
Fall—Judge Allen.
Catawba—Feb 20th 2 July 3d Oct 30th 2.
McDowell—†March 6th 2 †Sept 18th 2.
Burke—March 20th 2 Oct 2d 2.
Caldwell—April 2d 2 Oct 16th 2.
Ashe—April 24th ‡July 24th 2 Nov 13th.
Watauga—May 1st ‡Aug 7th Nov 20.
Mitchell—May 8th 2 Aug 21d 2 Nov 27th.
Yancey—May 22d Sept 4th 2.

ELEVENTH JUDICIAL DISTRICT.

Spring—Judge Coble.
Fall—Judge McNeill.
Union—*†Jan 30th 3 †for 2d 3d week *†Aug 22d 2.
Stanly—March 6th 2 Sept 4th 2.
Mecklenburg—†Jan 23d †March 20th 2 †Oct 2d 2 †June 5th †Dec 16th
Gaston—Feb 20th 2 Sept 18th 2.
Lincoln—April 3d 2 Oct 16th.
Cleveland—April 17th 2Oct 23d 2.
Rutherford—May 1st 2 Nov 6th 2.
Polk—May 15th Nov 21st.
Henderson—†May 22d 2 †Nov 27th 2.

TWELFTH JUDICIAL DISTRICT.

Spring—Judge Starbuck.
Fall—Judge Coble.
Madison—†Feb27th 2†July 21st 2.
Buncombe—†March 13th 3 †Aug 14th 3 †Dec 4th 2.
Transylvania—April 13th Sep 4th.
Haywood—†April 10th 2 †Sept 11th 2.
Jackson—April 24th 2 Sept 25th.
Macon—March 8th Oct 2d.
Clay—May 15th Oct 9th.
Cherokee—†May22d2*†Oct16th2.
Graham—June 5th 3 Nov 6th 2.
Swain—June 12th 3 Nov 20th 2.

CRIMINAL COURTS.

EASTERN DISTRICT.

Judge—Sutton of Fayetteville.

New Hanover—*Jan 2d March 13th Oct 9th.

Warren—*Jan 16th July 10th.

Vance—*Feb 14th.

Edgecombe—*Feb 13th *Nov 6th.

Craven—*Feb 20th Oct 2d.

Halifax—*Feb 29th *Dec 4th.

Mecklenburg—*April 10th *Sept 4th.

Robeson—April 17th *Oct 16th.

Cumberland—*Feb 6th*Sept 18th.

Wilson—*May 28th *Oct 17th Aug 21st.

Nash—*Jan 23 Sept 11th.

WESTERN DISTRICT,

Judge—Hamilton G Ewart of Hendersonville.

Solicitor—Robt S McCall Asheville.

Haywood—*Jan 9th *July 3d,

Buncombe—*Jan 23d April 24th *July 24th ⅜Oct 23d.

Madison—*Feb 20th June 12th Nov 13th.

Henderson—†Sept 11th April 10.

McDowell—*July 10th*Dec 11th.

*For criminal cases.

⅜†For civil cases alone.

(2)Means two weeks, etc.

‡For civil cases alone, except jail cases.

U. S. CIRCUIT AND DISTRICT COURTS.

Charles H. Simonton, Charleston, S. C., Judge of Fourth Circuit of U. S. Courts.

Nathan Goff, West Virginia, Judge of U. S. Circuit Court of Appeals for Fourth District.

WESTERN DISTRICT.—H. G. Ewart, Hendersonville, Judge; A. E. Haton, District Attorney; Spencer Blackburn, Assistant Attorney; S. L. Trogden, Clerk. *Greensboro*—Circuit and District—April 3d, October 2d. *Statesville*—Circuit and District—H. C. Cowles, Clerk; April 17th October 16th. *Asheville*—Circuit and District—C. B. Moore, Clerk; May 1st, November 6th. *Charlotte*—Circuit and District—H. C. Cowles, Clerk; June 12th, December 11th.

EASTERN DISTRICT.—T. R. Purnell, Judge; C. M. Bernard, Greenville, District Attorney; O. C. Spears and E. A. Johnson, Assistant Attorneys; W. C. Brooks, Deputy Clerk. *Elizabeth City*—District Court—April 17th, October 16th. *Newbern*—District Court—Geo Green, Deputy Clerk; Newbern, April 24th, October 23d. *Wilmington*—Circuit and District—N. J. Riddick, Clerk; V. Royster, Assistant Clerk in Raleigh; W. H. Shaw, Clerk of District and Deputy of Circuit Court at Wilmington; H. C. Dockery, Marshall; May 1st, October 30th. *Raleigh*—Circuit Court—N. J. Riddick, Clerk; V. Royster Clerk in Raleigh; W. H. Shaw, Clerk of District and Deputy of Circuit Court at Wilmington; H. C. Dockery, Marshall; Raleigh, May 29th, December 4th.

The following is the war chronology:

April 21—President signs order for North Atlantic Squadron to sail for Cuoa.

April 22—Squadron leaves Key West.

Apri 2?—President issued call for 125,000 volunteers.

April 24—Asiatic Squadron sails for the Philippines.

April 24—Spain declares war.

April 25—Congress declares war has existed since April 21.

April 27—Batteries at Matanzas bombarded.

April 28—Batteries at Cienfugos bombarded.

April 30—Batteries at Cabanas bombarded.

May 1—Spanish fleet at Manilla destroyed.

May 7—Mantanzas forts shelled.

May 9—Fight off Cardenas between the Winslow and three Spanish gunboats.

May 11—Ensign Worth Bagley and four sailors killed on the Winslow in an action off Cardenas, the first blood lost in the war. Also on the same day the attack was made on Cienfugos.

May 12—San Juan de Porto Rico bombarded.

May 12—Cardenas shelled.

May 13—Flying Squadron leaves Hampton Roads.

May 18—Flying Squadron reaches Key West.

May 18—Santiago bombarded.

May 19—Cervera's Squadron in Santiago harbor.

May 25—President issues second call for 75,000 volunteers.

May 25—First Manilla expedition leaves

May 31—Santiago forts bombarded.

June 3—Collier Merrimac sunk.

June 6—Bombardment of Santiago forts.

June 8—Shafter's force leaves Tampa.

June 8—Caimanera bombarded.

June 9—Marines land at Guantanamo.

June 11—Fight at Guantanamo; Spaniards repulsed.

June 14—Army sails from Tampa.

June 15. Spanish defeat at Guantanamo.

June 16—Fort Caimanera demolished.

June 19—Shafter's army arrives at Baiquiri.

June 21—Charleston captures the Ladrones.

June 22 and 23—Shafter's army lands.

June 23—Juragua captured.

June 24—Fight at La Quasina; Spaniards repulsed.

June 26—Cadiz fleet at Port Said.

June 26—Shafter occupies Sevilla.

June 27—Shafter within three miles of Santiago.

June 28—Third Manilla expedition sails.

June 29—First Manilla expedition arrives at Manilla.

June 30—Caney evacuated by Spaniards.

July 1—Outer defences of Santiago taken.

July 2—San Juan, near Santiago, taken.

July 3—Cervera's fleet destroyed

July 5—Camara's fleet at Suez.

July 6—Spanish cruiser Alfonso XII; destroyed.

July 7—Dewey captures Isla Grande and 1,300 prisoners.

July 8—Camara's fleet returned to Spain.

July 10—Bombardment of Santiago resumed; Linares refuses unconditional surrender.

July 10—Bombardment continued and investment completed.

July 13—Truce.

July 14—Santiago surrenders.

July 15—Spanish Cabinet declares martial law.

July 16—Gen. Shafter announces terms of Gen. Toral's surrender

July 17—American flag is raised over Santiago de Cuba and Gen. Kibben made military governor.

July 18—War council orders invasion of Porto Rico; Manzanillo bombarded.

July 19—British naval officers at Manilla promise help to Dewey.

July 20—Spanish cabinet reported as agreed to negotiate for peace.

July 21—Gen. Garcia withdraws his army from Shafter's support.

OFFICERS FROM ELECTION OF NOVEMBER, 1898—CORRECTED ANNUALLY.

COUNTY TOWN	CLERKS	REGISTERS	SHERIFFS	SUPERVISORS OF SCHOO
Graham,	J. D. Kernodle,	Chas O'Thompson,	L. B. McAdams,	Rev P H Fleming.
Taylorsville,	A. L. Watts,	V W Teague,	J Y Williams,	A. Frank Sharp.
Sparta,	L. N. Edwards,	S F Thompson,	Dr B Edwards	Prof S W Brown.
Wadesboro,				w D Redfearn.
Jefferson,	A. S. Ellis,	D A Osborne,	P G McNeill,	J w Jones.
Washington,	G. Wilkens,	Gilbert Rumley,	R T Hodges,	Dr Burton Suttley.
Windsor,	W. L. Lyon,	E E Etheridge,	T C Boone,	R w Askew.
Elizabethtown,	A. M. McNeill,	J S Williams,	S G Wooten,	D S Perry.
Southport,	Thos. L. Wines,	John W Brooks,	D R Walker,	Isaac Jennette.
Asheville,	T. C. Starnes,	J J Mackey,	R F Lee,	D L Ellis.
Morganton,	P. M. Patton,	J H Giles,	C M McDowell,	Rev R L Patton.
Concord,	J. M. Cook,	W E Johnson,	J Lawson Peck,	Prof H T Ludwig.
Lenoir,	J. V. McCall,	W D Ninish,	A. B. Boyd,	Prof R B Phillips.
Camden Court House.	R. L. Forbes,	Q B Garrett,	W S Bartlett,	C B Garrett.
Beaufort,	L. A. Garner,	W L Arrington,	A S Wells,	Joseph Pigott.
Yanceyville,	Thos. H. Harrison,	Joth T Groves,	J T Dombo,	A E Henderson.
Newton,	L. H. Phillips,	P M Dellinger,	J R Blackwelder,	R B Lineberry.
Pittsboro,	R. A. Dixon,	John T Paschal,	James J Johnson.	I M Lovingood.
Murphy,	S. W. Lovingood,	J C McDonald,	A J Martin,	w F watson.
Edenton,	H. C. Privatt,	M A Hughes,	A Q Elliott,	w J winchester.
Hayesville,	C. C. Standridge,	J O Sowell,	W H Hogsed,	J A Anthony.
Shelby,	L. J. Hoyle,	J F Roberts,	A B Sutle,	w H Sellars.
Whiteville,	H. C. Moffitt,	R L Powell,	J G Butler,	Rev johr S Long.
Newbern,	E. W. Carpenter,	John B Willis,	J L Hahn,	H l Everett.
Fayetteville,	A A McKeithen,	W H Bray,	George A Burns,	J w Ritter.
Currituck C. H.	E W Ansell,		R E Flora.	Lemuel Bassnight.
Manteo,		B O Morris,		Robert S Green.
Lexington,	W R Ellis,	B Frank Pearsall,	Jesse L Sheek,	C M Sheets.
Mocksville,	Herbert Smith,	John Suitt,	L Middleton,	Prof R w Millard.
Kenansville,	C B Green,	B I Dougan,	F D Markham,	C w Massey.
Durham,	Ed Pennington,	B F Byerly,	W L Stellings,	R M Davis.
Tarboro,	N S Wilson,	I T Clifton,	E T Knapps,	Dr A P Davis.
Winston,	W K Williams,	M A Carpenter,	H C Kearney,	B S Mitchell.
Louisburg,	C G Cornwell,	Lycurgus Holler,	W T Lovy,	L M Hoffman.
Dallas,	R V McElroy,	Robert B Slaughter,	R O Riddick,	John R walton.
Gatesville,	J G Hunt,	John B Mayes,	J A Ammons,	J N Moody.
Robbinsville.	John R Dale,	Charles A Lassiter,		Alexander Baker.
Oxford,	John J Nelson.	A G Kirkman,	B W Edwards,	Fred L Carr.
Snow Hill,				Prof J K wharton.
Greensboro,				col Aaron Prescott.
Halifax Court House.			J H Gilmer,	Rev J A Campbell.
Lillington,	J H Withers,	A O Holloway,	S A Solomon,	A Garner.
Waynesville,	N P Walker,	H B Noore,	W J Haynes,	R H Slaton
Hendersonville.	G M Pace.	W A Hood.	Jonathan Williams,	

No.	County	Town				
46	Hyde	Swan Quarter	R D Harris,	H W Brown,	T G Mann,	H L McGowan,
47	Iredell	Statesville	Jas. Hartness,	W W Turner,	J H Wycoff,	J A Butler,
48	Jackson	Webster	F K Alley,	James R Long,	William A Henson,	J H Painter,
49	Johnston	Smithfield	W S Stevens,	J W Stephenson,	J T Ellington,	Prof Ira T Turlington,
50	Jones	Trenton	S E Koonce,	W H Cox,	D H Harrison,	w H Hammond,
51	Lenoir	Kinston	H V Williams,	W D Suggs,	J O Wooten,	E A Simkins,
52	Lincoln	Lincolnton	A Nixson,	H A Self,	J K Kline,	J E Hoover,
53	Macon	Franklin	Lee Crawford,	H D Dean,	C T Keane,	J R Pendergrass,
54	Madison	Marshall	J H White,	Van B Davis,	K S Ramsey,	w P. Jervis,
55	Martin	Williamston	J A Hobbs,	W C Manning,	J C Crawford,	R. J. Peele,
56	McDowell	Marion	Thos Morris,	T W Wilson,	R L Nichols,	w F wood,
57	Mecklenburg	Charlotte	J A Russell,	A M McDonald,	A W Wollac,	R B. Hunter,
58	Mitchell	Bakersville	J O Bannan,	T B Garland,	R H Bradshaw,	Agustas Masters,
59	Montgomery	Troy	C A Armstrong,	W D Allen,	W D Clark,	George L Reynolds,
60	Moore	Carthage	D A McDonald,	N L McIntosh,	S S Jones,	Eugene M Cole,
61	Nash	Nashville	Thos Sills,	J A Whitaker,	W M Warren,	L M Conyers,
62	New Hanover	Wilmington	John D Taylor,	W H Biddle,	W G McRae,	M C S Noble,
63	Northampton	Jackson	J T Flythe,	Roberts,	F W Hargett,	Paul J Long,
64	Onslow	Jacksonville	John M Burton,	I E Ketchum,	John K Hughes,	A w Cooper,
65	Orange	Hillsboro	D H Hamilton,	John Lees,		John Thompson,
66	Pamlico	Bayboro	W H Jennings,	M B Culpepper,	N G Grandy,	D. F. Harris,
67	Pasquotank	Elizabeth City	W W Larkins,	J P Stringfield,	W W Alderman,	Gaston Pool,
68	Pender	Burgaw	R V Perry,	W R White,	A F Riddick,	T H w McIntyre,
69	Perquimans	Hertford	D W Bradsher,	H J Whitt,	J B Sims,	Francis Pickard,
70	Person	Roxboro	D O Moore,	T R Moore,	G M Mooring,	G F Holloway,
71	Pitt	Greenville	N B Thompson,	A L McMurray,	W O Robertson,	J R Single,
72	Polk	Columbus	G G Hendricks,	J T Winslow,	w F Redding,	S A Hudgin,
73	Randolph	Ashboro				N C English,
74	Richmond	Rockingham	W H Humphrey,	Joe Bale,	G B McLeod,	M N McIver,
75	Rockingham	Wentworth	J V Price,	J A Scales,	H W Hutcherson,	w R Surles,
76	Rowan	Salisbury	W G Watson,	N H Woodson,	J M Monroe,	E P Ellington,
77	Rutherford	Rutherfordton	M O Dickerson,	Jas P Jones,	E A Martin,	R G Kizer,
78	Sampson	Clinton	W R Pigford,	O P Herring,	J W Marshburn,	C C Gettys,
79	Stanly	Albemarle	R A Crowell,	I N Suggs,	G R McCain,	Street Brewer,
80	Stokes	Danbury	S O Petree,	I M Gordon,	R P Joyce,	J A Spence,
81	Surry	Dobson	O H Haynes,	T W Davis,	J M Davis,	Prof M T Chilton,
82	Swain	Bryson City	A J Hall,	A G De Hart,	O C Martin,	John w williams,
83	Transylvania	Brevard	T T Loftis,	Wm Henry,	N B McGaha,	J U Gible,
84	Tyrrell	Columbia				Judson Coon,
85	Union	Monroe	E A Armfield,	J M Stewart,	B A Horne,	James L Norman,
86	Vance	Henderson	Henry Perry,	Kenneth Edwards,	W H Smith,	Plummer Stewart,
87	Wake	Raleigh	W M Ross,	W H Hood,	M W Page,	A M Mattox,
88	Warren	Warrenton	W A White,	N F Thornton,	J B w Jones,	H w Norris,
89	Washington	Plymouth	W M Bateman,	W H Stall,	J L Phelps,	James R Rodwell,
90	Watauga	Boone		Jacob May,	w H Caloway,	w A Gibson,
91	Wayne	Goldsboro	J Y Ormand,	G O Kornegay,	B F Scott,	L H Michael,
92	Wilkes	Wilkesboro				K T Atkins,
93	Wilson	Wilson	J B Hardin,	Wm B Barnes,	W D P Sharp,	James H Foote,
94	Yadkin	Yadkinville	W A Hall,	J L Craton,	A P Woodruff,	James w Hayes,
95	Yancey	Burnsville	J B Ray,	J R Young,	w B wilson,	Rev J H Patterson,
						william McIntosh,

The Sun Life of Canada writes policies in amount from **$50** to **$50,000** on applicants from **1 year old up to 70.** Policies are Self-premium paying after two years.   J. R. JOHNSTON, Mgr. for North and South Carolina, Raleigh, N. C.

PUBLIC WORKS AND INSTITUTIONS.

NORTH CAROLINA COLLEGE OF AGRICULTURE AND MECHANIC ARTS, near Raleigh. Opened October 3, 1889. Col. J. C. L. Harris of Raleigh, President of Board of Trustees.
Alex. Q. Holliday, LL. D., President, assisted by 26 Professors.
[This is one of the Colleges that has a large future.]
THE N. C. AGRICULTURAL EXPERIMENT STATION is also connected with this College.

State Hospitals.

CENTRAL HOSPITAL, Raleigh. Dr. George L. Kirby, Superintendent.
STATE HOSPITAL, Morganton. Dr. P. L. Murphy, Superintendent.
EASTERN HOSPITAL, Goldsboro. (Colored). Dr. J. F Miller, Sup't.

STATE BOARD OF PHARMACY. E. V. Zoeller, Tarboro, President.
N. C. PHARMACEUTICAL ASSOCIATION. Will Yearby, Durham, Pres't.

State Government.

DANIEL L. RUSSELL, Governor. Salary, $3,000.
CHARLES A. REYNOLDS, Lieut. Governor, and Speaker of the Senate.
CHAS. H. MEBANE, Superintendent Public Schools.
CYRUS THOMPSON, Secretary of State. Salary, $2,000.

BETHEL HILL INSTITUTE,

BETHEL HILL, PERSON COUNTY, N. C.

CO-EDUCATIONAL.

A School of High Grade and Thorough Work.

BEST CHRISTIAN INFLUENCES. HEALTHFUL LOCATION. EIGHT TEACHERS. BOARD $6.70 PER MONTH. TUITION $1.00 TO $3.00.

For further information and catalogue, address

REV. J. A. BEAM,
Principal.

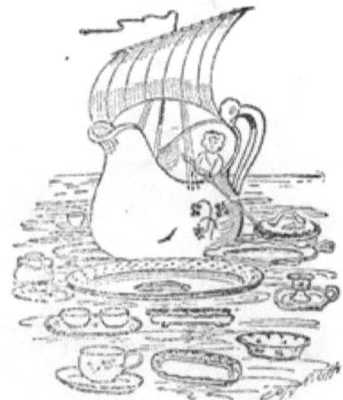

BRANSON'S SHORT CALENDAR FOR 1899.

JANUARY.

S	M	T	W	T	F	S
1	2	3	4	5	6	7
8	9	10	11	12	13	14
15	16	17	18	19	20	21
22	23	24	25	26	27	28
29	30	31				

FEBRUARY.

S	M	T	W	T	F	S
			1	2	3	4
5	6	7	8	9	10	11
12	13	14	15	16	17	18
19	20	21	22	23	24	25
26	27	28				

MARCH.

S	M	T	W	T	F	S
			1	2	3	4
5	6	7	8	9	10	11
12	13	14	15	16	17	18
19	20	21	22	23	24	25
26	27	28	29	30	31	

APRIL.

S	M	T	W	T	F	S
						1
2	3	4	5	6	7	8
9	10	11	12	13	14	15
16	17	18	19	20	21	22
23	24	25	26	27	28	29
30						

MAY.

S	M	T	W	T	F	S
	1	2	3	4	5	6
7	8	9	10	11	12	13
14	15	16	17	18	19	20
21	22	23	24	25	26	27
28	29	30	31			

JUNE.

S	M	T	W	T	F	S
				1	2	3
4	5	6	7	8	9	10
11	12	13	14	15	16	17
18	19	20	21	22	23	24
25	26	27	28	29	30	

JULY.

S	M	T	W	T	F	S
						1
2	3	4	5	6	7	8
9	10	11	12	13	14	15
16	17	18	19	20	21	22
23	24	25	26	27	28	29
30	31					

AUGUST.

S	M	T	W	T	F	S
		1	2	3	4	5
6	7	8	9	10	11	12
13	14	15	16	17	18	19
20	21	22	23	24	25	26
27	28	29	30	31		

SEPTEMBER.

S	M	T	W	T	F	S
					1	2
3	4	5	6	7	8	9
10	11	12	13	14	15	16
17	18	19	20	21	22	23
24	25	26	27	28	29	30

OCTOBER.

S	M	T	W	T	F	S
1	2	3	4	5	6	7
8	9	10	11	12	13	14
15	16	17	18	19	20	21
22	23	24	25	26	27	28
29	30	31				

NOVEMBER.

S	M	T	W	T	F	S
			1	2	3	4
5	6	7	8	9	10	11
12	13	14	15	16	17	18
19	20	21	22	23	24	25
26	27	28	29	30		

DECEMBER.

S	M	T	W	T	F	S
					1	2
3	4	5	6	7	8	9
10	11	12	13	14	15	16
17	18	19	20	21	22	23
24	25	26	27	28	29	30
31						

PRICE LIST.

Vol. 4.] 33 YEAR OF PUBLICATION. No. 3.]

BRANSON'S
AGRICULTURAL
ALMANAC

PRICE, 10 CENTS.

FOR THE YEAR OF OUR LORD

1900,

And until the 4th of July, the 124d year of American Independence.

Carefully Calculated for the Latitude and Longitude of Raleigh, by

LEVI BRANSON, A. M., D. D.

LEVI BRANSON, Publisher, Raleigh, N. C.

COPYRIGHT, 1900, BY LEVI BRANSON.

1. All men have faith in something, hence they work expecting results.—*Branson.*

TIME.

The calculations of this Almanac are made in mean solar or clock time, which is indicated by a well regulated watch or clock, and does not correspond with the Sun precisely, except on four days of the year.

Apparent time is that which makes the Sun come to the meridian at 12 o'clock. No good clock will run with the Sun; if set with the Sun on the 2d day of January, the clock will seem to be one minute too fast on the 3d of January.

To adapt the calculations of this Almanac to apparent time, use the minutes in the column marked "Sun slow" or "Sun fast;" add them when fast, subtract them when slow.

The calculations are made for the Latitude and Longitude of Raleigh, N. C., but the times phases &c., will vary only a few minutes for any part of North Carolina, South Carolina, Georgia, Tennessee or Virginia.

To know where the sign is, find the day of the month, and against the day in the column marked Moon's Signs you have the sign or place of the Moon, and then find he sign; it will give you the part of the body it is supposed to govern.

TWELVE SIGNS OF THE ZODIAC.

The Head and Face sign,   ♈ Aries the Ram......Ar.

♊ Arms.
Gemini...Gem.
Twins.

♋ Heart.
Leo.......Lion.
Lion.

♎ Reins.
Libra......Lib.
Balance.

♐ Thighs.
Sagittarius Sag.
Bowman.

♒ Legs.
Aquarius...Aq.
Waterman.

♉ Neck.
Taurus....Tau.
Bull.

♋ Breast.
Cancer....Can.
Crab.

♍ Bowels.
Virgo.....Vir.
Virgin.

♏ Loins.
Scorpio..Scorp.
Scorpion.

♑ Knees.
CapricornusCap.
Goat.

The ♓ Pisces the Fishes......Pisc.

SIGNS.

SPRING SIGNS.	Arises, or Ram. Taurus, or Bull. Gemini, or Twins.	AUTUMN SIGNS.	Libra, or Balance. Scorpio, or Scorpion. Sagittarius, or Bowman.
SUMMER SIGNS.	Cancer, or Crab-fish Leo, or Lion. Virgo, or Virgin.	WINTER SIGNS.	Capricornus, or Goat. Aquarius, or Waterman. Pices, or Fishes.

SIGNS OF THE PLANETS.

☀ Sun.   ☽ Moon.   ♀ Venus.   ♂ Mars.
♃ Jupiter.   ♄ Saturn.   ☌ In Conjunction.   ☐ Quadrature.
☿ Mercury.   ⛢ Uranus.   ♆ Neptune.   ☊ Ascending Node.
⊕ Earth.   ♆ Opposition. ☋ Decending Node.

MOON'S PHASES.

● New Moon.   ☽ First Quarter.   ○ Full Moon.   ☾ Last Quarter.

CHRONOLGICAL CYCLES AND ERAS.

Dominical Letter	G	Julian Period	6613
Epact	29	Jewish Era	5660
Golden Number	1	Era of Nabonassa	2647
Solar Cycle	5	Olympiads	2676
Roman Indiction	13	Mahommedan Era	1317

MOVABLE FEASTS OF THE CHURCH.

Epiphany	Jan. 6	Palm Sunday	April 8
Septuagesima Sunday	Feb. 11	Easter Sunday	April 15
Sexagesima Sunday	Feb. 18	White Sunday	June 3
Quinquagesima Sunday	Feb. 25	Trinity Sunday	June 10
Ash Wednesday, or Lent	Feb. 28	First Sunday in Advent	Dec. 2
St. Patrick's Day	March 17	Ancension Day	May 24
Good Friday	April 13	First Sunday in Lent	March 4

MORNING STARS.

Mercury will be Morning Star about April 22, August 19, and December 1. Venus will be Morning Star from July 8, till Sept. 15. Jupiter will be Morning Star till May 27, then from Dec. 14 to end of year.

EVENING STARS.

Mercury will be Evening Star about........March 8, July 4, and Oct. 29.
Venus will be Evening Star till ....July 3.
Jupiter will be Evening Star till...................................Dec. 14.

ECLIPSES.

In the year 1900 there will be three Eclipses—two of the *Sun* and one of the *Moon*.

I. *Total Eclipse of the Sun* May 28, visible to North America, and to many other parts of the world. The path of totality will run through Mexico, New Orleans, Mobile, Raleigh, Norfolk, and etc., with an average width of 50 miles, occuring as follows in *Eastern Standard Time*.
Begins in Raleigh ....7:37 A. M.
Total ....8:40 A. M.
Ends..10:10 A. M.
II. *A Partial Eclipse of the Moon*, June 12, visible to North and South America, Spain and Africa, as follows *Eastern Standard Time*.
Moon enters Shadow ....June 12, 10:24 P. M.
Middle of Eclipse..................................June 12, 10:28 P. M.
Leaves Shadow....................................June 12, 10:32 P. M.
Magnitude of Eclipse 0.001.
III. *An Annular Eclipse of the Sun*, November 22, invisible to North America.

TIDES.

The time of tides can readily be found for the following places by adding the hours and minutes opposite the names to the time when the Moon is South on the day to when the tide is sought. The time when the Moon is south is given in the Calendar for every day. The next tide can be foud very nearly by adding 12 hours and 29 minutes to the time of the one previous.

The tides are given in lical time—add 12 minutes for Eastern Standard:

	H. M.		H. M.
Boston	11 12	New York	8 13
Sandy Hook	7 29	Old Point	8 17
Baltimore	6 33	Washington City	7 44
Richmond	4 32	Hatteras Inlet	7 04
Beaufort	7 26	Bald Head	7 26
Southport	7 19	Wilmington	9 06
Charleston	7 26	Savannah	9 33

THE BELL BOOK AND STATIONERY CO.; 914 E. Main St., Richmond, Va.

THE FOUR SEASONS.

Spring commences...March 20, 8 P. M.
Summer commences...June 21, 4 P. M.
Autumn commences...September 23, 7 P. M.
Winter commences...December 22, 1 P. M.

HERSCHEL'S WEATHER PROGNOSTICATOR.

For Foretelling the Weather Through all the Lunations of the year.

This table and the accompanying remarks are the result of many years actual observation, the whole being constructed on a due consideration of the attractions of the Sun and Moon, in their several positions respecting the Earth, and, by simple inspection, it shows the observer what kind of weather will most probably follow the entrance of the Moon into any of its quarters, and that so near the truth as to be seldom or never found to fail.

If the new moon, first quarter, full moon, or last quarter, happen—	IN SUMMER.	IN WINTER.
Between midnight and 2 in the morning............	Fair	Hoar frost unless the wind is S. or S. W.
Between 2 and 4, morning	Cold, with frequent showers........	Snow and stormy.
Between 4 and 6, morning...	Rain............	Rain.
Between 6 and 8, morning...	Wind and rain......	Stormy.
Between 8 and 10, morning	Changeable	Cold rain if wind be W., snow if E.
Between 10 and 12 morning	Frequent Showers...	Cold and high wind.
Between 12 o'clock at noon and 2 in afternoon........	Very rainy........	Rain and snow.
Between 2 and 4, afternoon	Changeable	Fair and mild.
Between 4 and 6, afternoon	Fair	Fair.
Between 6 and 8, aftern'n	Fair if wind N. W.; rainy if S. or S. W.	Fair and frosty wind N. or N. E.; rain or snow if S. or S. W.
Between 8 and 10, afternoon	Ditto	Ditto
Between 10 and midnight...	Fair	Fair and frosty.

OBSERVATIONS.—1. The nearer the time for the Moon's change, first quarter, full and last quarter are to midnight, the fairer will be the weather during the next seven days.

2. The space for this calculation occupies from 10 at night until 2 next morning.

3. The nearer to midday or noon the phase of the Moon happens, the more foul or wet weather may be expected during the next seven days.

4. The space for this calculations occupies from 10 in the forenoon until 2 in the afternoon. These observations refer principally to the Summer, though they affect Spring and Autumn nearly in the same ratio.

5. The Moon's change, first quarter, full and last quarter happening during six of the afternoon hours, i. e., from 4 to 10, may be followed by fair weather, but this is mostly dependent on the wind, as is noted in the table.

6. Though the weather, from a variety of irregular causes, is more uncertain in the later part of Autumn, the whole of Winter and beginning of Spring, yet, in the main, the above observations will apply to those periods also.

7. To prognosticate correctly, especially in those cases where the wind is concerned, the observer should be in sight of a good vane, where the four cardinal points of the heavens are correctly placed.

STATISTICS OF LIBRARIES IN NORTH CAROLINA. 1899.

Through the untiring efforts of our efficient State Librarians, we are enabled to give correctly the great progress that has been made in our State in the last few years towards placing within the reach of the great masses of our people, useful information that has heretofore been beyond the reach of the common class of our citizens, by establishing public Libraries, accessible to all who are in search of useful knowledge,

NAMES OF LIBRARIES.	Where Located.	When Established.	No. of Vols.	Money Used Each Year.	Librarian.
State Library	Raleigh	1841	22,618	$ 500	Miles O Sherrell.
Female College	Asheville		1,000		
Asheville Library	Asheville		3,000	675	Miss F. L. Weddell
Bishop Atkinson Lib.	Asheville		2,400		Rev. A. H. Stubbs.
St. Mary's College	Belmont	1885	10,000		F. Bernard.
N. C. University	Chapel Hill	1790	36,000	1,000	R. H. Graves.
Biddle Univ'r'ty (col)	Charlotte		8,000		
Buckhorn Academy	Como		2,000		
Scotia Seminary	Concord	1870	1,000		
Davidson College Lib	Davidson	1887	12,000		F. F. Rowe.
Public School Library	Durham	1884	2,400		C. W. Toms.
Trinity College Lib.	W. Durham	1887	13,000		Geo. B. Pegram.
Elon College Library	Elon	1890	1,285		W P Lorance.
Cross Creek, I. O. O. F.	Fayetteville	1845	1,000		
Christian College Lib	Franklinton	1882	1,000		N. D. McReynolds.
Female College	Greensboro	1895	6,000		Dred Peacock.
State Normal College	Greensboro		3,000		
Guilford College Lib	Guilford Col	1837	4,000		Miss M. E Mendenhall
Shortia School	Highlands	1888	1,500		
Good Will Free Lib.	Ledger	1888	6,000		C. H. Wing.
Pioneer Library	Lenoir	1875	1,500		I. F. W. Harper.
N. C. College	Mt. Pleasant	1858	2,600		H. T. J. Ludwig.
Bap. Female Institute	Murfreesb'ro		1,000		
Collegiate Institute	Newbern		1,000		
Catawba College	Newton		2,500		
Oak Ridge Institute	Oak Ridge	1852	2,700	200	J. E. Holt.
A. & M. College	Raleigh	1890	3,300	200	A. Q. Holladay.
D. & D. Kelly Lib'ry	Raleigh	1877	2,500		
St. Mary's School	Raleigh		3,000		
Shaw University	Raleigh	1865	1,500		
Supreme Court Lib	aleigh		11,000		R. H. Bradley.
Rutherford Col. Lib.	R. College	1853	600		W. E. Abernathy..
Female College	Salem	1802	4,000		J. H. Clewell.
Livingston College	Salisbury		3,000		
Wake F. College Lib	Wake Forest	1833	15,500	485	W. L. Poteat.
Kab Library	Waynesville	1891	1,100	62	L. B. Lewis.
Wayne School	Waynesville	1886	3,000		T. G. Harbison.
Cassical School	Wilmington		2,000		
Library Association	Wilmington	1855	5,250	249	T. C. Diggs.
City School Library	Winston	1896	3,300	290	J. J. Blair.
College Library	Lenoir	1860	400		J. D. Minick.
A. & M College (col)	Greensboro	1894	2,600		J. H. M. Butler
Hickory Library	Hickory	1803	1,000		N. McComb.
Durham Library	Durham	1897	900		H. A. Forshee.
Morganton Library	Morganton	1878	1,000		Miss A. L. Avery.
Kinston Public Lib.	Kinston				D. T. H. Haughton.
Circulating Library	Charlotte				
S. A. L. Railroad	Raleigh				

48 in Libraries in all. Over 200,000 volumes of good books.

SEND YOUR PRINTING TO THE

Raleigh Christian Advocate,

For First-Class Work.

1st Month. JANUARY, 1900. 31 Days.

Moon's Phases.

	D.	H.	M.		D.	H.	M.
New Moon,	1	8	52 a.m.	Full Moon,	15	2	7 p.m.
First Quarter,	8	0	40 a.m.	Last Quarter	23	6	53 p.m.
				New Moon,	30	8	32 p.m.

Day of Month.	Day of Week.	Sun rises.	Sun sets.	Sun slow.	Sun's decline south.	ASPECTS OF PLANETS AND OTHER MISCELLANEOUS MATTER.	Moon's place.	Moon rises or sets.	Moon south.	High tides at Beaufort.
1	Mo	7 10	4 57	4	22 59	*New Year's Day.*	♐	5 12	0 12	7 26
2	Tue	7 10	4 58	4	22 54	Bat. of Trenton 1777	♐	6 27	1 11	8 28
3	We	7 10	4 59	5	22 48	☌ ♃ ♄ of Princeton 1777	♑	7 41	2 7	9 11
4	Thu	7 10	5 00	5	22 42	Vanderbilt Died 1877	♑	8 54	3 1	9 55
5	Fri	7 10	5 01	6	22 35	Brit. dest. Richm'd 1781.	♒	10 05	3 53	10 41
6	Sat	7 9	5 09	6	22 27	*Epiphany* ☌ ☿ ♃	♒	11 15	4 44	11 21
1.	First Sunday after Epiphany.					Day's length 9 hours 48 minutes.				
7	G	7 9	5 8	7	22 20	Liberia colonized '22	♓	morn	5 34	11 57
8	Mo	7 9	5 4	7	22 12	Bat of N. Orleans '15	♓	0 25	6 25	0 51
9	Tue	7 9	5 5	8	22 4	☿ in ♉ Napoleon 3 d. '73	♈	1 32	7 17	1 50
10	We	7 9	5 6	8	21 55	Stamp Act passed 1765	♈	2 38	8 10	2 52
11	Thu	7 9	5 7	8	21 46	Alabama seceded '61	♉	3 41	9 4	3 55
12	Fri	7 9	5 8	9	21 36	Gaston Co. formed '46	♉	4 39	9 57	4 57
13	Sat	7 9	5 9	9	21 26	☌ ♆ ☾ Fox died 1681	♊	5 32	10 49	5 53
2.	Second Sunday after Epiphany.					Day's Length 9 hours 56 minutes.				
14	G	7 9	5 10	9	21 15	Com'dore Maury b. 1806	♊	6 18	11 12	6 42
15	Mo	7 9	5 11	10	21 4	☌ ♂ ⊕ A. J. b. 1767	♊	rises	morn	7 24
16	Tue	7 8	5 12	10	20 53	Gibbon died 1794	♋	6 13	1 12	8 6
17	We	7 8	5 13	10	20 41	President Tyler died '62	♋	7 11	1 55	8 46
18	Tue	7 8	5 14	11	20 29	Daniel Webster b. 1782	♌	8 8	2 37	9 23
19	Fri	7 8	5 15	11	20 16	♀ in Aphelion	♌	9 05	3 17	9 51
20	Sat	7 7	5 16	11	20 3	Howard died 1790	♌	10 2	3 58	10 31
3.	Third Sunday after Epiphany.					Day's length 10 hours 2 minutes.				
21	G	7 7	5 16	12	19 50	Stonewall Jackson b. '24	♍	10 59	5 24	11 11
22	Mo	7 6	5 17	12	19 36	Byron born 1788	♍	11 56	6 11	11 31
23	Tue	7 6	5 18	12	19 22	Wm. Gastsn d. '44	♎	morn	7 1	0 16
24	We	7 5	5 19	12	19 8	Va. read'd to Con '70	♎	0 57	7 55	1 06
25	Thu	7 4	5 20	13	18 53	Fayetteville settled 1749	♎	1 59	8 52	2 02
26	Fri	7 3	5 21	13	18 38	☌ ♃ ♅ ☾ Gen. Gor. k. '85	♏	3 0	9 51	3 05
27	Sat	7 2	5 22	13	18 23	Audubon died '51	♏	4 1	10 51	4 11
4.	Fourth Sunday after Epiphany.					Day's length 10 hours 12 minutes.				
28	G	7 2	5 23	13	18 7	Tripple Alliance 1667	♐	4 57	11 50	5 25
29	Mo	7 2	5 23	13	17 51	Kansas admitted '61	♐	5 47	eve	6 16
30	Tue	7 2	5 24	14	17 34	☌ ♀ ♂ ☾ Sil. d c 1794	♑	sets	0 0	7 9
31	We	7 2	5 25	14	17 18	Corn. Laws ab. '49	♑	6 30	0 47	7 58

WEATHER CONJECTURES—January—1, 2, 3, 4, 5, 6, 7, stormy; 8, 9, 10, 11, 12, 13, 14, hoar frost unless the wind be South or Southwest; 15, 16, 17, 18, 19. 20, 21, 22, fair and mild; 23, 24, 25, 26, 27, 28, 29, fair and frosty if wind North or Northeast, rain or snow if South or Southwest; 30, 31, rain and snow.

"New Fruit" Handsomely Illustrated Book Sent Free to Fruit Raisers. Address F. Bright, Ellenboro, N. C.

Farmers should use "NATIONAL" Fertilizer for Tobacco; and "BEEF, BLOOD and BONE" brand for Cotton, Corn and Wheat. Strictly reliable. Ask your Fertilizer Merchant for them. Carefully prepared by

(See top 3d cover page.) *S. W. TRAVERS & CO., Branch, Richmond, Va.*

FARM AND GARDEN WORK FOR JANUARY.—Plant Peas, beens, beets, onions, Irish potatoes, horse radish; sow turnips, spinach, lettuce, radish, parsley, carrots, salsify.   Plant early peas; artichokes must now be dressed, also asparagus beds, this is the proper time to sow early spring tomatoes, etc.

NORTH CAROLINA COLLEGES, AND OTHER GRADUATING SCHOOLS.
(Names, Character and location.)

Asheville Female College (Methodist)	Asheville
Chowan Female Institute (Baptist)	Murfreesboro
Claremont Female College (Reformed Church of U. S.)	Hickory
Concordia College (Lutheran)	Conover
Davenport Female College (Methodist)	Lenoir
Davidson College (Presbyterian)	Davidson
Elon College (Christian)	Elon College
Greensboro Female College (Methodist)	Greensboro
Guilford College (Friends)	Guilford College
Hayesville College (Independent)	Hayesville
Judson College (Methodist)	Hendersonville
Kinston College (Independent)	Kinston
Louisburg Female College (Methodist)	Louisburg
Littleton Female College (Methodist)	Littleton
Mt. Amœna Seminary (Lutheran)	Mt. Pleasant
Mt. St. Joseph Academy (Catholic)	Asheville
North Carolina College (Lutheran)	Mt. Pleasant
North Carolina Agricultural and Mechanical College (State)	Raleigh
Oxford Female Seminary (Baptist)	Oxford
Oak Ridge Institute (Independent)	Oak Ridge
Peace Institute (Independent)	Raleigh
Rutherford College, Burke Co. (Independent)	Rutherford College
St. Mary's College (Catholic)	Belmont
Shelby Female College (Independent)	Shelby
St. Mary's School (Episcopal)	Raleigh
Salem Academy (Moravian)	Salem
St. Pauls Seminary (Lutheran Theological)	Hickory
State Normal and Industrial College (State)	Greensboro
Trinity College (Methodist)	Durham
University of North Carolina (State)	Chapel Hill
Weaverville College (Methodist)	Weaverville
Wake Forest College (Baptist)	Wake Forest
Elizabeth College (Lutheran)	Charlotte
Presbyterian College (Presbyterian)	Charlotte
Whitsett Institute (Independent)	Whitsett

COLORED SCHOOLS—Graduating.

Agricultural and Mechanical College (State)	Greensboro
Bennett Seminary (Methodist)	Greensboro
Biddle University (Presbyterian)	Charlotte
Building and Trade's College [Independent]	Southern Pines
Franklinton Christian College [Christian]	Franklinton
Kittrell College [A. M. E. C.]	Kittrell
Livingston College [Methodist]	Salisbury
Normal and Industrial College [Methodist]	Kittrell
Normal School [State]	Elizabeth City
Normal School [State]	Goldsboro
Normal School [State]	Salisbury
Normal School [State]	Plymouth
Normal School [State]	Fayetteville
Normal School [State]	Franklinton
Shaw University [Baptist]	Raleigh
St. Augustine Normal College [Episcopal]	Raleigh
Scotia Female Seminary [Presbyterian]	Concord
Slater Industrial Academy and Normal School [State]	Winston

1. The *mind crop* is the greatest crop that can be raised on any farm or in any State.—*Branson.*

2d Month.   FEBRUARY, 1900.   28 Days.

Moon's Phases.

	D. H. M.		D. H. M.
First Quarter,	6 11 23 a.m.	Last Quarter	22 11 44 a.m.
Full Moon,	14 8 50 a.m.		

Day of Month	Day of Week	Sun rises	Sun sets	Sun slow	Sun's decline South	ASPECTS OF PLANETS AND OTHER MISCELLANEOUS MATTER.	Moon's place	Moon rises or sets	Moon south	High tides at Beaufort
1	Thu	7 1	7 17	14 17	1	♂☿♀☾ Wash. Pres 1789		7 45	1 41	8 48
2	Fri	7 1	7 19	14 16	43	Peace Conference '65		9 0	2 35	2 33
3	Sat	7 0	7 01	14 16	26	♂☿♂R Barringer d. '95		10 11	3 27	10 17

5. Fifth Sunday after Epiphany.   Day's Length 10 hours 22 minutes.

Day of Month	Day of Week	Sun rises	Sun sets	Sun slow	Sun's decline South	ASPECTS OF PLANETS AND OTHER MISCELLANEOUS MATTER.	Moon's place	Moon rises or sets	Moon south	High tides at Beaufort
4	G	6 59	5 59	14 16	8	Rev. War End. 1783		11 21	4 20	11 6
5	Mo	6 58	5 58	14 15	50	*Branson's Nattivity 1832*		morn	5 13	11 33
6	Tue	6 58	5 34	14 15	31	Charles 2 died 1685		0 30	6 6	0 28
7	We	6 57	5 34	14 15	12	Suez Canal Com. '67		1 35	7 0	1 27
8	Thu	6 56	5 35	14 14	53	Gr'at'st Hal. L. South		2 35	7 54	2 32
9	Fri	6 55	5 36	14 14	34	♂☿✳Superior		3 29	8 46	3 37
10	Sat	6 54	5 37	14 14	15	Treaty of Paris 1763		4 17	9 36	4 37

6. Septuagesima Sunday.   Day's length 10 hours 36 minutes.

Day of Month	Day of Week	Sun rises	Sun sets	Sun slow	Sun's decline South	ASPECTS OF PLANETS AND OTHER MISCELLANEOUS MATTER.	Moon's place	Moon rises or sets	Moon south	High tides at Beaufort
11	G	6 53	5 38	14 13	55	Thos A. Edison b. '47		4 58	10 24	5 31
12	Mo	6 53	5 39	14 13	35	Seymour died '86		5 34	11 10	6 19
13	Tue	6 52	5 40	14 13	15	Richard Wagner died '83		6 6	11 53	7 0
14	We	6 51	5 41	14 12	55	*St. Valentine's Day*		rises	morn	7 35
15	Thu	6 50	5 42	14 12	34	U. S. M. bl'n up '98		6 58	0 35	8 14
16	Fri	6 49	5 43	14 12	13	Judge Battle buried '79		7 55	1 16	8 49
17	Sat	6 48	5 44	14 11	52	Columbia burned '65		8 52	1 57	9 24

7. Sexagesima Sunday.   Day's length 10 hours 48 minutes.

Day of Month	Day of Week	Sun rises	Sun sets	Sun slow	Sun's decline South	ASPECTS OF PLANETS AND OTHER MISCELLANEOUS MATTER.	Moon's place	Moon rises or sets	Moon south	High tides at Beaufort
18	G	6 47	5 45	14 11	31	Jefferson Davis inaug '61		9 50	2 38	9 57
19	Mo	6 46	5 46	14 11	10	Aaron Burr arrested '07		10 47	3 21	10 35
20	Tue	6 45	5 47	14 10	48	David Garrick b. 1716		11 47	4 6	11 19
21	We	6 43	5 48	14 10	26	Spinoza d. 1674		morn	4 54	11 43
22	Thu	6 42	5 48	14 10	5	*Washington b. 1732*		0 47	5 45	0 35
23	Fri	6 41	5 48	13	9 43	♂☿☽Bat. B. Vista '47		1 46	6 39	1 33
24	Sat	6 40	5 49	13	9 21	♂♄☽Monterey Sur. '46		2 42	7 35	2 40

8. Quinquagesima Sunday.   Day's length 11 hours 2 minutes.

Day of Month	Day of Week	Sun rises	Sun sets	Sun slow	Sun's decline South	ASPECTS OF PLANETS AND OTHER MISCELLANEOUS MATTER.	Moon's place	Moon rises or sets	Moon south	High tides at Beaufort
25	G	6 39	5 50	13	8 58	Battle of Montreal 1775		3 33	8 33	3 48
26	Mo	6 38	5 51	13	8 35	French Rep. founded '48		4 20	9 30	4 54
27	Tue	6 37	5 52	13	8 13	☿in♀☿in☋ Long b. '07		5 2	10 27	5 54
28	We	6 36	5 53	13	7 51	*Ashe Wednesday* ☐♃✳		5 39	11 33	6 45

WEATHER CONJECTURES—February—1, 2, 3, 4, 5, snow if wind from Southwest; 6, 7, 8, 9, 10, 11, 12, 13, cold and high wind; 14, 15, 16, 17, 18, 19, 20, 21, cold rain if wind be West; snow if from East; 22, 23, 24, 25, 26, 27, 28, cold and high wind.

FARM AND GARDEN WORK FOR FEBRUARY.—Continue to sow peas, and such vegetable as were omitted in January. Plant pole beans, first crop [in the low country]; full crop Irish Potatoes, beets and carrots, dress artichokes and aparagus. Tomatoes, peppers and cucumbers sow in hot beds; put out mangoes.

This is considered the opening month of the planter's year. Continue preparing as in January. Sow oats for a full crop in the low country; plant Irish potatoes; make up sprout beds for sweet potatoes. Plant Plant root crop of sweet potatoes.

BUREAU OF STATISTICS OF N. C. [Denominational.]

LEVI BRANSON, Secretary.

DENOMINATIONS.	Number Ministers.	Number Churches.	Number Members.
Methodist.—Methodist Episcopal Church, South..	684	1,334	136,557
Methodist Episcopal Church..	65	115	8,941
Methodist Church, Wesleyan	7	117	141
Methodist Protestant Church	64	208	16,416
African Methodist Episcopal Zion Church	240	526	121,154
African Methodist Episcopal	182	216	25,218
Colored Methodist Episcopal Church in America..	25	26	2,786
Methodist Episcopal, [col]	2	2	130
Baptist.—Missionary	840	1,628	158,892
Primitive	150	317	11,914
Free Will	160	168	10,224
Church of Christ	16	16	659
Old Two Seed	9	9	185
Seventh Day	1	1	10
Missionary. [col.]	765	1,190	129,265
Free Will, [col.]	10	25	1,640
Primitive, [col.]	15	20	1,000
Protestant Episcopal,-Protestant Episcopal, [white	96	190	15,439
Protestant Episcopal, [col.]	6	10	1,200
Presbyterian.—Presbyterian, [white]	150	350	32,482
Presbyterian, [col.]	173	306	17,851
Christian.—Christian, [white]	60	101	9,000
Christian, [col.]	50	53	3,746
Christian, Disciples of Christ, [white]	54	126	12,437
Christian, Disciples of Christ, [col.]	10	61	1,000
Congregational.—Congregational, [white]	4	4	1,000
Congregational, [col.]	21	39	2,087
Evangelical Lutheran	73	137	12,872
Universalist	3	3	255
Seventh Day Adventist	5	5	83
Reformed Church of U. S.	23	43	3,317
Later Day Saints	24	1	136
Friends	52	52	5,328
Dunkards	9	9	510
Moravians	7	19	3,548
Waldenses	1	1	275
Roman Catholic	24	24	2,640
Hebrews	4	4	386
Salvation Army	2	2	59
Advent Christian	18	18	1,549
Associate Reform	20	20	2,019

3d Month. **MARCH,** **31 Days.**

Address F. Bright Ellenboro, N. C.

Write for "New Fruit," A Hansomely Illustrated Book for Fruit Growers, Free.

Moon's Phases.

	D. H. M.		D. H. M.
New Moon,	1 6 25 a.m.	Full Moon,	16 3 12 a.m.
First Quarter,	8 0 34 a.m.	Last Quarter,	24 0 36 a.m.
		New Moon,	30 3 30 p.m.

Day of Month	Day of Week	Sun rises	Sun sets	Sun slow	Sun's decline South	ASPECTS OF PLANETS AND OTHER MISCELLANEOUS MATTER.	Moon's place	Moon rises or sets	Moon south	High tides at Beaufort
1	Thu	6 34	5 55	12 7	28	Bishop Andrew d '71		6 31	0 18	7 34
2	Fri	6 32	5 56	12 7	5	♂☿ CJWesley d 1791		7 46	1 13	8 22
3	Sat	6 30	5 57	12 6	42	Nevada admit'd '63		9 1	2 7	9 36

9. First Sunday in Lent. Day's length 11 hours 14 minutes.

Day of Month	Day of Week	Sun rises	Sun sets	Sun slow	Sun's decline South	ASPECTS OF PLANETS AND OTHER MISCELLANEOUS MATTER.	Moon's place	Moon rises or sets	Moon south	High tides at Beaufort
4	G	6 28	5 58	12 6	19	♂ ☿C—☿ in Peri		10 12	2 8	9 55
5	Mo	6 26	6 00	12 5	50	Ψ sta Addison b 1750		11 21	3 58	10 41
6	Tue	6 24	6 0	11 5	33	Battle of Pea Ridge 1862	morn		4 53	11 28
7	We	6 23	6 1	11 5	9	7 8 9 10 March Em. Days		0 26	5 48	12 7
8	Thu	6 22	6 1	11 4	46	☿ G'at'stE'gE ☿C		1 23	6 42	1 7
9	Fri	6 20	6 2	11 4	22	Bat of Vera Cruz '47		2 13	7 33	2 10
10	Sat	6 18	6 3	10 3	59	Bat of Manassa June '62		2 57	8 22	3 12

10. Second Sunday in Lent. Day's length 11 hours 36 minutes.

Day of Month	Day of Week	Sun rises	Sun sets	Sun slow	Sun's decline South	ASPECTS OF PLANETS AND OTHER MISCELLANEOUS MATTER.	Moon's place	Moon rises or sets	Moon south	High tides at Beaufort
11	G	6 17	6 4	10 3	35	William Barringer d '82		3 35	9 8	4 9
12	Mo	6 16	6 5	10 3	12	Hamelton died 1874		4 9	9 52	5 2
13	Tue	6 15	6 6	9 2	48	Pocahontas died 1660		4 37	10 34	5 48
14	We	6 14	6 6	9 2	24	☿ Gr'test Hel L N ☿ Sta		5 4	11 15	6 29
15	Thu	6 13	6 7	9 2	1	Ψ ☿ Cæsar As't'd B C 44		5 31	11 56	7 4
16	Fri	6 12	6 8	9 2	37	Nero died A D 37		rises	morn	8 38
17	Sat	6 9	6 9	8 2	13	St. Patrick's Day ☿ S		7 44	0 37	8 15

11. Third Sunday in Lent. Day's length 12 hours 8 minutes.

Day of Month	Day of Week	Sun rises	Sun sets	Sun slow	Sun's decline South	ASPECTS OF PLANETS AND OTHER MISCELLANEOUS MATTER.	Moon's place	Moon rises or sets	Moon south	High tides at Beaufort
18	G	6 8	6 10	8 0	50	♂ in Peri Suez C. c'ted '69		8 42	1 20	8 53
19	Mo	6 6	6 11	8 0	26	Livingston born 1813		9 41	2 4	9 30
20	Tue	6 4	6 12	7 0	2	Sun Enters aries Spring		10 40	2 51	10 9
21	We	6 3	6 12	7 0	21	Lucknow fell '58 [Com.		11 38	3 40	10 53
22	Thu	6 2	6 13	7	no'th	♂♃C—♂☿C		morn	4 32	11 33
23	Fri	6 0	6 13	7 1	8	Bat Winchester '62.		0 33	5 26	0 13
24	Sat	5 59	6 14	6 1	32	♂ ♄C—♂☿ ✳ inf'or		1 25	6 22	1 14

12. Fourth Sunday in Lent. Day's length 12 hours 18 minutes.

Day of Month	Day of Week	Sun rises	Sun sets	Sun slow	Sun's decline South	ASPECTS OF PLANETS AND OTHER MISCELLANEOUS MATTER.	Moon's place	Moon rises or sets	Moon south	High tides at Beaufort
25	G	5 58	6 15	6 1	55	♄ ✳ Thames Tun op '43		2 11	7 17	2 19
26	Mo	5 57	6 16	6 2	19	Earthquake in Cal. '72		2 54	8 13	3 26
27	Tue	5 55	6 17	5 2	42	♃ Sta. Vera Cruz cap '47		3 34	9 7	4 31
28	We	5 53	6 18	5 3	6	Davidson College op '37		4 9	10 1	5 30
29	Thu	5 51	6 18	5 3	29	♂ ☽C Brit Mus f'n'd 1753		4 43	10 55	6 23
30	Fri	5 50	6 19	4 3	52	♂ ☿C Alaska pur '67		sets	11 50	7 11
31	Sat	5 48	6 20	4 4	16	♂ ☿ S. M. Parrish d 1895		7 47	eve	7 57

WEATHER CONJECTURES—March—1, 2, 3, 4, 5, 6, 7, stormy, 8, 9, 10, 11, 12, 13, 14, 15, hoar frost unless wind be South or Southwest; 16, 17, 18, 19, 20, 21, 22, 23, snow and stormy; 24, 25, 26, 27, 28, 29, hoar frost unless wind be South or Southwest, 30, 31, fair and mild.

FARM AND GARDEN WORK FOR MARCH.—Plant bush squash, pumpkins, water and muskmelons, okra, Guinea squash or egg-plant, sugar beets, carrots, beans, peas, radishes, lettuce, corn, celery, [first crop] tanyah and mangoes in the low country and elsewhere as soon as danger from frost is over.

This is the first planting month for cotton, corn and rice. Plant your high lands first; leave the low lands for April. Plant rice about the 20th of the month.

NORTH CAROLINA COLLEGE OF AGRICULTURE AND MECHANIC ARTS.

Located in Raleigh on Hillsboro street, one and a half miles west of the capitol, nearly opposite the Fair Grounds. Incorporated in 1887. Opened October 1, 1889. Supported partly by the U. S. Government and partly by the State of North Carolina, The college owns 540 acres of land and twelve buildings. Tuition including room, fuel, lights etc., $30.00 a year, board $8.00 a month. One hundred and twenty scholarships are granted to deserving boys who are unable to pay. Nominations may be made by any member of the Legislator or by rhe County Board of Education in each county.

BOARD OF TTUSTEES:—W. S. Primrose, President, Raleigh, A. Leazer, Mooresville; H. E Fries, Salem, D. A. Tompkins, Charlotte, T. B. Twitty, Rutherfordton; Frank Wood, Edenton; J. C. L. Harriss, Raleigh, L. C. E C. Edwards, Oxford; John W. Harden, Raleigh; H. E. Bonitz, Wilmington; Matt Moore, Kenansville; J. Z. Waller, Burlington; W. H. Ragan, High Point; David Clark, Charlotte; R. L. Smith, Albemarle; P. J. Sinclair, Marion; J. B. Stokes, Windsor; W. J. Peele, Raleigh; E. Y. Webb; Shelby; W. C. Fields, Sparta, J. Frank Ray, Franklin; Geo. T. Winston, LL. D. Ex-officio, Raleigh.

FACULTY:—Geo. T. Winston, LL. D., President, W. F. Massey, C. E. Professor of Hohticulture, Arboriculture and Botany; W. A. Withers, A. M., Professor of Pure and Agaicultural Chemistry; D. H. Hill, A. M., Professor of English; W. C. Riddick, A. B., Professor of Civil Engineering and Mathematics; B. Irby, M. S., Professor of Agriculture; F. A. Weihe, M. E., Professor of Physics and Electrical engineering; C. W. Scribner, A. B., Professor of Mechanical Engineering; R. E. L. Yates, A. M., Instructor in Mathematics; Charles M. Pritchett, B. S., Instructor in Mechanical Engineering; Charles B. Fark, Superintendent of Shops; B. S. Skinner, Farm Superintendent; J. A. Bizzell, B. S., Instructor in Chemistry; Thomas L. Wright, B. S., Instructor in Mathematics; C. W. Hyams, Instructor in Botany; J. M. Johnson, B. S., Instructor in Agriculture; G. S. Fraps, B. S., Ph.D., Instructor in Chemistry; Lieut. John W. Stewart, U. S. Navy, retired, Instructor in Military Tactics; J. W. Carroll, B. S., Dairymen; H. W. Primrose, B S., Assistant in Chemistry; C. L. Mann, B. S., Assistant in Civil Engineering; B. F. Fennell, B. S., Assistant in Shop Work; N. R. Stansel, B. S., Assistant in Physics and Electrical Engineering; E. B. Owen, L. S., Librarian; Mrs. Sue Carroll, Matron; J. M. Fix, Bursar; Mrs. L. V. Darby, Stenographer.

NORTH CAROLINA AGRICULTURAL EXPERIMENT STATION.

The Station is a department of the Agricultural and Mechanical College and is managed by the same Board of Trustees. The station offices are in the main building of the college. The experiment work is carried on in the college Labratories and partly on the Experiment Station Farm west of the Fair Grounds and partly on the lands of the college.

EXPERIMENT STATION STAFF:—Geo. T. Winston, LL. D., Director; W. A. Withers, A. M., Chemist; B. Irby, M. S., Agriculturist; W. F. Massey, C. E., Horticulturist; Cooper Curtice, D. V. S., M. D., Veterinarian; G. S. Fraps, Ph. D., Assistant Chemist; H. W. Primrose, B. S., Assistant Chemist; Alex Rhodes, Assistant Horticulturist; C. W. Hyams, Assistant Botanist; J. M. Johnson, M. S., Assistant Agriculturist; B. S. Skinner, Farm Superintendent; J. M. Fix, Clerk and Bookkeeper; A. F. Bowen, Secretary; Mrs. L. V. Darby, Clerk and Stenographer.

4th Month. APRIL, 1900. **30 Days.**

Moon's Phases.

	D. H. M.		D. H. M.
☽ First Quarter,	6 3 54 p.m.	☾ Last Quarter,	22 9 33 a.m.
● Full Moon,	14 8 2 p.m.	◉ New Moon,	29 0 23 a.m.

Day of Month	Day of Week	Sun rises	Sun sets	Sun slow	Sun's decline south	ASPECTS OF PLANETS AND OTHER MISCELLANEOUS MATTER.	Moon's place	Moon rises or sets	Moon south	High tides at Beaufort
13.						**Fifth Sunday in Lent.** Day's length 12 hours 32 minutes.				
1	G	5 47	6 23	4 4	39	*April Fools Day.*	♐	8 59	1 42	8 48
2	Mo	5 46	6 24	5 5	2	♀ in Perihelion—♂♀☾	♐	10 47	2 39	9 35
3	Tue	5 44	6 25	5 5	25	♂☿♂Peter Cooper d '83	♐	11 9	2 39	10 23
4	We	5 42	6 26	5 5	48	♂☿☾Gen.Harrison d '71	♐	morn	3 37	11 18
5	Thu	5 41	6 27	3 6	11	Jefferson born 1773	♒	0 4	4 33	11 56
6	Fri	5 39	6 28	3 6	33	☿ Stationary	♒	0 43	6 17	0 43
7	Sat	5 38	6 29	6 6	56	☿ in ♒ PTB'rn'm d '91	♒	1 34	7 4	1 35
14.						**Palm Sunday.** Day's length 12 hours 39 minutes.				
8	G	5 36	6 30	7 7	18	Louisiana admitted 1812		2 9	7 49	2 38
9	Mo	5 35	6 31	7 7	41	Lee's Sur at Ap 1865		2 40	8 32	3 31
10	Tue	5 34	6 32	8 8	3	U.S. Bank inc'porated '16		3 8	9 13	4 21
11	We	5 33	6 32	8 8	25	Civil War began 1861		3 34	9 54	5 7
12	Thu	5 31	6 33	8 8	47	Fort Sumpter fell 1861		4 0	10 36	5 35
13	Fri	5 30	6 34	9 9	9	*Good Friday*	♈	4 27	11 18	6 30
14	Sat	5 28	6 35	9 9	30	♄ Stationary	♈	4 54	morn	7 6
15.						**Easter Sunday.** Day's length 12 hours 56 minutes.				
15	G	5 27	6 36	9 9	52	A. Johnson Pres. 1865		rises	0 2	7 43
16	Mo	5 26	6 37	10 10	13	French Evac. Mexico '67		8 33	0 49	8 26
17	Tue	5 24	6 38	10 10	44	☿ in Aphelion		9 32	1 38	9 8
18	We	5 23	6 39	10 10	55	♂☌☾ and ♂☌☾		10 28	2 29	9 50
19	Thu	5 22	6 40	11 11	16	Battle of Lexington 1775		11 21	3 22	10 49
20	Fri	5 21	6 41	11 11	37	♄☾ Ult to Spain 1898		morn	4 17	11 39
21	Sat	5 20	6 42	11 11	57	☿ Gr E W Sqd to Cuba'98		0 9	5 11	0 58
16.						**First Sunday after Easter.** Day's length 13 hours 11 minutes.				
22	G	5 18	6 43	12 12	17	Sq'd'n lv K West '98		0 51	6 5	0 54
23	Mo	5 17	6 44	12 12	37	Call 125,000 vol '98		1 29	6 58	1 58
24	Tue	5 15	6 45	12 12	57	♀ Gr Hel Lat N		2 5	7 51	3 2
25	We	5 14	6 46	13 13	17	U S dec war Spain '98		2 40	8 42	4 3
26	Thu	5 13	6 47	13 13	36	Gen Johnson at Dur'65		3 13	9 35	5 1
27	Fri	5 12	6 48	13 13	55	♂☿☾Mantanzas bom '98		3 48	10 29	5 57
28	Sat	5 11	6 49	14 14	14	♀ Gr E E Cings bom '98		4 23	11 22	7 48
17.						**Second Sunday after Easter.** Day's length 13 hours 26 minutes.				
29	G	5 10	6 50	14 14	33	Crimean war end '56		sets	ve	7 37
30	Mo	5 9	6 51	14 14	51	♂♀☿Wash. In 1789		8 52	1 20	8 28

WEATHER CONJECTURES—April—1, 2, 3, 4, 5, look for open weather; 6, 7, 8, 8, 10, 11, 12, 13, fair and mild; 14, 15, 16, 17, 18, 19, 20, 21, fair and frosty if wind be from North or Northeast; rain or snow if South or Southwest; 22, 23, 24, 25, 26, 27, 28, cold rain if wind be West—snow if East; 29, 30, hoar frost unless the wind is South or Southwest

FARM AND GARDEN WORK FOR APRIL:—Whatever has been omitted in March, do not neglect any longer. Sow green glazed cabbage, pickling cabbage, full crop of cauliflower and broccoli, okra, tomatoes; peppers, beets, Carrots, leeks, metons, cucumbers, celery.

Full crops of corn, cotton and rice should be put in during this month. Plant your lowland corn. Commence early to hoe your young cotton, and thin out to stand. Plant pumpkins for a field crop.

DEPARTMENT OF PUBLIC INSTRUCTION.

BY C. H. MEBANE, SUPERINTENDENT OF PUBLIC INSTRUCTION.

The Public Schools of North Carolina are under the supervision and general management of the Superintendent of Public Instruction. He is elected by the people just as the Governor and other State officials. His term of office is as same as the Governor—that is four years.

Our Common School system as it was then called went into operation in the year 1840. The schools were under the general management of a Literary board until the year 1852 when Calvin H. Wiley was elected as the first superintendent of Common Schools. Dr. Wiley labored faithfully for popular education for thirteen years. Even amidst the dark and gloomy years of the terrible war between the North and the South he was found at his post of duty.

We are beginning in the last few years to realize how great and how important his work was. From 1865 to 1868 we had no public schools as North Carolina during these years was ruled by Canby as a part of a military district.

Rev. S. S. Ashley, known among our people as a "carpet-bagger," came into office of Superintendent of Public Instruction in 1866 or 1869, being elected at the same time W. W. Holden wos elected governor.

During the year 1870 Mr. Ashley resigned and Alexander McIver was appointed to fill the vacancy. In 1872, Jas Reed, an aged man was elected, but died before he was inducted into office so Mr. McIver held on until 1875, when Stephen D. Pool was elected. He served until 1876 when he was forced to resign on account of mismanagement of Peabody Funds. Governor Brogden appointed John Pool to fill out the unexpired term of Stephen D. Pool.

John C. Scarboro was elected in August 1876 served until January 1885. S. M. Finger was elected in 1884, seaved until January 1893. John C. Scarborough was elected and served again from 1893 to 1897, when the present incumbent, C. H. Mebane, was elected.

Our educational progress has been slow but sure we think. We have suffered for want of funds, on account of what funds we have had being badly managed, on account of poorly prepared teachers, and last but by no means least on account of mean partisan politics. Our people are more interested in the cause of education now than ever before. Public sentiment is becoming more sympathetic and more interested.

But we are doing very little in comparison with what is before us to do. Let the parents into whose hands these lines fall be more concerned than ever before, not only for their own children but concerned for the education of their neighbors children.

Let no parent be deceived because he has done fairly well in the world with little or no education. Listen my friends while I tell you an awful truth. Your children if allowed to grow up in ignorance will be slaves to those who grow up in culture and intelligence. I am aware that the very idea of any parent's child being a slave is repulsive to such parent. *Intelligence will rule; ignorance must serve* in this life.

A boy who has his mind and hand trained so that he can take a piece of material in the rough worth twenty-five cents and make it worth a dollar, has power. A boy trained in agriculture so he knows how to make two bushels of wheat grow where only one grew before his power. A boy

[CONTINUED ON PAGE 17.]

5th Month. MAY, 1900. **31 Days.**

Moon's Phases.

	D. H. M.		D. H. M.
Fist Quarter,	6 3 30 a.m.	Last Quarter,	21 3 31 p.m.
Full Moon,	14 10 36 a.m.	New Moon,	28 9 59 a.m.

Day of Month.	Day of Week.	Sun rises.	Sun sets.	Sun slow.	Sun's decline south.	ASPECTS OF PLANETS AND OTHER MISCELLANEOUS MATTER.	Moon's place.	Moon rises or Sets.	Moon south.	High tides at Beaufort.
1	Tue	5 7	6 51	3 15	0	Dewey sinks S fleet '98		9 51	2 18	9 17
2	We	5 6	6 52	3 15	27	♂ ♅ ☾ and ♂ ♀ ☾		10 43	3 14	10 5
3	Thu	5 5	6 53	3 15	45	♂ ♋ ☾ Col dis Jam 1494		11 28	4 7	10 54
4	Fri	5 4	6 54	3 16	2	Ticonderago taken 1775		morn	4 57	11 45
5	Sat	5 8	6 55	4 16	20	Bat of Williamsburg 1862		0 7	5 44	0 11

18. Third Sunday after Easter. Day's length 13 hour 39 minutes.

6	G	5 3	6 56	4 16	37	Bat of Wilderness'64		0 40	6 28	1 1
7	Mo	5 2	6 57	4 16	53	♂ Gr Hel Lat S		1 9	7 10	1 54
8	Tue	5 1	6 58	4 17	10	Danta Corn 1265		1 36	7 51	2 44
9	We	5 0	6 59	4 17	26	Fight of Cardenas '98		2 2	8 32	3 33
10	Thu	4 59	7 00	4 17	41	*Con Memorial Day*		2 28	9 14	4 20
11	Fri	4 59	7 1	4 17	57	En W Bagley killed 1898		2 55	9 58	5 8
12	Sat	4 57	7 2	4 18	12	San Juan bomb 1898		3 25	10 43	5 54

19. Fourth Sunday after Easter. Day's length 13 hours 51 minutes.

13	G	4 56	7 3	4 18	27	Last Bat of Civil War '65		3 57	11 32	6 38
14	Mo	4 55	7 4	4 18	41	Jamestown set 1607		rises	morn	7 18
15	Tue	4 54	7 5	4 18	56	☉ ♂ ♃ ☾		8 22	0 24	8 4
16	We	4 53	7 6	4 19	10	1st ste'er c ocean 1819		9 18	1 17	8 40
17	Thu	4 53	7 6	4 19	23	♂ ♄ ☾ John Penn b 1741		10 7	2 12	9 37
18	Fri	4 52	7 7	4 19	36	Santiago bombarded '98		10 52	3 8	10 23
19	Sat	4 52	7 8	4 19	49	Sev Sq'd'n iu San Har'98		11 32	4 2	11 15

20. Fifth Sunday after Easter. Day's length 14 hours 4 minutes.

20	G	4 51	7 9	4 20	2	*Mecklenburg Ind 1775*		morn	4 56	11 42
21	Mo	4 50	7 10	4 20	14	N C Seceded '61		0 7	5 46	12 37
22	Tue	4 49	7 11	3 20	26	Victor Hugo d '85		0 40	6 37	1 34
23	We	4 48	7 12	3 20	38	Livingston d 1886		1 12	7 28	2 36
24	Thu	4 48	7 13	3 20	49	*Ascension Day*		1 45	8 19	3 36
25	Fri	4 48	7 13	3 21	0	Emerson b 1803		2 19	9 12	4 36
26	Sat	4 47	7 24	3 21	10	♂ ♂ ☾ - ♋ ☉ Calvin d 1564		2 57	10 7	5 35

21. Sunday after Ascension. Day's length 13 hours 52 minutes.

27	G	4 47	7 15	3 21	20	St Louis Cyclone '96		3 41	eve	6 30
28	Mo	4 47	7 16	3 21	30	✳ *Total Vis in N C*		sets	0 2	7 19
29	Tue	4 46	7 16	3 21	40	Rhode Island ad 1790		8 33	1 0	8 9
30	We	4 45	7 17	3 21	49	*Federal Memorial Day*		9 20	1 55	9 0
31	Thu	4 45	7 18	2 21	57	♀ greatest bril ♀ ☉ ✳		10 2	2 47	9 44

WEATHER CONJECTURES—May—1, 2, 3, 4, 5, fair; 6, 7, 8, 9, 10, 11, 12, 13, changeable, 14, 15, 16, 17, 18, 19, 20, frequent showers; 21, 22, 23, 24, 25, 26, 27, changeable; 28, 29, 30, 31, changeable.

Address F. Bright, Ellenboro, N. C.

Write for "New Fruit," A Hansomely Illustrated Book for Fruit Growers, Free.

FARM AND GARDEN WORK FOR MAY.—Plant snaps beans and squashes. Sow cabbage for winter use, cauliflower, broccoli, celery, beets, carrots, salsify. Plant cucumbers, melons and pumpkins for late crops. Gather herds for drying; always dry gently in the shade.

Look well to your hoeing and plowings. Continue to plant corn in low lands. Sow first crop of early cow peas. Rice planting is generally postponed until June, as the birds are very bad in May, and the May bird is exceedingly destructive.

LEE'S

PRACTICAL
BUSINESS
COLLEGE,

CHARLOTTE, N. C.,

Is thoroughly up-to-date in its equipment. Its courses of study are arranged with reference to the needs of the present advancing age, and are complete in every respect. Its methods of instruction are the most natural and practical known to the teaching profession, and consequently produce better results than any other methods, enabling pupils to accomplish more in one month than can be done in three by the antiquated methods of other colleges. Its faculty is composed of scholarly gentlemen, who are trained specialists and recognized leaders in educational thought. In fact this school offers unexcelled advantages to all young men and women who feel the great need of thorough training for the practical affairs of life, and to all persons who recognize the importance of keeping pace with the progress of the age in which we live.

Positions secured for the graduates of this institution free of charge.

The demand for expert stenographers is greater than we can supply.

For further information address

D. L. LEE, President.

6th Month. JUNE, 1900. 30 Days.

Moon's Phases.

	D. H. M.		D. H. M.
☽ First Quarter,	5 1 5 a.m.	☾ Last Quarter,	19 7 57 p.m.
Full Moon,	12 10 38 a.m.	New Moon,	26 8 27 p.m.

Day of Month.	Day of Week.	Sun rises.	Sun sets.	Sun slow.	Sun's decline South.	ASPECTS OF PLANETS AND OTHER MISCELLANEOUS MATTER.	Moon's place.	Moon rises or sets.	Moon south.	High tides at Beaufort.
1	Fri	4 44	7 18	2	22 6	Bat of Seven Pines '62	♋	10 38	3 36	10 26
2	Sat	4 44	7 19	2	22 13	Bat of Cold Harbor '64	♋	11 9	4 22	11 12
22.	White Sunday—Pentecost.					Day's length 14 hours 23 minutes.				
3	G	4 43	7 20	2	22 21	Hobson s'ks Merimac '98	♋	11 37	5 5	11 35
4	Mo	4 42	7 21	2	22 28	Mexican War dec '45	♌	morn	5 47	12 9
5	Tue	4 41	7 21	2	22 35	☽ Tel in China '71	♌	0 4	6 28	1 7
6	We	4 41	7 22	1	22 41	Pat Henry d 1799	♍	0 30	7 9	1 54
7	Thu	4 41	7 22	1	22 47	☌ ☿ ♆ 1st Am Cong 1765	♍	0 56	7 52	2 43
8	Fri	4 41	7 23	1	22 52	*June 8 9 Ember Days*	♍	1 24	8 37	3 36
9	Sat	4 41	7 23	1	22 57	Marines l Guantanimo'98	♎	1 56	9 24	4 26
23.	Trinity Sunday.					Day's length 14 hours 32 minutes.				
10	G	4 41	7 24	1	23 02	☿ Greatest Hel Lat N	♎	2 31	11 14	5 18
11	Mo	4 41	7 24	1	23 6	☌ ♃ ☾ Sp rep at Gaunt'98	♏	3 13	11 8	6 10
12	Tue	4 41	7 25	1	23 10	☌ ⛢ ☾—☾ *Par Ec*	♏	4 3	11 54	6 58
13	We	4 41	7 25	1	23 14	☌ ♄ ☾ Md char 1633	♐	rises	morn	7 44
14	Thu	4 41	7 26	1	23 17	U S Flag adopted 1777	♐	8 49	1 0	8 36
15	Fri	4 41	7 26	1	23 19	☿ Sta. Sp d'f't at G't 98	♐	9 30	1 56	9 23
16	Sat	4 41	7 27	1	23 22	Ft Caimanera demol '98	♑	10 9	2 51	10 9
24.	First Sunday after Trinity.					Day's length 14 hours 35 minutes.				
17	G	4 41	7 27	1	23 24	Bat of Bunker Hill 1775	♑	10 43	3 43	10 56
18	Mo	4 41	7 27	1	23 25	☌ ♆ ☉ Bat Waterloo 1815	♒	11 16	4 35	11 42
19	Tue	4 42	7 27	1	23 26	☾ ♀ in ♉ [R'c'd 1781	♒	11 48	5 25	12 14
20	We	4 44	7 28	1	23 27	Corn. Wallace ev	♓	morn	6 16	1 9
21	Thu	4 43	7 28	2	23 27	☉ enters cancer Sum C	♓	0 21	7 7	2 9
22	Fri	4 43	7 28	2	24 27	☌ ☿ ♀ Shafters A lands	♈	0 56	8 0	3 12
23	Sat	4 43	7 28	2	23 26	☍ ♄ ☉ Bat Chic'h'm '62	♈	1 36	8 55	4 16
25.	Second Sunday after Trinity.					Day's length 14 hours 37 minutes.				
24	G	4 43	7 29	2	22 25	☌ ♂ ☾ Carnot Ass '94	♉	2 23	9 51	5 18
25	Mo	4 43	7 29	3	23 23	Custer defeated 1876	♉	3 15	10 48	6 15
26	Tue	4 44	7 29	3	23 22	☌ ♆ ☾	♉	4 10		7 5
27	We	4 44	7 29	3	23 19	Bat of Gaines Mills 1862	♊	sets	eve	7 52
28	Thu	4 44	7 29	3	23 17	☌ ♀ ☾ 3d Manilla ex sails	♊	8 55	0 28	8 37
29	Fri	4 45	7 29	3	23 13	*St Peters* ☌ ☿ ☾ ['98	♋	9 9	2 15	9 19
30	Sat	4 45	7 29	4	23 10	Caney evac by Span. 98	♋	9 38	2 59	9 58

WEATHER CONJECTURES—June—1, 2, 3, 4, changeable, 5, 6, 7, 8, 9, 10, 11, 12, 13, 14, 15. 16, 17. 18, fair, 19, 20, 21, 22, 23, 24, 25, fair if wind Northwest, rain if South or Southwest, 26, 27, 28, 28, 30, fair if wind Northwest, rain if South or Southwest.

FARM AND GARDEN WORK FOR JUNE.—Sow full crops of cabbages for fall and winter use. Cauliflowers and broccoli may yet be sown, also a few carrots. Continue to sow tomatoes, okra, radishes, snap beans. Transplant leeks; pull and dry onions, garlic and aschalots. A few cucumbers and melons plant for a late crop, and a few ruta baga turnips.

Keed constantly at the plow and hoe; this is the most important grass month! If the vines from your sweet potato sprout bed are fit you can draw and plant out first good rain. Sow cow-peas between your corn hills and rows. The end of this month is a good time to put in the first crop of standing field peas.

[Continued from page 13.]

who thinks, who has ideas for the improvement of work along any line of science or art has power. Give the girls a chance too. Never before have there been so many vocations open to women. Teaching, Law, Medicine, Bookkeeping, Merchandise, and the highest and noblest of all the vocations of woman is the queen of the home. Give us intelligent, God-fearing mothers in our homes and we will soon become an intelligent people. If you cannot educate your boy and girl both, give the preference to the girl. The boy is the stronger and can help himself better than the girl.

We have a grand army of 628,480 children of school age in North Carolina. Let us all work together for the training of this mighty host into whose hands the destiny of Church and State will soon fall.

7th Month. JULY 1900. 31 Days.

Moon's Phases.

	D. H. M.		D. H. M.
☽ First Quarter,	4 7 13 p.m.	☾ Last Quarter.	9 31 57 a.m.
Full Moon,	12 8 22 a.m.	New Moon,	26 8 43 a.m.

Day of Month.	Day of Week.	Sun rises.	Sun sets.	Sun slow.	Sun's decline North.	ASPECTS OF PLANETS AND OTHER MISCELLANEOUS MATTER.	Moon's place.	Moon rises or sets.	Moon south.	High tides at Beaufort.
26.	Third Sunday after Trinity.					Day's length 14 hours 36 minutes.				
1	G	4 45	7 29	4	23 6	Battle of Santiago 1898		10 5	3 42	10 35
2	Mo	4 46	7 29	4	23 2	⊕ in Aph. Cev flt des '98		10 32	4 24	11 16
3	Tue	4 47	7 29	4	22 57	☿ in ☊ Monroe d 1831		10 57	5 5	12 37
4	We	4 47	7 29	4	22 52	*Ind Day 1776*		11 25	5 47	0 19
5	Thu	4 48	7 29	4	22 46	Cam flt at Suez '98		11 55	6 30	1 6
6	Fri	4 48	7 28	5	22 40	Sp Cr Al XII Des '98		morn	7 15	1 56
7	Sat	4 49	7 28	5	22 34	Haiwaii annexed '98		0 28	8 4	2 50
27.	Fourth Sunday after Trinity.					Day's Length 14 hours 33 minutes.				
8	G	4 50	7 28	5	22 27	☌ ♀ ☼ Inferior & ☌ ♃ ☾		1 5	8 56	3 48
9	Mo	4 50	7 28	5	22 20	☌ ♅ ☾ — ♄ in Aphelion		1 51	9 50	4 48
10	Tue	4 51	7 27	5	22 13	☌ ♄ ☾ Wy ad'm'd '90		2 45	10 46	5 46
11	We	4 52	7 27	5	22 5	Andrie Sts for N Pole '97		3 44	11 44	6 45
12	Thu	4 52	7 26	5	21 57	Erasmas died 1536		rises	morn	7 57
13	Fri	4 53	7 26	6	21 48	Gen Fremont d '90		8 7	0 41	8 19
14	Sat	4 53	7 25	6	21 39	Grt Fire in Chicargo '74		8 43	8 43	9 6
28.	Fifth Sunday after Trinity.					Day's length 14 hours 27 minutes.				
15	G	4 54	7 25	6	21 30	Battle of Vicksburg '62		9 18	2 29	9 50
16	Mo	4 55	7 24	6	21 20	*Santiago Surrendered '98*		9 51	3 21	10 35
17	Tue	4 55	7 24	6	21 10	☿ Stationary		10 24	4 13	11 12
18	We	4 56	7 23	6	20 59	Dean Stanly died 1881		10 50	5 4	11 52
19	Thu	4 57	7 23	6	20 49	♂ in ☋ Ingelow d '97		11 38	5 57	12 47
20	Fri	4 57	7 22	6	20 37	Spanish Cab Neg for P '98		morn	6 51	1 49
21	Sat	4 58	7 21	6	20 26	Garcia With. Army '98		0 20	7 46	2 54
29.	Sixth Sunday after Trinity.					Day's length 14 hours 20 minutes.				
22	G	5 59	7 20	6	20 14	☌ ♂ ☾ Napoleon 2d d '32		1 9	8 41	3 59
23	Mo	5 0	7 20	6	20 2	☌ ♆ ☾ — ♀ in Aphilion		2 4	9 36	5 1
24	Tue	5 1	7 19	6	19 50	☌ ♀ ☾ Boliver born 1783		3 1	10 30	5 59
25	We	5 2	7 18	6	19 37	Battle Lundys Lane 1814		4 1	11 21	6 89
26	Thu	5 3	7 17	6	19 23	Robert Fulton b 1765		sets	eve	7 01
27	Fri	5 3	7 17	6	19 10	☌ ☿ ☾ Powers b '05		7 38	0 55	7 41
28	Sat	5 3	7 16	6	19 56	M Montefiore d 1885		8 8	1 38	8 25
30.	Seventh Sunday after Trinity.					Day's length 14 hours 10 minutes.				
29	G	5 4	7 15	6	18 42	♃ Stationary—♀ Sta.		8 35	2 20	9 26
30	Mo	5 5	7 14	6	18 28	William Penn b 1718		9 1	3 1	10 00
31	Tue	5 6	7 13	6	18 13	Andrew Johnson d 1875		9 26	3 45	10 36

WEATHER CONJECTURES—July—1, 2, 3, fair if wind Northwest, rain if South or Southwest; 4, 5, 6, 7, 8, 9, 10, 11, fair if wind Northwest, rain if South or Southwest; 12, 13, 14, 15, 16, 17, 18, fair if wind Northwest, rain if South or Southwest; 19, 20, 21, 22, 23, 24, 25, fair; 26, 27, 28, 29, 30, 31, changeable.

FARM AND GARDEN WORK FOR JULY.—Sow cabbages, but protect from hot sun when young. Water at night. Plant snap beans and a few Irish potatoes. Continue to sow radishes, lettuce, endive, cresses, mustard and small salading. The early Dutch turnip is the best to sow for the first crop; follow with the yellow Swedish or ruta baga.

Now do not omit to sow full crops of standing cow-peas. Sow a few turnips, carrots and beets as field crops, though the hot suns are apt to destroy them, should they escape they will be fine, the next month is the best for these crops.

8th Month. AUGUST, 1900. 31 Days.

Moon's Phases.

	D. H. M.		D. H. M.
☽ First Quarter,	5 11 45 a.m.	☾ Last Quarter	17 6 46 a.m.
◉ Full Moon,	10 4 30 p.m.	● New Moon,	24 10 52 p.m.

Day of Month.	Day of Week.	Sun rises.	Sun sets.	Sun slow	Sun's decline North.	ASPECTS OF PLANETS AND OTHER MISCELLANEOUS MATTER.	Moon's place.	Moon rises or sets.	Moon south.	High tides at Beaufort.
1	We	5 6	7 12	6	17 58	☌☿☉ Inferior	[illegible]	9 54	4 25	11 17
2	Thu	5 7	7 11	6	17 43	Bat of Plevna 1877	[illegible]	10 26	5 9	11 38
3	Fri	5 8	7 10	6	17 27	☿ Greatest Hel L S	[illegible]	11 2	5 55	12 24
4	Sat	5 9	7 9	6	17 11	Ed Irving b 1792	[illegible]	11 43	6 45	1 14
31. Eighth Sunday after Trinity. Day's length 14 hours 0 minutes.										
5	G	5 10	7 8	6	17 55	☌♃☾—☌♅☾	[illegible]	morn	7 37	2 14
6	Mo	5 11	7 6	6	16 38	Ft Gaimes Sur 1864	[illegible]	0 31	8 32	3 16
7	Tue	5 11	7 5	5	16 22	☌♄☾—☌♂♆	[illegible]	1 27	9 28	4 20
8	We	5 12	7 4	5	16 0	Conovas assassinated '97	[illegible]	2 29	10 25	5 23
9	Thu	5 13	7 3	5	15 47	Dryden born 1631	[illegible]	3 33	11 21	6 23
10	Fri	5 14	7 2	5	15 30	☿ Stationary	[illegible]	rises	morn	7 9
11	Sat	5 14	7 0	5	15 12	Card Newman d '90	[illegible]	7 16	0 17	7 57
32. Ninth Sunday after Trinity. Day's length 13 hours 49 minutes.										
12	G	5 15	6 59	5	14 54	War U. S. & Spain en '98	[illegible]	7 49	1 11	8 45
13	Mo	5 16	6 58	5	14 36	Manilla surrendered '98	[illegible]	8 24	2 5	9 31
14	Tue	5 17	6 57	4	14 18	♀ greatest brilliancy	[illegible]	8 59	2 58	10 14
15	We	5 18	6 56	4	13 59	♀ greatest Hel Lat S	[illegible]	9 38	3 52	11 5
16	Thu	5 19	6 54	4	13 40	Napol'n at St Helena '15	[illegible]	10 21	4 46	11 32
17	Fri	5 19	6 53	4	13 21	♅ stationary	[illegible]	11 8	5 42	12 29
18	Sat	5 20	6 52	3	13 1	Ole Bull d 1880	[illegible]	11 59	6 38	1 33
33. Tenth Sunday after Trinity. Day's length 13 hours 34 minutes.										
19	G	5 21	6 51	3	12 42	☿ greatest E W—☌♆☾	[illegible]	morn	7 33	2 31
20	Mo	5 21	6 49	3	12 22	☌♂☾ Ben Harrison b '33	[illegible]	0 56	8 26	3 44
21	Tue	5 22	6 45	3	12 2	☌♀☾ Chat taken '63	[illegible]	1 55	9 17	4 43
22	We	5 23	6 42	3	11 42	☿ in ♌ J B Gough b '17	[illegible]	2 55	10 6	5 48
23	Thu	5 24	6 42	2	11 22	☌☿☾ Wm Herschel d '22	[illegible]	3 54	10 56	6 24
24	Fri	5 25	6 43	2	11 1	Daniel Webster d '52	[illegible]	4 54	eve	7 5
25	Sat	5 26	6 41	2	10 41	□♃☉ Hume d 1776	[illegible]	sets	0 18	7 41
34. Eleventh Sunday after Trinity. Day's length 13 hours 21 minutes.										
26	G	5 27	6 40	1	10 20	Louis Phillippe d 1850	[illegible]	7 5	1 0	8 17
27	Mo	5 27	6 39	1	9 59	☿ in Perihelion	[illegible]	7 31	1 41	8 54
28	Tue	5 28	6 38	1	9 38	Goethe born 1749	[illegible]	7 59	2 23	9 28
29	We	5 28	6 36	1	9 16	*Michælmas Day*	[illegible]	8 28	3 6	10 2
30	Thu	5 29	6 34	1	8 55	William Penn d 1718	[illegible]	9 2	3 51	10 42
31	Fri	5 30	7 32	0	8 33	□♅☉ Char Earthq'ke '86	[illegible]	9 40	4 38	11 22

WEATHER CONJECTURES—August—1, 2, changeable; 3, 4, 5, 6, 7, 8, 9, frequent showers; 10, 11, 12, 13, 14, 15, 16, fair, 17, 18, 19, 20, 21, 22, 23, wind and rain; 24, 25, 26, 27, 28, 29, 30, 31, fair.

FARM AND GARDEN WORK FOR AUGUST.—Transplant all kinds of cabbage, cauliflower and celery. Sow corrots and beets, turnips of all kinds, spinach, lettuce, radish and onions.

Now sow full crops of field turnips, carrots and beets, and such other crops as were omitted last month; strip fodder. Early rice will be fit to cut the last of this month. Look to it. This a good time to plant vines of the first slips, in order to procure seed potatoes for the next year's crops,

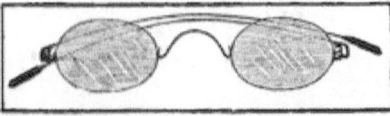

9th Month. SEPTEMBER, 1900. 30 Days.

Moon's Phases.

	D.	H.	M.			D.	H.	M.	
☽ Fist Quarter,	2	2	56	a.m.	☾ Last Quarter,	15	3	57	p.m.
● Full Moon,	9	0	6	a.m.	● New Moon,	23	2	57	p.m.

Day of Month.	Day of Week.	Sun rises.	Sun sets.	Sun slow.	Sun's decline south.	ASPECTS OF PLANETS AND OTHER MISCELLANEOUS MATTER.	Moon's place.	Moon rises or Sets.	Moon south.	High tides at Beaufort.
1	Sat	5 31	6 32	1	8 12	☌♃☾ Bat Chantilly '62	♏	10 24	5 28	1 01
35.	Twelfth Sunday after Trinity.						Day's length 13 hours 5 minutes.			
2	G	5 32	6 30	1	7 50	☌♅☾—♄ stationary	♏	11 14	6 20	12 55
3	Mo	5 33	6 28	2	7 28	☌♄☾ Atlanta cap'64	♐	morn	7 14	1 54
4	Tue	5 34	6 27	2	7 5	Frech Rep proclaimed'70	♐	0 12	8 9	2 48
5	We	5 35	6 25	2	6 43	J W Daniel born 1842	♑	1 16	9 5	3 54
6	Thu	5 35	6 24	2	6 31	☿ greatest Hel Lat N	♑	2 25	10 0	4 58
7	Fri	5 36	6 22	2	5 58	Whittier died 1892	♒	3 38	10 55	5 56
8	Sat	5 36	6 20	3	5 36	Bat Eutaw Springs 1781	♒	4 50	11 50	6 48
36.	Thirteenth Sunday after Trinity.						Day's length 12 hours 50 minutes.			
9	G	5 37	6 19	3	5 13	California ad 1850	♓	rises	morn	7 33
10	Mo	5 38	6 17	3	4 50	S S Cox died 1889	♓	6 56	0 44	8 22
11	Tue	5 39	6 15	4	4 28	Bat of Brandywine 1777	♓	7 34	1 40	9 10
12	We	5 39	6 14	4	4 5	R A Proctor died 1888	♈	8 16	2 36	9 55
13	Thu	5 40	6 13	4	3 42	☌☿☉ Sup. Wil'g'n d'52	♈	9 3	3 33	10 46
14	Fri	5 41	6 11	5	19	Humboldt born 1769	♉	9 56	4 31	11 36
15	Sat	5 42	6 10	5	56	J F Cooper b 1789	♉	10 52	5 27	12 14
37.	Fourteenth Suuday after Trinity.						Day's length 12 hours 35 minutes.			
16	G	5 43	6 8	5	2 32	☌♆☾ Moscow burn 1812	♊	11 50	6 22	1 15
17	Mo	5 44	6 6	6	2 9	♀ Greatest Elong W	♊	morn	7 14	2 18
18	Tue	5 44	6 5	6	1 46	☌♂☾ Boucicolt d 1890	♊	0 49	8 3	3 19
19	We	5 45	6 3	7	1 23	☌♀☾ Garfield d 1881	♋	1 49	8 50	4 15
20	Thu	5 45	6 1	7	0 59	Bat Chickamauga 1863	♋	2 47	9 34	5 5
21	Fri	5 46	6 0	7	0 36	□♄☉ Deut VIII–5	♌	3 45	10 17	5 51
22	Sat	5 47	5 58	8	sou'h	□♆☉ Bat Fishers Hill'64	♌	4 42	10 59	6 32
38.	Fifteenth Sunday after Trinity.						Day's length 12 hours 20 minutes.			
23	G	5 48	5 57	8	0 10	☉ *Ent Libra au.com.*	♌	5 38	eve	7 8
24	Mo	5 49	5 55	8	0 33	☌☿☾ Gen Hill d '89	♍	sets	0 22	7 43
25	Tue	5 50	5 54	9	0 57	Ethan Allen Cap 1777	♍	6 33	1 4	8 21
26	We	5 51	5 52	9	1 20	Daniel Boone d 1820	♎	7 4	1 49	8 38
27	Thu	5 51	5 51	9	1 44	Bat Pilot Knob 1864	♎	4 40	2 35	9 36
28	Fri	5 51	5 49	10	2 7	☌♃☾—☌♅☾	♎	8 21	3 23	10 16
29	Sat	5 51	5 47	10	2 30	*Michaelmas Day*	♏	9 9	4 14	11 1
39.	Sixteenth Sunday after Trinity.						Day's length 13 hour 3 minutes.			
30	G	5 53	5 45	10	2 54	☌♄☾	♏	10 3	5 6	11 29

WEATHER CONJECTURES—September—1, fair; 2, 3, 4, 5, 6, 7, 8, cold with freguent showers; 9, 10, 11, 12, 13, 14, fair; 15, 16, 17, 18, 19, 20, 21, 22, changeable, , 23, 24, 25, 26, 27, 28, 29, 30, changeable.

FARM AND GARDEN WORK FOR SEPTEMBER.—Now sow full crops of all kinds—turnips, onions, carrots, beets, cabbage, lettuce, cresses. Look after your mushroom beds. Hoe and thin your turnips. Continue to sow field turnips, carrots and beets. Southern seed is always better than the imported; those from the latter are apt to run to seed early in the spring, unless it be English seed. Prepare land for sowing rye in October. Pick cotton; harvest corn.

10th Month.   OCTOBER, 1900.   **31 Days.**

Moon's Phases.

	D. H. M.		D. H. M.
☽ First Quarter,	1 4 10 p.m.	☾ Last Quarter	15 4 51 a.m.
☽ Full Moon,	8 8 18 a.m.	☽ New Moon,	23 8 27 a.m.
		☽ First Quarter,	31 3 17 a.m.

Day of Month.	Day of Week.	Sun rises.	Sun sets.	Sun fast.	Sun's decline north.	ASPECTS OF PLANETS AND OTHER MISCELLANEOUS MATTER.	Moon's place.	Moon rises or sets.	Moon south.	High tides at Beaufort.
1	Mo	5 54	5 43	11	3 17	☽ Ψ Stationary	♐	11 2	5 59	12 21
2	Tue	5 55	5 42	11	3 40		♐	morn	6 52	0 19
3	We	5 56	5 39	11	4 4	Andre executed 1780	♑	0 6	7 46	2 22
4	Thu	5 57	5 39	12	4 27	R B Hayes born 1822	♑	1 14	8 39	3 27
5	Fri	5 58	5 38	12	4 50	Cornwallis defeated 1781	♒	2 25	9 32	4 29
6	Sat	5 59	5 36	12	5 13	Tennyson died 1892	♒	3 37	10 27	5 27

40. Seventheenth Sunday after Trinity. Day's length 11 hours 50 minutes.

Day of Month.	Day of Week.	Sun rises.	Sun sets.	Sun fast.	Sun's decline north.	ASPECTS OF PLANETS AND OTHER MISCELLANEOUS MATTER.	Moon's place.	Moon rises or sets.	Moon south.	High tides at Beaufort.
7	G	5 59	5 35	12	5 36	E A Poe died 1849	♒	4 52	11 22	6 22
8	Mo	6 0	5 33	13	5 39	☽ Bat Ft Pickens 1861	♒	rises	morn	7 10
9	Tue	6 1	5 32	13	6 22	☽ Galveston taken 1862	♓	6 8	0 19	7 59
10	We	6 2	5 30	13	6 45	☿ in Aphelion—♀ in ♌	♓	6 55	1 17	8 50
11	Thu	6 3	5 29	13	7 7	Dr Kane returned 1855	♈	7 46	2 16	9 40
12	Fri	6 4	5 27	14	7 30	R E Lee died 1870	♈	8 42	3 16	10 30
13	Sat	6 5	5 26	14	7 52	♂ ☿ ☾ Conover d 1822	♉	9 42	4 13	11 11

41. Eighteenth Sunday after Trinity. Day's length 11 hours 27 minutes.

Day of Month.	Day of Week.	Sun rises.	Sun sets.	Sun fast.	Sun's decline north.	ASPECTS OF PLANETS AND OTHER MISCELLANEOUS MATTER.	Moon's place.	Moon rises or sets.	Moon south.	High tides at Beaufort.
14	G	6 6	5 24	14	8 15	Josh Billing d 1885	♉	10 42	5 8	12 55
15	Mo	6 7	5 23	14	8 37	☾ Treaty Campo f 1797	♊	11 42	5 59	0 51
16	Tue	6 8	5 21	15	8 59	☾ ♂ ☾ A F Page d '99	♋	morn	6 47	1 47
17	We	6 9	5 19	15	9 21	C A Danna died 1897	♋	0 41	7 33	2 44
18	Thu	6 9	5 18	15	9 43		♌	1 40	8 16	3 48
19	Fri	6 10	5 17	15	10 5	☿ ☾—♂ ♃ ☽	♌	2 37	8 57	4 58
20	Sat	6 11	5 16	15	10 26	Froude died 1894	♍	3 33	9 39	5 13

42. Nineteenth Sunday after Trinity. Day's length 11 hours 13 minutes.

Day of Month.	Day of Week.	Sun rises.	Sun sets.	Sun fast.	Sun's decline north.	ASPECTS OF PLANETS AND OTHER MISCELLANEOUS MATTER.	Moon's place.	Moon rises or sets.	Moon south.	High tides at Beaufort.
21	G	6 12	5 15	15	10 48	Columbus Day	♍	4 28	10 20	5 55
22	Mo	6 13	5 13	15	11 9	Nana Sahib captured '74	♍	5 25	11 3	6 50
23	Tue	6 14	5 12	15	11 30	☽ Gen Jurat d 1771	♎	6 22	11 47	7 12
24	We	6 15	5 10	15	11 51	☽ Los Ang Mas 1873	♎	sets	eve	7 51
25	Thu	6 16	5 9	15	12 12	♂ ☿ ☾ Bat of Ballak 1854	♏	6 22	1 21	8 33
26	Fri	6 16	5 8	15	12 32	♂ ☾—♂ ♃ ☾ Hog d 1764	♏	7 7	2 10	9 14
27	Sat	6 17	5 7	15	12 53	I G Vassar d 1888	♏	7 58	3 2	9 56

43. Twentieth Sunday after Trinity. Day's length 10 hours 58 minutes.

Day of Month.	Day of Week.	Sun rises.	Sun sets.	Sun fast.	Sun's decline north.	ASPECTS OF PLANETS AND OTHER MISCELLANEOUS MATTER.	Moon's place.	Moon rises or sets.	Moon south.	High tides at Beaufort.
28	G	6 18	5 5	15	13 13	♄ ☾ Leviticus XIX—17	♐	8 55	3 54	10 42
29	Mo	6 19	5 4	15	13 33	☿ Greatest Elong E.	♐	9 56	4 46	11 26
30	Tue	6 20	5 3	15	13 53	☿ Greatest Hel Lat S	♑	11 0	5 38	12 00
31	We	6 21	5 2	15	14 12		♑	morn	6 29	0 51

WEATHER CONJECTURES—October—1, 2, 3, 4, 5, 6, 7, fair; 8, 9, 10, 11, 12, 13, 14, changeable; 15, 16, 17, 18, 19, 20, 21, 22, rain; 23, 24, 25, 26, 27, 28, 29, 30, changeable; 31, cold with frequent showers.

Elenboro.   Order more Owen Cherries; you can't get too many.—F. Bright,

FARM AND GARDEN WORK FOR OCTOBER.—You may make two sow"
ings of cabbage this month, and, if of English seed, they will not "run"
in the spring. Sow lettuce; hoe turnips and thin, put out leeks and
onions; sow principal crop of spinach; earth up celery.

Continue picking your cotton as it blows. Sow early rye, wheat and
barley. Dig your sweet potatoes when the weather becomes cool and
you expect frost.

11th Month. NOVEMBER, 1900. 30 Days.

Moon's Phases.

	D. H. M.		D. H. M.
Full Moon,	6 6 0 p.m.	New Moon,	12 2 17 a.m.
☾ Last Quarter,	13 9 37 p.m.	☽ First Quarter,	29 0 35 p.m.

Day of Month.	Day of Week.	Sun rises.	Sun sets.	Sun fast.	Sun's decline south.	ASPECTS OF PLANETS AND OTHER MISCELLANEOUS MATTER.	Moon's place.	Moon rises or sets.	Moon south.	High tides at Beaufort.
1	Thu	6 22	5 0	16	14 31	*Am Discovered 1492*	♑	0 7	7 21	1 55
2	Fri	6 23	4 59	16	14 50	Jenny Lind d 1887	♒	1 16	8 12	2 57
3	Sat	6 24	4 58	16	15 9	Louis Bonaparte d 1891	♒	2 27	9 5	3 57
44. Tewnty-first Sunday after Trinity. Day's length 10 hours 45 minutes.										
4	G	6 25	4 57	16	15 28	Peabody died 1889	♓	3 39	10 00	4 58
5	Mo	6 26	4 56	16	15 46	Guy Fawkes Day	♓	4 53	10 57	5 56
6	Tue	6 27	4 55	16	16 4	☌ ♀ ♄ Virginis	♈	6 7	11 56	6 49
7	We	6 28	4 54	16	16 22	*Braxton Craven d'82*	♉	rises	morn	7 47
8	Thu	6 29	4 53	16	16 40	Milton died 1674	♉	6 26	0 57	8 33
9	Fri	6 30	4 52	16	16 57	☌ ♆ ☾—☿ Sta	♉	7 26	1 57	9 24
10	Sat	6 31	4 51	16	17 14	Goldsmith born 1728	♊	8 28	2 55	10 12
45. 22nd. Sunday after Trinity. Day's length 10 hours 45 minutes.										
11	G	6 32	4 50	16	17 30	St of Wash ad 1889	♊	9 30	3 50	11 3
12	Mo	6 33	4 49	16	17 47	Proverbs III-13	♋	10 31	4 41	12 27
13	Tue	6 34	4 49	15	18 3	♀ in Perihelion	♋	11 30	5 28	1 20
14	We	6 35	4 48	15	18 18	☌ ♂ ☾ Mozart b 1719	♋	morn	6 12	1 9
15	Thu	6 36	4 47	15	18 34	Dom Pedro dethroned '89	♌	0 28	6 55	2 0
16	Fri	6 37	4 46	15	18 49	Ft Wash. taken 1776.	♌	1 26	7 36	2 51
17	Sat	6 38	4 46	15	19 4	Suez Canal opened 1869	♍	2 22	8 18	3 40
46. 23rd. Sunday after Trinity. Day's length 10 hours 19 minutes.										
18	G	6 39	4 45	15	19 18	☿ in ☊—☌ ♀ ☾	♍	3 18	9 0	4 29
19	Mo	6 40	4 45	14	19 32	Leg met in NewBern 1771	♍	4 14	9 43	5 16
20	Tue	6 41	4 44	14	19 46	☌ ☿ ✳ Inferior	♎	5 11	10 29	6 1
21	We	6 42	4 43	14	19 59	☌ ☿ ☾ Berlin decree 1886	♎	6 9	11 16	6 45
22	Thu	6 43	4 42	13	20 12	□ ♂ ✳ *Annu Eclipse*	♏	sets	eve	7 25
23	Fri	6 44	4 42	13	20 25	☌ ♅ ☾—☿ in P ☌ ♃ ☾	♏	5 54	0 58	8 10
24	Sat	6 44	4 42	13	20 37	☌ ♄ ☾ J Knox d 1572	♐	6 50	1 51	8 56
47. 24th. Sunday after Trinity. Day's length 10 hours 8 minutes.										
25	G	6 46	4 41	13	20 49	Bat Mis Ridge 1863	♐	7 51	2 43	9 40
26	Mo	6 47	4 40	12	21 0	Bishop Marvin d 1875	♑	8 54	3 35	10 25
27	Tue	6 48	4 40	12	21 12	Alex Dumas died 1895	♑	10 0	4 26	11 13
28	We	6 49	4 39	12	21 22	Wash Irving d 1859	♑	11 7	5 16	11 39
29	Thu	6 50	4 39	11	21 32	☽ ☿ Sta. H Greeley d '72	♒	morn	6 6	12 32
30	Fri	6 51	4 39	11	21 42	2d Samuel XXII—26	♒	0 14	6 57	1 27

WEATHER CONJECTURES—November—1, 2, 3, 4, 5, cold rain; 6, 7, 8, 9, 10, 11, 12 fair and frosty; 13, 14, 15, 16, 17, 18, 19, 20, 21, fair and frosty; 22, 23, 24, 25, 26, 27, 28, snow and stormy; 29, fair and frosty.

Farmers should use "NATIONAL" Fertilizer for Tobacco; and "BEEF, BLOOD and BONE" brand for Cotton, Corn and Wheat. Strictly reliable. Ask your Fertilizer Merchant for them. Carefully prepared by
(See top 3d cover page.) *S. W. TRAVERS & CO., Branch, Richmond, Va.*

Now is the time to set Owen Cherry Trees. Order them to-day. Address, F. Bright, Ellenboro, N. C.

FARM AND GARDEN WORK FOR NOVEMBER.—Sow your first crop of peas and a few turnips.   Plant out onions raised from seed in August and September.   Plant Windsor and long pod beans.   Dress asparagus and artichokes.

Sow full crops of rye, barley, wheat and other small grains.   Harvest your sweet potatoes.

12 Month. DECEMER, 31 Days.

Moon's Phases.

	D.	H.	M.		D.	H.	M.
Full Moon,	6	5	38 a.m.	New Moon,	21	7	1 p.m.
☾ Last Quarter,	13	5	42 p.m.	☽ First Quarter,	28	8	84 p.m.

Day of Month.	Day of Week.	Sun rises.	Sun sets.	Sun fast.	Sun's decline South.	ASPECTS OF PLANETS AND OTHER MISCELLANEOUS MATTER.	Moon's place.	Moon rises or sets.	Moon south.	High tides at Beaufort.
1	Sat	6 52	4 39	10	21 51	Prin Wales b 1844	♈	1 32	7 48	2 28
48. First Sunday in Advent.						Day's length 9 hours 58 minutes.				
2	G	6 53	4 39	10	22 0		♉	2 35	8 42	3 30
3	Mo	6 54	4 39	10	22 9	☿ Greatest Hel Lat N	♉	3 43	9 39	4 32
4	Tue	6 55	4 38	9	22 17	♀ Greatest Hel Lat N	♉	4 54	10 37	5 34
5	We	6 56	4 38	9	22 25	☌♅✳Gen Custar b '39	♉	6 5	11 38	6 32
6	Thu	6 57	4 38	8	22 32	Jefferson Davis d '89	♊	rises	morn	7 22
7	Fri	6 58	4 38	8	22 39	☌♆☾—☿ Gr E W	♊	6 7	0 37	8 15
8	Sat	6 59	4 38	8	22 45	Eli Whitney born 1765	♊	7 11	1 34	9 5
49. Second Sunday in Advent.						Day's length 9 hours 52 minutes.				
9	G	7 0	4 38	7	22 51	DeQuincy d 1859	♋	8 15	2 28	9 49
10	Mo	7 1	4 38	7	22 57	Mississippi admitted 1817	♋	9 16	3 19	10 33
11	Tue	7 2	4 38	6	23 2	Indianna admitted 1816	♋	10 16	4 5	11 18
12	We	7 2	4 39	6	23 6	☌♂☾Browning d 1889	♌	11 15	4 50	11 41
13	Thu	7 3	4 39	5	23 10	☾ Bat Fredericsb'g 62	♌	morn	5 32	12 27
14	Fri	7 3	4 39	5	23 14	*Halcyon Days begin*	♍	0 12	6 14	1 13
15	Sat	7 4	4 39	4	23 17	Sitting Bull Killed 1890	♍	1 8	6 55	2 1
50. Third Sunday in Advent.						Day's length 9 hours 46 minutes.				
16	G	7 4	4 40	4	23 20	☌♂ with Leonis	♎	2 4	7 38	3 51
17	Mo	7 4	4 40	3	23 22	Bathoven b 1770	♎	3 1	8 23	4 43
18	Tue	7 5	4 40	3	23 24	Gen Dahlgreen d 1889	♎	3 59	9 9	4 37
19	We	7 6	4 40	2	23 25	☌♀☾—♂♆✳	♏	4 57	9 58	5 29
20	Thu	7 7	4 41	2	23 26	☌☿☾—☌♅☾ ['76	♏	5 52	10 50	6 19
21	Fri	7 7	4 41	1	23 27	☌♃☾ Wrinchester	♏	6 45	11 43	7 5
22	Sat	7 8	4 42	1	nor'h	✳*ent cap win com*	♐	sets	eve	7 51
51. Fourth Sunday in Advent						Day's length 9 hours 34 minutes.				
23	G	7 8	4 42	0	23 26	Tornado in France 179	♐	6 45	1 30	8 38
24	Mo	7 9	4 43	0	23 25	Thackery d 1863	♑	7 51	2 23	9 23
25	Tue	7 9	4 43	1	23 24	*Christmas Day*	♑	8 58	3 14	10 7
26	We	7 9	4 44	1	23 22	☿ in ♉ S Girard d '39	♒	10 5	4 1	10 53
27	Thu	7 10	4 44	2	23 19	*St John Evangelist*	♒	11 14	4 54	11 37
28	Fri	7 10	4 45	2	23 16	McCaulay died 1859	♓	morn	5 44	0 8
29	Sat	7 10	4 45	3	23 13	☽ ☌♄✳Gladstone b'09	♓	0 25	6 36	1 2
52. Sunday after Christmas.						Day's length 9 hours 43 minutes.				
30	G	7 11	4 46	3	23 9	☌♃☿ Beaconsfield b '03	♈	1 32	7 30	2 3
31	Mo	7 11	4 56	4	23 5		♈	2 40	8 26	3 8

WEATHER CONJECTURES—December—1, 2, 3, 4, 5, fair and frosty; 6, 7, 8, 9, 10, 11, 12, rain; 13, 14, 15, 16, 17, 18, 19, 20, fair, 21, 22, 23, 24, 25, 26, 27, fair and frosty of wind North or Northeast; snow if South or Southwest; 28, 29, 30, 31, ditto.

$1,000 per acre on Cherries. Plant them freely. Best kind sold by P. Bright, Ellenboro, N. C.

Farmers should use "NATIONAL" Fertilizer for Tobacco; and "BEEF, BLOOD and BONE" brand for Cotton, Corn and Wheat. Strictly reliable. Ask your Fertilizer Merchant for them. Carefully prepared by

(See top 3d cover page.) *S. W. TRAVERS & CO., Branch, Richmond, Va.*

FARM AND GARDEN WORK FOR DECEMBER.—Plant peas of all kinds; set out onions, garlic, eschalots and cabbage. Sow a few lettuce, spinach, carrots and radishes. You may try a few Irish potatoes.

Finish picking cotton; get out crops of rice and prepare for market—Commence plowing, ditching, draining and manuring as early as possible for next year's crop.

SUPERIOR COURTS OF NORTH CAROLINA FOR 1900.

Adopted from N. C. Court Calendar of A. B. Andrews, Jr.

JUDGES.			SOLICITORS.		
NAMES.	DISTRICT.	RESIDENCE.	NAMES.	DISTRICT.	RESIDENCE
Geo. H. Brown,	1	Washington.	Geo. W. Ward,	1	Elizabeth City.
Henry R. Bryan.	2	New Bern	W. E. Daniel,	2	Weldon.
E. W. Timberlake,	3	Louisburg.	Lrrry I. Moore,	3	Greenville.
W. S. O'B. Robinson,	4	Goldsboro,	Edward W. Pon,	4	Smithfield.
Thos. J. Shaw,	5	Greensboro.	A. L. Brooks,	5	Greensboro.
O. H. Allen,	6	Kinston.	Rodolph Dufy.	6	Jacksonville.
Thos. A. McNeill,	7	Lumberton,	C. M. McLean,	7	Elizabethtown
A. L. Coble,	8	Statesville.	Wiley Rush,	8	Asheboro.
Henay R, Starbuck,	9	Winston.	M. L. Mott,	9	Wilkesboro.
Jacob W. Bowman,	10	Bakersville.	J. F. Spainhour,	10	Lenoir,
W. Alexander Hoke,	11	Lincolnton.	J. L. Webb,	11	Shelby.
Fred. Moore,	12	Asheville.	Sas. W. Ferguson,	12	waynesville.

Time of Holding Courts.

FIRST JUDICIAL DISTRICT.

Spring—Judge Coble.
Fall—McNeill.
Beaufort—‡Feb 19th (o) May 23th (o) Nov 26th (o).
Currituck—March 5th, Sept 3.
Camden—March 12th, Sept 10th.
Pasquotank—March 19th,† July 16th, Sept 17th, December 17th.
Chowan—April 2d, Oct 1st.
Perquimans—March 26th, Sept 24th.
Gates—April 9th, Oct 8th.
Hertford—April 16th, Oct 15th.
Washington—April 23d, Oct 22d.
Tyrrell—April 30th, Oct 29th.
Dare—May 7th, Nov. 5th.
Hyde—May 14th, Nov 12th,
Pamlico—May 21st, Nov 19.

SECOND JUDICIAL DISTRICT.

Spring—Starbuck.
Fall—Judge Coble.
Halifax—†March 5th (o) ‡Nov 19th.
Northampton—April 2d (o) Oct 22d (o).
Bertie—‡Feb 19th, April 30th (o) ‡Sept 10th, Nov 5th.
Craven—March 29th (o) †May 28th (o) †Nov. 26th (o).
Warren—†March 19th (o) †Sept 17th (o).
Edgecombe—†April 16th (o) †June 11th (o) ‡Oct 3d (o).

THIRD SUDICIAL DISTRICT.

Spring—Judge Bowman.
Fall—Starbuck.

Pitt—Jan 8th (o) ‡March 5th (o) April 2d (o) Sept 17th, Dec (o) 3 (o)
Franklin—Jan 22d (o) April 16th, (o) Oct. 15th (o).
Wilson—Feb. 5th (o) †May 14 th †Nov. 12 (o)
Vance—Feb 19th (o) May 21st (o) Oct. 1st (o).
Martin—March 19th (o) Sept 3d (o)
Nash—†April 30th (o) Nov 19th.

FOURTH JUDICIAL DISTRICT.

Spring—Judge Hoke.
Fall—Bowman.
Wake—*Jan 8th (o) †Feb 26th (o) †April 23d (o) *March 26th (o) July 9th (o) *Sept. 24th, Oct 22 (3).
Wayne—Jan. 22d (o) April 16th, Sept 10 (o) Oct. 15th.
Harnett—Feb 17th, Sept 3d ‡Nov 26th (o).
Johnston—March 12th (o) Aug 27th, Nov 12th (o),

FIFTH JUDICIAL DISTRICT.

Spring—Judge Moore.
Fall—Hoke.
Durham—Jan 19th (o) †March 26th (o) *May. 14ih, *Sept 3, †Oct 1st, (o).
Granville—Jan. 27th (o) April 23d (o) July 23d (o) Nov 17 (o) Nov 19th (o).
Chatham—Feb 12th, May 7th, Sept 17th (o).
Guilford—Feb 19th (o) June 4th (3) Aug 20 (o) Dec 3d (o).
Alamance—March 12th, May 21st, †Sept 10th, Nov. 5th.

Orange—March 19th †May 28th, Aug 6th, Oct 29th.

Caswell—April 9th, Oct 15th.

Person—April 16th, Aug 13th, Nov 12th.

SIX JUDICIAL DISTRICT.

Spring—Jude Brown.
Fall—Judge Moore.

Pender—March 5th Sept 10th (o)

Greene—Feb 26th Aug 27th Nov 26.

New Hanover—†Jan 22nd (o) †April 16th (o) †Sept 24th (o).

Lenoir—Jan 15th May 7th Aug 20th Nov 12th.

Duplin—Feb 19th Sep 3rd Dec. 3rd (o).

Sampson—Feb 5th (o) April 30th Oct 8th (o)

Carteret—April 2nd Oct 22nd Jones March 12th Oct 29th.

SEVENTH JUDICIAL DISTRICT.

Spring—Judge Bryan.
Fall—Judge Brown.

Columbus— March 12th Aug 13th Nov 8th Oct 22nd.

Anson—*Jan 8th †April 16th *Sept 3rd *Oct 29th.

Cumberland—†Feb 19th *†March 26th ⅔April 2 (o) †May 7th (o) †Sept 24 †Nov 12th (o).

Robeson—†Feb 12th †April 30th †July 23 †Oct 8th.

Richmond—†Jan 15th Tuesday (o) April 23rd †May 21nd *†Sept 10th Nov 5th.

Bladen—March 5th Tuesday Oct 1st Tuesday 13th.

Brunswick—March 19th Oct 15th

Moore—†Jan 29th (2) *April 2d (o) *†Aug 20th (o) Nov 26th.

EIGHTH JUDICIAL DISTRICT.

Spring—Judge Timberlake.
Fall—Judge Bryan.

Cabarrus—Jan 22d (o) April 23rd July 23rd (o) Oct 15th.

Iredell—Feb 5th (o) May 21st (o) Aug 6th (2) Nov 5th (2).

Rowan—Feb 19th (o) May 7th (o) Aug 20th (2) Nov 19th (o).

Davidson—March 5th (o) Sept 3rd (2).

Randolph—March 19th (o) July 9th (o) Dec 3rd (o).

Montgomery—Jan 10th April 16 Oct 1st (o).

Yadkin—April 30th Oct 22nd (o)

NINTH JUDICIAL DISTRICT.

Spring—Judge Robinson.
Fall—Judge Timberlake.

Alexander—Feb. 19 Aug 20.

Rockingham—March 5th (o) Aug 13th. Oct 29 (o).

Forsyth—†Feb. 26th May 14th (o). Nov. 26th (o).

Wilkes—March 19th May 28th (o) Aug. 27th (o).

Alleghany—March 26th April 3d Sept. 10th.

Davie—April 2th Oct. 25th (o).

Stokes—April 30th (o) Sep. 17th (o).

Surry—Nov. 12th (o) Oct. 1st (o).

TENTH JUDICIAL DISTRICT.

Spring—Judge Shaw.
Fall—Judge Robinson.

Catawba—Feb. 26th Aug. 6th (o) Nov. 19th (o).

McDowell—†April 9th (o) †July 23rd (o).

Burke—April 30th (o) Nov 5th(o).

Caldwell—March 2d Aug 20th (o) Oct. 16th (o).

Ashe—April 2d Feb. 17th (o) Nov 13th.

Watauga—March 26th Sep. 3d (o) Nov. 20.

Mitchell—Feb. 12th April 16th (o) Oct. 1st (o).

Yancey— May 14th (o) †*Oct. 15th (3).

ELEVENTH JUDICIAL DISTRICT.

Spring—Judge Allen.
Fall—Judge Shaw.

Union—*†Jan. 29th (3) †for 2d 3d weeks †*June 11th (o) *†Aug 20th (o) *Sept. 10th *Dec. 17th.

Stanly—March 5th (o) Sept. 3rd †Dec. 10th.

Mecklenburg—†Jan. 20th †March 19th (o) †Oct 1st (o) †June 4th †Dec 16th.

Gaston—Feb 19th (o) Sep 17th (o)

Lincoln—April 2nd (o) Oct 15th

Cleveland—April 16th (o) Oct 22nd (o).

Rutherford—April 30th (o) Nov 5th (2).

Polk—May 14th Nov. 19th.

Henderson—†May 21st (o) †Nov 26th (o).

TWELFTH JUDICIAL DISTRICT.

Spring—Judge McNeill
Fall—Judge Allen.

Madison—⅔Jan 22nd (o) ⅔July 23 Buncombe—⅔Feb 5th (3) * April 30th (o) Aug 13th (3) *Nov 12th (o).

Transylvania—Feb 22nd (o) Sep 3rd (o).

Haywood—*March 12th (o) *Sep 17th (2).

Jackson—March 26th (o) Oct 1st.

Macon—April 9th (o) Oct 8th.
Clay—April 23rd Oct 15th.
Cherokee—May 14th (o) *Oct 22nd (o).
Graham—May 28th Nov 5th
Swain—June 4th (3) Nov 26th (o)

CRIMINAL COURTS.

EASTERN DISTRICT.

Judge—Battle.

New Havover—March 12th *Mar 13th *June 4th (o) *Aug 6th Nov 19th.

Warren—*June 25th *Dec 10th.

Vance—*Feb 14th.

Edgecombe—*May 21st *Nov 12

Craven—*Feb 26th Aug 20th.

Halifax—*January 29th *May 7th *Oct 1st.

29th.

Mecklenburg—*January 8th (o) ※July 16 (o). *April 9th *Sept 24th ※Nov 26th.

Robinson— * April 16th *Oct 29th.

Cumberland — *January 1st *April 30th *Sept 17th.

Wilson—*June 18th *Oct 15th August 21st.

Nash—*Feb 5th *Aug 27th.

Northampton — * March 19th *Sept 3rd.

WESTERN DISTRICT.

Judge—Stevens.

Solicitor—Robt S McCall Asheville.

Buncombe—*Jan 15th (o) *April 23rd (o) *July 23rd †Oct 22.

Madison—*Feb 20th June 12th Nov 13th.

Henderson—†Sept 11th April 10.

McDowell—*July 10th *Dec 11th

———

*For criminal cases.
*†For civil cases alone.
(o) Means two weeks, etc.
‡For civil cases alone, except jail cases.
Scotland County Terms to be set by Governor.

U. S. CIRCUIT AND DISTRICT COURTS.

Charles H. Simonton, Charleston, S. C., Judge of Fourth Circuit of United States Courts.

Nathan Goff, West Virginia, Judge of U. S. Circuit Court of Appeals for Fourth District.

WESTERN DISTRICT.—H. G. Ewart, Hendersonville, Judge; A. E. Holton, District Attorney; Spencer Blackburn, Assistant Attorney; S. L, Trogden, Clerk. *Greensboro*—Circuit and District—April 2d, (o) October 1. *Statesville*—Circuit and District—H. C. Cowles, Clerk; April 16, (o) October 15. *Asheville*—Circuit and District—C. B. Moore, Clerk; May 7, (o) November 5. *Charlotte*——Circuit and District—H. C. Cowles, Clerk; June 4th, December 3.

EASTERN DISTRICT.—T. R. Purnell, Judge; C. M. Bernard, Greenville, District Attorney; O. C. Spears and E. A. Johnson, Assistant Attorneys; W. C. Brooks, Deputy Clerk. *Elizabeth City*—District Court—April 16, October 15. *New Bern*—District Court—George Green, Deputy Clerk; Newbern, April 23, October 22.—*Wilmington*—Circuit and District—J. B. Fortune, Clerk; V. Royster, Assistant Clerk, in Raleigh; W. H. Shaw, Clerk of District and Deputy of Circuit Court at Wilmington; H. C. Dockery, Marshal; April 30, October 29. *Raleigh*—Circuit and District—J. B. Fortune, Clerk; V. Royster. Clerk in Raleigh; W. H. Shaw, Clerk of District and Deputy of Circuit Court at Wilmington; H. C. Dockery, Marshal; Raleigh, May 28th, (o) December 3d.

SUPREME COURT OF NORTH CAROLINA.

Examiner's Applicants for license Monday, first week of term.

Cases Heard—First District, Monday, February 5th, September 24th; Second District, Monday, February 12th, October 1st. Third District, Monday, February 19th, October 8th. Fourth District, February 26th, October 15th. Fifth District, March 5th, October 21st. Sixth District, March 12, October 29. Seventh District, March 19, November 5th. Eighth District, March 26th, November 12th. Ninth District, April 2d, November 19. Tenth District, April 9th, November 26th. Eleventh District, April 16th, December 3d. Twelfth District, April 23d, December 10th. End of docket, etc., April 30th.

COUNTY OFFICERS CORRECTED FROM LAST ELECTION UP TO NOVEMBER, 1899.

	COUNTIES.	COUNTY TOWNS.	CLERKS	REGISTERS.	SHERIFFS.	SUPERVISORS OF SCHOOLS.
1	Alamance,	Graham,	J D Kerhodie,	Chas C Thompson,	L B McAdams,	Rev P H Fleming,
2	Alexander,	Taylorsville,	A L Watts,	V W Teague,	J V Williams,	A Frank Sharp,
3	Alleghany,	Sparta,	I N Edwards,	S F Thompson,	Dr R Edwards,	Prof S W Brown,
4	Ansou,	Wadesboro,	J C McLauchlin,	S A Benton,	J T Gaddy,	W D Redfearn,
5	Ashe,	Jefferson,	A S Ellis,	D A Osborne,	P G McNeill,	J W Jones,
6	Beaufort,	Washington,	G Wilkens,	Gilbert Rumley,	R T Hodges,	Dr Burton Stilley,
7	Bertie,	Windsor,	W L Lyon,	F E Etheridge,	T C Boone,	R w Askew,
8	Bladen,	Elizabethtown,	A M McNeill,	J S Williams,	S G Wooten,	D S Perry,
9	Brunswick,	Southport,	Thos L Wines,	John W Brooks,	D R Walker,	Isaac Jennette.
10	Buncombe,	Asheville,	T C Starnes,	J J Mackey,	R F Lee,	D L Ellis,
11	Burke,	Morganton,	P W Patton,	J H Giles,	C M McDowell,	Rev R L Patton,
12	Cabarrus,	Concord,	J M Cook,	W R Johnson,	J Lawson Peck,	Prof H T J Ludwig,
13	Caldwell,	Lenoir,	J V McCall,	W D Minish,	A H Boyd,	Prof E B Phillips,
14	Camden,	Camden C. H.,	R L Forbes,	C B Garrett,	W S Bartlett,	C B Garrett,
15	Carteret,	Beaufort,	L A Garner,	W L Arrington,	A S Welles,	Soseph Pigott,
16	Caswell,	Yanceyville,	Thos H Harrison,	John T Graves,	J T Domaho,	A E Henderson,
17	Catawba,	Newton,	L H Phillips,	P M Dellinger,	J R Blackwelder,	J D Rowe,
18	Chatham,	Pittsboro,	R A Dixon,	John T Paschal,	James J Johnson,	R B Lineberry,
19	Cherokee,	Murphy,	S W Lovingood,	J C McDonald,	A J Martin,	I M Lovingood,
20	Chowan,	Edenton,	H C Privatt,	M A Hughes,	A P Elliott,	W F Watson,
21	Clay,	Haysville,	C C Stanridge,	J O Scoggs,	W H Hogshed,	W J Winchester,
22	Cleveland,	Shelby,	L J Hoyle,	J F Roberts,	A B Suttle,	J A Anthony,
23	Columbus,	Whiteville,	H C Moffitt,	K L Fowell,	J G Butler,	W H Sellars,
24	Craven,	Newbern,	E W Carpeater,	John B Wils,	J L Hahn,	Rev John S Long,
25	Cumberland,	Fayetteville,	A A McKeithan,	Bynum,	George A Burns,	H T Everett,
26	Currituck,	Currituck C. H.,	E W Ansell,	W H Bray,	R E Flora,	J w Ritter,
27	Dare,	Mantes,	T S Meekins,	R W Smith,	T Cudworth,	Lemuel Bassnight,
28	Davidson,	Lexington,	H T Phillips,	S L Oweh,	T F S Dorsett,	Robert S Green,
29	Davie,	Mocksville,	W R Ellis,	R O Morris,	Jesse L Sheek,	C M Sheets,
30	Duplin,	Kenansville,	Herbert Smith,	B Frank Pearsall,	L Middleton,	Prof R w Millard,
31	Durham,	Durham,	C B Green,	John Suitt,	F D Markham,	C w Massey,
32	Edgecombe,	Tarboro,	Ed Pennington,	B L Dozan,	W L Stellings,	Dr A F Davis,
33	Forsyth,	Winston,	N S Wilson,	B F Byerly,	E T Knapps,	R M Davis,
34	Franklin,	Louisburg,	W K A Williams,	I T Clifton,	H C Kearney,	B S Mitchell,
35	Gaston,	Dallas,	C C Cornell,	M A Carpenter,	W T Love,	L M Hoffman,
36	Gates,	Gatesville,	W T Cross,	Lycurgus Hofler,	R O Riddick,	John R waltou,
37	Graham,	Robbinsville,	R V McElroy,	Robert B Slaughter,	J A Ammons,	J N Moody,
38	Granville,	Oxford,	J G Hunt,	John B Mayes,	S A Fleming,	Alexander Baker,
39	Greene,	Snow Hill,	John R Dale,	Chas A Lassiter,	B W Edwards,	Fred L Carr,
40	Guilford,	Greensboro,	John J Nelson,	A G Kirkman,	J H Gilmer,	Prof J R wharton,
41	Halifax,	Halifax C. H.,	S M Sary,	J H Norman,	J E. Honse,	Col Aaron Prescott,
42	Harnett,	Lillington,	J H Withers,	A C Holloway,	S A Soloman,	Rev J A Campbell,
43	Haywood,	Waynesville,	N P Walker,	H B Moore,	W J Haynes,	A Garner,
44	Henderson,	Hendersonville,	C M Pace,	W A Hood,	J S Mitchell,	R H Staton,
45	Hertford,	Winton,	I F Newsom,	S E Marsh,	T C Eaun,	P E Shaw
46	Hyde,	Swan Quarter,	R D Harlis,	R W Brown,	I H Wycoff,	H L McGowan
47	Iredell,	Statesville,	Jas Hartness,	W W Turner,	T C Hann,	J A Butler
48	Jackson,	webster,	F E Alley,	James R Long,	W A Hosson,	J H Painter,

No.	County	Seat					No.
63	Northampton,	Jackson,	J. T. Flythe,	E. E. Roberts,	W. H. Buffaloe,	Jaml I. Long.	63
64	Onslow,	Jacksonville,	John W. Burton,	I. R. Ketchum,	F. W. Hargett,	A. w. Cooper.	64
65	Orange,	Hillsboro,	D. H. Hamilton,	John Laws,	John K. Hughes,	John Thompson,	65
66	Pamlico,	Bayboro,	James R. Rice,	Alex Lee,	Wallace E. Hooker,	D. P. Harris,	66
67	Pasquotank,	Elizabeth City,	W. H. Jennings,	E. B. Culpeper,	N. G. Grandy,	Gaston Pool,	67
68	Pender,	Burgaw,	W. W. Larkins,	J. P. Stringfield,	w. w. Alderman,	T. H. w. McIntyre,	68
69	Perquimans,	Hertford,	E. V. Perry,	W. R. White,	A. F. Iddick,	Francis Pickard.	69
70	Person,	Roxboro,	D. W. Bradsher,	H. J. Whitt,	J. R. Sims,	G. F. Holloway.	70
71	Pitt,	Greenville,	D. C. Moore,	T. K. Moore,	G. M. Mooring,	J. R. Single.	71
72	Polk,	Columbus,	N. B. Thompson,	A. L. McMurray,	W. C. Robertson,	S. A. Hudgin.	72
73	Randolph,	Asheboro,	G. G. Hendricks,	J. Y. Winslow,	W. F. Redding,	N. C. English,	73
74	Richmond,	Rockingham,	W. T. Everett,	H. D. Gibson,	T. S. Wright,	M. N. McIver,	74
75	Robeson,	Lumberton,	W. H. Humphrey,	Joe Buic,	G. B. McLeod,	W. R. Surles.	75
76	Rockingham,	Wentworth,	J. V. Price,	J. A. Scales,	R. W. Hetcherson,	E. P. Ellington.	76
77	Rowan,	Salisbury,	W. G. Watson,	N. H. Woodson,	J. M. Monroe,	R. G. Kizer.	77
78	Rutherford,	Rutherfordton,	M. O. Dickerson,	Jas. P. Jones,	E. A. Marlin,	C. C. Gettys.	78
79	Sampson,	Clinton,	W. F. Pigford,	O. F. Herring,	J. W. Marshburn,	Street Brewer.	79
80	Scotland,	Laurinburg,	W. I. Everett,	H. D. Gibson,	J. S. Wright,	M. F. McIver.	80
81	Stanly,	Albemarle,	R. A. Crowell,	L. N. Sugg,	G. R. McCain,	J. A. Spence.	81
82	Stokes,	Danbury,	N. O. Petree,	T. W. Davis,	R. P. Joyce,	Prof. M. T. Chilton.	82
83	Surry,	Dobson,	C. H. Haynes,	A. G. De Hart,	J. M. Davis,	John W. williams.	83
84	Swain,	Bryson City,	A. J. Hall,	Wm. Henry,	V. B. EcGatlin,	J U. Gibbs.	84
85	Transylvania,	Brevard,	T. T. Loftis,	T. L. Jones,	F. L. Cohoon,	Judson Coon,	85
86	Tyrrell,	Columbia,	G. L. Linerman,	J. M. Stewart,	B. A. Horne,	James L. Norman.	86
87	Union,	Monroe,	E. A. Armfield,	Kenneth Edwards,	W. H. Smith,	R. F. Beasly.	87
88	Vance,	Henderson,	Henry Perry,	W. H. Hood,	M. W. Page,	A. M. Matics,	88
89	Wake,	Raleigh,	W. M. Russ,	M. F. Thornton,	J. B. W. Jones,	H. W. Norris.	89
90	Warren,	Warrenton,	W. A. White,	W. H. Stall,	J. L. Phelps,	James R. Kodwell.	90
91	Washington,	Plymouth,	W. M. Bateman,	Jacob May,	W. H. Caloway,	w. R. Chissom.	91
92	Watauga,	Boone,	J. F. Ormond,	G. C. Kornegay,	B. F. Scott,	L. H. Michael.	92
93	Wayne,	Goldsboro,	Linville Bumgarner,	E. M. Blackburn,	J. H. Johnson,	E. T. Atkins.	93
94	Wilkes,	Wilkesboro,	J. D. Bardin,	Wm. B. Barnes,	W. D. P. Sharp,	James H. Foote.	94
95	Wilson,	Wilson,	W. A. Hall,	J. L. Craton,	A. P. Woodruff,	James w. Hayes,	95
96	Yadkin,	Yadkinville,	J I. Ray,	J. R. Young,	W. B. Wilson,	Rev. J. H. Patterson.	96
97	Yancey,	Burnsville,				william McIntosh.	97

New Hanover in 1764.

[The following poem refers to the magnificent conduct of the brave people of New Hanover and Brunswick counties, when, soon after the inauguration after the iniquitous Stamp Act, the Diligence (an English sloop of war) entered the harbor of old Brunswick town for the purpose of landing stamp paper for the colony. It was a deed worthy of all fame, and still it is known and recognized by but few of the people of our country, or even of our State.]

Spoke the leader bold of men four-score—
In seventeen hundred and sixty-four—
To a sloop of war that sailed one day
Into the river, and—later—lay,
With colors afloat as the sun went down,
Within the harbor of Brunswick town:
"No England's George's ships land here
Their odious freight; we do not fear
The sceptered hand of a tyrant's power!
Make sail and away; delay one hour,
And your cursed ship shall strew the wave
With flaming brands!" Thus spoke the brave,
And, drawing nearer—with scarcely a sound—
They cut the cables that held her bound!

Ere the sun came up on the other side,
To redden the wave at the ebb of the tide,
The ship with its hateful cargo passed
Away out of sight of hull and of mast!

Hurrah for the men of Wilmington,
By whom this deed of glory was done!
Remember the men of old Brunswick tawn,
Who stood for the right as the sun went down.

Raleigh, N. C.   HUNTER L. HARRIS.

EDITORIAL NOTES.

1. THE BAPTIST FEMALE UNIVERSITY will be added to the lis of Graduating Schools on page seven next year,

2. WE GREATLY regret the absence of full reports from one or two of our State Schools in time to print the usual extended notice.

LEVI BRANSON, *Editor and Publisher.*

NOTE 2.—ONE OR TWO PUBLIC SCHOOLS FAILED TO REPORT IN TIME.

ABBA, FATHER.

I said one day to God, the Son,
"Thy will"—"Thy Father's will be done:"
He said, "A slave no longer be;
The Son of Man hath set the free."

Blest with a filial spirit now,
Before the Mercy seat I bow,
With offering of praise and prayer,
And know that I am welcome there.

Where once the dread Shekinah shoen
A rainbow girds the Jasper throne;
By faith I now draw near to Him
Who dwells between the cherubim.

—THEO. H. HILL.

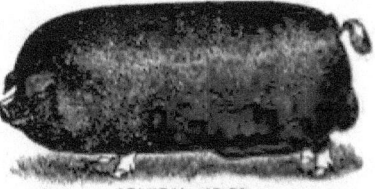

GOVERNMENT OF NORTH CAROLINA—1897-1901.

EXECUTIVE DEPARTMENT.

Daniel L. Russell, of New Hanover County, Governor, salary $3,000, and furnished house, fuel and lights.

Charles A. Reynolds, of Forsyth County, Lieutenant Governor and Speaker of the Senate.

Cyrus Thompson, of Onslow County, Secretary of State; salary $2,000 and fees; $1,000 additional assistance.

D. H. Senter, Clerk in Secretary of State's office.

Hal W. Ayer, of Wake County, Auditor; salary $1,500; additional for clerical assistance $1,000.

William H. Worth, of Wake County, Treasurer; salary $3,000.

E. O. Cole, Clerk in Treasurer's office.

Charles H. Mebane, of Catawba County, Superintendent of Public Instruction; salary $1,500; $500 per annum additional for extra clerical assistance.

Zebulon Vance Walser, of Davidson County, Attorney General, salary $2,000.

R. P. Buxton, Reporter to Supreme Court; salary $1,250.

B. S. Royster, of Granville County, Adjutant General; salary $400.

Miles O. Sherrell, Catawba County, State Librarian; salary $1,000.

R. C. Rivers, Wake County, Chief Clerk to Auditor; salary $1,000.

Baylus Cade, Franklin County, Private Secretary to Governor, salary $1,200.

Mrs. Sawyer, New Hanover County, Executive Clerk; salary $600.

J. B. Koonce, Jones County, Chief Clerk to Secretary of State; salary $1,000.

J. W. Denmark, of Wake County, Chief Clerk to Treasurer; salary $1,500.

S. L. Crowder, of Warren County, Teller; salary 750.

W. H. Worth, Treasurer *ex officio*, and Wm. H. Martin, of Wake County, Clerk for Charitable and Penal Institutions, salary $1,000.

C. C. Cherry of Edgecombe County, Superintendent of Public Buildings and Grounds, salary $600.

A. L. Moore, of Wake County, State Standard Keeper; salary $100.

STATE BOARD OF EDUCATION.

The Governor, Lieutenant Governor, Secretary of State, Treasurer, Auditor, Superintendent of Public Instruction and Atorney General constitute the Board.

STATE HOSPITAL, GEO. L. KIRBY, SUPERINTENDENT, RALEIGH, N. C.

Hon. W. H. Worth, Treasurer *ex officio*; W. H. Martin, Clerk to Treasurer *ex officio*; J. B. Bellamy, Keeper of Records.

RESIDENT OFFICERS.—Dr. George L. Kirby, Superiutendent, salary $2,800; term, six years from March 1, 1894. Dr. C. L. Jenkins, First Assistant Physician, salary $1,200; term, two years from March 1, 1897. Dr. Geo. Davis, salary $1,000; terms, two years from March 1, 1897. W. R. Crawford, Jr., Steward, salary $1,200; term, one year from March 1, 1897. Miss M. E. Whitaker, Matron, salary $600; term, one year from March 1, 1897.

BOARD OF DIRECTORS.—Capt. J. D. Biggs, President; J. B. Broadfoot, Fayetteville, N. C.; Dr. R. H. Speight, Edgecombe County; Dr. James McKee, Raleigh, N. C.; Geo. R. Curtis, Halifax County; J. B. Ballamy, Nash County; Wiley B. Fort, Wayne County; J. B. Barnes, Wilson, N. C.; Dr. R. H. Stancill, Margarettsville, N. C.

STATE BOARD OF PHARMACY.

E. V. Zoeller, Tarboro, President; W. H. Wearn. Charlotte; N. D. Fetzer, Concord; Wm. Simpson, Raleigh, Secretary and Treasurer; T. W. Hancock, Oxford.

NORTH CAROLINA PHARMACEUTICAL ASSOCIATION.

J. P. Stedman, Oxford, President; W. M. Yearby, Durham; J. B. Smith, Lexington, J. I. Johnson, Raleigh. Vice-Presidents; H. R. Horne, Fayetteville. Secretary; A. J. Cook, Fayetteville, Treasurer; J. H. Bobbitt, Chairman of Executive Committe, Raleigh.

STATE BOARD OF EXAMINERS.

C. H. Mebane, Chairman *ex officio*; W. L. Poteat, Wake Forest College; L. L. Hobbs, Guilford College; M. C. S. Noble, University of N. C.

OFFICERS OF STATE MEDICAL SOCIETY.

Dr. L. V. Pecot, Littleton, President; Dr. Geo. W. Pressley, Charlotte. Secretary.   Meeting in Asheville 1899.

STATE BOARD OF MEDICAL EXAMINERS.

Dr. D. T. Tayloe, Washington, President; Dr. Thos. E, Anderson Statesville, Secretary; Dr. Herbert Anderson. Wilson; Dr. W. H. H. Cobb Goldsboro; Dr. J. H. Way, Waynesville; Dr. Kemp. P. Battle, Raleigh Dr. E. C. Register, Charlotte.

Traveling expenses and $4.00 per day during session.

JACOB S. ALLEN, Jr., HARDWARE,

214 S. Wilmington, St., RALEIGH, N.C.

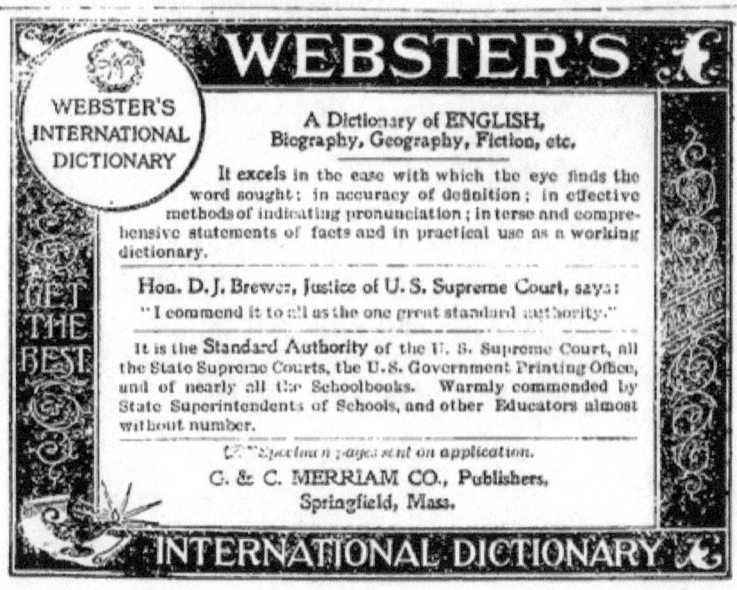

BRANSON'S SHORT CALENDAR FOR 1900.

JANUARY.						
S	M	T	W	T	F	S
	1	2	3	4	5	6
7	8	9	10	11	12	13
14	15	16	17	18	19	20
21	22	23	24	25	26	27
28	29	30	31			

FEBRUARY.						
S	M	T	W	T	F	S
				1	2	3
4	5	6	7	8	9	10
11	12	13	14	15	16	17
18	19	20	21	22	23	24
25	26	27	28			

MARCH.						
S	M	T	W	T	F	S
				1	2	3
4	5	6	7	8	9	10
11	12	13	14	15	16	17
18	19	20	21	22	23	24
25	26	27	28	29	30	31

APRIL.						
1	2	3	4	5	6	7
8	9	10	11	12	13	14
15	16	17	18	19	20	21
22	33	24	25	26	27	28
29	30					

MAY.						
	1	2	3	4	5	
6	7	8	9	10	11	12
13	14	15	16	17	18	19
20	21	22	23	24	25	26
27	28	29	30	31		

JUNE.						
					1	2
3	4	5	6	7	8	9
10	11	12	13	14	15	16
17	18	19	20	21	22	23
24	25	26	27	28	29	30

JULY.						
1	2	3	4	5	6	7
8	9	10	11	12	13	14
15	16	17	18	19	20	21
22	23	24	25	26	27	28
29	30	31				

AUGUST.						
		1	2	3	4	
5	6	7	8	9	10	11
12	13	14	15	16	17	18
19	20	21	22	23	24	25
26	27	28	29	30	31	

SEPTEMBER.						
						1
2	3	4	5	6	7	8
9	10	11	12	13	14	15
16	17	18	19	20	21	22
23	14	25	26	27	28	29
30						

OCTOBER.						
	1	2	3	4	5	6
7	8	9	10	11	12	13
14	15	16	17	18	19	20
21	22	23	24	25	26	27
28	29	30	31			

NOVEMBER.						
				1	2	3
4	5	6	7	8	9	10
11	12	13	14	15	16	17
18	19	20	21	22	23	24
25	26	27	28	29	30	

DECEMBER.						
						1
2	3	4	5	6	7	8
9	10	11	12	13	14	15
16	17	18	19	20	21	22
23	24	25	26	27	28	29
30	31					

PRICE, 10 CENTS

Vol. 4.]   34 YEAR OF PUBLICATION.   No. 4.]

BRANSON'S
AGRICULTURAL
ALMANAC

FOR THE YEAR OF OUR LORD
1901,

And until the 4th of July, the 125th year of American Independence.
FIRST YEAR OF 20TH CENTURY.

Carefully Calculated for the Latitude and Longitude of Raleigh, by

LEVI BRANSON, A. M., D. D.

LEVI BRANSON, Publisher, Raleigh, N. C.

TIME.

The calculations of this Almanac are made in mean solar or clock time,
which is indicated by a well regulated watch or clock, and does not correspond with the Sun precisely, except on four days of the year.

Apparent time is that which makes the Sun come to the meridian at
12 o'clock. No good clock will run with the Sun ; if set with the Sun
on the 2d day of January, the clock will seem to be one minute too fast
on the 3d of January.

To adapt the calculations of this Almanac to apparent time, use the
minutes in the column marked "Sun slow" or "Sun fast;" add them
when fast, subtract them when slow.

The calculations are made for the Latitude and Longitude of Raleigh,
N. C., but the times, phases, etc., will vary only a few minutes for any
part of North Carolina, South Carolina, Georgia, Tennessee or Virginia.

To know where the sign is, find the day of the month; and against the day in the
column marked Moon's Signs you have the sign or place of the Moon, and then find
the sign; it will give you the part of the body it is supposed to govern.

TWELVE SIGNS OF THE ZODIAC.

The Head and Face sign.   ♈ Aries the Ram......Ar.

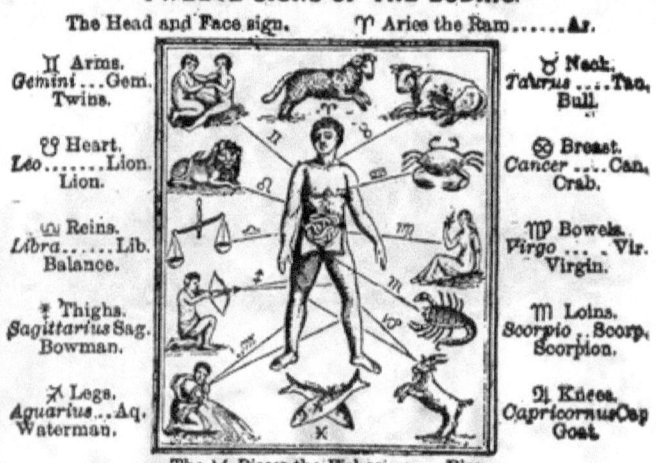

♊ Arms.
Gemini ...Gem.
Twins.

♌ Heart.
Leo.......Lion.
Lion.

♎ Reins.
Libra......Lib.
Balance.

♐ Thighs.
Sagittarius Sag.
Bowman.

♒ Legs.
Aquarius...Aq.
Waterman.

♉ Neck.
Taurus ....Tau.
Bull.

⊗ Breast.
Cancer ....Can.
Crab.

♍ Bowels.
Virgo ... Vir.
Virgin.

♏ Loins.
Scorpio .. Scorp.
Scorpion.

♑ Knees.
Capricornus Cap.
Goat.

The ♓ *Pisces* the Fishes ,.(....Pisc.

SIGNS.

SPRING SIGNS.	Aries, or Ram. Taurus, or Bull. Gemini, or Twins.	AUTUMN SIGNS.	Libra, or Balance. Scorpio, or Scorpion. Sagittarius, or Bowman.
SUMMER SIGNS.	Cancer, or Crab-fish Leo, or Lion Virgo, or Virgin.	WINTER SIGNS.	Capricornus, or Goat. Aquarius, or Waterman. Pisces, or Fishes.

SIGNS OF THE PLANETS.

☀ Sun.	☽ Moon.	♀ Venus.
♃ Jupiter.	♄ Saturn.	☌ In Conjunction.
☿ Mercury.	⛢ Uranus.	♆ Neptune.
⊕ Earth.	☍ Opposition.	☋ Descending Node.

♂ Mars.
□ Quadrature.
☊ Ascending Node.

MOON'S PHASES.

● New Moon.   ☽ First Quarter.   ● Full Moon.   ☾ Last Quarter.

Branson's Almanac is a household word.—*Truth.*

3. Some men have faith in the laws of health, and hence by obeying those laws they secure physical health and happiness.—*Branson.*

BRANSON'S NORTH CAROLINA ALMANAC. 3

CHRONOLGICAL CYCLES AND ERAS.

Dominical Letter	F	Julian Period	6614
Epact	10	Jewish Era	5661
Folden Number	2	Era of Nabonassa	2648
Solar Cycle	6	Olympiads.	2677
Roman Indiction	14	Mahommedan Era	1318

MOVABLE FEASTS OF THE CHURCH.

Epiphany	Jan. 6	Palm Sunday	March 31
Septuagesima Sunday	Feb. 3	Easter Sunday	April 7
Sexagesima Sunday	Feb. 10	White Sunday	May 26
Quinquagesima Sunday	Feb. 17	Trinity Sunday	June 2
Ash Wednesday, or Lent	Feb. 20	First Sunday in Advent	Dec. 1
St. Patrick's Day	Mar. 17	Ancension Day	May 16
Good Friday	April 15	First Sunday in Lent	Feb. 24

MORNING STARS.

Mercury will be Morning Star about April 4, August 2, and November 20. Venus will be Morning Star from April 30, till Sept. 15. Jupiter will be Morning Star till June 30.

EVENING STARS.

Mercury will be Evening Star about.................Feb. 19, and Oct. 12.
Venus will be Evening Star from.................................April 30.
Jupiter will will be Evening Star........................from June 30.

ECLIPSES.

In the year 1900 there will be two Eclipses of the Sun and one of the Moon, and a Lamar Appulse.

I. A Lumar Appulse May 3, 1901. Invisible in North America.

II. A Total Eclipse of the Snn, May 18, 1901, invisible in the United States.

III. A Partial Eclipse of the Moon, Oct. 27, visible to North and South America, except in Alaska.

IV. An Annular Eclipse of the Sun, November 11, invisible to North America.

TIDES.

The time of tides can readily be found for the following places by adding the hours and minutes opposite the names to the ◐ me when the Moon is South on the day to when the tide is sought. The time when the Moon is South is given to the Calendar for every day. The next tide can be found very nearly by adding 12 hours and 29 minutes to the time of the one previous.

The tides are given in local time—add 12 minutes for Eastern Standard.

	H. M.		H. M.
Boston	11 12	New York	8 13
Sandy Hook	7 29	Old Point	8 17
Baltimore	6 33	Washington City	7 44
Richmond	4 32	Hatteras Inlet	7 04
Beaufort	7 26	Bald Head	7 26
Southport	7 19	Wilmington	9 06
Charleston	7 26	Sauannah	9 33

2 A man in whose mind his own country is not *first* is a man who himself is not *worthy* to be first in another country.—*Branson.*

J. E. Bridgers, Merchant Tailor 216 Fayetteville St., Raleigh, N. C.

THE FOUR SEASONS.

Spring commences........ ....March 21, 1 P. M.
Summer commences ....June 21, 9 P. M.
Autumn commences............... ....September 23, 0 P. M.
Winter commences...... ....December 22, 6 A. M.

HERSCHELS WEATHER PROGNOSTICATOR.

For Fortelling the Weather Through all the Lunations of the year.

This table and the accompanying remarks are the result of many years actual observation, the whole being constructed on a due consideration of the attractions of the Sun and Moon, in their several positions respecting the Earth, and, by simple inspection, it shows the observer what kind of weather will most probably follow the entrance of the Moon into any of its quarters, and that so near the truth as to be seldom or never found to fail.

If the new moon, first quarter, full moon, or last quarter, hapen—	IN SUMMER.	IN WINTER
Between midnight and 2 in the morning............	Fair..................	Hoar frost unless the wind is S. or S. W.
Between 2 and 4, morning	Cold, with frequent showers..........	Snow and stormy.
Between 4 and 6, morning..	Rain	Rain.
Between 6 and 8, morning..	Wind and rain......	Stormy.
Between 8 and 10, morning	Changeable	Cold rain if wind be W., snow if E.
Between 10 and 12 morning	Frequent showers ...	Cold and high wind.
Between 12 o'clock at noon and 2 in afternoon........	Very rainy..........	Rain and Snow.
Between 2 and 4, afternoon	Changeable.........	Fair and mild.
Between 4 and 6, afternoon	Fair..........	Fair.
Between 6 and 8, aftern'n	Fair if wind N. W.; rainy if S. or S. W.	Fair and frosty wind N. or N. E.; rain or snow if S. or S. W.
Between 8 and 10, afternoon	Ditto..............	Ditto.
Between 10 and midnight..	Fair...............	Fair and frosty.

OBSERVATIONS.—1. The nearer the time for the Moon's change, first quarter, full and last quarter are to midnight, the fairer will be the weather during the next seven days.

2. The space for this calculation occupies from 10 at night until 2 next morning.

3. The nearer to midday or noon the phase of the Moon happens, the more foul or wet weather may be expected during the next seven days.

4. The space for this calculations occupies from 10 in the forenoon until 2 in the afternoon. These observations refer principally to the Summer, though they affect Spring ond Autumn nearly in the same ratio.

5. The Moon's change, ffrst quarter, full and last quarter happening during six of the afternoon hours, *i. e.*, from 4 to 10, may be followed by fair weather, but this is mostly dependent on the wind, as is noted in the table.

6. Though the weather, from a variety of irregular causes, is more uncertain in the later part of Autumn, the whole of Winter and beginning of Spring, yet, in the main, the above observations will apply to those periods also.

7. To prognosticate correctly, especially in those cases where the wind is concerned, the observer should be in sight of a good vane, where the four cardinal points of the heavens are correctly placed.

6. The Christian religion leads a man towards the cultivation of all his best capabilities.—*Branson.*

STATISTICS OF LIBRARIES IN NORTH CAROLINA, 1899.

Through the untiring efforts of our efficient State Librarian, we are enabled to give correctly the great progress that has been made in our State in the last few years towards placing within the reach of the great masses of our people, useful information that has theretofore been beyond the reach of the common class of our citizens, by establishing public Libraries, accessible to all who are in search of useful knowledge.

NAMES OF LIBRARIES.	Where Located.	When Estab-lished.	No, of Vols.	Money Used Each Year.	Librarian.
State Library	Raleigh	1841	22,618	$ 500.	Miles O. Sherrell.
Female College	Asheville		1,000		
Asheville Library	Asheville		3,000	675	Miss F. L. Weddell.
Bishop Atkinson Lib.	Asheville		2,400		Rev. A. H. Stubbs.
St. Mary's College	Belmont	1885	10,000		F. Bernard.
N. C. University	Chapel Hill	1790	36,000	1,000	R. H, Graves.
Biddle Univ'r'ty (col)	Charlotte		8,000		
Buckhorn Academy	Como		2,000		
Scotia Seminary	Concord	1870	1,000		
Davidson College Lib.	Davidson	1887	12,000		F. F. Rowe.
Public School Library	Durham	1884	2,400		C W. Toms.
Trinity College Lib.	W. Durham.	1887	13,000		Geo. B. Pegram.
Elon College Library.	Elon	1890	1,285		W. P. Lorance.
Cross Creek, I. O. O. F.	Fayetteville	1845	1,000		
Christian College Lib.	Franklinton	1882	1,000		N. D. McReynolds.
Female College	Greehsboro	1895	6,000		Dred Peacock.
State Normal College.	Greensboro		3,000		
Guilford College Lib.	Guilford Col.	1837	4,000		Miss M E Mendenhall
Shortia School	Highlands	1888	1,500		
Good Will Free Lib.	Ledger	1888	6,000		C. H. Wing.
Pioneer Library	Lenoir	1875	1,500		I. F, W, Harper.
N. C. College	Mt. Pleasant	1858	2,600		H. T. J. Ludwig.
Bap. Female Institute	Murfreesb'ro		1,000		
Collegiate Institute	Newbern		1,000		
Catawba College	Newton		2,500		
Oak Ridge Insitute	Oak Ridge	1852	2,700	100	J. F. Holt.
A. & M. College	Raleigh	1890	3,300	100	A. Q. Holladay.
D. & D. Kelly Library	Raleigh	1877	2,500		
St. Mary's School	Raleigh		3,000		
Shaw University	Raleigh	1865	1,500		
Supreme Court Lib.	Raleigh		11,000		R. H, Bradley.
Olivia Raney Library.	Raleigh	1899	6,000		Miss Jennie Coffin
Rutherford Col. Lib.	R. College	1853	600		W. E. Abernathy.
Female College	Salem	1802	4,000		J. H. Clewell
Livingston College	Salisbury		3,000		
Wake F. College Lib.	Wake Forest	1833	15,500	485	W, L. Poteat.
Rab Library	Waynesville	1891	1,100	62	L. B. Lewis,
Wayne School	Waynesville	1886	3,000		T. G. Harbison.
Classical School	Wilmington		2,000		
Library Association	Wilmington.	1855	5,250	249	T C. Diggs.
City School Library	Winston	1896	3,200	290	J. J. Blair,
College Library	Lenoir	1890	400		J. D, Minick.
A & M. College (Col)	Greensboro	1894	2,000		J. H. M. Butler.
Hickory Library	Hickory	1803	1,000		N. McComb,
Durham Library	Durham	1897	900		H. A. Forshee
Morganton Library	Morganton	1878	1,000		Miss A L Avery
Kinston Public Lib.	Kinston				D T H Haughton
Circulating Library	Charlotte				
S. A. L. Railroad	Raleigh				

49 in Libraries in all.   Over 216,000 volumes of good books

2. To give Advice unsolicited is delightful; it so magnifies our self-esteem. To receive advice unsolicited is humiliating, it so minifies our our own self esteem.—*Branson.*

1st Month. JANUARY. 31 Days.

Moon's Phases.

	D.	H.	M.		D.	H.	M.
Full Moon,	4	1	5 p.m.	New Moon.	20	1	27 a.m.
☾ Last Quarter,	12	3	30 a. m.	☽ First Quarter,	27	4	43 a.m.

School Furniture and Supplies of all Kinds. Chas. J. Parker, Manager, Raleigh, N. C.

Day of Month.	Day of week.	Sun rises.	Sun sets.	Sun slow.	Sun's decline South.	ASPECTS OF PLANETS AND OTHER MISCELLANEOUS MATTER.	Moon's place.	Moon rises or sets.	Moon South.
1	Tue	7 10	4 57	4	23 1	⊕ *in Perihelian New Year Day*		sets	9 23
2	We	7 10	4 58	4	22 56	☌♆☾&☌♀♅ Bat Trenton '77		4 52	10 22
3	Thu	7 10	4 59	5	22 50	Battle of Princeton 1777		5 52	11 20
4	Fri	7 10	5 0	5	22 45	Vanderbilt died 1877		rises	morn
5	Sat	7 10	5 1	6	22 38	☿ in Aphelion		5 56	0 15
(1.) Second Sunday after Christmas. Day's length 9 hours 53 minutes.									
6	F	7 9	5 2	6	22 31	EPIPHANY		7 0	1 7
7	Mo	7 9	5 3	6	22 24	☌☿♄ Liberia Colonized 1822		8 1	1 56
8	Tue	7 9	5 4	7	22 16	Battle New Orleans 1815		9 1	2 42
9	We	7 9	5 5	7	22 8	☌♂☾ Napoleon 3rd d 1873		9 59	3 26
10	Thu	7 9	5 6	8	22 0	Stamp Act passed 1765		10 56	4 9
11	Fri	7 9	5 7	8	21 50	Alabama seceded 1861		11 53	4 51
12	Sat	7 9	5 8	8	21 41	Gaston Co formed 1846		morn	5 33
(2.) First Sunday after Epiphany. Day's length 10 hours 6 minutes.									
13	F	7 9	5 9	9	21 31	♂ Stationary Fox died 1681		0 49	6 16
14	Mo	7 9	5 10	9	21 20	Commodore Maury b 1806		1 45	7 1
15	Tue	7 8	5 11	10	20 10	☌♀♃ Andrew Jackson b 1767		2 42	7 49
16	We	7 8	5 12	10	20 58	☌♅☾ Gibbon died 1794		4 39	8 39
17	Thu	7 8	5 13	10	20 47	☌♀☾ Pres Tyler died 1862		4 33	9 31
18	Fri	7 8	5 14	11	20 35	☌♄☾ Daniel Webster b 1782		5 24	10 25
19	Sat	7 8	5 15	11	20 22	☌☿☾ *Gen Robt E Lee's B Day*		6 13	eve
(3.) Second Sunday after Epiphany. Day's length 10 hours 8 minutes.									
20	F	7 7	5 15	11	20 10	♂ G Hel Lat N Howard d '90		sets	0 13
21	Mo	7 7	5 16	12	19 57	☍☌● S Jackson b 1824		6 46	1 7
22	Tue	7 6	5 17	12	19 42	Byron born 1788		7 53	1 59
23	We	7 6	5 18	12	19 0	William Gaston died 1844		9 3	2 50
24	Thu	7 5	5 19	12	19 15	♂ in Aphelion		10 14	3 42
25	Fri	7 4	5 20	13	19 0	☿ Sta. Fayetteville settled 1749		11 23	4 34
26	Sat	7 3	5 21	13	18 45	☌♆☾		morn	5 27
(4) Third Sunday after Epiphany. Day's length 10 hours 20 minutes.									
27	F	7 2	5 22	13	18 30	Audebon died 1851		0 32	6 22
28	Mo	7 2	5 23	13	18 15	☿ Greatest Hel Lat N		1 39	7 18
29	Tue	7 2	5 23	13	17 58	Kansas admitted 1861		2 43	8 14
30	We	7 2	5 24	14	17 42	Charles 1st beheaded 1647		3 44	9 11
31	Thu	7 2	5 25	14	17 26	Corn Laws abrogated 1849		4 38	10 6

For High Tides at Beaufort, see third page of the Almanac.

WEATHER CONJECTURES—January—1, 2, 3, 4, snow if wind South or Southwest; 5, 6, 7, 8, 9, 10, 11, 12, look for snow, 13, 14, 15, 16, 17, 18, 19, stormy and possibly snow; 20, 21, 22, 23, 24, 25, 26, look for hoar frost; 27, 28, 29, 30, 31, rain.

Farmers should use "NATIONAL" Fertilizer for Tobacco; and "BEEF, BLOOD and BONE" brand for Cotton, Corn and Wheat. Strictly reliable. Ask your Fertilizer Merchant for them. Carefully prepared by

(See top 3d cover page.) *S. W. TRAVERS & CO., Branch, Richmond, Va.*

FARM AND GARDEN WORK FOR JANUARY.—Plant peas, beans, beets, onions, Irish potatoes, horse radish; sow turnips, spinach, lettuce, raddish, parsley, carrots, salsify. Plant early peas; artichokes must now be dressed, also asparagus beds, this is the proper time to sow early spring tomatoes, etc.

NORTH CAROLINA COLLEGES, AND OTHER GRADUATING SCHOOLS.
(Names, Character and Location.)

Asheville Female College (Methodist)..................................Asheville
Baptist Female University (Baptist)..................................Raleigh
Chowan Female Institutue (Baptist)..................................Murfreesboro
Claremont Female College (Reformed Church of U. S.)..........Hickory
Concordia College (Lutheran) ....Conover
Eavenport Female College (Methodist)..................................Lenoir
Davidson College (Presbyterian)..................................Davidson
Elon College (Christian) ....Elon College
Greensboro Female College (Methodist) ....Greensboro
Guilford College (Friends)..................................Guilford College
Hayesville College (Independent) ....Hayesville
Judson College (Methodist)..................................Hendersonville
Kinston College (Independent)..................................Kinston
Louisburg Female College (Meteodist)..................................Louisburg
Littleton Female College (Methodist)..................................Littleton
Mt. Amœna Seminary (Lutheran)..................................Mt. Pleasant
Mt. St. Joseph Academy (Catholic)..................................Asheville
North Carolina College (Lutheran)..................................Mt. Pleasant
North Carolina Agricultural and Mechanical College (State).....Raleigh
Oxford Female Seminary (Baptist) ....Oxford
Oak Ridge Institute (Independent)..................................Oak Ridge
Peace Institute (Independent)..................................Raleigh
Rutherford College, Burke Co. (Methodist)..........Rutherford College
St. Mary's College (Catholic)..................................Belmont
Shelby Female College (independent) ....Shelby
St. Mary's School (Episcopal)..................................Raleigh
Salem Academy (Moravian)..................................Salem
St. Pauls Seminary (Lutheran Theological)..................................Hickory
State Normal and Industrial College (State) ....Greensboro
Trinity College (Methodist)..................................Durham
University of North Carolina (State)..................................Chapel Hill
Weaverville College (Methodist)..................................Weaverville
Wake Forest College (Baptist)..................................Wake Forest
Elizabeth College (Lutheran) ....Charlotte
Presbyteran College (Preibyterian)..................................Charlotte
Whitsett Institute (Independent) ....Whitsett

COLORED SCHOOLS—Graduating.

Agriculteral and Mechanical College (State)..................................Greensboro
Bennett Seminary (Methodist)..................................Greensboro
Biddle University (Presbyterian) ....Charlotte
Building and Trade's College (Independent)..................................Southern Pines
Franklinton Christian College (Christian)..................................Franklinton
Kittrell College (A. M. E. C.)..................................Kittrell
Livingston College (Methodist) ....Salisbury
Normal and Industrial College (Methodist)..................................Kittrell
Normal School (State)..................................Elizabeth City
Normal School (State)..................................Goldsboro
Normal School (State)..................................Salisbury
Normal School (State) ....Plymouth
Normal School (State) ....Fayetteville
Normal School (State) ....Franklinton
St. Augustine Normal College (Episcopal)..................................Raleigh
Shaw University (Baptist)..................................Raleigh
Scotia Female Seminary (Presbyterian) ....Concord
Slater Industrial Academy and Normal School (State)..................................Winston

12. To the end of life do your very best.—*Branson*.

2d Month. FEBRUARY, 1901, 28 Days.

Side margin (vertical): The Educational Bureau, Raleigh, N. C., Secures Positions for Competent Teachers. Established 1891.

Side margin (vertical, right): For High Tides at Beaufort see third page of Almanac.

Moon's Phases.

	D. H. M.		D. H. M.
Full Moon,	3 10 21 a. m.	New Moon,	18 9 37 p. m.
Last Quarter,	11 1 4 p. m.	First Quarter,	25 1 30 p. m.

Day of Month.	Day of Week.	Sun rises.	Sun sets.	Sun slow.	Sun's decline South.	ASPECTS OF PLANETS AND OTHER MISCELLANEOUS MATTER.	Moon's place.	Moon rises or sets.	Moon south.
1	Fri	7 1	5 27	14 17	09	Geo. Washington Pres. 1789		rises	10 58
2	Sat	7 1	5 29	14 16	52	Peace Conference 1865		6 24	11 48

(5.) Fourth Sunday after Epiphany. Day's length 10 hours 31 minutes.

3	F	7 0	5 31	14 16	34	Gov. Gobel of Ky d. 1900		7 14	morn
4	Mo	6 59	5 32	14 16	17	Rev. War ended 1783		8 7	0 35
5	Tue	6 58	5 33	14 15	59	*Branson Nativity 1832* ♂♂☾		8 46	1 20
6	We	6 58	5 34	14 15	40	Charles 2nd died 1685		9 29	2 3
7	Thu	6 57	5 34	14 15	22	Suez Canal Commenced 1867		10 12	2 46
8	Fri	6 56	5 35	14 15	03	Battle Roanoke Island 1862		10 54	3 28
9	Sat	6 55	5 36	14 14	44	General Hancock died 1886		11 37	4 11

(6.) Fifth Sunday after Epiphany. Day's length 10 hours 43 minutes.

10	F	6 54	5 37	14 14	24	Treaty of Paris 1763		eve	4 55
11	Mo	6 53	5 38	14 14	05	☾ Thomas A. Edison b. 1847		1 7	5 41
12	Tue	6 53	5 39	14 13	45	♂ ☍ ☾Seymour died 1886		1 55	6 29
13	We	6 52	5 40	14 13	25	W. J. Bryan spoke in Ral 1900		2 45	7 19
14	Thu	6 51	5 41	14 13	05	*St. Valentine's Day*		3 37	8 11
15	Fri	6 50	5 42	14 12	44	♂ ♄☾Main blown up 1898		4 31	9 5
16	Sat	6 49	5 43	14 12	24	Judge Battle buried 1879		5 26	9 59

(7.) Septuagesima Sunday. Day's length 10 hours 56 minutes.

17	F	6 48	5 44	14 12	3	♀ ☾Columbia burned 1865		6 19	10 53
18	Mo	6 47	5 45	14 11	42	☿ in Per. JDavis Pres. 1861		7 12	11 46
19	Tue	6 46	5 46	14 11	20	☿ Gre. Elong E. ♂ ☿☾		8 3	eve
20	We	6 45	5 47	14 10	59	David Garrick born 1716		8 59	1 33
21	Thu	6 43	5 48	14 10	37	♄♂☉Spinoza died 1674		9 52	2 26
22	Fri	6 42	5 48	14 10	15	*George Washington born 1732*		10 47	3 21
23	Sat	6 41	5 48	14 9	54	Battle of Buena Vasta 1847		11 43	4 17

(8.) Sexagesima Sunday. Day's length 11 hours 9 minutes.

24	F	6 40	5 49	14 13 9	32	♂ in Aphilion Monteray Su '46		morn	5 13
25	Mo	6 39	5 50	13 9	9	♀Sta'y B Montreal 1775		1 36	6 10
26	Tue	6 38	5 51	13 8	47	♂ ♅☾French Rep. F.1848		2 33	7 7
27	We	6 37	5 52	13 8	24	Longfellow born 1807		3 28	8 2
28	Thu	6 36	5 53	13 8	2	☿ Gr.Hel.Lat.N.Wingate d '79		4 20	8 54

WEATHER CONJECTURES—February—1, 2, 3, Rain , 4, 5, 6, 7, 8, 9, 10, 11, look for snow; 12, 13, 14, 15, 16, 17, 18, look for rain and snow; 19, 20, 21, 22, 23, 24, 25 snow if wind South or Southwest: 26, 27, 28, look for high wind

FARM AND GARDEN WORK FOR FEBRUARY.—Continue to sow peas, and such vegetable as were omitted in January. Plant pole beans, first crop (in the low country); full crop Irish potatoes, beets and carrots, dress artichokes and asparagus. Tomatoes, peppers and cucumbers sow in hot beds; put out mangoes.

This is considered the opening month of the planter's year. Continue preparing as in January. Sow oats for a full crop in the low country; plant Irish potatoes; make up sprout beds for sweet potatoes. Plant root crop of sweet potatoes.

BUREAU OF STATISTICS OF N. C. (Denominational.)
LEVI BRANSON, Secretary.

DENOMINATIONS.	Number Ministers.	Number Churches.	Number Members.
Methodist.—Methodist Episcopal Church, South.	679	1,338	137,129
Methodist Episcopal Church	65	115	8,941
Methodist Church, Wesleyan	7	117	131
Methodist Protestant Church	64	208	16,416
African Methodist Episcopal Zion Church	240	526	121,154
African Methodist Episcopal	182	216	25,213
Colored Methodist Episcopal Cnurch in America.	25	26	2,786
Methoeist Episcopal, (col)	2	2	130
Baptist.—Missionary	840	1,628	158,892
Primitive	150	317	11,914
Free Will	160	168	10,224
Church of Christ	16	16	659
Old Two Seed	9	9	185
Seventh Day	1	1	10
Missionary, (col)	765	1,190	129,265
Free Will, (col)	10	25	1,640
Primitive, (col)	15	20	1,000
Protestant Episcopal—Protestant Episcopal,(white)	107	224	10,439
Protestant Episcopal, (col)	6	10	1,200
Presbyterian—Presbyterian, (white)	150	350	32,482
Presbyterian, (col)	173	306	17,851
Christian.—Christian, (white)	60	101	9,000
Ohristian, (col)	50	53	3,746
Christian, Disciples of Christ, (white)	54	126	12,437
Christian, Disciples of Christ, (col)	10	61	1,000
Congregational.—Congregational, [white]	4	4	1,000
Congregational, [col]	21	39	2,087
Evangelical Lutheran	73	137	12,872
Universalist	3	3	255
Seventh Day Adventist	5	5	83
Reformed Church of U. S.	23	43	3,317
Later Day Saints	24	1	136
Friends	52	52	5,328
Drunkards	9	9	510
Moravians	7	19	3,548
Waldenses	1	1	275
Roman Catholic	24	24	2,640
Hebrews	4	4	386
Salvation Army	2	2	59
Advent Christian	18	18	1,549
Associate Reform	20	20	2,019

3d Month. MARCH, 1901. 31 Days.

Moon's Phases.

	D.	H.	M.			D.	H.	M.	
Full Moon,	5	2	56	a. m.	New Moon,	20	7	45	a. m.
Last Quarter,	13	7	58	a. m.	First Quarter	26	11	31	p. m.

Day of Month.	Day of Week.	Sun rises.	Sun sets.	Sun slow.	Sun's decline south	ASPECTS OF PLANETS AND OTHER MISCELLANEOUS MATTER	Moon's place.	Moon rises or sets.	Moon south.
1	Fri	6 34	5 55	13	7 39	Bishop Andrew died 1871.		morn	9 44
2	Sat	6 32	5 56	12	7 16	John Wesley died 1791.		5 10	10 31
9.	Quinquagesima Sundy.					Day's Length 11 hours 27 minutes.			
3	F	6 30	5 57	12	6 53	☌ ♂ ☾ Nevada admitted 1863.		5 57	11 16
4	Mo	6 28	5 58	12	6 30	Congress first met in N. Y. 1789		6 42	11 59
5	Tue	6 26	5 59	12	6 06	♀ in Ap'el'n--A'di'n b 1750		5 25	morn
6	We	6 24	6 0	12	5 44	Battle of Pea Ridge 1862		8 8	0 42
7	Thu	6 23	6 1	11	5 21	☌ ☿ ☉ Inferior □ ♅ ☉		8 51	1 25
8	Fri	6 22	6 1	11	4 57	William III died 1703		9 33	2 07
9	Sat	6 20	6 2	11	4 34	Battle of Vera Cruz 1847.		10 17	2 51
10.	Quadrigessima Sunday.					Day's Length 11 hours 45 minutes.			
10	F	6 18	6 3	11	4 11	Battle of Manassa 1862		11 02	3 36
11	Mo	6 17	6 4	10	3 47	Wm. Barringer died 1882		11 49	4 23
12	Tue	6 16	6 5	10	3 24	☌ ♅ ☾ & ☌ ☿ ♀ Hamil. d 1874		Eve	5 11
13	We	6 14	6 6	10	3 00	Pocahontas died 1660		1 27	6 1
14	Thu	6 13	6 6	9	2 36	☌ ♃ ☾ & ☌ ♄ ☾		1 59	6 33
15	Fri	6 12	6 7	9	2 13	Cæsar As't'd B. C. 44		3 11	7 45
16	Sat	6 11	6 8	9	1 49	Nero died A. D. 37		4 3	8 37
11.						Day's Length 12 hours 0 minutes.			
17	F	6 9	6 9	9	1 25	*St. Patrick's Day*		4 56	9 30
18	Mo	6 8	6 10	8	1 02	☌ ☿ ☾ Suz Canal compl'd 1869		5 49	10 23
19	Tue	6 6	6 11	8	0 38	☌ ♀ ☾ Livingstone died 1872		6 43	11 17
20	We	6 4	6 12	8	0 14	☉ *enters Aries Spring Com*		7 38	Eve
21	Thu	6 3	6 12	7	0 10	♅ Station'y Luknow fell 58		8 33	1 7
22	Fri	6 2	6 13	7	0 33	Stamp Act passed 1765		9 30	2 4
23	Sat	6 0	6 13	7	0 57	Battle of Winchester 1862		10 29	3 3
12.						Day's Length 12 hours 13 minutes.			
24	F	5 59	6 14	6	1 21	☿ in ☊ Qu'n Elizabeth d 1603		11 28	4 2
25	Mo	5 58	6 15	6	1 44	☌ ♆ ☾ Thames Tun op'd 1843		morn	5 0
26	Tue	5 57	6 16	6	2 08	Earthquake in Cal. 1843		1 23	5 57
27	We	5 55	6 17	6	2 31	♀ Gre. Hel. Lat. South		2 17	6 51
28	Thu	5 53	6 18	5	2 55	Davidson College op'd 1837		3 7	7 41
39	Fri	5 51	6 18	5	3 18	British Museum founded 1753		3 55	8 29
30	Sat	5 50	6 19	4	3 41	☌ ♂ ☾ Alaska purchased 1867		4 40	9 14
13	Palm Sunday.					Day's Length 12 hours 32 minutes.			
31	F	5 48	6 20	4	4 05	S. M Parish died 1895		5 24	9 57

WEATHER CONJECTURES—March—cold high wind from 1 to 5; 6, 7, 7, 8, 9, 10, 11, 12, 13, snow and stormy; 14, 15, 16, 17, 18, 19, 20, wind and rain; 21, 22, 23, 24, 25, 26, stormy, 27, 28, 29, 30, 31, fair and frosty.

See Botanic Blood Balm, Page 15.

For High Tides at Beaufort, see third page of the Almanac.

FARM AND GARDEN WORK FOR MARCH.—Plant bush squash, pumpkins, water and mushmelons, okra, Guinea squash or egg-plant, sugar beets, carrots, beans, peas, radishes, lettuce, corn, celery, [first crop] tanyah and mangoes in the low country and elsewhere as soon as danger from frost is over.

This is the first planting month for cotton, corn and rice. Plant your high lands first; leave the low lands for April· Plant rice about the 20th of the month.

NORTH CAROLINA COLLEGE OF AGRICULTURE AND MECHANIC ARTS.

Located in Raleigh on Hillsboro street, one and a half miles west of the capitol, nearly opposite tqe Fair Grounds. Incorporated in 1887. Opened October 1, 1889. Supported partly by the U. S. Government and partly by the State of North Carolina. The college owns 540 acres of lond and twelve buildings. Tuition including room, fuel, lights etc., $30.00 a year, board $8 00 a month. One hundred and twenty scholarships are granted to deserving boys who are unable to pay. Nominations may be made by any member of the Legislature or by the County Board of Education in each county.

BOARD OF TRUSTEES:—W. S. Primrose, President, Raleigh; A. Leazar, Mooresville; H. E. Fries, Salem; D. A Tompkins, Charlotte; T. B. Twitty, Rutherfordton; Frank Wood, Edenton; J. C. L Harris, Raleigh; L. C. Edwards, Oxford; John W. Harden, Jr., Raleigh; H. E. Bonitz, Wilmington; Matt Moore, Kenansville; J. Z. Waller, Burlington; W. H. Ragan, High Point; David Clark, Charlotte; R. L. Smith, Albemarle; P. J. Sinclair, Marion; J. B. Stokes, Windsor; W. J. Peele, Raleigh; E. Y. Webb, Shelby; W. C. Fields, Sparta; J. Frank Ray, Franklin; Geo. T. Winston, LL. D., Ex-officio, Raleigh

FACULTY.—Geo. T. Winston, LL. D., President, W. F. Massey, C. E. Professor of Horticulture, Arboricultuae and Botany; W. A. Withers, A. M., Professor of Pure and Agricultural Chemistry; D. H. Hill, A. M., Professor of English; W. C. Riddick, A. B. and C. E., Professor of Civil Engineering and Mathematics; B. Irby, M S., Professor of Agriculture; P. A. Weihe, M. E. and Ph. D., Professor of Physics and Electrical Engineering; C. W. Scribner, A. B. and M. E, Professor of Mechanical Engineering; Capt. F. E, Phelps, U. S. A. Retired, Professor Military Service and Tactics; R. E. I. Yates, A. M., Instructor in Mathematics; L. B. Abbott, C. E.. Instructor in Civil Engineering; Charles B. Park, Superintendent of Shops; V. W. Bragg, Superintendent Wood Shops; M. E Carter, Instructor in Wood Working; T. A. Chittenden, Instructor in Drawing; A. B. Hubard, Assistant Mechanical Engineering; B. S. Skinner, Farm Superintendent; J. A. Bizzell, B. S., Instructor in Chemistry; Thomas L. Wright, B. S, Instructor in English; C. W. Hyams, Instructor in Botany; J. M. Johnson, B. S, Instructor in Agriculture; G. S. Fraps, B. S., Ph. D., Instructor in Chemistry; J. W. Carroll, B. S.. Dairymen; N. R. Stansel, B. S., Assistant in Physics and Electrical Engineering; A. F. Brown, Registrant; E. B. Owen' L. S., Librarian and Assislant in English; Mrs. Sue Carroll, Matron; Henry W. Wilson, Instructor in Fertile Inductry: J. M. Fix, Bursar; Mrs L. V. Darby, Stenographer.

NORTH CAROLINA AGRICULTURAL EXPERIMENT STATION.

The Station is a department of Agricultural and Mechanical College and is managed by the same Board of Trustees. The station offices are in the main building of the college. The experiment work is carried on in the college Laboratories and partly on the Experiment Station Farm west of the Fair Grounds and partly on the lands of the college.

EXPERIMENT STATION STAFF.—George T. Winston, LL. D., Director; W. A. Withers, A. M., Chemist; B. Irby, M S Agriculturist; W. S. Massey, C. E., Horticulturist; G. S. Fraps, Ph. D., Assistant Chemist; W. A. Syme, Assistant Chemist; Alex Rhodes, Assistant Horticulturist; C. W. Hyames, Assistant Botanist; J. M. Johnson, M. S., Assistant Agriculturist; B. S. Skinner, Farm Superintendent; J N. Fix, Clerk and Bookkeeper; A. F. Bowen, Secretary; Mrs. L. V Darby, Clerk and Stenographer

4th Month.   APRIL, 1901.   30Days.

Moon's Phases.

	D. H. M.		D. H. M.
Full Moon,	3 8 12 p. m.	New Moon,	18 4 29 p. m.
Last Quarter	11 10 49 p. m.	First Quarter	25 11 7 p. m.

Day of Month.	Day of Week.	Sun rises.	Sun Sets.	Sun slow.	Sun's decline south.	ASPECTS OF PLANETS AND OTHER MISCELLANEOUS MATTER.	Moon's place.	Moon rises or sets	Moon south.
1	Mo	5 41	6 21	4	4 28	*April Fools Day*		morn	10 42
2	Tue	5 56	6 22	4	4 51	Wapale d 1797		6 49	11 23
3	We	5 44	6 23	5	5 14	E. West-P. Cooper d '88		7 5	morn
4	Thu	5 42	6 24	3	5 37	Sta. Gen. Harrison d '71		7 31	0 5
5	Fri	5 41	6 25	3	6 00	*Good Friday*		7 18	0 48
6	Sat	5 39	6 26	3	6 23	Battle of Shiloh 1862		8 59	1 33

14.   Easter Sunday.   Day's Length 13 hours 47 minutes.

7	F	5 38	6 27	2	6 45	Socrates d 338 B C		9 45	2 19
8	Mo	5 36	6 28	2	7 08	Lousiana admitted 1812		10 33	3 7
9	Tue	5 25	6 29	1	7 30	Lee Sur. Apomattax 1865		11 24	5 57
10	We	5 34	6 30	1	7 52	U S Bank incor. 1816		eve	4 45
11	Thu	5 33	6 31	1	8 14	Civil War began '61		1 12	5 36
12	Fri	5 31	6 31	1	8 36	Fort Sumpton fell 1861		1 3	6 27
13	Sat	5 30	6 12	1	8 58	Raleigh sur. to Sherman 1865		1 53	7 18

15.   First Sunday after Easter.   Day's Length 13 hours 5 minutes.

14	F	5 28	6 33	0	9 20	Lincoln assinated 1865		2 44	8 9
15	Mo	5 27	6 34	0	9 42	Andrew Jackson Pres. 1865		3 45	9 1
16	Tue	5 26	6 34	f't	10 03	Fren eva. Mexico 1867		4 27	9 54
17	We	5 24	6 35	0	10 24	Dr. Ben. Franklin d 1790		4 20	10 48
18	Thu	5 23	6 36	1	10 45	Luther at War's 1790		5 04	11 45
19	Fri	5 22	6 37	1	11 06			sets	eve
20	Sat	5 21	6 38	1	11 27	Ultimation to Spain 1898.		8 71	1 45

16.   Second Sunday after Easter.   Day's Length 13 hours 26 minutes.

21	F	5 20	6 39	1	11 47	U S squdrom sent to Cuba '98		9 72	2 46
22	Mo	5 18	6 40	1	12 08	Sq'd'n lv K West 1898		10 72	3 46
23	Tue	5 17	6 41	2	12 28	Call for 25,000 v2ls. 1898		11 69	4 43
24	We	5 16	6 41	2	12 48	Gr. Hel. Lal. S		morn	5 36
25	Thu	5 14	6 41	2	13 07	U S dec war Spain 1898		1 2	6 26
26	Fri	5 13	6 42	2	13 27	Pres. John. Dur. '65		1 52	7 14
27	Sat	5 12	6 43	2	13 46	Mantanzas bombarded 1898		2 39	7 57

17.   Third Sunday after Easter.   Day's Length 13 hours 33 minutes.

28	F	5 11	6 44	3	14 05	Ceuanfuzas bombarded 1898		3 23	8 39
29	Mo	5 10	6 45	3	14 24	Crimean war ended 1856		4 5	9 22
30	Tue	5 9	6 46	3	14 43	Sta, Superior		4 48	10 4

WEATHER CONJECTURES—April—1, 2, 3, frequent showers; 4, 5, 6, 7, 8, 9, 10, 11, rainy if wind 'south-west, 12, 13, 14, 15, 16, 17, 18, fair; 19, 20, 21, 22, 23, 24, 25, expect open weather; 26, 27, 28, 29, 30, expect wind and showers.

FARM AND GARDEN WORK FOR MAY.—Plant snap beans and squashes. Sow cabbage for winter use, cauliflower, broccoli, celery, beets, carrots, salsify. Plant cucumbers, melons and pumpkins for late crops. Gather herds for drying; always dry gently in the shade.

Look well to your hoeing and plowing. Continue to plant corn in low lands. Sow first crop of early cow peas. Rice planting is generally postponed until June, as the birds are very bad in May, and the May bird is exceedingly destructive.

Peele's Practical Business College, Raleigh, N. C., a Good School.

6th Month. JUNE, 1901. 30 Days.

Moon's Phases.

	D.	H.	M.		D.	H.	M.
☺ Full Moon,	2	4	44 a. m.	● New Moon,	16	8	25 a. m.
☾ Last Quarter,	9	4	52 p. m.	☽ First Quarter	23	3	51 p. m.

For High Tides at Beaufort, see third page of the Almanac.

Day of Month.	Day of Week.	Sun rises.	Sun sets.	Sun slow.	Sun's decline south.	ASPECTS OF PLANETS AND OTHER MISCELLANEOUS MATTER.	Moon's place.	Moon rises or sets.	Moon south.
1	Sat	4 44	7 18	2	12 02	☌ ♅ ☾ Battle of Seven Pines 62	♏	morn	11 49
(22.)						Day's Length 14 hours 45 minutes.			
2	F	4 44	7 19	2	22 10	Battle Cold Harbor 64	♐	7 15	morn
3	Mo	4 43	7 20	2	22 17	*Hobson Sinks Merimac* 98	♐	8 5	0 39
4	Tue	4 42	7 21	2	22 25	☌ ♃ ☾; ☌ ♄ ☾ Geo. I b 1738	♐	8 56	1 30
5	We	4 41	7 21	2	22 32	☍ ♅ ☉ Telegraph in China '71	♑	9 46	2 20
6	Thu	4 41	7 22	2	22 38	Santiago Fort Bombarded 1898	♑	10 36	3 10
7	Fri	4 41	7 22	1	22 44	1st American Congress 1765	♑	11 26	3 10
8	Sat	4 41	7 23	1	22 50	☌ ♅ ☿ Battle of Cross Key 62	♒	eve	4 48
(23.)	Whit Sunday.					Day's Length 15 hours 4 minutes.			
9	F	4 41	7 23	1	23 55	Dickens d 1870	♒	1 3	5 37
10	Mo	4 41	7 24	1	23 0		♒	0 53	6 27
11	Tue	4 41	7 24	1	23 5	J Q Adams b 1767	♓	2 44	7 18
12	We	4 41	7 25	1	23 9	William Cullen Bryant d 1878	♓	3 38	8 19
13	Thu	4 41	7 25	0	23 12	Gen Scott born 1786	♈	4 35	9 8
14	Fri	4 41	7 26	0	23 16	U S Flag adopted 1777	♈	5 34	10 2
15	Sat	4 41	7 26	f't	23 18	☿ Gre. Elong E. Ark. ad 36	♉	6 35	eve
(24.)	Trinity Sunday.					Day's Length 15 hours 8 minutes			
16	F	4 41	7 27	0	23 21	☌ ☿ ☾; ☌ ♀ ☾	♉	7 36	0 70
17	Mo	4 41	7 27	1	23 23	☌ ☿ ☾—Addison b. 1718	♈	8 35	1 9
18	Tue	4 41	7 27	1	23 25	Battle of Waterloo 1815	♊	9 31	2 5
19	We	4 42	7 27	1	23 26	Lord Cornwallace Evacuats	♋	10 23	2 57
20	Thu	4 43	7 28	1	23 27	☌ ☿ ☉; ☿ in ♉ [Rich 1781	♋	11 12	3 46
21	Fri	4 44	7 28	1	23 27	*Sun Enters Cancer Sum. Com.*	♋	11 58	4 32
22	Sat	4 43	7 28	2	23 27	☌ ♂ ☾ Shafter's Army land 98	♌	morn	5 15
(25.)	First Sunday after Trinity					Day's Length 14 hours 45 minutes.			
23	F	4 43	7 28	2	23 26	Stanhope Pullen d 1895	♌	0 41	5 58
24	Mo	4 43	7 29	2	23 26	*St. John Baptist Day*	♌	1 24	6 41
25	Tue	4 43	7 29	2	23 24	♀ in Perihelion—Cues. de. 76	♌	2 7	7 24
26	We	4 44	7 29	2	23 23	Cadiz Fleet at Port Said 1898	♍	2 50	8 9
27	Thu	4 44	7 29	3	23 21	Hiram Towers d 1873	♍	3 35	8 55
28	Fri	4 44	7 29	3	23 18	☿ Sta.—3rd Manilla Ex. sails	♍	4 21	9 43
29	Sat	4 45	7 29	3	23 15	☌ ♅ ☾ 1st Ex. ar. at Manilla 98	♏	5 9	10 33
(26.)	Second Sunday after Trinity.					Day's Length 14 hours 44 minutes.			
30	F	4 45	7 29	3	23 12	□ ♃ ☉; ☌ ☿ ♀ in Aphelion	♌	5 59	11 24

WEATHER CONJECTURES—June—1, 2, delightful; 3, 4, 5, 6, 7, 8, 9, expect rain; 10, 11, 12, 13, 14, 15, 16, fair and mild; 17, 18, 19, 20, 21, 22, 23, changeable; 23, 24, 25, 26, 27, 28, 29, 30, changeble.

Farmers should use "NATIONAL" Fertilizer for Tobacco; and "BEEF, BLOOD and BONE" brand for Cotton, Corn and Wheat. Strictly reliable. Ask your Fertilizer Merchant for them. Carefully prepared by

(See top 3d cover page.) *S. W. TRAVERS & CO., Branch, Richmond, Va.*

FARM AND GARDEN WORK FOR JUNE.—Sow full crops of cabbages for fall and winter use. Cauliflowers and broccoli may yet be sown, also a few carrots. Continue to sow tomatoes, okra, radishes, snap beans. Transplant leeks; pull and dry onions, garlic and eschalots. A few cucumbers and melons plant for a late crop, and a few ruta baga turnips.

Keep constantly at the plow and hoe; this is the most important grass month! If the vines from your sweet potato sprout bed are fit you can draw and plant out first good rain. Sow cow-peas between your corn hills and rows. The end of this month is a good time to put in the first crop of standing field peas.

7th Month. JULY, 1901. 31 Days.

Moon's Phases.

	D.	H.	M.		D.	H.	M.
Full Moon,	1	6	9 p.m.	New Moon,	15	5	2 p.m.
☾ Last Quarter,	8	10	12 p.m.	☽ First Quarter	23	8	50 a.m.
				Full Moon,	31	5	25 a.m.

Day of Month	Day of Week.	Sun rises.	Sun sets.	Sun slow.	Sun's decline north.	ASPECTS OF PLANETS AND OTHER MISCELLANEOUS MATTER.	Moon's place.	Moon rises or sets.	Moon south.
1	Mo	4 38	7 29	4	23 8	☌ ♃ ☾ & ☌ ♄ ☾ B. 7 Pines '62	♐	rises	morn
2	Tue	4 38	7 29	4	23 4	Bat Cold Harbor 1864	♐	7 52	0 15
3	We	4 39	7 29	4	23 0	⊕ in Aphelion.	♑	8 31	1 06
4	Thu	4 39	7 29	4	23 0	Mexican War declared 1845	♑	9 8	1 56
5	Fri	4 40	7 28	4	22 49	☍ ♄ ☉ Telegraph in China 1871	♒	9 42	2 46
6	Sat	4 40	7 28	5	22 44	Patrick Henry died 1799	♒	10 45	3 55
(27.)	Fifth Sunday after Trinity.					Day's length 14 hours 47 minutes.			
7	F	4 41	7 28	5	22 37	James Wright Moore d 1900	♓	10 48	4 25
8	Mo	4 41	7 28	5	22 31	Hon J J Davis d 1892	♓	11 23	5 15
9	Tue	4 42	7 27	5	22 24	Marines L Gaontanimo '98	♓	morn	6 07
10	We	4 42	7 27	5	22 17	Prof Ralph Grave died 1889	♈	0 0	7 0
11	Thu	4 43	7 26	5	22 9	J Q Adams born 1767	♈	0 43	7 57
12	Fri	4 44	7 26	5	22 1	☌ ☿ ☉ Inferior	♈	1 32	8 56
13	Sat	4 45	7 25	6	21 53	☌ ♆ ☾ Gen Fremont d 1890	♈	2 27	9 55
(28.)	Sixth Sunday after Trinity					Day's length 14 hours 40 minutes.			
14	F	4 45	7 25	6	21 44	Great Fire in Chicago 1874	♉	3 28	10 54
15	Mo	4 46	7 24	6	21 35	♃ in ☋ Bat Vicksburg 1862	♊	sets	11 51
16	Tue	4 47	7 24	6	21 25	Santiago Sur to US Ar 1898	♋	7 45	eve
17	We	4 48	7 23	6	21 15	☌ ♀ ☾ ♀ Gr Hel Lat S	♋	8 21	1 35
18	Thu	4 48	7 23	6	21 5	Dean Stanly died 1881	♌	8 53	2 24
19	Fri	4 49	7 22	6	20 54	Watauga county formed 1849	♌	9 23	3 9
20	Sat	4 50	7 22	6	20 43	Spanish Cab Neg for P 1898	♌	9 52	3 53
(29.)	Seventh Sunday after Trinity.					Day's length 14 hours 29 minutes.			
21	F	4 51	7 20	6	20 32	Gen D H Hill b 1821	♍	10 20	4 36
22	Mo	4 51	7 20	6	20 20	Napolean 2d died 1832	♍	10 50	5 19
23	Tue	4 52	7 19	6	20 8	☿ Sta	♍	11 23	6 3
24	We	4 53	7 19	6	19 56	Boliver born 1783	♎	11 59	6 49
25	Thu	4 54	7 18	6	19 43	Battle Lundy's Lane 1814	♎	morn	7 36
26	Fri	4 55	7 17	6	19 30	☌ ♅ ☾ Fulton born 1765	♏	0 40	8 25
27	Sat	4 56	7 16	6	19 17	Powers born 1805	♏	1 26	9 15
(30.)	Eighth Sunday after Trinity.					Day's length 14 hours 19 minutes.			
28	F	4 56	7 15	6	19 3	☌ ♃ ☾ & ☌ ♄ ☾ USF Porto Rico	♐	2 16	10 06
29	Mo	4 57	7 14	6	18 49	[1898	♐	3 12	10 58
30	Tue	4 58	7 13	6	18 35	Wm L Saunders b 1839	♐	4 12	11 50
31	We	4 59	7 12	6	18 20	Andrew Johnson d 1875	♑	rises	12 41

For High Tides at Beaufort, see third page of the Almanac.

WEATHER CONJECTURES—July—1, 2, changeable; 3, 4, 5 6, 7. fair if wind north or northwest; 8, 9, 10, 11, 12, 13, 14. expect fair weather; 15, 16, 17, 18, 19, 20, 21, 22, generally fair; 23, 24, 25, 26, 27, 28, 29, changeable; 30, 31 not settled.

FARM AND GARDEN WORK FOR JULY.—Sow cabbage, but protect from hot sun when young. Water at night, Plant snap beans and a few Irish potatoes. Continue to sow radishes, lettuce, endive, cresses, mustard and small salading. The early Dutch turnip is the best to sow for the first crop; follow with the yellow Swedish or rute baga.

Now do not omit to sow full crops of standing cow-peas. Sow a few turnips, carrots and beets as field crops, though the hot suns are apt to destroy them, should they escape they will be fine, the next month is the best for these crops.

THE NORTH CAROLINA COLLEGE

—OF—

Agriculture and Mechanic Arts

Offers a thorough practical education in all branches of Agriculture, in Cotton Manufacturing, in Civil, Mechanical and Electrical Engineering, in Architecture and in the Industrial Sciences, Chemistry, Biology and Physics. Regular courses, special courses. Total annual expenses, including board, fuel, lights, etc., $123. One hundred and twenty scholarships carrying free tuition and lodging are open to needy boys. Appointments made by any member of the Legislature.

Address,

President GEO. T. WINSTON,

WEST RALEIGH, N. C.

Peele's Practical Business College, Raleigh, N. C., a Good School.

20 BRANSON'S NORTH CAROLINA ALMANAC.

8th Month.   AUGUST, 1901.   31 Days.

Moon's Phases.

	D. H. M.			D. H. M.
☾ Last Quarter,	7 2 53 a. m.		☽ First Quarter, 22	7 44 a. m.
● New Moon,	14 3 19 a. m.		⊕ Full Moon, 29	3 13 p. m.

For High Tides at Beaufort, see third page of the Almanac.

Day of Month.	Day of Week.	Sun rises.	Sun sets	Sun slow.	Sun's decline North.	ASPECTS OF PLANETS AND OTHER MISCELLANEOUS MATTER.	Moon's place.	Moon rises or sets.	Moon south.
1	Thu	rises	7 14	6 18	05	☿ Greatest Elong. West	♌	eve	0 41
2	Fri	5 1	7 11	6 17	50	C B Aycock elected Gov 1900	♌	8 17	1 31
3	Sat	5 2	7 9	6 17	35	Gov Caswell born 1729	♍	8 51	2 21

(31.)   Ninth Sunday after Trinity.   Day's length 14 hours 5 minutes.

4	F	5 3	7 8	6 17	19	Mojor R S Tucker d 1894	♍	9 25	3 12
5	Mo	5 4	7 7	6 17	3	♂ in ♏ Bat Athens 1861	♍	10 2	4 04
6	Tue	5 4	7 6	6 16	47		♎	10 43	4 57
7	We	5 5	7 5	5 16	30	☾ John Wheeler d 1832	♎	11 30	5 52
8	Thu	5 6	7 4	5 16	13	☾ Joseph Davis died 1892	♎	morn	6 49
9	Fri	5 7	7 3	5 15	57	☿ in ♌ — ♂ ♅ ☾ Dryden b 1631	♎	0 21	7 47
10	Sat	5 8	7 2	5 15	39	Henderson Walker Gov 1699	♏	1 18	8 45

(32.)   Tenth Sunday after Trinity.   Day's length 12 hours 52 minutes.

11	F	5 9	7 1	5 15	21	Cardinal Newman d 1890	♏	2 20	9 41
12	Mo	5 10	6 59	5 15	3	♂ ☿ ☾War US & Spain En '98	♏	3 24	10 36
13	Tue	5 11	6 58	5 14	45	Manilla surrendered 1898	♐	4 28	11 26
14	We	5 12	6 56	4 14	27	● ☿ in Perihelion	♐	sets	0 16
15	Thu	5 13	6 55	4 14	8	Mrs Julia Bailey died 1900	♑	7 23	1 2
16	Fri	5 14	6 54	4 13	49	♂ ♀ ☾Legislature at N'bern '84	♑	7 53	1 47
17	Sat	5 15	6 53	4 13	30	Governor Hyde arrives 1710	♒	8 22	2 31

(33.)   Eleventh Sunday after Trinity.   Day's length 13 hours 6 minutes.

18	F	5 15	6 51	3 13	11	♂ ♂ ☾ Ole Bull d 1880	♒	8 51	3 14
19	Mo	5 16	6 50	3 12	52		♓	9 23	3 58
20	Tue	5 17	6 49	3 12	32	Harrison b 1833	♓	9 57	4 43
21	We	5 18	6 48	3 12	12	Capt TA Branson K in Bat 1864	♈	10 35	5 29
22	Thu	5 19	6 46	3 11	52	☿ Sta ♂☾ J B Gough b 1817	♈	11 18	6 17
23	Fri	5 20	6 45	2 11	32	☿ Greatest Hel Lat N	♉	morn	7 6
24	Sat	5 21	6 43	2 11	12	♂ ♃ ☾ Webster died 1852	♉	0 6	7 56

(34.)   Twelfth Sunday after Trinity.   Day's length 13 hours 20 minutes.

25	F	5 22	6 42	2 10	51	♂ ♄ ☾ Joe Turner in Ral 1870	♊	0 59	8 47
26	Mo	5 24	6 40	1 10	30	Louis Phillippe d 1850	♊	1 57	9 38
27	Tue	5 24	6 39	1 10	9	♂ ☿ ● Superior	♋	2 59	10 30
28	We	5 25	6 38	1	9 48	Goethe born 1749	♋	4 3	11 .21
29	Thu	5 26	6 36	1	9 48	● Brigham Young d 1877	♌	rises	0 13
30	Fri	5 26	6 34	1	9 6	♃ Sta Wm Penn d 1718	♌	6 48	0 35
31	Sat	5 27	6 32	0	8 44	Charleston Earthquake 1886	♍	7 24	1 5

WEATHER CONJECTURES—August—1, 2, 5, 4, 5, 6, expect good rains; 7, 8, 9, 10, 11, 12, 13, generally fair weather; 14, 15, 16, 17, 18, 19, 20, 21, cooler and showery; 22, 23, 24, 25, 26, 27, 28, expect rainy weather; 29, 30, 31, changeable.

FARM AND GARDEN WORK FOR AUGUST.—Transplant all kinds of cabbage, cauliflower and celery. Sow carrots and beets, turnips of all kinds, spinach, lettuce, radish and onions.

Now sow full crops of field turnips, carrots and beets, and such other crops as were omitted last month; strip fodder. Early rice will be fit to the cut last of this month. Look to it. This a good time to plant vines of the first slips, in order to procure seed potatoes for the next year's crops.

9th Month. SEPTEMBER, 1901. 30 Days.

Moon's Phases.

	D.	H.	M.			D.	H.	M.
☾ Last Quarter,	5	8	19 a. m.		☽ First Quarter	20	8	25 p.m.
● New Moon,	12	4	10 p. m.		○ Full Moon,	28	0	27 a. m.

Day of Month.	Day of Week.	Sun rises.	Sun sets.	Sun slow.	Sun's decline north	Aspects of Planets and Other Miscellaneous Matter.	Moon's place.	Moon rises or sets.	Moon south.
(35) Thirteenth Sunday after Trinity. Day's length 13 hours 2 minutes.									
1	F	5 28	6 30	0	8 22	Battle Chantilly 1862	♈	eve	morn
2	Mo	5 29	6 29	0	8 1		♈	8 42	2 51
3	Tue	5 30	6 28	1	7 39	Atlanta Taken 1864	♉	9 27	3 47
4	We	5 31	6 26	1	7 17	French Republic 1870	♉	10 18	4 44
5	Thu	5 32	6 25	1	6 54	☾ J W Daniel born 1842	♉	11 14	5 42
6	Fri	5 33	6 23	2	6 32	□♅☉	♉	morn	6 40
7	Sat	5 34	6 22	2	6 10	Whittier died 1892	♊	0 14	7 36
(36.) Fourteenth Sunday after Trinity. Day's length 12 hours 46 minutes.									
8	F	5 34	6 20	2	5 47	Battle Eutaw Springs 1781	♊	1 16	8 30
9	Mo	5 35	6 19	3	5 25	California admitted 1850--☿-☊	♋	2 19	9 21
10	Tue	5 36	6 17	3	5 2	S S Cox d 1889—☌♆☾	♋	3 21	10 10
11	We	5 37	6 16	3	4 39	Battle of Brandywine 1777	♌	4 23	10 56
12	Thu	5 38	6 14	4	4 16	● R A Proctor d 1888	♌	5 22	11 41
13	Fri	5 39	6 13	4	3 53	☌☿☾	♌	sets	eve
14	Sat	5 40	6 11	4	3 30	Humboldt b 1769 ☌☿☾--♄ Sta	♍	6 53	1 09
(37.) Fifteenth Sunday after Trinity. Day's length 12 hours 29 minutes.									
15	F	5 41	6 10	5	3 7	J F Cooper b 1789—☌♀☾	♍	7 24	1 53
16	Mo	5 41	6 8	5	2 44	Moscow burnt 1812	♎	7 58	2 37
17	Tue	5 42	6 6	5	2 21		♎	8 34	3 23
18	We	5 43	6 4	6	1 58	Dr. Harris d 1879	♎	9 14	4 9
19	Thu	5 44	6 3	6	1 34	Pres Garfield d 1881—☌♅☾	♏	9 59	4 57
20	Fri	5 45	6 1	6	1 11	☽ H H Helper d 1893	♏	10 49	5 46
21	Sat	5 46	6 0	7	0 48	☌♃☾—☌♄☾	♐	11 44	6 36
(38.) Sixteenth Sunday after Trinity. Day's length 12 hours 12 minutes.									
22	F	5 47	5 58	7	0 24	Battle Fishers Hill 1864	♐	morn	7 26
23	Mo	5 48	5 57	7	0 1	☉ *Enters Libra Autumn Com.*	♑	0 41	8 16
24	Tue	5 49	5 55	8	0 22	Gen Hill d 1889—□♆☾	♑	1 43	9 17
25	We	5 50	5 53	8	0 46	Ethan Allen Cap 1777	♑	2 48	9 58
26	Thu	5 51	5 51	9	1 9	Daniel Boone d 1820 ☿ in Aph	♒	3 57	10 50
27	Fri	5 52	5 50	9	1 33	○ Battle Pilot Knob 64	♒	5 7	11 44
28	Sat	5 52	5 48	9	1 56	Harvest Moon	♈	rises	morn
(39.) Seventeenth Sunday after Trinity. Day's length 11 hours 54 minutes									
29	F	5 53	5 47	10	2 19		♈	6 39	0 39
30	Mo	5 54	5 45	10	2 43	Legislature atFayetteville 1786	♉	7 22	1 36

For High Tides at Beaufort, see third page of the Almanac.

WEATHER CONJECTURES—September— 1, 2, 3, 4, fair if wind northwest; 5, 6, 7, 8, 9, 10, 11, changeable wether; 12, 13, 14, 15, 16, 17, 18, 19, fair; 20, 21, 22, 23, 24, 25, 26, 27, fair if wind south or southwest; 28, 29, 30, cool showers.

FARM ANE GARDEN WORK FOR SEPTEMBER.—Now sow full crops of all kinds—turnips, onions, carrots, beets, cabbage, lettuce, cresses. Look after your musnroom beds. Hoe and thin your turnips.

Continue to sow field turnips, carrots and beets. Southern seed is always better than the imported; those from the latter are apt to run to seed early in the spring, unless it be English seed. Prepare land for sowing rye in Octobar. Pick cotton; harvest corn.

10th Month. OCTOBER, 1901. 31 Days.

Moon's Phases.

	D. H. M.		D. H. M.
☾ Last Quarter	4 3 44 p. m.	☉ Full Moon,	20 0 49 p. m.
☽ New Moon,	12 8 3 a. m.	☽ First Quarter	27 9 58 a. m.

Day of Month	Day of Week.	Sun rises.	Sun Sets.	Sun fast.	Sun's decline north.	ASPECTS OF PLANETS AND OTHER MISCELLANEOUS MATTER.	Moon's place.	Moon rises or sets	Moon south.
1	Tue	5 55	5 43	10	3 6	Alex Holt d 1892	♐	rises	eve
2	We	5 56	5 42	11	3 29	Renan died 1892	♐	9 8	3 35
3	Thu	5 57	5 41	11	3 53	Andrew executed 1780	♑	10 8	4 34
4	Fri	5 58	5 39	11	4 16	☾ ☐ ♄ ☉ Bat Georgetown '77	♒	11 9	5 32
5	Sat	5 59	5 38	11	4 39	♅ Sta—Cornwallis de 1781	♒	morn	6 27

(40.) Eighteenth Sunday after Trinity. Day's length 11 hours 36 minutes.

6	F	6 0	5 36	12	5 2	Tenny died 1892	♒	0 12	7 19
7	Mo	6 1	5 35	12	5 25	Edgar Allen Poe d 1849	♒	1 15	8 8
8	Tue	6 2	5 33	12	5 48	Battle Fort Pickens 1861	♓	2 17	8 55
9	We	6 3	5 32	13	6 11	Galveston taken 1862	♓	3 18	9 39
10	Thu	6 4	5 30	13	6 34	♀ ☌ ♂ Geo V Strong d 1897	♓	4 16	10 23
11	Fri	6 5	5 29	13	6 57	Dr Kane returned 1855	♈	5 12	11 7
12	Sat	6 6	5 27	13	7 19	☿ Gretest Elong E	♈	sets	11 25

(41.) Nineteenth Sunday after Trinity Day's length 11 hours 19 minutes.

13	F	6 7	5 26	14	7 42	John Toomer died 1856	♉	5 57	11 50
14	Mo	6 8	5 24	14	8 4	♃ ☌ ☾ Josh Billing d 1885	♉	6 33	morn
15	Tue	6 9	5 23	14	8 26	♂ ☌ ☾ Koskiusko d 1817	♊	7 13	2 6
16	We	6 10	5 21	14	8 49	♂ ♀ ☾—♀ in Aphelion	♋	7 56	2 53
17	Thu	6 11	5 20	14	9 11	♂ ☌ ☾ Rev Jesse Rankin d 1877	♋	8 43	3 41
18	Fri	6 12	5 18	15	9 33	♂ ♃ ☾—♂ ♄ ☾ CA Danna d 1897	♌	9 34	4 30
19	Sat	6 13	5 17	15	9 54	J B Whitaker died 1892	♌	10 30	5 18

(42.) Twentieth Sunday after Trinity. Day's length 11 hours 1 minutes.

20	F	6 14	5 15	15	10 16	Froude died 1894	♌	11 30	6 7
21	Mo	6 15	5 14	15	10 38	☉ Columbus Day	♍	morn	6 56
22	Tue	6 16	5 13	15	11 0	Nana Sahib captured 1874	♍	0 31	7 46
23	We	6 17	5 12	16	11 20	Gen Jurat d 1771 Masten d '77	♎	1 35	8 36
24	Thu	6 18	5 10	16	11 41	☿ Sta—Water Mills inv AD 555	♎	2 42	9 28
25	Fri	6 19	5 9	16	12 2	Battle of Ballacklava 1854	♏	3 52	10 21
26	Sat	6 20	5 7	16	12 23	☾ Eclipsed: invisible here	♏	5 3	11 18

(43.) Twenty-first Sunday after Trinity. Day's length 10 hours 45 minutes.

27	F	6 21	5 6	16	12 43	☉ Vassar d 1888	♐	rises	eve
28	Mo	6 22	5 5	16	13 3	☾ Levicus XIX—17	♐	6 0	0 17
29	Tue	6 24	5 4	16	13 23	Raleigh beheaded 1618	♐	6 56	1 18
30	We	6 25	5 3	16	13 43	Hon Wm Hill died 1877	♐	7 55	2 20
31	Thu	6 26	5 1	16	14 3	♂ ♅ ☾ Rowan Governor 1753	♒	8 59	3 21

WEATHER CONJECTURES—October—1, 2, 3, fair, 4, 5, 6, 7, 8, 9, 10, 11, changeable; 12, 13, 14, 15, 16, 17, 18, 19, cold rain of wind be west, snow if east; 20, 21, 22, 23, 24, 25, 26, expect rain and snow; 27, 28, 29, 30, 31, changeable.

For High Tides at Beaufort see third page of Almanac.

FARM AND GARDEN WORK FOR OCTOBER.—You may make two sowings of cabbage this month, aud, if of English seed, they will not "run" in the spring. Sow lettuce: hoe turnips and thin, put out leeks and onions; sow principal crop of spinach; earth up celery.

Continue picking your cotton as it blows. Sow early rye, wheat and barley. Dig your sweet potatoes when the weather becomes cool and you expect frost.

11th Month. NOVEMBER, 1901, 30 Days.

Moon's Phases.

	D. H. M.		D. H. M.
☾ Last Quarter,	3, 2 16 p. m.	☽ First Quarter,	19 3.15 a. m.
● New Moon,	11 2 26 a. m.	◍ Full Moon,	25 8 9 p. m.

Day of Month.	Day of Week.	Sun rises.	Sun sets	Sun fast.	Sun's decline North.	ASPECTS OF PLANETS AND OTHER MISCELLANEOUS MATTER.	Moon's place.	Moon rises or sets.	Moon south.
1	Fri	6 27	5 0	16 14	22	America discovered 1492		10 03	4 19
2	Sat	6 28	4 59	16 14	41	Gen Bryan Grimes b 1828		11 8	5 13
(44.) 22d Sunday after Trinity.						Day's length 10 hours 21 minutes.			
3	F	6 29	4 58	16 15	0	☾ ♂ ☌ Clingman d 1897		morn	6 4
4	Mo	6 30	4 57	16 15	19	☌ ☿ ● Inferior— ☿ in ♌		0 10	6 52
5	Tue	6 31	4 56	16 15	38	GUY FAWKES DAY		1 11	7 38
6	We	6 32	4 55	16 15	56	H D Turner died 1867		2 9	8 21
7	Thu	6 34	4 54	16 16	14	♀ Gr Hel Lat S		3 6	9 5
8	Fri	6 35	4 53	16 16	31	Gov Dobbs died 1754		4 3	9 48
9	Sat	6 36	4 53	16 16	49	Dr S S Satchwell died 1892		4 59	10 31
(45.) 23rd Sunday after Trinity.						Day's length 10 hours 14 minutes.			
10	F	6 37	4 51	16 17	6	☿ in Perihelion—☌ ☿ ☾		5 55	11 16
11	Mo	6 38	4 50	16 17	23	Washington admitted 1889		sets	eve4
12	Tue	6 39	4 49	16 17	39	General Graham d 1836		5 53	0 42
13	We	6 40	4 48	15 17	55	☿ Sta—☌ ☌ ☾		6 39	1 37
14	Thu	6 41	4 47	15 18	11	A S Merrimon died 1892		7 30	2 25
15	Fri	6 42	4 47	15 18	27	☌ ♀ ☾—☌ ♃ ☾—☌ ♄ ☾		8 24	3 19
16	Sat	6 43	4 46	15 18	42	Donald W Bain d. 1892		9 21	4 5
(46.) 24th Sunday after Trinity.						Day's length 10 hours 2 minutes.			
17	F	6 45	4 46	15 18	57	Thomas Ruffin b 1787		10 19	4 50
18	Mo	6 46	4 45	15 19	11	☌ ♀ ♃—Dr R K Speed d 1898		11 21	5 37
19	Tue	6 47	4 44	14 19	26	☌ ♀ ♄ D McDonald d '77		morn	6 25
20	We	6 48	4 43	14 19	39	☿ Greatest Hel Lat N		0 25	7 14
21	Thu	6 49	4 43	14 19	53	☿ ♄ Elong W— B Decree 1886		1 31	8 5
22	Fri	6 50	4 42	13 20	6	Dr J H Smith died 1897		2 39	8 59
23	Sat	6 51	4 42	13 20	19	Dr R L Beal died 1891		3 49	9 55
(47.) 25th Sunday after Trinity.						Day's length 9 hours 49 minutes.			
24	F	6 52	4 41	13 20	31	Capt W F Avery died 1877		5 1	0 55
25	Mo	6 54	4 41	13 20	43	Battle Mission Ridge 1863		6 14	11 58
26	Tue	6 54	4 40	12 20	55	Wm Tryon Gov 1765		rises	morn
27	We	6 55	4 40	12 21	6	☌ ☿ ☾ B F Moore died 1858		6 39	1 1
28	Thu	6 56	4 39	12 21	17	☌ ♃ ♄ Geo W Blount d 1896		7 46	2 3
29	Fri	6 57	4 39	11 21	27	Isiah Mattin Gov 1771		8 55	3 1
30	Sat	6 58	4 39	11 21	37	SAINT ANDREWS		9 58	3 56

WEATHER CONJECTURES—November— 1, 2, changeable. 3, 4, 5, 6, 7. 8, 9, 10, cold rain; 11, 12, 13, 14, 15, 16, 17, 18, cold and showery; 19, 20, 21, 22, 23, 24, look for snow; 25, 26, 27, 28, 29. 30, fair if wind north-west, rain if wind south or southwest.

For High Tides at Beaufort, see third page of the Almanac.

FARM AND GARDEN WORK FOR NOVEMBER.—Sow your first crop of peas and a few turnips. Plant out onions raised from seed in August and September. Plant Windsor and long pod beans. Dress asparagus and artichokes.

Sow full crops of rye, barley, wheat and other small grains. Harvest your sweet potatoes.

THE UNIVERSITY OF NORTH CAROLINA

THE HEAD OF THE STATE'S
EDUCATIONAL SYSTEM.

TWEVE BUILDINGS

SIX SCIENTIFIC LABORATORIES.

ACADEMIC,
LAW,
MEDICAL,
PHARMACY
DEPARTMENTS.

FACULTY OF THIRTY-FIVE

STUDENTS NUMBER OVER 500.

Free tuition to teachers and ministers sons.
Scholarships and loans for the needy.
Address

F. P. VENABLE, President.

12th Month. DECEMBER. 31 Dasy.

Moon's Phases.

	D. H. M.		D. H. M.
☾ Last Quarter,	2 4 41 p. m.	☽ First Quarter,	18 3 27 p.m.
		◉ Full Moon,	25 7 7 a.m.
● New Moon.	10 9 47 p.m.	☾ Last Quarter,	30 10 59 a.m.

Day of Month.	Day of week.	Sun rises.	Sun sets.	Sun fast.	Sun's decline South.	ASPECTS OF PLANETS AND OTHER MISCELLANEOUS MATTER.	Moon's place.	Moon rises or sets.	Moon South.
(48) First Sunday in Advent.						Day's length 9 hours 41 minutes.			
1	F	6 9	4 40	11	21 47	Prince of Wales born 1844	♋	11 0	morn
2	Mo	7 0	4 39	11	21 56	☾ Jordan Womble Jr d 1890	♌	morn	5 35
3	Tue	7 1	4 38	10	22 5		♌	0 1	6 20
4	We	7 2	4 38	10	22 13	Dr Deems born 1820	♍	1 0	7 4
5	Thu	7 3	4 38	9	22 21	♀ Gre Elong E—Custar b 1839	♍	1 57	7 47
6	Fri	7 4	4 38	9	22 29	Jefferson Davis d 1889	♍	2 55	8 30
7	Sat	7 5	4 38	8	22 36	W W Vass died 1896	♎	3 51	9 14
(49.) Second Sunday in Advent.						Day's length 9 hours 32 minutes.			
8	F	7 6	4 38	8	22 42	Eli Whitney born 1765	♎	4 47	9 59
9	Mo	7 7	4 38	7	22 49	☌ ♂ ◉ - ☌ ☿ ☾ DeQuincy d 1859	♎	5 40	10 47
10	Tue	7 8	4 38	7	22 54	● Rev A W Mitler d 1892	♏	6 52	11 34
11	We	7 8	4 39	6	23 0	Indianna admitted 1816	♏	sets	eve
12	Thu	7 9	4 39	6	23 4	Robt Hancock d 1888	♐	6 19	1 12
13	Fri	7 10	4 39	5	23 9	☌ ♄ ☾—☌ ♃ ☾—Tombs d '84	♐	7 14	2 1
14	Sat	7 11	4 39	5	23 13	☌ ♂ ♄ *Halcyon Days begin*	♑	8 13	2 49
(50.) Third Sunday in Advent.						Day's length 9 hours 29 minutes.			
15	F	7 11	4 40	4	23 16	☌ ♀ ☾ J H Mills d 1898	♑	9 13	3 36
16	Mo	7 12	4 40	4	23 19	Mrs. S C White d 1881	♑	10 14	4 23
17	Tue	7 13	4 40	3	23 22	☌ ♂ ♃ Beethoven b 1770	♒	11 18	5 10
18	We	7 14	4 40	3	23 24	☽ ☌ ☿ ♅ Sir H Davy b 1779	♒	morn	5 58
19	Thu	7 14	4 41	2	23 25	J L Harris d 1874	♓	0 22	6 49
20	Fri	7 15	4 41	2	23 26	South Carolina seceded 1860	♓	1 29	7 41
21	Sat	7 15	4 42	1	23 27	☉ *Enters Cap winter com*	♈	2 38	8 38
(51.) Fourth Sunday in Advent.						Day's length 9 hours 16 minutes.			
22	F	7 16	4 42	1	23 27	☍ ♆ ☉ Dr Winchester d '76	♈	3 49	9 37
23	Mo	7 16	4 43	1	23 27	Grady died 1889	♉	4 58	10 39
24	Tue	7 17	4 43	[illegible]	23 26	☿ in Aphelion- Thackery d '63	♉	6 7	11 41
25	We	7 17	4 44	[illegible]	23 25	◉ *Christmas Day*	♊	rises	morn
26	Thu	7 18	4 44	1	23 23	Stephen Girard died 1831	♊	6 28	0 42
27	Fri	7 18	4 45	1	23 21	*St John Evangelist*	♋	7 37	1 41
28	Sat	7 18	4 46	2	23 18	McCauley died 1859	♋	8 43	2 35
(52.) First Sunday after Christmas.						Day's length 9 hours 29 minutes.			
29	F	7 18	4 47	2	23 15	Hon D F Caldwell d 1898	♌	9 47	3 26
30	Mo	7 19	4 47	3	23 11	Beaconsfield born 1803	♌	10 48	4 13
31	Tue	7 19	4 47	3	23 8	⊕ in Perihelion Walter d '77	♌	11 48	4 59

For High Tides at Beaufort, see third page of the Almanac.

WEATHER CONJECTURES—December—1, 2, changeable; 3, 4, 5, 6, 7, 8, 9, expect rain; 10, 11, 12, 13, 14, 15, 16, 17, fair and frosty if wind be north or northeast; rain or snow if south or southwest; 18, 19, 20, 21, 22, 23, 24, fair and mild; 25 26, 27, 28, 29, stormy; 30, 31 cold high wind.

FARM AND GARDEN WORK FOR DECEMBER —Plant peas of all kinds; set out onions, garlic, eschalots and cabbage. Sow a few lettuce, spinach, carrots and radishers. You may try a few Irish potatoes.

Einish pickking cotton; get out crops of rice and prepare for market. Commence plowing, ditching, draining and manuring as early as possible for next year's crop.

THE GENERAL ASSEMBLY OF NORTH CAROLINA

FOR 1901 AND 1902

Will be Overwhelmingly Democratic in the House and Senate.

HOUSE.

Alamance—Elijah Long, (D), McRays.

Alleghany—Joseph C Fields, (D), Amelia.

Ashe—Hiram Weaver, (R), Lansing.

Alexander—C J Carson, (R) Taylorsville.

Anson—L D Robinson, (D), Wadesboro.

Beaufort—B B Nicholson, (D.) Washington.

Bertie—F D Winston, (D) Windsor.

Bladen—E F McCullock, (D), White Oak.

Brunswick—Dr D B McNeill, (D), Supply.

Buncombe—Locke Craige, (D), Asheville; J C Curtis, (D), Luther.

Burke—J F Spainhour, (D), Morganton.

Camden—G C Barco, (D). Camden.

Chatham—R H Hayes, (D), Pittsboro; J D McIver, (D), Corinth.

Cumberland—E R McKethan, (D), Fayetteville; F R Hall, (D), Falcon.

Cabarrus—W H Morris, (D), Concord.

Caldwell—John B Isbell, (R), Lenoir.

Carteret—N W Taylor, (D), Beaufort.

Caswell—W S Wilson, (D), Gatewood.

Catawba—W B Gaither, (D), Newton.

Cherokee—W G Payne, (R), Hot House.

Chowan—W D Welch, (D), Glden.

Clay—R T Coleman, (R), Hayesville.

Cleveland—C R Hoey, (D), Shelby.

Columbus—D C Allen, (D), Amour.

Craven—H B Pierce, (D), Newbern.

Currituck—S M Beasley, (D), Poplar Branch.

Davidson—H H Hartley, (D), Tyro Shops.

Davie—C M Sheets, (R), Mocksville.

Dare—C T Williams, (D), Avon.

Duplin—D L Carlton, (D), Kenansville.

Durham—R G Russell, (D), South Lowell.

Edgecombe—E L Daughtridge, (D), Rocky Mount; B F Shelton, (D), Speed.

Forsyth—J B Whitaker, (D), Winston-Salem; F T Baldwin, (D), Winston-Salem.

Franklin—W H Yarborough, (D), Louisburg.

Gaston—O F Mason (D) Dallas.

Gates—L L Smith, (D), Gatesville.

Granville—A W Graham, (D), Oxford; W H P Jenkins. (D), Jeffreys.

Graham—W F Mauney, (D), Robbinsville.

Greene—F L Carr, (D), Castoria.

Guilford—T E Whitaker (D), Oak Ridge, Westcott Robinson, (D), High Point.

Halifax—F M Parker, (D), Enfield; W P White, (D), Hobgood.

Harnett—W A Stewart, (D), Dunn.

Haywood—Joe Collins, Ind.) D.), Waynesville.

Henderson—O V F Blythe, (R), Hendersonville.

Hertford—L J Lawrence, (D), Murfreesboro.

Hyde—Julius Mann, (D), Middleton.

Iredell—A D Watts, (D), Statesville; Dr S W Stevenson, (D), Mooresville.

Jackson—W E Moore, (D), Webster.

Johnston—Clarence Richdrdson, (D), Archer; John M Morgan, (D), Bvnson.

Jones—A H White, (D), Pollockville.

Lenoir—W W Carraway, (D), Kinston.

Lincoln—Jack Rheinhardt, (D), Rheinhardt.

Macon—

Madison—I N Ebbs, (R), Hot Springs.

Martin—H W Stubbs, (D) Williamston.

McDowell—M F Morphew, (D), Marion.

Mecklenburg—F M Shannonhouse, (D), Charlotte; C H Duls, (D), Charlotte; W E Ardrey, (D). Ardrey.

Mitchell—J E Burlison, (R), Spruce Pine.

Montgomery—R. N. Page (D), Bisco.

Moore—A A F Sewell, (D), Jonesboro.

Nash—C F Ellen, (D), Rocky Mount.

New Hanover—George Roundtree, (D), Wilmington; M S Willard, (D), Wilmington.

Northampton—F R Harris, (D), Jackson.

Onslow—Frank Thompson, (D), Jacksonville.

Orange—S M Gattis, (D), Hillsboro.

Pasquotank—T P Nash, (D), Elizabeth City.

Pender—J R Bannerman, (D), Banuerman's.

Polk—John W McFarland, (R), Poors Ford.

Pamlico—George Dees, (D), Vanceboro.

Perquimans—Thomas R Ward, (D), Belvidere.

Person—W T Bradshaw, (D), Roxboro.

Pitt—W J Nichols, (D), Greenville; Thomas H Barnhill, (D), Grindoll.

Randolph—John T Brittain, (D), Asheboro; Charles Ross, (D), Asheboro.

Richmond—A J Little, (D) Rockingham.

Robeson—G B Patterson, (D), Maxton; J S Oliver, (D), Affinity.

Rockingham—J Robert Garrett, (D), Thompsonville; J H Lane, (D), Leaksville.

Rowan—R Lee Wright, (D), Salisbury; L H Rothrock, (D), Rockwell.

Rutherford—J F Alexander, (D), Forest City.

Sampson—W Y Duncan, (P), Clinton; E B Owen, (P), Clinton.

Stanly—W E Blalock, (D), Norwood.

Stokes—Riley J Petree, (R), Germanton.

Surry—Brim, (R).

Scotland—Hector McLean, (D), Lauriuburg.

Swain—Republican.

Transylvania—R H Zachary, (D), Jeptha.

Tyrrell—August W Owens, (D), Columbia.

Union—R S Bivens, (D), Monroe.

Vance—W B Daniel, (D), Epsom.

Wake—E C Beddingfield, (D), Neus : John P Pearson, (D), Apex; R N Simms. (D), Raleigh.

Warren—S G Daniel (D), Littleton.

Washington—Thomas W Blount, (D), Roper.

Watauga—W H Calloway, (R).

Wayne—W R Allen, (D), Goldsboro; George E Hood, (D), Goldsboro.

Wilson—H. G. Connor, (D), Wilson.

Wilkes—H L Green, (D). Wilkesboro, and one Republican.

Yadkin—Republican.

Yancey—Republican.

SENATE.

First District—(Currituck, Camden, Pasquotank, Hertford, Gates, Chowan, Perquimans)—W H Bray, (D), Shawboro; S C Vann, (D), Edenton.

Second District—(Tyrrell, Washington, Martin, Dare, Beaufort,

Hyde, Pamlico)—I W Miller, (D),
Bayboro; H S Ward, (D), Plymouth.

Third District — (Northampton,
Bertie)—S J Calvert, (D), Jackson.

Fourth District—(Halifax)—E L
Travis, (D), Halifax.

Fifth District — (Edgecombe)—
R H Speight, (D), Wrendale.

Sixth District--(Pitt)--F G James,
(D), Greenville.

Seventh District--(Wilson, Nash,
Franklin—T M Arrington, (D),
Rocky Mount; J E Woodard, (D),
Wilson.

Eighth District—(Craven, Jones,
Carteret, Lenoir, Onslow, Greene)
—J E W Sugg. (D), Snow Hill, T
D Warren, (D), Trenton.

Ninth District—(Duplin, Wayne,
Pender)—B F Aycock, (D), Fremont, J T Foy, (D), Burgaw.

Tenth District—(New Hanover,
Brunswick)—George L Morton,
(D), Wilmington

Eleventh District—(Warren and
Vance)—John E Burroughs, (D),
Dabney.

Twelfth District—(Wake)—N B
Broughton, (D), Raleigh.

Thirteenth District--(Johnston)--
Allan K Smith, (D), Smithfield.

Fourteenth District— (Sampson,
Harnett, Bladen—George H. Currie, (D). Clarkton; Populist. Blrden
county.

Fifteenth District—(Columbus,
Robeson)—Joseph A Brown, (D),
Chadbourn; Stephen Maintyre,
(D), Lumberton.

Sixteen District—(Cumberland)
—James D McNeill, (D), Fayetteville.

Seventeen District—(Granville,
Person)—James A Long, (D). Roxboro.

Eighteenth District—(Caswell,
Alamance, Orange, Durham)—R
W Scott, (D), Melville; Howard
Foushee, (D), Durham.

Nineteenth District—(Chatham)
—Henry A London, (D), Pittsboro.

Twentieth District—(Rockingham)- William Lindsay, (D), Reidsville.

Twenty-first district—(Guilford)
James D Glenn, (D), Greensboro.

Twenty-second District—(Randolph, Moore)—W P Wood, (d),
Asheboro.

Twenty-third district — (Richmond, Scotland; Montgomery, Anson, Union)—Cameron, Morrison.
(d), Rockingham; J A Leak, (d),
Wadesboro.

Twenty-fourth district—(Cabarrus and Stanly)—H C McAllister,
(d), Mt Pleasant.

Twenty-fifth district —(Mecklenburg)—S B Alexander, (d), Charlotte

Twenty-sixth district—(Rowan,
Davidson)—John S Henderson, (d),
Salisbury; John C Thomas, (d),
Midway.

Twenty.seventh district — (Iredell Davie, Yadkin)—J C Pinnix.
(r), ——; Stikeleather, (p), Marber.

Twenty-eighth district—(Stokes,
Surry)—S E Marshall, (r), White
Plains.

Twenty-ninth district—(Catawba, Lincoln, Alexander, Wilkes)—
Thomas J Dula, (r), Wilkesboro:
J O McIntosh, (p), Lincolnton.

Thirtieth district—(Alleghany,
Ashe, Watauga.), L. McLeod, (r),
Rutherfordton.

Thirty-first district—(Caldwell,
Burke. McDowell, Mitchell, Yancey)—Van Miller, (r). Lenoir; Marion Buchanan, (r), Bakersville.

Thirty-second district—(Gaston,
Cleveland, Rutherford, Polk)—M
H Justice, (d), Rutherfordton, F
Y Webb, (d), Shelby.

Thirty-third district--)Buncombe,
Madison, Haywood)—J M Gudger,
(d), Asheville; W W Stringfield,
(d), Waynesville.

Thirty-fourth district—(Henderson, Transylvania, Jackson, Swain)
—James M Candler, (r). ——.

Thirty-fifth district — (Macon,
Cherokee, Clay, Graham)--Joel L.
Crisp, (r), Stecoah.

FARM AND GARDEN WORK FOR APRIL.—Wnatever has been omitted in March, do not neglect any longer. Sow green glazed cabbage, pickling cabbage, full crop of cauliflower and broccoli, okra, tomatoes; peppers, beets, carrots, leeks, metons, cucumbers, celery.

Full crops of corn, cotton and rice should be put in during this month Plant your lowland corn. Commence early to hoe your young cotton, and thin out to stand. Plant pumpkins for a field crop.

THE UNIVERSITY OF NORTH CAROLINA.

Located in Chapel Hill, Orange County, twenty-eight miles northwest of Raleigh.

Chartered in 1898, founded in 1793, opened 1795. It now has 512 students and 25 instructors. The equipment includes twelve large buildings, six scientific laboratories, library of 32,000 volumes, campus of sixty acres with ample athletic grounds, gymnasium, etc. Perfect sanitation, baths, closets, etc. Tuition $60 a year, total expenses $200 to $300. Scholarships and loans for the needy Law school 80, medical school 44, pharmacy 20. A summer school for teachers is conducted each July. It enrolled 161 teachers in 1899. The faculty includes 35 professors and instructors. Many students support themselves by labor, the total amount earned being about $5 009. The University is non-political and non-sectarian.

FACULTY.—Francis Preston Venable, Ph. D., President of the University; Kemp Plummer Battle, LL. D., Alumni Professor of History; Charles Baskerville, Ph. D.; Smith Professor of General and Analytical Chemistry; Joseph Austin Holmes, S. B., State Geologist, Lecturer on Geology of Carolina; Joshua Walker Gore, C. E , Professor of Physics; James Mac-Rae, LL. D., Professor of Law; Thomas Hume, D. D., LL. D., Professor of English Language and Literature; Eban Alexander, Ph. D., Professor of Greek ; William Cain, C. E , Professor of Mathematics ; Richard Henry Whitehead, M. D., Professor of Anatomy and Pathology; Henry Horace Williams, A. M., B. D., Professor of Philosophy; Henry Van Peters Wilson, Ph. D., Professor of Biology; H. F. Linscott, Ph. D., Professor of Latin Language and Literature; Collier Cobb, A. M., Professor of Geology; A. S Wheeler, Ph. D., Assistant Professor of Chemistry; Charles Staples Mangum, M. D., Professor of Physiology and *Materia Medica*; Edward Vernon Howell, A. B., Ph. G., Professor of Pharmacy; Thomas J. Wilson, Jr., Ph. D., Associate Professor of Classical Philology; M. C. Noble, Professor of Pedagogy; Thomas Ruffin Ph. B,, Assistant Professor of Law.

INSTRUCTORS.—Archibald Henderson, A. B. Instructor in Mathematics; Jacob Warshaw, A. B., Instructor in Modern Languages; Edward K. Graham, A. B., Instructor in English; W. R. Weeks, Director of Gymnasium.

ASSISTANTS IN LABORATORIES.—J. E. Mills, Ph. D., Assistant in Chemistry; T. D. Rice, Assistant in Geology; J. E. Latta, Assistant in Physics; C. A. Shore, Assistant in Biology; W. M. McNider, Assistant in Biology.

OFFICERS.—Walter D. Toy, M. A., Secretary of the Faculty; Eben Alexander, Ph D., LL. D., Supervisor of the Library, W. S. Bernard. Librarian; Eugene Lewis Harris, Ph. B. Registrar; Willie Thomas Patterson. Bursar.

2. A man in whose mind his own country is not *first*, is a man who himself is not *worthy* to be first in another country.—*Branson.*

CHARLES PEARSON, Architect, Raleigh, N. C.   Correspondence Solicited.

COUNTY OFFICERS CORRECTED FROM LAST ELECTION UP TO NOVEMBER, 1900.

	COUNTIES.	COUNTY TOWNS.	CLERKS.	REGISTERS.	SHERIFFS.	SUPERVISORS OF SCHOOLS.
1	Alamance,	Graham,	J D Kerhodle	Chas C Thompson	L B McAdams	Rev W S Love
2	Alexander,	Taylorsville,	A L Watts	V W Teague	J Y Williams	A Frank Sharp
3	Alleghany,	Sparta,	I N Edwards	E Thompson	D R Edwards	Prof S W Brown
4	Anson,	Wadesboro,	J C McLauchlin	S A Fenton	J T Gaddy	W D Redfearn
5	Ashe,	Jefferson,	A S Ellis	D A Osbonne	P G McNeill	J W Jones
6	Beaufort,	Washington,	G Wilkens	Gilbert Rumley	R T Hodges	Rev Nat Harding
7	Bertie,	Windsor,	W L Lyon	E E Etheridge	T C Bond	R W Askew
8	Bladen,	Elizabethtown,	A M McNeill	J S Williamson	C W Lyon	J L Currie
9	Brunswick,	Southport,	Thos L Wines	C Ed Taylor	D R Walker	R Vance Leonard
10	Buncombe,	Asheville,	T C Starnes	J J Mackey	R F Lee	H O Hauk
11	Burke,	Morganton,	P W Patton	J H Giles	C M McDowell	Herbert Houk
12	Cabarrus,	Concord,	J M Cooke	W R Johnson	J Lawson Peck	C B Miller
13	Caldwell,	Lenoir,	J V McCall	W L Minish	A H Boyd	Prof H B Phillips
14	Camden, C. H.,	Camden, C. H.,	R L Forbes	C B Garrett	W S Bartlett	Chas H Spencer
15	Carteret,	Beaufort,	L A Garner	W L Arrington	S T Hancock	Joseph Pigott
16	Caswell,	Yanceyville,	Dr J G Hunt	J B Mayes	S A Fleming	A Baker
17	Catawba,	Newton,	L H Phillips	P M Dellinger	J W Backwelder	A P Whisenhunt
18	Chatham,	Pittsboro,	R H Dixon	W E Brooks	James J Johnson	T H Hancock
19	Cherokee,	Murphy,	S W Lovingood	T C McJonald	A J Martin	W R Johnson
20	Chowan,	Edenton,	H C Privatt	M A Hughes	A P Elliott	R H Willis
21	Clay,	Hayesville,	C C Standridge	M M Burns	John A Chambers	T H Hancock
22	Cleveland,	Shelby,	L J Hoyle	J F Roberts	A B Suttle	J A Anthony
23	Columbus,	Whiteville,	H C Moffitt	R L Powell	J G Butler	L W Stanly
24	Craven,	Newbern,	E W Carpenter	John B Willis	J L Hahn	Rev John S Long
25	Cumberland,	Fayetteville,	A A McKeithan	J A McPherson	George A Burns	Z B Newton
26	Currituck,	Currituck, C. H.,	E W Ansell	E N Williams	R E Flora	F B Anson
27	Dare,	Manteo,	T S Meekins	R W Smith	A H Ethridge	F P Gates
28	Davidson,	Lexington,	H T Phillips	S L Owen	T F S Dorsett	P L Lunsford
29	Davie,	Mocksville,	A C Grant	B O Morris	Jesse L Sh ek	J D Hodges
30	Duplin,	Kenansville,	Herbert Smith	B Frank Pearsall	L Middleton	S W Clements

No.	County	Town				
31	Durham,	Durham,	C B Green	John E Suit	F D Markham	C W Massey
32	Edgecombe,	Tarboro,	Ed Pennington	B L Dougan	W L Stellings	F S Wilkinson
33	Forsyth,	Winston,	N S Wilson	B F Byerly	E T Knapps	Dr A P Davis
34	Franklin,	Louisburg,	W K A Williams	J F Clifton	H C Kearney	R R White
35	Gaston,	Dallas,	C C Cornell	M A Carpenter	W T Love	L M Hoffman
36	Gates,	Gatesville,	W T Cross	Lycurgus Hoffler	R O Riddick	John R Walton
37	Graham,	Robbinsville,	R V McElroy	Robert B Slaughter	J A Ammons	J W Moody
38	Granville,	Oxford,	J G Hunt	John B Mayes	S A Fleming	Alexander Baker
39	Greene,	Snow Hill,	John R Dale	Chas A Lassiter	B W Edwards	M P Davis
4	Guilford,	Greensboro,	John J Nelson	A G Kirkman	James F Jordan	J R Wharton
41	Halifax,	Halifax, C. H.,	S M Gary	J H Norman	J E H use	Col Aaron Prescott
42	Harnett,	Lillington,	J H Withers	A C Holloway	S A Solomon	Rev J A Black
43	Haywood,	Waynesville,	N P Walker	H B Moore	W M Hanson	A J Garner
44	Henderson,	Hendersonville,	C M Pace	W A Hood	Jonathan Williams	Jas M Jastire
45	Hertford,	Winton,	J F Newsom	S E Marsh	I S Mitchell	J C Scarboro
46	Hyde,	Swan Quarter,	Reuban D Harris	Geo W Brown	A L Catrell	J M Watson
47	Iredell,	Statesville,	Jas Hartness	W W Turner	J H Wycoff	J A Butler
48	Jackson,	Webster,	F E Alley	James R Long	W A Hanson	J N Wilson
49	Johnston,	Smithfield,	W S Stevens	J W Stephenson	T Ellington	Prof Ira T Turlington
50	Jones,	Trenton,	S E Koonce	W H Cox	D H Harrison	W H Hammond
51	Lenoir,	Kinston,	H V Williams	W D Suggs	J C Wooten	G W Howard
52	Lincoln,	Lincolnton,	Lee Crawford	H A Self	J K Kline	G T Heafner
53	Macon,	Franklin,	J H White	D W Blain	T B Hughn	J R Pendergrass
54	Madison,	Marshall,	J A Hobbs	Van B Davis	R S Ramsey	J M James
55	Martin,	Williamston,	Thos Morris	W C Manning	J C Crawford	R J Peele
56	McDowell,	Marion,	J A Russell	T W Wilson	Frank H Stedman	Rev W H Wood
57	Mecklenburg,	Charlotte,	J C Bauman	A M McDonald	N W Wallace	R B Hunter
58	Mitchell,	Bakersville,	C A Armstrong	T B Garland	R H Bradshaw	Agustus Masters
59	Montgomery,	Troy,	D A McDonald	W D Allen	W D Clark	D W Cochran
60	Moore,	Carthage,	Thos Sills	A L McIntosh	S M Jones	T M Lundey
61	Nash,	Nashville,	John D Taylor	J A Whitaker	W M Warren	W S Wilkinson
62	New Hanover,	Wilmington,	J T Flythe	W H Biddle	Wm M F Bargin	Washington Catlelett
63	Northampton,	Jackson,	John W Burton	M F Stancell	W H Joyner	Paul J Long
64	Onslow,	Jacksonville,	D H Hamilton	I E Ketchum	F W Hurgett	A W Cooper
65	Orange,	Hillsboro		John Laws	John K Hughes	John Thompson

	COUNTIES.	COUNTY TOWNS.	CLERKS.	REGISTERS.	SHERIFF.	SUPERVISOR OF SCHOOLS.	
66	Pamlico,	Bayboro	James R Rice	Alex Lee	Wallace E Hooker	M W Ball	66
67	Pasquotank,	Elizabeth City	W H Jennings	E B Culpeper	N G Grandy	S L Sheep	67
68	'ender,	Burgaw	W W Larkins	J P Stringfield	W W Alderman	T H W McIntyre	68
69	Perquimans,	Hertford	E V Perry	W R White	A F Riddick	W G Gaither	69
70	Person,	Roxboro	D W Braisher	H J Whitt	J K Simms	G F Holloway	70
71	Pitt,	Greenville	N B Hampton	T R Moore	G M Mooring	W H Ragsdale	71
72	Polk,	Columbus	N B Thompson	A L McAlarny	W C Robertson	W M Justice	72
73	Randolph,	Asheboro	G G Hendrick	J T Winslow	W F Redding	W C Hammer	73
74	Richmond,	Rockingham	W T Everett	H D Gibson	T S Wright	J H Walsh	74
75	Robeson,	Lumberton	W H Humphrey	Joe Buie	G B McLeod	M Shephard	75
76	Rockingham,	Wentworth	J V Price	I A Scales	R W Hutcheson	E P Ellington	76
77	Rowan,	Salisbury	M O Dickerson	N H Woodson	J M Monroe	R G Kizer	77
78	Rutherford,	Rutherfordton	W R Pigford	Jas P Jones	E A Martin	A L Rucker	78
79	Sampson,	Clinton	W I Everett	O F Herring	J W Marshburn	Street Brewer	79
80	Scotland,	Laurinburg	R A Crowell	H D Gibson	T S Wright	W F McIver	80
81	Stanly,	Albemarle	N O Petree	I N Suggs	G R McCain	C C Black	81
82	Stokes,	Danbury	C H Haynes	I M Gordion	R P Joyce	W B Harris	82
83	Surry,	Dobson	A J Hall	T W Davis	J M Davis	Rev J H Lewellyn	83
84	Swain,	Bryson City	T T Loftis	A G De Hart	C C Martin	L Leeman	84
85	Transylvania,	Brevard	G L Linerman	Wm Henry	V B McGatha	W L Carmichael	85
86	Tyrrell,	Columbia	E A Armfield	T L Jones	F L Cohoon	Bailing me	86
87	Union,	Monroe	Henry Perry	J M Stewart	B A Horne	A M Craxton	87
88	Vance,	Henderson	W M Rass	Kenneth Edwards	W H Smith	Rev Gideon McDray	88
89	Wake,	Raleigh	W A White	W H Hood	M W Page	Rev W G Clements	89
90	Warren,	Warrenton	W M Bateman	M F Thornton	J B W Jones	James R Ro well	90
91	Washington,	Plymouth	J H Bingham	W H Stall	J L Phelps	B F Hassell Jr	91
92	Watauga,	Boone	J F Ormond	Jacob May	W H Caloway	B B Daugherty	92
93	Wayne,	Goldsboro	Linville Bumgarner	G C Kornegay	B F Scott	E T Atkin-on	93
94	Wilkes,	Wilkesboro	J D Bardin	E M Blackburn	J H Johnson	C C Wright	94
95	Wilson,	Wilson	W A Hall	Wm B Barnes	W D P Sharp	James W Hayes	95
96	Yadkin,	Yadkinville	J B Ray	J L Craton	A P Woodruff	E G M ers	96
97	Yancey,	Burnsville		J R Young	W B Wilson	Wm D Peterson	97

SUPERIOR COURTS OF NORTH CAROLINA FOR 1901.

Adopted from N. C. Court Calendar of A. B. Andrews, Jr.

JUDGES.

NAMES.	DISTRICT.	RESIDENCE.
Geo. H. Brown, Jr.,	1	Washington.
Henry R. Bryan,	2	New Bern.
E. W. Timberlake,	3	Louisburg.
W. S. O'B. Robinson	4	Goldsboro.
Thos. J. Shaw,	5	Greensboro.
Owen H. Allen,	6	Kinston.
Thos. A. McNeill,	7	Lumberton.
A. M. Coble,	8	Statesville.
Henry S. Starbuck,	9	Winston.
W. B. Council,	10	Boone.
W. Alexander Hoke,	11	Lincolnton.
Fred. Moore,	12	Asheville.

SOLICITORS.

NAMES.	DISTRICT.	RESIDENCE.
Geo. W. Ward,	1	Elizabeth City.
W. E. Daniel,	2	Weldon.
Larry I. Moore,	3	Greenville.
	4	Smithfield.
A. L. Brooks,	5	Greensboro.
Rudolph Duffy,	6	Cather'n Lake
C. M. McLean,	7	Elizabethtown
Wiley Rush.	8	Asheboro.
M. L. Mott.	9	Wilkesboro.
M. Henshaw,	10	Lenoir.
J. L. Webb,	11	Shelby.
Jas. W. Fergusou,	12	Waynesville.

Time of Holding Courts.

FIRST JUDICIAL DISTRICT.

Spring—Judge Allen.
Fall—Judge Shaw.
Beaufort—‡Feb 18 (2) May 27th (2) Nov. 25th.
Currituck—March 4 Sept 1st (1)
Camden—March 4, Sept 11.
Pasquotank—March 18th †July 10th, Sept 17th, December 16.
Chowan—April 1st, September 30th.
Perquimans—March 25th, September 23.
Gates—April 3d, Oct. 7th.
Hertford—April 22d, Oct. 22nd
Washington—April 3d, Oct. 4th.
Tyrrell—April 21st Oct. 28th
Dare—May 6th, Nov. 4th.
Hyde—May 13th, Nov. 11th.
Palmico—May 20th, Nov. 16th.

SECOND JUDICIAL DISTRICT.

Spring—Judge McNeil.
Fall—Judge Allen.
Halifax—†March 4th, (2) †Nov. 18th (2).
Northampton—April 1st (2) Oct 21st.
Bertie—‡Feb 18th, April 29th (2) ‡Sept. 9th, Nov. 5.
Crraven—Jan. 28th (2) †May 27 (2)‡Nov. 25th (2).
Werren—†March 18 (2) †Sept. 16th (2).
Edgecombe — †April 5th (2) †June 10th (2). Oct. 3d (2).

THIRD JUDICIAL DISTRICT.

Spring—Judge Coble.
Fall—Judge McNeil.

Pitt—Jan. 7 (2) †March 4 (2) Apr. 1st (2) Sept. 16th (2) Dec. 2 (2).
Franklin—Jan. 21 (2) April 15th (2) Oct. 14 (2)
Wilson—Feb. 4 (2) †May 13th, †Nov. 11th (2).
Vance—Feb. 18th (2) May 20th Sept. (2).
Martin—March 12th (2) Sept. 2d (2).
Nash—†April 29th (2) Nov. 18th (2).

FOURTH JUDICIAL DISTRICT.

Spring—Judge Starbuck.
Fall—Judge Coble.
Wake—*Jan. 7th (2) †Feb 25th (2) †April 22 (2) *March 25(2) July 8 (2) *Sept. 23d (2) Oct. 21 (3).
Wayne—Jan. 21st (2) April 15th, Sept 9th (2) Oct. 14th.
Harnett—Feb. 18th, Sept. 2d, ‡Nov. 25th (2).
Johnston—March 11th (2) Aug 26th, Nov. 11th (2).

FIFTH JUDICIAL DISTRICT.

Spring—Judge Council.
Fall—Judge Starbuck.
Durham—Jan. 14th (2) †March 25th (2) †May 13th (2) *Sept. 2d. †Sept. 30th (2)
Granville—Jan. 28th (2) April 22d (2) July 22d (2) Nov. 18th (2)
Chatham—Feb 11th, May 6th. Sept 16th (2).
Guilford—Feb. 12th (2), June 3d (3) Aug. 19th, Dec. 2 (2).
Alamance—March 11, †May 20th 20th, †Sept. 9th, Nov. 4th.

Orange—March 18th †May 27th, Aug 15, Oct 28th.

Caswell—April 8th, Oct. 14th.

Person—April 15th, Aug. 12th, Nov. 11th.

SIXTH JUDICIAL DISTRICT.

Spring—judge Hoke.
Fall—Judge Council.
Pendor—March 15th, Sept. 9th, (2).

Greene—Feb. 25th. Aug. 26, Nov. 25th.

New Hanover—Jan. †21,(2 †April 15th, (2), †Sept. 23d,

Lenoir—Jan. 14th, May 6(2) August 19th, Nov. 11th.

Duplin—Feb. 18th, Sept. 2d, Dec. 2d (2).

Sampson, Feb. 4th (2), April 29, Oct. 7th (2).

Carteret, April 1st, Oct. 21st, Jones March 25th, Oct 28th.

Onslow, April 8th, Nov. 4th.

SEVENTH JUDICIAL DISTRICT.

Spring, Judge Fred. Moore.
Fall, Judge Hoke.
Columbus, March 11th, August 12th, Nov. 7th, Oct. 21st.

Anson. *7th †April 15th, *Sept. 2d, †Oct. 28th.

Cumberland, †Feb. 18th, *†Mar. 25th, ¾April 2d, (2) †May 6th(2) †Sept. 25th Nov 11th (11th (2).

Robeson, †Feb 11th †April 29 †July 22 †Oct. 7th.

Richmond, †Jan. 16th, Tuesday (2) Nov. 4th, April 23d †May 20th *†Sept. 7th, Nov. 4th.

Bladen, March 4th, Tuesday, Sept. 30th (2)

Brunswick, March 18th, October 14th.

Moore, †Jan. 28th (2) *April 1 *†Aug. 19th (2) Nov. 25th.

Scotland, Terms to be set by the Governor.

EIGHTH JUDICIAL DISTRICT.

Spring, Judge G. H Brown.
Fall, Judge Fred. Moore.
Cabarrus, Jan. 21st (2) April 23d July 22 (2) Oct. 14th

Iredell, Feb. 4th (2) May 20th (2). Aug. 5th [2] Nov. 4th (2).

Rowan, Feb. 18th [2] May 6th [2], Aug. 19th [2] Nov. 18th [2].

Davidson, March 4th, [2] Sept. 2d [2].

Randolph, March 18th [2] July 8th [2]. Dec. 2d [2].

Montgomery. *Jan. 7th, April 15th Sept. 30th [2]

Yadkin, April 29th, Oct. 21 [2]

NINTH JUDICIAL DISTRICT

Spring, Judge Bryan.
Fall, Judge Brown.
Alexander, Feb. 18th, Aug. 19th.

Rockingham, March 4th [2], Aug 12th, Oct. 28ih [2].

Forsyth, †Feb. 25th *May 13th [2] Nov. 25th [2].

Wilkes, March 25th. May 27th [2] Aug .26th (2).

Alleghany, March 25th, Sept. 9

Davie, April 1.(2) Oct. 24th [2].

Stokes, April 27th [2] Sept. 16th [2].

Surry, †April 15th [two] †Sept. 30 [two] Nov. 11 [two].

TENTH JUDICIAL DISTRICT.

Spring, Judge Timberlake.
Fall, Judge Bryan.
Catawba, Mar. 4th [two] Aug. 5th [two] Nov. 18th [two].

McDowell, †April 15th [two] †July 22d [two]

Burke, April 6th [two] Nov 4th [two]

Caldwell, †March 18th, [two.] August 17th [two] Oct 15th [two].

Ashe, April 8th, Feb. 19th [2] Sept. 16th [two].

Watauga, April 1st [two] Sept. 2d [two]. Sep 2 (2)

Mitchell Feb. 18th, April 4th, Sept. 30th [two].

Yancey, May 20th [two] †*Oct. 14th [three]

ELEVENTH JUDICIAL DISTRICT.

Spring, Judge Robinson.
Fall, Judge Timberlake.
Union, *†Jan. 28th [three] †for 2d 3d weeks †*June 10th [two] *†Aug. 19th [two] *Sept. 9th, Dec. 16.

Stanly—Mar. 4 (2) *Sep 2 Dec 9

Mecklenburg, Jan 21st † March 13th, [two] †June 3d [two] Sept. 30th [two].

Gaston, Feb. 18th [two] Sept. 16 [two]

Lincoln, April 1st (two) October 15th.

Cleveland, April 15(two) October 21st (two).

Rutherford, April 29th (two) November 4th (two).

Polk. May 13th Nov 18th.

Henderson. †May 20th two Nov 25th two.

TWELFTH JUDICIAL DISTRICT.

Spring. Judge Shaw.
Fall. Judge Robinson.

Madison. ⅔Jan 21st two ⅔July 23 three.

Buncombe. ⅔Feb 4th three *Apr 29th two Aug 12th three Nov 11th two.

Transylvania. Feb 25th two Sept 2d two.

Haywood. *March 11th two *Sep 16th two.

Jackson. March 25th two, Sept 30th.

Macon. April 8th two Oct 7th.

Clay. April 22 Oct 14th.

Cherokee. May 13th two October 21st.

Graham. May 27th Nov 4th.

Swain. June 3d three November 25th two.

CRIMINAL COURTS.

EASTERN DISTRICT.

Judge. Aug. M. Moore.

New Hanover. March 11th *June 3d two *Aug 5th Nov 18th.

Warren. *June 24th *December 9th.

Vance. *Feb 14th.

Edgecombe. *May 30th *Nov 11.

Craven. *Feb 26th Aug 19th.

Halifax. *Jan 25th *May 6th Sep 3oth.

Mecklenburg. *January 7th two *July 15th two *April 8 *Sept 23d *Nov 25th.

Robeson. *April *Oct 25th.

Cumberland Dec 31st, 1900 *Apr 29th *Sept 16th.

Wilson. *June 17th *Oct 14th.

Nash. *Feb 4th *Aug 26th.

Northamptou. *March 15 *Sept 2d.

WESTERN DISTRICT.

Judge. Stevens.

Solicitor. Robt S McCall, Asheville.

Buncombe. *Jan 14th [o] *April 22d [o] *July 22d Oct 21st.

Madison. *Feb 19th June 11th Nov 12th.

Henderson. †Sept 10th, April 9.

McDowell. July 9th *Dec 16th.

———

*For criminal cases only.

†For civil cases only.

[2] or [two] Means two weeks, etc.

Scotland County Terms to be set by Governor.

U. S. CIRCUIT AND DISTRICT COURTS.

Charles H. Simonton, Charleston, S. C., Judge of Fourth Circuit of United States Courts.

Nathan Goff, West Virginia, Judge of the U. S. Circuit Court of Appeals for Fourth district.

WESTERN DISTRICT.—James E. Boyd, Greensboro, Judge; A. E Holton, District Attorney; Spencer Blackburn, Assistant Attorney; S. L. Trodgen, Clerk. *Greensboro*—Circuit and District—April 1st. two, October 7th. *Statesville*—Circuit and district, H. C. Cowles. Clerk; April 15. (2) October 21st. *Asheville*—Circuit and district, C. B. Moore, Clerk; May 6th, two, November 4th. *Charlotte*—Circuit and district, H. C, Cowles, Clerk; June 3d, December 2d

EASTERN DISTRICT.—T. R. Purnell, Judge; C. M. Bernard, Greenville, District Attorney; O. C. Spears and E. A Johnson, Assistant Attorneys; John P. Overman, Deputy Clerk. *Elizabeth City*---District Court, April 15th, October 21st. *New Bern*---District Court, George Green, deputy clerk; New Bern, April 22d, October 23d. *Wilmington*----Circuit and district; H. L Grant, clerk; George Tonnoffski. assistant clerk, in Raleigh; W. H. Shaw, clerk of district and deputy of Circuit Court at Wilmington; H. C Dockery, marshal; April 29th, November 24th. *Raleigh*---Circuit and district; N. J. Riddick, clerk, in Raleigh; W. H .Shaw, clerk of district and deputy of Circuit Court at Wilmington; H. C. Dockery, marshal; Raleigh, May 27th, two, December 2d.

SUPREME COURT OF NORTH CAROLINA.

Examiner's Applicants for license Monday, first week of term. Court meets 1st Monday in February and last Monday in September of each year.

Cases Heard: First district Monday, February 5th, September 24th. Second district, Monday, February 12th, October 1st. Third district, Monday, February 19th, October 8th. Fourth district, February 26th, October 15th. Fifth district, March 5th, October 21st. Sixth district, March 12th, October 29th. Seventh district, March 19th, November 5th. Eighth district, March 26th, November 12th. Ninth district, April November 19th. Tenth district, April 9th, November 26th. Eleventh district, April 16th, December 3d. Twelfth district, April 23d, December 10th. End of docket, etc., April 30th

CIRCUIT COURT OF APPEALS.

U. S. FOURTH CIRCUIT.—The Circuit Court of Appeals meets in Richmond, Va., February 2d, May 7th and November 3d. Chief Justice Fuller presides. Circuit Judges: Nathan Goff and Charles H. Simonton. Two district judges are designated at each term. Maryland, West Virginia and Virginia, North and South Carolina complete the circuit.

GOVERENMENT OF NORTH CAROLINA.

EXECUTIVE DEPARTMENT.

Charles B. Aycock, of Wayne County. Governor, salary $3,000, and furnished house, fuel and lights.

W. D. Turner, of Iredell County, Lieutenant-Governor and President of the Senate.

T. M. Pearsall, Private Secretary to the Governor, salary $1,200 and commissions.

J. Bryan Grimes, of Pitt County Secretary of State, salary $2,000 and certain fees, and $1,000 extra for clerical assistance.

Chief Clerk to Secretary of State, salary $1,000.

B. F. Dixon, of Cleveland county, Auditor, salary $1,500, and $1,000 extra for clerical assistance.

Hiliary T. Hudson. Chief Clerk to Auditor, salary $1,000.

B. R. Lacy, of Wake county, Treasurer, salary $3,000.

--, County, Chief Clerk to Treasurer, salary $1,500.

-------------------------------------- County, Clerk for Charitable amd Penal Institutions, salary $1,000.

-------------------------------------- County, Teller of the Treasury Department, salary $750.

Thomas F. Toon, of Robeson county, Superintendent of Public Instruction, salary $1,500, and $500 per annum for travelling expenses.

Robert D. Gilmer, of Haywood county, Attorney General, salary $2,000 and $600 for clerical assistance.

B. S. Royster, Granville county, Adjutant General, salary $1,000.

M. O. Sherrill, Catawba county, State Librarian, salary $1,000.

-------------------------------------- County. Executive Clerk, salary $600.

C. C. Cherry, of Edgecombe county, Superintendent of Public Buildings and Grounds, salary $850.

A. L. Moore, of Wake county, State Standard Keeper, salary $100.

N. C. BOARD OF CORPORATION COMMISSIONERS.

Commissioners.—Franklin McNeill, New Hanover county. Chairman; term expires January, 1907. Sam. L. Rogers, Macon county, term expires

1905. D. H. Abbott, Pamlico county; term expires April 1, 1903; salary $2,000 each. Henry C. Brown, Surry county, regular Clerk, salary ....
Miss Riddick, Stenographer, salary ......

Regular session of the Court are held at Raleigh. Special sessions are also held at other places, under such regulations as made by the Commission.

Offices of the Commissioners are located in the Agricultural Building.

BUREAU OF LABOR AND PRINTING.

Henry B. Varner, Commissioner, Davidson county. salary $1,500 ....
.... Assistant Commissioner, ... county, , salary $900.

NORTH CAROLINA GEOLOGICAL SURVEY.

J. A. Holmes, State Geologist; J. V. Lewis, Assistant Geologist, in charge of corundum and building stone investigation; W. W. Ashe, Forester; E. W. Myers, Assistant, in charge of water power investigation: Joseph H. Pratt, Mineralogist. The general office of the Survey is in the Agricultural Building, Raleigh.

BOARD OF INTERNAL IMPROVEMENTS.

Members of the Board are elected biennially by the General Assembly, and to consist of one member from each Congressional district, as follows: 1st district, E. F. Lamb; 2d district, J. W. Grainger; 3d district, W. J. Adams; 4th district, Armistead Jones; 5th district, C. M. Parks; 6th district, R. D. Caldwell; 7th district, A. H. Boyden; 8th district, Clement Manlp; 9th district, W. T. Lee. Armistead Jones; President; E. F. Lamb, Secretary.

STATE BANK EXAMINERS.

The Examiners are appointed by the Corporation Commission, and are as follows: Dr. George F. Lucas, of Pender county; W. B. Shaw, of Vance county; Arthur E. Rankin, of Bunbombe county. They examine the State and private banks only, and are subject to the control of the Corporation Commission.

STATE INSURANCE DEPARTMENT.

Office in Capitol Building James R. Young, of Vance county, Insurance Commissioner, salary $2,000; W. W. Wilson, of Wake, Clerk, salary $1,000. Term of office for two years, elected by the last Legislature.

STATE BOARD OF EDUCATION.

The Governor, Lieutenant-Governor, Secretary of State, Treasurer, Auditor, Superintendent of Public Instruction and Attorney General constitute the S ate Board of Education.

SHELL FISH COMMISSION OF NORTH CAROLINA.

Chief Commissioner, Theo. White, He tford, Perquimans county. Appointed Shell Fish Commissioner by the Governor February, under the act of General Assembly, 1897. Term of office four years; salary $900. Associate Commissioner not appointed.

The Professor of Biology at the University (Prof. H. V. Wilson) is ex officio an Associate Commissioner, but without additional salary.

BOARD OF PUBLIC BUILDINGS AND GROUNDS.

The Governor, Secretary of State, Treasurer, and Attorney General.

GOVEROR'S COUNCIL.

The Secretary of State, Treasurer, Auditor, and Superintendent of Public Instruction.

STATE HOSPITAL, GEO L. KIRBY SUPERINTENDENT, RALEIGH, N. C.

B. R. Lacy, Treasurer, *ex officio;* Geo. L. Kirby, M. D., Superintendent; C. L. Jenkins, M. D., First Assistant Physician; E. B. Ferrebee, Second Assistant Physician; W. R. Crawford, Jr., Steward; Miss M. E. Whitaker, Matron.

BOARD OF DIRECTORS.—J. D. Biggs, [President, Williamston, J. C.; Broadfoot, Fayetteville, N. C., Dr. James McKee, Raleigh, N. C., Geo. B. Curtis, Enfield. N. C.; J. C. Bellamy, Whitaker's, N. C; W. B. Fort, Pikeville, N. C., Frank Barnes, Wilson, N. C.; Dr. R. H. Stancell, Margarettesville, N. C.; James G. Kenan, Kenansville, N. C.

EXECUTIVE COMMITTEE.—James McKee, Chairman; W. B. Fort, R. H. Stancell.

 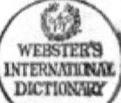

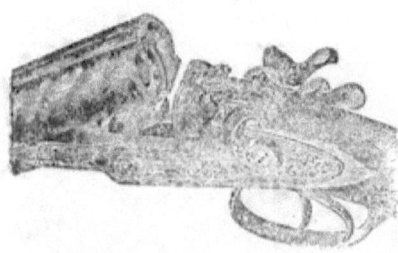

PRICE, 10 CENTS.

Vol. 4.] 35 YEAR OF PUBLICATION. [No. 5.

BRANSON'S
AGRICULTURAL
ALMANAC

FOR THE YEAR OF OUR LORD
1902,

And until the 4th of July, the 126th year of American Independence.

SECOND YEAR OF 20TH CENTURY.

Carefully Calculated for the Latitude and Longitude of Raleigh, by

LEVI BRANSON, A. M., D. D.

LEVI BRANSON, Publisher, Raleigh, N. C.

TIME.

The calculations of this Almanac are made in mean solar or clock time which is indicated by a well regulated watch or clock, and does not cor respond with the Sun precisely, except on four days in the year.

Apparent time is that which makes the Sun come to the meredian a 12 o'clock.   No good clock will run with the Sun; if set with the Sun on the 2d day of January, the clock will seem to be one minute too fast on the 3d of January,

To adapt the calculations of this Almanac to apparent time, use the minutes in the column marked "Sun slow" or "Sun fast;" add them when fast, subtract them when slow.

The calculations are made for the Latitude and Longitude of Raleigh N. C., but the times, phases, etc., will vary only a few minutes for any part of North Carolina, South Carolina, Georgia, Tennessee or Vir ginia.

To know where the sign is, find the day of the month; and against the day in the col umn marked Moon's Signs, you have the sign or place of the moon, and then find the sign it will give you the part of the body it is supposed to govern.

TWELVE SIGNS OF THE ZODIAC.

The Head and Face sign.   ♈ Aries the Ram......**Ar.**

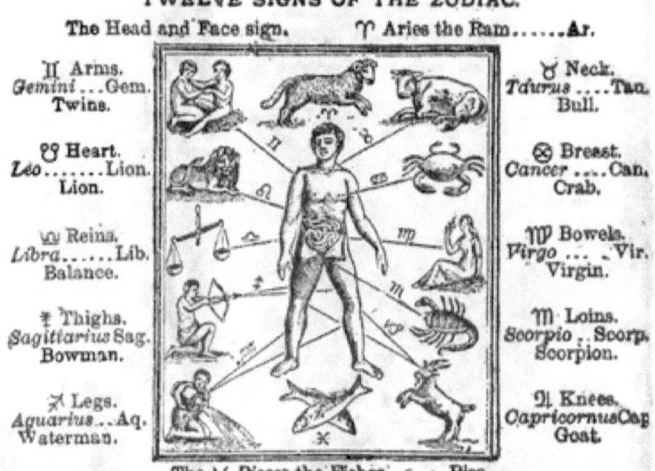

♊ Arms.
Gemini ... Gem.
Twins.

♉ Neck.
Taurus ....Tau.
Bull.

♌ Heart.
Leo ....Lion.
Lion.

⊗ Breast.
Cancer ....Can.
Crab.

♎ Reins.
Libra ......Lib.
Balance.

♍ Bowels.
Virgo ... Vir.
Virgin.

♐ Thighs.
Sagittarius Sag.
Bowman.

♏ Loins.
Scorpio . Scorp.
Scorpion.

♒ Legs.
Aquarius ...Aq.
Waterman.

♑ Knees.
Capricornus Cap
Goat.

The ♓ *Pisces* the Fishes., ...Pisc.

SIGNS.

SPRING SIGNS.	♈ Arises, or Ram. ♉ Taurus, or Bull ♊ Gemini, or Twins.	AUTUMN SINGS.	♎ Libra, or Balance. ♏ Scorpio, or Scorpion. ♐ Sagittarius, or Bowman
SUMMER SIGNS.	♋ Cancer, or Crab-fish. ♌ Leo, or Lion. ♍ Virgo, or Virgin.	WINTER SIGNS.	♑ Capricornus, or Goat. ♒ Aquarius, or Waterman ♓ Pisces, or Fishes.

SIGNS OF THE PLANETS.

☀ Sun.   ☽ Moon.   ♀ Venus.   ♂ Mars.
♃ Jupiter.   ♄ Saturn.   ☌ In Conjunction.   ☐ Quadrature.
☿ Mecury.   ♅ Uranus.   ♆ Neptune.   ☊ Ascending Node
⊕ Earth,   ☍ Opposition.   ☋ Descending Node.

MOON'S PHASES.

● Few Moon.   ☽ First Quarter.   ⊕ Full Moon.   ☾ Last Quarter

Branson's Almanac is a *household word.*—"*Truth.*"

3. Some men have faith in the laws of health, and hence by obeying those laws they secure physical health and happiness.—*Branson.*

CHRONOLOGICAL CYCLES AND ERAS.

Dominical Letter	E	Julian Period	6615
Epact	10	Jewish Era	5662
Folden Number	2	Era of Nabonassa	2649
Solar Cycle	6	Olimpiads	2677
Roman Indication	14	Mahommedan Era	1318

MOVABLE FEASTS OF THE CHURCH.

Epiphany	Jan. 6	Palm Sunday	March 23
Septnagessimer Sunday	Feb. 3	Easter Sunday	March 30
Sexagesima Sunday	Feb. 2	White Sunday	May 18
Quinquagesima Sunday	Feb. 9	Trinity Sunday	May 25
Ash Wednesday, or Lent	Feb. 20	First Sunday in Advent	Dec. 1
St. Patrick's Day	Mar. 17	Ascension Day	May 16
Good Friday	April 15	First Sunday in Lent Feb.	24

MORNING STARS.

Murcury will be Mosning Star about April 4, August 2, and November 20. Venus will be morning Star from April 30 till September 15. Jupiter will be morning Star till June 30.

EVENING STARS.

Murcury will be Evening Star about ....Feb. 16, and Oct. 12.
Venus will be Evening Star from...................................April 30
Jupiter will be Evening Star....................................From June 30

ECLIPSES.

In the year 1902 there will be five eclipses, three of the Sun, and two of the Moon.

I. A Partial Eclipse of the Sun, April 8th, 2h. 53m., P. M. visible at Washington.

II. Total Eclipse of the Moon, April 22—7h. P. M., invisible in the United States.

III. A Partial Eclipse of the Sun May 7, 10:12 p, m., invisible in North Carolina.

IV. A Partial Eclipse of the Moon, Oct. 17th, 6h 10m. A. M.—duration 5 hours and 33 minutes—Visible in North and South America.

V A partial Eclipse of the Sun, Oct. 31 7h. 28m. A. M. lasting 4 hours and 4 minutes. Invisible.

TIDES.

The time of tides can readily be found for the following places by adding the hours and minutes opposite the names to the time when the Moon is south on the day to when the tide is sought The time when the Moon is south is given in the calendar for every day. The next tide ban be found very nearly by adding 12 hours and 29 minutes to the time of the one previous.

The tides are given in local time—add 12 minutes for Eastern Standard

	H. M.		H. M.
Boston	11 12	New York	8 13
Sandy Hook	7 29	Old Point	8 17
Baltimore	6 33	Washington City	7 44
Richmond	4 32	Hatteras Inlet	7 04
Beaufort	7 26	Bald Head	7 26
Southport	7 19	Wilmington	9 06
Charlaston	7 26	Savannah	9 33

2. A man is whose mind his own country is not *first* is a man who himself is not *worthy* to be first in another country.—*Branson.*

THE FOUR SEASONS.

Spring commences..March 21, 8 A. M.
Summer commences....................................June 22, 4 A. M.
Autumn commences..............................September 23, 7 P. M.
Winter commences ....December 22, 1 P. M.

HERSCHELS WEATHER PROGNOSTICATOR.

For Foretelling the Weather Through all the Lunations of the year.

This table and the accompanying remarks are the result of many years actual observation, the whole besng constructed on a due consideration of the attractions of the Sun and Moon, in their several positions respecting the Earth, and, by simple inspection, it shows the observer what kind of whether will most probably follow the entrance of the Moon into any of its quarters, and that so near the truth as to be seldom or never found to fail.

If the new moon, first quarter, full moon, or last quarter, hapen—	IN SUMMER.	IN WINTER.
Between midnight and 2 in the morning............	Fair............	Hoar frost unless the wind is S. or S. W.
Between 2 and 4, morning	Cold, with frequent showers...........	Snow and stormy.
Between 4 and 6, morning..	Rain	Rain.
Between 6 and 8, morning..	Wind and rain......	Stormy.
Between 8 and 10, morning	Changeable.........	Cold rain if wind be W., snow if E.
Between 10 and 12 morning	Frequent showers....	Cold and high wind.
Between 12 o'clock at noon and 2 in afternoon.......	Very rainy.......... Changeable.........	Rain and Snow. Fair and mild.
Between 2 and 4, afternoon	Fair..................	Fair
Between 4 and 6, aftern'n	Fair if wind N. W., rainy if S or S W	Fair and frosty wind N. or N. E.; rain or snow if S or S. W.
Between 8 and 10, afternoon	Ditto...............	Ditto.
Between 10 and midnight..	Fair................	Fair and frosty.

OBSERVATIONS—1. The nearer the time for the Moon's change, first quarter, full and last quarter are to midnight, the fairer will be the weather during the next seven days.

2. The space for this calculation occupies from 10 at night until 2 next morning,

3. The nearer to midday or noon the phase of the Moon happens, the more foul or wet weather may be expected during the next seven days.

4. The space for this calculation occupies from 10 in the forenoon until 2 in the afternoon.   These observations refer principally to the Summer, though they affect Spring and Autum nearly in the same ratio.

5. The Moon's change, first quarter, full and last quarter happening during six of the afternoon hours, *i. e.*; from 4 to 10, may be followed by fair weather, but this is mostly dependent on the wind, as is noted in the table.

6. Though the weather, from a variety of irregular causes, is more uncertain in the later part of Autumn, the whole of Winter and beginning of Spring, yet, in the main, the above observations will apply to those periods also.

7. To prognosticate correctly, especially in those cases where the wind is concerned, the observer should be in sight of a good vane, where the four cardinal points of the heavens are correctly placed.

6. The Christian religion leads a man towards the cultivation of all his best capabilities.—*Branson.*

STATISTICS OF LIBRARIES IN NORTH CAROLINA, 1901.

Through the untiring efforts of our efficient State Librarian, we are enabled to give correctly the great progress that has been made in our State in the last few years towards placing within the reach of the great masses of our people, useful information that has theretofore been beyond the reach of the common class of our citizens, by establishing public Libraries, accessible to all who are in search of useful knowledge.

NAME OF LIBRARIAN.	Where Located.	When Established.	Number of Volumes.	Money Used Each Year.	Librarian.
State Library	Raleigh	1841	22,618	$ 800	Miles O. Sherrell.
Female College	Asheville		1 000		
—sheville Library	Ashrvile		3 000	750	Miss F. L. Weddell.
Bishop Atkinson Lib.	Asheville		2,400		Rev. A. H. Stubbs.
St. Mary's College	Belmont	2885	10,000		F. Bernard.
N. C. University	Chapel Hill	2790	36,000	2,000	R. H. Graves.
Biddle University (col.)	Charlotte		8,000		
Buckhorn Academy	Como		2,000		
Scotia Seminary	Concord	1870	1,000		
Davidson College Lib.	Davidson	1887	12,000		F. F. Rowe.
Public School Library	Durham	1884	2,400		C. W. Toms.
Trinity College Library	W. Durham	1887	13 000		Geo. B. Pegram.
Elon College Library	Elon	1890	1,285		W. P. Lorance.
Cross Creek, I. O. O. F.,	Fayetteville	1845	1,000		
Christian College Lib.	Franklinton	1882	1 000		N. D. McReynolds.
Female College	Greensboro	1895	6,000		Dred Peacock.
State Normal College	Greensboro		3,000		
Guilford College Lib.	Guilford Col	1837	4 000		Miss M. E. Mendenhall.
Shortia School	Highlands	1888	1 500		
Good Will Face Lib	Ledger	1888	6,000		C. H. Wing.
Pioneer Library	Lenoir	1875	1,500		J. F. W. Harper.
N. C. College	Mt Pleasant	1838	2,000		H. T. J. Ludwig.
Baptist Female Institute	Murfreesboro,		1,000		
Collegiate Institute	Newbern		1 000		
Catawba College	Newton		2,000		
Oak Ridge Institute	Oak Ridge	1852	2,700	200	J. F. Holt.
A. & M. College	Raeigh	1890	3,300	200	A. Q. Holladay.
D. & D. Kelly Library	Raleigh	1877	2,500		
St. Mary's School	Raeigh		3,000		
Shaw University	Rreigh	1865	1,500		
Supreme Court Library,	Raleigh		11 000		R. H. Bradley
Olivia Raney Library	Raleigh	1899	6,000		Miss Jennie Coffin.
Rutherford College Lib.	R. College	1853	600		W. E. Abernathy.
Female College	Salem	1892	4,000		J. H. Clewell.
Livingston College	Salisbury		3,000		
Wake Forest Col. Lib	Wake Forest	1833	15,500	485	W. L. Poteat.
Rab Library	Waynesville	1894	1,100	62	L. B. Lewis.
Wayne School	Waynesvil e	1896	3,000		T. C. Harbison.
Classical School	Wilmington		2,000		
Library Association	Wilmington	1855	5,250	249	T. C. Diggs.
City School Library	Winston	1856	3,200	230	J J Blair.
College Library	Lenoir	1890	400		J. D. Minick.
A. & M. College [col.	Greensboro	1894	2,600		J. H M Butler.
Hickory Library	Hickory	1863	1,000		N. McComb
Durham Library	Durham	1897	900		H. A Foushee
Morganton Library	Morganton	1878	1,000		Miss A L very!.
Kinston Public Library	Kinston				D. T H. Haughton.
Circulating Library	Charlotte				
S. A. L. Railroad	Raleigh				

49 in Dibraries in all.   Over 216,000 volumes of good books.

2. To give advice unsolicited is delightful; it so magnifies our self-esteem To receive advice unsolicited is humiliating, it so miniges our own self-esteem.—*Branson*

1st Month. JANUARY 1902. 31 Days.

Moon's Phases.

	D. H. M.		D. H. M.
New Moon,	9 4 6 p. m.	Full Moon,	23 6 58 p.m.
First Quarter,	15 13 50 a. m.	Last Quarter,	31 8 0 a.m.

Day of Month.	Day of Week.	Sun Rises.	Sun Sets.	Sun Slow.	Sun's decline South.	ASPECTS OF PLANETS AND OTHER MISCELLANEOUS MATTER.	Moon's place.	Moon rises or sets.	Moon south.
1	We	7 10	4 59	4	23 03	*New Year's Day.*	[illegible]	sets	morn
2	Thu	7 10	5 00	4	22 58	☌ ☿ ☉ Superior; ♀ in ☊	[illegible]	9 26	2 00
3	Fri	7 10	5 01	4	22 52	Battle of Friceton 1777	[illegible]	9 55	2 49
4	Sat	7 10	5 02	4	22 46	Com. Vanderbilt d. 1877.	[illegible]	11 05	3 39
(1) First Sunday in New Year.						Day's length 9 hours 53 minutes.			
5	E	7 10	5 3	5	22 40		[illegible]	11 56	4 30
6	Mo	7 9	5 4	6	22 33	☌ ☿ ♄ *Epiphany.*	[illegible]	rises	5 23
7	Tue	7 9	5 4	6	22 26	☌ ♅ ☾—Liberia Colonized 1822	[illegible]	1 42	6 16
8	We	7 9	5 6	7	22 26	Battle New Orleans 1815.	[illegible]	2 35	7 09
9	Thu	7 9	5 6	7	22 10	☌ ♄ ☉ Saperior ☌ ♄ ☾	[illegible]	3 01	7 35
10	Fri	7 9	5 8	7	22 01	☿ Gt Hel Lat S:	[illegible]	3 02	8 02
11	Sat	7 9	5 8	8	22 52	☌ ♂ ☾; Alabama Seceded 1861	[illegible]	5 01	8 55
(2) First Sunday after Epiphany.						Day's length 10 hours 1 minute.			
12	E	7 9	5 9	8	21 43	Gaston County formed 1846.	[illegible]	5 13	9 47
13	Mo	7 9	5 10	9	21 33	☌ ☿ ☾; ☿ Gr Hel Lat S.	[illegible]	6 04	10 38
14	Tue	7 9	5 11	9	21 23	*Aycock Inaug Gov N. C. 1901*	[illegible]	sets	11 30
15	We	7 8	5 12	10	21 12	☌ ♃ ☉ Sup. A Jackson b. 1767	[illegible]	7 49	eve
16	Thu	7 8	5 13	10	21 01	T H Selby died 1880.	[illegible]	8 44	1 18
17	Fri	7 8	5 14	10	20 50	W R. Tucker died 1889	[illegible]	9 41	2 15
18	Sat	7 8	5 15	10	20 38	Daniel Webster born 1782	[illegible]	10 41	3 15
(3) Second Sundɑy after Epiphany.						Day's length 10 hours 8 minutes.			
19	E	7 8	5 16	11	20 26	Q Victoria ill at Osborne house	[illegible]	11 43	4 17
20	Mo	7 7	5 16	11	20 13	Howard d 1890.	[illegible]	00 48	5 22
21	Tue	7 7	5 17	11	20 00	☌ ♆ ☾ Stonewall Jackson b1824	[illegible]	01 52	6 26
22	We	7 7	5 18	12	19 46	☌ ☿ ♂ *FM.Simons Sinator1901*	[illegible]	2 55	7 39
23	Thu	7 6	5 19	12	19 33	William Gaston died 1844	[illegible]	reses	8 70
24	Fri	7 6	5 20	12	19 19	Salem Academy Estab 1804	[illegible]	4 53	9 21
25	Sat	7 4	5 20	12	19 04	Dr G A Foote died 1899.	[illegible]	5 47	10 22
(4) Third Sunday after Epiphany.						Day's length 10 hours 18 minutes.			
26	E	7 3	5 21	13	18 49	Olivia Raney Lib open 1901	[illegible]		11 13
27	Mo	7 2	5 22	13	18 34	Audebon died 1851	[illegible]		12 02
28	Tue	7 2	5 23	13	18 18	Judge Sewell died 1835	[illegible]		12 51
29	We	7 2	5 24	13	18 03	John Rex died 1835	[illegible]		morn
30	Thu	7 2	5 25	13	17 46	Charles 1st beheaded 1647	[illegible]		2 27
31	Fri	7 2	5 26	14	17 30	Stanley, Henry died 1812.	[illegible]		

WEATHER CONSECTURE—January—1, 2, 3, 4, 5, 6, 7, 8 Cold and some high wind; 9, 10, 11, 12, 13, 14, 15, 16 Hoar frost unless the wind is from South or Southwest; 17, 18, 19 20, 21, 22, 23, 24, 25, 26, 27, 28, Stormy; 29, 30, 31 Cold and stormy.

FAM AND GARDEN WORK FOR JANUARY.—Plant peas, beans, beets, onions, Irish potatoes, horse radish; sow turnips, spinach, lettuce, raddish, parsley, carrots, salsify. Plant early peas; artichokes must now be dressed, also asparagus beds, this is the proper time to sow early spring tomatoes, etc.

NORTH CAROLINA COLLEGES, AND OTHER GRADUATING SCHOOLS.
(Names, Character and Location.)

Asheville Female College (Methodist)........................Asheville
Baptist Female University (Baptist)........................Raleigh
Cata ba College........................Newton
Chowan Female Institute (Baptist).........................Mnrfreesboro
Claremont Female College (Reformed Church of U. S.).........Hickory
Concordia College (Lutheran)........................Conover
Davenport Female College (Metho list)........................Lenoir
Davidson College (Presbyterian)........................Davidson
Elon College (Christian)........................Elon College
Greensboro Female College (Methodist)........................Greensboro
Guilford College (Friends)........................Guilford College
Hayesville College (Independent)........................Hayesville
Judson College (Methodist)........................Hendersonville
Kinston College (Independent)........................Kinston
Louisburg Female College (Methodist........................Louisburg
Littleton Female College (Methodist)........................Littleton
Mt. Amœna Seminary (Lutheran)........................Mt. Pleasant
Mt. St. Joseph Academy (Catholic)........................Asheville
North Carolina College (Lutheran)........................Mt Pleasant
North Car lina Agricultural and Mechanical College (State)....Raleigh
Oxford Female Seminary (Baptist)........................Oxford
Oak Ridge Institute (Independent)........................Oak Ridge
Peace Institute (Independent)........................Raleigh
Rutherford College, Burke Co., (Methodist).........Rutherford College
St. Mary's College (Catholic)........................Belmont
Shelby Female College (Independent)........................Shelby
St. Mary's School (Episcopal)........................Raleigh
Salem Academy (Moravian)........................Salem
St. Pauls Seminary (Lutheran Theological)........................Hickory
State Normal and Industrial College (State)........................Greensboro
Trinity Coll ge (Methodist)........................Durham
University of North Carolina (State)........................Chapel Hill
Weaverville College (Methodist)........................Weaverville
Wake Forest College (Baptist)........................Wake Forest
Elizabeth College (Lutheran)........................Charlotte
Presbyteran College (Presbyterian)........................Charlotte
Whitsett Institute (Independent)........................Whitsett

COLORED SCHOOLS—Graduating.

Agricultural and Mechanical College (State)........................Greensboro
Bennett Seminary (Methodist)........................Greensboro
Biddle University (Presbyterian)........................Charlotte
Building and Trade's College (Independent)........................Southern Pines
Franklinton Christian College (Christian)........................Franklinton
Kittrell College (A. M. E. C.)........................Kittrell
Normal School (State)........................Elizabeth City
Normal School (State)........................Goldsboro
Normal School (State)........................Salisbury
Normal School (State)........................Plymouth
Normal School (State)........................Fayetteville
Normal School (State)........................Franklinton
St. Augustine Normal College (Episcopal)........................Raleigh
Shaw University (Baptist)........................Raleigh
Scotia Female Seminary (Presbyterian)........................Concord
Slater Industrial Academy and Normal School (State).........Winston.

2nd Month. FEBRUARY 1902. 28 Days.

Moon's Phases.

	D. H. M		D. H. M.
New Moon,	8 8 13 a. m.	Full Moon,	22 7 25 a.m.
Last Quarter 15 4 48 a. m.			

For High Tides at Beaufort. See third page of the Almanac.

Day of Month.	Day of Week.	Sun rises.	Sun sets.	Sun slow.	Sun's decline south.	ASPECTS OF PLANETS AND OTHER MISCELLANEOUS MATTER.	Moon's place.	Moon rises or sets.	Moon south.
1	Sat	7 1	5 27	14	17 13	☌ ☿ ♀: ☿ in ♌	♎	rises	morn
(5)					Sexagesima Sunday.		Day's length 10 hours 27 minutes.		
2	E	7 1	5 28	14	16 56	Peace Conference 1865	♏	06 28	5 02
3	Mo	7 0	5 28	14	16 39	☿ Gr. Elong. E; ♂ in Perih'n	♏	01 01	5 35
4	Tue	6 59	5 29	14	16 29	Rev War ended 1783	♐	2 14	6 48
5	We	6 58	5 30	14	16 03	♀ in Peri; ☌ ♀ ♂ Birthday 1832	♐	3 07	7 41
6	Thu	6 58	5 31	14	15 45	☿ in Peri; ☌ ♄ ☾; ☌ ♃ ☾	♐	4 01	5 35
7	Fri	6 57	5 32	14	15 26	Suez Canal Com'ced 1867	♑	4 27	9 01
8	Sat	6 56	5 33	14	15 07	Bat Roanoke Island 1862	♑	4 54	9 28
(6)					Quinqua-esima Sunday.		Day's length 10 hours 39 minutes.		
9	E	6 55	5 34	14	14 48	☌ ♀ ☾; ☿ Sta ☌ ☿ ☾	♒	5 46	10 20
10	Mo	6 54	5 35	14	14 28	Treaty of Paris 1763	♒	6 39	11 13
11	Tue	6 53	5 36	14	14 10	Thos A Edison b 1847.	♒	sets	eve
12	We	6 52	5 37	14	13 50	☌ ☿ ♂; Dr J Manning d 1899	♒	9 24	1 58
13	Thu	6 51	5 38	14	13 30	Governor Walker d 1704	♓	10 23	2 57
14	Fri	6 50	5 39	14	13 10	St. Valentine's Day	♓	10 33	2 57
15	Sat	6 50	5 40	14	12 49	Steamship Main blo'n up 1898	♓	11 23	3 57
(7)					Quadrigessima Sunday.		Day's length 10 hours 52 minutes.		
16	E	6 49	5 41	14	12 29	☿ Gr Hel Lat N.	♓	12 25	4 59
17	Mo	6 48	5 42	14	12 07	☌ ♃ ☾; ☿ ☉ Inferior	♈	rises	7 04
18	Tue	6 47	5 43	14	11 47	Bryant died 1878	♈	2 30	8 03
19	We	6 46	5 44	14	11 26	H Vaughan died 1886	♉	3 29	8 03
20	Thu	6 45	5 45	14	11 04	David Garrick b 1716	♉	4 27	9 01
21	Fri	6 43	5 46	14	10 42	Spinza died 1674	♊	5 22	9 56
22	Sat	6 42	5 47	14	10 21	Washington Birthday 1732	♊	6 15	10 49
(8)					Fifth Sunday before Easter.		Day's length 11 hours 7 minutes.		
23	E	6 41	5 48	13	9 59	Bat Buena Vesta 1847	♊	sets	11 40
24	Mo	6 40	5 48	13	9 37	Monteray Surrendered 1846	♋	7 26	morn
25	Tue	6 39	5 49	13	9 15	Battle of Montreal 1775	♋	8 45	1 19
26	We	6 38	5 50	13	8 53	♀ Gr Hel Lat N.	♋	9 34	2 08
27	Thu	6 37	5 51	13	8 30	Longfellow born 1807	♌	10 24	2 58
28	Fri	6 36	5 52	13	8 08	Dr Wingate died 1879	♌	11 16	3 50

WEATHER CONJECTURES—February—1, 2, 3, 4, 5, 6 Cold and windy; 7, 8, 9, 10, 11, 12, 13 Bracing and good; 14, 15, 16, 17, 18, 19, 20 Hoar frost, unless the wind is South or Southwest; 21, 22, 23, 24! 25, 26, 27, 28 Stormy.

FARM AND GARDEN WORK FOR FEBRUARY.—Continue to sow peas, and such vegetable as were omitted in January. Plant pole beans, first crop (in the low country); full crop Irish potatoes, beets and carrots, dress artichokes and asparagus. Tomatoes, peppers and cucumbers sow in hot beds ; put out mangoes.

This is considered the opening month of the planter's year. Continue preparing as in January. Sow oats for a full crop in the low country ; plant Irish potatoes ; make up sprout beds for sweet potatoes. Plant root crop of sweet potatoes.

North Carolina College of Agriculture and Mechanic Arts.

Located in Raleigh near the Fair Grounds, on Hillsboro road. Thorough practical and liberal education offered in all branches of Engineering and the Mechanic Arts, in Cotton manufacturing, in Chemistry, and in Agriculture. Tuition $20 a year, board $8 a month. 325 students, 30 teachers, 120 scholarship in Agriculture, 120 scholarship in Mechanical Arts. Full courses of study, four years, furnishing complete education and conferring degrees ; short courses (mainly practical work) two years, special courses, in carpentry, in machine shop, in engine and boiler tending, and in machine drawing and dressing, (3 to 9 monhs)

BOARD OF TRUSTEES

S. L. PATTERSON, Commissioner, *ex officio* Chairman.

First District	J. B. COFFIELD.
Second District	E. L. DAUGHTRIDGE.
Third District	WM. DUNN.
Fourth District	C. N. ALLEN.
Fifth District	J. S. CUNINGHAM.
Sixth District	A. T. McCALLUM.
Seventh District	J. P. McRAE.
Eighth District	L. G. WAUGH.
Ninth District	W. A. GRAHAM.
Tenth District	A. CANNON.

HOWARD BROWNING

J. R. JOYCE.

G. E FLOW

J. C. RAY.

FACULTY

Geo T. Winston, A. M, and LL. D., President and Professor of Political Economy ; W. A. Withers, A. M., Professor of Pure and Agricultural Chemistry ; D. A. Hill, A. M., Professor of English ; W. C. Riddick, A. M. and C. E., Professor of Civil Engineering and Mathematics ; F. A. Wishe, M. E. and Ph. D., Professor of Electrical Engineering and Physics ; C. W. Burkett, Ph. D., Professor of Agriculture ; T. M. Dick. Assistant Engineer U. S. N. Retired, Professor of Mechanical Engineering ; Tait Butler, D V. M., Professor of Veterinary Science and Animal Husbandry ; Henry M Wilson, A. B., Professor of Textile Industry ; F, E Philps, Captain U. S. A. retired, Professor of Military Science and Tactics ; F. L. Stevens, Ph D., Instructor in Biology ; R. E. L. Yates, A. M., Assistant Professor of Mathematics ; G. S. rraps, B. S. and Ph D., Assistant Professor of Chemistry ; C. B. Park, Superintendent of Shops ; T. A. Chittenden, B. S., Instructor in Drawing ; V. W. Bragg, Instructor in Wood Working ; M E. Carter ; Instructor in Wood Working ; Oliver Carter, Instructor in Forge Shop ; E. B. Owen, B. A , Instructor in English ; Alexander Rhodes, Instructor in Horticulture ; William A.

Peele's Practical Business College, Raleigh, N. C., a Good School.

10 BRANSON'S NORTH CAROLINA ALMANAC.

3d Month. MARCH, 1902. 31 Days.

Moon's Phases.

	D. H. M.		D. H. M.
◔ Last Quarter,	2 5 31 a. m.	◑ First Quarter, 16	5 4 p. m.
● New Moon,	9 9 42 p. m.	○ Full Moon,	23 10 13 p. m.

Day of Month.	Day of Week.	Sun Rises.	Sun Sets.	Sun Slow.	Sun's decline south.	ASPECTS OF PLANETS AND OTHER MISCELLANEOUS MATTER.	Moon's place.	Moon rises or sets.	Moon south.
1	~at	6 34	5 53	12	7 45		♒	12 06	4 40
(9)						Fourth Sunday before Easter. Day's length 11 hours 22 minutes.			
2	E	6 32	5 54	12	7 22	☿ stationary; ♂ ☾	♒	00 58	5 52
3	Mo	6 30	5 56	12	6 59	☾ ☾W. C. Stronach d '01	♒	1 51	6 25
4	Tue	6 28	5 57	12	6 36	*Wm. McKinley* inaug. 1901	♓	2 44	7 18
5	We	6 26	5 58	12	6 13	♂ ♄ ☾ ☿ sta. Addison b 1750	♓	3 37	8 11
6	Thu	6 24	5 59	11	5 50	♀ sta. ♂ ♃ ☾ Bat Pearidge 1862	♈	4 30	9 04
7	Fri	6 23	6 00	11	5 27	♂ ♀ ☾ Am Bib Soc founded 1804	♈	5 23	9 57
8	Sat	6 22	6 01	11	5 03	♂ ♀ ☾ William III died 1703	♉	6 27	10 51
(10)						Third Sunday before Easter. Day's length 11 hours 22 minutes			
9	E	6 20	2 11		4 40	Battle of Vera Cruz 1847	♉	5 33	9 57
10	Mo	6 18	3 10		4 16	♂ ♂ ☾; Ψ sta.	♊	7 11	11 45
11	Tue	6 17	4 10		4 53	♀ in ♉ Wm. Barringer d 1882	♋	rises	even
12	We	6 16	5 10		3 29	☐ ☾ ● Seymour died 1886	♋	9 04	1 38
13	Thu	6 14	6 9		3 06	Pocahontas died 1660	♌	10 04	2 38
14	Fri	6 13	6 9		2 42	N. C. Leg. ad. 1901 to April 3	♌	11 05	3 39
15	Sat	6 12	7 9		2 18	Battle Guilford C. H. 1781	♌	12 07	4 41
(11)						Second Sunday before Easter. Day's length 11 hours 57 minutes.			
16	E	6 11	6 08	7	1 55	♂ ♀ ☾; ♀ Gr Elong W	♍	1 09	5 43
17	Mo	6 09	6 09	8	1 31	*St Patrick's Day*	♎	2 11	6 45
18	Tue	6 08	6 10	8	1 07		♎	3 10	7 44
19	We	6 06	6 12	8	0 44		♏	4 07	8 41
20	Thu	6 04	6 13	7	0 20	☐Ψ☾; ☿ greatest brilliancy	♏	5 01	9 35
21	Fri	6 03	6 13	7	uorth	⊙ enters *Aries—Spring com*	♐	5 54	10 28
22	Sat	6 02	6 13	7	0 00		♐	6 39	11 19
(12)						Sunday before Easter. Day's length 12 hours 14 minutes.			
23	E	5 00	6 14	7	0 51	Judge Ruffin b 1786	♐	7 35	morn
24	Mo	5 59	6 15	6	1 15	Seat of gov. Raleigh 1788	♑	8 24	12 58
25	Tue	5 58	6 16	6	1 38	Dec of war with Spain 1898	♑	9 24	1 48
26	We	5 57	6 17	6	2 02	Thames tunnel opened 1843	♒	10 04	2 38
27	Thu	5 55	6 18	5	2 26	☿ sta. Earthquake in Cal. '43	♒	10 54	3 28
28	Fri	5 53	6 19	5	2 49	*Good Friday*	♒	11 45	4 19
29	Sat	5 51	6 20	5	3 12	♂ ♂ ⊙ ~up	♓	12 37	5 11
(13)						Easter Sunday. Day's length 12 hours 30 minutes.			
30	E	5 50	6 20	4	3 36	♂ ☾ ☾ Alaska pur by U S '67	♓	1 29	6 03
31	Mo	5 48	6 21	4	3 59	S M Parish d 1895	♓	2 21	6 55

WEATHER CONJECTURES—March—1, 2, 3, 4, 5, 6, 7, 8, rain, 9, 10, 11, 12, 13, 14, 15, rain or snow if wind south or southwest; 16, 17, 18, 19, 20, 21, 22. cold high winds; 23 24. 25, 26, 27, 28, 29, 30, cold and brisk wind.

For High Tides at Beaufort, see third page of the Almanac.

FARM AND GARDEN WORK FOR MARCH.—Plant bush squash. pumkins, wat-r and mushmelons, okra. Guinea squash or egg-pl-nt, sugar beets, carrots, beans teas. radishes. lettuce, corn, celery. [first crop] tanyah and mangoes in the low country and elsewhere as soon as danger from frost is over.

This is the first planting month for cotton, corn and rice. Plant your high lands first ; leave the low lands for April. Plant rice about the 20th of the month.

Syme, B. S., Instructor in Chemistry ; Chas. L. Fish, B. S., Instructor in Civil Engineering and Mathematics ; W. S. Sturgill, B. E., Instructor in Mathematics ; Thomas Nelson, Instructor in Carding and Spinning ; A. F. Bowen, Bursar ; E. B. Owen, Librarian ; Mrs. D. Lewis, Matron , Mrs. L. V. Darby, Stenographer.

N. C. AGRICULTURAL EXPERIMENT STATION.

The station is a department of the Agricultural and Mechanical College and is managed by the same board of Trustees. The station offices are in the main building of the College, and in the building of the Department of Agriculture. The experiment work is carried on in the College laboratories and partly on the Experiment Station Farms, and partly on the lands of the College.

EXPERIMENT STATION STAFF:

B. W. KILGORE, M. S.,	State Chemist.
W. A. WITHERS, A. M.,	Chemist
C. W. BURKETT, Ph. D.	Agriculturist.
W. F. MASSEY, C. E.	Horticulturist.
TAIT BUTLER, D. V. M.	Veterinariau.
G. S. FRAPS, Ph. D.	Assistant Chemist
ALEX. RHODES	Assistant Horticulturist.
FRANKLIN SHERMAN	Entomoligist.
B. S. SKINNER	Farm Superintendent.
A. F. BOWEN	Secretary and Bursar
MRS. L. V. DARBY	Stenographer.

The University of North Carolina.

Located in Chapel Hill, Orange County, twenty-eight miles northwest of Raleigh.

Chartered in 1788, founded in 1795, opened 1793. It now has 527 students and 25 instructors. The equipment includes twelve large buildings, six scientific laboratories, library of 32,000 volumes, campus of sixty acres with ample athletic grounds, gymnasium, etc. Perfect sanitation, baths, closets, etc. Tuition $60 a year, total expenses $200 to $300. Scholarships and loans for the needy Law school 80, medical school 44, pharmacy 36. A summer school for teachers is conducted each July. It enrolled 256 teachers in 1899. The faculty includes 35 professors and instructors. Many students support themselves by labor, the total amount earned being about $5,000. The University is non-political and non-sectarian.

FACULTY.—Francis Preston Venable, Ph. D., President of the University ; Kemp Plummer Battle, LL. D., Alumni Professor of History; Charles Baskerville, Ph. D.; Smith, Professor of General and Analytical Chemistry; Joseph Austin Holmes, S. B., State Geologist, Lecturer on Geology of Carolina ; Joshua Walker Gore, C. E., Professor of Physics; James Mac-Rae, LL. D., Professor of Law; Thomas Hume. D. D., LL. D., Professor of English Language and Literature ; Eben Alexander, Ph. D., Professor of Greek ; William Cain. C. E., Professor of Mathematics ; Richard Henry Whitehead, M. D., Professor of Anatomy and Pathology ; Henry Horace Williams, A. M., B. D. Professor of Philosophy ; Henry Van Peters Wilson, Ph. D., Professor of Biology ; H. F. Linscott, Ph. D., Professor of Latin Language and Literature ; Collier Cobb, A. M., Professor of Geology ; A. S. Wheeler ; Ph. D., Assistant Professor of Chemistry ; Charles Staples Mangum, M. D., Professor of Physiology and

4 Month. APRIL, 1902. 30 Days.

Moon's Phases.

	D. H. M.		D. H. M.
☾ Last Quarter	1 1 16 a. m.	New Moon,	8 8 42 a. m.
Full Moon,	12 1 41 p. m.	☽ First Quarter,	15 0 11 a. m.

Day of Month	Day of Week.	Sun rises.	Sun sets.	Sun slow.	Sun's decline North.	ASPECTS OF PLANETS AND OTHER MISCELLANEOUS MATTER.	Moon's place.	Moon rises or se's.	Moon south.
1	Tue	5 46	6 22	4	4 22	☌ ♅ ☾-*April Fools Day.*	[illegible]	rises	morn
2	We	5 44	6 23	3	4 45	☌ ♄ ☾ Richm'd Evacu '65	[illegible]	4 05	8 39
3	Thu	5 42	6 24	·	5 08	☌ ♃ ☾ Peter Cooper d 1888	[illegible]	4 58	9 32
4	Fri	5 41	6 25	3	5 31	Gen Harrison d 1871	[illegible]	5 50	10 24
5	Sat	5 40	6 26	2	5 54	☌ ♀ ☾ Jefferson born 1743	[illegible]	6 44	11 18
(14)	First Sunday after Easter.					Day's length 12 hours 47 minutes'			
6	E	5 39	6 26	2	6 17	Col McRay d 1879	[illegible]	7 39	eve5
7	Mo	5 38	6 27	2	6 40	☌ ☿ ☾ *Eclipse of Sun In. here*	[illegible]	8 01	0 31
8	Tue	5 36	6 28	2	7 02	First Set. in N. C 1663	[illegible]	8 37	1 11
9	We	5 34	6 29	1	7 25	*H. Blount Lec. in Ral 1901*	[illegible]	9 37	2 14
10	Thu	5 33	6 30	1	7 47	U S Bank 1816	[illegible]	10 40	3 18
11	Fri	5 32	6 31	1	8 09	☿ Greatest Hel Lat S	[illegible]	11 44	4 1
12	Sat	5 31	6 ·2	1	8 31	Fort Sumpton fell 1862	[illegible]	00 48	5 22
(15)	Second Sunday after Easter.					Day's length 13 hours 3 minutes.			
13	E	5 30	6 33	0	8 53	☌ ♆ ☾ Ral taken Sherman, '65	[illegible]	1 51	6 25
14	Mo	5 28	6 33	fast	9 13	Lincoln assassinated 1865	[illegible]	2 52	7 26
15	Tue	5 27	6 34		9 36	Andrew Johnson Pres 1865.	[illegible]	3 50	8 24
16	We	5 26	6 34	0	9 58	French evacuated Mexico 1867	[illegible]	4 45	9 19
17	Thu	5 24	6 35	1	10 19	Ben Franklin d 1790	[illegible]	5 37	10 11
18	Fri	5 23	6 36	1	10 40	□ ♄ ☉: Luther at Worms 1521	[illegible]	6 28	11 02
19	Sat	5 22	6 37	1	11 01	Dr. J. W. Alston d 1891	[illegible]	7 17	11 51
(16)	Third Sunday after Easter.					Day's length 13 hours 17 minutes			
20	E	5 2	6 38	1	11 22	Ultimation to Spain 1898	[illegible]	8 06	even
21	Mo	5 20	6 39	1	11 42	Squdron sent to Cuba 1898	[illegible]	8 56	1 30
22	Tue	5 18	6 40	2	12 03	*Moon Eclipse Inv at Wash'ton*	[illegible]	9 45	2 19
23	We	5 17	6 41	2	12 23	Call for 25,000 volunteers	[illegible]	10 35	3 09
24	Thu	5 15	6 41	2	12 43	♀ in ☋. Dr McKee d 1875	[illegible]	11 26	4 00
25	Fri	5 14	6 42	2	13 03	♀ Gr. Elongation West	[illegible]	11 58	4 52
26	Sat	5 13	6 43	2	13 22	☌ ♅ ☾ Gen Jo Johnson sur Dur	[illegible]	1 10	5 44
(17)	Fouth Sunday after Easter					Day's length 13 hours 31 minutes'			
27	E	5 12	6 43	3	13 41	Mantanzas bumbarded 1898	[illegible]	2 01	6 35
28	Mo	5 11	6 44	3	14 00	☌ ☿ ☉ Superior.	[illegible]	2 53	7 27
29	Tue	5 10	6 45	3	14 19	☌ ♄ ☾ Crimeam War e 1856	[illegible]	3 44	8 18
30	We	5 09	6 46	3	14 38	☿ in ☊ Washington in 1789	[illegible]	4 35	9 09

For High Tides at Beaufort, see third page of the Almanac.

WEATAER CONJECTURES—April—1, 2, 3 4. 5. 6, look for snow and storm; 7. 8. 9. 10, 11, 12, changeable; 13. 14. 15. 16. 17, 18, 19. 20. 21. fair, unless the wind is south or southwest; 22, 23. 24. 25, 26, 27, 28, 29, expect much rain.

FARM AND GARDEN WORK FOR APRIL.—Whatever has been omitted in March, do not neglect any longer. Sow green glazed cabbage, pickling cabbage, full crop of cauliflower and broccoli, okra, okra, tomatoes; peppers, beets, Carrots; leeks, melons, cucumbers, celery.

Full crops of corn, cotton and rice should be put in during this month. Plant your lowland corn. Commence early to hoe your young cotton, and thin out to stand. Plant pumkins for a field crop.

Materia Medica ; Edward Vernon Howell, A. B., Ph. G., Professor of Pharmacy ; Thomas J. Wilson, Jr., Ph. D., Associate Professor of Classical Philology ; M. C. Noble, Professor of Pedagogy ; Thomas Ruffin Ph. B., Associate Professor of Law ; J. H. Manning, M. D., Professor of Physiology ; C. L. Roper, A. M., Associate Professor of Economics ; J. D. Brewer, Ph. D , Associate Professor of Romance Languages.

INSTRUCTORS.—Archibald Henderson, Ph. D., Instructor in Mathematics ; Edward K. Graham, A. B., Instructor in English ; E. V. D. Steinen, Director of Gymnasium ; J. E. Mills, Ph. D., Physical Chemistry ; C. A. Shore, B. S. Biology ; J. E. Latta, A. M. Physics ; W. S. Bernard, A. B. Greek ; G. M. McKie, Expression.

ASSISTANTS IN LABORATORIES.—Palmer Cobb, Modern Languages , B. F. Page, Pharmacy ; R. N. Duffy and M. H. Stacy, Mathematics ; R. G. Lassiter and R. A. Lichtenthacler, Geology ; R. O. E. Davis, R. S. Drane and H. H. Bennett, Chemistry ; D. S. Thompson, Biology ; J. R. Hall, English ; M. D. MacNider, Anatomy.

OFFICERS.—Walter D. Toy, M. A., Secretary of the Faculty ; Eben Alexander, Ph. D., LL. D., Supervisor of the Library, L R. Wilson, Librarian ; Eugene Lewis Harris, Ph. B. Registrar , Willie Thomas Patterson, Bursar

BE CONTENT.

By MRS. HATTIE DAVIS COOLEY, Nashville, N. C.

(Written for the *Dispatch*.)

If we always had the sunshine,
 And we never had the rain;
If life held naught but pleasure,
 And we never knew a pain;
If our hearts were always happy,
 Ever joyous, ever bright;
If we always had the daytime,
 And we never had the night;
Why, our eyes would soon get weary,
 And our limbs would tired grow,
And the sunshine look as dreary
 As the winter, frost, and snow.

Why, it is the brightest sunbeams
 That the deepest shadows cast;
And the greatest of all trials
 Are as trifles when they're past.
It is pain that makes us helpless,
 Makes us turn to God above;
'Tis not joy, but grief and anguish,
 Binds our hearts in perfect love.
Let us, then, always remember
 That the storms of life are few,
That the loveliest, sweetest flowers
 Are the flowers wet with dew.

5th Month. MAY, 1902. 31 Days.

Moon's Phases.

	D. H. M.		D. H. M.
New Moon,	7 8 37 p. m.	Full Moon,	22 5 28 a. m.
☽ First Quarter,	14 8 31 a. m.	☾ Last Quarter,	30 6 52 a. m.

For High Tides at Beaufort, see third page of the Almanac.

Day of Month	Day of Week.	Sun Rises.	Sun Sets.	Sun Fast	Sun's decline north.	ASPECTS OF PLANETS AND OTHER MISCELLANEOUS MATTER.	Moon's place.	Moon rises or sets.	Moon south.
1	Thu	5 07	6 47	3	14 56	☌♃☾ Dewey sunk Span F '98	♒	5 26	10 00
2	Fri	5 06	6 48	3	15 14	S H Young died 1882	♒	6 18	10 52
3	Sat	5 05	6 49	3	15 32	Jacksonville dest'd by fire 1901	♓	7 12	11 46
(18)	Rogation Sunday.					Day's length 13 hours 45 minutes.			
4	E	5 04	6 49	3	15 50	☌♀☾ Dr Wm G. Hill d 1877	♓	8 07	0 41
5	Mo	5 03	6 50	4	16 07	☿ in Peri. Bat Williamsb'g '62	♓	9 06	1 40
6	Tue	5 03	6 50	4	16 24	Battle of Wilderness 1864	♉	10 08	2 42
7	We	5 02	6 51	4	16 41	☌♂☾; □♃☉; ☉ eclip., inv	♉	10 38	3 12
8	Thu	5 01	6 52	4	16 58	♄ stationary; ☌☿☾ Ascension	♉	11 14	3 47
9	Fri	5 00	6 53	4	17 14	Battle Spottsylvania C H 1863	♉	sets	1 53
10	Sat	4 59	6 54	4	17 30	☌♆☾ *Confederate Mem Day*	♊	1 25	5 59
(19)	Sixth Sunday after Easter.					Day's length 13 hours 56 minutes.			
11	E	4 58	6 54	4	17 46	*Chang and Eng born* 1811	♊	2 29	7 03
12	Mo	4 57	6 55	4	18 01	Wor. Bagley k at Cardenas 1898	♋	3 30	8 04
13	Tue	4 56	6 56	4	18 16	Last battel of Civil War 1865	♋	4 27	9 01
14	We	4 55	6 57	4	18 31	Battle of Risaca, Ga., 1864	♌	5 21	9 55
15	Thu	4 54	6 58	4	18 46	☿ Gr. Hel. Lat. N.	♌	6 13	10 47
16	Fri	4 53	6 59	4	19 00	First steamer crossed ocean 1819	♌	7 02	11 36
17	Sat	4 52	7 00	4	19 14	John Penn born 1741	♍	rises	morn
(20)	Whit Sunday--Pentecost.					Day's length 12 hours 9 minutes.			
18	E	4 52	7 01	4	19 27	Matamoras fell 1846	♍	8 40	1 14
19	Mo	4 52	7 01	4	19 40	Vicksburg defended 1863	♍	9 29	2 03
20	Tue	4 51	7 02	4	19 63	*Mecklenburg Dec. of Ind. 1775*	♎	10 18	2 52
21	We	4 50	7 03	4	20 06	N Carolina seceded 1861	♎	11 09	3 43
22	Thu	4 49	7 03	3	20 18	David Livington d 1886	♏	12 00	4 34
23	Fri	4 48	7 04	3	20 30	☌♅☾ Col Buck Tucker d 1882	♏	00 52	5 26
24	Sat	4 48	7 05	3	20 41	♄ in ☋ Leo H Heartt d 1889	♐	1 44	6 18
(21)	Trinity Sunday.					Day's length 14 hours 17 minutes.			
25	E	4 48	7 05	3	20 52	Emerson born 1803	♐	2 45	7 09
26	Mo	4 47	7 06	3	21 03	John Calvin died 1664	♐	3 26	8 00
27	Tue	4 47	7 07	3	21 13	☌♄☾ Dr Jas Stewart d 1892	♑	4 17	8 51
28	We	4 46	7 08	3	21 23	☿ Gr Elong E; ♀ in Aphilion	♒	4 27	9 41
29	Thu	4 46	7 09	3	21 33	☌☿♆ Rhode Island ad 1790	♒	5 57	10 31
30	Fri	4 45	7 10	3	21 42	☾ *Federal Decoration Day*	♓	sets	eve
31	Sat	4 45	7 11	2	21 51	Battle Fair Oaks 1862	♓	7 41	00 15

WEATHER CONJECTURES—May—1, 2, 3, 4, 5, 6 **Fair**; 7, 8, 9, 10, 11, 12, 13 **Rain, Rain, Rain**; 14, 15, 16, 17, 18, 19, 20 **Changeable**, 21, 22, 23, 24, 25, 26, 27, 28, 29 **look for rain**; 30, 31 rain.

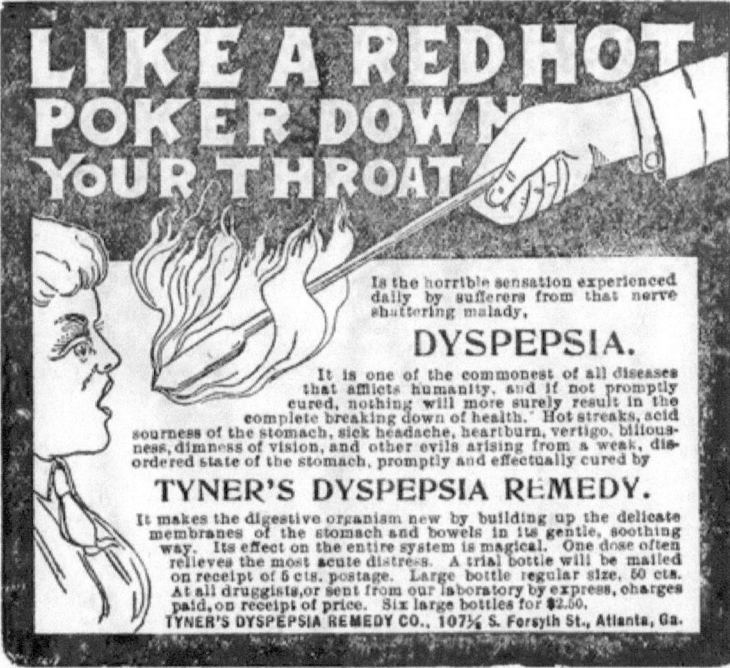

6th Month. **JUNE, 1902.** **30 Days.**

Moon's Phases.

		D.	H.	M.			D.	H.	M.	
◉New Moon,		6	1	3	a.m.	◑Full Moon,	20	9	8	p.m.
☽First Quarter		12	6	46	p.m.	☾Last Quarter	28	4	44	p.m.

Day of Month.	Day of Week	Sun Rises.	Sun Sets.	Sun Fast	Sun's decline south.	ASPECTS OF PLANETS AND OTHER MISCELLANEOUS MATTER.	Moon's place.	Moon rises or sets.	Moon south.
(22)	First Sunday after Trinity.					Day's length **14 hours** 27 **minutes.**			
1	E	4 44	7 11	2	22 00	Battle of Seven Pines 1862	[illegible]	sets	even
2	Mo	4 44	7 11	2	22 08	Battle of Cold Harbor 1864	[illegible]	9 36	2 10
3	Tue	4 43	7 12	2	22 16	☌♀☾Hobson sks Merrimac '98	[illegible]	10 39	3 13
4	We	4 42	7 12	2	22 23	☌♂☾ Dr Wm G Hill d 1877	[illegible]	11 44	4 18
5	Thu	4 44	7 13	2	22 30	Battle of Williamsburg 1862	[illegible]	12 26	5 00
6	Fri	4 41	7 13	1	22 37	♃ sta.; ♂ in ♌	[illegible]	rises	5 26
7	Sat	4 41	7 14	1	22 43	☌♆☾; ☿ in ♉	[illegible]	1 58	6 32
(23)	Second Sunday after Trinity.					Day's length **14 hours** 33 minutes.			
8	E	4 41	7 14	1	22 49	Battle or Cross Keys 1862	[illegible]	3 03	7 37
9	Mo	4 41	7 15	1	22 54	☿ sta.; ☍♂☉	[illegible]	4 04	8 38
10	Tue	4 41	7 15	1	22 59	Dickens died 1870	[illegible]	5 01	9 35
11	We	4 41	7 16	1	23 04	L L Polk died 1892	[illegible]	5 55	10 29
12	Thu	4 41	7 16	slow	23 08	N C R R chartered 1848	[illegible]	6 46	11 20
13	Fri	4 41	7 16		23 11	James H Horner d 1892	[illegible]	7 36	morn
14	Sat	4 41	7 17	1	23 15	U S flag adopted 1777	[illegible]	8 24	0 58
(24)	Third Sunday after Trinity.					Day's length **14 hours** 36 minutes.			
15	E	4 41	7 17	1	23 18	John D Eccles died 1857	[illegible]	9 03	1 47
16	Mo	4 41	7 17	1	23 20	Cornwallace evac Richm'd 1781	[illegible]	10 02	2 36
17	Tue	4 41	7 18	1	23 22	☿ in Aphelion	[illegible]	10 53	3 27
18	We	4 41	7 19	1	23 24	Battle of Waterloo 1815	[illegible]	11 43	4 17
19	Thu	4 42	7 19	1	23 26		[illegible]	00 35	5 09
20	Fri	4 43	7 19	1	23 26	♀ Gr. Hel. Lat. S.	[illegible]	1 27	6 01
21	Sat	4 44	7 19	2	23 27	Shafter's army lands 1898	[illegible]	2 19	6 53
(25)	Fourth Sunday after Trinity.					Day's length 14 hours 36 minutes			
22	E	4 43	7 19	2	23 27	*Sun enters Cancer—Sum. com.*	[illegible]	3 10	7 44
23	Mo	4 43	7 19	2	23 27	☌♄☾; ☌♆☉ Sup.; ☌☿☉ In.	[illegible]	4 00	8 35
24	Tue	4 43	7 19	2	23 26	*St. John Bagtist Day*	[illegible]	4 51	9 25
25	We	4 43	7 19	3	23 25	☌♃☾ Custer defeated 1876	[illegible]	5 41	10 15
26	Thu	4 44	7 19	3	23 23	Louis Bonaparte died 1846	[illegible]	6 31	11 05
27	Fri	4 44	7 20	3	23 21	Big fire in Raleigh 1883	[illegible]	7 24	11 56
28	Sat	4 44	7 20	3	23 19	Third Manilla ex, sails '98	[illegible]	8 15	even
(26)	Fifth Sunday after Trinity.					Day's length 14 hours 35 **minutes.**			
29	E	4 45	7 20	3	26 16	1st Manilla ex. ar. Manilla 1898	[illegible]	9 10	1 44
30	Mo	4 45	7 20	4	13 13	Montezuma died 1430	[illegible]	10 09	2 43

For High Tides at Beaufort, see third page of Almanac.

WEATHER CONJECTURES—June—1, 2, 3, 4, 5 **Cloudy—some rain;** 6, 7, 8, 9, 10, 11 **Fair and warm;** 12, 13, 14, 15, 16, 17, 18, 19 **very rainy;** 20, 21, 22, 23, 24, 25, 26, 27, Fair, if wind **from Northwest; Rainy if wind be from South or Southwest**: 28, 29 very rainy.

FARM AND GARDEN WORK FOR JUNE – S w full crops of cab-
bag s for fall and winter use. Caul fl wers and broccoli may be
sown, also a few carrots. Continue to sow tomatoes, okra, radishes, snap beans. Transplant leeks; pull and dry onions, garlic
and esch lots. A few cucumbers and melons plant for a late
crop, and a few ruta baga turnips.

Keep constantly at the plo w and hoe; this is the most important grass month! If the vines from your swee t p tato sprout
bed are fit you can draw and plant out first goo l rain So w cow
peas betw en your corn hills and rows. The end of this month
is a good time to put in the first crop o standing field peas.

Peele's Practical Business College, Raleigh, N. C., a Good School.

18 BRANSON'S NORTH CAROLINA ALMANAC.

7th Month.   JULY, 1902.   31 Days.

Moon's Phases.

	D. H. M		D. H. M.
New Moon,	5 7 51 a. m.	Full Moon,	20 11 37 a. m.
First Quarter	12 7 38 a. m.	L st Quar er,	27 0 6 a. m.

Day of Month.	Day of Week.	Sun rises.	Sun sets.	Sun slow.	Sun's decline ' orth.	ASPECTS OF PLANETS AND OTHER MISCELLANEOUS MATTER.	Moon's place.	Moon rises or sets.	Moon south.
1	T e	4 38	7 29	4 28	09	♂ ♀ ☾		rises	eve
2	We	4 38	7 29	4 23	05	Battle of Cold Harbor 1864		11 5	4 58
3	Thu	4 39	7 29	4 23	01	Vis. White Lake. Bladen co. N C		0 32	5 58
4	Fi	4 49	7 29	4 22	56	Mexican War de '45 ♂ ♃ ☾		12 0	6 30
5	Sat	4 40	7 28	4 22	51	Telegraph in China 1871		1 04	7 04
(2)	Sunday.					Day's length 14 hours 47 minutes.			
6	E	4 40	7 28	5 22	45			2 08	8 08
7	M.	4 41	7 28	5 22	39	Jame Wright Mo re d 1900		3 08	9 08
8	Tue	4 41	7 28	5 22	32	Hon J J Davis d 1892		4 05	10 05
9	We	4 42	7 27	5 22	26	Marines l'd t Guantanimo '98		4 59	10 59
10	Thu	4 42	7 27	5 22	18	rof Ralph Graves d 1889		5 51	11 51
11	Fr	4 42	7 26	5 22	11	J Q Adams b 1767		6 40	eve
12	at	4 43	7 2	5 22	03	Battle Bayyou 1590		8 31	1 30
(28)	Sunday					Day's length 14 hours 40 minutes.			
13	E	4 45	7 25	6 21	55	Ge Fremont d 1890		8 35	2 20
14	Mo	4 46	7 25	6 21	46	Santiago surrendered 1898		9 10	3 10
15	T e	4 46	7 24	6 21	37	♂ ♀ ♅ B t of Vicksburg 1862		10 00	4 01
16	We	4 47	7 24	6 21	27	Toral sur. San i go 1898		1 52	4 52
17	Thu	4 48	7 23	6 21	17	♂ ♄ Am fl g rais'd in San. '98		11 40	4 43
18	Fri	4 48	7 23	6 21	07	Dean St nly d 1881		sets	6 36
19	S t	4 49	7 22	6 20	58	Watauga co n'y formed 1849		1 12	7 27
(29)	Sunday.					Day's length 14 hou s 29 minutes.			
20	E	4 50	7 22	6 2	46	♂ ♄ ☾		2 03	8 19
21	Mo	4 51	7 21	6 20	3	Gen D H Hill born 1821		3 00	9 09
22	Tue	4 51	7 20	6 20	23	♂ ♃ ☾ Napoleon 2d d 1832		4 00	10 00
23	We	4 52	7 19	6 20	11	♂ ♂ ♅ Bolivar b 1788		4 35	10 50
24	Thu	4 53	7 19	6 19	39	Elec sto m at Fayetteville 1901		5 40	11 40
25	Fri	4 54	7 18	6 19	46	Re urned home 1901		6 30	morn
26	S t	4 55	7 17	6 19	33	☿ in ☊ S an Cab sues for p. '98		7 1	1 26
(3)	Sunday.					Day's length 14 hours 19 minutes.			
27	E	4 56	7 16	6 19	20	♂ ♀ ♅ Powers b 1805		8 11	2 22
28	Mo	4 56	7 15	6 19	06			9 06	3 21
29	Tue	4 57	7 14	6 18	53			10 08	4 23
30	We	4 58	7 13	6 18	38	Wm L Saunders b 1837		11 12	5 27
31	Th	4 59	7 12	6 18	24	♂ ♀ ♂ ♂ ♀ ☾ A Johnson d 1875		00 20	6 32

WEATHER CONJECTURES—July—1, 2, 3, 4, expect fair weather; 5, 6, 7, 8, 9, 10, 11, rainy; 12, 13. 14, 15, 16, 17, 18, 19, changeable; 20, 21, 22, 23, 24, 25, 26, frequent showers; 27, 28, 29. 30, 31, expect more ain.

FARM AND GARDEN WORK FOR JULY —Sow cabbage, but protect from hot sun when young. Water at night. Plant sna beans a d a few Irish potatoes Continue to sow radishes, le tuce, endive, cress-s, mustard and small salading The early Dutch turnip is the one to sow for the first crop; follow with the yellow Swedish or ruta baga.

Now do not omit to sow full crops of standing cow-peas. Sow a few turnips, carrots and beets as field crops, though the hot suns are apt to destroy them should they escape they will be fine, the next month is the best for these crops.

8th M.th.   AUGUST, 1902.   31 Days.

Moon's Phases.

	D. H. M.		D. H. M.
☽ New Moon,	2 3 9 p. m.	☽ Full Moon,	19 0 55 a. m.
☽ First Quarter,	10 11 16 p. m.	☾ Last Quarter,	26 5 56 a. m!

Day of Month.	Day of Week.	Sun rises.	Sun se's.	S n s ses.	Su 's echne S uh.	ASPECTS OF PLANETS AND OTHER MISCELLA- NEOUS MATTER.	Moon's place.	Moon rises or se s.	Moon south.
1	Fri	5 00	7 14	6 18	09	☽ C ʁ Aycock elect Gᴏv '9⊙	♒	rises	3 37
2	Sat	5 01	7 .1	6 17	54	♂ ☿ ℂ	♒	3 32	8 39
(31) Sun ay.						Day's l e g h 14 m e 5 nets .			
3	E	. 02	7 09	6 17	38	♂ ☿ ℂ Gov Casw l b 1729	♓	2 30	7 3
4	Mo	5 03	7 08	6 17	23	Maj R S Tucker died 1894	♓	4 32	9 38
5	Tue	5 0	7 07	6 17	07	♂ ♃ ⊙ Bat of Athen 1861	♈	5 30	10 34
6	We	5 04	7 .6	6 16	51	ʁ C Branson born 1851	♈	3 13	11 28
7	Thu	5 0	7 06	5 16	34	John Wheeler d 1832	♉	6 04	12 19
8	Fri	5 06	7 04	5 16	17	Spanish Armada destroy'd 1588	♉	7 01	morn
9	Sat	5 07	7 3	5 16	0	Dryden born 1681	♉	8 00	2 01
(32) S da.						Days en h 12 m 5 mins.			
10	E	5 08	7 04	5 15	43	☽ B ttle O k Hill 18.1	♊	8 5	2 51
11	Mo	5 09	7 01	5 15	2	Ψ Gr. H l. Lat. N.	♊	9 40	3 42
12	Tue	5 10	6 59	5 15	08	♂ ont E Le-d 1870	♋	10 35	4 33
13	We	5 1	6 58	5 4	49	♂♂ ℂ C nov d 1822	♋	11 2	5 2
14	Thu	5 12	5 56	4 14	3	Battle of Hastings 1066	♋	00 16	6 16
15	Fri	5 13	6 55	4 14	13	♀ in ♋ N pol on b 1769	♌	1 c8	7 08
16	Sat	5 14	5 51	4 13	54	♂ b ℂ Leg a Newbeto 1784	♌	1 59	7 59
(33) Sunday.						Day s len 1 13 mins 6 mins es.			
17	E	5 15	6 53	4	3 35	Burgoyne urrenders 1777	♍	2 50	8 51
18	Mo	5 15	6 51	4 13	16	♂ ♃ ℂ Cor stone U S cap 1790	♍	3 28	9 42
19	Tue	5 16	6 50	. 2	56		♎	4 2ι	10 33
20	We	5 17	6 4	3 12	37	☽ Harrison b 1838	♎	5 15	11 24
21	Thu	5 18	6 48	3 12	1	apt T A Branson k in bat 1864	♎	6 15	eve
22	Fri	5 19	6 46	. 11	57	J B G ugh b 1817	♏	7 10	1 10
23	Sat	5 20	6 45	2 11	37	C m Perry d 1820	♏	8 05	2 05
(34) Sunday.						Day s length 13 h rs 20 minutes.			
24	E	5 21	6 43	2 11	16	Daniel Webster d 1852	♐	9 00	3 03
25	Mo	5 2	6 42	2 10	56	Jo Turne 's triumph in Ral. '70	♐	10 03	4 03
26	Tue	5 23	6 40	2 10	35	☽ ♂ st Louis chillippd '50	♐	11 00	5 05
27	We	5 24	5 39	1 10	35		♐	00 08	6 c8
28	Thu	5 2	6 38	1	9 53	Go th born 1 49	♒	1 10	7 10
29	Fri	5 26	6 36	1	9 32	Br gham Young d 1877	♒	2 12	8 12
30	Sat	5 6	6 4	1	9 1	♂♂ ℂ Wm P nn d 1 18	♓	3 10	9 11
(35) Sunday						Day's l ngth 13 ho rs 2 minutes.			
31	E	5 27	6 32	0	8 49	♂ ♀ ℂ Charlesto earthq'ke '86	♓	0 00	10 08

WEATHER CONJECTURES—August—1, 2, v riable; 3 4. 5. 6. 7, 8 9,
carry yo r umbrella; 10 11, 12. 13, 14. 15, 16. 17. most y f ir; 18, 19,
2 , 21 22, 23, 24, expect fair weath r; 25, 26, 27, 28, 29, 30, 31, clean
your rubbers.

For High Tides at Beaufort, see third page of the Almanac.

FARM AND GARDEN WORK FOR AUGUST.—Transplant all kinds of cabbage, cauliflower and celery. Sow carrots and beets, turnips of all kinds, spinach, lettuce, radish and onions.

Now sow full crops of field turnips, carrots, and beets, and such other crops as were omitted last month; strip fodder. Early rice will be fit to cut last of this month. Look to it. This a good time to plant vines of the first slips, in order to procure seed potatoes for the next year's crops.

Peele's Practical Business College, Raleigh. N. C., a Good School.

9th Month. SEPTEMBER, 1902. 30 Days.

Moon's Phases.

	D.	H.	M.		D.	H.	M.
New Moon,	2	0	11 a. m.	Full Moon,	17	1	15 p. m.
First Quarter,	9	5	7 p. m.	Last Quarter,	24	11	23 a. m.

Day of Month.	Day of Week.	Sun Rises.	Sun Sets.	Sun Slow.	Sun's decline north.	ASPECTS OF PLANETS AND OTHER MISCELLANEOUS MATTER.	Moon's place.	Moon rises or sets.	Moon south.
1	Mo	5 28	6 30	0	8 2	Battle of Ox Hil l 1862		mo n	no'th
2	Tue	5 29	29		8 6	Atlanta captured 1864		5 40	11 02
3	We	5 30	6 28	1	7 44	☌ ☿ ☾; ☿ in ♉		5 50	11 55
4	Thu	5 31	5 26	1	7 22	French Republic 1870		6 00	even
5	Fri	5 32	6 25	1	7 00	J W Daniel born 1842		7 40	1 51
6	Sat	5 33	5 23	2	6 37	McKinley ass by Cz lgosz 1901		8 30	2 30
(36)	Sixth Sunday after Trinity.					Day's length 12 hours 45 minutes.			
7	E	5 34	6 22		6 15	Whittier died 1892		9 20	3 21
8	Mo	5 31	6 20	2	5 52	Destruction Jerusalem A D 70		10 10	4 12
9	Tue	5 35	6 19	3	5 30	☌ ♂ ☾		11 0	5 04
10	We	5 36	6 17	3	5 07	□ ♂ ☉ Sunset Cox d 1889		even	5 55
11	Thu	5 37	6 16	3	4 44	Battle of Brandywine 1777		0 4	6 47
12	Fri	5 38	6 14	4	4 22	☌ ♄ ☾ Bat of Chapultiepc '47		1 38	7 39
13	Sat	5 3	6 13	4	3 59	☿ in phelion—B t Quebec '50		2 30	8 30
(37)	Seventh Sunday after Trinity.					Day's length 12 hours 31 minutes.			
14	E	5 40	6 11	4	3 36	Pres McKinley d in Buff. 1901		3 2	9 21
15	Mo	5 41	6 10	5	3 13	Gen Scott took Mexico 1847		4 12	10 12
16	Tue	5 41	6 08	5	2 50	Leon Cz lgosz on trial 1901		5 00	11 04
17	We	5 42	6 08	5	2 26	♀ in Perihelon		6 10	morn
18	Thu	5 43	6 04	6	2 03			7 0	00 51
19	Fri	5 44	6 04	6	1 40	Dr Harris died 1879		7 45	01 47
20	Sat	5 45	6 01	6	1 17	President Arthur inaug 1881		8 00	02 45
(38)	Eighth Sunday after Trinity.					Day's length 12 hours 14 minutes.			
21	E	5 46	6 00	7	0 53	Battle of Fish r s Hil 1864		9 20	3 45
22	Mo	5 57	5 58	7	0 30	Mrs J A McDonald d in Dur '01		10 40	4 46
23	Tue	5 48	5 57	7	0 07	☉ enters ♎ *Autumn Com*		11 43	5 49
24	We	5 49	5 55	8	0 17	☌ ♆ ☾ Ge D H Hill d '89		morn	6 50
25	Thu	5 50	5 53	8	so'th	May. Powell ass. in Ral. '01		1 51	7 51
26	Fri	5 51	5 51	9	1 04	♄ sta. Daniel Boon d 1820		2 49	8 49
27	Sat	5 52	5 50	9	1 27	□ ♆ ☉ J C S Lumsden d 1901		3 46	9 46
(39)	Ninth Sunday after Trinity.					Day's length 11 hours 56 minutes.			
28	E	5 52	5 48	9	1 5	Wreck on S A L near Cam. 1901		4 40	10 40
29	Mo	5 53	5 47	10	2 14			5 33	11 33
30	Tue	5 54	5 45	10	2 37	☌ ♀ ☾ Leg met at Fayette. '86		6 25	12 25

For High Tides at Beaufort, see third page of the Almanac.

WEATHER CONJECTURES—September—1, warm; 2, 3, 4, 5, 6 7, 8, expect frequent showers; 9, 10, 11, 12, 13, 14, 15, 16, fair if wind northwest, rainy if south or southwest.

FARM AND GARDEN WORK FOR SEPTEMBER.—Now sow full crops of all kinds—turnips, onions carrots, beets, cabbage, lettuce, cresses. Look after your mushroom beds. Hoe and thin your turnips.

Continue to sow field turnips, carrots and beets. Southern seed is always better than the imported; those from the latter are apt to run to seed early in the spring, unless it be English seed. Prepare land for sowing rye in October. Pick cotto ; harvest corn.

10 h Month. OCTOBER, 1902. 31 Days.

Moon's Phases.

	D. H. M.		D. H. M.
New Moon,	1 0 1 p.m.	Full Moon,	16 0 53 a.m.
First Quarter	9 0 12 p.m.	Last Quarter,	23 5 50 p.m.
		New Moon,	31 3 5 a.m.

Day of Month.	Day of Week.	Sun Rises.	Sun Sets.	Sun Fast	Sun's decline north.	ASPECTS OF PLANETS AND OTHER MISCELLANEOUS MATTER.	Moon's place.	Moon rises or sets	Moon south.
1	We	5 55	5 43	10	3 0	Alex Holt d ed 1892	♍	rises	morn
2	Thu	5 56	5 42	11	3 24	Thos C Powell mar. 1901	♍	5 35	0 25
3	Fri	5 57	5 41	11	3 47	A dre ex. '8 . ☿ Gr. Hi . L S.	♍	7 16	1 16
4	at	5 58	5 40	11	4 10	B ttle of Geo getown 1777	♎	8 40	2 59
(40) Ninete nt Sunday after Tri ity. Day's length 11 hours 40 minutes.									
5	E	5 59	5 39	11	4 33	Cornwallis sur endered 1781	♎	8 9	2 59
6	Mo	6 00	5 37	12	4 57	Hawthorn prea. in Ral. 1901	♏	9 51	3 51
7	Tue	6 01	5 35	12	5 20	Edg r Allen Poe died 1849	♏	10 42	4 42
8	Ve	6 02	5 53	12	5 43	Bat f Fort Fish r 1861	♐	11 34	2 34
9	Thu	6 03	5 32	13	6 05	♀ Gr. Hel. Lat. N.	♐	sets	5 26
10	Fri	6 04	5 30	13	6 28	☌ ♄ ☾ Geo. V. Stron d. 1897.	♐	1 18	7 17
11	at	6 05	5 29	13	6 51	☌ ♃ ☾ Dr. Kane returned 1855	♑	2 08	8 08
(41) Tw ntieth Sunday after T init . Day's length 11 hours 26 minutes.									
12	E	6 06	5 7	13	7 14	Robert E Lee died 870	♒	2 58	8 58
13	Mo	6 07	5 26	14	7 36	John Toomer died 1856	♒	3 49	9 49
14	Tue	6 08	5 25	14	7 59	Josh Bil ings died 1885	♓	4 4	10 40
15	We	6 09	5 23	14	8 21	□ ♄ ☉ Koskiusk d 1817	♓	5 30	11 22
16	Thu	6 10	21	14	8 43	Noah Whee er di d 1758	♓	6 10	even
17	Fri	6 1	5 20	14	9 05	Dr Miller in Ra e gh 1901	♈	7 22	1 22
18	Sat	6 12	5 18	15	9 27	C A Dana died 1397	♈	8 21	2 20
(42) Twenty-first Sunday af er T in ty. Day's length 11 hours 4 minutes.									
19	E	6 13	17	15	9 48	☌ ☿ ☉ inf rior.	♉	1 21	3 21
20	Mo	6 14	5 16	1	10 11	Fro e died 1894	♉	10 23	4 24
21	Tue	6 1	5 14	15	10 32	☌ ♆ ☾ *Colum us Day*	♊	11 28	5 28
22	We	6 16	13	15	10 54	Non Saml captured 1874	♊	0 41	6 31
23	Thu	6 17	5 12	16	11 15	♀ in ☊	♋	1 5	7 53
24	Fri	6 18	5 10	16	11 36	*Great State Fair 1901*	♋	2 42	9 32
25	Sat	6 19	5 09	16	11 57	Newbern settled 1712	♌	3 28	9 28
(43) T enty-second Sundayafte Trinity Day's length 10 hours 47 minutes									
26	E	6 20	5 07	16	so'th	J siah Turner died 19 1	♌	rises	10 22
27	Mo	6 21	5 06	16	0 38	☿ in Perihelion Vassar d 1888	♌	5 15	11 15
28	Tue	6 22	5 05	6	1 19	☿ sta. Leviticus xix : 17	♍	6 00	morn
29	We	6 24	5 04	16	1 39	☌ ☿ ☾ Ra'e gh b headed 1618	♍	6 57	0 57
30	Thu	6 25	5 03	16	1 38	*Sun eclipsed*, invis. in N C	♍	7 4	1 47
31	Fri	6 26	5 02	16	1 58	S a n seizes Virginius 1873	♍	8 35	2 38

For High Tides at Beaufort, See third page of the Almanac.

WEATHER CONJECTURES—October—1 2 3, 4, 5, 6, 7, 8, variable; 9, 10, 11, 12, 13, 14, 15, rathe unfavorab'e to farmers; 16, 17 18, 19, 20, 21, 22, expect go d weather; 23, 24, 25, 26, 27, 28, 29, 30, fair a d mild; 31, moderate.

FARM AND GARDEN WORK FOR OCTOBER — You may make two
sowings of cabbage this month, a d, if f E glish seed, they will not
"run" in the spring. Sow lettuce; hoe turnips and thin, put out leeks
and o ions; sow principal crop of spinach; earth up cel ry.

Continue picking your cotton as it opens. Sow early rye, wheat and
barley, Dig your sweet potato s when the weather becomes cool and
you expect frost.

Peele's Practical Business College, Raleigh, N. C., a Good School.

26 BRANSON'S NORTH CAROLINA ALMANAC.

11th Month. NOVEMBER, 1902. 30 Days.

Moon's Phases.

	D. H. M.		D. H. M.
New Moon,	1 3 5 a. m.	Full Moon,	15 11 58 a. m.
First Quarter, 8	7 22 a. m.	Last Quarter, 22	2 39 a. m.
		New Moon,	29 8 56 p m.

Day of Month	Day of Week	Sun Rises	Sun Sets	Sun low.	Sun's decline North.	ASPECTS OF PLANETS AND OTHER MISCELLANEOUS MATTER.	Moon's place.	Moon rises or sets	Moon south.
1	at	6 27	5 or	16	11 18	☐♃☉ America dis. 1492	♋	r se-	morn
(44) Twenty third Sunday fie trin t . Day's length 10 hours 29 mins.									
2	E	6 28	4 59	16	14 37	Gen Bry on Grimes born 1828	♋	10 22	16 22
3	Mo	6 29	4 58	16	14 56	✶☾ Gen Clingman d 1897	♌	11 14	17 14
4	Tue	6 30	4 57	1	14 15	☿ Gr. Elon. W.	♌	2 05	18 05
5	We	6 31	4 56	16	15 33	Guy Fawkes Day	♍	12 57	18 57
6	Thu	6 32	4 55	16	15 51	✶♄☾ H D Turner d 1867	♍	1 47	19 47
7	Fri	6 33	4 54	16	16 09	☿ Gr. Hel. Lat N.	♎	2 37	20 37
8	Sat	6 34	4 53	16	16 27	☽ Gov Dobbs died 1754	♎	3 26	21 26
(45) Twent to r h Sunday after Tr ni y. Day's length 10 hours 28 mins.									
9	E	6 35	4 53	16	16 44	Dr S S Satchwell died 1892	♏	4 16	22 16
10	Mo	6 36	4 51	16	17 02		♏	5 07	23 07
11	Tue	6 37	4 51	16	17 18	State of Washington ad. 1889	♐	5 59	23 59
12	We	6 38	4 49	1	17 35	G n Graham died 1836	♐	6 2	eve
13	Thu	6 39	4 48	15	17 51		♑	7 50	1 50
14	Fri	6 40	4 47	15	18 07	☹ Judge A S Merrimon d 1892	♑	set	2 51
15	Sat	6 41	4 47	15	18 23		♒	9 54	3 54
(46) Twenty-fifth Sunday after Trinity. Day's length 10 hours 6 minutes.									
16	E	6 42	4 46	15	18 38	Don d W Barn died 1842	♒	11 00	5 00
17	Mo	6 43	4 46	15	18 53	Tho Ruffin born 1787	♒	rises	6 06
18	Tue	6 44	4 45	15	19 08	♂♆☾ Dr R K Speed d 1898	♓	1 10	7 10
19	We	6 45	4 44	14	19 22	D McMonald died 1877	♓	2 12	8 12
20	Thu	6 47	4 43	14	19 36		♈	3 11	9 11
21	Fri	6 49	4 43	14	19 50	☽	♈	4 06	10 06
22	Sat	6 50	4 42	13	20 03	Dr J H Smith died 1897	♉	5 00	11 00
(47) Twenty-sixth Sunday after Trini y. Day's length 9 hours 53 mins.									
23	E	6 51	4 42	13	20 16	♂☾ Dr R L Beal died 1891	♉	5 50	11 50
24	Mo	6 52	4 41	13	20 08	Cap. W F Avery died 1877	♊	6 40	morn
25	Tue	6 53	4 41	1	20 40		♊	7 31	1 31
26	We	6 54	4 40	2	20 52	Wm Tr on Gov. of N C 1765	♊	sets	2 21
27	Thu	6 55	4 40	12	21 03	B F Moore died 1868	♋	3 12	3 12
28	Fri	6 56	4 39	12	21 14	☉♂☿☉ Superior	♋	2 03	4 03
29	Sat	6 57	4 39	11	21 25	♂♀☾ Jo Martin Gov. 1771	♌	2 19	4 19
(48) Twenty-seve th Sund v after Trinity. Day's length 9 hours 37 mins.									
30	E	6 58	4 39	11	21 35	Saint Andrews	♌	2 55	4 55

WEATHER CONJECTURES—November—1, 2, 3, 4, 5, 6 good; 7, 8, 9, 10, 11, 12, 13. very rainy; 14, 15, 16, 17, 18, 19. 20, 21, expect fair weather mostly; 22, 23. 24, 25, 26, 27. cold with frequent showers; 28, 29, 30, fair if wind northwest; rainy if south or southwest.

For High Tides at Beaufort, see third page of the Almanac.

FARM AND GARDEN WORK FOR NOVEMBER —Sow your first crop of peas and a few turnips. Plant out onions raised from seed in August and September. Plant Windsor and long pod beans. Dress asparagus and artichokes

Sow full crops of rye, barley, wheat and other small grains. Harvest your sweet potatoes.

The Conquered Banner.

By Father Ryan.

Furl that Banner, for 'tis weary,
Round its staff 'tis drooping dreary,
    Furl it, fold it, it is best;
For there's not a man to wave it,
And there's not a sword to save it,
And there's not one left to lave it
In the blood which heroes gave it;
And its foes now scorn and brave it;
    Furl it, hide it—let it rest.

Take the Banner down, 'tis tattered,
Broken is its staff and shattered,
And the valiant hosts are scattered,
    Over whom it floated high;
Oh! 'tis hard for us to fold it,
Hard to think there's none to hold it,
Hard that those who once unrolled it,
    Now must furl it with a sigh.

Furl that Banner—furl it sadly—
Once ten thousands hailed it gladly,
And ten thousands wildly, madly,
    Swore it would forever wave;
Swore that foeman's sword could never
Hearts like theirs entwined dissever,
'Till that flag would float forever
    O'er their freedom or their grave.

Furl it, for the hands that grasped it,
And the hearts that fondly clasped it,
    Cold and dead are lying low;
And the Banner it is trailing
While around it sounds the wailing
    Of its people in their woe;
For though conquered they adore it,
Love the cold, dead hands that bore it,
Weep for those who fell before it—
Pardon those who trailed and tore it—
And oh! wildly they deplore it,
    Now to furl and fold it so.

Furl that Banner, true, 'tis gory,
Yet 'tis wreathed around with glory,
And 'twill live in song and story,
    Though its folds are in the dust;
For its fame on brightest pages,
Penned by poets and by sages,
Shall go sounding down the ages—
    Furl its folds though now we must.

Furl that Banner, softly, slowly,
Treat it gently—it is holy—
    For it droops above the dead;
Touch it not—unfold it never,
Let it droop there furled forever,
    For its people's hopes are dead.

12th Month. DECEMBER, 1902. 31 Days.

Moon's Phases.

	D	H	M.		D.	H.	M.
☽ First Quarter,	8	o	18 a. m.	☾ Last Quarter,	21	2	52 p m.
Full Moon,	14	10	39 p. m.	New Moon,	29	4	17 p. m.

Day of Month.	Day of Week.	Sun Rises.	Sun Sets.	Sun Fast	Sun's decline south.	ASPECTS OF PLANETS AND OTHER MI CELLANEOUS MATTER.	Moon's place.	Moon rises or sets.	Moon south.
1	Mo	6 09	4 40	11	21 45	Prince of Wales born 1844	[illegible]	rises	morn
2	Tue	7 00	4 39	11	21 54	Jordan Womble, Sr., d 1890	[illegible]	11 47	6 38
3	We	7 01	4 38	10	22 03	☌ ♄ ☾ [*Shout the glad tidings*]	[illegible]	morn	7 29
4	Thu	7 01	4 38	10	22 11	D D·ems o n 1820	[illegible]	2 19	8 19
5	Fri	7 03	4 38	9	22 9	♀ in ☋; ☌ ♃ ☾	[illegible]	3 08	9 08
6	Sat	7 04	4 38	9	22 27	Jefferson Davis died 1889	[illegible]	3 57	9 57
(49) Advent Sunday.						Day's length 9 hours 33 minutes			
7	E	7 05	4 38	8	22 34	W W Vass died 1896	[illegible]	4 46	10 46
8	Mo	7 06	4 38	8	22 4	☽ Eli Whitney born 1765	[illegible]	5 35	11 35
9	Tue	7 07	4 38	7	22 47	De Quincey died 1859	[illegible]	6 25	eve
10	We	7 08	4 38	7	22 53	☿ in Aphelion	[illegible]	sets	1 21
11	Thu	7 08	4 39	6	22 58	☌ ♀ ♅; I diana admitted 1816	[illegible]	8 18	2 18
12	Fri	7 09	4 39	6	22 03	☌ ☿ ☉ Supe io	[illegible]	9 20	3 19
13	Sat	7 10	4 39	5	23 08	Robert Toombs died 1884	[illegible]	10 2	4 24
(50) Second Sunday in Advent.						Day's length 9 hours 28 minutes.			
14	E	7 11	4 39	5	23 12	☌ ♅ ☉ uperi r	[illegible]	11 31	5 31
15	Mo	7 11	4 40	4	23 15	☌ ♆ ☾ J H Mills d 1898	[illegible]	12 38	6 38
16	Tue	7 12	4 40	4	23 18	Mrs S C White d 1881	[illegible]	rises	7 44
17	We	7 13	4 40	3	23 21	Beethoven born 1770	[illegible]	2 46	8 46
18	Thu	7 14	4 40	3	23 23	Sir Humphre Davy b 1779	[illegible]	3 45	9 45
19	Fri	7 14	4 41	2	23 25	J L Harris d ed 1874	[illegible]	4 40	10 41
20	Sat	7 15	4 41	2	23 26	South Carolina ·ece ed 1860	[illegible]	5 34	11 34
(51) Third Sunday in Advent.						Day's length 9 hours 27 minutes.			
21	E	7 15	4 42	1	23 27	☾	[illegible]	6 30	morn
22	Mo	7 16	4 42	1	23 27	☌ ☿ ♀; *Sun enters Cap*	[illegible]	7 15	1 15
23	Tue	7 16	4 43	1	23 2	G ad died 1889	[illegible]	8 00	2 06
24	We	7 17	4 43	[illegible]	23 26	☍ ♆ ☉	[illegible]	8 56	2 56
25	Thu	7 17	4 44	[illegible]	23 2[illegible]	*Christmas Day*	[illegible]	9 47	3 47
26	Fri	7 18	4 44	1	23 23	Stephen Girard died 1831	[illegible]	10 38	4 33
27	Sat	7 18	4 45	1	23 21	*St. John Evangelist*	[illegible]	11 30	5 30
(52) First Sunday after Christmas						Day's length 9 hours 28 minutes.			
28	E	7 18	4 46	2	23 19	☌ ♅ ☾ McC u ey died 1859	[illegible]	eve	6 21
29	Mo	7 18	4 47	2	23 16	Hon D F Caldwell d 1898	[illegible]	0 50	6 50
30	Tue	7 19	4 47	3	23 12	☌ ♀ ☾; ☌ ☿ ☾	[illegible]	1 12	7 12
31	We	7 19	4 47	3	23 08	Johnson born 1809	[illegible]	2 03	8 03

For High Tides at Beaufort, see third page of Almanac.

WEATHER CONJECTURES—December—1, 2, 3, 4, 5, 6, rain if wind south or southwest; 7, 8, 9, 10, 11, 12, 13, fair; 14 15, 16, 17, 18, 19, 20, showry; 21, 22, 23, 24, 25, 26, 27, 28, very rainy; 29, 30, 31, fair.

FARE AND GARDEN W RK DE EMBER —Plant peas f allkinds, set
out onions, garlic. es h lo's and cabbage. S w a few le.tuce, spinach,
carrots and rad shes. You may try a few Irish potato s.

Finish icking cotton: et out crops of rice a d prepare for market
C mmence plowing, ditching, draini .g and manuring as e rly as possible
for next year'g crop.

EDITORIAL.

We are a native of Randolph county, North Carolina,
and we had the good fortune to have been born just *one
hundred years later* than George Washington. Now, if
any one of the readers of BRANSON'S ALMANAC is curious
to know our age he can find out by referring to the life of
Mr. Washington, who was a *very worthy* young man.
You ought to read his life anyway.   BRANSON'S ALMANAC
has been published steadily since 1865, hence you can see
that the ALMANAC is not so old as to be in its *dotage*.   We
offer here A FRIENDLY GREETINS to all our READERS. We
are hoping to occupy a place in the CHIMNEY CORNER of
every home in our NATIVE STATE.

A HAPPY NEW YEAR TO YOU! and may you continue to
read our Almamac for ONE HUNDRED YEARS TO COME.

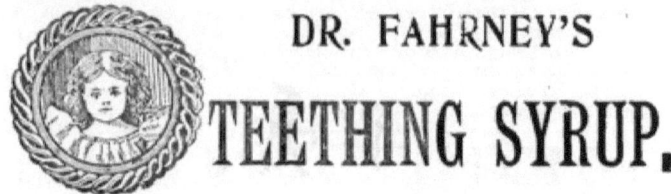

FREE TO YOU!
A Splendid Portrait of President McKinley.

The cut shown on this page is a *miniature* copy of a portrait of President McKinley, which the UNION GOSPEL NEWS has had made especially for its subscribers. The original is a photograph taken at the White House last year by Parker, the Washington photographer, at the request of President McKinley himself, and pronounced by him to be his favorite picture. During the year he ordered twenty-five dozen to be presented to friends.

The small cut serves to show the pose and gives some idea of the face, but in the large portrait the high-light on the face and the rugged grandeur of the features are brought out by the artist in such a way as to make the portrait simply GRAND. The full size portrait is a very fine half-tone engraving 9 x 11 inches, printed on the very finest coated paper 14 x 17 inches in size. It is all ready for framing. A copy of this magnificent portrait will be mailed free to all who send 50 cents for a year's subscription to the UNION GOSPEL NEWS, a weekly undenominational paper. Coin or stamps accepted. Order at once.

Address, THE UNION GOSPEL NEWS,
Cleveland, Ohio.

Be sure to mention Branson's Almanac.

· COUNTY OFFICERS.

CORRECTED FROM LAST ELECTION UP TO NOV., 1901.

COUNTIES	COUNTY TOWNS	CLERKS.	REGISTERS.
Alamance,	Graham,	J. D. Kernodle,	Chas C. Thompson
Alexander,	Taylorsville,	A L. Watts,	J C. Bel.
Alleghany,	·parta,	J. N. Edwards	·. F Thompson,
Arson,	Wadesboro,	J. C. Mc auchlin,	S A Benton,
Ashe.	Jefferson,	A. S. Eller,	D A O borne,
Beaufort,	Washi gton,	L B. Mayo,	Gilbert Rumley,
Bertie,	Windsor,	W. L Lyon,	E E. Ethe idge,
Bladen,	Eliz bethtown,	A. M. M Ne ll,	J.S Williamson,
Brunswick,	S uthport,	Thos. L. Wines,	C. El. Taylor,
Buncombe,	Ashe i le,	Marcus Erwin,	J J. Mackey,
Burke,	Morganton,	P. W Patton,	J H Giles,
Cabarrus,	Conco d,	J M. Cooke,	W. R. Johnson,
Caldwell,	Lenoir,	J V. McC ll,	W. L Minish,
Camden,	Camden, C. H.,	R. L. Forbes,	C. B. G rrett,
Carter t,	Beaufo t,	L A. Garner,	W. L. Arlington,
Caswe'l,	Yanceyville,	Thos. H. Harrison,	A. W I inch,
Catawba,	Newton,	L H. hillips,	P. M. Dellinger,
Chatham,	Pittsboro,	R. H Dixon,	W. E. Brooks,
Cherokee,	Murphy,	S. W. Lovingood,	T. C McDonald,
Chowan,	Edenton,	H. C. Privat,	A. J. Bynum,
Clay,	Haysville,	C. C Standridge,	M. M. Bunch,
Cleveland,	Shelby,	L. J. Hoyle,	J F. Robert·,
Columbus,	Whiteville,	H C. Moffitt;	R. Q. owell,
Craven,	Newb rn,	W. M. atson,	E. M. Green,
Cumberland,	Fayett ville,	Al A. McKeiihan,	J. A. McPhe son,
Currituck,	ur ituck, C. H	E W Ansell	E. W Wi liams,
Dare,	Manteo,	T. S Me kins,	R. W. Smith,
Davidson,	exington,	H. T Phillips,	S. L. Owen,
Davie,	Mocksi le,	A G. Grant,	B. O Morris,
Duplin,	Kenansville,	Her ert Smith,	B Frank P arsall,
Durham,	Durh m,	C B. Green,	John E. Suitt,
E lgecombe,	Tarboro,	Ed Pennington,	H. S. Barns,
Fo syth,	Wins on,	N. S Wilson,	W W. Lindsey,
Franklin,	Lo i burg,	W. K A Williams	M. S. lifton,
Gaston,	Dallas,	C C. Cornwall,	M. A. Carpe ter,
Gates,	Gatesville,	W T. Cross,	Lycurgus Hofler,
Graham,	Robb nsville,	R. V. McElroy,	R bt S. Slaughter,
G anville,	Oxford,	J G. Hunt,	John B. Maves,
Gre ne,	Snow Hill,	John R. Dale,	Charles A. Lassiter
Guilford,	Gr ensboro,	J hn J. Nelson,	A. G. Kirkman,
H lifax,	Halifax, C. H,	S. M. Oary,	J H. Norman,
Harnett,	Lillington,	J, H. Withers,	A. C. Ho ioway,
Haywood,	Way esville,	·. P. Walter,	H. B, Moore,
He derson,	Hendersonville,	C M. Pace,	W A. Hood,
Hertford,	Winton,	Thos L. Boon,	J T. Free nan,
Hyde,	Swan Quarter,	Reuben D. Harris,	Geo. W. Brown,
Iredell,	Statesville,	James Hertness,	W. W Turn r,
J ckson,	Webster,	F. E. Alley,	Jame R. l ong,
Johnso ,	Smithfiel l,	W. S, Stevens,	J. W. Stephenson,

COUNTY OFFICERS.

CORRECTED FROM LAST ELECTION UP TO NOV., 1901.

COUNTIES	COUNTY TOWNS	CLERKS.	REGISTERS.
Jones,	Trenton.	S. E. Koonce,	Z. Brock,
Lenoir,	Kinston,	Plato Collins,	W. D. Suggs,
Lincoln,	Lincolnton,	A. Nixon,	H. A. Self,
Macon,	Franklin,	Lee Crawford,	D. W. Bain.
Madison,	Marshall,	J. H. White,	Van B. Davis,
Martin,	Williamston,	J. A. Hobbs,	W. C. Manning,
McDowell,	Marion,	Thos Morris,	T. W. Wilson,
Mecklenburg,	Charlotte,	J. A. Russell,	A. M. McDonald
Mitchell,	Bakersville,	J. C. Bowman,	T. B. Garland,
Montgomery,	Troy,	C. A. Armstrong,	W. D. Allen,
Moore,	Carthage,	D. A. McDonald,	A. L. McIntosh,
Nash,	Nashville,	Thos. A Sills,	J. A. Whitaker,
New Hanover,	Wilmington,	John D. Taylor,	W. H. Biddle,
Northampton,	Jackson,	J. T. Flythe,	M. E. Stancill,
Onslow,	Jacksonville,	John W. Burton,	I. E. Ketchum.
Orange,	Hillsboro,	D. H. Hamilton,	John Laws,
Pamlico,	Bayboro,	James R. Rice.	Z V. Rowles,
Pasquotank,	Elizabeth City,	W. H. Jennings,	S. C. Spence,
Pender,	Burgaw,	W. W. Larkins,	J B. Black,
Perquimans,	Hertford,	L. V. Perry,	R. R. Knowles,
Person,	Roxboro,	D. W. Bradsher,	W. E Webb,
Pitt,	Greenville,	D. C. Moore,	T. R Moore,
Polk,	Columbus,	N. B. Hampton,	A. L McMurray.
Randolph,	Asheboro,	G. G. Hendrick,	J. P. Burrows,
Richmond,	Rockingham,	W. I. Everett,	N. Buie,
Robeson,	Lumberton,	W. H. Humphrey,	W. S. Thomas,
Rockingham,	Wentworth,	J. V. Price,	J. A. Scales,
Rowan,	Salisbury,	W. G. Watson,	A. L. Smoot,
Rutherford,	Rutherfordton,	M O. Dickerson,	G. H. Russell,
Sampson,	Clinton,	W. R. Pigford,	James P. Jones,
Scotland,	Laurinburg,	W. I. Everett,	R. A. Ingram,
Stanly,	Albemarle,	R. A. Crowell,	W. T. Harkabee
Stokes,	Danbury,	N. O. Petree,	I. M. Gordon,
Surry,	Dobson,	C. H. Haynes,	T. W Davis,
Swain,	Bryson City,	A. J, Hall,	A. G. DeHart,
Transylvania,	Brevard,	T. T. Loftis,	Wm. Henry.
Tyrrell,	Columbia,	G. L. Liverman,	T. L. Jones,
Union,	Monroe,	E. A. Armfield,	J. M. Stewart,
Vance,	Henderson,	Henry Perry,	Kenneth Edwards
Wake,	Raleigh,	W. M. Russ,	J. T. Bernard,
Warren,	Warrenton,	W. A. White,	John A. Dowtin,
Washington,	Plymouth,	W. M Bateman,	F. R. Johnson,
Watauga,	Boone,	J. H. Bingham,	Jacob N. May,
Wayne,	Goldsboro,	J. F. Ormond,	G. C Kornegay,
Wilkes,	Wilkesboro,	Lin. Bumgarner,	E. M. Blackburn
Wilson,	Wilson,	J. D. Bardin,	Wm. B. Barnes,
Yadkin,	Yadkinville,	W. A. Hall,	J L. Cravon,
Yancey,	Burnsville,	J. B. Ray,	W. F. Adkins,

SUPERIOR COURTS OF NORTH CAROLINA FOR 1902.

FIRST JUDICIAL DISTRICT.

Solicitor—George W. Ward, Elizabeth City.

Spring Term—1902.—Judge Geo. A. Jones, Franklin.

Fall—Judge Frederick Moore, Asheville.

Beaufort—Feb 10 (2) †April 14 (1) *May 12 (1) *†Oct 15 (2) *†† December 1 (3)

Currituck—Feb 24 (1) Sept 1 (1).

Camden—March 3 (1) Sept 8 (1).

Pasquotank—Mar 10 (2) *†May 26 (2) Sept 15 (1) Nov 17 (1).

Perquimans—March 24 (1) Sept 22 (1).

Chowan—March 31 (1) Sept 29 (1).

Gates—April 7 (1) Oct 6 (1)

Washington—April 21 (1) Oct 27 (1).

Tyrrell—April 28 (1) Nov 3 (1).

Hyde—May 5 (1) Nov 24 (1).

Dare—May 19 (1) Nov 10 (1).

SECOND JUDICIAL DISTRICT.

Solicitor—Walter E. Daniels, Wilson

Spring Term—1902.—Judge Geo. H. Brown, Washington.

Fall—Judge Geo. Jones, Franklin.

Halifax—Jan 20 (2) April 7 (2) Aug 18 (1) Nov 24 (2).

Northampton—†Feb 3 (1) March 24 (2) ‡Sept 1 (1) Oct 24 (2).

Warren—Feb 10 (1) May 12 (1) Sept 15 (2).

Bertie—Feb 17 (1) Sept 28 (2) ‡Sept 8 (1) Nov 10 (2).

Hertford—*Feb 24 (1) April 21 (1) *Aug 11 (1) Oct 20 (1).

THIRD JUDICIAL DISTRICT

Solicitor—L. I. Moore, Greenville.

Spring Term—1902.—Judge F. D. Winston, Windsor.

Fall—Judge George H. Brown, Washington.

Pitt—March 17 (2) April 21 (2) Jan 13 (2) Sept 1 (2) Oct 13 (2).

Craven—†Feb 10 (2) April 7 (1) †May 5 (2) *Aug 18 (1) †Sept 15 (2) *Nov 10 (1) †Nov 17 (1).

Greene—Feb 24 (1) Aug 5 (1) Dec 1 (2).

Carteret—March 10 (1) Sept 29 (1).

Jones—March 31 (1) Nov 3 (1).

Pamlico—April 14 (1) Oct 6 (1).

FOURTH JUDICIAL DISTRICT.

Solicitor Charles C. Daniels, Wilson.

Spring Term—1902.—Judge H. R. Bryan, New Bern.

Fall—Judge Francis D. Winston, Windsor.

Franklin—‡Jan 20 (2) April 14 (2) Oct 13 (2).

Wilson—*†Feb 3 (2) †May 12 (1) *Sept 1 (1) †Nov 10 (2) *Dec 8 (1).

Vance—Feb 17 (2) May 19 (2) Sept 29 (2).

Edgecombe—March 3 (1) †Mar 31 (2) †Sep 8 (2) nOct 27 (2)

Martin—March 17 (1) Sept 15 (2).

Nash—March 10 (1) April 28 (2) Aug 25 (1) Nov 24 (1).

FIFTH JUDICIAL DISTRICT

Solicitor—Radolph Duffy, Catharine Lake.

Spring Term—1902.—Judge E. W. Timberlake, Louisburg.

Fall—Judge Henry R. Bryan, New Bern.

New Hanover—*Jan 6 (2) †Jan 27 (1) *Mar 24 (1) †April 7 (1) *May 26 (1) *26 (1) *July 7 (1) *Aug 11 (1) †Oct 6 (2), *Nov 3 (2) *Nov 24 (2).

Duplin—Feb 10 (1) May 5 (1) Aug 25 (1) Dec 1 (2).

Lenoir—March 10 (2) April 28 (1) Nov 10 (2)

Sampson—Feb 17 (2) May 12 (2) Sept 22 (2).

Pender—March 3 (1) Sept 1 (1) Dec 15 (1).

Onslow—Jan 20 (1) July 14 (2) Oct 20 (2).

SIXTH JUDICIAL DISTRICT.

Solicitor—Armistead Jones, Raleigh.

Spring Term—1902.—Judge Oliver H. Allen, Kinston.

Fall—Judge E. W. Timberlake, Louisburg.

Wake—*Jan 6 (2) †Feb 24 (2)

*March 24 (2) †April 21 (2) *July 7 (2)*Sept 22 (2) †Oct 20 (3).

Wayne—Jan 20 (2) April 14 (1) Sept 8 (2) Nov 24 (1).

Harnett—Feb 10 (2) Aug 25 (1) ‡Nov 10 (2).

Johnston—March 10 (2) Sept 1t (1) Dec 1 (2).

SEVENTH JUDICIAL DISTRICT.

Solicitor—Colin M. McLean, Elizabethtown.

Spring Term—1902.—Judge W. S. O'B Robinson, Goldsboro.

Fall—Judge A. H. Allen, Kinston.

Columbus—Feb 24 (1) April 14 (1) Sept 1 (1) Nov 24 (1).

Cumberland—*Jan 13 (1) ‡Feb 17 (1) †March 24 (1) *April 21 (1) †May 5 (2) *Aug 25(1) nnOct 20 (2) *Nov 7 (1).

Robeson—†Feb 3 (2) †March 31 (2) *May 19 (1).

Bladen—Marc 3 (2) Oct 6 2).

Brunswick—March 17 (1) Sept 22 (1).

EIGHTH JUDICIAL DISTRICT.

Solicitor—L. D. Robinson, Wadesboro.

Sring Term—19 1.—Judge Thos. A. McNeal, Lumberton

Fall—Judge W. S. O'B. Robinson, Goldsboro.

Chatham—Feb 3 (1) May 5 (1) †Aug 4 (1) Nov 10 (1)

Moore—†Jan 20 (2) *April 21 (1) †May 12 (1) Aug 11 (1) *Sept 15 (1) *Dec 1 (1):

Scotland—†March 10 (1) April 28 (1) †Oct 27 (1) †Eov 17 (1).

Anson—*Feb 10 (1) †April 14 (1) *Sept 8 (1) †Oct 6 (1)

Union—*Feb 17 (2) †March 17 (2) *July 28 (1) *Aug 18 (2) †Oct 13 (2) *Nov 24 (1)

Richmond—*March 3 (1) †Mar 31 (2) *Sept 1 (1) Sept 22 (2).

NINTH JUDICIAL DISTRICT.

Solicitor—Aubry L. Brooks, Greensboro.

Spring Term—1902.—Judge Walter H Neal Laurinburg.

Fall—Jude Thomas A. McNeal, Lumberton.

Durham—*J n 6 (2) †Jan 20 (2) †March 17 (2) *May 12 (1) *Aug 25 (1) †Sept 29 (2) *Dec 1 (1)

Guilford—*Jan 13 (1) †Feb 10 (2) †April 14 (1) *May 5 (1) †June 9 (2) †Aug 18 (1) †Sept 15 (2) †*Oct 20 (2) †Dec 8 (2).

Granville—Feb 3 (1) April 21 (2) July 28 (1) Nov 17 (2).

Alamance—Feb 24 (2) †May 26 (1) *Sept 1 (2) aNov 3 (1).

Orange—March 10 (1) nMay 19 (1) Aug 4 (1) Oct 13 (1).

Person—April 7 (1) Aug 11 (1) Nov 10 (1).

TENTH JUDICIAL DISTRICT.

Solicitor—Wiley Rush, Asheboro.

Spring Term—1902. Judge Thos. J. Shaw, Greensboro.

Fall—Judge Walter H. Neal, Laurinburg

Montgomery—*Jan 20 (1) nApr 14 (1) S pt 22 (1).

Iredell—Jan 27 (2) May 19 (2) Aug 4 (2) Nov 3 (2).

Rowan—Feb 10 (2) May 5 (2) Sept 1 (2) Nov 17 (2).

Davidson—Feb 24 (2) nApril 21 (2) Aug 18 (2).

Stanly—aMarch 10 (1) aJuly 14 (1) aSept 15 (1) Dec 15 (1).

Randolph—March 17 (2) July 21 (2) Dec 1 (2).

Davie—March 31 (2) Oct 6 (2).

Yadkin—April 28 (1) Oct 20 1.

ELEVENTH JUDICIAL DISTRICT.

Solicitor—M. L. Mott, Wilkesboro.

Spring Term—1902.—Judge Albert L. Coble, Statesville.

Fall—Judge Thos. J. Shaw, Greensboro.

Forsyth—aFeb 10 (2) nMarch 10 (2) May 19 (2) aJuly 21 (1) nSept 8 (2) *Oct 6 (1) nDec 1 (2).

Wilkes—Jan 27 (2) Aug 4 (2) nOct 20 (2).

Rockingham—Feb 24 (2) July 28 "1" Nov 3 "2".

Alleghany—March 24 "1" Aug 18 "1".

Caswell—April 14 "1" Oct 13 "1".

Surry—April 21 "2" nAug 25 "2" Nov 17 "2".

Stokes—May 5 "2" Sept 22 "2"

TWELFTH JUDICIAL DISTRICT.

Solicitor—Jas L. Webb, Waynesville.

Spring Teem—1902.—Judge Albert L. Coble, Statesville.

Fall—Judge Henry B. Starbuck, Winston

Mecklenburg—*n*Jan 13 "*2*" *a*Feb 10 "*2*" *a*March 10 "*2*" *a*April *21* "*2*" *a*June *2* "*2*" *July *14* "*2*", *Aug *11* "*2*" *a*Sep 22 "*2*" *a*Oct 6 "*2*" *a*Nov *24* "*2*".

Cleveland—March 24 "*2*" July *28* "*2*" Nov 3 "*2*".

Gaston—Feb *24* "*2*" May *19* "*2*". Sept 8 "*2*" Nov *17* "*2*".

Lincoln—April 7 "*2*" Sept *1* "*1*" Dec 8 "*1*".

Cabarrus—Jan *27* "*2*" May 5 "*2*" Aug 25 "*1*" Oct *20* "*2*".

THIRTEENTH JUDICIAL DISTRICT.

Solicitor—Moses N. Harshaw, Lenoir.

Spring Term—1902.—Judge W. A. Hoke, Lincolnton.

Fall—Judge Henry R. Starbuck, Greensboro.

Catawba—Feb 3 "*2*" *n*May 5 "*2*" July 7 "*2*" Oct 27 "*2*".

Alexander—Feb 17 "*1*" Sept 29 "*1*"

Caldwell—Feb 24 "*2*" Sept *15* "*2*" *n*Nov *24* "*2*".

Mitchell—March *10* "*2*" *n*May *19* "*2*" Sept *1* "*2*" Nov *10* "*2*".

Watauga—March 24 "*2*" June *2* "*1*" Aug 4 "*1*".

Ashe—April *21* "*2*" July *21* "*2*" Oct *13* "*2*".

FOURTEENTH JUDICIAL DISTRICT

Solicitor—J. F. Spainhour, Morganton.

Spring Term—1902.—Judge W. B. Council, Boone.

Fall—1902.—Wm. A. Hoke, Lincolnton.

Yancey— April 21 (2) Bec. 1 (2). McDowell—Feb. 17 (2) August 4 (2) October 20 (2).

Henderson—*March 3 (2) ††May 12 (2) *September 15 (2) ††May 3 (2).

Rutherford—March 10 (2) Septe ber 1 (2) November 17 (2).

Polk—March 24 (2) Sept. 29 (1). Burke—August 7 (2) ‡June 2 (2) ‡August 18 (2) October 6 (2).

FIFTEENTH JUDICIAL DISTRICT.

Solicitor—Jas. M. Gudger, Asheville.

Spring Term—1902.—Judge M. H. Justice, Rutherfordton.

Fall—Judge W. B. Council, Boone.

Buncombe—*Feb 3 (2) †March 10 (4)*a* Apr 21 (2) †May 26 (4) *July 28 (2) †Sept 8 (6) Nov 10 (2) †Dec 1 (2).

Madison—Feb 24 (2) ††May 5 (3) Aug 11 (2) *Oct 20 (3).

Transylvania—April 7 (2) Aug 25 (2) Nov 24 (1).

SIXTEENTH JUDICIAL DISTRICT.

Solicitor—James W. Furguson, Waynesville.

*Spring Term—1902—*Judge Frederick Moore, Asheville.

Fall—Judge M. H. Justice, Rutherfordton.

Haywood—Feb 3 (2) May 5 (2) Sept 22 (2).

Jackson—Feb 17 (2) May 19 (2) Oct 6 (2).

Swain—March 3 (2) July 21 (3) Oct 20 (2).

Graham—March 17 (2) Sept 1 (2).

Cherokee—March 31 (2) Aug 4 (2) Nov 3 (2).

Clay—April 14 (1) Sept 15 (1).

Macon—April 21 (2) Aug 18 (2) *n*Nov 17 (2).

---

* and *a* For criminal cases only.
† and *n* For civil cases only.
(2) or "2".Means two weeks, etc.
‡Civil and judicial cases.

SUPREME COURT OF NORTH CAROLINA.

Emaminer's Applicants for license Monday, **first** week of term. Court meets 1st Monday in February and last Monday in August of each year.

Cases Heard First district Monday, February 4th, August 26th. Second district, Monday, February 11th, September 2nd. Third district, Monday, February 18th, September 9th. Fourth district, February 25th, September 16th. Fifth district, March 4th. Sixth district, March 11th, September 30th. Seventh district, March 18th, October 7th. Eigth district, March **26th**, November 12th. Nineth district, April 1st, October 21st. Tenth district, April 8th, October 28th. Eleventh district, April 15th, November 4th. Twelfth district, April 22nd, November 1st. Thirteenth district, April 29th, November 18th, Fourteenth district, May 6th, **Nov.** 25th. Fifteenth district, May 13th, December 2nd. Sixteenth district, May 20th, December 9th. End of docket, etc., April 30th.

Courts meets in Raleigh 1st Monday in February, and 4th Monday in August of each year.

U. S. CIRCUIT AND DISTRICT COURTS.

Charles H Simonton, Charleston, S. C., **Judge of** Fourth Circuit of United States Cour s.

Nathan Goff, West Virginia, Judge of the U. S Circuit **Court of Appleals for the Fourth district.**

WESTERN DISTRICT.—James E Boyd, Greensboro, Judge; **A. E. Holton**, District Attorney; Spencer Blackburn, Assistant Attorney; **S. L.** Trodgen, Clerk. *Greensboro*—Circuit and District—April 31st two October 6th. *Statesville*—Circuit and District, H C. Cowles, Clerk; April 3rd "3" October 6th. *Asheville*—Circuit and District, Chas. F. McKesson, Clerk; May 5th, (two) November 7th *Charlotte*—Circuit and District, H. C. Cowles, Clerk; June 2nd, December 1st.

EASTERN DISTRICT.—T. R. Purnell, Judge; C. M. Bernard, Greenville, District Attorney; O. C. Spears and E. A Johnson, Assistant Attorneys; John P. Overman, Deputy Clerk *Elizabeth*—District Court, George Green, Deputy Clerk; New Bern, April 14th October 20th. *Wilmington*—Circuit and District; H. L. Grant Clerk; George Tonnoffski, Assistant Clerk, in Raleigh; W. H. Shaw, Clerk and Deputy of Circuit Court at Wilmington; H. C. Dockery, Marshal; April 29th, November 24th. *Raleigh*—Circuit and District; N. J. Riddick Clerk, in Raleigh; W. H. Shaw, Clerk of district and Deputy of Circuit Court at Wilmington; H. C. Dockery, Marshal; Raleigh, May 22nd "two," December 2nd.

U. S. CIRCUIT COURT APPEALS.

U. S FOURTH CIRCUIT.—The Circuit Court of appeals meets **in Richmond**, Va., February 2, May, and November 7. Chief Justice F. I. Osborn presides Circuit Judges : Nathan Goff and Charles H. Simonton. Two district judges are designated at each term. Maryland, West Virginia and Virginia, North and South Carolina complete the circuit.

GOVERNMENT OF NORTH CAROLINA.

EXECUTIVE COMMITTEE.

Charles B. Aycock, of Wayne County, Governor, salary 4,000, and **furnished** house, fuel and lights.

W. D. Turner, of Iredell County, Lieutenant-Governor and President of the Senate. Salary Same as a Senator.

P. M Pearsall, Private Secretary to the Governor, salary 1,200 and **commissions.**

J. Bryan Grimes, of Pitt County, Secretary of the State, salary $2,000 and certain fees, and $1,000 extra for the clerical assistance.

Chief Clerk to Secretary of State, salary $1,000.

B. F. Dixon, of Cleveland County, Auditor, salary $1,500, and $2,500 extra for clerical assistance.

Hilary T. Hudson, Chief Clerk to Auditor, salary $1,000.

B. R. Lacy, of Wake County, Treasurer' salary $3,000.

W. F. Moody of Mecklenburg County, Chief Clerk to Treasurer salary $1,500.

J. P. Arrington of Nash County, Clerk for Charitable and Penal Institution, salary $1,000.

C. F. Glenn of Forsythe County, Teller of the Treasury Department, salary $750.

Thomas F. Toon, of Roberson County, Superintendent of Public Instruction, salary $1,500, and $500 per annum for traveling expenses, 1,000 extra for Clerk.

Robert D. Gilmer, of Haywood County, Attorney General, salary $2,000 and $600 for clerical assistance.

B. S. Royster, Granville County, Adjutant General, salary $1,000.

M. O. Sherrill, Catawba County, State Librarian, salary $1,250, Assistant Librarian, Marshall D. L. Haywood, Wake County, salary, $300.

Miss Julia Howell, Wayne County, Executive Clerk, salary $600.

C. C. Cherry, of Edgecombe County, Superintendent of Public Buildings and Grounds, salary $600.

L. W. Lancaster, of Wake County, State Standard Keeper, salary $100.

N. C. BOARD OF CARPORATION COMMISSIONERS.

Commissioners.—Franklin McNeill, New Hanover County. Chairman; terms expires January, 1907. Sam. L. Rogers, Macon County, term expires 1905. D. H. Abbott, Pamlico County; term expires April 1, 1903; salary $2,000 each. Henry C. Brown, Surry County, regular Clerk, salary......., Miss Riddick. Stenographer, salary......

Regular sessions of the Court are held at Raleigh, First Wednesday of each month. Special sessions are also held at other places, under such regulations as made by the Commissions.

Officers of the Commissoners are locatee in the Agricultural Building.

BUREAU OF LABOR AND PRINTING.

Heury B. Varner, Commissioner, Davidson County, salary $1,500, W. E. Faison, Assistant Commissioner, Wake County, salary $900.

NORTH CAROLINA GEOLOGICAL SURVEY.

J. A. Aolmes, State Geologist, J. V. Lewis, Assistant Geologist, in charge of corundum and building stone investigation: W. W. Ashe, Forestor; E. W. Myers, Assistant, in charge of water power investigation; Joseph H. Pratt, Mineralogist. The general office of the Survey is in the Agricultural Building, Raleigh.

BOARD OF INTERNAL IMPROVEMENTS.

Members of the Borad are appointed by the Governor and confirmed by the Senate, and to consist of Gov. C. B. Aycock, *ex-offieio* chairman; B. W. Ballard, Franklinton; B. C. Beckwith, Raleigh.

STATE BANK EXAMINERS.

The Examiners are appointed by the Corporation Commission, and are as follows: Dr George F. Lucas, of Pender County; W B. Shaw, of Vance County; Arthur E. Rankin, of Bunbombe County. They examine the State and private banks only, and are subject to the control of the Corparation Commission.

STATE INSURANCE DEPARTMENT.

Office in Capitol Building. James R. Young, of Vance County, Insurance Commissioner, salary $2,000, Clerk salary $750. Term of office for two years, elected by the last Legislature.

STATE BOARD OF EDUCATION.

The Governor, Lieutenant-Governor, Secretary of State, Treasurer. Auditor. Superintendent of Public Instruction and Attorney General constitute the State Board of Education.

SHELL FISH COMMISSION OF NORTH CAROLINA.

Chief Commissioner, W. M. Webb, Carteret county; appointed Shell Fish Commissioner by the Governor, in February, under the act of General Assembly, 1901. Term of office, four years; salary, $900. Associate Commissioner not appointed.

The Professor of Biology at the University (Prof. H. V. Wilson) is *ex officio* an Associate Commissioner, but without additional salary.

BOARD OF PUBLIC BUILDINGS AND GROUNDS.

The Governor, Secretary of State, Treasurer and Attorney General.

GOVERNOR'S COUNCIL.

The Secretary of State, Treasurer, Auditor, and Superintendent of Public Instruction

STATE HOSPITAL, JAMES M'KEE, M. D., SUPERINTENDENT, RALEIGH, N. C.

R. B. Lacy, Treasurer, *ex officio;* James McKee, M. D., Superintendent; C. L. Jenkins, E. B. Ferebee, Physicians; W. R. Crawford, Jr., Steward; Miss M E. Whitaker, Matron; Miss S. Timberlake, Secretary to Board of Directors, and Stenographer.

BOARD OF DIRECTORS.—J. D. Briggs, President, Williamston; J. B. Broadfoot, Fayetteville, Dr. R. H. Stancell, Margarettsville; F. W. Barnes, Wilson; W. B Fort, Pikeville; S O. Middleton, Hallsville; Edwin Smith, Godwin; W. H. Nicholson Louisburg; L. J. Picot, Littleton, N. C.

EXECUTIVE COMMITTEE.—Dr. R. H Stancell, Chairman; W. B. Fort, W. H. Nicholson.

When is a plant like a soldier? When it begins to shoot.

Why is a whisper forbidden in polite society? Because it is not aloud.

What is the difference between the House of Commons and the House of Lords? One has ability—the other nobility.

Whatsoever thy hand findeth to do, do it with thy might.—Ecclesiates 9:10.

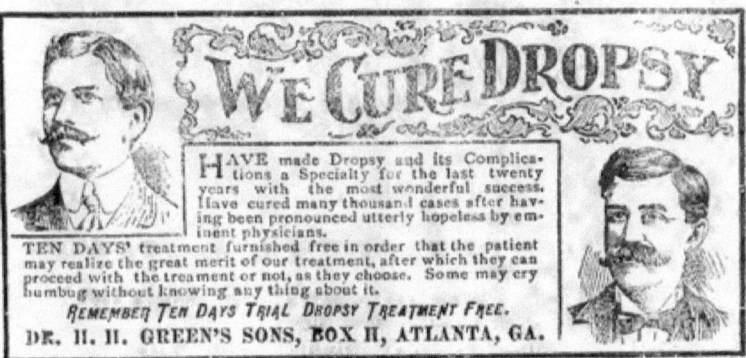

"FINIS."

What ! here so soon ?
  Sunset and night ?
Why, I have work to do that needs the noon,
  And day's broad light.
See, on the palette, there, the colors are but set,
The canvas still unwet,
  And it is night.

How shall it rise—
  That heavenly strain—
On heavenly wings, to woo the listening skies
  To earth again ?
While lies the violin here, untouched, unstrung;
The sweetest notes unsung,
  And it is night.

How sweet 'twould be,
  My work all done—
To sit at eve, my threshold on, and see stars, one
    by one
  Flash into the dark heaven.   Oh, happy rest !
  My folded hands how blest,
    But—'tis already night !

—SUSAN MARGARET WHITAKER, *Raleigh, N. C.*

PRICE, 10 CENTS.

Vol. 4.]   35th YEAR OF PUBLICATION.   [No. 6.

BRANSON'S

AGRICULTURAL

ALMANAC

(FOR THE SOUTHERN STATES)

FOR THE YEAR OF OUR LORD

1903

And until the 4th of July, the 127th Year of American Independence.

THIRD YEAR OF 20TH CENTURY.

Carefully Calculated by LEVI BRANSON, A. M., D. D.

LEVI BRANSON, Publisher, Raleigh, N. C.
WILLIAM C. SMITH, Publisher, Atlanta, Ga.

GET THE BEST AND STICK TO IT—NO OTHER LIKE IT.

1—All men have faith in something, hence they work expecting results.—*Branson.*

TIME.

The calculations for this Almanac are made in mean solar or clock time,
which is indicated by a well regulated watch or clock, and does not correspond with the Sun precisely, except on four days in the year.

Apparent time is that which makes the Sun come to the meredian at
12 o'clock.   No good clock will run with the Sun; if set with the Sun on
2d day of January, the clock will seem to be one minute too fast on the
3d of January.

To adapt the calculations of this Almanac to apparent time, use the
minutes in the column marked "Sun slow" or "Sun fast;" add them
when fast, subtract them when slow.

The calculations are made for the Latitude and Longitude of Raleigh,
N. C., but the times, phases, etc., will vary only a few minutes for any
part of the Southern States.

To know where the sign is, find the day of the month; and against the day in the
column marked Moon's Signs, you have the sign or place of the moon, and then find
the sign; it will give you the part of the body it is supposed to govern.

TWELVE SIGNS OF THE ZODIAC.

The Head and Face sign.   ♈ Aries the Ram......**Ar.**

♊ Arms.
Gemini ...Gem.
Twins.

♌ Heart.
Leo.......Lion.
Lion.

♎ Reins.
Libra......Lib.
Balance.

♐ Thighs.
Sagittarius Sag.
Bowman.

♒ Legs,
Aquarius...Aq.
Waterman.

♉ Neck.
Taurus ....Tau.
Bull.

♋ Breast.
Cancer ....Can.
Crab.

♍ Bowels.
Virgo ... Vir.
Virgin.

♏ Loins.
Scorpio ..Scorp.
Scorpion.

♑ Knees.
Capricornus Cap
Goat.

The ♓ Pisces the Fishes.....Pisc.

SIGNS.

SPRING SIGNS. { ♈ Arises, or Ram
♉ Taurus, or Bull
♊ Germini, or Twins.

SUMMER SIGNS. { ♋ Cancer or Crab-fish.
♌ Leo, or Lion.
♍ Virgo, or Virgin.

AUTUMN SIGNS. { ♎ Libra, or Balance.
♏ Scorpio, or Scor ion.
♐ Sigittarius, or Bowman

WINTER SIGNS. { ♑ Capricornus, or G at
♒ Aquarius, or Waterman
♓ Pisces, or Fishes.

SIGNS OF THE PLANETS.

☼ Sun.   ☽ Moon.   ♀ Venus.   ♂ Mars.
♃ Jupiter.   ♄ Saturn.   ☌ In Conjunction   ☐ Quadrature
☿ Mercury.   ♅ Uranus.   ♆ Neptune.   ☋ Ascending Node.
⊕ Earth.   ☍ Opposition.   ☋ Descending Node.

MOON'S PHASES.

◐ New Moon.   ☽ First Quarter.   ◑ Full Moon.   ☾ Last Quarter.

Branson's Almanac is a *household word.*—" *Truth.*"

3.—Some men have faith in the laws of health, and hence by obeying those laws they secure physical health and happiness.—*Branson*.

CHRONOLOGICAL, CYCLES AND ERAS.

Dominical Letter	D	Julian Period	6616
Epact	2	Jewish Era	5662
Golden Number	4	Era of Nabonassa	2650
Solar Cycle	8	Olimpiads	2678
Roman Indication	1	Mahommedan Era	1319

MOVABLE FEASTS OF THE CHURCH.

Epiphany	Jan. 6	Palm Sunday	April 5
Septuagessima Sunday	Feb. 8	Easter Sunday	April 12
Sexagessima Sunday	Feb. 15	White Sunday	May 18
Quinquagessima Sunday	Feb. 22	Trinity Sunday	June 7
Ash Wednesday, or Lent	Feb. 25	First Sunday in Advent	Nov. 29
St. Patrick's Day	March 17	Ascension Day	May 21
Good Friday	April 10	First Sunday in Lent	Feb. 24

MORNING STARS.

Mercury will be Morning Star from February 10 to June 3, July 26 to October 3.

Venus will be Morning Star after November 25 till September 17.

Jupiter will be Morning Star till February 19 and after June.

EVENING STARS.

Mercury will be Evening Star until February 2 and October 12.

Venus will be Evening Star until September 17 and April 3.

Jupiter will be Evening Star from February 19 and after June.

ECLIPSES FOR 1903.

I.   An Annular Eclipse of the Sun March 28, invisible at Washington.

II.   A Partial Eclipse of the Moon April 11, partly visible at Washington and in the Eastern portion of North America.

III.   A Partial Eclipse of the Sun, invisible in America.

IV.   A Partial Eclipse of the Moon October 6, invisible at Washington, but visible in Europe, Africa and the Pacific Ocean.

TIDES.

The time of tides can readily be found for the following places by adding the hours and minutes opposite the names to the time when the Moon is south on the day to when the tide is sought. The time when the Moon is south is given in the calendar for every day. The next tide can be found very nearly by adding 12 hours and 29 minutes to the time of the one previous.

The tides are given in local time—add 12 minutes for Eastern Standard

	H. M.		H. M.
Boston	11 12	New York	8 13
Sandy Hook	7 29	Old Point	8 17
Baltimore	6 33	Washington City	7 44
Richmond	4 32	Hatteras Inlet	7 04
Beaufort	7 26	Bald Head	7 26
Southport	7 19	Wilmington	9 06
Charleston	7 26	Savannah	9 33

2.   A man in whose mind his own country is not *first* is a man who himself is not *worthy* to be first in another country.—*Branson*.

THE FOUR SEASONS.

Spring commences ....March 21, 2 P. M.
Summer commences................................June 22, 11 A. M.
Autumn commences.............................September 24, 1 A. M.
Winter commences................. ....December 22, 4 P. M.

HERSCHEL'S WEATHER PROGNOSTICATOR,

For Fortelling the Weather Through all the Lunations of the Year.

This table and the accompanying remarks are the result of many years
actual observation, the whole being constructed on a due consideration
of the attractions of the Sun and Moon in their several positions respecting the Earth, and, by simple inspection, it shows the observer what
kind of weather will most probably follow the entrance of the Moon into
any of its quarters, and that so near the truth as to be seldom or never
found to fail.

If the new moon, first quarter, full moon, or last quarter, happen—	IN SUMMER	IN WINTER
Between midnight and 2 in the morning.............	Fair...............	Hoar frost unless the wind is S. or S. W.
Between 2 and 4 morning	Cold, with frequent showers..........	Snow and stormy.
Between 4 and 6 morning..	Rain	Rain.
Between 6 and 8 morning..	Wind and rain......	Stormy.
Between 8 and 10 morning	Changeable	Cold rain if wind be W., snow if E.
Between 10 and 12 morning	Frequent showers...	Cold and high wind.
Between 12 o'clock at noon	Very rainy.........	Rain and snow.
and 2 in afternoon......	Changeable.......	Fair and mild.
Between 2 and 4 afternoon	Fair	Fair.
Between 4 and 6 aftern'n	Fair if wind N. W., rainy if S. or S.W.	Fair and frosty wind N. or N. E.; rain or snow if S. or S. W.
Between 8 and 10 afternoon	Ditto	Ditto.
Between 10 and midnight	Fair	Fair and frosty.

OBSERVATIONS—1. The nearer the time for the Moon's change, first
quarter, full and last quarter are to midnight, the fairer will be the
weather during the next seven days.
2. The space for this calculation occupies from 10 at night until 2 next
morning.
3. The nearer to midday or noon the phase of the Moon happens, the
more foul or wet weather may be expected during the next seven days.
4. The space for this calculation occupies from 10 in the forenoon until
2 in the afternoon. These observations refer principally to the Summer,
though they affect Spring and Autumn nearly in the same ratio.
5. The Moon's change, first quarter, full and last quarter happening
during six of the afternoon hours, i. e.: from 4 to 10 may be followed by
fair weather, but this is mostly dependent on the wind, as is noted in the
table.
6. Though the weather, from a variety of irregular causes, is more uncertain in the latter part of Autumn, the whole of Winter and beginning
of Spring, yet, in the main, the above observations will apply to those
periods also.
7. To prognosticate correctly, especially in those cases where the wind
is concerned, the observer should be in sight of a good vane, where the
four cardianl points of the heavens are correctly placed.

EDITORIAL.

We are a native of Randolph county, North Carolina, and we had the good fortune to have been born just *one hundred years later* than George Washington. Now, if any one of the readers of BRANSON'S ALMANAC is curious to know our age he can find out by referring to the life of Mr. Washington, who was a *very worthy* young man. You ought to read his life anyway. BRANSON'S ALMANAC has been published steadily since 1865, hence you can see that the ALMANAC is not so old as to be in its *dotage*. We offer here a FRIENDLY GREETING to all our READERS. We are hoping to occupy a place in the CHIMNEY CORNER of every home in our NATIVE STATE.

NOTE—The Agricultural Almanac is now issued in Atlanta, Ga., the Metropolis of the South. Those most convenient to Atlanta can order Almanacs or ads. from our Atlanta publisher, William C. Smith, 19 S. Fourth street. I expect to supply my North Carolina customers from Raleigh as heretofore.   LEVI BRANSON.

A HAPPY NEW YEAR TO YOU! and may you continue to read our Almanac for ONE HUNDRED YEARS TO COME.

MOON'S PHASES.

	BOSTON D. H. M.	NEW YORK D. H. M.	CHICAGO D. H. M.
F.Q.	6 4 56 A.	6 4 56 A.	6 3 56 A.
F.M.	13 9 17 M.	13 9 17 M.	13 8 17 M.
L.Q.	20 6 49 M.	20 6 49 M.	20 5 49 M.
N.M.	28 11 39 M.	28 11 39 M.	28 10 39 M.

D. M.	D. W.	Aspects of Planets and other Miscellaneous Matter	MOON'S SIGNS.	LATITUDE Of New York City, Phila., N. J., Pa., Del., Md., Va., W. Va., Ohio, Illinois, Ind., Neb., Cal. Sun rises. H. M.	Sun sets. H. M.	Moon sets. H. M.	SUN SLOW. M.	LATITUDE Of Charleston, N. Car., S. Car., Ga., Fla., Ala., Miss., Tenn., Ark., La., Tx., N. Mex., Ariz. Sun rises. H. M.	Sun sets. H. M.	Moon sets. H. M.
1	Th	*New Year's Day.*	♑	7 25	4 43	7 35	3	7 3	5 5	7 47
2	Fr	☌ ♃ ☾	♑	7 25	4 44	8 32	4	7 3	5 6	8 42
3	Sa	⊕Battle of Priceton, 1777	♒	7 25	4 45	9 34	4	7 3	5 6	9 39
1. 2d Sunday after Christmas. Luke 2. 9h. 21m. Day's Length, 10h. 4m.										
4	Su	Com. Vanderbilt d. 1877	♒	7 25	4 46	10 35	5	7 3	5 7	10 35
5	M	☌ ☿ ♄	♒	7 25	4 47	11 32	5	7 3	5 8	11 30
6	Tu	☽ *Epiphany.*	♓	7 25	4 48	morn	6	7 3	5 9	morn
7	W	Liberia coloniz'd 1822	♓	7 25	4 49	0 38	6	7 3	5 10	0 31
8	Th	♀ in Apelion ; battle of	♈	7 25	4 50	1 43	7	7 3	5 10	1 32
9	Fr	[New Orleans 1815	♈	7 24	4 51	2 50	7	7 3	5 11	2 35
10	Sa		♉	7 24	4 52	3 58	8	7 3	5 12	3 40
2. 1st Sunday after Epiphany. Luke 2. 9h. 29m. Day's Length, 10h. 11m.										
11	Su	○ Ala. seceded 1861	♉	7 24	4 53	5 5	8	7 2	5 13	4 45
12	M	☌ ♆ ☾	♊	7 24	4 54	6 6	8	7 2	5 14	5 46
13	Tu	♂ in Apelion	♊	7 23	4 55	rises.	9	7 2	5 15	rises.
14	W	Gov. Aycock inaug. 1901.	♋	7 23	4 56	6 39	9	7 2	5 16	6 52
15	Th	Andrew Jackson b 1767	♋	7 23	4 57	7 52	9	7 2	5 16	8 0
16	Fr	L. H. Selby died 1880	♌	7 22	4 58	9 3	10	7 2	5 17	9 7
17	Sa	☿ Greatest Elang East	♌	7 22	4 59	10 9	10	7 2	5 18	10 9
3. 2d Sunday after Epiphany. John 2. 9h. 40m. Day's Length, 10h. 17m.										
18	Su	☌ ♂ ☾ Dan'l W'r b 1782	♍	7 21	5 1	11 12	10	7 2	5 19	11 7
19	M	☿ in ☊ Q. Vic. d 1902	♍	7 21	5 2	morn	11	7 1	5 20	morn
20	Tu	☾ ♂ ♄ ☉ Howard d 1890	♍	7 20	5 3	0 17	11	7 1	5 21	0 7
21	W	Stonewall Js'n b 1824	♎	7 20	5 4	1 18	11	7 1	5 22	1 6
22	Th	Sen. Simmons elected 1901	♎	7 19	5 5	2 17	12	7 1	5 23	2 1
23	Fr	☿ in Per ☿ Stationary	♏	7 18	5 7	3 12	12	7 0	5 24	2 54
24	Sa	☌ ♅ ☾ Sal. Acd. es'd 1851	♏	7 18	5 8	4 5	12	7 0	5 25	3 45
4. 3d Sunday after Epiphany. Matt. 8. 9h. 52m. Day's Length, 10h. 26m.										
25	Su		♐	7 17	5 9	4 54	12	7 0	5 26	4 34
26	M	☌ ☿ ☾—☌ ♀ ☾	♐	7 16	5 10	5 38	13	6 59	5 27	5 19
27	Tu		♐	7 16	5 11	6 19	13	6 59	5 28	6 1
28	W	● ☌ ☿ ☾—☌ ♄ ☾	♑	7 15	5 13	sets	13	6 59	5 29	sets
29	Th		♑	7 14	5 14	6 27	13	6 58	5 30	6 36
30	Fr	☌ ♀ ♃—♀ gre'st lat. S.	♒	7 13	5 15	7 27	13	6 57	5 31	7 33
31	Sa		♒	7 12	5 16	8 28	14	6 56	5 32	8 30

Weather for January.—1, 2, 3, 4, 5, 6 hoar frost; 7, 8, 9, 10, 11, 12 snow, if wind is from the east; 13, 14, 15, 16, 17, 18 stormy; 19, 20, 21, 22, 23, 24, 25, 26, 27, 28 cold, high winds; 29, 30, 31 snow, if wind be from the east.

FARM AND GARDEN WORK FOR JANUARY.—Plant peas, beans, beets, onions, Irish potatoes, horseradish; sow turnips, spinach, lettuce, raddish, parsley, carrots, salsify. Plant early peas; artichokes must now be dressed, also asparagus beds; this is the proper time to sow early spring tomatoes, etc.

NORTH CAROLINA COLLEGES AND OTHER GRADUATING SCHOOLS.

(Names, Character and Location.)

Asheville Female College (Methodist) ....Asheville
Baptist Female University (Baptist).........................Raleigh
Catawba College ... .Newton
Chowan Female Institute (Baptist).....................Murfreesboro
Claremont Female College (Reformed Church of U. S.).......Hickory
Concordia College (Lutheran)...............................Conover
Davenport Female College (Methodist) ....Lenoir
Davidson High School (Presbyterian) ....Davidson
Elon College (Christian).........................Elon College
Greensboro Female College (Methodist)...................Greensboro
Guilford College (Friends)................... Guilford College
Hayesville College (Independent) ....Hayesville
Judson College (Methodist)   ....Hendersonville
Kinston College (Independent) ....Kinston
Louisburg Female College (Methodist)......................Louisburg
Littleton Female College (Methodist).......................Littleton
Mt. Omœna Seminary (Lutheran) ....Mt. Pleasant
Mt. St. Joseph Academy (Catholic) ....Asheville
North Carolina College (Lutheran)..................Mt. Pleasant
N C. Agricultural and Mechanical College (State) ....Raleigh
Oxford Female Seminary (Baptist).........................Oxford
Oak Ridge Institute (Independent).....................Oak Ridge
Peace Institute (Independent)..........................Raleigh
Rutherford College, Burke Co. (Methodist)........Rutherford College
St. Mary's College (Catholic) ....Belmont
Shelby Female College (Independent)......................Shelby
St. Mary's School (Episcopal) ....Raleigh
Salem Academy (Moravian) ....Salem
St Paul's Seminary (Lutheran Theological)..................Hickory
State Normal and Industrial College (State) ....Greensboro
Trinity College (Methodist)...........................Durham
University of North Carolina (State) -----..........Chapel Hill
Weaverville College (Methodist)..........................Weaverville
Wake Forest College (Baptist)........................Wake Forest
Elizabeth College (Lutheran) ....Charlotte
Presbyterian College (Presbyterian)..... ....Charlotte
Whitsett Institute (Independent).... ....Whitsett
Eastern Carolina Female College (Disciples of Christ)..........Wilson

COLORED SCHOOLS—Graduating.

Agricultural and Mechanical College (State)...............Greensboro
Bennett Seminary (Methodist)..........................Greensboro
Biddle University (Presbyterian)..........................Charlotte
Building and Trade's College (Independent)...........Southern Pines
Franklinton Christian College (Christian).................Franklinton
Kittrell College (A. M. E. C.)...........................Kittrell
Normal School (State)........................Elizabeth City
Normal School (State)..........................Goldsboro
Normal School (State)...........................Salisbury
Normal School (State) .. ..Plymouth
Normal School (State) ....Fayetteville
Normal School (State)   ....Franklinton
St. Augustine Normal College (Episcopal) ....Raleigh
Shaw University (Baptist).... . ... ..Raleigh
Fotia Female Seminary (Presbyterian).......................Concord
er Industrial Academy and Normal School (State) ....Winston

MOON'S PHASES.

☾	BOSTON D. H. M.	NEW YORK D. H. M.	CHICAGO D. H. M.
F.Q.	5 5 12 M.	5 5 12 M.	5 4 12 M.
F.M.	11 7 58 A.	11 7 58 A.	11 6 58 A.
L.Q.	19 1 23 M.	19 1 23 M.	19 0 23 M.
N.M.	27 5 20 M.	27 5 20 M.	27 4 20 M.

D. M.	D. W.	Aspects of planets and other Miscellaneous Matter	MOON'S SIGNS.	LATITUDE Of New York City, Phila., N. J., Pa., Del., Md., Va., W. Va., Ohio, Illinois, Ind., Neb., Cal. Sun rises. H. M.	Sun sets. H. M.	Moon sets. H. M.	SUN SLOW. M.	LATITUDE Of Charleston, N. Car., S. Car., Ga., Fla., Ala., Miss., Tenn., Ark., La., Tx., N. Mex., Ariz. Sun rises. H. M.	Sun sets. H. M.	Moon sets. H. M.
5. 4th Sunday after Epiphany.		*Matt. 8.*		*10h. 6m.*		*Day's Length, 10h. 37m.*				
1	Su	☌ ☿ ☉ Inferior	♒	7 11	5 17	9 26	14	6 56	5 33	9 25
2	M	☿ Gr Hel Lat North	♓	7 10	5 18	10 28	14	6 55	5 34	10 22
3	Tu	Gen. R. Baringer d 1895	♓	7 9	5 20	11 32	14	6 54	5 34	11 23
4	W	Galvani d 1770	♈	7 8	5 21	morn	14	6 54	5 35	morn
5	Th	Branson's b'day 1832	♈	7 7	5 22	0 38	14	6 53	5 36	0 24
6	Fr	Suez Canal com 1867	♉	7 6	5 24	1 43	14	6 52	5 37	1 26
7	Sa	Pope Pius IX d 1878	♉	7 5	5 25	2 47	14	6 51	5 38	2 28
6. Septuagesima Sunday.		*Matt. 20.*		*10h. 22m.*		*Day's Length, 10h. 49m.*				
8	Su	☌ ♆ ☾ b Roanoke I 1862	♊	7 4	5 26	3 50	14	6 50	5 39	3 30
9	M	Gen Hancock d 1886	♊	7 2	5 27	4 46	14	6 50	5 40	4 27
10	Tu	Treaty of Paris 1763	♋	7 1	5 28	5 37	14	6 49	5 41	5 21
11	W	Thos. Edison b 1847	♋	7 0	5 29	rises.	14	6 48	5 42	rises.
12	Th	Pres. Seymour d 1886	♌	6 59	5 31	6 37	14	6 47	5 43	6 44
13	Fr	☌ ☿ ♄ Fern Wood d 1881	♌	6 57	5 32	7 49	14	6 46	5 44	7 50
14	Sa	♀ st *St. Valentine's Day*	♌	6 56	5 33	8 53	14	6 45	5 44	8 51
7. Sexagesima Sunday.		*Luke 8.*		*10h. 40m.*		*Day's Length, 11h. 1m.*				
15	Su	☌ ♂ ☾ Fire in Dur. 1881	♍	6 55	5 35	10 1	14	6 44	5 45	9 53
16	M	Judge Battle buried 1879	♍	6 53	5 36	11 4	14	6 43	5 46	10 53
17	Tu		♎	6 52	5 37	morn	14	6 42	5 47	11 51
18	W	♂ station'y Luther d 1546	♎	6 51	5 38	0 6	14	6 41	5 48	morn
19	Th	☌ ♃ ☉ *Lent begins*	♏	6 50	5 39	1 4	14	6 40	5 49	0 47
20	Fr	Sen Douglas d 1895	♏	6 49	5 40	1 58	14	6 39	5 50	1 39
21	Sa	☌ ♅ ☾ Gov Clark d 1874	♏	6 48	5 43	2 48	14	6 38	5 50	2 29
8. Quinquagesima Sunday.		*Luke 18.*		*10h. 56m.*		*Day's Length, 11h. 14m.*				
22	Su	*Washington's Birthday*	♐	6 47	5 43	3 34	14	6 37	5 51	3 15
23	M	Battle Buena Vista 1847	♐	6 45	5 45	4 16	14	6 36	5 52	3 58
24	Tu	Monteray surrend'd 1846	♑	6 44	5 46	4 55	13	6 35	5 53	4 39
25	W	☌ ♄ ☾ also ☌ ♀ ☾	♑	6 43	5 48	5 28	13	6 34	5 54	5 15
26	Th	☿ in ☋—☌ ♃ ☾	♑	6 42	5 49	6 1	13	6 32	5 55	5 52
27	Fr	☿ Gr Elong West	♒	6 40	5 50	sets	13	6 31	5 55	sets
28	Sa	Dr Wingate d 1879	♒	6 37	5 51	7 18	13	6 30	5 56	7 18

WEATHER FOR FEBRUARY.—1, 2, 3, 4, 5, 6, 7, 8, 9, 10 rainy; 11, 12, 13, 14, 15, 16, 17, 18 snow, if wind south or southwest; 19, 20, 21, 22, 23, 24, 25, 26 hoar frost; 27, 28 expect frost.

☞ FARM AND GARDEN WORK FOR MARCH.—Plant bush squash, pumpkins, water and muskmelons, okra, Guinea squash or egg-plant, sugar beets, carrots, beans, peas, radishes, lettuce, corn, celery (first crop), tanyah and mangoes in the low country and elsewhere as soon as danger of frost is over.

This is the first planting month for cotton, corn and rice. Plant your high lands first; leave the low lands for April. Plant rice about the 20th of the month.

THAT WONDERFUL TOP DRAWER.

If anything is *lost* from cellar to garret,
　Needed by master or even wood sawer,
Very likely you'l find it, most surely you'll find it,
　In the *top drawer*, that HANDY *top drawer*.

If anything is *wanted*, in cellar or garret,
　To mend the door latch, or dress the hall floor,
Go look for it quickly—yes, quickly look for it—
　In the *top drawer*, that SHALLOW *top drawer*.

If anything is *shaky*, in cellar or garret,
　And needs tying up to make it last more,
Go find a good string—yes, also a stringlet—
　Right in the *top drawer*, that STRINGY *top drawer*.

If anything is *broken* in cellar or garret,
　And needs to be mended to look like of yore,
You'll find scraps of glue, also a gimlet,
　Down in the *top drawer*, that LOVELY *top drawer*.

If anything is *found*, from cellar to garret,
　Not needed at once, nor yet for an hour,
Where will you put it?—say, where will you put it?
　Surely in the *top drawer*, that WONDERFUL *top drawer*.
　　　　　　　　　　　　　　　　　—*Branson.*

WHEN EASTER COMES.

A friend of the *Boston Transcript*, "E. M. H.," writes: "I was attracted by the suggestion in your paper to-day to compose a rhyme which would give the reasons for the movable nature of the Easter feast." The following clever rhymes are added　They should be taught in the primary schools :

" Thirty days hath September,"
　Every person can remember;
But to know when Easter comes,
　Puzzles even scholars some.

When March the twenty-first is past,
　Just watch the silvery moon,
And when you see it full and round,
　Know Easter'll be here soon.

After the moon has reached its full,
　Then Easter will be here
The very Sunday after,
　In each and every year.

And if it hap on Sunday
　The moon should reach its height,
The Sunday following this event
　Will be the Easter bright.

The waltz had its beginning in Germany.

From Poland came the stately polonaise, or polacca and mazourka.

MOON'S PHASES.	BOSTON D. H. M.	NEW YORK D. H. M.	CHICAGO D. H. M.
F.Q.	4 8 51 A.	4 8 51 A.	4 7 51 A.
F.M.	11 7 18 A.	11 7 18 A.	11 6 18 A.
L.Q.	19 4 30 A.	19 4 30 A.	19 3 30 A.
N.M.	27 8 31 M.	27 8 31 M.	27 7 31 M.

D. M.	D. W.	Aspects of Planets and other Miscellaneous Matter	MOON'S SIGNS.	LATITUDE Of New York City, Phila., N. J., Pa., Del., Md., Va., W. Va., Ohio, Illinois, Ind., Neb., Cal. — Sun rises. H. M.	Sun sets. H. M.	Moon sets. H. M.	SUN SLOW. M.	LATITUDE Of Charleston, N. Car., S. Car., Ga., Fla., Ala., Miss., Tenn., Ark., La., Tx., N. Mex., Ariz. — Sun rises. H. M.	Sun sets. H. M.	Moon sets. H. M.
1	W	*All Fools Day*	♈	5 43	6 25	10 32	4	5 49	6 20	10 14
2	Th	Richmond, Va., surd 1865	♉	5 41	6 26	11 34	4	5 48	6 20	11 15
3	Fr	☌ ♆ ☾ P Cooper d1888	♉	5 40	6 27	morn	4	5 46	6 21	morn
4	Sa	Gen. Harrison d 1871	♊	5 38	6 28	0 33	3	5 45	6 22	0 14
14. Palm Sunday.		*Matt. 27.*		*12h. 53m.*		*Day's Length, 12h. 38m.*				
5	Su	Jefferson born 1743	♊	5 36	6 29	1 26	3	5 44	6 22	1 8
6	M	Battle of Shiloh 1862	♋	5 35	6 30	2 12	3	5 42	6 23	1 57
7	Tu	Socrates d B. C. 333	♋	5 33	6 31	2 54	2	5 41	6 24	2 43
8	W	De Medica d 1492	♌	5 32	6 32	3 30	2	5 40	6 25	3 24
9	Th	R. E. Lee sur 1865	♌	5 30	6 33	4 5	2	5 39	6 25	4 2
10	Fr	☌ ♂ ☾ *Good Friday*	♍	5 28	6 35	4 41	2	5 37	6 26	4 42
11	Sa	☾ in Par Eclp, vis	♍	5 27	6 36	rises.	1	5 36	6 27	rises.
15. Easter Sunday.		*John 20.*		*13h. 12m.*		*Day's Length, 12h. 52m.*				
12	Su	☌ ☿ ☉ sup *Easter Monday*	♍	5 25	6 37	7 32	1	5 35	6 27	7 22
13	M	Raleigh sur 1865	♎	5 24	6 38	8 35	1	5 34	6 28	8 20
14	Tu	Lincoln Assinated 1865	♎	5 22	6 39	9 35	0	5 32	6 29	9 18
15	W	Andrew Johnson ing 1865	♏	5 21	6 40	10 30	0	5 31	6 29	10 11
16	Th	☌ ♅ ☾ M Arnold d 1865	♏	5 19	6 41	11 21	ft	5 30	6 30	11 1
17	Fr	☿ in ☊ Dr Frank'n d 1790	♐	5 18	6 42	morn	0	5 29	6 31	11 47
18	Sa	M Luther at Worms 1521	♐	5 16	6 43	0 6	0	5 28	6 32	morn
16. Low Sunday.		*John 20.*		*13h. 29m.*		*Day's Length, 13h. 6m.*				
19	Su	[First newspaper	♐	5 15	6 44	0 47	1	5 26	6 32	0 29
20	M	☌ ♄ ☾ in U. S. 1704	♑	5 13	6 45	1 24	1	5 25	6 33	1 9
21	Tu	☿ in Perhelion	♑	5 12	6 46	1 57	1	5 24	6 34	1 46
22	W	Oklahoma opened 1889	♒	5 10	6 47	2 29	1	5 23	6 35	2 20
23	Th	☌ ♄ ☾ Cervantes d 1616	♒	5 9	6 48	2 58	2	5 22	6 35	2 54
24	Fr	Dr. McKee d 1875	♒	5 8	6 49	3 28	2	5 21	6 36	3 27
25	Sa	Dr. Aldert Smedes d 1877	♓	5 6	6 50	4 4	2	5 20	6 36	4 6
17. 2d Sunday after Easter.		*John 10.*		*13h. 46m.*		*Day's Length, 13h. 18m.*				
26	Su	Gen Johns'n sur 1865	♓	5 5	6 51	4 37	2	5 19	6 37	4 43
27	M	Emerson d 1882	♈	5 3	6 52	sets	2	5 18	6 38	sets
28	Tu	☌ ♀ ☾ Monroe b 1758	♈	5 2	6 53	8 19	2	5 17	6 39	8 3
29	W	☌ ♀ ☾ Louisia ceded 1803	♉	5 1	6 54	9 24	3	5 16	6 40	9 6
30	Th	♀ in Perihelion	♉	4 59	6 55	10 27	3	5 15	6 41	10 7

WEATHER FOR APRIL.—1, 2, 3, 4, 5, 6, 7, 8, 9, 10 changeable; 11, 12, 13, 14, 15, 16, 17 18 fair, if wind northwest, rain, if wind south or southwest; 19, 20, 21, 22, 23, 24, 25, 26 fair; 27, 28, 29, 30 fair, if wind northwest, rainy, if south or southwest.

FARM AND GARDEN WORK FOR APRIL.—Whatever has been omitted in March, do not neglect any longer. Sow green glazed cabbage, pickling cabbage, full crop of cauliflower and broccoli, okra, tomatoes, peppers, beets, carrots, leeks, melons, cucumbers, celery.

Full crops of corn, cotton and rice should be put in during this month. Plant your lowland corn. Commence early to hoe your young cotton, and thin out to stand. Plant pumpkins for a field crop.

MOON'S PHASES.

	BOSTON D. H. M.	NEW YORK D. H. M.	CHICAGO D. H. M.
F.Q.	4 2 26 M.	4 2 26 M.	4 1 26 M.
F.M.	11 8 18 M.	11 8 18 M.	11 7 18 M.
L.Q.	19 10 18 M.	19 10 18 M.	19 9 18 M.
N.M.	26 5 50 A.	26 5 50 A.	26 4 50 A.

D. M.	D. W.	Aspects of Planets and other Miscellaneous Matter	Moon's Signs.	Latitude of New York City, Phila., N. J., Pa., Del., Md., Va., W. Va., Ohio, Illinois, Ind., Neb., Cal. — Sun rises. H. M.	Sun sets. H. M.	Moon sets. H. M.	Sun Fast. M.	Latitude of Charleston, N. Car., S. Car., Ga., Fla., Ala., Miss., Tenn., Ark., La., Tx., N. Mex., Ariz. — Sun rises. H. M.	Sun sets. H. M.	Moon sets. H. M.
1	Fr	☿ Gr Hel Lat North	♊	4 58	6 56	11 22	3	5 14	6 41	11 4
2	Sa	(May day)	♊	4 56	6 57	morn	3	5 13	6 42	11 56
18. 3d Sunday after Easter. John 16. 14h. 3m. Day's Length. 13h. 33m.										
3	Su		♋	4 55	6 58	0 12	3	5 12	6 42	morn
4	M		♋	4 54	6 59	0 56	3	5 11	6 43	0 42
5	Tu		♌	4 53	7 0	1 34	3	5 10	6 44	1 25
6	W		♌	4 52	7 2	2 8	3	5 9	6 45	2 4
7	Th	☌ ♂ ☾	♌	4 51	7 3	2 41	4	5 8	6 45	2 40
8	Fr		♍	4 50	7 4	3 16	4	5 7	6 46	3 19
9	Sa		♍	4 49	7 5	3 48	4	5 6	6 47	3 56
19. 4th Sunday after Easter. John 16. 14h. 19m. Day's Length, 13h. 42m.										
10	Su	☿ Gr Elang E, ☌ Stat'y	♎	4 47	7 6	4 22	4	5 5	6 47	4 33
11	M		♎	4 46	7 7	rises.	4	5 4	6 48	rises.
12	Tu		♏	4 45	7 8	8 20	4	5 4	6 49	8 2
13	W		♏	4 44	7 8	9 13	4	5 3	6 50	8 54
14	Th		♏	4 43	7 9	10 1	4	5 2	6 50	9 42
15	Fr	☌ ♅ ☾	♐	4 42	7 10	10 44	4	5 1	6 51	10 26
16	Sa	☌ ♀ ♆	♐	4 41	7 11	11 22	4	5 1	6 52	11 7
20. Rogation Sunday. John 16. 14h. 31m. Day's Length, 13h. 53m.										
17	Su		♑	4 41	7 12	11 59	4	5 0	6 53	11 45
18	M	☌ ♄ ☾	♑	4 40	7 13	morn	4	4 59	6 53	morn
19	Tu		♑	4 39	7 14	0 29	4	4 59	6 54	0 20
20	W	♄ Stationary	♒	4 38	7 15	0 59	4	4 58	6 55	0 52
21	Th	☌ ♃ ☾ *Ascension Day*	♒	4 37	7 15	1 28	4	4 58	6 55	1 25
22	Fr	☿ Gr Hel Lat N, ☿ Sta'y	♓	4 37	7 16	2 0	4	4 57	6 56	2 1
23	Sa		♓	4 36	7 17	2 33	4	4 56	6 57	2 38
21. Sunday after Ascension. John 15-16. 14h. 43m. Day's Length, 14h. 1m.										
24	Su		♈	4 35	7 18	3 7	3	4 56	6 57	3 15
25	M	☿ in ☋	♈	4 35	7 19	3 45	3	4 55	6 58	3 58
26	Tu		♈	4 34	7 20	4 29	3	4 55	6 59	4 46
27	W		♉	4 34	7 21	sets	3	4 55	6 59	sets
28	Th	☌ ☿ ☾	♉	4 33	7 21	9 13	3	4 54	7 0	8 53
29	Fr	☌ ♆ ☾	♊	4 33	7 22	10 7	3	4 54	7 1	9 50
30	Sa	☌ ♀ ☾	♊	4 32	7 23	10 55	3	4 54	7 1	10 40
22. Whit Sunday. John 14. 14h. 52m. Day's Length, 14h. 9m.										
31	Su	Fenian raid, 1866.	♋	4 32	7 24	11 36	3	4 53	7 2	11 25

Weather for May.—1, 2, 3 cold, with frequent showers; 4, 5, 6, 7, 8, 9, 10 cold rains; 11, 12, 13, 14, 15 changeable; 16, 17, 18 variable; 19, 20, 21, 22, 23, 24, 25 frequent showers; 26, 27, 28, 29, 30, 31 look for heavy rains.

See Dr. Green's Sons Ad. on Page 39.

FARM AND GARDEN WORK FOR MAY.—Plant snap beans and squashes. Sow cabbage for winter use, cauliflower, broccoli, celery, beets, carrots, salsify. Plant cucumbers, melons and pumpkins for late crops. Gather herbs for drying; always dry gently in the shade.

Look well to your hoeing and plowing. Continue to plant corn in low lands. Sow first crop of early cow peas. Rice planting is generally postponed until June, as the birds are very bad in May, and the May bird is exceedingly destructive.

Government of North Carolina.

EXECUTIVE DEPARTMENT.

Charles B. Aycock, of Wayne county, Governor; salary $4,000 and furnished house, fuel and lights.

P. M. Pearsall, of Craven county, Private Secretary to the Governor; salary $1,200 and commissions.

W. D. Turner, of Iredell county, Lieutenant-Governor and President of the Senate.

Miss Julia Howell, of Wayne county, Executive Clerk, salary $600.

J. Bryan Grimes, of Pitt county, Secretary of State; salary $2,000 and certain fees, and $1,000 extra for clerical assistance.

Geo. W. Norwood, of Wake county, Chief Clerk to Secretary of State; salary $1,000.

W. S. Wilson, of Caswell county, Corporation Clerk; salary $1,200.

Mrs Mary G. Smith, stenographer.

B. F. Dixon, of Cleveland county, Auditor; salary $1,500, and $1,000 extra for clerical assistance.

Hilary T. Hudson, Cleveland county, Chief Clerk to Auditor; salary $1,000.

W. H. Bain, of Wake county, Pension Clerk; salary $750.

Mrs. F. W. Smith, of Wake county, stenographer; salary $500.

B. R. Lacy, of Wake county, Treasurer; salary $3,000.

W F. Moody, of Mecklenburg county, Chief Clerk to Treasurer; salary $1,500.

J. P. Arrington, of Nash county, Clerk for Charitable and Penal Institutions; salary $1,000.

P. B. Fleming, Franklin county, Teller of the Treasury Department; salary $750.

Miss M. F. Jones, of Buncombe county, stenographer; salary $720.

J. Y. Joyner, Guilford county, Superintendent of Public Instruction; salary $1,500, and $500 per annum for traveling expenses.

John Duckett, of Robeson county, Clerk; salary $1,000.

Robt. D. Gilmer, of Haywood county, Attorney-General; salary $2,000.

Miss Sarah Burkhead, of Columbus county; salary $600.

B. S. Royster, Granville county, Adjutant-General; salary $600.

M. O. Sherrill, Catawba county, State Librarian; salary $1,250.

Miss Carrie E. Broughton, Assistant Librarian; salary $300.

C. C. Cherry, Edgecombe county, Superintendent of Public Buildings and Grounds; salary $850.

L. W. Lancaster, Wake county, State Standard Keeper; salary $100.

N. C. BOARD OF CORPORATION COMMISSIONERS.

Commissioners.—Franklin McNeill, New Hanover county, Chairman; term expires January, 1907. Sam L. Rogers, Macon county; term expires 1905. D. H. Abbott, Pamlico county; term expires April 1, 1903—salary $2,500 each. Henry C. Brown, Surry county, Clerk, salary $1,500; Miss Riddick, Wake county, stenographer, salary $600.

Regular sessions of the court are held at Raleigh. Special session are also held at other places, under such regulations as made by the Commission.

Offices of the Commissioners are located in the Agricultural Building.

MOON'S PHASES.

	BOSTON D. H. M.	NEW YORK D. H. M.	CHICAGO D. H. M.
F.Q.	2 8 24 M.	2 8 24 M.	2 7 24 M.
F.M.	9 10 8 A.	9 10 8 A.	9 9 8 A.
L.Q.	18 1 44 M.	18 1 44 M.	18 0 44 M.
N.M.	25 1 11 M.	25 1 11 M.	25 0 11 M.

LATITUDE Of New York City, Phila., N. J., Pa., Del., Md., Va., W. Va., Ohio, Illinois, Ind., Neb., Cal.

LATITUDE Of Charleston, N. Car., S. Car., Ga., Fla., Ala., Miss., Tenn., Ark., La., Tx., N. Mex., Ariz.

D. M.	D. W.	Aspects of Planets and other Miscellaneous Matter	Moon's Signs	Sun rises. H. M.	Sun sets. H. M.	Moon sets. H. M.	Sun Slow. M.	Sun rises. H. M.	Sun sets. H. M.	Moon sets. H. M.
1	M	Battle of Seven Pines 1862	♋	4 31	7 25	morn	3	4 53	7 2	morn
2	Tu	Marietta capt'd 1864	♌	4 31	7 25	0 12	2	4 53	7 3	0 5
3	W	☌ ☿ ☉ Inf., ☌ ♂ ☾	♌	4 30	7 26	0 45	2	4 52	7 3	0 43
4	Th	☿ in Aphelion	♍	4 30	7 27	1 20	2	4 52	7 4	1 22
5	Fr	Telegraph in China 1871	♍	4 29	7 27	1 51	2	4 52	7 4	1 58
6	Sa	Patrick Henry died 1799	♎	4 29	7 28	2 24	2	4 52	7 5	2 33
23. Trinity Sunday.		*John 3.*		*14h. 59m.*		*Day's Length, 14h. 13m.*				
7	Su	Robert Bruce died 1329	♎	4 29	7 28	2 56	2	4 52	7 5	3 10
8	M	Battle of Cross Keys 1862	♎	4 28	7 29	3 35	1	4 51	7 6	3 51
9	Tu	Georgia chart'd 1732	♏	4 28	7 29	rises.	1	4 51	7 6	rises.
10	W	☌ ⛢ ☾ Dickn's d 1870	♏	4 28	7 30	7 57	1	4 51	7 7	7 38
11	Th	Gen Sher. at Kens'w 1864	♐	4 28	7 30	8 41	1	4 51	7 7	8 22
12	Fr	N. C. R. R. chart'd 1848	♐	4 28	7 31	9 22	1	4 51	7 8	9 5
13	Sa	□ ♃ ☉ Gen. Scott b 1786	♑	4 28	7 31	9 59	0	4 51	7 8	9 44
24. 1st Sunday after Trinity.		*Luke 16.*		*15h. 4m.*		*Day's Length, 14h. 17m.*				
14	Su	☌ ♄ ☾ U. S. Flag ad 1777	♑	4 28	7 32	10 31	0	4 51	7 8	10 20
15	M	☿ Stationary; ☌ ⛢ ☉	♑	4 28	7 32	11 2	sl	4 51	7 9	10 53
16	Tu	Cornwallis ev. Rich. 1781	♒	4 28	7 32	11 30	0	4 51	7 9	11 25
17	W	☌ ♃ ☾ Addison d 1719	♒	4 28	7 33	11 58	0	4 51	7 10	11 58
18	Th	Bat of Waterloo 1815	♓	4 28	7 33	morn	1	4 51	7 10	morn
19	Fr	Council of Nice 325	♓	4 28	7 33	0 33	1	4 51	7 10	0 35
20	Sa		♓	4 28	7 34	1 3	1	4 52	7 11	1 10
25. 2d Sunday after Trinity.		*Luke 14.*		*15h. 5m.*		*Day's Length, 14h. 19m.*				
21	Su	Shafter's Army lands 1898	♈	4 29	7 34	1 39	1	4 52	7 11	1 50
22	M	☉ Sun enters ♋	♈	4 29	7 34	2 18	2	4 52	7 11	2 33
23	Tu	Bat Chickahom. 1862	♉	4 29	7 35	3 6	2	4 52	7 11	3 23
24	W	*St. John Bap. Day*	♉	4 29	7 35	4 10	2	4 53	7 11	4 19
25	Th	☌ ☿ ☾; ♂ in ♉	♊	4 30	7 35	sets	2	4 53	7 11	sets
26	Fr	☌ ♆ ☾ L Bonapart d 1846	♊	4 30	7 35	8 46	2	4 53	7 11	8 30
27	Sa	☿ Gr Elon West	♋	4 30	7 35	9 32	3	4 53	7 12	9 19
26. 3d Sunday after Trinity.		*Luke 15.*		*15h. 4m.*		*Day's Length, 14h. 18m.*				
28	Su	☌ ♀ ☾ 3d Man ex s'd 1898	♋	4 31	7 35	10 11	3	4 54	7 12	10 3
29	M	Henry Clay died 1852	♌	4 31	7 35	10 46	3	4 54	7 12	10 43
30	Tu	Montezuma died 1430	♌	4 32	7 35	11 24	3	4 54	7 12	11 24

Weather for June.—1, 2, 3, 4, 5, 6, 7, 8 changeable; 9, 10, 11, 12, 13, 14, 15, 16, 17 expect fair weather; 18, 19, 20, 21, 22, 23, 24 fair; 25, 26, 27, 28, 29, 30 more fair weather.

See Dr. Green's Sons Ad. on Page 39.

FARM AND GARDEN WORK FOR JUNE.—Sow full crops of cabbage for
fall and winter use. Cauliflower and broccoli may be sown, also a few
carrots. Continue to sow tomatoes, okra, radishes, snap beans. Transplant leeks; pull and dry onions, garlic and eschalots. A few cucumbers
and melons plant for a late crop, and a few ruta baga turnips.

Keep constantly at the plow and hoe; this is the most important grass
month. If the vines from your sweet potato sprout beds are fit you can
draw and plant out first good rain. Sow cow peas between your corn
hills and rows. The end of this month is a good time to put in the first
crop of standing field peas.

BUREAU OF LABOR AND PRINTING.

Henry B. Varner, of Davidson county, Commissioner; salary $1,500.
W. E. Faison, of Wake county, Assistant Commissioner; salary $900.
Miss Daisy Thompson, of Wake county, stenographer

NORTH CAROLINA DEPARTMENT OF AGRICULTURE.

Located at Raleigh, in the department building especially constructed
for the purpose.

Officers.—S. L. Patterson, of Caldwell county, Commissioner, salary
$2,000; T. K. Bruner, of Rowan county, Secretary, salary $1,500; W. A.
Graham, of Lincoln county, Inspection Clerk, salary $900; H. P. Dortch,
of Wayne county, Inspection Clerk, salary $900; Miss L. D. Rives, of
Nash county, stenographer, salary $600. During the fertilizer season a
number of inspectors are emplyed, who draw samples of all fertilizer on
sale in the State for analyzation.

Analytical Division.—B. W. Kilgore, State Chemist, salary $2,500;
W. M. Allen, First Assistant, salary $1,200; C. B. Williams, Second As-
sistant, salary $1,200; S. E. Asbury, Third Assistant, $900; W. G. Haywood, Fourth Assistant, salary $720; F. C. Lamb, Fifth Assistant, salary
$720; Miss Mamie Birdsong, of Wake county, stenographer, salary $800.

Biological Division.—Dr. Tait Butler, State Veterinarian, salary $2,000
and traveling expenses; Frank Sherman, Jr., Entomologist, salary $1,200;
Gerald McCarthy, Botanist and Biologist, salary $1,200.

The Department is maintained by a tonnage tax of 20 cents per ton on
fertilizers. The fund arising from this charge is used to defray the expenses of the Department.

State Museum.—In the Agricultural building, embracing geology,
mineralogy, forestry, agriculture and natural history, under the control
of the Board of Agriculture. J. A. Holmes, T. K. Bruner and H. H.
Brimley are Directors. H. H. Brimley is Curator, salary $1,200; Miss A.
Lewis, Usher, salary, $480.

State Board of Agriculture.—S. L. Patterson, ex officio, Chairman;
J. S. Cunningham, Cunningham; A. T. McCallum, Red Springs; W. A.
Graham, Machpelah; P. B. Kennedy, Daltonia; E. L. Daughtridge,
Rocky Mount; William Dunn, New Bern; J. P. McRae, Laurinburg;
A. Cannon, Horse Shoe; J. B. Coffield, Everetts, C. N. Allen, Auburn;
Howard Browning, Littleton; J. C. Ray Boone; G. Ed. Flow, Monroe;
J. R. Joyce, Reidsville.

NORTH CAROLINA GEOLOGICAL SURVEY.

J. A. Holmes, State Geologist; W. W. Ashe, Forester; E. W. Myers,
Engineer, in charge of water-power investigation; Jos. H. Pratt, Mineralogist; R. H. Sykes, Secretary. The general office of the Survey is in the
Agricultural Building, Raleigh. The office work of the Survey is done
mainly at Chapel Hill.

BOARD OF INTERNAL IMPROVEMENTS.

Members of the Board are appointed by the Governor. The present
Board, appointees of Governor Aycock, are: B. C. Beckwith, of Raleigh,
and B. W. Ballard, of Franklinton.

STATE INSURANCE DEPARTMENT.

Office is in Capitol Building. James R. Young, of Vance county, Insurance Commissioner, salary $2,000. Nominated by the Governor and

MOON'S PHASES.

☽	BOSTON D. H. M.	NEW YORK D. H. M.	CHICAGO D. H. M.
F.Q.	1 4 2 A.	1 4 2 A.	1 3 2 A.
F.M.	9 0 43 A.	9 0 43 A.	9 11 43 M.
L.Q.	17 2 24 A.	17 2 24 A.	17 1 24 A.
N.M.	24 7 46 M.	24 7 46 M.	24 6 46 M.
F.Q.	31 2 15 M.	31 2 15 M.	31 1 15 M.

D. M.	D. W.	Aspects of Planets and other Miscellaneous Matter	☽ Moon's Signs	Latitude of New York City, Phila., N. J., Pa., Del., Md., Va., W. Va., Ohio, Illinois, Ind., Neb., Cal. — Sun rises H. M.	Sun sets H. M.	Moon sets H. M.	Sun Slow M.	Latitude of Charleston, N. Car., S. Car., Ga., Fla., Ala., Miss., Tenn., Ark., La., Tx., N. Mex., Ariz. — Sun rises H. M.	Sun sets H. M.	Moon sets H. M.
1	W	☌ ♂ ☾	♍	4 32	7 35	11 56	3	4 55	7 12	11 59
2	Th	⊕ in Aphelion	♍	4 33	7 34	morn	4	4 55	7 12	morn
3	Fr	Bat of Cold Harbor 1864	♎	4 33	7 34	0 27	4	4 56	7 12	0 36
4	Sa	*Independence Day 1776*	♎	4 34	7 34	1 1	4	4 56	7 12	1 13
27. 4th Sunday after Trinity.		*Luke 6.*		*15h. 0m.*		*Day's Length,*		*14h. 14m.*		
5	Su	Telegraph in China 1871	♎	4 34	7 34	1 37	4	4 57	7 11	1 52
6	M	□ ♅ ☉ Hamlin d 1891	♏	4 35	7 33	2 16	4	4 57	7 11	2 34
7	Tu	☌ ♅ ☾ Sheridan d 1876	♏	4 36	7 33	2 59	5	4 58	7 11	3 18
8	W	Hon. J. J. Davis d 1892	♐	4 36	7 33	3 45	5	4 58	7 11	4 4
9	Th	♀ Gr Elong E	♐	4 37	7 32	rises.	5	4 59	7 11	rises.
10	Fr	Ralph Graves d 1889	♐	4 38	7 32	8 0	5	4 59	7 10	7 44
11	Sa	☌ ♄ ☾ J Q Adams b 1767	♑	4 38	7 32	8 34	5	4 59	7 10	8 21
28. 5th Sunday after Trinity.		*Luke 5.*		*14h. 52m.*		*Day's Length,*		*14h. 10m.*		
12	Su	☌ ☿ ♆ Bat Bayou 1690	♑	4 39	7 31	9 5	5	5 0	7 10	8 56
13	M	Gen Fremont died 1890	♒	4 39	7 31	9 33	5	5 1	7 9	9 27
14	Tu	☿ in ☊; ♃ Stationary	♒	4 40	7 30	10 1	6	5 1	7 9	9 59
15	W	☌ ♃ ☾ Bat Vicksb'g 1862	♒	4 40	7 30	10 32	6	5 2	7 9	10 34
16	Th	Toral sur'd Santiago 1898	♓	4 41	7 29	11 3	6	5 2	7 8	11 9
17	Fr	☿ in ☋	♓	4 42	7 29	11 36	6	5 3	7 8	11 45
18	Sa	☿ in Perihelion	♈	4 42	7 28	morn	6	5 4	7 8	morn
29. 6th Sunday after Trinity.		*Matt. 5.*		*14h. 44m.*		*Day's Length,*		*14h. 3m.*		
19	Su	E. P. Roe died 1888	♈	4 43	7 27	0 12	6	5 4	7 7	0 25
20	M	Battle of Winchester 1864	♉	4 44	7 27	0 55	6	5 5	7 7	1 11
21	Tu	Battle of Bull Run 1862	♉	4 45	7 26	1 44	6	5 6	7 6	2 3
22	W	☌ ♆ ☾	♊	4 45	7 25	2 41	6	5 6	7 6	3 1
23	Th	Bolivar born 1783	♊	4 46	7 24	3 47	6	5 7	7 5	4 5
24	Fr	☌ ☿ ☾	♋	4 47	7 23	sets	6	5 8	7 4	sets
25	Sa	Battle Lundy's Lane 1714	♋	4 48	7 22	8 5	6	5 8	7 4	7 55
30. 7th Sunday after Trinity.		*Mark 8.*		*14h. 32m.*		*Day's Length,*		*13h. 54m.*		
26	Su	☌ ☿ ☉ Superior	♌	4 49	7 21	8 44	6	5 9	7 3	8 38
27	M	☌ ♀ ☾ Prin Louisa m '89	♌	4 50	7 19	9 18	6	5 10	7 2	9 17
28	Tu		♍	4 51	7 18	9 56	6	5 10	7 2	9 59
29	W	☿ Gr Hel Lat N; ☍ ♄ ☉	♍	4 52	7 18	10 29	6	5 11	7 1	10 36
30	Th	☌ ♂ ☾ Wm. Penn d 1718	♍	4 54	7 17	11 2	6	5 11	7 0	11 13
31	Fr		♋	4 55	7 16	11 38	6	5 12	7 0	11 52

Weather for July.—1, 2, 3, 4, 5, 6, 7, 8 rain; 9, 10, 11, 12, 13, 14, 15, 16 very rainy; 17, 18, 19, 20, 21, 22, 23 rain; 24, 25, 26, 27, 28, 29, 30 wind and rain; 31 fair.

FARM AND GARDEN WORK FOR JULY —Sow cabbage, but protect from hot sun when young. Water at night. Plant snap beans and a few Irish potatoes. Continue to sow radishes, lettuce, endive, cresses, mustard and small salading. The early Dutch turnip is the one to sow for the first crop; follow with the yellow Swedish or ruta baga.

Now do not omit to sow full crops of standing cow peas. Sow a few turnips, carrots and beets as field crops, though the hot suns are apt to destroy them; should they escape they will be fine; the next month is the best for these crops.

---

confirmed by the Senate. D. H. Milton, Rockingham county, Clerk. salary $700. Term of office for four years. Miss. I. M. Montgomery, of Wake County, stenographer.

STATE BOARD OF EDUCATION.

The Governor, Lieutenant-Governor, Secretary of State, Treasurer, Auditor, Superintendent of Public Instruction and Attorney-General constitute the State Board of Education.

STATE OYSTER COMMISSON.

This Commission was established by the Legislature of 1901. The Commissioner and five Inspectors are appointed by the Governor. W. M. Webb, Morehead City, Commissioner, salary $700 and traveling expenses. The following are the Inspectors appointed for the five counties, each receiving a salary of $400. Hyde, Seth Gibbs, Middleton; Beaufort, Geo. H. Hill, Washington; Dare, I. H. Scarborough, Jr., Avon; Pamlico, Paul Woodard, Pamlico; Carteret, J. W. Mason, Atlantic. Each of the counties have a sub-Inspector, salary $30 per month during the oyster season. The sub-Inspectors are appointed by the Oyster Commissioner.

The object of the Commission is to have general control over the oyster industry, and to see that the laws regulating the same are enforced.

GOVERNOR'S COUNCIL.

The Secretary of State, Treasurer, Auditor and Superintendent of Public Instruction. .

North Carolina Court Calendar for 1903.

FIRST JUDICIAL DISTRICT.

Beaufort county—February 9th (2)†; April 13th†; May 11th*; October 19 (2)*†; December 7th (3)*††.

Currituck county—February 23d; September 7th.

Camden county—March 2d; September 14th.

Pasquotank—March 9th (2); May 25 (2)₄†; September 14th; November 23d.

Perquimans county—March 23d; September 28th.

Chowan county—March 30th; October 5th.

Gates county—April 6th; October 12th.

Washington county—April 20th; November 2d.

Tyrell county—April 27th; November 9th.

Hyde county—May 4th; November 30th.

Dare county—May 18th; November 16th.

SECOND JUDICIAL DISTRICT.

Halifax county—January 19th (2); April 6th (2); August 24th (2); November 30th (2).

Northampton county—February 2d‡; March 23d (2); September 7th‡; November 2d.

Warren county—February 9th; May 11th; September 21st (2).

Bertie county—February 16th‡; April 27th (2); September 14th‡; November 16th (2).

Hertford county—February 23d*; April 20th; August 17th*; October 26th.

MOON'S PHASES.

	BOSTON D. H. M.	NEW YORK D. H. M.	CHICAGO D. H. M.
F.M.	8 3 54 M.	8 3 54 M.	8 2 54 M.
L.Q.	16 0 22 M.	16 0 22 M.	15 11 22 A.
N.M.	22 2 51 A.	22 2 51 A.	22 1 51 A.
F.Q.	29 3 34 A.	29 3 34 A.	29 2 34 A.

D. M.	D. W.	Aspects of Planets and other Miscellaneous Matter.	Moon's Signs.	Latitude of New York City, Phila., N. J., Pa., Del., Md., Va., W. Va., Ohio, Illinois, Ind., Neb., Cal. — Sun rises. H. M.	Sun sets. H. M.	Moon sets. H. M.	Sun Slow. M.	Latitude of Charleston, N. Car., S. Car., Ga., Fla., Ala., Miss., Tenn., Ark., La., Tx., N. Mex., Ariz. — Sun rises. H. M.	Sun sets. H. M.	Moon sets. H. M.
1	Sa	C. B. Aycock el Gov 1900	♎	4 56	7 15	morn	6	5 13	6 59	morn
31. 8th Sunday after Trinity. Matt. 7. 14h. 17m. Day's Length, 13h. 44m.										
2	Su		♏	4 57	7 14	0 16	6	5 14	6 58	0 33
3	M	☌♅☾ Crown Pt tkn 1759	♏	4 58	7 13	0 58	6	5 14	6 57	1 16
4	Tu	Tilden died 1886	♐	4 59	7 12	1 43	6	5 15	6 56	2 3
5	W	Battle of Athens 1861	♐	5 0	7 11	2 32	6	5 16	6 55	2 51
6	Th		♐	5 1	7 9	3 25	6	5 16	6 55	3 43
7	Fr	☌♄☾ J. Wh'er d 1882	♑	5 2	7 8	4 19	6	5 17	6 54	4 35
8	Sa	Span Amada ds 1588	♑	5 3	7 7	rises.	6	5 18	6 53	rises.
32. 9th Sunday after Trinity. Luke 16. 14h. 1m. Day's Length, 13h. 34m.										
9	Su	O'Riley d 1890	♒	5 4	7 5	7 33	5	5 18	6 52	7 30
10	M	Battle of Oak Hill 1861	♒	5 5	7 4	8 6	5	5 19	6 51	8 3
11	Tu	☌♃☾ Card New'n d 1896	♒	5 6	7 3	8 37	5	5 20	6 50	8 37
12	W	♀ Greatest Brillancy	♓	5 7	7 1	9 8	5	5 21	6 49	9 12
13	Th	Conova died 1822	♓	5 8	7 0	9 38	5	5 21	6 48	9 45
14	Fr	Battle of Hasting 1066	♈	5 9	6 59	10 12	5	5 22	6 47	10 23
15	Sa	Napoleon born 1769	♈	5 10	6 58	10 51	4	5 23	6 46	11 6
33. 10th Sunday after Trinity. Luke 19. 13h. 45m. Day's Length, 13h. 22m.										
16	Su	Senator Hill d 1832	♈	5 11	6 56	11 36	4	5 23	6 45	11 54
17	M	Burgoyne sur 1777	♉	5 12	6 54	morn	4	5 24	6 43	morn
18	Tu	Cor-stone U. S. cap. 1790	♉	5 13	6 53	0 27	4	5 25	6 42	0 46
19	W	☌ ♆ ☾ Bat of Grav 1870	♊	5 14	6 52	1 26	4	5 25	6 41	1 46
20	Th	Harrison born 1838	♊	5 15	6 51	2 32	3	5 26	6 40	2 50
21	Fr	♀ in Aphelion	♋	5 16	6 49	3 43	3	5 26	6 39	3 58
22	Sa	☿ in ☋	♋	5 17	6 47	4 57	3	5 27	6 38	5 7
34. 11th Sunday after Trinity. Luke 18. 13h. 28m. Day's Length, 13h. 9m.										
23	Su	Com Perry died 1820	♌	5 18	6 46	sets	3	5 28	6 37	sets
24	M	Daniel Webster died 1852	♌	5 19	6 44	7 53	2	5 29	6 35	7 53
25	Tu	☌ ☿ ☾; ☌ ♀ ☾; ♀ Sta'y	♍	5 20	6 43	8 28	2	5 29	6 34	8 32
26	W	Battle of Dresden 1813	♍	5 21	6 41	9 1	2	5 30	6 33	9 10
27	Th	☌♂☾ Sir R. Hill d 1879	♎	5 22	6 40	9 37	2	5 31	6 32	9 49
28	Fr	☌ ☿ ♀ 1 Cab Mes 1858	♎	5 23	6 39	10 15	1	5 31	6 31	10 31
29	Sa	Bat of Granston 1862	♏	5 24	6 37	10 57	1	5 32	6 29	11 14
35. 12th Sunday after Trinity. Mark 7. 13h. 10m. Day's Length, 12h. 55m.										
30	Su	☌ ♅ ☾	♏	5 25	6 35	11 40	1	5 33	6 28	11 59
31	M	☿ in Aphelion; ♅ Sta'y	♏	5 26	6 33	morn	0	5 33	6 27	morn

Weather for August.—1, 2, 3, 4, 5, 6, 7 cool, with frequent showers; 8, 9, 10, 11, 12, 13, 14, 15 fair; 16, 17, 18, 19, 20, 21 changeable; 22, 23, 24, 25, 26, 27, 28 variable; 29, 30, 31 changeable.

FARM AND GARDEN WORK FOR AUGUST.—Transplant all kinds of cabbage, cauliflower and celery. Sow carrots and beets, turnips of all kinds, spinach, lettuce, radish and onions.

Now sow full crops of field turnips, carrots and beets, and such other crops as were omitted last month; strip fodder. Early rice will be fit to cut last of this month. Look to it. This is a good time to plant vines of the first slips, in order to procure seed potatoes for the next year's crops.

THIRD JUDICIAL DISTRICT.

Pitt county—January 12th (2); March 16th (2); April 20th (2); September 7th (2); October 19th (2)†.

Craven county—February 9th†; April 6th; May 4th (2)†; August 24th*; September 21st (2)†; November 16th*; November 23d†.

Green county—February 23d; August 31st; December 7th (2).

Carteret county—March 9th; October 5th.

Jones county—March 30th; November 9th.

Pamlico county—April 13th; September 14th.

FOURTH JUDICIAL DISTRICT.

Franklin county—January 19th (2)‡; April 13th (2); October 19th (2).

Wilson county—February 2d (2)*†; May 11th†; September 7th*; November 16th (2)†; December 14th*.

Edgecombe county—March 2d; March 30th (2)†; September 14th; November 2d (2)†.

Nash county—March 9th; April 27th (2); August 31st; November 30th (2).

Martin county—March 16th (2); September 21st (2).

Vance county—May 18th; February 16th (2); October 5th (2).

FIFTH JUDICIAL DISTRICT.

New Hanover county—January 5th (2)*; January 26th (2)†; March 23d*; April 6 h (2)†; May 25th*; July 13th*; August 17th*; October 12th (2)†; November 9th*; November 30*.

Onslow county—January 19th (2); July 20th (2)†*; October 26th.

Duplin county—February 9th (1); May 4th (1); August 31st (1); December 7th (2).

Sampson county—February 16 (2); May 11th (2); September 28th (2).

Pender county—March 2d (2); September 7th (2); December 21st (1).

Lenoir county—March 9th (2); April 27th; November 16th (2).

SIXTH JUDICIAL DISTRICT.

Wake county—January 5th (2)*; February 23d (2)†; March 23d (2)†; April 20th (2)†; July 13th (2)*; September 28th (2)*; October 26th (3)†.

Wayne county—January 19th (2); April 13th; September 14th (2); November 30th.

Harnett county—February 9th (2); August 31st; November 16th (2)‡.

Johnston county—March 9th (2); September 7th; December 7th (2).

SEVENTH JUDICIAL DISTRICT.

Cumberland county—January 12th; February 16th (2); March 23d (2)†; April 27th; May 4th†, August 31st*; October 26th†; November 23d*.

Robeson county—February 2d (2)*; March 20th (2)†; May 18th; July 27th*; September 14th (2)†; November 9th (2)*; December 7th.†

Columbus county—February 23d; April 13th; September 7th; November 30th.

Bladen county—March 2d (2); October 12th (2).

Brunswick county—March 16th; September 28th.

EIGHTH JUDICIAL DISTRICT.

Moore county—January 9th (2)†; April 20th*; May 11th (2)†; August 17th*; September 21st†; December 7th*.

SEPTEMBER 1903

MOON'S PHASES.

	BOSTON D. H. M.	NEW YORK D. H. M.	CHICAGO D. H. M.
F.M.	6 7 20 A.	6 7 20 A.	6 6 20 A.
L.Q.	14 8 14 M.	14 8 14 M.	14 7 14 M.
N.M.	20 11 31 A.	20 11 31 A.	20 10 31 A.
F.Q.	28 8 8 M.	28 8 8 M.	28 7 8 M.

D. M.	D. W.	Aspects of Planets and other Miscellaneous Matter.	MOON'S NODE	LATITUDE Of New York City, Phila., N. J., Pa., Del., Md., Va., W. Va., Ohio, Illinois, Ind., Neb., Cal.			SUN FAST.	LATITUDE Of Charleston, N. Car., S. Car., Ga., Fla., Ala., Miss., Tenn., Ark., La., Tx., N. Mex., Ariz.		
				Sun rises. H. M.	Sun sets. H. M.	Moon sets. H. M.	M.	Sun rises. H. M.	Sun sets. H. M.	Moon sets. H. M.
1	Tu	♂ ♄ ☾ Bat Ox Hill 1862	♐	5 27	6 31	0 28	0	5 34	6 26	0 48
2	W	Atlanta captured 1864	♐	5 28	6 30	1 19	0	5 35	6 24	1 37
3	Th		♑	5 29	6 28	2 13	0	5 35	6 23	2 30
4	Fr	French Rep. form'd 1870	♑	5 30	6 27	3 8	1	5 36	6 22	3 22
5	Sa	Confeds invaded Md 1862	♑	5 31	6 25	4 6	1	5 36	6 20	4 16

36. 13th Sunday after Trinity. Luke 10. 12h. 52m. Day's Length, 12h. 42m.

6	Su	◉ McKinley as'd 1901	♒	5 32	6 24	rises.	1	5 37	6 19	rises.
7	M	◉ ♂ ♃ ☾; ☿ Gr El E	♒	5 33	6 22	6 38	2	5 38	6 18	6 38
8	Tu	Destruc. of Jeru. A. D. 70	♓	5 34	6 20	7 12	2	5 38	6 16	7 15
9	W	Sebastopol Fell 1855	♓	5 35	6 18	7 42	2	5 39	6 15	7 49
10	Th	Sunset Cox died 1889	♓	5 36	6 17	8 15	3	5 39	6 14	8 25
11	Fr	America discovered 1492	♈	5 37	6 15	8 51	3	5 40	6 12	9 5
12	Sa	♂ ♃ ◉ ; ♀ Gr Hel Lat S	♈	5 38	6 14	9 34	3	5 41	6 11	9 50

37. 14th Sunday after Trinity. Luke 17. 12h. 33m. Day's Length, 12h. 28m.

13	Su	☾ Bat of Quebec 1850	♉	5 39	6 12	10 21	4	5 42	6 10	10 39
14	M	☾ Pres McKin'y d 1901	♉	5 40	6 10	11 15	4	5 42	6 8	11 34
15	Tu	♂ ♅ ☾; ☐ ♄ ◉	♊	5 41	6 9	morn	5	5 43	6 7	morn
16	W	Farenheit died 1736	♊	5 42	6 7	0 16	5	5 44	6 6	0 35
17	Th	♂ ◉ Inferior	♋	5 43	6 5	1 23	5	5 44	6 4	1 39
18	Fr	Fugitive Slave Act 1850	♋	5 44	6 4	2 33	6	5 45	6 3	2 47
19	Sa	Pres Arthur Inaug'd 1881	♋	5 45	6 2	3 45	6	5 46	6 2	3 54

38. 15th Sunday after Trinity. Matt. 6. 12h. 14m. Day's Length, 12h. 14m.

20	Su	♂ ♀ ☾; ☿ Stat'y	♌	5 46	6 0	5 0	6	5 46	6 0	5 4
21	M	◉ Total Ec ◉ inv here	♍	5 47	5 59	sets	7	5 47	5 59	sets
22	Tu		♍	5 48	5 57	6 57	7	5 48	5 58	7 4
23	W	◉ Sun enters Lebra	♎	5 49	5 55	7 32	7	5 48	5 56	7 42
24	Th	Gen D. H. Hill d 1889	♎	5 50	5 54	8 9	8	5 49	5 55	8 24
25	Fr	♂ ♂ ☾	♎	5 51	5 52	8 51	8	5 49	5 54	9 8
26	Sa	♂ ♅ ☾ D'l Booue d 1820	♏	5 52	5 50	9 35	8	5 50	5 52	9 53

39. 16th Sunday after Trinity. Luke 7. 11h. 55m. Day's Length, 12h. 0m.

27	Su	Strasburg sur 1870	♏	5 53	5 48	10 21	9	5 51	5 51	10 40
28	M	☽ Bishop Randle d 1873	♐	5 54	5 47	11 12	9	5 51	5 50	11 30
29	Tu	◉	♐	5 55	5 45	morn	9	5 52	5 48	morn
30	W	☐ ♅ ◉; ♂ ♄ ☾	♑	5 56	5 43	0 5	10	5 53	5 47	0 23

WEATHER FOR SEPTEMBER.—1, 2, 3, 4, 5, fair, if wind northwest; 6, 7, 8, 9, 10 11, 12, 13 changeable; 14, 15, 16, 17, 18, 19 not settled; 20, 21, 22, 23, 24, 25, 26, 27 fair; 28, 29, 30 unsettled.

FARM AND GARDEN WORK FOR SEPTEMBER.—Now sow full crops of all kinds—turnips, onions, carrots, beets, cabbage, lettuce, cresses. Look after your mushroom beds. Hoe and thin your turnips.

Continue to sow field turnips, carrots and beets. Southern seed are always better than the imported; those from the latter are apt to run to seed early in the spring, unless it be English seed. Prepare land for sowing rye in October. Pick cotton and harvest corn.

Chatham county—February 2d; May 4th; August 10th†; November 16th.

Anson county—February 9th*; April 13th†; September 14th*; October 12th†.

Union county—February 16th (2)*; March 16 (2)†; August 3d (1)*; August 24th (2)*†; October 9th (2)†*; November 30th (1)*.

Richmond county—March 2d*; March 30th (2)†; September 7th*; September 28th (2).

Scotland county—March 9th†; April 27th*; November 23d*.

NINTH JUDICIAL DISTRICT.

Durham county—January 5th*; January 19th*; March 16th; †May 11th*; August 31st*; December 7th*.

Guilford county—January 12th*; February 9th†; April 13th†; May 4th*; June 8th†; August 24th*; September 21st†; October 26*; November 2d†; December 14th.†

Granville county—February 2d (1); April 20th (2); August 3d (1); November 23d (2).

Alamance county— February 23d†; May 25th†; September 7th (2)†; November 9th*.

Orange county—March 9th; May 18th†; August 4th; October 19th.

Person county—April 6th; August 17th; November 16th.

TENTH JUDICAL DISTRICT.

Montgomery county—January 19th*; April 13th; †September 28th (2).

Iredell county—January 26th (2); May 18th; August 10th (2); November 9th (2).

Rowan county—February 9th (2); May 4th (2)*†; September 7th (2); November 23d (2)*†.

Davidson county—February 23d (2); April 20th†; August 31st (2).

Stanley county—March 9th*; July 20th†; September 21st*; December 21st†.

Randolph county—March 16th (2); July 27th (2); December 7th.

Davie county—March 30th (2); October 12th (2).

Yadkin county—April 29th (2); October 26th (2).

ELEVENTH JUDICIAL DISTRICT.

Forsyth county—February 9th (2)*; March 9th (2)†; May 18th (2); July 27th*; September 14th (2)†; October 12th*; December 7th (2)†.

Wilkes county—January 26th (2); August 10th (2); October 26th (2)†.

Rockingham county—February 23d (2); August 3d; November 9th (2).

Alleghany county—March 23d; August 24th.

Caswell county—April 13th; October 19th.

Surry county—April 20th†; August 31st (2)†; November 23d (2).

Stokes county—May 4th (2); September 28th (2).

TWELFTH JUDICIAL DISTRICT.

Mecklenburg county—January 12th (2); February 9th (2)*; March 9th (2)†; April 20th; June 1st*; June 29th (2)*; July 20th (2)†; August 17th*; September 28th*; October 12th (2)†; November 30th*.

Cabarrus county—January 26th (2); May 4th (2); August 31st; October 26th (2).

Gaston county—February 23d (2); May 18th; September 14th (2); November 23d.

Cleveland county—March 23d (2); August 3d (2); November 9th (2).

Lincoln county—April 7th (2); September 7th; November 14th.

MOON'S PHASES.

	BOSTON D. H. M.	NEW YORK D. H. M.	CHICAGO D. H. M.
F.M.	6 10 24 M.	6 10 24 M.	6 9 24 M.
L.Q.	13 2 56 A.	13 2 56 A.	13 1 56 A.
N.M.	20 10 30 M.	20 10 30 M.	20 9 30 M.
F.Q.	28 3 32 M.	28 3 32 M.	28 2 32 M.

				LATITUDE Of New York City, Phila., N. J., Pa., Del., Md., Va., W. Va., Ohio, Illinois, Ind., Neb., Cal.				LATITUDE Of Charleston, N. Car., S. Car., Ga., Fla., Ala., Miss., Tenn., Ark., La., Tx., N. Mex., Ariz.		
D. M.	D. W.	Aspects of Planets and other Miscellaneous Matter.	MOON'S SIGNS.	Sun rises. H. M.	Sun sets. H. M.	Moon sets. H. M.	SUN FAST. M.	Sun rises. H. M.	Sun sets. H. M.	Moon sets. H. M.
1	Th	[illegible]	♑	5 57	5 42	1 0	10	5 54	5 46	1 15
2	Fr	Gen'l Assem at Ed'n 1722	♑	5 58	5 40	1 57	10	5 54	5 44	2 9
3	Sa	☌ ☿ ☾ Inferior	♒	5 59	5 38	2 55	11	5 55	5 43	3 4
40. 17th Sunday after Trinity. Luke 14. 11h. 37m. Day's Length, 11h. 46m.										
4	Su	☾ ♃ ☾ Bat G'town 1777	♒	6 0	5 37	3 55	11	5 56	5 42	3 59
5	M	Par Eclp of Moon	♓	6 1	5 35	4 55	11	5 56	5 40	4 55
6	Tu	♀ Stationary	♓	6 2	5 33	rises.	12	5 57	5 39	rises.
7	W	Bat of Saratoga 1777	♓	6 3	5 32	6 16	12	5 58	5 38	6 24
8	Th	♄ Stationary	♈	6 4	5 30	6 52	12	5 58	5 36	7 5
9	Fr	♆ Stationary	♈	6 5	5 29	7 32	12	5 59	5 35	7 48
10	Sa	☿ in ☊ Stuart r'd Tenn62	♉	6 6	5 28	8 19	13	6 0	5 34	8 37
41. 18th Sunday after Trinity. Matt. 22. 11h. 19m. Day's Length. 11h. 32m.										
11	Su	☿ Stationary	♉	6 7	5 26	9 11	13	6 1	5 33	9 30
12	M	☌ ♆ ☾ R E Lee d 1870	♊	6 8	5 24	10 9	13	6 1	5 32	10 28
13	Tu	John Toomer d 1856	♊	6 9	5 22	11 12	14	6 2	5 30	11 30
14	W	☿ in Perihelion	♋	6 11	5 21	morn	14	6 3	5 29	morn
15	Th	Josh Billings d 1885	♋	6 12	5 19	0 19	14	6 4	5 28	0 34
16	Fr	Napoleon of St H 1815	♌	6 13	5 18	1 29	14	6 4	5 27	1 39
17	Sa	☌ ☿ ♀ ☾	♌	6 14	5 16	2 39	14	6 5	5 26	2 45
42. 19th Sunday after Trinity. Matt. 9. 11h. 0m. Day's Length, 11h. 18m.										
18	Su	☿ Gr Elong W	♌	6 15	5 15	3 51	15	6 6	5 24	3 52
19	M	☌ ☿ ☾ Bat H. Run 1864	♍	6 16	5 13	4 57	15	6 7	5 23	4 54
20	Tu	Grace Darl'g d 1842	♍	6 17	5 12	6 6	15	6 7	5 22	5 58
21	W	Bat Ball's Bluff 1861	♎	6 18	5 11	sets	15	6 9	5 21	sets
22	Th	Bat of Maryville Ark 1864	♎	6 20	5 10	6 43	15	6 8	5 20	6 59
23	Fr		♏	6 21	5 8	7 26	15	6 10	5 19	7 44
24	Sa	☌ ♂ ♅; ☌ ♅ ☾; ♀ G B	♏	6 22	5 6	8 13	16	6 10	5 18	8 32
43 20th Sunday after Trinity. Matt. 22. 10h. 42m. Day's Length, 11h. 6m.										
25	Su	☿ Gr Hel Lat N	♐	6 23	5 5	9 3	16	6 11	5 17	9 22
26	M	□ ♄ ☉ Sal'y ld off 1753	♐	6 24	5 4	9 55	16	6 12	5 16	10 13
27	Tu	Vassar died 1888	♐	6 25	5 2	10 49	16	6 13	5 15	11 5
28	W	☌ ♄ ☾	♑	6 26	5 1	11 45	16	6 14	5 14	11 59
29	Th	Sir W Ral'gh bd 1618	♑	6 27	5 0	morn	16	6 15	5 13	morn
30	Fr	Gambrella born 1838	♒	6 29	4 59	0 43	16	6 15	5 12	0 52
31	Sa	☌ ♃ ☾ Gen Scott rd 1861	♒	6 30	4 57	1 41	16	6 16	5 11	1 48

☞ WEATHER FOR OCTOBER.—1, 2, 3, 4, 5 open weather; 6, 7, 8, 9, 10, 11, 12 frequent showers; 13, 14, 15, 16, 17, 18 changeable; 19, 20, 21, 22, 23, 24 frequent showers, 25, 26, 27 more rain; 28, 29, 30, 31 cold, with frequent showers.

See Dr. Green's Sons Ad. on Page 39.

FARM AND GARDEN WORK FOR OCTOBER.—You may make two sowings of cabbage this month, and, if of English seed, they will not "run" in the spring. Sow lettuce; hoe turnips and thin; put out leeks and onions: sow principal crops of spinach; earth up celery.

Continue picking your cotton as it opens. Sow early rye, wheat and barley. Dig your sweet potatoes when the weather becomes cool and you expect frost.

THIRTEENTH JUDICIAL DISTRICT.

Catawba county—February 2d (2); May 4th (2)†; July 13th (2); November 2d (2).

Alexander county—February 16th; October 5th.

Caldwell county—February 23d (2)*; September 21st (2)*; November 30th (2)†.

Mitchell county—March 9th (2); May 18th (2); September 7th (2); November 16th (2).

Watauga county—March 23d (2); June 1st (2); August 10th (2).

Ashe county—April 20 (2); July 27th (2); October 19th (2).

FOURTEENTH JUDICIAL DISTRICT.

McDowell county—February 16th (2); August 10th (2); October 26th.

Henderson county—March 2d (1)*; May 11th (2)†*; September 21st (2)*; November 9th (2)†*.

Rutherford county—March 9th (2); September 7th (2); November 23d (2).

Polk county—March 23d (2); October 25th.

Burke county—April 6th (2); June 1st (2)†*; August 24th (2)†*; October 12th (2).

Yaucey county—April 20th (3); December 7th (2).

FIFTEENTH JUDICIAL DISTRICT.

Buncombe county—February 2d (3)*; March 9th (4)†; April 20th (2); May 25th (4)†; August 3d (2); September 14th (6)†; November 16th† December 7th (2).†

Madison county—February 23d (2)*; May 4th (3)*†; August 17th (2)†.

Transylvania county—April 6th (2); August 31st (2); November 30th.

SIXTEENTH JUDICIAL DISTRICT.

Haywood county—February 2d (2); May 4th (2); September 28th (2).

Jackson county—February 16th (2); May 18th (2); October 12th (2).

Swain county—March 2d (2); July 27th (2)†; October 26th (2).

Graham county—March 16th (2); September 7th (2).

Cherokee county—March 30th (2); August 10th (2); November 9th (2).

Clay county—April 13th; September 21st.

Macon county—April 20th (2); August 24th (2); November 23d (2)†.

NOTE.—*Criminal cases only. †Civil cases only. ‡Civil and jail cases. *†First week criminal; second week civil cases. *††First week criminal; two weeks civil cases.

Supreme Court of North Carolina.

Walter Clark, of Raleigh, Chief Justice; Walter A. Montgomery, of Raleigh, Associate Justice; Robert M. Douglas, of Greensboro, Associate Justice; H. G. Conner, of Wilson, Associate Justice; Platt D. Walker, of Charlotte, Associate Justice; Thomas S. Kenan, of Raleigh, Clerk; J. L. Seawell, of Raleigh, Office Clerk; Robert H. Bradley, of Raleigh, Marshal and Librarian; Zeb. V. Walser; of Lexington, Reporter.

Court meets at Raleigh on the first Monday in February and the fourth Monday in August of each year. Appeals are called as follows: (Tuesday)

DISTRICT.	SPRING TERM.	FALL TERM.
First	February 3d	August 25th.
Second	February 10th	September 1st.

MOON'S PHASES.

☽	BOSTON D. H. M.	NEW YORK D. H. M.	CHICAGO D. H. M.
F.M.	5 0 27 M.	5 0 27 M.	4 11 27 A.
L.Q.	11 9 46 A.	11 9 46 A.	11 8 46 A.
N.M.	19 0 10 M.	19 0 10 M.	18 11 10 A.
F.Q.	27 0 37 M.	27 0 37 M.	26 11 37 A.

D. M.	D. W.	Aspects of Planets and other Miscellaneous Matter.	MOON'S SIGNS.	LATITUDE Of New York City, Phila., N. J., Pa., Del., Md., Va., W. Va., Ohio, Illinois, Ind., Neb., Cal. Sun rises. H. M.	Sun sets. H. M.	Moon sets. H. M.	SUN FAST. M.	LATITUDE Of Charleston, N. Car., S. Car., Ga., Fla., Ala., Miss., Tenn., Ark., La., Tx., N Mex., Ariz. Sun rises. H. M.	Sun sets. H. M.	Moon sets. H. M.
44. 21st Sunday after Trinity.		*John 4.*		*10h. 25m.*		*Day's Length, 10h. 53m.*				
1	Su	Gen McClellan com 1861	♒	6 31	4 56	2 42	16	6 17	5 10	2 44
2	M		♓	6 32	4 55	3 40	16	6 18	5 9	3 39
3	Tu	Gen Clingman d 1897	♓	6 33	4 54	4 41	16	6 19	5 8	4 35
4	W	Peabody d 1869	♈	6 35	4 53	5 44	18	6 20	5 7	5 35
5	Th	○ *Guy Fawlkes Day*	♈	6 36	4 52	rises.	16	6 21	5 6	rises.
6	Fr	Lincoln elected 1860	♉	6 37	4 50	6 14	16	6 22	5 6	6 32
7	Sa	♀ in ☊	♉	6 38	4 49	7 5	16	6 23	5 5	7 24
45. 22d Sunday after Trinity.		*Matt. 18.*		*10h. 9m.*		*Day's Length, 10h. 40m.*				
8	Su	☌ ♆ ☾ Milton d 1694	♉	6 39	4 48	8 2	16	6 24	5 4	8 22
9	M	♃ Stationary	♊	6 40	4 47	9 6	16	6 24	5 3	9 24
10	Tu	Martin Luther born 1483	♊	6 42	4 46	10 11	16	6 25	5 2	10 27
11	W	☾ State Wash. ad 1889	♋	6 43	4 45	11 19	16	6 26	5 2	11 31
12	Th	Gen Graham d 1836	♋	6 44	4 44	morn	16	6 27	5 1	morn
13	Fr	Fall of Meteors 1833	♌	6 45	4 43	0 29	16	6 28	5 0	0 36
14	Sa	Hershel born 1738	♌	6 46	4 43	1 38	16	6 29	5 0	1 41
46. 23d Sunday after Trinity.		*Matt. 23.*		*9h. 55m.*		*Day's Length, 10h. 29m.*				
15	Su	☌ ♀ ☾	♍	6 47	4 42	2 44	15	6 30	4 59	2 43
16	M	Sherman's March 1864	♍	6 48	4 41	3 49	15	6 31	4 59	3 44
17	Tu	☿ in ☋ Suez Canal o 1869	♎	6 50	4 40	4 58	15	6 32	4 58	4 48
18	W	☌ ☿ ☾	♎	6 51	4 40	6 4	15	6 33	4 58	5 50
19	Th	●	♏	6 52	4 39	sets	15	6 34	4 57	sets
20	Fr		♏	6 53	4 38	6 4	14	6 34	4 57	6 23
21	Sa	☌ ♅ ☾; ☌ ☿ ☉ Superior	♏	6 55	4 38	6 51	14	6 35	4 56	7 11
47. 24th Sunday after Trinity.		*Matt. 9.*		*9h. 41m.*		*Day's Length, 10h. 20m.*				
22	Su	☌ ♂ ☾ Jos Graham d 1836	♐	6 56	4 37	7 44	14	6 36	4 56	8 2
23	M	Gov Ellis born 1820	♐	6 57	4 37	8 38	14	6 37	4 56	8 55
24	Tu	☌ ♄ ☾	♑	6 58	4 36	9 33	13	6 38	4 56	9 48
25	W	Isaac Watts died 1748	♑	6 59	4 36	10 31	13	6 39	4 55	10 42
26	Th	Bishop Marvin d 1875	♑	7 0	4 36	11 28	13	6 40	4 55	11 36
27	Fr	☽ ☿ in Aphelion; ☌ ♃ ☾	♒	7 1	4 35	morn	13	6 41	4 55	morn
28	Sa	♀ Gr Elong West	♒	7 2	4 35	0 27	12	6 42	4 54	0 31
48. 1st Sunday in Advent.		*Matt. 21.*		*9h. 31m.*		*Day's Length, 10h. 12m.*				
29	Su	Savannah taken 1778	♓	7 3	4 34	1 26	12	6 42	4 54	1 26
30	M	*St. Andrew's Day*	♓	7 4	4 34	2 22	11	6 43	4 54	2 19

WEATHER FOR NOVEMBER.—1, 2, 3, 4, 5, 6, 7, 8, 9, 10 fair; 11. 12, 13, 14, 15, 16, 17, 18 open weather; 19, 20, 21, 22 changeable; 23, 24, 25, 26, 27, 28, 29, 30 fair.

FARM AND GARDEN WORK FOR NOVEMBER.—Sow your first crop of peas and a few turnips. Plant out onions raised from seed in August and September. Plant Windsor and long pod beans. Dress asparagus and artichokes.

Sow full crops of rye, barley, wheat and other small grains. Harvest your sweet potatoes.

DISTRICT.	SPRING TERM.	FALL TERM.
Third	February 16th	September 8th.
Fourth	February 23d	September 15th.
Fifth	March 3d	September 22d.
Sixth	March 10th	September 29th.
Seventh	March 17th	October 6th.
Eighth	March 24th	October 13th.
Ninth	April 7th	October 27th.
Tenth	March 3 th	October 20th.
Eleventh	April 14th	November 3d.
Twelfth	April 21st	November 10th.
Thirteenth	April 28th	November 17th.
Fourteenth	May 5th	November 24th.
Fifteenth	May 12th	December 1st.
Sixteenth	May 19th	December 8th.

Applicants for license are examined on the first day of each term.

MOON'S PHASES.	BOSTON D. H. M.	NEW YORK D. H. M.	CHICAGO D. H. M.
F.M.	4 1 13 A.	4 1 13 A.	4 0 13 A.
L.Q.	11 5 53 M.	11 5 53 M.	11 4 53 M.
N.M.	18 4 26 A.	18 4 26 A.	18 3 26 A.
F.Q.	26 9 22 A.	26 9 22 A.	26 8 22 A.

D. M.	D. W.	Aspects of Planets and other Miscellaneous Matter.	Moon's Signs.	Latitude of New York City, Phila., N. J., Pa., Del., Md., Va., W. Va., Ohio, Illinois, Ind., Neb., Cal. — Sun rises. H. M.	Sun sets. H. M.	Moon sets. H. M.	Sun Fast. M.	Latitude of Charleston, N. Car., S. Car., Ga., Fla., Ala., Miss., Tenn., Ark., La., Tx., N. Mex., Ariz. — Sun rises. H. M.	Sun sets. H. M.	Moon sets. H. M.
1	Tu	Prince of Wales d 1844	♓	7 5	4 34	3 26	11	6 44	4 54	3 19
2	W	51st Cong. opened 1890	♈	7 6	4 34	4 31	11	6 45	4 54	4 20
3	Th		♈	7 7	4 33	5 36	10	6 46	4 54	5 21
4	Fr	○	♉	7 8	4 33	rises.	10	6 46	4 54	rises.
5	Sa		♉	7 9	4 33	5 50	10	6 47	4 54	6 10
49. 2d Sunday in Advent.		*Luke 21.*		*9h. 23m. Day's Length, 10h. 6m.*						
6	Su	☌ ♆ ☾ Jeff Davis d 1889	♊	7 10	4 33	6 54	9	6 48	4 54	7 12
7	M	□ ♃ ☉	♊	7 11	4 33	8 1	9	6 49	4 54	8 17
8	Tu	☌ ☿ ♅ E Whitney b 1765	♋	7 12	4 33	9 9	8	6 50	4 54	9 23
9	W	Milton born 1608	♋	7 13	4 33	10 20	8	6 51	4 54	10 28
10	Th	☾ Dumas d 1870	♌	7 13	4 33	11 30	7	6 51	4 54	11 35
11	Fr	♀ in Perihelion	♌	7 14	4 33	morn	7	6 52	4 54	morn
12	Sa	Cromwell Protector 1653	♍	7 15	4 33	0 37	7	6 53	4 55	0 37
50. 3d Sunday in Advent.		*Matt. 11.*		*9h. 18m. Day's Length. 10h. 1m.*						
13	Su	Robt Tombs d 1885	♍	7 16	4 34	1 40	6	6 54	4 55	1 36
14	M	☌ ♀ ☾ *Halcion Days beg*	♎	7 17	4 34	2 48	6	6 54	4 55	2 39
15	Tu	Sitting Bull killed 1890	♎	7 18	4 34	3 52	5	6 55	4 55	3 40
16	W	Boston Tea Party 1773	♎	7 18	4 35	4 55	5	6 55	4 56	4 40
17	Th	● ☿ in ☊	♏	7 19	4 35	5 54	4	6 56	4 56	5 36
18	Fr	☌ ♅ ☉	♏	7 20	4 35	6 50	4	6 57	4 57	6 31
19	Sa		♐	7 20	4 36	sets	3	6 57	4 57	sets
51. 4th Sunday in Advent.		*John 1.*		*9h. 15m. Day's Length, 10h. 0m.*						
20	Su	☌ ☿ ☾; ☌ ♂ ♄	♐	7 21	4 36	6 29	3	6 58	4 58	6 47
21	M	☌ ♅ ☾	♑	7 21	4 37	7 23	2	6 58	4 58	7 39
22	Tu	☌ ♄ ☾; ☌ ♂ ☾; ♂ in Per	♑	7 21	4 38	8 19	2	6 59	4 58	8 32
23	W	☉ enters ♑ winter beg	♑	7 22	4 38	9 16	1	6 59	4 59	9 26
24	Th		♒	7 22	4 39	10 16	1	7 0	5 0	10 21
25	Fr	☌ ♃ ☾ *Xmas Day*	♒	7 23	4 39	11 13	0	7 0	5 0	11 15
26	Sa	☽ Stephen Girard d 1731	♒	7 23	4 40	morn	sl	7 1	5 1	morn
52. 1st Sunday after Christmas.		*Luke 2.*		*9h. 18m. Day's Length, 10h. 0m.*						
27	Su	☍ ♆ ☉ *St. John Evang't*	♓	7 23	4 41	0 10	1	7 1	5 1	0 9
28	M		♓	7 24	4 42	1 9	1	7 1	5 2	1 3
29	Tu	W. E. Gladstone b 1809	♈	7 24	4 42	2 11	2	7 2	5 3	2 2
30	W	Bat of Vicksburg 1861	♈	7 24	4 43	3 15	2	7 2	5 3	3 1
31	Th		♉	7 24	4 43	4 20	3	7 2	5 4	4 3

Weather for December.—1, 2, 3 fair; 4, 5, 6, 7, 8, 9, 10 changeable; 11, 12, 13, 14, 15, 16, 17 expect rain; 18, 19, 20, 21, 22, 23, 24, 25 fair, if wind northwest, rainy if wind from south or southwest; 26, 27, 28, 29, 30, 31 fair, if wind be from northwest, rainy, if wind from south or southwest.

FARM AND GARDEN WORK FOR DECEMBER.—Plant peas of all kinds; set out onions; garlic, eschalots and cabbage. Sow a few lettuce, spinach, carrots and radishes. You may try a few Irish potatoes.

Finish picking cotton; get out crops of rice and prepare for market. Commence plowing. ditching, draining and manuring as early as possible for next year's crop.

General Assembly of North Carolina—Session of 1903.

SENATE.

First District—(Camden, Chowan, Currituck, Gates, Hertford, Pasquotank, Perquimans—two Senators)—C. S. Vann, D., Edenton; P. W. McMullan, D., Elizabeth City.

Second District—(Beaufort, Dare, Hyde, Martin, Pamlico, Tyrell, Washington—two Senators)—S. S. Mann, D., Swan Quarter; J. A. Spruill, D., Columbia.

Third District—(Bertie, Northampton—one Senator)—C. W. Mitchell, D., Aulander.

Fourth District—(Halifax—one Senator)—E. L. Travis, D., Halifax.

Fifth District—(Edgecombe—one Senator)—Donnell Gilliam, D., Tarboro.

Sixth District—(Pitt—one Senator)—A. L. Blow, D., Greenville.

Seventh District—(Franklin, Nash, Wilson—two Senators)—John E. Woodard, D., Wilson; R. B. White, D., Franklinton.

Eighth District—(Carteret, Craven, Greene, Jones, Lenoir, Onslow—two Senators)—T. D. Warren, D., Trenton; John A. Pollock, D., Kinston.

Ninth District—(Wayne—one Senator)—D. J. Aaron, D., Mt. Olive.

Tenth District—(Duplin, Pender—one Senator)—A. D. Hicks, D., Faison.

Eleventh District—(Brunswick, New Hanover—one Senator)—George H. Bellamy, D., El Paso.

Twelfth District—(Bladen, Columbus—one Senator)—J. A. Brown, D., Whiteville.

Thirteenth District—(Robeson—one Senator)—Thomas McBryde, D., Lumberton.

Fourteenth District—(Cumberland—one Senator)—James M. Lamb, D., Fayetteville.

Fifteenth District—(Harnett, Johnston, Sampson—two Senators)—C. W. Richardson, D., Selma; H. L. Godwin, D., Dunn.

Sixteenth District—(Wake—one Senator)—H. E. Norris, D., Raleigh.

Seventeenth District—(Vance, Warren—one Senator)—H. B. Hunter, Jr., D., Afton.

Eighteenth District—(Granville, Person—one Senator)—A. A. Hicks, D., Oxford.

Nineteenth District—(Alamance, Caswell, Durham, Orange—two Senators)—W. N. Pritchard, D., Chapel Hill; R. L. Walker, D., Milton.

Twentieth District—(Rockingham—one Senator)—A. J. Burton, D., Reidsville.

Twenty-first District — (Guilford—one Senator)—J. D. Glenn, D., Greenboro.

Twenty-second District—(Chatham, Moore, Richmond, Scotland—two Senators)—H. A. London, D., Pittsboro; U. L. Spence, D., Carthage.

Twenty-third District—(Montgomery, Randolph—one Senator)—N. M. Thayer, D., Eldorado.

Twenty-fourth District—(Anson, Davidson, Stanly, Union two Senators)—R. F. Beasley, D., Monroe; S. H. Milton, D., Albemarle.

Twenty-fifth District—(Cabarrus, Mecklenburg—two Senators)—H. N. Pharr, D., Charlotte; John P. Allison, D., Concord.

Twenty-sixth District—(Rowan—one Senator)—J. S. Henderson, D., Salisbury.

Twenty-seventh District—(Forsyth—one Senator)—F. T. Baldwin, D., Winston-Salem.

Twenty-eighth District—(Stokes, Surry—one Senator)—S. E. Marshall, R., White Plains.

Twenty-ninth District—(Davie, Wilkes, Yadkin)—J. Q. Holton, R., Yadkinville.

Thirtieth District—(Iredell—one Senator)—R. B. McLaughlin, D., Statesville.

Thirty-first District—Catawba, Lincoln—one Senator)—J. F. Reinhardt, D., Reinhardt.

Thirty-second District—(Gaston—one Senator)—S. J. Durham, D., Bessemer City

Thirty-third District—(Cleveland, Henderson, Polk, Rutherford—two Senators)—C. R. Hoey, D., Shelby; T. T. Ballenger, D., Tryon.

Thirty-fourth District—(Alexander, Burke, Caldwell, McDowell—two Senators)—E. J. Justice, D., Marion; W. A. Conley, Ind. Dem., Marion.

Thirty-fifth District—(Alleghany, Ashe, Watauga—one Senator)—H. Montgomery Wellborn, R., Transou.

Thirty-sixth District—(Madison, Mitchell, Yancey)—Zeb Wilson, R., Burnsville. Deceased. Election ordered for successor.

Thirty-seventh District—(Buncombe—one Senator)—C. A. Webb, D., Asheville.

Thirty-eighth District—(Haywood, Jackson, Swain, Transylvania—one Senator)—James H. Cathey, D., Sylva.

Thirty-ninth District—(Cherokee, Clay, Graham, Macon—one Senator)—J. L. Crisp, R., Stecoah.

HOUSE.

Alamance—R. W. Scott, D., Melville.
Alexander—Dr. C. J. Carson, R., Taylorsville,
Alleghany—R. A. Doughton, D., Sparta.
Anson—J. A. McRae, D., White Store.
Ashe—John D. Thomas, D., Jefferson.
Beaufort—B. F. Sugg, D., Washington; F. B. Hooker, D., Idalia.
Bertie—D. W. Britton, D., Rosemead.
Bladen—Forney Willis, D , Dublin.
Brunswick—W. H. Phillips, D., Shallotte.
Buncombe—J. C. Curtis, D., Luther; Theo. F. Davidson, D., Asheville.
Burke—J. Ernest Erwin, D., Morganton.
Cabarrus—C. H. Hamilton, D., Coddle.
Caldwell—W. C. Newland, D., Lenoir.
Camden—M. B. Hughes, D., Camden.
Carteret—J. W. Mason, D , Atlantic.
Caswell—John F. Walters, D., Blanch.
Catawba—W. A. Self, D , Hickory.
Chatham—W. D. Siler, D., Siler City.
Cherokee—W. M West, R., Murphy,
Chowan—W. T. Woodley, Jr., D., Amboy.
Clay—O. L. Anderson R., Hayesville.
Cleveland—W. A. Goode, D., Waco.
Columbus—J. M. Shipman, D., Elkton.
Craven—Owen H Guion, D., New Bern.
Cumberland—V. C. Bullard, D., Fayetteville; J. W. Moore, D., Raeford.
Currituck—S. M. Beasley, D., Poplar Branch.
Dare—R. B. Etheridge, D., Manteo.
Davidson—Harlee McCall, D., Lexington.
Davie —A. T. Grant, Jr., R., Mocksville.
Duplin—D. L. Carlton, D , Kenansville.
Durham—Jones Fuller, D., Durham.
Edgecombe—E. L. Daughtridge, D., Rocky Mount; B. F. Shelton, D., Speed.
Forsyth—B. S. Nissen, D., Winston Salem; John D. Waddell, D., Salem Chapel.
Franklin—I. G. Riddick, D., Youngsville.
Gaston—W. T. Love, D., Gastonia; J. F. Leeper, D., Belmont.
Gates—L. L. Smith, D., Gatesville.

Graham—T. A. Morphew, D., Robbinsville.
Granville—A. W. Graham, D., Oxford.
Greene—F. L. Carr, D., Castoria.
Guilford—T. E. Whitaker, D., Oak Ridge; Wescott Roberson, D., High Point.
Halifax—W. P. White, D., Hobgood; W. F. Parker, D., Enfield.
Harnett—T. W. Harrington, D., Harrington.
Haywood—M. D. Kinsland, D., Sonoma.
Henderson—J. R. Freeman, R., Hendersonville.
Hertford—Jno. E. Vann, D., Winton.
Hyde—W. H. Lucas, D., Middleton.
Iredell—S. W. Stevenson, D., Mooresville; A. D. Watts, D., Statesville.
Jackson—C. C. Cowan, D., Webster.
Johnston—E. S. Abell, D.; Smithfield; Jos. Wood, D., Benson.
Jones—A. H. White, D., Pollocksville.
Lenoir—Shade Wooten, Sr., D., LaGrange.
Lincoln—A. L. Quicknel, D., Lincolnton.
Macon—H. H. Jarrett, R., Franklin.
Madison—Lewis Hamlin, R., Marshall
Martin—Harry W. Stubbs, D., Williamston.
McDowell—Thomas Morris, Ind. Dem., Marion.
Mecklenburg—H. Q. Alexander, D., Tampa; R. C. Freeman, D., Dixie; Thomas Gluyas, D., Bristow.
Mitchell—J. C. Bowman, R., Bakersville.
Montgomery—C. T. Luther, D., Troy.
Moore—E. J Harrington, D., Jessup.
Nash—R. H. Ricks, D., Rocky Mount.
New Hanover—Geo. L. Morton, D., Wilmington.
Northampton—B. S. Gay, D., Jackson.
Onslow—W. M. Thompson, D., Richlands.
Orange—S. M. Gattis, D., Hillsboro
Pamlico—R. L. Woodard, D., Bayboro.
Pasquotank—W. H. Hinton, D., Elizabeth City.
Pender—J. H. Foy, D., Scott's Hill.
Perquimans—E. G. Simpson, Ind. Dem., Belvidere.
Person—W. A. Warren, D., Bushy Fork.
Pitt—Henry T. King, D., Greenville; J. B. Little, Pactolus.
Polk—J. P. Morris, D, Columbus
Randolph—J. T. Brittain, D., Asheboro; D. I. Offman, D., Liberty.
Richmond—A. S. Dockery. D., Rockingham.
Robeson—Geo. H. Hall, D., Red Springs, E. J. Britt, D., Lumberton.
Rockingham—Ira P. Humphrey, D., Wentworth; Jno. T. Price, D., Geneva.
Rowan—Walter Murphy, D., Salisbury; Burton Craige, D., Salisbury.
Rutherford—W. F. Rucker, D., Rutherfordton.
Sampson—W. Y. Duncan, R., Clinton; E. B. Owen, R., Clinton.
Scotland—J.-C. McNeill, D., Laurinburg.
Stanly—J. R., Price, D., Albemarle.
Stokes—Julius H. Kruger, R., King.
Surry—John H. Dobson, R., Dobson.
Swain—A. J. DeHart, R., Loreta.
Transylvania—E. A. Aiken, R., Brevard.
Tyrrell—Ab. Alexander, R., Columbia.
Union—E. S. Williams, D., Monroe; C. N. Simpson, D., Monroe.
Vance—W. B. Daniel, D., Epsom.
Wake—J. C. Drewry, D., Raleigh; F. H. Whitaker, D., Raleigh; A. B. Hunter, D., Apex.
Warren—S. G. Daniel, D., Littleton.
Washington—T W. Blount, D., Roper.
Watauga—Lindsay H. Michael, R., Virgil.
Wayne—H. B. Parker, Jr., D., Goldsboro; A. T. Uzzell, D., Goldsboro.
Wilkes—J. Q. A. Bryan, R., Trap Hill; S. W. Pegram, R., Dellaplane.
Wilson—S. H. Crocker, D., Stantonsburg.
Yadkin—Frank Benbow, Y., Yadkinville.
Yancey—J. Bis Ray, D., Burnville.

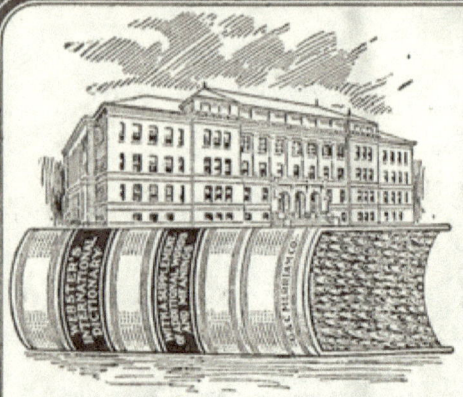

COUNTY OFFICERS
FOR NORTH CAROLINA.

CORRECTED FROM LAST ELECTION UP TO NOVEMBER, 1902.

COUNTIES	COUNTY TOWNS	CLERKS	REGISTERS
Alamance	Graham	J. D. Kernodle	Chas. C. Thompson
Alexander	Taylorsville	A. L. Watts	J. C. Bell
Alleghany	Sparta	J. N. Edwards	S. F. Thompson
Anson	Wadesboro	J. C. McLauchlin	S. A. Benton
Ashe	Jefferson	A. S. Eller	D. A. Osborne
Beaufort	Washington	L. B. Mayo	Gilbert Rumley
Bertie	Windsor	W. L. Lyon	E. E. Etheridge
Bladen	Elizabethtown	A. M. McNeill	J. S. Williamson
Brunswick	Southport	Thos. L. Wines	C. Ed. Taylor
Buncombe	Asheville	Marcus Erwin	J. J. Mackey
Burke	Morganton	P. W. Patton	J. H. Giles
Cabarrus	Concord	J. M. Cooke	W. R. Johnson
Caldwell	Lenoir	J. V. McCall	W. L. Minish
Camden	Camden C. H.	R. L. Forbes	C. B. Garrett
Carteret	Beaufort	L. A. Garner	W. L. Arrington
Caswell	Yanceyville	Thos. H. Harrison	A. W. Finch
Catawba	Newton	L. H. Phillips	P. M. Dellinger
Chatham	Pittsboro	R. H. Dixon	W. E. Brooks
Cherokee	Murphy	S. W. Lovingood	T. C. McDonald
Chowan	Edenton	H. C. Privatt	A. J. Bynum
Clay	Haysville	C. C. Standridge	M. M. Bunch
Cleveland	Shelby	L. J. Hoyle	J. F. Roberts
Columbus	Whiteville	H. C. Moffitt	R. Q. Howell
Craven	Newbern	W. M. Watson	E. M. Green
Cumberland	Fayetteville	Al. A. McKeithan	J. A. McPherson
Currituck	Currituck C. H.	E. W. Ansell	E. W. Williams
Dare	Manteo	T. S. Meekins	R. W. Smith
Davidson	Lexington	H. T. Phillips	S. L. Owen
Davie	Mocksville	A. G. Grant	B. O. Morris
Duplin	Kenansville	Herbet Smith	B. Frank Pearsall
Durham	Durham	C. B. Green	John E. Suitt
Edgecombe	Tarboro	Ed Pennington	H. S. Barnes
Forsyth	Winston	N. S. Wilson	W. W. Lindsey
Franklin	Louisburg	W. K. A. Williams	M. S. Clifton
Gaston	Dallas	C. C. Cornwall	M. A. Carpenter
Gates	Gatesville	W. T. Cross	Lycurgus Hofler
Graham	Robbinsville	R. V. McElroy	Robt. S. Slaughter
Granville	Oxford	J. G. Hunt	John B. Mayes
Greene	Snow Hill	John R. Dale	Chas. A. Lassiter
Guilford	Greensboro	John J. Nelson	A. G. Kirkman
Halifax	Halifax C. H.	S. M. Oary	J. H. Norman
Harnett	Lillington	J. H. Withers	A. C. Holloway
Haywood	Waynesville	S. P. Walter	H. B. Moore
Henderson	Hendersonville	C. M. Pace	W. A. Hood
Hertford	Winton	Thos. L. Boon	J T. Freeman
Hyde	Swan Quarter	Reuben D. Harris	Geo. W. Brown
Iredell	Statesville	James Hertness	W. W. Turner
Jackson	Webster	F. E. Alley	James R. Long
Johnston	Smithfield	W. S. Stevens	J. W. Stephenson

COUNTY OFFICERS

FOR NORTH CAROLINA.

CORRECTED FROM LAST ELECTION UP TO NOVEMBER, 1902.

COUNTIES	COUNTY TOWNS	CLERKS	REGISTERS
Jones	Trenton	S. E. Koonce	Z. Brock
Lenoir	Kinston	Plato Collins	W. D. Suggs
Lincoln	Lincolnton	A. Nixon	H. A. Self
Macon	Franklin	Lee Crawford	D. W. Bain
Madison	Marshall	J. H. White	Van B. Davis
Martin	Williamston	J. A. Hobbs	W. C. Manning
McDowell	Marion	Thos. Morris	T. W. Wilson
Mecklenburg	Charlotte	J. A. Russell	A. M. McDonald
Mitchell	Bakersville	J. C. Bowman	T. B. Garland
Montgomery	Troy	C. A. Armstrong	W. D. Allen
Moore	Carthage	D. A. McDonald	A. L. McIntosh
Nash	Nashville	Thos. A. Sills	J. A. Whitaker
New Hanover	Wilmington	John D. Taylor	W. H. Biddle
Northampton	Jackson	J. T. Blythe	M. F. Stancill
Onslow	Jacksonville	John W. Burton	I. E. Ketchum
Orange	Hillsboro	D. H. Hamilton	John Laws
Pamlico	Bayboro	James R. Rice	Z. V. Rowles
Pasquotank	Elizabeth City	W. H. Jennings	S. C. Spence
Pender	Burgaw	W. W. Larkins	J. B. Black
Perquimans	Hertford	L. V. Perry	R. E. Knowles
Person	Roxboro	D. W. Bradsher	W. E. Webb
Pitt	Greenville	D. C. Moore	T. R. Moore
Polk	Columbus	N. B. Hampton	A. L. McMurray
Randolph	Asheboro	G. G. Hendrick	J. P. Burrows
Richmond	Rockingham	W. I. Everett	N. Buie
Robeson	Lumberton	W. H. Humphrey	W. S. Thomas
Rockingham	Wentworth	J. V. Price	J. A. Scales
Rowan	Salisbury	W. G. Watson	A. L. Smoot
Rutherford	Rutherfordton	M. O. Dickerson	G. L. Russell
Sampson	Clinton	W. R. Pigford	James P. Jones
Scotland	Laurinburg	W. I. Everett	R. A. Ingram
Stanly	Albemarle	R. A. Crowell	W. T. Harkabee
Stokes	Danbury	N. O. Petree	I. M. Gordon
Surry	Dobson	C. H. Haynes	T. W. Davis
Swain	Bryson City	A. J. Hall	A. G. DeHart
Transylvania	Brevard	T. T. Loftis	Wm. Henry
Tyrrell	Columbia	G. L. Liverman	T. L. Jones
Union	Monroe	E. A. Armfield	J. M. Stewart
Vance	Henderson	Henry Perry	Kenneth Edwards
Wake	Raleigh	W. M. Russ	J. J. Bernard
Warren	Warrenton	W. A. White	John A. Dowtin
Washington	Plymouth	W. M. Bateman	F. R. Johnson
Watauga	Boone	J. H. Bingham	Jacob N. May
Wayne	Goldsboro	J. F. Ormond	G. C. Kornegay
Wilkes	Wilkesboro	Lin Bumgarner	E. M. Blackburn
Wilson	Wilson	J. D. Bardin	Wm. B. Barnes
Yadkin	Yadkinville	W. A. Hall	J. L. Crapon
Yancey	Bernsville	J. B. Ray	W. F. Adkins

8. A man in whose mind his own country is not *first*, is a man who himself is not *worthy* to be first in another country.—*Branson*.

BUREAU OF STATISTICS OF NORTH CAROLINA.

(DENOMINATIONAL)

LEVI BRANSON, SECRETARY.

DENOMINATION.	Number Ministers	Number Churches	Number Members
White.			
Methodist Episcopal Church, South..............	661	1,520	128,691
Methodist Episcopal Church....	65	115	8,941
Wesleyan Methodist Church......................	7	7	141
Methodist Protestant Church	64	208	16,416
Christian (Followers of James O'Kelly)........ ..	60	101	9,000
Evangelical Lutheran..........................	73	130	12,872
Presbyterian..................................	149	336	30,278
Universalists ....:	3	3	255
Protestant Episcopal	96	184	9,025
Missionary Baptist	*722	1,538	148,693
Primitive Baptist............................	150	317	11,914
Seventh Day Adventist........................	5	5	83
Free-Will Baptist	160	168	10,224
Baptist Church of Christ.......	16	16	659
Old Two-Seed Baptist	9	9	183
Disciples of Christ (Campbellites)...............	93	186	12,437
Seventh Day Baptist	1	1	10
Reformed Church of United States..........	17	40	3,140
Church of Jesus Christ of Latter Day Saints	24	1	136
Friends	52	52	5,328
Dunkards	9	9	510
Moravians	7	19	3,548
Waldenses	1	1	215
Roman Catholics	24	24	2,640
Hebrews	4	4	386
Salvation Army.............................	2	2	59
Advent Christian Church.....................	18	18	1,549
Associate Reformed	20	20	2,109
Colored.			
Missionary Baptist	*572	1,131	109,871
African M. E. Zion Church.......	150	526	121,154
African M. E. Church.	240	147	16,156
Colored M. E. Church in America	25	26	2,786
Methodist Episcopal	2	2	130
Protestant Episcopal	6	10	1,200
Congregational	20	20	1,002
Christian	50	53	3,746
Free-Will Baptist	10	25	1,640
Primitive Baptist	16	20	1,000
Presbyterian, North	173	306	17,851

*Quoted from Minutes Baptist State Convention, December, 1895.

The University of North Carolina.

Located in Chapel Hill, Orange county, twenty-eight miles northwest of Raleigh.

Chartered in 1789, founded in 1793, opened 1795. It now has 575 students and 64 in the faculty. The equipment includes fifteen buildings, eleven scientific laboratories, library of 40,000 volumes, campus of sixty acres, with ample athletic grounds, gymnasium, etc. Perfect sanitation, baths, closets, etc. Tuition $60 a year, total expenses $200 to $300. Scholarships and loans for the needy. Law school 66, medical school 81, pharmacy 41. A summer school for teachers is conducted in June and July. The faculty includes 64 professors and instructors. Many students support themselves by labor, the total amount earned being about $5,000. The University is non-political and non-sectarian.

FACULTY.

Francis Preston Venable, Ph. D., President and Professor of Theoretical Chemistry.

Kemp Plummer Battle, LL. D., Alumni Professor of History.

Joseph Austin Holmes, S. B., State Geologist, Lecturer on the Geology of North Carolina.

Joshua Walker Gore, C. E., Physics.

Thomas Hume, D. D., LL. D., English Literature.

Walter Dallam Toy, M. A., Germanic Languages and Literatures.

Eben Alexander, Ph. D., LL. D., Greek Language and Literature.

William Cain, C. E., Mathematics.

Richard Henry Whitehead, A. B., M. D., Anatomy and Pathology.

Henry Horace Williams, A. M., B. D., Philosophy.

Henry Van Peters Wilson, Biology.

J. E. Duerden, Ph. D., Acting Professor of Biology.

Collier Cobb, A. M., Geology and Mineralogy.

Charles Staples Mangum, A. B., M. D., Materia Medica, and Instructor in Anatomy.

Edward Vernon Howell, A. B., Ph. G., Pharmacy.

Marcus Cicero Stephens Noble, Pedagogy.

Henry Farrar Linscott, Ph. D., Latin Language and Literature.

James Cameron MacRae, LL. D., Law.

Charles Baskerville, Ph. D., Smith Professor of General and Analytical Chemistry.

Isaac Hall Manning, M. D., Physiology, and Instructor in Bacteriology.

Charles Alphonzo Smith, Ph. D., English Language.

Hubert Ashley Royster, A. B., M. D., Dean of the Medical Department at Raleigh, Gynaecology.

Augustus Washington Knox, M. D., Surgery.

Wisconsin Illinois Royster, M. D., Practice of Medicine.
Richard Henry Lewis, A. B., M. D., Diseases of the Eye and Ear.
Kemp Plummer Battle, Jr., A. B., M. D., Diseases of the Nose and Throat.
Andrew Watson Goodwin, M. D., Physical Diagnosis and Dermatology.
Henry McKee Tucker, M. D., Pediatrics and Obstetrics.
James William McGee, Jr., M. D., Chief of Dispensary.
Robert Sherwood McGeachy, A. B., M. D., Surgery and Gynaecology.

ASSOCIATE PROFESSORS.

Thomas Ruffin, D. C. L., Law.
Alvin Sawyer Wheeler, Ph. D., Organic Chemistry.
Charles Lee Raper, Ph. D., Economics and History.
James Dowden Bruner, Ph. D., Romance Languages and Literatures.
W. C. Coker, Ph. D., Botany.
Thomas James Wilson, Jr., Ph. D., Latin.
Archibald Henderson, Ph. D., Mathematics.

INSTRUCTORS.

George McFarland McKee, Expression and in English.
James Edward Mills, Ph. D., Physical Chemistry.
Clarence Albert Shore, S. M., Biology.
William Stanley Bernard, A. B., Greek.
Edward von den Steinen, Physical Culture.
Marvin Hendrix Stacy, Ph. B., Mathematics.

ASSISTANTS.

Ivey Foreman Lewis, Fred Moir, Hanes, Biology.
Royall Oscar Eugene Davis, Ph. B., Hazell Holland, and Hugh Hammond Bennett, Chemistry.
George Phifer Stevens, A. B, Mathematics.
William DeBerniere MacNider, B. S., Clinical Pathology.
William Moncure, Jr.; M. D., Dispensary.
Robt. Arthur Lichtentraeler, S. B., and Robt. Gilliam Lassiter, Geology.
William Morgan Perry, Pharmacy.
Marshal Capon Gutherie, Jr., Anatomy.
Henry Richard McFayden, Physics.

OFFICERS.

Walter Dallan Toy, M. A., Secretary of the Faculty.
Eben Alexander, Ph. D., LL. D., Supervisor of the Library.
Louis Round Wilson, M. A., Librarian
Willie Thomas Patterson, Bursar.
Charles Thomas Woollen, Registrar.
John Frank Pickard, Superintendent of Buildings.

N. C. College of Agriculture and Mechanic Arts.

Located in Raleigh, near the Fair Grounds, on Hillsboro road. Thorough practical and liberal education offered in all branches of Engineering and the Mechanic Arts, in Cotton Manufacturing, in Chemistry, and in Agriculture. Tuition $20 a year, board $8 a month; 325 students, 30 teachers, 120 scholarships in agriculture, 120 scholarships in mechanical arts. Full courses of study, four years, furnishing complete education and conferring degrees; short courses (mainly practical work) two years; special courses in carpentry, in machine shop, in engine and boiler tending, and in machine drawing and designing (3 to 9 months).

BOARD OF TRUSTEES

S. L. PATTERSON, Commissioner, *ex officio*, Chairman.

First District..J. B. COFFIELD
Second District...E. L. DAUGHTRIDGE
Third District...WM. DUNN
Fourth District..C. N. ALLEN
Fifth District...J. S. CUNINGHAM
Sixth District...A. T. McCALLUM
Seventh District...J. P. McRAE
Eighth District...L. G. WAUGH
Ninth District...W. A. GRAHAM
Tenth District...A. CANNON

HOWARD BROWNING.   J. R. JOYCE.
G. E. FLOW.   J. C. RAY.

FACULTY

Geo. T. Winston, A. M. and LL. D., President, and Professor of Political Economy; W. A. Withers, A. M., Professor of Pure and Agricultural Chemistry; D. A. Hill, A. M., Professor of English; W. C. Riddick, A. M. and C. E., Professor of Civil Engineering and Mathematics; F. A. Weihe, M. E. and Ph. D., Professor of Electrical Engineering and Physics, C. W. Burkett, Ph. D., Professor of Agriculture; T. M. Dick, Assistant Engineer U. S. N. (retired), Professor of Mechanical Engineering; Tait Butler, D. V. M., Professor of Veterinary Science and Animal Husbandry; Henry M. Wilson, A. B., Professor of Textile Industry; F. E. Phelps, Captain U. S. A. (retired), Professor of Military Science and Tactics; F. L. Stevens, Ph. D., Instructor in Biology; R. E. L. Yates, A. M., Assistant Professor of Mathematics; G. S. Fraps, B. S. and Ph. D., Assistant Professor of Chemistry; C. B. Park, Superintendent of Shops; T. A. Chittenden, B. S., Instructor in Drawing; V. W. Bragg, Instructor in Wood Working; M. E. Carter, Instructor in Wood Working; Oliver Carter, Instructor in Forge Shop; E. B. Owen, B. A., Instructor in English; Alexander Rhodes, Instructor in Horticulture; William A. Syme, B. S., Instructor in Chemistry; Chas. L. Fish, B. S., Instructor in Civil Engineering and Mathematics; W. S. turgill, B. E., Instructor in Mathematics; Thomas Nelson, B. S., Instructor in Carding and Spinning; A. F. Bowen, Bursar; E. B. Owen, Librarian; Mrs. D. Lewis, Matron; Mrs. L. V. Darby, Stenographer.

N. C. AGRICULTURAL AND EXPERIMENT STATION.

This Station is a department of the Agricultural and Mechanical College and is managed by the same Board of Trustees. The station officers are in the main building of the College and in the building of the Department of Agriculture. The experiment work is carried on in the College laboratories and partly on the Experiment Station farms and partly on the lands of the College.

een's Sons Advertisement on top of page 42

EXPERIMENT STATION STAFF :

B. W. KILGORE, M. S., State Chemist and Director.
W. A. WITHERS, A. M., Chemist.
C. W. BURKETT, Ph. D., Agriculturist.
W. F. MASSEY, C. E , Horticulturist.
TAIT BUTLER, D. V. M., Veterinarian.
G. S. FRAPS, Ph. D., Assistant Chemist.
ALEX RHODES, Assistant Horticulturist.
FRANKLIN SHERMAN, Entomologist.
B. S. SKINNER, Farm Superintendent.
A. F. BOWEN, Secretary and Bursar.
MRS. L. V. DARBY, Stenographer.

At Crown Point, N. Y., there is a handsome granite monument which was erected to the memory of a horse. The horse was "Old Pink," and the monument was erected by General John Hammond, who rode the old war-horse during the Civil War.

The Congo river, in Africa, is fifteen miles wide in some places. Steamers often pass each other, but out of sight.

INTERESTING ITEMS.

Brick is made from slag.
Pekin has 15,000 police.
Russia has railway schools.
Electric tanning is increasing.
Winnepeg car fare is 2 cents.
Japan has 100 national banks.
We export hops to Germany.
Texas is first in cattle and cotton
Liverpool has an electric elevated.
'Frisco is the leading whaling port.
The States have 1050 savings banks.
Our wool crop is 364,156,666 pounds.
New York city has 30,000 Hebrews.
A ton of diamonds is worth $35,000,000.
Germany's navy employs 18,051 men.
Submarine cables stretch 140,400 miles.
Florida raises 50 varieties of oranges.
The States contain 15,000,000 horses.
Uncle Sam leads the world in wheat output.
Blankets were named after the inventor.
Arizona ranks fifth in silver production.
Germany has 5,000,000 savings bank depositors.
Paper can be made from the standing tree in the space of 24 hours.
In Paris the undertaking business is monopolized by the city government.

Almost five-eights of the steamers in the world are under the British flag.

The diamond has been found on all continents and in almost every country in the world.

In India and Ceylon tea leaves are rolled by machinery, but in China it is done by hand.

About 74 per cent. of the value of the exports of the United States comes from the farms.

Edison claims to have in his laboratory every substance, organic and inorganic, in the world.

Twenty-five thousand persons in the United States, it has been estimated, own $31,500,000,000 worth of property.

A single shovel in the Lake Superior region mines loads on the cars in a single day 3,100 tons of iron ore.

An advocate of electrical cooking claims that of every 100 tons of coal used in cooking 96 tons go to waste.

It is unlawful in Norway for an alehouse keeper to employ any woman other than his wife in the serving of drinks.

In order to protect an invention all over the world no less than sixty-four patents are required at cost of about $7,500.

Aluminum is destined soon to take the place of lead and copper to a large degree, as well as iron when it becomes cheap enough.

The Christian religion leads a man towards the cultivation of all his best capabilities.—*Branson.*

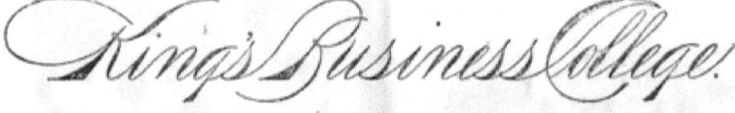

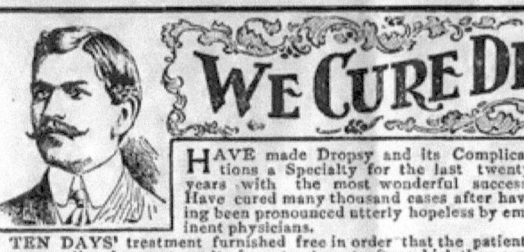

Lee's Prepared Agricultural Lim

For Peanuts, Cotton, Corn, Wheat, Oats, Clover and other Grasses and a Permanent Improver of the Land. It has been on the market over a quarter of a century and is as popular as ever.

LEE'S EXCELSIOR TOBACCO FERTILIZER equal to any, for Heavy Tobacco.

Our SPECIAL WHEAT FERTILIZER has the praise of all who used it. One customer writes us that he made 36½ bushels of wheat to the acre with it.

SPECIAL CORN FERTILIZER. We are Southern Sales Agents for CAYUGA BLUE LAND PLASTER, a superior article. Mr. J. M. Fisher says he used it on Corn and Peanuts and it acted finely on both. Every one who used it on Clover and Grass was highly pleased with it.

We are General Agents for BLACK DEATH BUG KILLER which is certain death to tobacco worms and potato bugs, and all insects that feed on the leaves of plants or fruit trees. We are prepared to furnish Sifters and Patent Improved Hand Machines for distributing it.

Write for circulars,   Address,

A. S. LEE & SON, Richmond, Va.

www.ingramcontent.com/pod-product-compliance
Lightning Source LLC
Chambersburg PA
CBHW052330110726
47901CB00005B/1188